THE GIRL
IN THE
WOODS

Camilla Lackberg is a worldwide bestseller renowned for her brilliant contemporary psychological thrillers. Her novels have sold over 20 million copies in 55 countries with translations into 37 languages.

www.camillalackberg.com

Also by Camilla Lackberg

Short stories

CAMILLA LACKBERG

THE GIRL
IN THE
WOODS

Translated from the Swedish by
Tiina Nunnally

HarperCollins*Publishers*

HarperCollins*Publishers* Ltd
1 London Bridge Street,
London SE1 9GF

www.harpercollins.co.uk

This paperback edition 2018
1

First published in Great Britain in 2018 by HarperCollins*Publishers*

Copyright © Camilla Lackberg 2017
Published by agreement with Nordin Agency, Sweden
Translation copyright © Tiina Nunnally 2017

Originally published in 2017 by
Bokförlaget Forum, Sweden, as *Häxan*

Camilla Lackberg asserts the moral right to
be identified as the author of this work

A catalogue record for this book is available from the British Library

ISBN: 978-0-00-751840-1 (PB b-format)
ISBN: 978-0-00-828860-0 (PB a-format)

Set in Meridien by Palimpsest Book Production Ltd, Falkirk, Stirlingshire

Printed and bound in the UK by CPI Group (UK) Ltd, Croydon CR0 4YY

MIX
Paper from
responsible sources
FSC™ C007454

This book is produced from independently certified FSC™ paper to ensure
responsible forest management.

For more information visit: www.harpercollins.co.uk/green

For Polly

�֎

It was impossible to know what sort of life the girl would have had. Who she would have become. What kind of work she might have done, who she would have loved, mourned, lost and won. Or whether she would have had children and if so who they might have become. It was not even possible to imagine how she might have looked as a grown woman. At the age of four nothing about her was finished. Her eyes had changed from blue to green, her dark hair she'd had at birth was now light, though with a touch of red in the blond, and no doubt the colour would have changed again. That was especially difficult to determine at the moment. She was lying face down at the bottom of the lake. The back of her head was covered with thick, congealed blood. Only the strands floating outward from her skull revealed the subtle hues in her fair hair.

There was nothing particularly gruesome about this scene with the girl. It was no more gruesome than if she had not been lying there in the water. The sounds from the woods were the same as always. The light filtered through the tree branches the same way it always did at this time of day. The water rippled gently around her, the surface disturbed only when a dragonfly occasionally landed, spreading tiny rings in its wake. The transformation had begun, and gradually she would

1

become one with the woods and the water. If no one found her, nature would run its usual course until she became part of it.

So far no one knew she was gone.

✤

'Do you think your mother will wear white?' Erica asked as she turned to look at Patrik lying next to her in bed.

'Ha, ha. Very funny,' he said.

Erica laughed and poked him in the side.

'Why is it so hard for you to accept that your mother's getting married? Your father remarried a long time ago, and there was nothing strange about that, right?'

'I know I'm being silly,' said Patrik, shaking his head as he swung his legs off the bed and started putting on his socks. 'I like Gunnar, and I think it's great my mother won't have to live alone any more, but . . .'

He stood up and pulled on his jeans.

'It feels a little odd, to be honest. Mamma has lived alone for as long as I can remember. I suppose you could say there's some sort of mother-and-son thing going on, for some reason it feels . . . strange, Mamma getting married again.'

'You mean it feels strange that she and Gunnar are having sex?'

Patrik raised his hands to cover his ears.

'Stop!'

Laughing, Erica tossed a pillow at him. He instantly threw it back, and all-out war ensued. Patrik flung himself on top of her, but the wrestling quickly turned to caresses and heavy breathing. She moved her hands to his fly and undid the top button.

'What are you guys doing?'

Maja's bright voice made them both stop and turn towards the open doorway. Maja was not the only one standing there. She was flanked by her little twin brothers, who were happily staring at their parents on the bed.

'We're just tickling each other,' said Patrik, out of breath, as he sat up.

'You need to fix the lock on the door!' Erica hissed, pulling up the covers to hide her bare breasts.

She sat up and managed to smile at her children.

'Why don't you go downstairs and start breakfast. We'll be there in a minute.'

By now Patrik had put on the rest of his clothes, and he shooed the kids ahead of him.

'If you can't fix the lock yourself, you could ask Gunnar. He always seems ready with his tools. Assuming he's not busy with something else with your mother, that is.'

'Cut it out,' laughed Patrik, leaving the room.

With a smile on her face, Erica sank back on the bed. She could allow herself a few more minutes before getting up. Not having a set schedule was one of the benefits of being her own boss, though it might also be regarded as a disadvantage. Making her living as an author required stamina and self-discipline, and sometimes it could be a little lonely. Yet she loved her job. She loved writing and bringing to life the stories and fates she chose to depict. She loved all the poking around and research as she tried to work out what had actually happened and why. She'd been longing to sink her teeth into the case she was working on right now. The case of little Stella, who had been kidnapped and killed by Helen Persson and Marie

Wall, had affected her deeply. It was still affecting everybody in Fjällbacka.

And now Marie Wall was back. The celebrated Hollywood actress was in Fjällbacka to star in a film about Ingrid Bergman. The whole town was buzzing with rumours.

Everyone had known at least one of the girls or their families, and everyone had been equally upset on that July afternoon in 1985 when Stella's body was found in the small lake.

Erica turned on to her side and wondered if the sun had been as hot back then as it was today. She'd have to look that up when it was time for her to walk the few metres across the hall to her home office. But not quite yet. She closed her eyes and dozed off as she listened to Patrik and the kids talking in the kitchen downstairs.

Helen leaned forward as she looked around. She propped her sweaty hands on her knees. A personal record today, even though she had gone out running later than usual.

The sea shimmered clear and blue in front of her, but inside her a storm was raging. Helen straightened up and stretched, wrapping her arms around her torso. She couldn't stop shaking. 'Someone just walked across my grave.' That's what her mother always used to say. And maybe there was something to it. Not that anyone was walking across *her* grave. But maybe across somebody's grave.

Time had lowered a veil; the memories were now so hazy. What she did remember were the voices of all those people who wanted to know exactly what had happened. They'd said the same thing over and over until she no longer knew what was their truth and what was hers.

Back then it had seemed impossible to come back and build a life here. But all the whispering and shouts had diminished over the years, transformed into low murmurs until at last they ceased altogether. She'd felt as if she was once again a natural part of life.

And now the gossip was going to start again. Everything was going to be dredged up. As so often happens in life, several events had coincided. She'd been sleeping badly for weeks, ever since receiving the letter from Erica Falck, telling her she was writing a book and would like to meet with Helen. She'd been forced to renew the prescription for the pills she'd managed to do without for so many years. She needed the pills to deal with the next piece of news: Marie was back.

Thirty years had passed. She and James had been living quietly, without drawing attention, and she knew that was what James preferred. Eventually all the talk will stop, he'd said. And he was right. Their dark moments didn't last long, provided she made sure everything went as smoothly as possible. And she'd been able to ward off the memories. Until now. Images began flashing through her mind. She could see Marie's face so clearly. And Stella's happy smile.

Helen turned her eyes towards the sea again, trying to focus on the waves slowly rolling in. But the images refused to loosen their grip. Marie was back, and with her came disaster.

'Excuse me, where can I find the loo?'

Sture offered a look of encouragement to Karim and the others who had gathered for Swedish lessons in the refugee centre in Tanumshede.

Everyone repeated the phrase, doing the best they could. 'Excuse me, where can I find the loo?'

'How much does this cost?' Sture went on.

Again they repeated in unison. 'How much does this cost?'

Karim struggled to connect the sounds Sture was uttering as he stood at the blackboard with the text in his book. Everything was so different. The letters they were supposed to read, the sounds they were supposed to make.

He glanced around the room at the valiant group of six students. Everyone else was either outside in the sun playing ball or inside lying in bed. Some people tried to sleep away the days and the memories, while others sent emails to friends and relatives who were still alive and possible to reach, or they surfed the Internet for news reports. Not that there was much information to be gleaned. The government broadcast nothing but propaganda, and the news organizations around the world had a hard time getting their correspondents into the country. Karim had been a journalist in his former life, and he understood the difficulties of reporting accurate and updated news from a country at war like Syria, which had been ravaged both from within and without.

'Thank you for inviting us over.'

Karim snorted. Now there was a phrase he'd never use. If there was one thing he'd quickly learned, it was that Swedes were a reserved people. They'd had no contact whatsoever with any Swedes, except for Sture and the others who worked for the refugee centre.

It was as if they'd ended up in a separate little land inside the country, isolated from the rest of the world. Their only companions were each other, along with their memories of Syria. Some of the memories were good, but most of them were bad. Those were the ones many people relived over and over again. For his part, Karim tried to suppress all of it. The war that had become their daily existence. The long journey to the promised land in the north.

He'd made it here, along with his beloved wife Amina

and their two precious children Hassan and Samia. That was the only thing that mattered. He'd managed to bring them to safety and give them an opportunity for a future. The bodies floating in the water sometimes forced their way into his dreams, but when he opened his eyes they were gone. He and his family were here in Sweden. Nothing else was important.

'How do you say when you have sex with someone?'

Adnan laughed at his own words. He and Khalil were the youngest of the men here. They sat next to each other and egged each other on.

'Show some respect,' Karim said in Arabic, glaring at them.

He shrugged an apology as he looked at Sture, who gave a slight nod.

Khalil and Adnan had come here on their own, without family, without friends. They'd managed to escape Aleppo before it got too dangerous to flee. They'd had to decide between leaving and staying. Both could be deadly.

Karim couldn't muster any anger toward them, despite their blatant lack of respect. They were children, frightened and alone in a strange country. Their cockiness was all they had. Everything here was unfamiliar to them. Karim had spent some time talking to them after the lessons. Their families had collected all the money they could find to make it possible for the two young men to leave Syria. A lot was riding on the boys' shoulders. Not only had they been thrown into a foreign world, they were also obligated to create a life for themselves here so they could rescue their families from the war. Karim understood them, but it still was not acceptable for them to show such lack of respect for their new homeland. No matter how scared the Swedes were of the refugees, they had welcomed them and provided them with shelter and food. Sture came here in his spare time, struggling to teach them how to ask for the price of things and how to find a loo. Karim might not understand the Swedes, but he was eternally grateful for what they'd done for his family. Not everyone shared his attitude, and those who displayed no respect for their new country ruined things for them all, making the Swedes regard them with suspicion.

'How nice the weather is today,' said Sture, carefully enunciating the words as he stood at the blackboard.

'How nice the weather is today,' Karim repeated, smiling to himself.

After two months in Sweden, he understood why the Swedes were so grateful every time the sun came out. 'What bloody awful weather,' was one of the first phrases he'd learned to say in Swedish. Though he still hadn't fully mastered the pronunciation.

'How often do you think people have sex at their age?' Erica asked, taking a sip of her sparkling wine.

Anna's laugh made the other customers in Café Bryggan turn to stare at them.

'Are you serious, Sis? Is that what you go around thinking about? How many times Patrik's mother is getting laid?'

'Yes, but I'm thinking about it in a broader context,' said Erica, eating another spoonful of her cioppino. 'How many years are left for a good sex life? Do people lose interest somewhere along the way? Do they replace their sexual desires with an irresistible urge to do crossword puzzles or Sudoku and eat sweets, or does it remain constant?'

'Hmm . . . I don't know.'

Anna shook her head and leaned back in an attempt to find a more comfortable position. Erica felt a lump form in her throat. It wasn't long ago that they'd both been involved in the horrible car accident that had caused Anna to lose the baby she was expecting. She would always have the scars on her face, but soon she would give birth to the child she and Dan had created from their love. Sometimes life could be truly surprising.

'For instance, do you think—'

'If you're about to say "Mamma and Pappa", I'm going to get up and leave right now,' said Anna, holding up her hand. 'That's not something I even want to think about.'

Erica grinned.

'Okay, I won't use our parents as an example, but how often do you think Kristina and Bob the Builder have sex?'

'Erica!' Anna covered her face with her hands and again shook her head. 'You need to stop calling poor Gunnar "Bob the Builder" just because he happens to be such a nice handy guy.'

'Okay, let's talk about the wedding instead. Have you been summoned to give your opinion about the dress? I can't be the only one who has to pretend to be enthusiastic and approving when she shows me one hideous matronly gown after another.'

'Yup, she asked me too,' said Anna, struggling to lean forward to eat her open-face shrimp sandwich.

'Why don't you balance the plate on your belly?' Erica suggested with a smile that was rewarded with a glare from Anna.

No matter how much Dan and Anna had longed for this baby, it wasn't much fun being pregnant in the intense summer heat, and Anna's belly was huge.

'Couldn't you try steering her in the right direction?' Erica went on. 'Kristina has such a great figure. She has a smaller waist and nicer boobs than me, but she doesn't dare show them off. Think how beautiful she'd look in a lacy, low-cut sheath dress!'

'Keep me out of it if you're going to try to give Kristina some sort of makeover,' said Anna. 'I'm planning to tell her she looks fantastic no matter what she shows me.'

'You're such a chicken!'

'You can take care of your own mother-in-law, and I'll take care of mine.'

Anna took a bite of her shrimp sandwich, savouring the taste.

'Right – like Esther's difficult to get on with,' said Erica, picturing Dan's sweet mother, who would never express the slightest criticism or offer any conflicting opinions.

This was something Erica knew from personal experience, because a long time ago she and Dan had been an item.

'No, you're right. I'm lucky to have her,' said Anna, then swore when she dropped her sandwich on her dress.

'Hey, don't worry about it. Nobody'll even notice – they'll be too busy looking at your enormous bazookas,' said Erica, pointing at Anna's breasts, which currently required a bra with size G cups.

'Shut up.'

Anna did her best to wipe the mayonnaise off her dress. Erica leaned forward, took her little sister's face in her hands, and kissed her on the cheek.

'What's that for?' asked Anna in surprise.

'Love you, that's all,' said Erica lightly, raising her glass. 'To us, Anna. To you and me and our crazy family. To everything we've been through, to everything we've survived, and to not having any more secrets between us.'

Anna blinked a few times before raising her glass of cola to drink a toast with Erica.

'To us.'

For a moment Erica thought she glimpsed a dark glint

in Anna's eyes, but the next second it was gone. She must have imagined it.

Sanna leaned over the Philadelphus coronarius and breathed in the scent. This time it didn't soothe her as it usually did. Customers were walking around, picking up pots and placing potting soil in their trolleys, but she hardly noticed. The only thing she could see was Marie Wall's phoney smile.

Sanna couldn't for the life of her fathom what Marie thought she was doing, coming back after all these years. As if it weren't bad enough having to run into Helen in town and being forced to nod a greeting.

She had accepted that Helen lived close by, that any moment she might catch sight of her. She could see the guilt in Helen's eyes and how it was eating her up more and more as the years passed. But Marie had never shown any remorse, and her smiling face could be seen in every celebrity magazine.

And now she was back. Phoney, beautiful, laughing Marie. They'd been in the same class at school, and Sanna had always looked with envy at Marie's thick lashes and her long blond hair curling down her back, but she'd also seen the darkness inside her.

Thank goodness Sanna's parents wouldn't have to see Marie's smile here in town. Sanna was thirteen when her mother died from liver cancer, and she was fifteen when her father passed away. The doctors hadn't been able to give a precise cause of death, but Sanna knew what it was. He had died from grief.

Sanna shook her head, feeling a headache coming on.

They had forced her to move in with her mother's sister, Aunt Linn, but she'd never felt at home there. Linn and Paul's own children were several years younger than Sanna, and they didn't have a clue what to do with an orphaned teenager. They hadn't been mean or treated her badly, they'd done the best they could, but they'd remained strangers to her.

Sanna had chosen to attend a community college specializing in horticulture far away, and she found a job soon after graduating. She'd supported herself ever since. She ran this small garden centre on the outskirts of Fjällbacka. She didn't earn a lot, but it was enough to make a living for herself and her daughter. And that was all she needed.

Her parents had been transformed into the living dead when Stella was found murdered, and she understood why. Certain people were born with a brighter light than others, and Stella had been one of them. Always happy, always cheerful, always offering kisses and hugs to everyone. If Sanna could have died instead of Stella on that hot summer morning, she would have gladly taken her place.

But Stella was the one who was found in the lake. After that, nothing was left.

'Excuse me, but are there any roses that are easier to take care of than others?'

Sanna gave a start and looked up at the woman who had come over without her noticing.

The woman smiled, and the furrows on Sanna's face relaxed.

'I love roses, but I'm afraid I don't have green fingers.'

'Is there a specific colour you'd like?' asked Sanna.

She was an expert at helping people find the plants best suited to them. Certain people did better with flowers that needed a lot of care and attention. They were able to make orchids thrive and blossom, and they'd have many happy years together. Other people could barely even take care of themselves, so they needed plants that were tolerant and strong. Not necessarily cacti – those she saved for the worst cases – but she might suggest, for instance, a Peace Lily or a philodendron. And she took pride in always pairing the right plant with the right person.

'Pink,' said the woman dreamily. 'I love pink.'

'In that case, I have the perfect rose for you. It's called a burnet rose. The most important thing to remember is to give it some extra attention when you plant it. Dig a deep hole and soak the soil with water. Add a little ferti-lizer – I'll give you the right kind – before you put in the rosebush. Fill in the hole and water it again. Watering is very important in the beginning when the roots are taking hold. Once it's established, it's more a matter of regular maintenance so the rosebush doesn't dry out. And cut it back every year in early spring, when buds are starting to appear on the birch trees.'

The woman cast an adoring glance at the rosebush Sanna placed in her trolley. She understood completely. There was something special about roses. She often compared people to flowers. If Stella had been a flower, she would definitely have been a rose. Rosa Gallica. Lovely, magnificent, with layer upon layer of petals.

The woman cleared her throat.

'Is everything all right?' she asked.

Sanna shook her head, realizing that once again she'd got lost in memories.

'Yes, I'm fine, just a little tired. This heat . . .'

The woman nodded at her vague reply.

Actually everything was not all right. Evil had returned. Sanna could sense it as clearly as she smelled the fragrance from the roses.

Being on holiday with children couldn't really be classi-fied as relaxing, thought Patrik. It was an odd combination of all that was wonderful and yet completely exhausting. Especially when he had sole responsibility for all three kids while Erica went to lunch with Anna. Against his better judgement, he'd taken them to the beach to keep them from climbing the walls at home. It was usually easier to prevent them from fighting if they were fully occupied, but he'd forgotten how the beach could make things more difficult. For a start, there was always the risk of drowning. Their house was in Sälvik, right across from the bathing area, and many times he'd woken in a cold sweat after dreaming that one of the kids had slipped out and wandered down to the sea. Then there was the sand. Noel and Anton insisted not only on throwing sand at other children, which earned Patrik angry looks from other parents, but they also, for some inexplicable reason, enjoyed stuffing sand in their mouths. The sand was one thing, but Patrik shuddered to think of all the other nasty things going into their little mouths along with it. He'd already taken a cigarette butt out of Anton's sandy fist, and it was only a matter of time before a piece of glass followed. Or a pinch of discarded snuff.

Thank God for Maja. Sometimes Patrik felt guilty his little girl took on so much responsibility for her younger brothers, but Erica always claimed Maja enjoyed doing it. Just as Erica had enjoyed taking care of her own little sister.

Right now Maja was watching the twins so they didn't go too far out in the water. If they did, she hauled them back towards shore with a firm hand, checking to see what they'd put in their mouths, and brushing off the other children when her little brothers threw sand at them. Sometimes Patrik wished she wasn't always so dutiful; he worried she'd have plenty of ulcers ahead of her if she continued to be such a conscientious child.

Ever since the heart trouble he'd experienced a few

years back, he knew how important it was to take care of himself, allowing time to rest and unwind. But it was questionable whether being on holiday with the kids fit the bill. Much as he loved his children, on days like these he longed for the peace and quiet of the Tanumshede police station.

Marie Wall leaned back in her deckchair and reached for her drink. A Bellini. Champagne and peach juice. Well, not like at Harry's in Venice, unfortunately. No fresh peaches here. She had to make do with the cheap champagne the skinflints at the film company had put in her fridge, mixed with ProViva peach juice. She had demanded that the ingredients for Bellinis should be here when she arrived and it seemed this was the best they could come up with.

It was such a strange feeling to be back. Not back in the house, of course. It had been demolished long ago. She couldn't help wondering whether the people who owned the new house built on that plot were haunted by evil spirits after everything that had gone on there. Probably not. No doubt the evil had gone to the grave with her parents.

Marie took another sip of her Bellini. She looked around and wondered where the owners of this house had gone. A week in August with fantastic summer weather should have been the time when they got the most enjoyment out of a house that must have cost them millions, both to buy and to renovate, even if they didn't spend much time in Sweden. Presumably they were at their chateau-like property in Provence, which Marie had found when she googled their name. Rich people seldom settled for anything less than the best. Including summer houses.

Yet she was grateful to them for renting out their house. This was where she retreated each day the moment filming was finished. She knew it couldn't last. Some day she was bound to run into Helen, and she'd no doubt be struck by how much they had once meant to each other, and how much had changed since. But she wasn't yet ready for that.

'Mamma!'

Marie closed her eyes. Ever since Jessie was born, she'd tried in vain to get her to use her first name instead of that dreadful label. But the child had insisted on calling her 'Mamma', as if by doing so she might change Marie into one of those dowdy earth-mother types.

'Mamma?'

The voice was right behind her, and Marie realized she couldn't hide.

'Yes?' she said, reaching for her glass.

The bubbles prickled her throat. Her body grew softer and more pliant with every sip.

'Sam and I were thinking of going out in his boat for a while. Is that okay?'

'Sure,' said Marie, taking another sip.

She peered at her daughter from under the brim of her sun hat. 'What do you want?'

'Mamma, I'm fifteen,' said Jessie with a sigh.

Good God, Jessie was so pudgy it was hard to believe she was her daughter. Thank goodness she'd at least managed to meet a boy since they'd arrived in Fjällbacka.

Marie sank back and closed her eyes, but only for a second.

'Why are you still here?' she asked. 'You're blocking the sun, and I'm trying to get a tan. I need to go back to filming after lunch, and they want me to have a natural tan. Ingrid Bergman looked as brown as a gingerbread biscuit when she spent her summers on the island of Dannholmen.'

'I just . . .' Jessie began, but then she turned on her heel and left.

Marie heard the front door slam. She smiled to herself. Alone at last.

Bill Andersson opened the lid of the basket and took out one of the sandwiches Gun had made. He glanced up before swiftly shutting the lid. The seagulls were quick, and if he didn't watch out they would steal his lunch. Here on the pier, he was particularly vulnerable.

Gun poked him in the side.

'I think it's a good idea, after all,' she said. 'Crazy, but good.'

Bill closed his eyes for a moment as he took a bite of his sandwich.

'Do you mean that, or are you only saying it to make your husband happy?'

'Since when do I say things to make you happy?' Gun replied, and Bill had to admit she was right.

During the forty years they'd been together, he could recall only a few times when she had not been brutally honest.

'Well, I've been thinking about this ever since we saw that documentary, *Nice People*, about the Somali bandy team that lives and trains here in Sweden. In my opinion, something similar ought to work here too. I talked with Rolf at the refugee centre, and they're not having much fun up there. People are such cowards, they don't dare approach the refugees.'

'I get treated like an outsider in Fjällbacka because I'm from Strömstad,' said Gun, reaching for another fresh roll, bought at Zetterlinds, and slathering it with butter. 'If locals treat people from the next county as foreigners, it's no surprise they're not exactly welcoming the Syrians with open arms.'

'It's about time everybody changed their attitude,' said Bill, throwing out his hand. 'These people have come with their children, fleeing from war and misery, and they've had a terrible journey getting here. So the locals need to start talking to them. If Swedes can teach people from Somalia to ice-skate and play bandy, surely we should be able to teach Syrians to sail. Isn't Syria on the coast? Maybe they already know how to sail.'

Gun shook her head. 'I have no idea, sweetheart. You'll have to google it.'

Bill reached for his iPad, which he'd put down after completing their morning Sudoku puzzle.

'I'm right, Syria does have a coastline, but it's hard to know how many of these people lived near the sea. I've always said, *anybody* can learn to sail. This will be a good chance to prove I'm right.'

'But wouldn't it be enough for them to sail for fun? Why do they need to compete?'

'According to the documentary, those Somalis were motivated by accepting a real challenge. It became a kind of statement for them.'

Bill smiled. It felt good to express himself in a way that sounded both knowledgeable and reasonable.

'Okay, but why does it have to be a – what was it you said? A "statement"?'

'Because it won't have any impact otherwise. The more people who get inspired, like I was, the more it will have a ripple effect, until it becomes easier for refugees to be accepted by society.'

In his mind, Bill pictured himself instigating a national movement. This was the way all big changes started. Something that began with the Somalis entering the world bandy championships and continued with the Syrians competing in sailing contests could lead to anything at all!

Gun placed her hand on his and smiled at him.

'I'll go and talk to Rolf today and set up a meeting at the centre,' said Bill, reaching for another roll.

After a moment's hesitation he picked up a second roll and tossed it to the seagulls. After all, they too were entitled to food.

Eva Berg pulled up the stalks and placed them in the basket next to her. As usual, her heart skipped a beat when she looked out across the fields. All this was theirs. The history of the place had never troubled them. Neither she nor Peter was especially superstitious. Yet when they bought this farm ten years ago there had been a lot of talk about all the misfortunes that had struck the Strand family, the former owners. But from what Eva understood, a single tragic event had caused all the other troubles. The death of little Stella had brought about the sad chain of events that had befallen the Strand family, and that had nothing to do with this farm.

Eva leaned forward to look for more weeds, ignoring the ache in her knees. For her and for Peter, their new home was paradise. They were from the city, if Uddevalla could be called a city, but they'd always dreamed of living in the country. The farm outside Fjällbacka had seemed perfect in every respect. The fact that the asking price was so low because of what had happened here simply meant it was within their budget. Eva hoped they had been able to fill the place with enough love and positive energy.

Best of all was the way Nea was thriving here. They'd named her Linnea, but ever since she was tiny, she'd called herself Nea, so it was only natural for Eva and Peter to call her that too. She was now four years old and so stubborn and headstrong that Eva was already dreading her teenage years. But it seemed she and Peter were not going to have more children, so they'd at least be able to focus all their attention on Nea when the time came. At the moment, those days seemed very far away. Nea ran around the farm like a little ball of energy, with her fluff of blond hair, which she'd inherited from Eva, framing her bright face. Eva was always worried that the child would get sunburned, but she merely seemed to get more freckles.

Eva sat up and used her wrist to wipe the sweat from her forehead, not wanting to smudge her face with the dirty gardening gloves she wore. She loved weeding the vegetable garden. It was such a refreshing contrast to the work of her office job. She took a childish pleasure in seeing the seeds she'd sown become plants that grew and flourished until they could be harvested. Their garden was intended only for their own use, since the farm couldn't provide them with an income, but they were able to meet much of their household needs with a vegetable garden, a herb garden, and a field of potatoes. Yet occasionally she felt guilty about how well they were doing. Her life had turned out better than she'd ever imagined. She needed nothing more than Peter, Nea, and their home on this farm.

Eva began pulling up carrots. Off in the distance she saw Peter approaching on the tractor. His regular job was working for the Tetra Pak company, but he spent as much of his free time as possible on the tractor. This morning he'd gone out early, long before Eva was awake, taking along a sack lunch and a Thermos of coffee. A small wooded area belonged to the farm, and he'd decided to clear out the underbrush, so she knew he'd bring back firewood for the winter. He'd no doubt be sweaty and filthy, with aching muscles and a big smile.

She put the carrots in her basket and pushed it aside. The carrots were for the supper she'd cook this evening. Then she took off her gardening gloves and dropped them next to the basket before she headed towards Peter. She squinted her eyes, trying to catch sight of Nea on the tractor. She'd probably fallen asleep, as she always did.

It had been an early start for the child, but she loved going to the woods with Peter. She loved her mother, but she adored her father.

Peter drove the tractor into the farmyard.

'Hi, honey,' said Eva after he switched off the engine.

Her heart beat faster when she saw his smile. Even after all these years he could still make her weak at the knees.

'Hi, sweetheart! Have the two of you had a good day?'

'Er, um . . .'

What did he mean by 'the two of you'?

'What about the two of you?' she said.

'What?' said Peter, giving her a sweaty kiss on the cheek.

He looked around.

'Where's Nea? Is she taking an afternoon nap?'

There was a great rushing in Eva's ears, and as if from far away she heard herself say:

'I thought she was with you.'

They stared at each other as their world split apart.

THE STELLA CASE

Linda glanced at Sanna as she sat beside her, bouncing in the passenger seat of the car.

'What do you think Stella will say when she sees all the clothes you've bought?'

'I think she'll be happy,' said Sanna with a smile, and for a moment she looked like her cheerful little sister. Then she frowned in that typical way of hers. 'But maybe she'll be jealous too.'

Linda smiled as she drove into the farmyard. Sanna had always been such a considerate big sister.

'We'll have to explain to her that she'll get lots of nice clothes when she starts school too.'

She'd hardly stopped the car before Sanna jumped out and opened the back door to take out all the shopping bags.

The front door of the house opened, and Anders came out on to the porch.

'Sorry we're a little late,' said Linda. 'We had to stop for a bite to eat.'

Anders gave her an odd look.

'I know it's dinnertime soon, but Sanna had her heart set on going to a café,' Linda went on, smiling at her daughter, who gave her father a quick hug before running inside the house.

Anders shook his head.

'It's not that. I just . . . Stella hasn't come home.'

'She hasn't?'

The look on Anders's face made her stomach knot.

'No, and I rang both Marie and Helen. They weren't home either.'

Linda let out a sigh and shut the car door.

'Oh, I'm sure they must've forgotten about the time. You'll see. You know how Stella is. She probably wanted to walk through the woods and show them everything.'

She kissed Anders on the lips.

'I expect you're right,' he said, but he didn't look convinced.

The phone was ringing, so Anders hurried into the kitchen to take the call.

Linda frowned as she leaned down to take off her shoes. It wasn't like Anders to get so upset. But he'd had a full hour to wonder what might have happened to the girls.

When she straightened up, she found Anders standing in front of her. The expression on his face brought back the knot in her stomach full force.

'That was KG on the phone. Helen is back home now, and they're about to eat dinner. KG rang Marie's house, and according to him, both girls claim they dropped Stella off around five.'

'So what are you saying?'

Anders pulled on his trainers.

'I've searched everywhere on the farm, but maybe she went back to the woods and got lost.'

Linda nodded.

'We need to go out and look for her.'

She went over to the bottom of the stairs and called to their elder daughter.

'Sanna? Pappa and I are going out to look for Stella.

She's probably over in the woods. You know how much she loves being there. We'll be back soon!'

Then she looked at her husband. She didn't want him to let on to Sanna how uneasy they both felt.

Half an hour later they could no longer hide their concern from each other. Anders was gripping the steering wheel so tightly, his knuckles were white. After searching the woods next to their property, they'd driven back and forth along the road, slowly passing all the places where they knew Stella usually went. But they hadn't seen any trace of her.

Linda put her hand on Anders's knee.

'We should head home now.'

Anders nodded and looked at her. The worry in his eyes was a frightening reflection of her own.

They needed to ring the police.

Gösta Flygare riffled through the stack of papers in front of him. It was a Monday in August, so the stack wasn't very big. He had no complaints about working in the summertime. Aside from playing a few rounds of golf, he had nothing better to do. Occasionally Ebba came to visit him, but with a new baby to care for, she couldn't get away very often. He understood that. What mattered to him was knowing he had a standing invitation to visit Ebba in Gothenburg, and the invitation was genuinely meant. Even a small dose of what had now become his family was better than nothing. And it was best if Patrik, who had young children, was able to take time off in the middle of the summer. He and Mellberg could sit here like a pair of old horses and handle whatever business came in. Martin dropped by once in a while to check on the 'old guys', as he jokingly said, but Gösta thought the real reason was that he needed company. Martin hadn't met anyone new since Pia died, which was a shame. He was a fine young man. And his daughter needed a maternal influence. Annika, the police station's secretary, sometimes took the child home with her, giving the excuse that Tuva could play with her own daughter, Leia. But it wasn't enough. The child needed a mother. But Martin wasn't ready for a new relationship, and that was that. Love could not be forced, and for Gösta there had only ever been one woman. Yet he thought Martin was a little too young to feel the same way.

He realized it wasn't easy to find a new love. It was impossible to control such feelings, and the choices were limited since they lived in such a small town. Besides, Martin had been somewhat of a Don Juan before he met Pia, so there was always the risk it would be a second-time around with certain women. And in Gösta's opinion, trying a second time rarely worked out if the first time hadn't been successful. But what did he know? The love of his life had been his wife Maj-Britt, with whom he'd shared all his adult years. There had never been anyone else, either before or after.

The shrill ringing of the phone roused Gösta from his brooding.

'Tanumshede police station.'

He listened intently to the voice on the line.

'We're on our way. What's the address?'

Gösta wrote it down, hung up the phone, and then rushed into the next room without bothering to knock.

Mellberg gave a start, waking from a sound sleep.

'What the hell?' he said, staring at Gösta, frantically pushing his comb-over back into place.

'A missing child,' said Gösta. 'Four years old. She's been gone since this morning.'

'This morning? And the parents are only calling us now?' said Mellberg, jumping up from his chair.

Gösta glanced at his watch. It was a little after three p.m.

They didn't get a lot of cases involving missing children. In the summer, the police mostly dealt with drunks, burglaries and break-ins, assault and battery incidents, and sometimes rape.

'Each one thought she was with the other parent. I told them we'd leave immediately.'

Mellberg stuck his feet in his shoes, which he'd discarded on the floor next to his desk. His dog Ernst, who was also awake now, wearily lowered his head having concluded that the commotion had nothing to do with the possibility of going out for a walk or getting something to eat.

'Where is it we're going?' asked Mellberg, hurrying after Gösta, who was headed for the garage.

'The Berg farm,' said Gösta. 'Where the Strand family used to live.'

'Bloody hell,' said Mellberg.

He'd only heard about the old case, which had happened long before he came to Fjällbacka. But Gösta had been here back then, and for him the situation seemed all too familiar.

'Hello?'

Patrik had brushed off his hand before he took the call, but the phone still got sand on it. With his free hand he motioned for the kids to come over and then he got out a packet of Marie biscuits and a container of apple slices. Noel and Anton lunged for the biscuits, each trying to grab the packet away from his brother, until it fell on the sand sending biscuits spilling out. Other parents were staring at them, and Patrik could literally feel them snorting. He could understand their reaction. He thought that he and Erica were both relatively competent parents, yet sometimes the twins behaved as if they'd been brought up by wolves.

'Just a second, Erica,' he said. With a sigh he picked up a couple of biscuits and blew off the sand.

Noel and Anton had already eaten so much sand, a little more wasn't going to hurt them.

Maja picked up the container of apple slices and set it

on her lap as she sat down to survey the bathing area. Patrik looked at her slender back and her hair curling damply at the nape of her neck. She looked so lovely as she sat there, even though he, as usual, had failed to pull her hair into a proper ponytail.

'All right, I can talk now. We're down at the beach, and we just had a little biscuit incident I had to take care of.'

'Okay,' said Erica. 'Is everything good apart from that?'

'Everything's great,' he lied as he again tried to wipe the sand off by rubbing his hands on his swim trunks.

Noel and Anton picked up the biscuits from the sand and continued eating them, causing an audible crunching sound to issue from their mouths. A seagull circled overhead, waiting for the toddlers to take their eyes off the biscuits for a second. But the gull wasn't about to get any of the treats. The twins could finish off an entire packet of Marie biscuits in world-record time.

'I'm finished with lunch now,' said Erica. 'Shall I come over and join you?'

'Sure, do that,' said Patrik. 'Could you bring some coffee in a Thermos? I'm such a novice at these kinds of outings, I forgot to bring any coffee.'

'No problem. Your wish is my command.'

'Thanks, sweetheart. You have no idea how much I've been longing for a cup of coffee.'

He smiled as he ended the call. After five years of marriage and three children, he could still feel butterflies in his stomach whenever he heard his wife's voice on the phone. Erica was the best thing that had ever happened to him. Well, aside from the children. Then again, without Erica he wouldn't have any children.

'Was that Mamma?' asked Maja, shading her eyes with her hand as she turned to look at him.

Dear God, she looked so much like her mother from

certain angles. And that made Patrik very happy. Erica was the most beautiful woman he knew.

'Yup, that was Mamma. She's on her way here.'

'Yay!' shouted Maja.

'Hold on, someone's ringing me from the station. I have to take this call,' said Patrik, using a sandy finger to push the green button on his mobile.

Gösta's name had appeared on the display, and Patrik knew his colleague wouldn't call to disturb his holiday unless it was something important.

'Hi, Gösta,' he said. 'One minute. Maja, could you give the boys some pieces of apple? And take away that old lollypop stick Noel is about to stuff in his mouth. Thanks, sweetie.'

He raised the mobile to his ear again.

'Sorry, Gösta. I'm listening now. I'm at the beach in Sälvik with the kids, and chaos doesn't come close to describing things.'

'I'm sorry to bother you when you're on holiday,' said Gösta, 'but I was thinking you might want to know we've received a report of a missing child. A little girl has been missing since this morning.'

'Since this morning?'

'Yes, we don't have any further information yet, but Mellberg and I are on our way to see her parents right now.'

'Where do they live?'

'That's the thing. She disappeared from the Berg farm.'

'Oh, shit,' said Patrik, his blood turning cold. 'Wasn't that where Stella Strand used to live?'

'Yes, that's the place.'

Patrik looked at his own children who were now playing relatively peacefully in the sand. The mere thought of one of them going missing made him break out in a sweat. It didn't take him long to make up his mind. Even though Gösta hadn't specifically asked for his help, Patrik knew he would like someone to assist him other than Mellberg.

'I'll come,' he said. 'Erica should be here in fifteen minutes or so, and then I can leave.'

'Do you know where the farm is?'

'I do,' replied Patrik.

He knew all right. Lately, at home, he'd been hearing a lot about that particular farm.

Patrik pressed the red button to end the call and leaned forward to pull all three children close. They protested, and he got completely covered with sand. But he didn't care.

'You look a little funny,' said Jessie.

The wind kept blowing her hair into her face, and she reached up to brush it back.

'What do you mean by "funny"?' said Sam, squinting up at the sun.

'Well, you're not exactly a . . . boating type.'

'So what does a boating type look like?'

Sam turned the wheel to avoid another sailboat.

'Oh, you know what I mean. They wear deck shoes with tassels, navy-blue shorts, a polo shirt, and a crew-neck sweater draped over their shoulders.'

'And a captain's hat, right?' Sam added with a little smile. 'How do you happen to know what a boating type looks like, anyway? You've hardly ever been out on a boat.'

'Sure, but I've seen films. And pictures in magazines.'

Sam pretended not to know what she was talking about.

Of course he didn't look like a typical boating type. With his ragged clothes, his raven-black hair, and kohl-rimmed eyes. With dirt under his fingernails that were bitten to the quick. But she hadn't meant it as a criticism. Sam was the cutest guy she'd ever seen.

Jessie shouldn't have said that stuff about boating types. Every time she opened her mouth she said something stupid. That's what everyone had told her at the series of boarding schools she'd attended. They all said she was stupid. And ugly.

And they were right. She knew that.

She was fat and clumsy. Her face was spotty, and her hair always looked greasy, no matter how often she washed it. Jessie felt tears well up in her eyes, but she quickly blinked them away so Sam wouldn't notice. She didn't want to disgrace herself in front of him. He was the first friend she'd ever had. And the only one, ever since the day when he'd come over to her as she stood in a queue outside the Central Kiosk in town. He'd told her he knew who she was, and then she'd realized who he was.

And who his mother was.

'Shit, how come there are so many people out here,' said Sam, looking for an inlet that didn't have two or three boats moored or anchored off shore.

Most of the best places were already taken by morning.

'Fucking swimmers,' he mumbled.

He managed to find a sheltered cleft on the back side of Långskär Island.

'Okay, we're going to pull in here. Could you jump ashore with the mooring line?'

Sam pointed to the rope lying on the deck in the bow of the boat.

'Jump?' said Jessie.

Jumping was not something she ever did. And definitely not from a boat on to slippery rocks.

'It's not hard,' said Sam calmly. 'I'll stop the boat right before we get there. Crouch down in the bow so you can jump ashore. It'll be fine. Trust me.'

Trust me. Was she even capable of such a thing? Trust someone? Trust Sam?

Jessie took a deep breath, crawled forward to the bow, took a tight grip on the rope, and crouched down. As the island got closer, Sam slowed their approach, and they slid gently and quietly towards the rocks where they would moor. Much to her own surprise, Jessie leapt from the boat on to the rocks, landing lightly, and still holding the rope in her hand.

She'd done it.

It was their fourth trip to the Hedemyr department store in two days, but there wasn't much else to do in Tanumshede. Khalil and Adnan sauntered around the top floor among all the clothing and accessories on display. In the beginning Adnan had a hard time dealing with all the looks levelled at them, and the suspicion. By now he'd accepted that they attracted attention. They didn't look like Swedes or talk like Swedes or move like Swedes. He probably would have stared too if he'd seen a Swede in Syria.

'What the hell are you looking at?' snapped Adnan in Arabic, turning towards a woman in her seventies who was staring at them.

No doubt she was keeping an eye on them to make sure they didn't shoplift. Khalil could have told her that they would never take anything that didn't belong to them. They wouldn't dream of it. They weren't brought up like that. But when she snorted and headed for the stairs to the ground floor, he realized it would be pointless.

'What kind of people do they think we are? It's always the same thing.'

Adnan continued cursing in Arabic and waving his arms around so he almost knocked over a lamp on a nearby shelf.

'Let them think whatever they like. They've probably never seen an Arab before,' said Khalil.

Finally he got Adnan to smile. Adnan was two years younger, only sixteen, and sometimes he still seemed like a boy. He couldn't control his emotions; they controlled him.

Khalil hadn't felt like a boy for a long time now. Not since the day when the bomb killed his mother and little brothers. The mere thought of Bilal and Tariq brought tears to his eyes, and Khalil quickly blinked them away so Adnan wouldn't notice. Bilal was always getting into mischief, but he was such a happy kid, it was hard to be mad at him. Tariq was always reading and filled with curiosity; he was the boy everyone said would be something great one day. In a split second they were gone. Their bodies were found in the kitchen, with their mother lying on top of the boys. She hadn't been able to protect them.

Clenching his fists, Khalil looked around, thinking about how his life was now. He spent his days in a small room in the refugee centre, or he roamed through the streets in this strange little town where they'd landed. Such a quiet and desolate place, lacking all smells and sounds and colours.

The Swedes went about in their own world, barely even greeting one another, and they seemed almost frightened if anyone addressed them directly. They all spoke so quietly, without gesturing.

Adnan and Khalil went downstairs and out into the summer heat. They paused on the pavement outside the department store. It was the same thing every day. So difficult to find anything to occupy their time. The walls of the refugee centre seemed to close in, as if trying to suffocate them. Khalil didn't want to seem ungrateful. Here in Sweden he had a roof over his head and food in his belly. And he was safe. There were no bombs falling here. People lived without the threat of either soldiers or terrorists. Yet even in safety it was hard to live a life in limbo. Without a home, without anything to do, without purpose.

This was not living. It was merely existing.

Adnan sighed as he stood next to Khalil. In silence they headed back to the refugee centre.

Eva stood as if frozen to the spot, hugging her arms around her torso. Peter kept rushing around. He'd searched everywhere at least four or five times, lifting up bedclothes, moving the same boxes, calling Nea's name over and over. But Eva knew it was pointless. Nea wasn't here. She could feel her absence in her body.

She squinted her eyes, noticing a dot way off in the distance. A dot that got bigger and bigger, becoming a white splotch as it approached. Eva realized it must be the police. Soon she could clearly see the blue and yellow markings on the car, and a chasm opened inside her. Her daughter was missing. The police were here because Nea was missing. She'd been missing since this morning. Her brain struggled to take in the fact she'd been missing since the morning. How could they have been such bad parents not to notice their four-year-old had been gone all day?

'Are you the one who called?'

An older man with silver hair had got out the police car and now came over to her. She nodded mutely, and he reached out to shake her hand.

'Gösta Flygare. And this is Bertil Mellberg.'

An officer about the same age but significantly heavier shook her hand as well. He was sweating copiously and raised his arm to wipe his brow on his shirtsleeve.

'Is your husband here?' asked the thinner officer with greyer hair as he scanned the yard.

'Peter!' called Eva, alarmed at how weak her voice sounded.

She tried again, and Peter came rushing out of the woods.

'Have you found her?' he shouted.

Then he caught sight of the policemen and his heart sank.

It all seemed so unreal to Eva. This couldn't be happening. She expected to wake up at any second, relieved to find she'd simply been dreaming.

'Why don't we sit down and talk over a cup of coffee?' said Gösta calmly as he touched Eva's arm.

'Of course. Come in. We'll sit in the kitchen,' she said as she led the way.

Peter stayed where he was, standing in the middle of the farmyard, his long arms hanging limply at his sides. She knew he wanted to keep searching, but she couldn't handle this conversation on her own.

'Peter, come on.'

With heavy steps he followed his wife and the police inside. Turning her back on the others, Eva began fiddling with the coffee machine, but she was very aware of the officers' presence. Their uniforms seemed to fill the whole room.

'Milk? Sugar?' she asked them, and both nodded.

She got out the milk and sugar as her husband stood in the doorway.

'Sit down,' she told him, a bit sharply, and he obeyed.

As if on autopilot, she set the table with coffee mugs, spoons, and a packet of Ballerina biscuits she found in the cupboard. Nea loved Ballerina biscuits. The thought made Eva flinch, and she dropped a spoon on the floor. Gösta bent down to pick it up, but she beat him to it. She put the spoon in the sink and took a new one out of the silverware drawer.

'Shouldn't you be asking us questions?' said Peter, keeping his gaze fixed on his hands. 'She's been missing since this morning, and every second counts.'

'We'll wait for your wife to sit down, and then we'll start,' said Gösta with a nod towards Eva.

She poured coffee for all of them and sat down.

'When did you last see the little girl?' asked the fat officer as he reached for a biscuit.

Eva felt a rush of anger. She'd put the biscuits on the table because it was expected when guests came over, but it infuriated her to see him munching on a chocolate biscuit as they answered questions about Nea.

Eva took a deep breath, knowing she was being irrational.

'Last night. She went to bed at the usual time. She has her own bedroom, and I read her a good-night story and then turned off the light and closed the door.'

'And you didn't see her after that? She didn't wake up during the night? Neither of you went to check on her? You didn't hear anything?'

Gösta's voice was so gentle, she could almost ignore the fact that his colleague had helped himself to another biscuit.

Peter cleared his throat.

'No. She always sleeps through the night. I was the first one up this morning. I was going to drive the tractor over to the woods, so I just had a quick cup of coffee and a piece of toast. Then I left.'

There was a pleading tone to his voice. As if there might be some answer to be found in what he'd said. Eva reached out to put her hand on his. It felt as cold as her own.

'And you didn't see Linnea at that time? In the morning?'

Peter shook his head.

'No, the door to her room was closed. I tiptoed past as quietly as I could so I wouldn't wake her. I wanted Eva to be able to sleep a little longer.'

She squeezed his hand. That was Peter in a nutshell. Always so considerate. Always thinking of her and Nea.

'What about you, Eva? Tell us about your morning.'

Gösta's gentle voice made her feel like crying.

'I woke up late, it was already half past nine. I can't remember the last time I slept so late. The whole house was quiet, and the first thing I did was go to check on Nea. The door to her room was open, and her bed was unmade. She wasn't there, so I just assumed . . .'

Eva couldn't hold back a sob. Peter placed his other hand on top of hers and gave it a squeeze.

'I assumed she must have gone with Peter out to the woods. She loves doing that, and she often goes with him. So it wasn't strange and I didn't think for a second . . .'

Eva could no longer hold back the tears. She reached up to wipe them away.

'I would have assumed the same thing,' said Peter, and again squeezed his wife's hand.

She knew he was right. And yet. If only she had . . .

'Could she have gone to visit a friend?' asked Gösta.

Peter shook his head.

'No, she always stays here on the farm. She has never even tried to go beyond our property.'

'There's always a first time,' said the fat officer. He'd been sitting so quietly as he ate one biscuit after another that Eva practically jumped when he spoke. 'Maybe she ran into the woods.'

Gösta gave Bertil Mellberg a look that Eva couldn't decipher.

'We'll organize a search party,' he said.

'Do you think that's what happened? She got lost in the woods?'

The woods went on forever. The very thought of Nea lost in there made Eva feel sick with apprehension. They had never worried such a thing might happen. And Nea had never gone off on her own. But maybe they'd been naive. Naive and irresponsible. Allowing a four-year-old girl to run free on the farm when it was right next to a big woods. Nea was lost, and it was all their fault.

As if Gösta could read Eva's mind, he said:

'If she's in the woods, we'll find her. I'm going to make a few phone calls right now, and we'll start the search in no time. We'll have a search party organized within the hour, so we can make maximum use of the daylight.'

'Will she make it through a night out there on her own?' asked Peter in a toneless voice.

His face was deathly pale.

'The nights are still warm,' Gösta assured him. 'She's not going to freeze, but we'll do everything we can to find her before it gets dark.'

'What was she wearing?' asked Mellberg, reaching for the last biscuit on the plate.

Gösta looked surprised.

'That's a good question. Do you know what clothes she had on when she disappeared? Even though you didn't see her this morning, maybe you could check to see if any of her clothes are missing.'

Eva nodded and stood up to go to Nea's room. At last, here was something concrete she could contribute.

But at the door to the bedroom she hesitated. She took several deep breaths before she could push it open. Everything looked exactly the same as always, which made it even more heartbreaking. The wallpaper with pink stars, with little pieces missing where Nea had picked at the paper. The teddy bears piled up at the end of the bed. The bedclothes decorated with pictures of Elsa from the film *Frozen*. The Olaf doll that always lay on the

39

pillow. The hanger with . . . Eva stopped short. She knew exactly what Nea had on. To make sure she peeked inside the wardrobe and then looked around the room. No, she didn't see it anywhere. She hurried back downstairs.

'She's wearing her Elsa dress.'

'What does an Elsa dress look like?' asked Gösta.

'It's a blue princess dress. With a picture of the princess on the front. Elsa, from *Frozen*. She loves *Frozen*. And she probably has on her *Frozen* knickers too.'

Eva realized that things she took for granted, as the parent of a young child, might be completely foreign to someone else. She'd watched that film at least a hundred times. It was on twice a day, every day, year round. Nea loved it more than anything, and she could perform the whole 'Let It Go' scene. Eva forced back a sob. She could picture Nea so clearly as she whirled around wearing her blue dress and the long white gloves, dancing as she sang all the lyrics. Where was she? And why were they just sitting here?

'I'll go and make those phone calls. Then we'll start the search,' said Gösta, as if he'd heard her silent scream.

All she could muster was a nod. She looked at Peter. Both of them were thinking the same dark thoughts.

BOHUSLÄN 1671

It was an overcast November morning, and Elin Jonsdotter shivered as she sat next to her daughter in the clattering wagon. The vicarage, which they were gradually approaching, was beginning to look more like a castle compared with the little house where she and Per had lived in Oxnäs.

Britta had been fortunate. That had always been true. As their father's favourite, Elin's little sister had received all manner of advantages during their childhood, and there had never been any doubt that she would find a good husband. And their father had been right. Britta had married the vicar and moved into the vicarage, while Elin had been forced to settle for Per the fisherman. But Elin had no complaints. Per might have been poor, but a kinder person could not be found on this earth.

A heavy feeling settled in her chest at the thought of Per. But she gave herself a shake and plucked up her courage. There was no use shedding any more tears over something she could not change. God had wanted to test her, and now she and Märta would have to try to survive without Per.

She had to admit, it had been most generous of Britta to offer her a position as a maid at the vicarage, as well as a roof over their heads. Even so, Elin felt a great sense of unease as Lars Larsson drove into the yard, their few possessions piled in the wagon. Britta had not been a particularly nice child, and Elin doubted that age would have made her any kinder. But she could ill afford to turn down the offer. As tenants in the coastal area they had merely leased the fields. When Per died, the farmer had said they could stay until the end of the month, but then they would have to leave. As a poor widow without a home or any means of support, she would have to rely on the goodwill of others. And she had heard that Britta's husband Preben, who was the vicar in Tanumshede, was a pleasant and amiable man. She had seen him only at church services. She had not been invited to Britta's wedding, and of course she and her family had never been invited to visit the vicarage. But she recalled that he had kind eyes.

When the wagon came to a halt and Lars muttered that they should climb down, she pulled Märta close for a moment. Everything would be fine, she told herself. But a voice inside her was saying something else entirely.

❖

Martin gave the swing another push. He couldn't help smiling at Tuva's happy shriek.

He was feeling better with every day that passed, and he realized this was largely due to his daughter Tuva. Right now she was on summer holiday from pre-school, and he had a couple of weeks off, so they were spending every second together. And it had done both of them a world of good. Ever since Pia died, Tuva had slept in his bed, and every night she fell asleep leaning against his chest, often in the middle of a story. He would slip out of bed when he was sure she was sleeping and go sit in front of the TV for another hour or two, drinking a cup of the calming tea he'd bought at a health-food shop. Annika was the one who had suggested in the wintertime he should try to find some soothing natural herb or supplement for those times when sleep evaded him. He didn't know whether it was a placebo effect or the tea was actually working, but he'd been able to get some sleep. And maybe that's what had made all the difference, enabling him to cope with the loss. It never went away entirely, but the edges had gradually worn smooth, and he could even allow himself to think of Pia without falling apart. He tried to tell Tuva about her mother.

They would talk about her and look at photographs. Tuva was so young when Pia died that she had very few memories of her mother. He wanted to tell her as much about Pia as he could.

'Pappa, push me higher!'

Tuva shrieked with joy when he gave the swing an even harder push, and she soared higher.

Her dark hair flew around her face and, as had happened so many times before, Martin was struck by how much the little girl looked like Pia. He got out his mobile to film her, backing up to get everything in the frame. When his heels bumped into something, he heard a loud cry. Startled, he glanced behind him and caught sight of a toddler who was screaming to high heaven as he held a sandy toy spade in his hand.

'Oh, sorry,' said Martin, kneeling down to comfort the boy.

He glanced around, but none of the other adults showed any sign of coming over, so he ruled them out as the kid's parents.

'Shhh, don't worry, we'll find your mamma and pappa,' he consoled the toddler, who merely screamed even louder.

A short distance away, over by some shrubbery, he saw a woman about his own age who was talking on her mobile. He tried to catch her eye, but she seemed upset. She was speaking angrily and motioning with her free hand. He waved to her, but she still didn't notice. Finally he turned to Tuva, whose swing was losing momentum now that he wasn't pushing it.

'Wait here. I have to take this baby over to his mamma.'

'Pappa kicked the baby,' said Tuva loudly, but he shook his head at her words.

'No, Pappa didn't kick the baby. Pappa— Oh, never mind, we'll talk about it later.'

Martin picked up the screaming boy, hoping he could make it over to the woman before she noticed that a strange man was carrying her son. But he needn't have worried. She remained completely immersed in her phone conversation. He felt a trace of annoyance as he watched her talking and gesticulating when she should be keeping an eye on her child. The boy was now screaming loud enough to pierce his eardrums.

'Excuse me,' he said when he reached the woman, and she stopped in mid-sentence.

She had tears in her eyes, and mascara was running down her cheeks.

'I have to go now. YOUR son is unhappy!' she said, and ended the call.

She wiped her eyes and held out her arms towards the boy.

'I'm sorry, I stepped back and didn't see him behind me,' said Martin. 'I don't think he's hurt, but I probably scared him a bit.'

The woman hugged the boy.

'Don't worry. He's at that age when he's scared of strangers,' she said, blinking away the last of her tears.

'Are you all right?' he asked. She blushed at the question.

'Oh my God, how embarrassing to stand here crying in broad daylight. And I wasn't watching Jon either. I'm sorry. I must seem like the world's worst mother.'

'No, no, don't say that. He was doing fine. Are you sure you're okay?'

Martin didn't mean to pry, but she looked so miserable.

'Well, it's not like somebody died, or anything. It's just that my ex is such an idiot. His new girlfriend apparently isn't interested in the "baggage" of his marriage, so he's cancelled the three days he was supposed to have Jon. And his excuse was that she "was looking forward to the two of them spending some alone-time together".'

'How pathetic,' said Martin, irate on her behalf. 'What an arsehole!'

She smiled and he felt his gaze drawn to her dimples.

'So what about you?'

'Oh, I'm okay,' he replied, and she laughed.

'No, I meant which one is yours?'

She nodded towards the playground, and he slapped his hand to his forehead.

'Oh, right. That's what you meant. Well, my daughter's over there – the little girl on the swing who's looking a bit grumpy about not swinging any more.'

'Oops. You'd better go over and give her swing a push. Or is her mother here too?'

Martin blushed. Was she flirting with him? He caught himself hoping she was. He didn't know what to say in reply, but he realized he might as well tell her the truth.

'No, I'm a widower,' he said.

'Oh, forgive me,' she said, putting her hand to her mouth. 'Trust me to go and make some crass remark like "it's not like somebody died".'

She touched his arm, and he gave her as reassuring a smile as he could muster. Something inside him didn't want her to be sad or upset. He wanted to hear her laugh. He wanted to see those dimples again.

'It's okay,' he said and felt her relax.

Behind him, Tuva was calling: 'Pappaaaa!' Her voice was getting shriller and more demanding.

'Looks like you'd better go over and give your little girl's swing a push,' the woman said, wiping the snot and sand off Jon's face.

'Maybe I'll see you here again,' said Martin.

He could hear the hope in his voice. She smiled, and her dimples were even more visible than before.

'Sure, we come here often. In fact, we'll probably be

back tomorrow,' she said. Martin nodded happily as he started backing away to rejoin Tuva.

'We'll most likely see you then,' he said, trying not to grin too much.

He took another step and felt his heels bump into something. This was immediately followed by a piercing shriek. Over by the swings he heard Tuva sigh.

'Pappa, watch out . . .'

In the midst of the chaos Martin's mobile rang. He pulled it out of his pocket and checked the display: *Gösta*.

'Where on earth did you find this person?'

Marie pushed away the woman who'd spent the past hour making up her face and turned to look at the film director, Jörgen Holmlund.

'Yvonne is really good at her job,' said Jörgen with that irritating quaver in his voice. 'She's worked on most of my films.'

Behind her, Yvonne was quietly sobbing. The headache that had plagued Marie since she arrived at her trailer was getting worse.

'I'm supposed to be Ingrid Bergman down to her fingertips in every single scene. She was always flawless. I can't look like one of the Kardashians. Contouring? Have you ever heard of anything so dreadful! My features are perfect. I don't need fucking contouring!'

She pointed at her face, which had distinct patches of white and dark brown.

'They'll be blended together. It's not going to look like that when I'm finished,' said Yvonne, so faintly Marie barely heard her.

'I don't give a shit. My features don't need fixing!'

'I'm sure Yvonne can do it over,' said Jörgen. 'Just tell her what you want.'

Beads of sweat had formed on his forehead even though it was cool inside the trailer.

The big film team and the production office were being housed at TanumStrand, a tourist and conference centre situated between Fjällbacka and Grebbestad. But on location in Fjällbacka, various trailers served as the make-up and wardrobe quarters.

'Okay, take it off and start over. Then we'll see,' she said, and she couldn't help smiling when she saw how relieved Yvonne looked.

During her early days in Hollywood, Marie had always complied with other people's wishes, doing whatever was asked of her. But she was a different person nowadays, and she knew how her role should be shaped, how she should look.

'We need to be ready in an hour, at the latest,' said Jörgen. 'We're going to film some of the easier scenes this week.'

Marie turned to look at him. Yvonne had used a damp cloth to remove an hour's worth of work in ten seconds, and her face was clean of all make-up.

'You mean we're doing the cheaper scenes this week? I thought we had a green light from everybody.'

She couldn't keep the concern from creeping into her voice. This was not one of those obvious film projects with investors queuing up in their eagerness to be part of it. The film climate had changed in Sweden, with priorities shifting to indie films, while the bigger pictures went begging. This project had already come close to folding several times.

'They're still having discussions about . . . priorities . . .' Again the irritating quaver in his voice. 'But that's nothing for you to worry about. Concentrate on doing an amazing job on the scenes we film. That's the only thing you need to think about.'

Marie turned back towards the mirror.

'There are lots of reporters who want to interview you,' said Jörgen. 'About your connection to Fjällbacka, and the fact this is the first time you've been back in thirty years. I can understand if it feels . . . uncomfortable to talk about that time, but if you'd like to—'

'Go ahead and schedule them,' said Marie without taking her eyes off the mirror. 'I have nothing to hide.'

If there was one thing she'd learned, it was that any publicity was good publicity. She smiled at herself in the mirror. Maybe the damned headache was finally starting to fade.

After relieving Patrik, Erica had packed up the children and then they slowly walked up the hill towards home. Patrik had taken off as soon as she arrived, and she'd noticed a trace of worry in his eyes. Erica shared his concern. Just considering the possibility of something happening to a child was like falling into an abyss.

She had given her own kids a few extra kisses when they reached home. She put the twins down for their afternoon nap and turned on the DVD player so Maja could watch *Frozen*. Now she was sitting in her home office. When Patrik had told her the name of the farm where the missing girl lived and the uncanny similarity in age, Erica had immediately felt a pressing need to go over her research material. She was a long way from being ready to start writing the book, but her desk was covered with maps, photocopies of newspaper articles, and hand-written notes about Stella's death. She sat for a moment, staring at the piles of papers. At this stage, she was still gathering facts, making no effort to shape, arrange, or sort through all the material. That would be the next step in the long and winding path that would lead to a completed book. She reached for the copy of an article and studied the two girls in the black-and-white photographs. Helen and Marie. Their expressions sullen and truculent. It was difficult to tell whether she was seeing anger or fear in their eyes. Or evil, as many people had claimed. But Erica had a hard time believing children could be evil.

The same kind of speculation occurred in all the famous cases where children committed horrible acts: Mary Bell, who was only eleven when she killed two children. The murderers of three-year-old James Bulger. Pauline Parker and Juliet Hulme, the two girls in New Zealand who killed Pauline's mother. Erica loved the Peter Jackson film *Heavenly Creatures*, which was based on the case. After the event, people would say things like: 'She was always such a horrible child.' Or: 'I saw the evil in his eyes even when he was young.' Neighbours, friends, and even family members had been more than willing to give their views on such cases, pointing to factors they believed indicated some innate evil. But surely a child couldn't be evil. Erica was more apt to believe what she'd read somewhere: 'evil is the absence of goodness'. A person was undoubtedly born with a tendency towards one or the other, but whether that tendency was enhanced or diminished would depend on where and how the individual was raised.

For that reason she needed to find out as much as she could about the two girls in the photographs. What sort of children were Marie and Helen? How had they been brought up? She wasn't planning to settle for what other people knew about them and their families. She was equally interested in what had gone on behind closed doors. What sort of values had been instilled in the girls? Were they treated well? What had they learned about the world prior to that terrible day in 1985?

Eventually both girls had retracted their confessions and stubbornly insisted on their innocence. Even though most people had remained convinced Helen and Marie were guilty, there had been plenty of speculation. What if someone else was responsible for Stella's death? An opportunist killer. And what if an opportunity had once again presented itself? It couldn't be a coincidence that a girl of the same age should disappear from the very same farm. What were the odds of that happening? There had to be a connection between the two events. What if the police had missed a clue the killer had left behind, and what if the perpetrator, for some reason, had decided to strike again? Maybe inspired by Marie's return? But if so, why? And were other girls in danger?

If only she'd made more progress in her research. Erica got up from her desk. The heat was stifling in her office, so she leaned across to open the window. Outside, life was going on as usual. The sounds of summer reached her. Children shrieking and laughing down at the beach. Seagulls screeching as they hovered over the water. The wind rustling the crowns of the trees. Outside, everything seemed idyllic. But Erica hardly noticed.

She sat back down and began sorting through the materials she'd collected. But she hadn't even started on the interviews. She had a long list of people she planned to talk to, and naturally Marie and Helen were at the top of the list. She'd already tried to approach Helen, sending her several letters without receiving a response, and she'd been in contact with Marie's PR agent. On the desk were copies of various interviews Marie had given about the Stella case, so Erica didn't think the actress would be averse to talking to her. In fact, it was commonly thought that Marie's career would not have taken off as it had if the news about her past hadn't been leaked to the press after she'd appeared in small roles in a few minor productions.

If there was one thing Erica had learned from the previous books she'd written about true crime cases, it was that people had a deep-seated longing to speak out, to tell their story. Almost without exception.

She switched on the ringer on her mobile in case Patrik happened to call, though he'd probably be too busy to keep her updated. She had offered to help search, but he'd said they would have more than enough volunteers, and it would be better if she stayed with the children. Erica had voiced no objections. From downstairs in the living room she could hear that the film had reached the point where Elsa had built an entire castle out of ice. Erica slowly put down the papers she was holding. It had been far too long since she'd kept Maja company in front of the TV to watch a film. I'll just have to put up with that ego-tripping princess, she thought as she stood up. Besides, Olaf is so charming. The reindeer too, for that matter.

'What have you arranged so far?' asked Patrik, getting right to the point when he arrived at the farm.

Gösta stood outside the farmhouse, next to a group of wooden patio furniture painted white.

'I rang Uddevalla and they're sending a helicopter.'

'What about the Coast Guard?'

Gösta nodded. 'Everybody has been notified, and help is on the way. I phoned Martin and asked him to get together some volunteers for the search party. He got right on it, calling people in Fjällbacka, so we should have lots of people here very soon. And our colleagues from Uddevalla are bringing the search dogs.'

'So what do you think?' said Patrik, keeping his voice low because the girl's parents were standing a short distance away, holding on to each other.

'They want to go out and search on their own,' said Gösta, who had noticed Patrik looking at the couple. 'But I told them they needed to wait until we get organized, otherwise we might end up squandering resources if we have to go looking for them too.'

He cleared his throat.

'I don't know what to think, Patrik. Neither of them has seen the little girl since she went to bed last night, which was around eight o'clock. And she's so young: four years old. If she'd been anywhere close by, she would have showed up sometime during the day. If nothing else, she would have come home when she got hungry. So she must have got lost. Or . . .'

He left the word dangling in the air.

'It's such a strange coincidence,' said Patrik. Thoughts he didn't want to acknowledge kept creeping into his mind.

'I know. The same farm,' said Gösta, nodding. 'And the girl is the same age. It's impossible not to think about that.'

'I assume we're not working solely on the premise that she got lost. Right?'

Patrik was careful not to look at the parents as he spoke.

'Right,' said Gösta. 'As soon as possible we'll start talking to all the neighbours around here, at least those who live along the road leading to the farm. We need to find out whether they saw anything last night or today. But first we need to focus on the search. It gets dark a lot sooner now that it's August, and I can't stand the thought of her sitting somewhere in the woods, all alone and scared. Mellberg wants us to contact the media, but I think it would be better to wait.'

'Good God, yes. But of course that's what he'd want,' said Patrik with a sigh.

Their boss was looking quite full of himself as he welcomed the volunteers who were starting to arrive.

'Okay, we need to get organized. I brought along a

map of the area surrounding the farm,' said Patrik, and Gösta's face lit up.

'Let's divide the search area into sections,' he said, taking the map from Patrik.

He placed it on the patio table, took a pen from his shirt pocket, and began drawing.

'What do you think? Is this about the right size section for a group? If we assign three or four people to each group?'

'Sure, that's good,' said Patrik, nodding.

Over the past few years he and Gösta had worked well together, and even though Patrik's usual partner was Martin Molin, he enjoyed teaming up with the older police officer. That had not been the case back in the days when Gösta's partner was Ernst, their now deceased colleague. But it turned out it actually was possible to teach an old dog new tricks. Gösta's mind still had a tendency to drift to the golf course instead of focusing on police work, but when it really mattered, like now, his mind was razor-sharp and completely focused.

'Want to give everyone a briefing?' asked Patrik. 'Or do you want me to do it?'

He didn't want to tread on his colleague's toes by taking over.

'You do it,' said Gösta. 'The main thing is to prevent Bertil from saying anything.'

Patrik nodded. It was seldom a good idea to allow Mellberg to speak to the public. Invariably he'd upset or offend someone, and they'd have to waste time on crisis-management instead of getting on with the task at hand.

He glanced over at Nea's parents, who were now standing in the middle of the farmyard, still holding on to each other.

'I'll go say hello to the parents first,' he said. 'Then I'll brief everybody who's here so far, and we'll have to repeat the briefing as more people arrive. Volunteers are going to be turning up the whole time, so it'll be impossible to get everyone together at once. And we need to see about getting the search under way as soon as possible.'

He cautiously approached the girl's parents. It was always difficult to deal with family members at times like this.

'I'm Patrik Hedström. From the police,' he said, shaking hands with them. 'As you can see, we've started bringing in volunteers for the search party, and I'm planning to give them a quick run-down on what's happening so we can begin the search.'

He realized he sounded very official, but that was the only way he could keep his own emotions in check and focus on what needed to be done.

'We've called our friends, and Peter's parents, who are in Spain, said they'd be here,' Eva explained quietly. 'We told them it wasn't necessary, but they're terribly worried.'

'We have search dogs on the way from Uddevalla,' said Patrik. 'They'll need an item that belongs to your daughter . . .'

'Nea,' said Eva, swallowing hard. 'Her name is actually Linnea, but we call her Nea.'

'Nea. Nice name. Do you have something belonging to Nea that the dogs can sniff so they'll be able to track her scent?'

'The clothes she wore yesterday are in the hamper. Would that do?'

Patrik nodded.

'Perfect. Could you go and get them? And would you mind making some coffee for the volunteers?'

He could hear how stupid it sounded to suggest serving coffee, but he had two reasons for making the request. He wanted to be undisturbed while he was giving the volunteers instructions, and he wanted to keep the parents occupied. That usually made things easier.

'Shouldn't I go with them?' said Peter. 'On the search, I mean?'

'We need you to stay here. When we find her, we have to know where you are, so it's best if you stay here at the farm. We'll have more than enough volunteers out there.'

Peter seemed to hesitate, so Patrik placed his hand on the man's shoulder.

'I know how hard it must be to stay here and wait. But believe me, that's the most useful thing you can do.'

'Okay,' said Peter quietly. Then he and Eva headed for the house.

Patrik gave a loud whistle to draw the attention of the three dozen or so people who had already gathered in the farmyard. A man in his twenties who was filming the scene stuffed his mobile in his pocket.

'In a few minutes we'll be sending you off to start searching. Every minute counts when such a young child is missing. We're looking for Linnea, known as Nea, who is four years old. We don't know exactly how long she's been missing, but her parents haven't seen her since they put her to bed last night around eight o'clock. Each thought she was with the other parent all day today, an unfortunate misunderstanding, so it wasn't until about an hour ago that they discovered she was missing. One of the theories we're working on, and it's the most likely one, is that the little girl has got lost in the woods.'

He pointed towards Gösta, who was still standing next to the patio table with the map spread out in front of him.

'We're going to divide you up into groups of three or four, and then my colleague Gösta will assign you to a specific area. We don't have any extra maps to give you, so you'll have to do the best you can. Perhaps use your mobile phone to take a picture of your section on the map so you can keep tabs on your search area.'

'We can also pull up a GPS map of the area,' said a bald man, holding up his phone. 'If anyone needs a good app, come and see me before we leave, and I'll show you which is the best one. I always use a GPS map on my mobile when I go hiking in the woods.'

'Thanks,' said Patrik. 'After you've been assigned a search area, I'd like you to walk about an arm's length apart. And move slowly. I know it can be tempting to try to search the area as fast as possible, but there are so many places in the woods where a little four-year-old might be hidden, or . . . uh . . . might hide, so it's better to take your time.'

He raised his fist to his mouth and coughed. 'If you should . . . find something,' he said and paused.

He didn't know how to go on, and he was hoping the people gathered here would understand without him being more specific. He started over.

'If you should find something, please do not touch or move anything. It might be a clue, or, well, something else.'

A few people nodded, but most kept their eyes fixed on the ground.

'So stay where you are and phone me immediately. Here's my number,' he said, taping a big piece of paper with his number to the wall of the barn. 'Go ahead and type it into your mobile. Everybody understand? Stay where you are and phone me. Don't do anything else. Okay?'

An older man at the back raised his hand. Patrik recognized the man. His name was Harald, and he'd owned the bakery in Fjällbacka for years.

'Is there any . . .' He stopped and tried again. 'Is there

57

any chance this is not a coincidence? With the farm, I mean? And the little girl? And what happened . . .'

He didn't need to say anything more. Everybody understood exactly what he was getting at. Patrik wasn't sure how to reply.

'We're not ruling out anything,' he said at last. 'But for the moment, the most important thing is to search the woods nearby.'

Out of the corner of his eye, Patrik saw Nea's mother come out the front door carrying a bundle of clothes in her arms.

'All right. Let's get going.'

The first group of four went over to Gösta to get their assigned area. A helicopter could be heard approaching above the treetops. It wouldn't have any trouble landing because there was plenty of space on the farm. People began heading for the woods, and Patrik watched them go. Behind him he heard the helicopter make its landing, and at the same time the police vehicle bringing the dogs from Uddevalla turned into the farmyard. If the girl was out there in the woods, they would find her. He was convinced of that. But there was another possibility: she hadn't got lost. And that's what scared him.

THE STELLA CASE

They'd been searching for the girl all night. More and more had joined the search, and Harald could hear people all around him in the woods. The police had done a good job, and there was no lack of volunteers. The family was well liked, and everyone knew the little girl with the reddish blond hair. She was the kind of child who refused to give up until she won a smile from anyone she happened to meet in the shops.

He felt bad for the parents. His own kids were grown now; two of his sons were helping to search. He'd closed the bakery. It wasn't a busy time anyway, since the summer holidays were mostly over and there were long intervals during the day when the bell over the door didn't ring. Although he would have closed even if there was a flood of customers. He felt a pain in his chest at the mere thought of the horror Stella's parents must be going through right now.

Harald randomly poked at the bushes with the stick he carried. Their task was not an easy one. The woods covered a big area, yet how far could the little girl have gone on her own? If she was even in the woods at all. This was only one of the possibilities the police were considering. Her face had appeared on all the news broadcasts, because it was just as likely she could have been coaxed into a car. If so, she'd be miles away by this time. But Harald refused to think about that. Right now his task was to help search the woods, along with all the others whose footsteps and voices he could hear through the branches.

For a moment he paused to breathe in the forest scent. He rarely ventured into the outdoors these days. The last few decades he'd been busy with the bakery and his family, but when he was a young man he'd spent a lot of time outdoors. He promised himself to get back in the habit. Life was short. The past day had been a constant reminder there was no way of knowing what lay around the corner.

Only a few days ago Stella's parents had no doubt thought they knew what to expect from life. They had lived each day without pausing every other moment to rejoice at what they had. Same as most people. It wasn't until something happened that people stopped to treasure every second they had with those they loved.

He set off again, walking very slowly, one metre after another. Up ahead he caught a glimpse of water in between the trees. They had received detailed instructions about what to do if they came upon a pond or lake. They were supposed to notify the police, so they could drag the water or send divers in if it was deep. The water he was looking at right now was calm and smooth, except for a few dragonflies landing on the surface, spreading tiny little rings around them. That's all he saw. The only other thing visible to the naked eye out on the small lake was a tree trunk that had fallen into the water, felled by wind or lightning several years earlier. He went closer and saw that the roots of the trunk were still clinging to the shore. Cautiously he climbed up on the broken tree.

He saw nothing but the calm surface of the water. Then he slowly lowered his gaze to look down at his feet. That's when he noticed the hair. The reddish blond hair floating like seaweed in the murky water.

Sanna was standing in the middle of an aisle in the Konsum supermarket. During the summer she usually kept the garden centre open as long as possible, but today she hadn't been able to keep her mind on her customers. For once all the questions about how often geraniums needed to be watered seemed too stupid for words.

She gave herself a shake and looked around. Vendela was supposed to come back from staying with her father today, and Sanna wanted to make sure she had plenty of her favourite foods and snacks on hand. One week her daughter was vegan, the next she would eat only hamburgers, and after that she might be on a diet and merely gnaw on a carrot while Sanna babbled on about how young girls needed to eat or risk succumbing to anorexia. Nothing was permanent, nothing was the way it used to be.

She wondered whether Niklas had the same problems with their daughter. Taking turns having Vendela stay with them every other week had worked out well for many years. But now Vendela seemed to have discovered the leverage she wielded. If she didn't like the food, she would say it was better at her father's place, and that he let her hang out with Nils in the evenings. Sometimes

Sanna felt utterly exhausted, and she wondered why she'd ever thought the early years of Vendela's life had been demanding; the teenage years seemed to be ten times worse.

It was as if her daughter had turned into a stranger. Vendela always used to be on at her mother the minute she spotted her sneaking a smoke behind the house, and she'd frequently lectured her about the risk of cancer. But lately Sanna had noticed that Vendela's clothes reeked of cigarette smoke.

Sanna glanced around at the shelves and finally made up her mind. She'd go for something safe. Tacos. And she bought both ground beef and tofu, just in case this turned out to be a vegan week.

These teenage phases had passed Sanna by; she'd grown up too fast for that. Stella's death, and all the awful things that followed, had catapulted her straight into adulthood. There had been no opportunity for teen angst, no parents to make her roll her eyes.

She'd met Niklas at the community college. They moved in together when she got her first job. Eventually they had Vendela – and Sanna had to admit the pregnancy had been an accident. The fact their relationship had failed was her fault, not his. Niklas was a good man, but she'd never been able to let him fully into her heart. Loving someone, no matter whether it was a spouse or a daughter, hurt too much. That was something she'd learned early on.

Sanna put tomatoes, cucumbers, and onions in her trolley and headed for the checkout.

'I suppose you've heard the news,' said Bodil as she began scanning the prices of each item Sanna placed on the conveyor belt.

'No, what's going on?' asked Sanna as she picked up a soda bottle and placed it flat on the belt.

'You didn't hear about the little girl?'

'What little girl?'

Sanna was listening with only half an ear. She was already regretting her decision to buy Coke for Vendela.

'The one who's disappeared. From your old farm.'

Bodil couldn't keep the excitement out of her voice. Sanna froze, holding the bag of Tex-Mex shredded cheese in her hand.

'Our farm?' she said, hearing a rushing sound in her ears.

'Yes,' said Bodil, continuing to scan the items without noticing that Sanna had stopped unloading her trolley. 'A four-year-old girl disappeared from your old farm. My husband went out to join the search party in the woods. I heard lots of people have turned up to help.'

Sanna slowly set the bag of cheese on the belt. Then she headed for the door, leaving her groceries behind. Her purse too. Behind her, she heard Bodil calling her name.

Anna leaned back in her chair and looked at Dan, who was sawing a board in half. Right now, in the worst of the summer heat, he'd decided it was the perfect time to get started on the 'new deck' project. They'd been talking about it for three years, but apparently it couldn't be put off any longer. She guessed his male nesting instincts had come into play. Her own nesting instincts had taken a different form. She'd been going through the clothing in all the wardrobes in the house. The kids had started hiding their favourite clothes, fearing they'd end up among the garments she was planning to give away.

Anna smiled at Dan as he worked in the heat. She realized that for the first time in ages she was actually enjoying life. Her small decorating business wasn't exactly ready to be launched on the stock market, but she'd won the trust of many of the discriminating summer visitors, and she was now having to turn away customers because she was too busy. And the baby was growing inside her. They'd decided not to find out the gender, so for now they simply called the child 'baby'. The other children were eagerly involved in trying to come up with a name, but with suggestions like 'Buzz Lightyear', 'RackarAlex', and 'Darth Vader', they hadn't been much help. And one night a grumpy Dan had quoted Fredde from the TV show *Solsidan*: 'We each made a list of suggested names, and then we took the one at the top of Mickan's.' All because she'd dissed his suggestion that, if the baby was a boy, they should call him Bruce after Bruce Springsteen. Dan claimed her choice, Philip, made it sound as if the kid was going to be born wearing a navy pea jacket. So that's how things stood. The birth was only a month away, and they still hadn't decided on a single name for a boy or a girl.

But it'll all work out, thought Anna as Dan came over to her. He leaned down and kissed her on the lips. He was sweaty and tasted of salt.

'So here you sit, relaxing,' he said, patting her belly.

'Yup. The kids have all gone out to visit friends,' she said, taking a sip of her iced coffee.

She'd heard it said pregnant women shouldn't drink too much coffee, but she needed some sort of treat for herself now that alcohol and unpasteurized cheese were both forbidden.

'I practically died at lunch today when my sister sat there sipping a big, cold glass of bubbly,' she moaned. Dan squeezed her shoulder.

He sat down next to her and leaned back with his eyes closed, enjoying the late afternoon sun.

'Soon, sweetheart,' he said, stroking her hand.

'I'm going to bathe in wine after the birth,' she sighed, as she too closed her eyes.

Then she remembered that pregnancy hormones put her at risk for brown spots. With a muttered curse she opened her eyes and put on her broad-brimmed hat.

'Shit. I can't even sunbathe,' she cursed.

'What?' said Dan drowsily, and she realized he was about to fall asleep in the sun.

'Nothing, sweetheart,' she said, although she suddenly had an irresistible urge to kick him in the shin, purely for being a man and not having to endure the pains of pregnancy or give up anything.

It was so fucking unfair. As for those women who sighed dreamily about how *wonderful* it was to be pregnant and what a *gift* it was to be the one who brought children into the world – well, she'd like to punch them. Hard.

'People are idiots,' she muttered.

'What?' Dan said again, this time sounding even drowsier.

'Nothing,' she said, pulling the brim of her hat down over her eyes.

What was she thinking about before Dan came over and interrupted her? Oh, right. How wonderful life was. And it was. In spite of the pregnancy pains and everything else. She was loved. She was surrounded by family.

She took off the hat and lifted her face to the sun. To hell with brown spots. Life was too short not to enjoy the sun.

Sam wished he could stay here forever. Ever since he was a kid, he'd loved it here. The heat from the rocks. The gurgling of the water. The screech of the seagulls. Out here he could escape from everything. He could close his eyes and let it all slip away.

Jessie was lying next to him. He could feel the warmth of her body. A miracle, that's what she was. The fact she'd come into his life at this particular moment. Marie Wall's daughter. What an irony of fate.

'Do you love your parents?'

Sam opened one eye and squinted at her. She was lying on her front with her chin propped on one hand, staring at him.

'Why are you asking?'

It was an intimate question. Especially since they'd known each other only a short time.

'I've never met my father,' she said, looking away.

'How come?'

Jessie shrugged.

'I don't know. I guess my mother didn't want me to. I'm not sure she even knows who my father is.'

Sam reached out his hand to touch her arm. She didn't flinch, so he left it there. Her eyes brightened.

'What about you? Do you have a good relationship with your parents?'

He'd been feeling so safe and calm, but now that disappeared. Yet he understood why she would ask, and he somehow felt he owed her an answer.

'My father, he's . . . well, he's been in the war. Sometimes he's gone for months at a time. And sometimes he brings the war home with him.'

Jessie leaned closer, resting her head on his shoulder.

'Has he ever . . .'

'I don't want to talk about it. Not yet.'

'What about your mother?'

Sam closed his eyes, letting the sunlight warm him.

'She's okay,' he said at last.

For a few seconds he thought about what he was refusing to think about, and he squeezed his eyes shut even tighter. Then he opened his eyes and fumbled in his pocket for the cigarettes he'd brought along. He took out two, lit both of them, and handed one to Jessie.

Calm spread through his body, the buzzing faded from inside his head, and the memories were carried away by the smoke. He leaned forward and kissed Jessie. At first she froze. From fear. From surprise. Then he felt her lips soften and let him in.

'Oh, how adorable!'

Sam gave a start.

'Look at the little lovebirds!'

Nils came sauntering down from the rocks with Basse and Vendela in tow. As always. They didn't seem to be capable of surviving without each other.

'So who's this?' Nils sat down right next to Sam and Jessie, staring at her intently as she pulled up her bikini top. 'Looks like you've found yourself a girlfriend, Sam.'

'I'm Jessie,' she told him, holding out her hand, which Nils ignored.

'Jessie?' said Vendela behind him. 'You must be Marie Wall's daughter.'

'Aha. The daughter of your mother's pal. The Hollywood star.'

Nils was now looking at Jessie with interest as she kept on tugging at her bikini top. Sam wanted to protect her from their prying eyes. He wanted to put his arms around her and tell her to pay them no mind. Instead he reached for her T-shirt.

'I guess it's no surprise that the two of you would find each other,' said Basse, giving Nils a poke in the side.

His voice was a shrill, feminine falsetto, but no one ever teased him about it for fear of drawing the wrath of Nils. His real name was Bosse, but in middle school he'd got everyone to call him Basse instead, because it sounded cooler.

'Yeah, I guess it's not really that strange,' said Nils, looking from Jessie to Sam.

'Okay, I'm fucking hungry,' he said. 'Let's get out of here.'

Vendela smiled at Jessie. 'See you later.'

Sam looked at them in surprise. Was that it?

Jessie leaned towards him.

'Who were those guys?' she said. 'They're weird. Nice, but weird.'

Sam shook his head.

'They're not nice. Not at all.'

He pulled his mobile out of his pocket, opened the photo file, and skimmed through the videos. He knew why he'd saved this particular video. It was a reminder of what people could do to each other. And to him. But he'd never planned to show it to Jessie. Enough people had already seen it.

'They posted this on Snapchat last summer,' he said, handing his mobile to Jessie. 'I managed to film it before it was removed.'

Sam looked away as Jessie clicked on the start button. He didn't need to watch it. When he heard the voices the whole scene clearly unfolded in his mind.

'You're so out of shape!' Nils had shouted. 'Wimpy like a girl. Swimming is good exercise.'

Nils had headed for Sam's boat, which was moored not far from where it was today.

'You can swim back to Fjällbacka. It'll build muscles.'

Vendela laughed as she filmed everything with her camera. Basse came running alongside Nils.

Nils tossed the mooring line into the boat, then set his foot on the bow and gave it a push. The small wooden boat began slowly backing away from the island, but it got caught in a current a few metres out, and the distance increased rapidly.

Nils turned towards the camera, grinning broadly.

'Have a nice swim.'

At that point the video ended.

'Holy shit,' said Jessie. 'Holy shit.'

She looked at Sam with tears in her eyes.

He shrugged.

'I've been through worse.'

Jessie blinked away her tears. He suspected that she too had survived worse experiences. He put his hand on her shoulder and felt how she was shaking. But he could also feel the bond between them. And what united them.

One day he would show her his notebook and share all his thoughts with her. Including his big plan. One day everyone would see.

Jessie wrapped her arms around his neck. She smelled so wonderful, of sun and sweat and marijuana.

It was getting late, but still light, like a memory of the sun that had shone all day from a clear blue sky. Eva looked towards the farmyard where the shadows were beginning to lengthen. Cold fingers seemed to clutch at her heart as she thought about Nea, who always hurried inside before dark fell.

People were coming and going out there. Voices mixed with barking from the dogs as they took turns to search. The ice-cold fingers again clutched at her heart.

The older officer, Gösta, came in the front door.

'I was thinking of having a cup of coffee, and then I'll go back out.'

Eva got up to pour him some coffee. She'd made countless pots of coffee over the past few hours.

'Nothing yet?' she asked, even though she knew the answer.

If he had any news, he would have told her at once instead of asking for coffee. But there was something comforting and soothing about asking the question.

'No, but we've got a big team out there searching. It feels like all of Fjällbacka has turned out.'

Eva nodded, trying to compose herself before speaking.

'Yes, everyone has been amazing,' she said, sinking down on her chair. 'Peter went out to join the search too. I couldn't keep him away.'

'I know.' Gösta sat down across from her. 'I saw him in one of the search groups.'

'What . . .' The words stuck in her throat. 'What do you think happened?'

She didn't dare look at Gösta. Various scenarios, each one worse than the last, kept running through her mind. Whenever she tried to seize hold of one of them, wanting to understand, the pain was so great she could hardly breathe.

'There's no use in speculating,' said Gösta gently, reaching out to place his hand on hers. His calm concern slowly warmed her.

'But she's been missing such a long time now.'

Gösta squeezed her hand.

'It's summer and it's warm outside. She's not going to freeze. The woods cover a large area, there's a lot of territory to search, and we simply need a few more hours. I'm sure we'll find her, and she'll be scared and upset, but no harm done. Okay?'

'Except . . . that's not what happened to the other little girl.'

Gösta pulled away his hand and took a sip of coffee.

'That was thirty years ago, Eva. Another lifetime, another era. It's pure coincidence that you're living on this farm, and it's pure coincidence that your daughter is the same age. Four-year-olds get lost. They're filled with curiosity and, from what I understand, your daughter is a lively little girl with an adventurous streak. Which means it's probably not so strange that she couldn't resist venturing into the woods. Obviously it didn't turn out the way she'd expected, but we're going to find her. There are so many of us searching.'

He stood up.

'Thanks for the coffee. I'll head back out now. We'll keep searching all night, but it would be a good idea for you to get some sleep.'

Eva shook her head. How could she sleep while Nea was out there in the woods?

'I didn't think you'd want to,' said Gösta, 'but at least I tried.'

She stared at the door after he closed it behind him. She was alone again. Alone with her thoughts and the cold fingers gripping her heart.

BOHUSLÄN 1671

Elin leaned forward to make Britta's bed. Then she straightened up and pressed her hand to her lower back. She was not yet accustomed to sleeping on the hard bed in the maid's quarters.

As she looked down at the comfortable bed where Britta slept, she allowed herself to feel something like envy, but only for a moment. With a shake of her head, she reached for the empty pitcher on the night table.

It had come as a surprise to discover that her sister did not share either a bedroom or a bed with her husband. But it was not her place to judge. For her part, she had always thought the best time of day was when she could climb into bed next to Per. Resting safely in his arms had made her feel that she and Märta would never come to harm in the world.

How wrong she had been.

'Elin?'

She started when she heard the gentle voice of the master of the house. She had been so lost in her own thoughts that she nearly dropped the pitcher.

'Yes?' she said, pausing to collect herself before turning around.

His kind blue eyes were fixed on her, and she felt the blood rush to her face. Quickly she lowered her eyes.

She did not know how to behave around her sister's husband. Preben was always so kind to her and Märta. He was both a vicar and master of the house. And she was merely a servant in her sister's employ. A widow living on the mercy of a household that was not her own.

'Lill-Jan says you can cure milk fever. My best milk cow is afflicted.'

'Is it Stjärna?' asked Elin, keeping her eyes fixed on the floor. 'The boy mentioned something about it this morning.'

'Yes, Stjärna. Are you busy or might you come with me to have a look at her?'

'Yes, of course I will come.'

She set the pitcher on the night table and silently followed Preben out to the cowshed. Stjärna lay on the stable floor at the very back, bellowing. She was clearly in pain and unable to stand. Elin nodded to the boy named Lill-Jan who stood nearby, looking dismayed.

'Go to the kitchen and get me some salt.'

She squatted down and cautiously caressed the cow's soft muzzle. Stjärna's eyes were wide with fear.

'Will you be able to help her?' asked Preben quietly as he too patted the brown-and-white spotted cow.

For a second their hands touched. Elin swiftly pulled hers away, as if she had been bitten by a snake. Again she felt the blood rush to her face, and she noticed a slight flush on the master's face before he straightened up as Lill-Jan returned, out of breath.

'Here you are,' said the boy with that lisp of his, and he handed the container of salt to Elin.

She poured a mound of salt into the palm of her left hand. With the index finger of her right hand she stirred

74

the salt in a clockwise direction as she loudly spoke the words her maternal grandmother had taught her:

'*Our Lord Jesus, he journeys far and wide, curing pox and blight, water bane and all manner of banes between heaven and earth. In God's name, amen.*'

'Amen,' said Preben, and Lill-Jan hurried to chime in. Stjärna bellowed.

'What happens now?' asked Preben.

'All we can do now is wait. Praying over salt most often will do the trick, but it can take time, and it also depends on how bad the fever is. But have a look at her early in the morning. I think this will have helped.'

'Hear that, Lill-Jan?' said Preben. 'Look in on Stjärna as soon as you get up in the morning.'

'That I will, master,' said Lill-Jan, backing his way out of the cowshed.

Preben turned to Elin.

'Where did you learn such things?'

'From my grandmother,' said Elin tersely.

She could still feel the touch of his hand.

'What else can you cure?' asked Preben, leaning against one of the stalls.

She scraped her toe on the ground, pausing before she answered.

'Most things as long as the pain is not too far gone.'

'Both people and animals?' asked Preben curiously.

'Yes,' replied Elin.

It surprised her that Britta had never mentioned this to her husband. Yet the boy Lill-Jan had heard rumours about Elin's skills. Perhaps that was not so strange, after all. When they lived together under their father's roof, her sister had always spoken scornfully about Elin's grandmother and her wisdom.

'Tell me more,' said Preben as he headed for the door.

Elin followed reluctantly. It was not proper for her to

be chatting with the master of the house in this manner, and it was all too easy for gossip to begin spreading on the farm. But Preben was the one in charge, so she had no choice but to follow him. Britta was standing outside, her arms hanging at her sides, a dark look on her face. Elin's heart sank. This was what she had feared. He risked nothing, but she could easily land in disfavour. And Märta along with her.

Her trepidation about how it might be to live at the mercy of her younger sister had been fully realized. Britta was a stern and unkind mistress, and both she and Märta had felt the sting of her sharp tongue.

'Elin has been helping me with Stjärna,' said Preben, calmly meeting his wife's eye. 'Now she is on her way to set the dinner table for us. She suggested that we might spend some time together, you and I, since I have been away so much lately, tending to church business.'

'Did she now?' said Britta, still suspicious, though not quite as stern as usual. 'Well, that was a good suggestion.'

She briskly took hold of Preben's arm.

'I have been missing my lord and master terribly, and I think he has been neglecting his wife of late.'

'My dear wife is perfectly right about that,' he replied, heading for the house along with Britta. 'But we will now make amends. Elin said we might sit down at the table in half an hour's time, which suits me well, as I will have time to wash and dress properly so I will not appear like a shabby ruffian next to my beautiful wife.'

'Oh, come now, you can never look shabby,' said Britta, slapping him on the shoulder.

Elin walked behind them, forgotten for the moment, and sighed with relief. The darkness she had glimpsed in Britta's eyes was all too familiar. She knew her sister would not hesitate to do harm to anyone she thought had wronged her. But this time Preben had saved her and Märta, and she would remain eternally grateful to him for that, even though he should not have placed her in this situation to begin with.

She picked up her pace and hurried to the kitchen. She had only half an hour to set out the food and ask the cook to prepare something special. She smoothed her apron, feeling again the warmth of Preben's hand.

'What are you doing, Pops?'

Bill had been so immersed in the text he was writing that he gave a start when his son spoke. He almost knocked over his cup, and some of the coffee sloshed over the side on to his desk.

He turned to look at Nils, who was standing in the doorway.

'I'm working on a new project,' he said, turning the computer screen so Nils could see.

'"Nicer People",' read Nils aloud.

Underneath the text was a picture of a sailboat ploughing its way through the water.

'I don't get it.'

'Don't you remember that documentary we saw? The Filip and Fredrik film, *Nice People*?'

Nils nodded.

'Oh, yeah. Those black guys who wanted to play bandy.'

Bill grimaced.

'The Somalis who wanted to play bandy. Don't call them "black guys".'

Nils shrugged.

Bill peered at his son standing there in the dim light

of the room with his hands in his pockets and his blond fringe hanging in his eyes. Nils had come along late in their lives. Unplanned and, to be honest, not particularly welcome. Gun had been forty-five when Nils was born, while he was almost fifty, and Nils's two older brothers were in their late teens. Gun had insisted they keep the child, saying there had to be some meaning behind her pregnancy. But Bill had never developed the same connection with Nils as he had with the older boys. He hadn't really tried. He hadn't wanted to change nappies or sit in the sandbox or read the first-grade maths book for the third time.

Bill turned back to the computer screen.

'This is a media presentation. My thought is to do something that will be a positive way of helping the refugees in the area become part of Swedish society.'

'Are you going to teach them how to play bandy?' asked Nils, his hands still in his pockets.

'Don't you see the sailboat?' Bill pointed at the screen. 'They're going to learn to sail! And then we'll compete in the Dannholmen regatta.'

'The Dannholmen regatta isn't exactly the same thing as the bandy world championship those blacks competed in,' said Nils. 'Not the same league at all.'

'Don't call them blacks!' said Bill.

Nils was undoubtedly trying to provoke him.

'I know the Dannholmen regatta is a significantly smaller event, but it has great symbolic importance around here, and it will attract a lot of media attention. Especially now they're making that film here.'

Nils snorted. 'I don't know if they're really refugees at all. Only people who have money can make their way up here. I read that on the Internet. And those so-called refugee kids have beards and moustaches.'

'Nils!'

Bill looked at his son, whose face was now flushed with indignation. It was like looking at a stranger. If he didn't know better, he'd think his son was . . . a racist. But that wasn't possible. Teenagers knew so little about the ways of the world. All the more reason to promote this type of project. Most people were basically good at heart. They just needed to be educated, given a little push in the right direction. Nils would soon realize how wrong he was.

Bill heard his son leave the room and close the door behind him. Tomorrow was the start-up meeting, and he needed to have everything ready for the press. This was going to be big. Really big.

'Hello?' called Paula as she and Johanna came in the door with three suitcases and two prams. She was carrying the baby, balanced on her hip.

Paula smiled at Johanna as she set down the heaviest suitcase. A holiday on Cyprus with a three-year-old and an infant probably hadn't been the smartest plan, but they'd survived.

'I'm in the kitchen!'

Paula relaxed as soon as she heard her mother's voice. If Rita and Bertil were home, she could leave the kids with them so she and Johanna could unpack in peace and quiet. Or else they could forget about unpacking until tomorrow and instead stretch out on the bed to watch a film until they fell asleep.

Rita gave them a smile as they came into the kitchen. There was nothing strange about her cooking in their kitchen as if it were her own. Rita and Bertil lived in the flat upstairs, but ever since the kids were born, the boundaries between the two flats had disappeared to such an extent that they might as well have installed a direct staircase from one to the other.

'I made enchiladas. I thought you'd be hungry after the trip. How did things go?'

She reached out her arms to take Lisa.

'Fine. Or rather, not so great,' said Paula, gratefully handing over the baby. 'Shoot me if I ever start talking again about how wonderful it would be to go away for a week with the kids.'

'It was your idea,' muttered Johanna as she tried to wake Leo, who had fallen asleep.

'It was nuts,' said Paula, taking a pinch of melted golden cheese from the top of one of the enchiladas. 'Kids everywhere, grown people dressed up like cuddly toys walking around in the heat and singing some sort of battle song.'

'I don't think you could really call it a battle song,' said Johanna, laughing.

'Okay, but it was indoctrination from some kind of sect. If I'd been forced to listen to it one more time I was going to go over and strangle that big hairy bear.'

'Tell her about the chocolate fountain,' said Johanna.

Paula groaned.

'Oh my God. Every night they had a buffet, specially designed for kids, so there were tons of pancakes, meatballs, pizza, and spaghetti. And a chocolate fountain. One boy made quite an impression. Everyone knew this kid's name was Linus, because his mother ran around the whole time yelling: "No, no, Liiinus! Don't do that, Liiinus! Stop kicking that girl, Liiinus!" Meanwhile the boy's father was busy chugging down the beer, starting right after breakfast. And on the last day . . .'

Johanna couldn't help giggling as Paula picked up a plate, helped herself to an enchilada, and sat down at the kitchen table.

'On the last day,' she went on, 'Linus ran right into that huge chocolate fountain and knocked it over. There was chocolate everywhere! And he threw himself down in it and began smearing chocolate all around, while his mother jumped up and down, completely hysterical.'

She took a big bite of her food and sighed. This was the first taste of anything spicy all week.

'Uncle Bertil?' said Leo, starting to wake up as Johanna held him.

'Yes, where is Bertil?' asked Paula. 'Has he already fallen asleep in front of the TV?'

'No,' said Rita. 'He's working.'

'This late?'

Bertil rarely worked nights.

'Yes, he had to go. But you're still on maternity leave,' said Rita, casting a hesitant look at Johanna.

She knew it hadn't been easy to get her daughter to take time off, and Johanna was still worried that Paula might go back to work too soon. The plan was for the family to spend the whole summer together.

'So what's going on?' asked Paula, putting down her knife and fork.

'They went out to search for someone who's gone missing.'

'Who's missing?'

'A child,' said Rita, avoiding her eye. 'A four-year-old girl.'

She knew her daughter all too well.

'How long has the little girl been missing?'

'Since last night, but the parents didn't discover she was gone until this afternoon, so the search has only been going on for a couple of hours.'

Paula cast a pleading look at Johanna, who glanced at Leo and nodded.

'Go. They'll need all the help they can get.'

Paula got up and gave her partner a kiss on the cheek. 'Love you. I'll be back soon.' She went into the hall and pulled on a lightweight jacket. 'Where are they?' she asked her mother.

'On a farm. Bertil called it the Berg farm.'

'The Berg farm?'

Paula abruptly stopped what she was doing. She knew that farm well. And its history. And she was too much of a cynic to believe in coincidences.

Karim knocked hard on the door. He knew Adnan was inside, and he had no intention of leaving until he opened the door. The years they'd spent in a world where a knock on the door could spell death, for themselves or a family member, meant that many refugees were reluctant to open the door. Karim pounded on the door again. Finally it opened.

When he saw Adnan staring at him wide-eyed, he was almost sorry he'd knocked so hard.

'I just talked to Rolf, and he said all of Fjällbacka is out looking for a missing girl. We need to help.'

'A girl? A child?'

'Yes. Rolf said she's four years old. They think she might be lost in the woods.'

'Of course we'll help.' Adnan turned to look back inside the room as he reached for his jacket. 'Khalil, come here!'

Karim backed up a few steps.

'We need you to help round everyone up. Tell them we'll meet up at the kiosk. Rolf has promised to drive us there.'

'Sure. And we'd better hurry. A little girl shouldn't be all alone in the woods at night.'

Karim continued knocking on doors, and he heard Khalil and Adnan doing the same. After a while they'd gathered fifteen others to help out. Rolf would have to make two or three trips to get them all there, but that wasn't a problem. He was a nice person. He wanted to help.

For a moment Karim felt uncertain. Rolf was nice, and he knew them. But how would the other Swedes react when they turned up? A bunch of roaches from the refugee centre. He knew that's what people called them. Roaches. Or wogs. But a child was missing, and it was everyone's responsibility to find her. It didn't matter whether she was Swedish or Syrian. Somewhere a mother was crying in despair.

When Rolf pulled up in his car, Karim, Adnan, and Khalil were waiting along with Rashid and Farid. Karim glanced at Rashid. His children were back in Syria. Rashid met Karim's eye. He didn't know whether his own children were still alive, but tonight he was going to help search for a Swedish little girl.

It was blissfully quiet now the kids were in bed. Sometimes Erica felt guilty about how much she enjoyed the peace in the evenings. When Maja was little she'd joined the web forum Family Life in an attempt to find like-minded people and to get things off her chest. She thought she couldn't be the only one who was experiencing a conflict between being a mother and needing time to herself once in a while. But she'd received such a hate-filled response when she'd honestly written about her feelings that she'd never gone back to the forum. She'd been caught off guard by the curses and insults other mothers had hurled at her, just because she didn't love every minute she spent breastfeeding, getting up in the middle of the night, changing nappies, and listening to her baby crying. She'd been told she should not have had a child, that she was an egotistical and self-absorbed bitch because she felt the need for time on her own. Erica could still feel the anger surging inside her at the thought of those women judging her because she didn't act and feel the same as them. Why can't everyone do whatever is best for them? she wondered as she sat on the sofa with a glass of red wine, trying to relax in front of the TV.

Her thoughts soon turned to another mother. Nea's mother, Eva. She could only imagine what anguish she must be feeling right now. Erica had sent Patrik a text to ask again whether she could help. She could get Kristina to come over to look after the kids. But he had told her they already had all the volunteers they needed, and she would be more useful staying at home with the children.

Erica didn't know the Bergs, and she'd never been to their farm. Wanting to describe the setting as precisely as possible, she'd thought about going out there to have a look around and take a few pictures, but so far she hadn't done it. There were old photographs available, so she knew exactly how the farm had looked when the Strand family lived there. Yet it was always a different experience to visit a location in person, to take in the atmosphere and get a feeling for how life on the farm must have been.

She'd enquired about the Berg family and learned they'd moved here from Uddevalla, looking for peace and quiet in the country and a good place for their daughter to grow up. Erica sincerely hoped their dream would be realized, that she'd soon get a text from Patrik saying they'd found the child in the woods, scared and lost, but alive. Yet she had a bad feeling that was not how this would end.

She swirled the red wine in her glass. She'd treated herself to a good Amarone in spite of the oppressive evening heat. Most people drank chilled rosé wines in the summer, or white wine served with ice cubes. But she didn't care for either white or rosé wines. She preferred sparkling wines or intense red wines, no matter what the season. That said, she couldn't tell the difference between an expensive champagne and a cheap Spanish cava, so as Patrik liked to joke, she was a cheap date.

She felt guilty, sitting in comfort and drinking wine when a four-year-old girl, in the best-case scenario, was lost in the woods. But that was how her mind worked. It was too awful to dwell on all the bad things that might happen to a child, so she subconsciously turned her thoughts to something banal and meaningless. That was a luxury Nea's mother couldn't afford at the moment. She and her husband had found themselves caught in a living nightmare.

Erica straightened up and set her wine glass on the coffee table. She reached for her notebook. Over the years she'd got in the habit of always having paper and pen nearby. She liked to jot down whatever thoughts and ideas popped into her head, and she made lists of things she needed to do in order to move forward with her book. That was what she wanted to do now. All her instincts told her that Nea's disappearance was somehow connected to Stella's death. She'd spent the past few weeks loafing. Summertime laziness and sunshine had taken over, and she hadn't made the sort of progress she'd hoped with her book. Now she was going to set her mind to it. That way, if the worst happened, she might be able to offer help, based on what she'd learned about the previous case. Maybe she could find the link that she was sure existed.

Erica glanced at her mobile. Still no word from Patrik. Then she began feverishly jotting down notes.

THE STELLA CASE

She knew even before they reached her. The heavy footsteps. Their eyes fixed on the ground. They didn't have
to say a word.

'Anders!' she screamed, and her voice was so shrill.

He came rushing out of the house, but stopped abruptly
when he saw the police officers.

He fell to his knees on the gravel. Linda rushed over
to him, put her arms around him. Anders had always
been so big and strong, but right now she was the one
who had to keep them both going.

'Pappa? Mamma?'

Sanna stood in the doorway. The light from the kitchen
lit up her blond hair like a halo.

'Did they find Stella, Mamma?'

Linda couldn't meet her daughter's eye. She turned
towards one of the officers. He nodded.

'We've found your daughter. I'm afraid she's . . . she's
dead. We're so sorry.'

He stared down at his shoes and swallowed hard to
hold back the tears. He was as pale as a ghost, and Linda
wondered whether he'd seen Stella. Seen the body.

'But how can she be dead? That can't be true. Mamma?
Pappa?'

She heard Sanna's voice behind her, rattling off questions. But Linda had no answers to give her. Nor any solace to offer. She knew she ought to let go of Anders and take her daughter in her arms. But only Anders understood the pain she now felt in every fibre of her body.

'We want to see her,' she said, finally making herself raise her head from Anders's shoulder. 'We have to see our daughter.'

The taller of the two officers cleared his throat.

'And you will. But first we have to do our job. We have to find out who did this.'

'What do you mean? It was an accident, surely?'

Anders pulled away from Linda and stood up.

The tall policeman quietly replied.

'I'm afraid this was no accident. Your daughter was murdered.'

The ground suddenly rose up towards Linda. She didn't even have time to be surprised before everything went black.

❦

Only twenty more to go.

James Jensen was hardly out of breath as he did the next push-up. The same routine every morning, in summer as well as winter. On Christmas Eve and on Midsummer Eve. These sorts of things had meaning. Routines had meaning. Consistency. Order.

Ten left.

Helen's father had understood the meaning of routines. James still missed KG, although the feeling was a form of weakness he normally didn't allow himself. KG had suffered a heart attack almost ten years ago, and no one had ever been able to take his place.

The last one. James got up after his hundred push-ups. A long life spent in the military had taught him the value of being in top physical condition.

James glanced at his watch: 08.01. He was behind schedule. When he was home he always had breakfast at eight o'clock sharp.

'Breakfast is ready!' called Helen, as if she'd read his mind.

James frowned. The fact she was calling him meant she'd noticed he was late.

He used a towel to dry off the sweat, then left the

deck and went into the living room. The kitchen was right next door, and he could smell bacon cooking. He always ate the same breakfast. Scrambled eggs and bacon.

'Where's Sam?' he asked as he sat down and started in on the eggs.

'He's still sleeping,' said Helen as she served him the bacon, which was perfectly crisp.

'It's eight o'clock and he's still asleep?'

Annoyance crept over him, as it always did when he thought about Sam. Sleeping past eight in the morning? He'd always been up by six in the summertime, and then he'd worked until late in the evening.

'Go wake him,' he said, taking a swig of coffee, but the next instant he spat it out. 'What the hell? No milk?'

'Oh, sorry,' said Helen, taking the cup from his hand.

She poured the coffee into the sink, refilled it, and added a dash of whole milk.

Now it tasted the way it should.

Helen hurried out of the kitchen. He could hear her rushing up the stairs, followed by a murmur of voices.

His annoyance returned. The same annoyance he felt when he was deployed with a unit and one or more of the soldiers tried to downplay or avoid situations out of fear. He couldn't understand that kind of behaviour. If a man chose to join the military, especially in a country like Sweden where it was completely voluntary to deploy to a war zone in another country, then he should do the job he'd been assigned. Fear was something you left at home.

'Where's the fire?' grumbled Sam as he came sauntering into the kitchen, his black hair standing on end. 'Why do I have to get up at this hour of the morning?'

James clenched his fists under the table.

'In this house we don't sleep away the day,' he said.

'But I couldn't find a summer job, so what the hell am I supposed to do?'

'No swearing!'

Both Helen and Sam flinched. For a moment anger made everything go black before his eyes, and James forced himself to take several deep breaths. He had to maintain control, both over himself and over his family.

'At nine hundred hours we'll meet out back for target practice.'

'Okay,' said Sam, looking down at the table.

Behind him Helen was still cringing.

They'd been walking all night. Harald was so tired he could hardly see straight, but he had no intention of going home. That would mean giving up. Whenever the fatigue got the better of him, he'd returned to the farm for a short break to warm up and drink some coffee. Each time he'd found Eva Berg sitting mutely in the kitchen, her face grey with worry. That was enough for him to go back out to rejoin the search party.

He wondered whether the others knew who he was. And what role he'd played thirty years ago. He was the one who had found the other little girl. People who had lived in Fjällbacka back then knew about it, of course, but he didn't think Eva and Peter did. At least, he hoped not.

When they were assigned search areas, he had deliberately chosen the area with the lake where he'd found Stella. And that was the first place he'd gone to search. The small lake had dried up long ago, leaving behind only a patch of wooded land. But the old tree trunk was still there. The huge tree had clearly withstood a good deal of wind and weather, and it looked more brittle and drier than thirty years earlier. But he found no little girl lying there. He caught himself heaving a sigh of relief.

The search party had regrouped several times during the night. Some people had gone home to get a few hours' sleep, then come back and joined different groups. New volunteers had also arrived as the summer night gave way to morning. Those who had not gone home to rest included the men and boys from the refugee centre. Harald had chatted with them as they searched. They spoke in halting Swedish while he tried out his halting English. But somehow they'd managed to communicate.

He was now part of a small group that included the man who had introduced himself as Karim, and Johannes Klingsby, a local builder whom Harald had hired whenever he needed renovations done at the bakery. They were moving slowly and resolutely through the woods as the sun broke through and the day brightened. The police officers in charge of the search had reminded them several times during the night not to hurry. It was best to make their way forward carefully and methodically.

'We've been searching this area all night,' said Johannes. 'She can't have gone this far.'

He threw out his hands.

'Last time we spent twenty-four hours searching,' said Harald.

Once again he pictured Stella's body in his mind.

'What?' asked Karim in English, shaking his head. It was hard for him to understand Harald's broad Bohuslän accent.

'Harald was the one who found the dead girl in the woods, thirty years ago,' Johannes explained in English.

'Dead girl?' said Karim, stopping. 'Here?'

'Yes. Four years old, same as this girl.'

Johannes held up four fingers.

Karim looked at Harald, who nodded quietly.

'Yes. It was right over here. But there was water back then.'

He was ashamed of his poor English, but Karim nodded.

'There,' said Harald, pointing at the tree trunk. 'It was not a big lake, it was a . . . the Swedish word is "tjärn".'

'A small lake, more like a pond,' Johannes chimed in.

'Yes, yes. A pond,' said Harald. 'A pond over there by that tree, and the girl was dead.'

Karim slowly walked towards the tree. He squatted down and placed his hand on the trunk. When he turned to look at the other men, his face was so pale that Harald took a step back.

'Something is under the tree. I can see a hand. A small hand.'

Harald staggered back another step. Johannes leaned over a bush, and they soon heard him sobbing. Harald met Karim's eye and saw a reflection of his own despair. They needed to call the police.

Marie held the script on her lap as she tried to learn her lines for the upcoming scene, but she couldn't concentrate. The scene was going to be filmed indoors, in the big industrial warehouse in Tanumshede. Inside, they'd constructed a number of sets, almost like mini-worlds, ready for the actors to enter. For the most part, the rest of the filming would be done on location, on the island of Dannholmen. Ingrid Bergman had spent a great deal of time on the island when she was married to the theatre director Lars Schmidt. She'd carried on visiting Dannholmen long after she and Lars were divorced.

Marie stretched out her arms and shook her head. She wanted to be rid of all the thoughts that had started haunting her when people began talking about the missing girl. All those memories of a laughing Stella running ahead of her and Helen.

Marie sighed. She was here now, about to play her dream role. This was what she'd been working towards for so many years; it was the thing that had kept her going after the roles in Hollywood dried up. She'd earned this part, and she was a good actress. It didn't take much effort for her to immerse herself in a role, pretending to be someone else; after all, she'd had plenty of practice, ever since she was a child. Lying or acting – there was so little difference between the two. She'd learned to master both early on.

If only she could stop thinking about Stella.

'How does my hair look?' she asked Yvonne.

The make-up artist approached nervously and came to such an abrupt halt she almost stumbled. She surveyed Marie from head to toe, then removed a comb stuck in the bun at the nape of her neck and smoothed a few stray strands of hair. She handed Marie a mirror and waited for her to inspect the results.

'It looks fine,' said Marie, and the tense, anxious look on Yvonne's face vanished.

Marie turned towards the designated wardrobe area where Jörgen was arguing with Sixten, who was in charge of lighting.

'Are you ready for me yet?' she asked.

'Give us another fifteen minutes!' called Jörgen.

His frustration was obvious in his voice. Marie knew why. Delays cost money.

Once again she wondered how things were going with the finance for the film. This wasn't the first time she'd worked on a film that started shooting before the money was in place, and on those previous occasions the plug had been pulled on the entire production. Nothing was certain until they passed the point when the film had already cost so much that it wouldn't be feasible to stop. But they weren't there yet.

'Excuse me, but could I ask you a few questions while you're waiting?'

Marie looked up from her script. A man in his thirties was looking at her with a big smile on his face. Obviously a reporter. Normally, she would never agree to an interview that hadn't been scheduled in advance, but his skin-tight T-shirt showed off well-toned muscles that made her reluctant to dismiss him out of hand.

'Sure, ask away. I'm only sitting here waiting.'

Thankfully, Ingrid had always been stylish, so the shirt she was wearing for today's scene was particularly flattering.

The guy with the six-pack introduced himself as Axel, a reporter from *Bohusläningen*. He began with several banal questions about the film and her career before he got to what was clearly the purpose of the interview. Marie leaned back and crossed her long legs. The past had served her career well.

'So how does it feel to be back here? Oh, I almost said "back at the scene of the crime", but let's call that a Freudian slip. Because you and Helen have always maintained your innocence.'

'We *were* innocent,' said Marie, noting with satisfaction that the young reporter couldn't stop staring at her décolletage.

'Even after you were found guilty of the crime?' said Axel, making an effort to tear his gaze away from her chest.

'We were children and completely incapable of committing such a crime, even though we were charged and convicted. Witch hunts still go on, even in this day and age.'

'So what was it like for you, in the years that followed?'

Marie tossed her head. She would never be able to describe those years to him. He'd probably grown up with two perfect parents who helped him with everything, and he now lived with a significant other and their kids. She glanced at his left hand. A wife, not a significant other, she corrected herself.

'It was . . . educational,' she said. 'I plan to write about it in detail in my memoirs some day. It's not something I can describe in a few sentences.'

'Since you mention your memoirs, I've heard that the local author, Erica Falck, is planning to write a book about the murder and about you and Helen. Are you cooperating with her? And have you and Helen approved the book?'

Marie hesitated before answering. Erica had contacted her, but she was in negotiations with one of the big book publishers in Stockholm regarding her own version of the story.

'I haven't yet decided whether to cooperate,' she said, signalling that she had no intention of answering any more questions on that topic.

Axel took the hint and changed the subject.

'I assume you've heard about the little girl who's been missing since yesterday? From the same farm where Stella was living when she disappeared.'

'A strange coincidence, but no more than that. The girl probably just got lost somewhere.'

'Let's hope so,' said Axel.

He glanced down at his notebook, but at that moment Jörgen motioned for Marie. PR was great, but right now she wanted to go into the Dannholmen living room set and put on a brilliant performance. She had to convince the backers that this film was going to be a hit.

She shook hands with Axel, holding his hand a little longer than necessary as she thanked him for the interview. She began walking towards Jörgen and the rest of the team, but then stopped and turned around. Axel's tape recorder was still rolling, and Marie leaned forward and in a hoarse voice spoke a few numbers into the microphone. She glanced at Axel.

'That's my phone number.'

Then she turned away and stepped into the 1970s,

entering the set of the windswept island that had been Ingrid Bergman's paradise on earth.

As soon as Patrik took the call from an unknown number, he knew this would be the news they'd been dreading. He listened to the voice on the other end of the line, then motioned to Gösta and Mellberg who were standing a short distance away talking to the dog handlers.

'Yes, I know where it is,' he said. 'Don't touch a thing. Not a thing. Wait there until we arrive.'

By the time he ended the call, Mellberg and Gösta had joined him. There was no need to say a word. One look at his expression told them all they needed to know.

'Where is she?' Gösta asked.

His eyes were fixed on the farmhouse where Nea's mother was standing in the kitchen making more coffee.

'The same place where the other girl was found.'

'Bloody hell!' said Mellberg.

'But we already searched that area. Several groups have searched it,' said Gösta with a frown. 'How could they have missed her?'

'I don't know,' said Patrik. 'That was Harald on the phone – the man who owns Zetterlind bakery. It was his group that found her.'

'The same guy who found Stella,' said Gösta quietly.

Mellberg stared at him.

'That's quite a coincidence. What are the odds that the same person, after a thirty-year gap, would find a second murdered little girl?'

Gösta waved his hand dismissively.

'We checked him out the first time, but he had an airtight alibi. He had nothing to do with the murder.' He looked at Patrik. 'Because this is murder, right? Not an accident? Considering that she was found at the same spot, it seems more than likely we're talking about murder.'

Patrik nodded.

'We'll need to wait and see what the techs say, but Harald said she was naked.'

'Bloody hell,' said Mellberg again, his face turning pale.

Patrik took a deep breath. The morning sun had begun its climb upward, and the temperature had already risen so much that his shirt was sticking to his body with sweat.

'I suggest we split up. I'll go and meet Harald at the site where the girl was found. His group is waiting there. I'll take some crime scene tape with me and cordon off the area. Bertil, ring Torbjörn in Uddevalla and ask him to come out here as fast as possible with a forensic team. When the search parties get back here, tell them the search has been called off. We don't want any volunteers going out searching again. And tell the dog handlers and the helicopter pilots they can stop looking. Gösta, could you . . .'

Patrik fell silent, giving his colleague a troubled look. Gösta nodded.

'I'll do it,' he said.

Patrik didn't envy him the task. But it was only logical for him to ask Gösta to do it. He'd had the most contact with Nea's parents, and Patrik knew he would be able to deal with the situation.

'And ring the pastor too,' said Patrik. Then he turned to Mellberg. 'Bertil, go get Nea's father as soon as he comes back with his group, so he doesn't hear the news before Gösta has a chance to speak to him.'

'That won't be easy,' said Mellberg, grimacing.

Beads of sweat had formed on his upper lip.

'I know. The news is going to spread like wildfire, but do your best.'

Mellberg nodded. Patrik left his colleagues and headed for the woods. He still couldn't understand it. The place where Stella had been found thirty years ago had been the first location they'd searched. Yet somehow they had missed her.

After walking for ten minutes he caught sight of the three men who were waiting for him. In addition to Harald, there were two younger men, one of whom looked like a foreigner. Patrik shook hands and greeted them. Not one of them wanted to meet his eye.

'Where is she?' he asked.

'Under the big tree trunk over there,' said Harald, pointing. 'That's why we didn't see her at first. There's a hollow space underneath, and someone stuffed her body into it. You can only see her if you go close and move the tree trunk.'

Patrik nodded. That explained it. But he cursed himself for not giving the order to search the area more thoroughly.

'You know she's back, right? For the first time since she was sent away.'

Patrik didn't have to ask who Harald meant. Everybody in town was aware of Marie Wall's return, especially since she'd come back under such dramatic circumstances.

'Yes, we know,' he said without speculating any further about what her return might mean.

But the thought had already occurred to him. It was certainly a strange coincidence, to say the least: no sooner had Marie returned than another little girl from the same farm turned up murdered, in the exact same spot where Stella was found.

'I'm going to cordon off the area, and in a while our forensics team will inspect the crime scene.'

He set down the bag he was carrying and took out two big rolls of blue-and-white police tape.

'Should we go back?' asked the younger man, who'd introduced himself as Johannes.

'No, I'd like all of you to stay. Try not to move around

99

too much. The techs will want to examine your clothing and shoes, since you've been walking around the crime scene.'

The man who seemed to be a foreigner looked puzzled. Harald turned to him and said in halting English:

'We stay here. Okay, Karim?'

'Okay,' said the man with a nod. Patrik realized he was one of the men Rolf had brought from the refugee centre.

No one spoke for a few minutes. They were all struck by the surreal contrast between the reason for their presence and the idyllic surroundings. The birds carried on chirping merrily, as if nothing had happened, as if the dead body of a four-year-old girl wasn't lying just metres away. The birdsong was accompanied by the rustle of the gentle breeze in the treetops. At this time of day, with the sun's rays penetrating the trees to light the glade where they stood, it was heartbreakingly beautiful. Patrik's gaze settled on a patch of chanterelles. Under normal circumstances, his heart would have leapt with excitement at the prospect of harvesting a few to take home. But right now picking mushrooms was the furthest thing from his mind.

Patrik began unwinding the tape. The only thing he could do for the little girl was to carry out his job to the best of his ability. So he worked in silence, and tried to avoid looking at the tree trunk.

Eva was standing at the sink, rinsing out the coffee pot. She'd lost count of how many pots she'd made during the night. The sound of someone quietly clearing his throat made her turn around. When she saw the look in Gösta's eyes and his tense posture, the coffee pot slipped out of her grasp. The sound of breaking glass was instantly followed by a scream that sounded so close, yet so far away. A scream of grief and loss beyond all comprehension.

The scream came from her own lips.

She fell into Gösta's arms. His hold on her was the only thing keeping her from collapsing. She gasped for breath as Gösta stroked her hair. She wished Nea was here, laughing as she ran around the room. She wished Nea had never been born, wished she'd never produced a child who would then be taken from her.

Now all was lost. Everything had died with Nea.

'I've notified the pastor,' said Gösta, leading her over to a kitchen chair.

He must see how broken I am inside, thought Eva, since he's treating me so carefully.

'Why did you do that?' she asked, genuinely confused.

What could a pastor do for her now? She'd never had a strong religious faith. And a child should be with her parents, not with some god up in heaven. What could a pastor say that she and Peter would find the least bit consoling?

'Peter?' she said, her voice sounding parched and brittle.

Even her voice had died with Nea.

'They're looking for him. He'll be here soon.'

'No,' she said, shaking her head. 'Don't do it. Don't tell him.'

Let him stay out there in the woods, she thought. Let him still have hope. Peter was the only one left now. She had died with Nea.

'He has to be told, Eva,' said Gösta, putting his arm around her again. 'There's no way to avoid it.'

Eva nodded as she leaned against Gösta. Of course Peter couldn't keep wandering through the woods like some kind of forest creature. They had to tell him, even though that would mean he too would die.

She pulled away from Gösta and leaned forward to lay her head on the table. She'd been awake for twenty-four hours. Hope and fear had kept her going. Now all she wanted was to sleep and escape everything. Pretend it was all a bad dream. Her body relaxed, the wooden tabletop felt as soft as a pillow under her cheek. She slipped further and further away. A warm hand was cautiously patting her back. Warmth spread through her body.

Then someone came in the front door. She didn't want to open her eyes. She didn't want to see Peter standing there. But Gösta gave her shoulder a squeeze, and she had to do it. She looked up and met Peter's gaze, which was just as shattered as her own.

BOHUSLÄN 1671

The cow named Stjärna had recovered by the time Lill-Jan went to see to her the next morning. Preben said nothing to Elin about it, but he looked at her with new interest. She felt him watching her as she prepared breakfast. Britta had been in an unusually good mood when Elin helped her sister to dress. But she was always happiest on Sundays. She loved sitting at the very front of the church during the services, wearing her best clothes and with her hair beautifully coiffed. She loved seeing the pews fill with the members of Preben's congregation.

It was not a long walk from the vicarage to the church, and the servants went as a group. Preben and Britta had gone ahead in the horse-drawn wagon so Britta's fine clothes would not be soiled by muck and mire.

Elin held Märta's hand in a tight grip. The girl scampered more than she walked, and her blond plaits bounced against the back of the old cloak she wore. It was freezing cold, and Elin had carefully stuffed paper inside Märta's shoes to keep her feet warm and dry, but also because the shoes were hand-me-downs from one of the maids whose feet were much bigger. But Märta did not complain. Shoes were shoes, and she had already learned to be happy with what she had.

Elin's heart lifted when she saw the church looming before them as they reached Vinbäck. The newly built tower was a stately sight, and the metal roof gleamed in the winter sun. A cemetery wall made of red-painted planks surrounded the church, and there were three big brick entrances with roof tiles, and iron gates to prevent livestock from wandering into the cemetery.

Merely stepping inside the churchyard made Elin's heart sing, and when they entered the church itself she took a deep breath and allowed the silent atmosphere to seep inside her.

She and Märta took seats at the very back. There were forty-eight pews in all, but lately they were never filled. The crowds of people who had once flocked to the coastal area during the great herring era a hundred years earlier were now only a memory. Elin's maternal grandmother had told her about the old days, recounting stories she had heard from her own parents and grandparents. Back then, everything had been different. The herring was so abundant they hardly knew what to do with all the fish, and people had come from all over Sweden to settle in the area. But the herring had disappeared and war and famine had depleted the land. Now only the stories remained. And many pews stood empty, while the rest were occupied by the listless, pale, and gaunt residents of Bohuslän. Looking at their faces, Elin saw a defeated people, devoid of hope.

The church had windows only on the south wall, but the light streaming in was so lovely that she felt tears well up in her eyes. The pulpit was also on the south side. The murmuring among the congregation faded as Preben climbed the stairs to the pulpit.

The service began with a hymn, and Elin put extra effort into the song, as she usually did, since she knew she had a beautiful singing voice. It was a small vanity she allowed herself because Märta loved to hear her sing.

She tried hard to understand what Preben was saying. Swedish was the only language permitted in the church, both for the sermon and the prayers. This was a great burden for most members of the congregation, since they were more accustomed to speaking Danish and Norwegian.

But he had a lovely voice. Elin closed her eyes and immediately felt the warmth of Preben's hand. She opened her eyes and forced herself to stare at the back of Britta's head, at the very front of the church. Britta wore her hair in a beautiful plait that Elin had fixed for her that morning. The white collar of her dress was freshly starched. She was nodding as Preben preached.

Elin forced her thoughts away from the sound of Preben's voice and the memory of his hand touching hers. He was Britta's husband, yet she was sitting here in God's house thinking these forbidden thoughts. It would come as no surprise if lightning struck the church and killed her on the spot, as punishment for her ungodliness. She squeezed Märta's hand and made herself listen, trying to understand the words issuing from the pulpit. Preben was talking about the great turmoil spreading across their kingdom and their parish, and about their countrymen who were carrying on a brave fight against the devil by seeking out his envoys and bringing them to trial. The congregation listened as if mesmerized. The devil was as much a part of their daily lives as God was. Satan was omnipresent – danger lurked in the eyes of cats, in the ocean deep, in the raven perched in the tree. Satan was as real as a father or a brother, or the neighbour living next door. The fact that the evil one could not be seen by the naked eye made him even more dangerous, and constant vigilance was required.

'So far we have been spared,' said Preben, his voice resounding so beautifully between the stone walls. 'But it is only a matter of time before Satan sinks his claws into children and women in our little corner of the world as well. So I beseech you to be watchful. The signs will be evident. Keep God's watchful eye on your wife, your daughter, your maids, your neighbour, your mother-in-law, and your sister. The sooner we find these brides of the devil who dwell among us, the sooner we can strike back and prevent Satan from claiming a foothold here.'

Everyone nodded, an agitated rosy flush appearing on their cheeks. Any of the children who sniggered received a sharp poke in the side, a tug on their hair, or a box on the ear.

The rest of the church service was over much too soon. It was a break from the daily routine, a time for everyone to rest and turn their attention to the needs of their soul.

Elin stood up and took a firm grip on Märta's hand so she would not get lost in the crowd of people all trying to leave at once. When they stepped outside, she shivered in the cold.

'Pox upon you!' a voice cried behind her.

Elin turned in surprise, but when she saw who had cursed her she lowered her eyes. It was Ebba of Mörhult, the widow of Claes who had perished along with Per and the others on the fishing boat. Ebba was one of the reasons she had not been able to stay in Fjällbacka but had been forced instead to accept Britta's offer. Ebba's hatred towards her knew no bounds, since she blamed Elin for what happened. And Elin knew why the woman felt that way, even though the words she had called to Per on that fateful morning had not caused the boat to sink. Elin's words had not drowned Per and his men; it was the fault of the storm that had suddenly overtaken them.

Yet things had not gone well for Ebba after Claes died, and she blamed her misfortune on Elin.

'Ebba, not on the church grounds, not on sacred soil,'

Helga Klippare admonished her younger sister, drawing her away.

Elin gave Helga a grateful look and quickly moved off with Märta before the confrontation turned into an even bigger spectacle. People had turned to stare at her, and she knew that many thought Ebba's accusations were justified. But Helga had always been a kind and fair woman. She was the one, after all, who had helped bring Märta into the world on that spring morning eight years ago. The birth of every child in the area had been overseen by Helga, who was skilled at midwifery. It was also rumoured that she secretly helped poor girls who had landed in trouble, but that was not something Elin fully believed.

With heavy steps she headed back towards the vicarage. The bliss she had felt after the church service was gone, and the memories of that unhappy day made her drag her feet on the short walk home. Usually she tried not to dwell on the past. Even God could not undo what was done. And to some extent Per had only himself to blame. His pride had caused him to fall. It was something she had warned him against ever since she agreed to marry him, but he had refused to listen. And now he and the others lay at the bottom of the sea as prey for the fish, while she and her daughter trudged along as lowly servants, heading for her sister's home. She would spend the rest of her life knowing that she had sent off her husband with harsh words the last time she saw him. Words that Ebba, and God knew how many others from Fjällbacka, now held against her.

It all began with a cask of salt. Word had come that henceforth all trade with foreign lands must be conducted via Gothenburg, and Bohuslän had been forbidden to carry on trade with Norway or any of the other countries with which they had successfully conducted business in the past. This had further increased the poverty of the region, and a great animosity arose against the powers that had so blithely arrived at this decision. Not everyone abided by the rules, and coastal patrols were kept busy confiscating goods that had not been properly cleared by customs. Elin had many times urged Per to obey the regulations; not doing so would only bring misfortune upon their heads. And Per had nodded, assuring her that he agreed.

So when the customs official Henrik Meyer knocked on the door one afternoon in early September, she was not concerned as she let him enter their home. But one look at Per sitting at the kitchen table made her realize she had made a grave mistake. It took Meyer only a few minutes to find the illegal cask of salt in the back of the tool cupboard. Elin understood at once what this meant, causing her to clench her fists in the pockets of her tunic. She had warned Per so many times not to do anything foolish. Yet he could not resist.

She knew him so well. He had that unabashed look of pride in his eyes that shone through the poverty and lent him a tenacious strength. The mere fact that he had courted her testified to the courage he possessed, which most others certainly lacked. He had not known that her father cared little about her fate. In Per's eyes, she was the daughter of a wealthy man and should have been beyond his reach. But that same audacity, that same pride and strength, had now brought them to ruin.

When the customs official entered their small home, he announced that in three days he would return to confiscate the boat Per had spent so many years toiling to make his own, even though the fishing was meagre and starvation was a constant threat. The boat was his, yet he had risked everything for the sake of a cask of salt, which he had illegally purchased in Norway.

Elin was furious. Angrier than she had ever been before. She wanted to hit him, scratch out his green eyes and tear out his blond hair. His cursed pride was about to rob them of everything. How would they support themselves now? She always took whatever work she could find, but she was unable to bring in many *riksdaler*, and it would not be easy for Per to get hired as crew on someone else's boat now they were forbidden from trading with foreign goods. And the fishing was no longer profitable.

Per had reached out to put his hand on her shoulder, but she had shrugged it off and turned her back to him. Then she had wept bitter tears. From anger and from fear. Outside their small home the wind was blowing harder, and when Per got out of bed at dawn, she sat up and asked where he was going.

'We are going out in the boat,' he replied, pulling on his trousers and shirt.

Elin had merely glared at him as Märta slept soundly on the bench in the kitchen.

'In this weather? Are you out of your mind?'

'If they are going to take away my boat in three days' time, we need to do all we can before then,' he said, putting on his coat.

Elin hurriedly dressed and followed him out of the house. He did not stop long enough to eat anything. He seemed in such a hurry to go out into the stormy weather, it was as if the devil were on his heels.

'You must not go out today!' she shouted, trying to be heard over the roar of the wind. As she pursued him down the street, curious neighbours emerged to watch. Ebba of Mörhult's husband Claes came out too, with an equally furious wife running after him.

'You will bring death upon yourselves if you go out in this weather!' screamed Ebba shrilly as she tugged at Claes's jacket.

He pulled free and snarled at her: 'We have no choice if you want the children to have food to eat.'

Per nodded to Claes, and the two of them headed for the spot where the boat was moored. Elin watched his broad back retreating, and fear sunk its claws into her so fiercely that she could hardly breathe. At the top of her lungs she yelled:

'Have it your way then, Per Bryngelsson. Let the sea take you and your cursed boat, because I do not want you any more.'

She noticed Ebba's frightened expression as she turned away. With her skirts flapping around her legs, Elin rushed back inside. As she threw herself on to the bed to weep, she had no idea how those words would continue to haunt her, even into death.

✤

Jessie turned over in bed. Her mother had left for the film shoot before six a.m., and Jessie was enjoying having the house to herself. She stretched out her arms, then sucked in her stomach. It felt wonderfully smooth. Not at all fat and doughy the way it normally did. It was flat and smooth, like Vendela's.

But eventually she had to exhale, making her stomach bulge out. She removed her hand in disgust. She hated her stomach. She hated her whole body and everything else in her life. The only thing she didn't hate was Sam. She could still taste his kiss on her lips.

Jessie sat up and swung her legs over the side of the bed. She could hear the water lapping below the house. She pushed aside the curtains. Brilliant sunshine again. She hoped Sam would want to go out in the boat today too, in spite of the video he'd shown her.

She'd known kids like Nils, Basse and Vendela all her life, at various schools, in different countries in different parts of the world. She knew what they wanted. And what they were capable of doing.

Yet for some reason they didn't seem interested in doing anything to her.

Jessie had always known the moment when news about

her mother began to spread through a new school. First the smiles, the pride at having the daughter of a film star at their school. But that changed as soon as somebody googled her mother's name and found out who she was: the murderer who became an actress. Then came the stares. And the whispering. She would never be one of the popular girls – because of the way she looked and because of who she was.

Her mother didn't understand. For her, attention was always a good thing. No matter how bad the situation was for Jessie at school, she had to hang on in there until her mother started making a new film somewhere else.

It was the same for Sam. What had happened to their mothers thirty years ago hovered like a dark cloud over both of them.

Jessie went to the kitchen and opened the fridge. As usual, there was no food, just bottles of champagne. Eating was never a priority for her mother. She was too concerned about keeping her slim figure to take any interest in food. Jessie survived on the generous monthly allowance her mother gave her, spending most of the money on fast food and sweets.

She ran her hand over the bottles, feeling the cold glass under her fingertips. She took one out of the fridge – it was surprising how heavy it was – and set it on the marble countertop. She had never tasted champagne, but her mother – *Marie* – drank it all the time.

She tore off the metal wrapper and for several seconds stared at the wire surrounding the cork before she cautiously took it off. She pulled at the cork but didn't hear the familiar 'pop'. It seemed to be firmly wedged in the top of the bottle. Jessie glanced around before recalling the way Marie always wrapped a dishtowel around the cork in order to pull it out. Jessie reached for one of the white kitchen towels, then twisted the cork at the same time as she pulled on it. Finally it began to come loose. Another tug and Jessie heard the 'pop' as the cork flew out of the bottle.

Foam gushed out, and Jessie hurriedly stepped back to avoid being drenched with champagne. Quickly she poured some of the bubbly into a water glass she found on the counter. Hesitantly she took a sip and then grimaced. It tasted awful. But Marie usually added juice, which probably made it taste better, and she always used proper champagne glasses. Jessie took a tall, slender glass from the cupboard and then found the only container of juice in the fridge. She had no idea how much juice to use, but she filled the glass two-thirds full with champagne before adding peach juice. The concoction threatened to overflow, so Jessie slurped it up. Now it tasted much better. It was actually good.

Jessie put the open bottle back in the fridge along with the juice and then took her glass out to the dock in front of the house. Her mother was going to be away filming all day, so she could do whatever she liked.

She reached for her mobile. Maybe Sam would come over and have some champagne.

'Knock, knock?' Erica called through the open door, which was framed by an enormous trellis of pink climbing roses. They smelled marvellous, and she'd spent a few minutes admiring them.

'Come in!' said a cheerful voice from somewhere inside, so Erica took off her shoes in the hall and went in.

'Oh my, is that really you?' said a woman in her sixties when she saw Erica. She was holding a dishtowel in one hand and a plate in the other.

Erica always felt strange when people recognized her even though they'd never met. The success of her books had made her somewhat of a celebrity, and occasionally she was even stopped on the street by someone wanting to take her picture or ask for an autograph.

'Hi. Yes, I'm Erica Falck,' she said, shaking hands with the woman.

'Viola,' said the woman, giving her a big smile.

She had a delicate network of laughter lines at her eyes, revealing that she smiled often.

'Do you have a few minutes?' asked Erica. 'I'm working on a book about one of your father's old cases, and since he's no longer with us—'

'You thought you'd find out what I know,' Viola interjected, smiling again. 'Come in. I was just making a fresh pot of coffee. And I think I know which case you're talking about.'

Viola led the way to the kitchen, which was off the hallway. A bright and airy room with watercolour paintings on the walls offering spots of colour. Erica paused to admire one of the paintings. She didn't know much about art, nor was she particularly interested, but it was clear the artist was talented and she felt drawn to the image.

'What lovely paintings,' she said, looking at them one after the other.

'Thank you,' said Viola, blushing. 'It has long been a hobby of mine, but recently I've started exhibiting a few of them. And it turns out people actually want to buy my work. I have a show on Friday at Stora Hotel, if you'd like to come.'

'I may just do that. I can see why people like them. They're wonderful,' said Erica as she sat down at the big white kitchen table which was positioned in front of a huge mullioned window.

She loved old windows. There was something about the irregularity of the glass that made them seem much more alive than modern factory-made windows.

'Milk?' asked Viola, and Erica nodded.

114

'Please.'

Viola brought over a sponge cake from the counter and cut two thick slices. Erica could feel her mouth watering.

'I assume you want to talk about my father's investigation into little Stella's murder,' said Viola as she sat down across from Erica.

'Yes. I'm writing about the case, and your father Leif is an important piece of the puzzle.'

'It's been nearly fifteen years since Pappa died. I suppose you know that he committed suicide. It was a terrible shock, even though we should have known it might happen. He'd been terribly depressed ever since our mother passed away from lung cancer. He said he no longer had any reason to live. But I remember that up until his death he talked a lot about that particular case.'

'Do you recall what he said?'

Erica resisted the impulse to close her eyes out of sheer pleasure as she took a big bite of sponge cake. The butter and sugar melted in her mouth.

'It was so long ago, I can't remember the details. Maybe they'll come back to me if I give it some thought. But I do remember that the case bothered him. He was starting to have doubts.'

'Doubts about what?'

'About whether those girls really did it.'

Viola looked pensive as she took a sip of coffee from the white ceramic mug.

'You mean he thought they were innocent?'

This was news to Erica. Her pulse quickened. After living with a police officer for many years, she knew that gut instincts often turned out to be right. If Leif had doubted the girls' guilt, he must have had good reason.

'Did he say why he was having doubts?'

Viola held her coffee mug in both hands, caressing the grooves on the sides with her thumbs.

'No,' she said, frowning. 'He never mentioned anything specific. But I suppose it didn't help that both girls retracted their confessions and continued to proclaim their innocence all these years.'

'But no one believed them,' said Erica, recalling the many articles she'd read about the case, and the response from local residents whenever the case happened to come up in conversation.

Everybody seemed to be in agreement: the girls had killed Stella.

'Right before he died, he started talking about re-opening the case, but he killed himself before he could do anything. Besides, he was retired, so he would have had to persuade the new chief of police, who I don't think would have been especially keen on the idea. The case was solved. The question of guilt had been established, even though there was never a proper trial because the girls were so young.'

'I don't know whether you've heard, but . . .' Erica began, glancing at her mobile. Still no word from Patrik. 'A little girl went missing yesterday afternoon, or possibly even since the night before, from the same farm where Stella lived.'

Viola stared at her.

'What? No, I haven't heard a thing. I've been in my studio, working on the paintings for my show. What happened?'

'They don't know yet. They've been out searching since yesterday afternoon. My husband is a police officer, so he's involved in the search.'

'Oh no. Good gracious.'

Viola was struggling to find the right words. No doubt she was experiencing the same flood of emotions that Erica had on hearing the news.

'It's a strange coincidence,' said Erica. 'Too strange. And the girl is the same age as Stella. Four years old.'

'Oh, dear God,' said Viola. 'Maybe she just got lost. That farm is in a rather remote spot, isn't it?'

'Yes, it is. I hope that's what happened.'

But Erica could see Viola wasn't convinced either.

'Did your father write down any notes on the case? Do you think he might have saved some of the investigative materials at home?'

'Not that I'm aware of,' replied Viola. 'My two brothers and I took care of Pappa's estate after he died, but I can't recall seeing anything. I can check with my brothers, but I don't think there were any notebooks or case files. If there were, I'm afraid we must have thrown them out. None of us are sentimental about saving things. We believe we keep our memories in here.'

She placed her hand on her heart.

Erica knew what she meant and wished she was the same way. She had a hard time getting rid of things with sentimental value, and Patrik was always joking that he was married to a hoarder.

'Please do ask them. And here's my phone number, in case you happen to find anything. Or if you remember something your father said about the case. Anything at all. Don't hesitate to phone, no matter how insignificant it might seem. You never know.'

Erica took a business card from her purse and handed it to Viola, who studied it for a moment before setting it on the table.

'Such awful news about that little girl. I hope they find her,' she said, shaking her head.

'I hope so too,' replied Erica, again glancing at her mobile.

Still no message from Patrik.

'Well, thank you,' she said, getting up to leave. 'I'll try to stop by the gallery on Friday if I can. I love your paintings.'

'I hope to see you then,' said Viola, blushing at Erica's praise.

As Erica headed for her car, the scent from the roses lingered in her nostrils. And Viola's words rang in her ears.

Leif had harboured doubts that Marie and Helen were guilty.

It felt as if they'd been waiting for an eternity, but an hour after Mellberg made the call, Torbjörn Ruud and his team of technicians from Uddevalla came walking through the woods. Patrik ushered them towards the tree trunk a couple of metres inside the area he had cordoned off.

'Oh hell,' said Torbjörn. Patrik nodded.

He knew crime scene techs had seen just about everything, and over time they couldn't help but become inured to the horror. But dead children never ceased to affect them. The contrast between the vitality of a young child and the utter finality of death felt like a punch in the solar plexus.

'Is that where she is?' asked Torbjörn.

'Under the tree trunk,' Patrik confirmed. 'I haven't gone over to check. I wanted to wait for you to get here so as to avoid having anyone else walking through the site. According to the men who found her, there's a hollow space, and her body was shoved inside. That's why we didn't find her earlier, even though we searched this area several times.'

'Are those the men who found her?'

Torbjörn pointed at Harald, Johannes and Karim, who were standing a short distance away.

'Yes. I asked them to stay here, so you could make sure nothing at the crime scene came from them. I assume you'll want to photograph their shoes to identify which footprints are theirs.'

'That's right,' said Torbjörn. He rattled off some instructions to one of the techs he'd brought along. Then he put on a protective suit and pulled plastic coverings over his shoes. Patrik did the same.

'Come on,' said Torbjörn when they were both ready.

Patrik took a deep breath and followed him over to the tree. He steeled himself for what they were about to see, but the sight still upset him so much that for a moment he froze. The first thing he saw was a child's hand. As he'd been told, the little girl's naked body had been stuffed into a hollow in the ground underneath the tree. She was curled up as if in a foetal position. Her face was turned towards them, though partially hidden by her hand, which was black with dirt. Her blond hair was covered with dirt and leaves, and Patrik had to stop himself from bending down to brush off the debris. Who could have done such a thing? What kind of person would do that? Fury rushed through his veins, giving him the strength to do what he had to do. It helped him to remain cold and professional, putting his own feelings aside until later. He owed it to the little girl and her parents. And after many years of working together, he knew Torbjörn would be doing the same.

They squatted down next to each other and took in all the details. The child's body was mostly hidden from view, making it impossible to tell the cause of death. That would come later. What mattered at the moment was securing any evidence the perpetrator might have left behind.

'I'll step away for a while and let your team get to work,' said Patrik. 'Let me know when we can lift her out. I want to help.'

Torbjörn nodded, and signalled for the techs to move in and begin the meticulous task of collecting evidence from the area surrounding the tree. It was a task that could not be hurried. The smallest strand of hair, a cigarette butt, a piece of plastic, everything found in the area would have to be photographed, placed in plastic bags, and labelled. Any footprints in the loose soil would have to be lifted by pouring a viscous substance into the indentation; once the substance hardened, the techs could remove the entire footprint and take it back to the lab for comparison. It was time-consuming work, and having participated in a number of homicide investigations, Patrik had learned to curb his impatience and allow Torbjörn and his team to do their job in peace. The evidence they collected would be vital when the murderer was brought to trial. If anything was lost due to carelessness, it might harm their case.

Patrik stepped beyond the cordoned-off area and took up position a short distance away. Right now he didn't have the energy to talk to anyone. He needed to gather his thoughts and prepare for what had to be done. The first twenty-four hours of an investigation were crucial; they needed to trace witnesses before they had time to forget what they'd seen, and to ensure that evidence was gathered before it could be erased or damaged by the elements, or by the perpetrator returning to remove all traces. A lot could happen in twenty-four hours, so it was important to prioritize. In theory, Mellberg, as the station chief, should have been in charge of this, but in practice the responsibility fell on Patrik's shoulders.

He got out his mobile to text Erica and let her know he'd be late. She'd be wondering what was going on, and he trusted her to be discreet and keep the news to herself until he gave her the all clear. But there was no reception, so he put his phone back in his pocket. He'd ring her later.

It was hot. He closed his eyes and turned his face towards the sun. The sounds from the woods blended with the murmured conversations of the techs. Patrik thought about Gösta. He wondered how he was doing, and he was grateful he wasn't the one who had to tell Nea's parents.

A mosquito landed on his bare arm. He opened his eyes, but resisted the impulse to kill it, swatting it away instead. There had been enough death for one day.

It was all so surreal. Here he stood in the middle of a Swedish wood with people he'd never met before.

This was not the first time Karim had seen a dead body. When he was imprisoned in Damascus, a dead man had been dragged from the cell right in front of his eyes. And during the journey across the Mediterranean Sea, he'd seen dead children floating next to the boat.

But this was different. He'd come to Sweden because it was a country with no dead children. Yet a dead girl was lying only a few metres away.

Karim felt someone touch his arm. It was the older man named Harald, the one with the kind brown eyes who spoke English with such a strong Swedish accent that Karim found it difficult to understand. But he liked the man. They had passed the time by chatting. When neither of them could find the right words, they had resorted to gesturing and miming. And the younger guy, Johannes, had helped Harald find the English words that eluded him.

For the first time since arriving in Sweden, Karim had found himself talking about his family and homeland. He was aware of the longing in his own voice as he spoke of the city he'd left behind, maybe never to return. But he knew the picture he presented was not entirely accurate. The place and people he longed for had nothing to do with terrorism.

How could any Swede comprehend what it was like to spend your days constantly looking over your shoulder, fearful that at any moment someone might betray you?

It might be a friend, a neighbour, even a family member – the government had eyes everywhere. Everyone was trying to protect their own interests, everyone did whatever was necessary to save their own skin. Everyone had lost somebody. Everyone had seen loved ones die, and that meant they would do anything to protect whoever they had left. As a journalist, he'd been especially targeted.

'You okay?' asked Harald, his hand still resting on Karim's arm.

Karim could see his own thoughts mirrored in the other man's face. He had let down his guard, revealing the longing and frustration, and it unnerved him. He slammed the lid shut on his memories.

'I'm okay. I'm thinking about the girl's parents,' he said, seeing for a second the faces of his own children.

Amina was probably worried by now, and her uneasiness always affected the children. But there was no reception out here, so he hadn't been able to phone her. She would be cross when he returned. Amina was always angry whenever she felt anxious. But it didn't matter. She was even more beautiful when she was angry.

'Those poor people,' said Harald, and Karim saw that his eyes were shiny with tears.

A short distance away the men in white plastic overalls were kneeling on the ground near the little girl, carrying out their work. One of the techs had photographed Karim's shoes. He'd also taken pictures of the shoes Johannes and Harald were wearing. And he'd pressed tape against their clothing, then carefully placed the pieces of tape in plastic bags, which he sealed and labelled. Karim understood why he did this, even though he'd never seen it happen before. The technicians wanted to rule out any traces that he and the two other men might have left behind when they entered the area where the little girl lay.

Johannes said something in Swedish to the older man, and they both nodded. Johannes then translated:

'We thought maybe we could ask the policeman if we can go home now. They seem to be done with us.'

Karim nodded. He wanted to get away from this place where the dead girl lay. Away from the sight of her blond hair and her little hand covering her face. Away from where she had been stuffed into a hollow in the ground, lying in a foetal position.

Harald went to talk to the officer standing on the other side of the police tape. They spoke for a moment in low voices, and then Karim saw the policeman nod.

'We can go,' said Harald when he rejoined the others.

Karim noticed he had started to shake, now that the tension had eased. He wanted to go home. Back to his children. And to Amina's flashing eyes.

Sanna closed her eyes at the sound of Vendela pounding up the stairs. She had a splitting headache today, and she couldn't help flinching when the door slammed. She could picture the wood panelling cracking.

All Sanna had done was suggest that Vendela should go with her to the garden centre. Vendela had never been exactly thrilled about being there, but nowadays she seemed to regard it as a form of punishment. Sanna knew she ought to take a sterner hand with Vendela, but she just didn't have the energy. It felt as if all her strength had vanished when she heard about Nea's disappearance.

The sound of throbbing bass came from upstairs now, so loud it made the walls vibrate. Sanna wondered how her daughter planned to spend the day. She mostly seemed to hang out with those two boys, and they were probably not the best companions for her. A fifteen-year-old girl and two boys the same age could only mean trouble.

Sanna pushed aside her breakfast plate. Vendela had

eaten only an egg. The bread she'd always had for breakfast, ever since she was little, contained too much sugar for Vendela these days. Sanna toasted a slice of the bread and spread on a thick layer of orange marmalade. She was already so late that five more minutes would make no difference.

She didn't mind that Vendela was in one of her defiant moods today. At least it was a distraction from thoughts of Nea. And she hadn't had time to think about Stella. But now, as she sat alone in the kitchen, all the memories came flooding in. She remembered that day down to the smallest detail. How happy she'd been to go with her mother to Uddevalla to buy new clothes for school. How she'd felt torn between joy at having a shopping expedition with her mother and envy of Stella, who had those two cool older girls babysitting her. But her jealousy was forgotten as soon as they had waved goodbye and she and her mother drove off in the Volvo, headed for the big city.

On their way home, she kept glancing in the back seat at the shopping bags with her new clothes. Such amazing clothes. She'd been so happy it was all she could do to sit still. Her mother had scolded her, but she'd been laughing as she did so.

That was the last time she ever saw her mother laugh.

Sanna set the rest of her toast on the table. The bread seemed to swell inside her mouth. She remembered getting out of the car and seeing her father's expression when he greeted them. Nausea suddenly overwhelmed Sanna, and she had to rush for the toilet, making it there just in time. Pieces of orange marmalade floated in the toilet bowl, and she began to retch again.

Afterwards she sank on to the cold tile floor, shaking all over.

Upstairs, the music was still thudding.

*   *   *

The bullet slammed into one of the targets nailed to a tree in the forest glade behind their yard.

'Good,' said James curtly.

Sam had to force himself not to smile. This was the only thing for which he ever received praise. It seemed his only talent as a son was being a good shot.

'You're getting better and better,' James told him, giving a satisfied nod as he peered over the rims of his sunglasses.

He wore aviator shades. Sam thought his father looked like a parody of an American sheriff.

'See if you can hit the target from a little further away,' said James, motioning for Sam to back up.

Sam moved away from the tree.

'Steady your hand. Exhale at the precise moment you squeeze the trigger. Focus.'

James had trained elite Swedish military units for years, and Sam knew his father was a highly respected professional. That he was also a cold bastard probably added to his reputation, but it made Sam long for the next time James would be deployed abroad.

The months when James was away, often to unknown destinations, seemed like a breath of fresh air to Sam. Both he and his mother were more relaxed. She laughed more, and Sam loved seeing her happy. As soon as James stepped in the door, the laughter vanished, and she went out running more often. She lost weight, but instead of looking healthier, she just looked stressed. Sam hated that version of his mother as much as he loved the happier one. He knew he was being unfair, but she was the one who had chosen to have a child with that man. Sam refused to call him Father. Or Pappa.

He quickly fired off a few shots. He knew his aim was right on.

James nodded with satisfaction.

'Hell, if only you had a backbone, I could make a fine soldier out of you,' said James, chuckling.

Helen came into the backyard.

'I'm going out for a run,' she called to James and Sam, but neither of them answered.

Sam thought she'd already left. She usually went running right after breakfast in order to avoid the worst heat of the day, but it was nearly ten o'clock.

'Back up another couple of metres,' said James.

Sam knew he'd be able to hit the target, even at that distance. He'd been practising at greater distances during the periods when James was away. But for some reason he didn't want to show his father exactly how good a shot he was. He didn't want to give him the satisfaction of thinking his son had inherited something from him. He didn't deserve any credit. Everything in Sam's life was in spite of James, not thanks to him.

'Nice!' his father shouted when he made the next series of shots.

That was something Sam hated. The way James would switch to English, speaking with a distinct American accent. He had no American ancestors; his grandfather had been a fan of James Dean when he was young. But James had spent so much time with Americans that he'd picked up their accent. Thick and mushy. Sam found it embarrassing every time James failed to speak Swedish.

'One more time,' said James in English, as if he could read Sam's thoughts and wanted to provoke him.

Sam aimed the gun at the target and pulled the trigger. Bullseye.

BOHUSLÄN 1671

'The girl was inside the big house yesterday. And you know what I have said about that, Elin!'

Britta's words were spoken harshly, and Elin bowed her head.

'I will speak to her,' she said quietly.

Britta swung her legs over the side of the bed.

'We are receiving a special visitor today,' she went on. 'Everything must be perfect. Have you washed and starched my blue dress? The silk brocade?'

She stuck her feet into the slippers next to the bed. Their warmth was welcome. Even though the vicarage was a more splendid house than any Elin had ever seen, it was still cold and draughty, and the floor was ice-cold in the wintertime.

'Everything is ready and waiting,' replied Elin. 'We have scrubbed every nook and cranny of the house, and Boel from Holta arrived yesterday and has already begun to prepare the food. She will start by serving stuffed codheads, followed by capon with gooseberries as the main course, and bread custard for dessert.'

'Excellent,' said Britta. 'Harald Stake's envoy should be served a meal befitting a lord. After all, Harald Stake is the governor of the county of Bohuslän, and he has been ordered by the king himself to speak to the vicars about this plague of witchcraft. Only a few days ago, Preben told me of a witch who has been imprisoned in Marstrand.'

Britta's cheeks had flushed crimson with indignation.

Elin nodded. People could talk of nothing else these days. The recently formed witchcraft council had busied itself imprisoning witches all over Bohuslän and soon the trials would begin. All over Sweden, strong measures were being taken against this wickedness. Elin shuddered. Witches and sorcerers. Travels to Blåkulla, witch mountain, and alliances with the devil himself. It appalled her that such evil existed so close to home.

'I heard from Ida-Stina that it is because of you that Svea of Hult is now with child,' said Britta as Elin helped her dress. 'Whatever it is you did for her, I want you to do the same for me.'

'I can do only what my maternal grandmother taught me,' said Elin, tightly lacing Britta's bodice in the back.

She was not surprised by the request. Britta was nearing twenty, and she and Preben had been married for two years, yet her belly had not yet swollen with child.

'Do whatever you did for Svea. It is time for me to give Preben a child. He has started asking when this might happen.'

'I made Svea a herbal mixture from one of Grandmother's recipes,' said Elin, as she began brushing Britta's long hair.

The two sisters were very different in appearance. Elin had inherited her mother's blond hair and pale blue eyes. Britta had dark hair, and her dark blue eyes were like those of the woman who had taken Elin's mother's place even before she died. Gossiping tongues in the village still whispered that Elin's mother Kerstin had died of a broken heart. Even if this were true, Elin wasted no time thinking about it. Their father had died a year ago, and Britta was the only one who could save her and Märta from death by starvation.

'She also taught me certain words to speak,' said Elin cautiously. 'If you are not opposed, I could prepare the mixture for you and say the appropriate prayers. I have everything I need to brew the concoction. I dried plenty of herbs during the summer so that I would have enough to last the winter.'

Britta waved her slender white hand dismissively.

'Do as you please. I need to give birth to a child for my husband or risk bringing misfortune upon us.'

Elin was about to say in that case perhaps it would be a good idea for her to share the marriage bed with him. But she was wise enough to keep quiet. She had seen the consequences of arousing Britta's ire. For a moment she wondered how a man as kind as Preben could have married someone like Britta. No doubt their father had had a hand in it, eager as he was to see his daughter make a good match.

'You may go now,' said Britta, standing up. 'I am sure there must be countless things you need to attend to before Stake's envoy arrives. And speak to that girl of yours, or I shall have to let the rod do the talking.'

Elin nodded, though her sister's threat of beating Märta made her blood boil. So far Britta had not lifted a hand against the girl, but when she did, Elin knew she would not be able to answer for her actions. She would have to impress upon her daughter the importance of heeding her warning not to enter the big house.

Elin went out to the yard and looked around uneasily.

'Märta?' she called.

Britta took a dim view of any servant who spoke too loudly. Yet another thing to remember if Elin did not want to fall into disfavour.

'Märta?' she called a little louder as she went into the stable.

This was the most likely place to find Märta, but she wasn't there either. Unfortunately, Elin's daughter had inherited not only her father's green eyes, but also his stubbornness. The girl never seemed to listen to her mother's admonitions.

'We are here,' she heard a familiar voice say.

Preben. She stopped abruptly.

'Come over here, Elin,' he said kindly from the darkness of the last stall.

'Yes, come here, Mother,' said Märta eagerly.

Elin hesitated but then picked up her skirts to avoid soiling the hem with muck from the ground and quickly moved in the direction of their voices.

'Look, Mother,' said Märta, awe in her voice.

She was sitting at the very back of an empty stall, holding three kittens on her lap. They looked to be no more than a day old. They were turning their heads back and forth, blind to the world. Next to Märta sat Preben. He too had a lapful of kittens.

'Truly one of God's miracles,' he said, petting a tiny grey kitten.

The creature meowed pitifully, rubbing its head on his sleeve.

'Here, take one, Mother,' said Märta, handing Elin a black-and-white spotted kitten that flailed its paws in the air.

Elin hesitated. She looked over her shoulder. Britta would not be pleased to find her and Märta here. And with Preben.

'Sit down, Elin.' Preben gave her a small smile. 'My dear wife is fully occupied with preparations for our grand visitor this evening.'

Still Elin hesitated. But unable to resist the helpless

appeal of the black-and-white kitten, she reached out and took it from Märta, then sat down on the straw and set the kitten on her lap.

'The vicar says I can choose one to be mine, all mine.'

Märta gave Preben a delighted look. Elin glanced at him as well. He was smiling – a smile that reached all the way to his blue eyes.

'You must baptize the kitten too,' he said. 'But as we have agreed, this must be a secret, just between the two of us.'

He held a finger to his lips and gave the girl a solemn look. Märta nodded, her expression equally solemn.

'I will tell no one. It will be my most precious secret,' she said, looking at the kittens. 'That is the one I want.'

She stroked the head of a tiny grey kitten. It was the smallest of the litter. Elin looked over at Preben, trying to shake her head without drawing Märta's attention. The poor little thing looked so scrawny, she doubted it would survive. But Preben calmly returned her look.

'Märta has a fine eye for cats,' he said, scratching the grey kitten behind the ear. 'I would have made the very same choice.'

Märta gave the vicar a look that Elin had not seen since misfortune had befallen them, and it made her heart ache. Per was the only one who had ever received such looks from Märta. Yet there was something about Preben that reminded her of Per. A kindness in his eyes that was soothing and invited trust.

'Her name will be Viola,' said Märta, 'since violets are my favourite flowers.'

'A splendid name,' said Preben.

He looked at Elin. They had to hope the kitten did not turn out to be a male.

'Märta wants to learn to read,' said Preben, patting the

girl's blond head. 'My parish clerk gives the children lessons twice a week.'

'I do not see what use she would have for that,' said Elin.

If there was one thing life had taught her, it was that womenfolk did best not to draw attention. Or to entertain great hopes. Disappointment was all they could expect in life.

'She must be able to read her catechism,' said Preben, and Elin felt ashamed.

How could she argue with the vicar? If he thought it beneficial or even advisable for her daughter to learn to read, who was she to object?

'In that case, Märta may attend the lessons,' said Elin, bowing her head.

She herself had never learned to read. She had managed to handle the repeated catechism questions because she had learned everything by rote.

'That is decided then,' said Preben happily, giving Märta one last pat on the head.

He stood up and brushed the straw from his trousers. Elin tried not to look at him. There was something about him that attracted her, and she was ashamed the thought had even entered her mind. Preben was her sister's husband and the vicar of the church. To feel anything but gratitude and reverence for such a man was a sin, and she deserved God's punishment.

'I suppose I had better go in and help Britta with the preparations now, before she runs all the servants ragged,' he said cheerfully. Then he turned to Märta. 'Take care of Viola now. You have a good eye for who needs a helping hand.'

'Thank you,' said Märta, giving Preben such an adoring look that Elin's heart melted.

And ached. The longing she felt for Per struck her with

such force she had to turn away. Listening to Preben's retreating footsteps, she banished the memories from her mind. Per was gone. There was nothing to be done about it. She and Märta had only each other now. And Viola.

'This is a very sad day,' said Patrik, looking around at his colleagues in the conference room.

No one spoke, no one looked at him. He supposed that, like him, they were thinking about their own children. Or grandchildren.

'Bertil and I are cancelling all leave. As of now, everyone is back on the job,' he said. 'I hope you will understand.'

'I think I speak for everybody here when I say you couldn't keep us away,' said Paula.

'That's what I thought,' replied Patrik, moved by his colleagues' response. Even Mellberg was eager to get to work.

'So let's tend to the practical matters first. I know that several of you have children who aren't in school at the moment.'

He looked at Martin as he said this.

'Pia's parents will take care of Tuva while I'm at work.'

'Good,' said Patrik.

Since no one else spoke, he assumed that Paula and Annika had also made arrangements at home. The death of a child took priority over everything else. It was all hands on deck, and he knew they had many hours of work ahead of them.

'Gösta, how are the parents doing?' asked Patrik, sitting

down in a chair next to the whiteboard at the front of the room.

'As well as could be expected,' said Gösta, blinking several times. 'The pastor came over, and I called in the doctor as well. When I left, both parents had been given a sedative to help them sleep.'

'Do they have any relatives who can come over?' asked Annika, who had a big family and was used to having lots of people around, lending their support in a crisis.

'Eva's parents are dead. Peter's parents live in Spain, but they're on a plane as we speak. They should be here in a few hours.'

'What has Torbjörn told you so far? How is their work coming along?' asked Martin, reaching for the large Thermos jug that Annika had filled with coffee before the meeting began.

'The girl's body is being taken to Gothenburg for the post-mortem,' said Patrik quietly.

The memory of lifting Nea's small body out from underneath the tree trunk would stay with him forever. Wild animals had not been able to reach her as she lay there in the hollow, but insects had poured out when they lifted her. Images flashed through his mind in rapid progression; he knew the same sequence would be replayed in his mind every night for the foreseeable future. He had observed many post-mortems in the course of his career, so he was familiar with what went on. All too familiar. He didn't want to picture the little girl lying naked and exposed on the steel table. He didn't want to know where Pedersen would make the incisions, how her organs would be removed, how everything that had once given her life would be weighed and measured. He didn't want to know how the stitches would then form a 'Y' on her chest.

'How did it go at the crime scene?' Gösta asked. 'Did they find anything useful?'

Patrik gave a start as he tried to shake off the visions of Nea on the autopsy table.

'They collected a lot of material, but we don't know yet how significant it will be.'

'What sort of things did they find?' Martin wanted to know.

'Footprints, though they might be from the three men who found her or the previous search parties. Everyone who took part in the search has been asked to provide footprints. Did any of you search that particular area? If so, we need footprints from you too.'

'No, none of us was in the area where the girl was found,' said Gösta, helping himself to a cup of coffee.

'Okay, footprints. What else?' asked Paula.

'I'm not sure. The techs were putting a lot of things in plastic bags, but I won't know the details until Torbjörn's report comes in. He doesn't like to give out any information until he's had a chance to take a close look at all the collected material.'

Mellberg stood up and went over to the window.

'Damn, it's hot in here.'

He tugged at his shirt collar as if he couldn't breathe. There were big patches of sweat under his arms, and his comb-over had slid down over one ear. He opened the window. The traffic noise was a little intrusive, but no one objected to having fresh air sweep through the stuffy room. Ernst, the station's dog, had been lying at Mellberg's feet, panting. Now he got up and padded over to the window to sniff at the air.

'So Torbjörn didn't tell you anything?' asked Paula.

Patrik shook his head. 'No, we'll have to wait for his preliminary report. And I need to find out from Pedersen when we can expect the results of the post-mortem. I'm afraid there are other cases ahead of this one, but I'll talk to him and see what he can do.'

'You were there at the scene. Did you notice anything?' Paula persisted. 'Anything on her body or—'

Martin grimaced.

'No. And it's not worth speculating until Pedersen has time to examine her.'

'Are there any obvious suspects?' asked Martin, tapping his pen on the table. 'What do we know about the parents? It wouldn't be the first time parents killed their own child and then tried to make it look like someone else had done it.'

'I have a hard time believing that, in this case,' said Gösta, setting down his cup so hard the coffee sloshed over the side.

Patrik held up his hand.

'At this point there's no reason to believe Nea's parents are in any way involved. But Martin's right – we can't rule out the possibility. We need to talk to them as soon as we can, partly to find out whether they have an alibi, and partly to find out whether they have any information that might help us move forward with the investigation. But I'm inclined to agree with Gösta. At this stage, nothing points towards them.'

'Since the girl was naked, maybe we ought to look into whether any paedophiles have been seen in the area of the farm,' Paula suggested.

Silence settled over the room. Nobody wanted to think about what this suggestion implied.

'I'm afraid you're right,' Mellberg said after a moment. 'But how do we go about that?'

He was still sweating buckets and panting as heavily as Ernst.

'There are thousands of tourists here right now,' he went on. 'How can we tell whether there are any sex offenders or paedophiles among all those people?'

'We can't. But we can dig out the reports of suspected

sex offenders who may have turned up here this summer. Wasn't there a woman who came in this week to report a guy who was secretly taking pictures of kids at the beach?'

'Yeah,' said Patrik with a nod. 'I took the report. Glad you thought of that, Annika. Could you go through all the reports we've taken since May? Pull out anything of interest. Better to cast a broad net, and later we can narrow it down.'

'I'm on it,' she said, writing a note to herself.

'So we need to talk about the elephant in the room,' said Paula, refilling her cup from the Thermos.

A hissing sound issued from the Thermos pump, indicating it was almost empty. Annika got up to refill it. Coffee was the fuel they all needed at the moment.

'I know what you're talking about,' said Patrik, looking a little uncomfortable. 'The Stella case. Helen and Marie.'

'Yes,' said Gösta. 'I was working here at the station thirty years ago. Unfortunately, I don't remember all the details. It was a long time ago, and Leif turned over all the routine stuff to me while he handled the investigation and interviews. But I do recall what a shock it was to the whole town when Helen and Marie, having admitted to killing Stella, later retracted their confessions. To my mind, it's no coincidence that Nea disappeared from the same farm and was found in the same place. Or the fact that this should happen right when Marie comes back here after a thirty-year absence.'

'I agree,' said Mellberg. 'We need to talk to both of them. Even though I wasn't here for that investigation, I heard a lot of talk about the case. And I've always thought it was especially horrifying that such young girls would kill a child.'

'Both of them have maintained their innocence all these years,' Paula pointed out.

Mellberg snorted. 'In that case, why did they confess in the first place? Personally, I've never doubted those two girls killed Stella. And it doesn't take an Einstein to put two and two together when the same thing happens again, now they're back together for the first time in thirty years.'

'We need to be careful not to rush to judgement,' said Patrik. 'But I agree we need to talk to both of them.'

'I think it's crystal clear,' Mellberg went on. 'Marie comes back, she and Helen are united, another murder occurs.'

Annika came back into the room, bringing the Thermos filled with coffee.

'Did I miss anything?'

'We were only saying that we need to consider possible similarities with the 1985 case. And we'll have to interview Helen and Marie.' Patrik looked at the whiteboard. 'Annika, could you try to find the interview files and the rest of the case notes and evidence? I know it won't be easy, considering what a mess it is in the archives, but give it a try.'

Annika nodded and made another note on her pad.

For a moment Patrik sat in silence, pondering whether what he was about to say had been properly thought through. But if he said nothing, it would undoubtedly come up in some other context, and then he'd be criticized for not mentioning it to his colleagues.

'Regarding the Stella case . . .' he said, pausing before going on. Then he tried again. 'Well, the thing is, Erica has started work on her next book. And . . . she has decided to write about that particular case.'

Mellberg sat up straight. 'She's going to have to put that on hold for a while,' he said. 'We have enough to worry about without your wife running around and getting in the way. This is police business, not a matter for civilians who have neither the training nor the experience of the police force.'

Patrik had to stop himself from pointing out that Erica had been of far more help than Mellberg in solving their last few big cases. He knew it would do no good to insult Mellberg. His boss had the greatest faith in his own talents, albeit he was alone in that regard. Patrik had learned to work around him instead of with him. He also knew from experience that it would serve no purpose to tell Erica not to research the Stella case. Once she started poking around, she wouldn't rest until all her questions were answered. But that wasn't something he needed to tell his colleagues. He surmised that everyone other than Mellberg was well aware of this.

'Fine,' he said. 'I'll tell Erica. But she has already done a lot of research, so I was thinking we might use her as a resource. What would you think if I invited her over this afternoon so she could tell us what she knows about the case?'

'I think that's a brilliant idea,' said Gösta. Everyone except Mellberg nodded agreement.

But Bertil knew when he was outnumbered and muttered: 'I suppose that's all right.'

'Good. I'll talk to her as soon as we finish the meeting,' said Patrik. 'Maybe you could add whatever details you do remember from the investigation, Gösta.'

Gösta nodded. His wry smile indicated there wasn't much he'd be able to recall.

'So, what else is on the list of things we need to do?' asked Patrik.

'The press conference,' said Mellberg, looking more cheerful.

Patrik frowned but he knew he had to choose his battles. Mellberg would be allowed to handle the press conference. They would just have to cross their fingers that he didn't manage to do any damage in the process.

'Annika, could you call a press conference for this afternoon?'

'Okay,' she said, making a note of the request. 'Before or after Erica has been here?'

'Let's do it before,' said Patrik. 'Preferably two o'clock. I'll ask Erica to be here around three thirty.'

'I'll tell the reporters two o'clock. The phone has been ringing nonstop, so it'll be nice to be able to tell them something.'

'We all need to be aware that this is going to turn into a real media circus,' said Patrik.

He shifted in his seat. Unlike Mellberg, who relished being in the spotlight, he viewed media interest as nothing more than a hindrance. Though on rare occasions media reports did lead to important tips from the public, more often than not the negative effects far outweighed the positive.

'Don't worry. Leave it to me,' said Mellberg happily, leaning back in his chair. Ernst was once again draped over his feet under the table. Even though it must have been like wearing a pair of warm wool socks, Mellberg let him stay. Erica was fond of saying that Mellberg's love for the big, shaggy dog was one of his few redeeming qualities.

'Be sure to weigh every word you say,' Patrik reminded him, fully aware that Mellberg usually allowed the words to spill out, free and uncensored, and without any thought for the consequences.

'I have a lot of experience dealing with the press corps. During my days in Gothenburg—'

'Great,' Patrik cut in. 'We'll leave it to you then. Maybe you and I could do a brief run-through beforehand, discuss what we want to emphasize and what we should keep to ourselves. Okay?'

Mellberg huffed. 'As I said, during my days in Gothenburg—'

'How should we divide up the work?' asked Martin, heading off Mellberg's diatribe.

Patrik gave him a grateful look. 'I'll talk to Torbjörn and Pedersen and find out when we might expect to get more information from them.'

'I'll talk to Nea's parents,' said Gösta. 'But I'll give the doctor a call first to check how they're doing.'

'Do you want to take someone with you?' asked Patrik. He could only imagine what Eva and Peter must be going through.

'No, I can handle it alone. Better to use our resources on other things,' said Gösta.

'I can talk to the girls who were convicted of killing Stella,' said Paula. 'Or "women", I suppose I should say. They're not girls any more.'

'I'll go with you,' said Martin, raising his hand like a schoolboy.

'Good.' Patrik nodded. 'But wait until Erica has been here and given us more meat on the bone, so to speak. Use the time until then to knock on doors in the area around the farm. When people live in a remote spot like that, they tend to keep an eye out for anything unusual and any strangers who happen by. So it's worth talking to the neighbours.'

'Okay,' said Paula. 'We'll drive out there and have a chat with the closest neighbours.'

'I'll hold the fort here,' said Patrik. 'The phone keeps ringing, and I want to review our plans for the investigation before the press conference.'

'And I need to get ready,' said Mellberg, reaching up to pat his hair in place.

'All right. We've got a lot of work to do,' said Patrik, signalling the meeting was over.

The small conference room was now unbearably stuffy and hot. He was desperate to get out of there, and he suspected his colleagues felt the same way.

The first thing he did was ring Erica. He wasn't sure it was wise to let her get involved in the investigation, but as he saw it, he had no choice. On the other hand, it would be a real bonus if she had information that could help them find Nea's killer.

The first kilometre was always tough, in spite of all the years she'd been running. But after that it got easier. Helen felt her body respond and her breathing became more regular.

She had started running as soon as the court hearing was over. The first day she ran five kilometres to rid her body of all the frustration. The pounding of her footsteps on the gravel, the wind blowing through her hair, the sounds all around her – those were the only things that could silence the rest of the world.

She ran a little further each time, and she got better and better. Over the years she'd run in more than thirty marathons. But only in Sweden. She dreamed of being in a marathon in New York, Sydney, or Rio, but she was grateful that James at least let her take part in the Swedish races.

The fact that she was allowed to cultivate this interest of hers, allowed to spend a couple of hours every day on her running, was solely because he appreciated the discipline of the sport. It was the only thing he respected about her – that every morning she ran tens of kilometres, that her psyche was able to conquer the limitations of her body. But she could never explain to anyone how, when she ran, everything that had happened was erased, becoming hazy and distant, nothing more than a dream she had once had.

In her peripheral vision she saw the house built on

the site where Marie's childhood home had once stood. By the time Helen returned to Fjällbacka, the new house was already there. Her parents chose to move away immediately after everything fell apart. Her mother, Harriet, couldn't handle all the gossip, the surreptitious stares, and the whispering.

James and her father, KG, had seen each other often until KG died. Sometimes she and Sam would go along when James drove to Marstrand, but only so Sam could visit his grandparents. Helen had no wish to see either of her parents. They had failed her when she needed them most, and that was something she could never forgive.

Her legs were starting to tighten, and she reminded herself to correct her stride. Like so much else, she'd had to struggle to develop a good stride. Nothing had ever come naturally to her.

No, now she was lying to herself. Until that day, life had been easy, they had still been a family. She couldn't recall any problems or setbacks. Nothing but bright summer days and the scent of her mother's perfume when she tucked her in at night. And love. She remembered the love.

She picked up speed in order to drown out her thoughts. All those thoughts that running usually erased. Why were they appearing in her mind now? Was she going to have to give up even this temporary reprieve? Had Marie's return ruined everything?

With each breath, Helen noticed how different everything felt. Her lungs were straining, and in the end she had to stop. Her legs felt so tight, and her body was weak from lactic acid. For the first time her body had defeated her will.

Helen didn't notice she was falling until she landed on the ground.

*　*　*

144

Bill looked around the restaurant in the TanumStrand hotel and conference centre. Only five people had turned up. He saw five weary faces. He knew they had been out searching for little Nea all night. He and Gun had talked about it on their way over, wondering whether they should postpone the meeting. But Bill was convinced this was exactly what was needed at the moment.

Yet it had never occurred to him that only five people would come.

Rolf had arranged for Thermoses of coffee and rolls with cheese and paprika to be set on a side table, and Bill had already helped himself. He took a sip of coffee. Gun sat on a chair next to him, sipping her coffee as well.

Bill looked from the exhausted faces to Rolf, who was standing at the entrance to the restaurant.

'Maybe you'd like to introduce everyone?' he asked.

Rolf nodded.

'This is Karim. He came here with his wife and two children. He worked as a journalist in Damascus. Then we have Adnan and Khalil, sixteen and eighteen, respectively. They came to Sweden alone and have become friends at the refugee centre. And this is Ibrahim, the oldest of the group.' Rolf switched to English. 'How old are you, Ibrahim?'

The man next to Rolf had a big beard. Smiling, he held up five fingers.

'Fifty.'

'That's right. Ibrahim is fifty, and he arrived here with his wife. Finally, we have Farid. He came to Sweden with his mother.'

Bill nodded to the man with the shaved head and the huge body. He looked to be in his thirties and, judging by his girth, he spent a large part of his time eating. Bill thought it might be tricky to get the weight distribution right in a sailboat with someone who weighed at least three times as much as the others, but they'd find a way. He needed to stay positive. If he hadn't stayed positive he never would have survived that time when his boat capsized off the coast of South Africa and the great white sharks began circling.

'And my name is Bill,' he said, speaking slowly and clearly. 'I'm going to speak Swedish with you as much as possible.'

He and Rolf had agreed that would be best. The whole point was for the refugees to learn the language so they could more rapidly become part of society.

Everyone except Farid had a puzzled expression. He replied in broken but understandable Swedish:

'I am the only one who understands Swedish okay. I have been here the longest and I have studied hard, very hard. I can maybe help to translate in the beginning. So the boys will understand?'

Bill nodded. That seemed sensible. All the new words and specialized sailing terms would be challenging even for a native Swede. Farid switched to Arabic and quickly explained what Bill had said. The others nodded.

'We try . . . understand . . . Swedish . . . and learn,' said the man named Karim.

'Great! Excellent!' said Bill, giving them a thumbs up. 'Do all of you know how to swim?'

He made swimming motions with his arms, and Farid repeated his question in Arabic. The five men spoke among themselves, then Karim replied for all of them, again in laborious Swedish.

'We can . . . that is why we take this course. Otherwise not.'

'Where did you learn to swim?' asked Bill, both relieved and surprised. 'Have you spent a lot of time on the coast?'

Farid quickly translated. His words were greeted with laughter.

'At the leisure centre,' he said with a smile.

'Oh, of course.'

Bill felt stupid. He didn't dare glance at Gun sitting next to him, but he could hear her trying not to snort. He probably needed to do some reading about Syria, so he wouldn't seem like such an ignorant fool. He'd visited many parts of the world, but for him their country was only a blank patch on the map.

He reached for another roll. It had a thick layer of butter, just the way he liked it.

Karim raised his hand, and Bill gave him a nod.

'When . . . when we begin?'

Karim said something in Arabic, and Farid added: 'When do we begin sailing?'

Bill threw out his hands.

'There's no time to lose. The Dannholmen regatta takes place in only a few weeks, so we start tomorrow! Rolf will give you a lift to Fjällbacka, and we'll begin at nine o'clock. Bring warm clothes with you. It's colder out on the water than on shore when the wind is blowing.'

When Farid had translated, the others looked a bit uneasy. But Bill gave them an encouraging look and what he hoped was a winning smile. This was going to be great, just great. No problems at all. It was all good.

'Thanks for letting the kids hang out here for a while,' said Erica as she sat down across from Anna on the partially finished deck.

She had gratefully accepted the offer of iced tea. The heat was oppressive, and the AC wasn't working properly in her car. She felt as if she'd been wandering in the desert for forty days. She reached for the glass Anna had filled from the carafe and downed the iced tea in one long swig. Anna laughed and refilled her glass. Now that Erica had quenched the worst of her thirst, she could drink the rest of her tea more slowly.

'It was fine,' said Anna. 'The kids were so sweet I hardly even noticed them.'

Erica grinned. 'Are you sure you're talking about my kids? Maja can be quite docile, but I wouldn't call those two little rascals "sweet".'

Erica wasn't kidding. When the twins were younger, they'd been very different from each other. Anton had been calmer and more introverted, while Noel was the one who always made a fuss and got into mischief. Now both of them had entered a period when they were filled with such an excess of energy that it was frequently too much for her. Maja had never gone through anything like that. She hadn't even been particularly obstinate when she was a toddler, so Erica and Patrik had not been prepared for this. And it was double trouble, since they were twins. Erica would have loved to leave the children with Anna for the rest of the day, but her sister looked so tired that she couldn't ask any more of her today.

'So how did it go?' Anna said, leaning back in her Baden Baden deckchair with the gaudy, sun-patterned cushion.

Anna hated the sight of those cushions every time they sat outside on the deck, but Dan's mother had made them, and she was such a nice person that Anna couldn't bring herself to replace them. In that respect Erica was lucky. Patrik's mother, Kristina, would never dream of sewing or doing any other type of handiwork.

'It was pretty hopeless,' said Erica gloomily. 'Her father died so long ago, and she didn't remember much. And she didn't think he'd saved any of the investigative materials. But she did say something interesting. She told me Leif had started to doubt whether they actually did it.'

'You mean he thought the girls weren't guilty after all?' said Anna, swatting away a horsefly.

Erica kept her eye on the fly. She hated all wasps and flies.

'Uh-huh. She said he wasn't convinced they did it, especially towards the end of his life.'

'I thought they confessed,' said Anna, again swatting at the fly. But it was merely dazed and continued attacking her the second it recovered. 'My God, get away from me!'

Anna got up and reached for a magazine on the table. She rolled it up and swung at the fly, mashing it against the wax tablecloth.

Erica couldn't help smiling at her hugely pregnant little sister going after that fly. Not an easy task for Anna at the moment.

'Go ahead and smirk,' said Anna peevishly as she wiped the sweat from her forehead before she sat down again. 'Now where were we? Oh, right. Those girls confessed, didn't they?'

'Yes, they did, and it was their confession that got them convicted. Since they were so young, they didn't receive a sentence, but the matter of their guilt was outlined in a statement at the court hearing.'

'But what if they *weren't* guilty?' said Anna, staring at Erica. 'What a tragedy that would be. Two thirteen-year-old girls whose lives were destroyed. Doesn't one of them live around here? That's awfully brave of her, if you ask me.'

'I know. She moved back after a few years in Marstrand. You can imagine what the locals were saying about her at first, so it must have been hell. But after a while all the talk died down.'

'Have you met her yet? For your book?'

'No. I sent her several requests for an interview, but

she never answered. So I was thinking of going to see her. To find out whether she'd agree to talk to me.'

'How do you think your work on the book is going to be affected by what's happened?' asked Anna quietly. 'To the little girl, I mean.'

Erica had phoned to tell Anna about Nea as soon as she heard that the girl's body had been found. News of the child's death would spread like wildfire through the whole community.

'I'm not sure,' said Erica hesitantly as she helped herself to more iced tea. 'Maybe people will be more inclined to talk now, or maybe the opposite. We'll soon find out.'

'What about Marie? Our glamorous Hollywood star? Is she willing to be interviewed?'

'I've been corresponding with her publicist for the past six months. My guess is, she has her own book deal in the works, and she's not sure whether my book will help or hinder sales. But I'm going to pay her a visit, regardless.'

Anna looked askance. Erica knew the thought of contacting complete strangers and trying to persuade them to talk was her sister's worst nightmare.

'Let's talk about something more pleasant, okay?' said Erica. 'We need to arrange a bachelorette party for Kristina.'

'Of course we do,' said Anna, laughing so hard her huge belly bounced. 'But what do you do when the bride is a bit . . . past the usual age? All the traditional games like getting her to sell kisses at a booth don't seem appropriate, not to mention making her skydive or bungee-jump.'

'You're right. I can't imagine Kristina doing any of those things,' said Erica. 'Why don't we just invite a bunch of her friends and spend a nice evening together? How about dinner at Café Bryggan? Good food, good wine. It can be as simple as that.'

'Sounds like a great idea,' said Anna. 'Though we should still come up with some kind of fun kidnapping plan.'

Erica nodded.

'Sure, otherwise it's not a real bachelorette party! And by the way, when is Dan going to make a respectable woman of you?'

Anna blushed.

'You can see how I look at the moment. We've agreed to have the baby first. Then we'll start thinking about a wedding.'

'So when do you think—' Erica began, but she was interrupted by 'Mambo No. 5' playing on her mobile.

'Hi, sweetheart,' she said when she saw the name on the display.

She listened to what Patrik was saying, giving only a few brief remarks in reply.

'No problem. Don't worry about the kids. See you later.'

She ended the call and put her mobile back in her purse. Then she looked at Anna. She knew it was asking a lot to get her sister to babysit the kids again, but she had no choice. Kristina was in Uddevalla all afternoon, so she couldn't ask her.

'Okay,' said Anna. 'I can watch the kids for you. How long will you be gone?' She laughed when she saw Erica's embarrassed expression.

'Could I drop them off again around three? Patrik wants me to come over to the station to tell them about the Stella case. I have to be there at three thirty. So I should be back here by five or five thirty. Will that work?'

'That's fine,' said Anna. 'Your kids are better behaved with me than with you.'

'Oh, come on,' said Erica, blowing her sister a kiss.

But it couldn't be denied that Anna had a point. The children had behaved like angels.

* * *

'What do you think they're scared of?'

Sam realized he had started to slur his words. The combination of sun and champagne had gone straight to his head. He was holding the glass in his left hand. His right hand ached after the morning's target practice.

'Scared of?' said Jessie.

She too was slurring her words. She'd had several glasses before he arrived and they were now on the second bottle.

'Won't your mother notice some bottles are missing?' he asked, motioning with the glass.

The golden bubbles sparkled when the sunlight hit the glass. He'd never thought about how beautiful champagne was. On the other hand, he'd never seen it close up.

'Oh, don't worry. She won't care,' replied Jessie, tossing her head. 'As long as there's still some left for her.'

She reached for the bottle.

'But what did you mean about being scared? I don't think they're scared of us.'

'Of course they're fucking scared,' said Sam, holding out his glass.

The foam reached the top and spilled over the rim, but he merely laughed and licked the champagne off his hand.

'They know we're not like them. They sense . . . they can sense the darkness inside us.'

'Darkness?'

She studied him in silence. He loved the contrast between her green eyes and blond hair. He wished she would realize how beautiful she was. He looked beyond her weight and the spots. He had recognized himself in her when he saw her at the Centrum kiosk. He knew they both shared that lost feeling. And he saw in her the same darkness.

'They know we hate them. They see all the hatred

they've already created in us, but they can't help themselves, they keep pouring it on, keep creating something they won't be able to control.'

Jessie giggled.

'My God, you sound so pretentious. *Skål!* We're sitting here in the sunshine, on the dock next to a luxury villa, we're drinking champagne, and we're having a fucking great time.'

'You're right.' He smiled as their glasses clinked. 'We're having a fucking great time.'

'Because we deserve it,' Jessie said, stumbling over her words. 'You and me. We fucking deserve it. We're better than them. They're nothing compared to us.'

She raised her glass so abruptly that half the champagne spilled out, landing on her bare stomach.

'Oops,' she said, giggling.

She reached for a towel, but Sam stopped her. He looked around. The dock was hidden by a fence, and the boats out in the water were a good distance away. They were alone in the world.

He knelt down in front of her, between her legs. She looked down at him with excitement. Slowly he licked the champagne off her skin. He sucked up the bubbly that had filled her navel and then ran his tongue over her sun-warmed skin. She tasted of champagne and sweat. He raised his eyes and looked at her. Keeping his eyes fixed on hers, he reached for the edge of her bikini bottoms and slowly pulled them down. When he began licking her, he heard her panting breaths mixing with the sound of the seagulls screeching overhead. They were alone. All alone in the world.

THE STELLA CASE

Leif Hermansson took a deep breath before he stepped inside the small interview room at the police station. Helen Persson and her parents, KG and Harriet, were waiting inside. He knew the parents – everyone in Fjällbacka did – though they were no more than chance acquaintances. It was different with Marie Wall's parents. The police in Tanumshede had had countless opportunities to meet them over the years.

Leif wasn't happy about being police chief. He didn't enjoy supervising others or having to make the decisions. But he was too good at his job, and it had got him promoted. Of course it was only the police station in Tanumshede; he had politely but firmly turned down all opportunities that would have meant moving somewhere else. He had been born in Tanumshede, and that was where he intended to stay until the very end.

Days like today made him hate being the boss. The responsibility of having to find the perpetrator, male or female, who had killed a little girl, rested heavily on his shoulders.

He opened the door to the dreary room with the grey-painted walls, allowing his eyes to rest for a moment on Helen's slumped figure as she sat at the table. Then he nodded to Harriet and KG, seated on either side of their daughter.

'Is it really necessary for us to have this talk here at the station?' asked KG.

He was chairman of the Rotary Club and a big shot within the local business community. His wife Harriet was always impeccably dressed, with her hair styled and her nails exquisitely manicured. But Leif had no idea what she did with her time other than taking care of her appearance and attending meetings of the Home and School Association. She always seemed to be at KG's side at various functions and parties, always laughing and with a martini in her hand.

'We thought it would be easier for you to come to us,' said Leif, signalling an end to that discussion.

How the police chose to do their job was their own concern, and he had a feeling that KG would try to take over if he didn't keep tight control of the conversation.

'It's the other girl you should be talking to,' said Harriet, tugging at her freshly ironed white blouse. 'Marie. She comes from that dreadful family.'

'We have to talk to both girls, since all indications are that they were the last ones to see Stella alive.'

'But Helen has nothing to do with this. Surely you understand that.'

KG was so indignant, his moustache quivered.

'We're not saying they had anything to do with the girl's death, but they were the last ones to see her, and we need to go over the chain of events if we're going to find the perpetrator.'

Leif glanced at Helen. She was sitting in silence, staring down at her hands. She had dark hair like her mother. She was pretty in a quiet, ordinary sort of way. Her shoulders were tensed, and she was plucking at her dress.

'Helen, can you tell me in your own words what

happened?' he said gently, surprised to feel a certain tenderness for the girl.

She looked so vulnerable and frightened, and her parents seemed much too focused on themselves to notice their daughter's terror.

Helen glanced at her father, who nodded curtly.

'We promised Linda and Anders to babysit Stella. We live nearby, and sometimes we go over there to play with Stella. They said they'd give us twenty kronor so we could go to the kiosk with Stella and buy ice cream.'

'When did you pick her up?' asked Leif.

The girl looked up at him.

'I think it was around one. I went over there with Marie.'

'Marie,' snorted Harriet, but Leif raised his hand to silence her.

'So it was around one o'clock.'

Leif jotted down the time in the notebook in front of him. The tape recorder was silently running in the background, but taking notes helped him to organize his thoughts.

'Yes, but Marie would know better than me.'

Helen shifted position.

'Who was at home when you picked her up?'

Leif stopped writing and smiled at Helen, but she still refused to meet his eye as she picked invisible lint off her white summer dress.

'Her mother. And Sanna. They were about to leave when we got there. She gave us the money so we could pay for the ice cream. Stella was really happy. She was jumping up and down.'

'Did you leave at once? Or did you stay at the farm for a while?'

Helen shook her head and a lock of her dark hair fell into her face.

'We played on the farm. Jumped rope with Stella. She

likes it when we each take one end of the rope so she can jump. But she kept stumbling and getting tangled up, so we got tired of the game.'

'What did you do then?'

'We took her with us and walked to Fjällbacka.'

'That must have taken quite a while.'

Leif made a quick calculation. It would take him personally about twenty minutes to go from the Strand farm to the centre of town. With a four-year-old in tow, it would take much longer. The child would want to smell the grass and pick flowers and then she'd get a pebble in her shoe, or she'd have to pee, and her legs would get so tired that she wouldn't want to go any further. Walking from the farm to Fjällbacka with a four-year-old would take for ever.

'We took a pushchair with us,' said Helen. 'The kind you can fold up so it gets really small.'

'A collapsible pushchair,' said Harriet.

Leif gave her a look that stopped her from saying anything else.

Helen cast a quick glance at her mother.

Leif put down his pen.

'So how long did it take you to get there? With Stella in the pushchair.'

Helen frowned.

'It took ages. It's a gravel road up to the main road, and it's hard to steer a pushchair on gravel. The wheels kept getting stuck.'

'But approximately how long did it take?'

'Maybe forty-five minutes? But we didn't check the time. We don't have watches.'

'You do have a watch,' said Harriet. 'You just refuse to wear it. But I'm not surprised that other girl doesn't have one. If she did, it probably would have been a stolen watch.'

'Mamma! Don't say that!'

Helen's eyes flashed.

Leif looked at Harriet.

'If you don't mind, let's stick to the matter in hand.'

He nodded at Helen.

'Then what? How long did you stay in Fjällbacka with Stella?'

Helen shrugged.

'I don't know. We bought ice cream and sat on the wharf for a while, but we didn't let Stella go near the edge because she can't swim, and we didn't have any life jackets with us.'

'Very smart,' said Leif with a nod.

He made a note to speak to Kjell and Anita who owned the kiosk to see if they recalled seeing the girls and Stella yesterday.

'So you ate your ice cream and sat on the wharf. Did you do anything else?'

'No. After a while we started walking back. Stella was tired. She fell asleep in the pushchair.'

'So you spent about an hour in Fjällbacka? Does that sound right?'

Helen nodded.

'Did you go the same way back?'

'No, on the way back Stella wanted to go through the woods, so she got out of the pushchair and we walked the rest of the way through the woods.'

Leif jotted down a few notes.

'And when you got back, what time do you think it was?'

'I don't know, but it took about the same amount of time to walk home.'

Leif looked down at the notes he'd written. If the girls arrived at the farm around one, played for twenty minutes or so, then walked to Fjällbacka in forty minutes, spent an hour there and then walked back in forty minutes, it would have been about 15.40 when they got home. Although considering Helen's less than precise sense of time, he couldn't rely on that, so he wrote '15.30–16.15' in his notebook and drew a circle around it. Even that time frame might not be reliable.

'What happened once you got home with Stella?'

'We saw her father's car in the yard, so we assumed he was home. And when we saw Stella running towards the house, we left.'

'But you didn't see her father? You didn't see her go inside the house?'

'No.'

Helen shook her head.

'Did the two of you go straight home?'

'No . . .'

Helen glanced at her parents.

'What did you do?'

'We went over to the lake behind Marie's farm and went swimming.'

'We've told you before you're not allowed—'

A look from Leif stopped Harriet.

'About how long were you there?'

'I don't know. But I was home for dinner at six.'

'Yes, she was,' said KG, nodding. 'Though she didn't tell us anything about going swimming. She said they'd been babysitting little Stella the whole time.'

He glared at his daughter, who was still looking down at her dress.

'Obviously we noticed that her hair was wet, but she said they'd been running through the sprinkler with Stella.'

'It was stupid to lie. I know that,' said Helen. 'But I'm not supposed to go there. They don't like me to go anywhere with Marie, but that's just because of her family, and she can't help who her parents are, can she?'

Again her eyes flashed.

'That girl is made of the same stuff as her family,' said KG.

'She's just . . . a little tougher than others,' said Helen in a low voice. 'But maybe there's a good reason for her to be that way. Have you ever thought about that? She didn't choose to grow up in that family.'

'Let's all calm down,' said Leif, holding up his hands.

Even though their argument told him something valuable about their family dynamics, this wasn't the right time or place to be airing such matters.

He read aloud from his notes.

'Does that match more or less what you remember about yesterday?'

Helen nodded.

'Yes, it does.'

'And Marie will tell me the same thing?'

For a moment he thought he saw a glimmer of uncertainty in her eyes. Then she replied calmly:

'Yes, she will.'

✤

'How are you doing?' asked Paula, giving Martin a searching look as they drove.

He wondered how long everyone was going to keep worrying about him.

'Things are good,' he said, surprised to hear that he actually meant it.

His grief at losing Pia would never disappear completely. He would always wonder what their life together might have been, and he'd see her like a shadowy presence at all the important occasions in Tuva's life. Even at the less important occasions, for that matter. After Pia died, people told him a time would come when he'd be able to enjoy life again. That one day he would feel happy and find himself laughing. That his grief would never go away, but he'd learn to live with it, to walk side by side with his sorrow. At the time, when he was wandering in darkness, it had seemed impossible. In the beginning he frequently seemed to be taking one step forward and two steps back, but after a while it became two steps forward and one step back. Until gradually all movement was forward.

Martin's thoughts turned to the mother he'd met at the playground yesterday. To be honest, he'd been thinking about her a lot. He realized he should have asked for her phone number. Or at least found out her name. But it was easy to think of things after the event. He'd felt flustered when he realized he'd like to see her again. As luck would have it, they lived in a small community, and he'd been hoping to see her at the playground today. That was his plan, anyway, until Nea was found murdered, and he'd been forced to end his holiday and go back to work.

Guilt flooded over him. How could he be thinking about a woman at a time like this?

'You look happy, but also a little worried,' said Paula, as if she'd read his thoughts.

Before he could stop himself, he told her about the woman at the playground. He nearly missed the exit and had to turn the wheel hard to the left.

'Aha,' said Paula. 'She's so cute you can't even drive when you think about her!' She reached for the grab-handle above the car window.

'You probably think I'm a real idiot,' Martin said, blushing so much that his freckles were even more noticeable against his pale skin.

'I think it's great,' said Paula, patting his leg. 'And don't feel guilty. Life has to go on. And if you're feeling good, then you'll do a better job. So find out who she is and give her a call. We're not going to be able to work round the clock. If we get too tired we'll only make mistakes.'

'You're probably right,' said Martin, wondering how he should go about finding her.

He knew the name of her son. That was always a start. Tanumshede wasn't a big place, so he should be able to find her. Provided she wasn't a tourist just passing through. What if she didn't even live in the area?

'Aren't we going to stop somewhere?' said Paula as he drove past the first house they'd seen since turning on to the gravel road.

'What? Oh, sorry,' he said, blushing again.

'I'll help you track her down later,' Paula told him with a grin.

Martin pulled into the driveway of an old, red-painted house with white trim and lots of gingerbread details. He found himself sighing from sheer envy. This was exactly the sort of house he'd dreamed of owning. He and Pia had been saving up for a house, and had almost scraped together enough for a down payment. Every evening they would search the property websites, and they'd even gone to their first viewing. But then came the cancer diagnosis. The money was still in his savings account. His dream of buying a house had died with Pia, along with all his other dreams.

Paula knocked on the door of the house.

'Hello?' she called after a moment.

She glanced at Martin, found the door was unlocked, and stepped into the entryway. In a big city it would have been unthinkable to do such a thing, but here few people ever locked their doors, and friends would often simply go inside. The woman who now came towards them didn't seem the least bit startled to hear the voices of strangers in her front hall.

'Oh, hello. Looks like the police are paying me a visit, am I right?' she said, giving them a smile.

She was so short and tiny and wrinkled that Martin was afraid the draught coming in from the front door might blow her over.

'Come in. I'm watching the third round between Alexander Gustafsson and Daniel Cormier,' she said.

Martin gave Paula a puzzled look. He had no clue what the old lady was talking about. He had very little interest in sports. Occasionally he might watch a football match if Sweden was in the semi-finals for the European or world championships, but that was about it. And he knew

Paula was even less interested in sports, if such a thing were possible.

'Whatever it is you want, it'll have to wait. Have a seat on the sofa,' the woman told them, pointing at a rose-patterned sofa upholstered in some sort of shiny fabric.

Slowly she lowered herself on to a big wingback chair with a footstool placed right in front of the huge TV. To his surprise, Martin saw that the 'match' she was watching consisted of two men in a cage going at each other like crazy.

'Gustafsson had him in an arm lock in the second round, and Cormier nearly caved, but the bell rang just as he was about to give up. And now in the third round Gustafsson is looking tired, while Cormier is recharged. But I haven't given up yet. Gustafsson has a fierce fighting spirit, and if he can only get him down on the ground, I think he'll take it home. Cormier is strongest when he's on his feet, but not as sharp on the ground.'

Martin found himself speechless as he stared at the woman.

'Mixed Martial Arts, right?' asked Paula. 'MMA?'

The woman looked at her as if she were an idiot.

'Of course it's MMA. What did you think it was? Hockey?'

She chuckled. Martin noticed a glass of whisky on the table next to her chair. When I'm her age, he thought, I'm going to treat myself to whatever I want, and whenever I want it, and never mind what might be considered sensible.

'It's a title match,' said the woman, her eyes fixed on the TV. 'They're fighting for the world championship. It's been billed as the match of the year. So you'll have to excuse me if I can't give you my full attention right now. I don't want to miss this.'

She reached for her glass and took a swig of whisky. On the TV screen the big blond guy knocked down the dark-skinned man with the bizarrely wide shoulders and then pounced on top of him. To Martin it looked like an assault that would have earned him several years in jail in real life. And what about those ears? What had those guys done to their ears? They were big and thick and looked like badly shaped lumps of clay. He suddenly understood what people meant by 'cauliflower ears' when they talked about fighters.

'Three minutes to go,' said the woman, taking another swig of her drink.

Martin and Paula exchanged glances. He could see she was trying hard not to laugh. This was the last thing they'd expected.

Suddenly the woman shouted and leapt up from her chair.

'YES!'

'Did he win?' asked Martin. 'Did Gustafsson win?'

The blond giant was racing around the cage like a lunatic. He jumped up on the edge and screamed. Apparently, he was the winner.

'Cormier got beat. He had him in a rear neck choke, and he finally gave up.'

She downed the last of her whisky.

'Is he the one they've been writing about in all the papers? The Mole – isn't that what they call him?' asked Paula, looking pleased she'd remembered that much.

'The Mole? No, he's called The Mauler!' the woman snorted. 'Gustafsson is one of the best in the world. Surely you know that – it's common knowledge.'

She got up to go to the kitchen.

'I'm going to make some coffee. Would you like some?'

'Yes, please,' said both Martin and Paula.

Having a cup of coffee was part of what they did when

165

they were out talking to people. If they had a lot of interviews in one day, it was sometimes hard to get to sleep at night.

They got up and followed the woman into the kitchen. Martin realized they hadn't even introduced themselves.

'Sorry, we didn't get a chance to tell you our names. I'm Martin Molin, and this is Paula Morales. We're from the Tanumshede police station.'

'Dagmar Hagelin,' said the woman cheerfully as she set a kettle on the hob. 'Have a seat at the table. It's more pleasant. I only use the living room when I want to watch TV. I prefer to spend most of my time in here.'

She pointed to the worn wooden table, which was covered with crossword puzzles. Quickly she gathered them all up and set the pile on the window ledge.

'A workout for the brain. I'll be ninety-two in September, so I need to keep exercising the old noggin, else dementia will creep in faster than you can say . . . Oh, er, I forget.'

She laughed merrily at her own joke.

'How did you get interested in MMA?' asked Paula.

'My great-grandson is involved at the elite level. He doesn't compete in the UFC yet, but it's only a matter of time. He's good, and he's ambitious.'

'I see. But it's still a little . . . um, unusual,' Paula ventured.

Dagmar didn't reply at once. She took the kettle off the hob using a crocheted potholder and set it on the table on top of a cork trivet. Then she got out three sweet little cups made of delicate porcelain with a pink pattern and gold rims. She put them on the table and sat down to serve the coffee. Only then did she speak.

'We've always been very close, Oscar and I, so I started going to his matches. And it's easy to get caught up in the whole thing. You can't help it. I was quite a successful track-and-field athlete in my younger days, so I can relate to the tension and excitement.'

She pointed to a black-and-white photograph on the wall of a young and sporty-looking woman on her way over the high-jump bar.

'That's you?' said Martin, impressed as he tried to match the image of the tall, slender, and muscular young woman with the tiny, stooped grey-haired granny sitting across from him.

Dagmar seemed to know what he was thinking and gave him a big smile.

'Even I have a hard time believing that's me. But the strange thing is, I feel the same way inside as I did back then. Sometimes I'm shocked when I look at myself in the mirror, and I find myself saying: "Who's this old lady?"'

'How long were you involved in sports?' asked Paula.

'Not long, compared to athletes today, but too long for those days. When I met my husband, I had to put sports aside, and then I had a child and a house to take care of. But I'm not blaming my daughter. That's the way things were. She's a fine person. She wants me to come and live with her when I can't take care of the house any more. She's getting on in years herself. She'll be sixty-three this winter, so I think we'd get along all right if we ended up under the same roof.'

Martin took a sip of coffee from the delicate cup.

'It's Kopi Luwak coffee,' said Dagmar when she saw the look of pleasure on his face. 'My eldest grandchild imports it to Sweden. It's made from coffee beans eaten by civet cats. The civets poop out the beans, which are then gathered, washed, and roasted. It's not cheap. Usually costs about six hundred kronor per cup, but as I said, Julius imports the coffee, so he gets it for a better price, and sometimes he gives me some. He knows I love it. You'll never taste better coffee.'

Martin looked at the coffee aghast, but then shrugged and took another sip. He didn't care where it came from when it tasted so divine. He hesitated for a moment but decided it was time to move on from the small talk.

'I don't know whether you've heard the news,' he said, leaning forward. 'But a little girl was found murdered up here in the woods.'

'I heard. My daughter came by and told me,' said Dagmar, her expression darkening. 'That sweet little blonde girl who was always running around like a tornado. I still go out for a long walk every day, and I often go past the Berg farm. I'd often see her out in the yard.'

'When did you last see her?' asked Martin, taking another sip of coffee.

'Hmm . . . when was it?' said Dagmar, looking pensive. 'Not yesterday, but the day before, I think. On Sunday.'

'What time of day?' asked Paula.

'I always take my walk in the morning before it gets too hot. She was out in the yard, playing. I waved to her as I walked past, like I always do, and she waved back.'

'So that was Sunday morning?' said Martin. 'But not since then?'

Dagmar shook her head.

'No. I didn't see her yesterday.'

'Did you happen to see anything that struck you as unusual? The smallest detail could be important. So even if something seems trivial to you, better to tell us and we'll decide whether it's significant or not.'

Martin drank the rest of his coffee. He felt so clumsy holding the fragile little cup in his hand. He set it carefully down on the saucer.

'No, I can't say I recall anything that would be of interest. I have a good view out the kitchen window when I'm sitting here, but I don't remember seeing anything special.'

'If you happen to think of something later on, don't hesitate to phone us,' said Paula, getting up after casting an enquiring glance at Martin, who nodded.

She put her business card on the table and pushed in her chair.

'Thanks for the coffee,' said Martin. 'It was excellent and also . . . an experience.'

'Precisely the way things in life should be,' replied Dagmar with a smile.

He glanced again at the photo of the beautiful young athlete and saw the same glint in her eye as in the eyes of ninety-one-year-old Dagmar. He recognized that glint. Pia had had it too: joie de vivre.

With great care he closed the lovely old front door behind him.

Mellberg stretched as he sat at the head of the conference table. An impressive group of reporters had gathered. Not only from the local papers, but from the national media as well.

'Is it the same perpetrator?' asked Kjell from *Bohusläningen*.

Patrik was keeping a close eye on Mellberg. He would have preferred to take over, but Mellberg had put his foot down. A press conference was his moment in the spotlight, and he wasn't about to give up the opportunity. This was in stark contrast to his readiness to step aside when it came to anything that resembled hard work.

'We can't rule out the possibility of a link to the Stella case, but we're not going to get locked into any one theory,' said Mellberg.

'But surely it's not a coincidence,' Kjell insisted.

His dark beard now had a few streaks of grey.

'As I said, we will of course investigate every angle, but when something seems too obvious, there's a risk we might not look into other possibilities.'

Good answer, Mellberg, thought Patrik with surprise. Maybe he'd actually learned a few things along the way.

'Though clearly it does seem a strange coincidence that the film star should come back here right before this happens,' said Mellberg. All the reporters began feverishly taking notes.

Patrik had to clench his fists to stop himself from slapping his forehead. He could already guess what the evening headlines would be.

'So, are you planning to question Marie and Helen?' asked a hack from one of the evening papers.

The younger reporters were always the most persistent. Hungry to establish themselves at the paper and prepared to do whatever it took to make their name.

'Yes, we plan to talk to them,' Mellberg confirmed. It was obvious he was enjoying all the attention.

He gladly turned his face towards the cameras aimed at him, reaching up to make sure his comb-over was in place.

'So are they your prime suspects?' asked a young female reporter from the other big evening paper.

'Well, I mean . . . No, I wouldn't exactly say that . . .'

Mellberg scratched his head and seemed to realize he might have turned the conversation in the wrong direction. He looked at Patrik, who cleared his throat and said:

'We have no suspects at this stage of the investigation. As Bertil Mellberg said, we're not ruling anything out yet. We're waiting for the technical report, and we're carrying out interviews on a broad front, talking to people who might provide information regarding the time period when Nea disappeared.'

'So you think it's merely coincidence that a girl from the same farm disappears and is found dead in the same place as Stella, during the same week when one of the individuals convicted in the Stella case comes back here for the first time in thirty years?'

'The most obvious connections are not always the most significant,' he replied to the follow-up question. 'So it would not be wise for us to get locked into one theory right now. As Mellberg has already pointed out.'

Kjell from *Bohusläningen* raised his hand to indicate he had another question.

'How did the girl die?'

Mellberg leaned forward.

'As Patrik Hedström mentioned, we haven't yet received the technical report, and the post-mortem hasn't been done. So at this time we can't address that question.'

'Is there a risk other children might be murdered?' Kjell went on. 'Should parents in the area keep their children inside? As you might expect, rumours have been spreading, and people are scared.'

Mellberg paused before answering. Patrik discreetly shook his head, hoping his boss would get the message. There was no reason to frighten the local population.

'At the present time there is no reason for concern,' Mellberg said. 'We're putting all our resources into this investigation. We will find out who killed Linnea Berg.'

'Was she killed in the same way as Stella?'

Kjell wasn't giving up. The other journalists looked from him to Mellberg. Patrik crossed his fingers that Mellberg would stand firm.

'As I said, we won't know until we have the results of the pathology report.'

'But you're not denying it?' the young hack chimed in.

In his mind Patrik again pictured the body of the little girl, lying exposed and alone on the cold autopsy table. He couldn't help snapping, 'We've already told you that we won't know anything until we get the pathology report!'

The young reporter retreated, looking offended.

Kjell raised his hand again. This time he looked straight at Patrik.

'I've heard your wife is writing a book about the Stella case. Is that true?'

Patrik had known the question would come, but he still felt unprepared for it. He looked down at his clenched fists.

'For some reason, my wife refuses to discuss her projects, even with the excellent resources she has at home,' he said, drawing a ripple of laughter from the reporters. 'So I've only heard a few things about it in passing. I don't know how far along she is in her research. I'm usually kept out of the creative process, and I don't get involved until she asks me to read the completed manuscript.'

That wasn't entirely true, but almost. He knew roughly what stage Erica had reached in the project, but only because of a few casual remarks she'd let slip. She was always reluctant to talk about her books while she was working on them, and he usually got involved only if she needed to ask him about any police-related issues. But she rarely supplied any context when putting her questions, so they were little help in getting a sense of the book itself.

'Could that have been a contributing factor? For another murder?'

The young woman from the evening paper was looking at him expectantly, and he could see the gleam in her eye. What the hell did she mean? Was she saying his wife might have provoked the death of the little girl?

He was about to open his mouth to deliver a scathing reply when he heard Mellberg's calm admonition:

'I consider that question both tasteless and irrelevant. And no, there is nothing to suggest any connection what-soever between Erica Falck's book and the murder of

Linnea Berg. And if you can't refrain from such out-
rageous questions during the next' – Mellberg glanced at
his watch – 'ten minutes that remain of this press conference, I won't hesitate to cut it short. Understood?'

Patrik exchanged astonished glances with Annika. And
to his great surprise, the journalists behaved themselves
for the rest of the press conference.

After Annika had ushered everyone out, overriding
their mild protests and attempts to ask a few more questions, Patrik and Mellberg remained behind in the
conference room.

'Thank you,' said Patrik simply.

'I'll be damned if I'll let them go after Erica,' muttered
Mellberg, and turned away.

He called to Ernst, who had been lying under the table
where Annika had set out coffee for the reporters, and
then left the room.

Patrik laughed quietly to himself. Amazing. The old
guy had a streak of loyalty in him after all!

BOHUSLÄN 1671

Elin had to admit that Britta looked enchanting. Her dark eyes were beautifully offset by the blue fabric of her gown, and her hair had been brushed to a glossy sheen. She wore her hair loose, held back from her face by a lovely silk ribbon. It was not often that they received such a grand visitor. Actually never, if truth be told. Such dignitaries had no reason to visit a simple vicarage in Tanumshede parish, but the king's edict issued to Harald Stake, governor of Bohuslän, had been quite clear. All the representatives of the church in the county were to be involved in the battle against sorcery and the forces of evil. The government and the church had joined together to fight the devil, and for that reason the vicarage in Tanumshede was to be honoured with a visit. The message was to be spread to all corners of the realm; that was what the king had decreed. And Britta was quick to understand and exploit the opportunity. They would offer the very best in food, lodging, and conversation during Lars Hierne's visit. He had politely suggested he might stay at the local inn, but Preben had told him that would be out of the question. At the vicarage they would be delighted to receive such an esteemed guest. Even though the inn had a separate section for noble and refined guests, the Tanumshede vicarage would see to it that the governor's envoy would be offered all the comforts he might desire.

Britta and Preben were waiting at the door when the carriage arrived. Elin and the other servants kept to the background, their heads bowed and their eyes fixed on their feet. Everyone had been ordered to appear neat and tidy, dressed in clean clothing. And the girls had all combed their hair so carefully that not a strand escaped from beneath their kerchiefs. The air was filled with the fresh scent of soap and the pine boughs the servant boy had used to decorate the rooms that morning.

When the vicar and his wife were seated at the table with their guest, Elin poured wine into the big tankards her father had always used to serve wine when she was growing up. They had been passed on to Britta as a wedding gift. When she married, Elin had received several of the tablecloths her mother had embroidered. Her father had not wanted the finer things from his home to end up in the poor hovel of a fisherman. And Elin had actually agreed with his decision. What would she and Per have done with such frills and finery? Those things were better suited to the vicarage than Elin's simple home. But she treasured her mother's tablecloths. She kept them in a small chest along with the herbs she gathered and dried every summer. She always wrapped the herbs in paper so as not to stain the white cloths.

Ever since she was little, Märta had been sternly warned never to open the chest. Elin did not want her child's sticky fingers touching her mother's tablecloths, but the admonition was also because some of the herbs could be poisonous if not handled properly. Her maternal grandmother had taught her the uses of the various herbs, along with the words of supplication to be used. There could be no confusion, or disaster might ensue. Elin was ten years old when her grandmother began teaching her, and she had decided to wait until Märta was the same age before she passed on her knowledge.

'Oh, how terrible it is with all these wives of the devil,' said Britta, giving Lars Hierne a gentle smile.

Enchanted, he stared at her lovely features glowing in the light of the many tallow candles. Britta had chosen well when she decided to wear the blue brocade dress; the fabric gleamed and sparkled against the backdrop of the dark walls in the vicarage dining room, making Britta's eyes look as blue as the sea on a sunny day in July.

Elin silently wondered how Preben was reacting to the way their visitor was immodestly staring at his wife, but he appeared completely unaffected. He seemed to pay no attention at all. Instead, Elin felt him looking at her, and she quickly lowered her gaze. She had already noticed that he too looked exceptionally stylish. When he was not wearing his clerical garb, he dressed most often in dirty work clothes. For a man of his position, he had an odd fondness for doing manual labour on the farm and taking care of the livestock. On her very first day at the vicarage, Elin had asked one of the other maids about this and was told it was indeed strange, but the master often worked side by side with his servants. They had simply grown accustomed to this unusual behaviour. Yet the maid had gone on to say that the mistress did not favour her husband's conduct, which had led to many quarrels at the farm. When the maid suddenly realized who Elin was, her whole face turned red. This sort of response occurred frequently. Elin held a strange position on the farm, since she was both a maid and the sister of the vicar's wife. She belonged and yet did not belong. When she entered the servants' quarters the others would often stop talking and refuse to look in her direction. In that sense, she felt even lonelier, but it did not greatly concern her. She had never been friends with many women, most of whom she regarded as spending far too much time gossiping and squabbling.

'Yes, these are troubling times,' said Lars Hierne. 'Yet we are fortunate to have a king who refuses to turn a blind eye, a king who dares to enter the battle against the evil forces we are now fighting. This has been a difficult year for the realm, and the ravages of Satan have been greater than for many generations. The more of these women we can find and bring to trial, the faster we can quell the devil's power.'

He took a bite of bread and ate it with pleasure. Britta's gaze was fixed on his lips, and her face shone with both fascination and alarm.

Elin listened closely as she carefully refilled his tankard with wine. The first course had been served, and Boel of Holta need not feel shame for the meal she had prepared. They were all eating with great appetite, and Lars Hierne praised the food many times, which caused Britta to modestly throw out her hands.

'But how can you be certain these women are part of the devil's web?' asked Preben as he leaned back in his chair, holding the tankard in his hand. 'We have not yet found the need to bring anyone to trial here in our district, but I doubt we will be spared. Though so far we have merely heard rumours and loose talk about how others have set about the task.'

Lars Hierne tore his eyes away from Britta and turned to Preben.

'It is actually a very simple and straightforward process to establish whether someone is a witch – or a sorcerer, for that matter. We must not forget that women are not the only ones who may succumb to Satan's temptations. Although it is more common for womenfolk, since they are more susceptible to the devil's enticements.'

He gave Britta a solemn look.

'To determine whether the accused is indeed a witch, we first subject her to the water test. She is bound, hand and foot, and thrown into deep water.'

'What happens next?'

Britta leaned forward. She seemed to find the subject fascinating.

'If she floats, she is a witch. I am proud to say that so far we have not subjected a single innocent woman to an unjust accusation. They have all floated like birds. And with that, they have revealed their true nature. Afterwards they are offered the chance to confess and receive God's forgiveness.'

'And have they confessed? The witches you have seized?'

Britta leaned even closer, and the flames from the candles cast dancing shadows over her face.

Lars Hierne nodded.

'Oh yes, they have all confessed. Some have required . . . persuasion in order to elicit a confession. Where a woman has been long under Satan's power or deeply in thrall to the evil one, his hold may be greater. But in the end they all confess. And upon confessing they have been executed according to the decree of both king and God.'

'You are carrying out a most important task,' said Preben, nodding pensively. 'Yet I dread the day when we must carry out such a painful duty here in our parish.'

'Yes, it is indeed a heavy cross to bear, but we must have the courage to take on whatever obligations Our Lord asks of us.'

'In truth, in truth,' said Preben, raising the tankard to his lips.

The next course was now brought to the table, and Elin hurried to pour more red wine. All three had already had a good deal to drink, and a slight haze had appeared in their eyes. Again Elin felt Preben looking at her, and she took great pains not to meet his eye. A shiver raced down her spine, and she nearly dropped the pitcher she was holding. Her grandmother used to call such a feeling a premonition of trouble brewing. But Elin convinced herself it was merely a gust of wind from a gap in the window frame.

Later, when she went to bed, however, the feeling returned. She drew Märta closer on the narrow cot they shared, in an attempt to fend it off, but the feeling stayed with her.

✤

Gösta was glad he wasn't expected to attend the press conference. It was nothing but show and spectacle, in his opinion. He always had the feeling the journalists were there to find fault and stir up trouble rather than to communicate with the public and contribute to the investigation. But maybe he was a cynic. When you'd been in the job as long as he had, cynicism became a habit that was hard to break.

Even though he was happy not to participate in the press conference, the prospect of interviewing Eva and Peter filled him with dread. According to the doctor, although badly shaken they'd be up to answering his questions. Gösta remembered when he and Maj-Britt lost their little son and how grief had paralysed them for a long time afterwards.

He saw Paula and Martin's car parked outside a small red-painted house with white trim. He hoped they were having some luck with their door-to-door enquiries. Out in the country, neighbours tended to keep a close eye on any goings on. His own place was in a slightly out of the way location, near the Fjällbacka golf course, and he often found himself sitting in the kitchen, staring out the window at passers-by. Another habit he'd picked up over the years. He had a clear memory of his father sitting at the kitchen table and staring out the window. As a boy he'd thought it silly, but now he understood why his father had done it. There was something soothing about simply looking out the window. Not that he'd ever tried any of that meditation nonsense, but he could imagine there were certain similarities.

He turned on to the track leading up to the farm. Yesterday the yard had been bustling with activity, but now it was empty and desolate. Not a soul in sight. And it was quiet. Very quiet. The blustery wind from earlier in the morning had subsided now that the sun had passed its zenith. The air was shimmering with heat.

A jump rope was lying on the ground near the barn, and Gösta carefully avoided stepping on a hopscotch game scratched into the dirt. It was already partially erased and no doubt wouldn't last much longer. Nea must have traced the outline with the toe of her little foot, or maybe her parents had helped her draw it.

Gösta paused a moment to look at the house. Nothing about the farm gave any indication of the tragedy that had played out here. The old barn was slightly more crooked and tilting than he remembered from thirty years ago, but the farmhouse was freshly painted and in good repair, and the flowers in the garden were more abundant than ever. Clothes had been hung up to dry at one end of the yard, and he saw a child's garments that would never be worn again. His throat tightened and he had to cough. Then he walked towards the house. No matter what his own feelings might be, he had a job to do. If someone had to talk to the parents, he was the right person to do it.

'Knock, knock. May I come in?'

The kitchen door was ajar, so he pushed it open. An older and significantly tanner version of Peter got up from the table and came to shake his hand.

'I'm Bengt,' he said solemnly.

A thin woman who was equally tan also stood up. She had sun-bleached hair worn in a pageboy style. She introduced herself as Ulla.

'The doctor told us you'd be coming over,' said Bengt.

His wife sat down again. The table was covered with crumpled pieces of paper.

'Yes, I asked him to tell you, so my visit wouldn't be unexpected,' replied Gösta.

'Have a seat. I'll get Eva and Peter,' said Bengt quietly as he headed for the stairs. 'They've been resting.'

Ulla looked at Gösta with tears in her eyes as he sat down across from her.

'Who could do such a thing? She was so little . . .'

She reached for a roll of kitchen towels on the table and tore off a piece to wipe her eyes.

'We will do our best to find out who did it,' said Gösta, clasping his hands on the table.

Out of the corner of his eye he saw Bengt coming down the stairs, with Eva and Peter behind him. They were moving slowly, and Gösta felt the lump in his throat grow.

'Would you like some coffee?' asked Eva mechanically.

Ulla jumped up.

'Sit down, honey. I'll get it.'

'But I can . . .' said Eva, turning towards the counter.

Ulla gently pushed her daughter-in-law over to the table.

'No, you sit down. I'll make the coffee,' she said and began looking through the cupboards.

'The filter is in the right-hand cupboard above the sink,' said Eva, about to get up again.

Gösta placed his hand on her trembling arm.

'Your mother-in-law will manage,' he said.

'So you wanted to talk to us?' said Peter, taking Ulla's place at the table.

He looked at all the crumpled balls of paper, as if he couldn't understand what they were doing there.

'Has something happened?' asked Eva. 'Do you know anything? Where is she?'

Her voice was toneless, but her lips quivered.

'We don't have any new information yet, but believe me everyone is working very hard, and we're doing everything we can. Nea is in Gothenburg now. You'll be able to see her later, if you like, but not just yet.'

'What will they . . . what will they do with her?' asked Eva, giving Gösta a look that cut right through him.

He tried not to grimace. He knew all too well what would be done to her little body, but that wasn't something a mother needed to hear.

'Eva, don't ask him that,' said Peter, and Gösta noticed that he too was shaking.

He wasn't sure whether it was from shock or because the shock was leaving Peter's body. Everyone reacted differently, and over the years he'd seen as many reactions as victims of crimes.

'I'm afraid I need to ask you a few questions,' said Gösta, nodding his thanks as Ulla set a cup of coffee in front of him.

She seemed calmer now that she had a task to do. Both she and Bengt looked more composed as they sat down at the table.

'Anything that will help. We'll answer any questions you have. But we don't know anything. We can't understand how this could have happened. Who could have . . .'

Peter's voice broke, and a sob escaped his lips.

'We'll take this one step at a time,' Gösta said calmly. 'I know you've already answered a number of questions, but we'll go through everything again. It's important for us to be as thorough as possible.'

Gösta placed his mobile on the table and, after receiving

a nod from Peter, he switched on the recording function.

'When was the last time you saw her?' he asked. 'Try to be as precise as possible.'

'It was Sunday night,' said Eva. 'Day before yesterday. I read her a story after she put on her nightgown and brushed her teeth at eight o'clock. And I read for maybe half an hour. It was her favourite book, the one about the little mole who gets poop on his head.'

Eva wiped her nose. Gösta reached for the roll of kitchen towels and tore off a piece for her. She blew her nose.

'So it was sometime between eight thirty and eight forty-five?' he asked, and Eva looked at her husband, who nodded.

'Yes. That's about right.'

'What about later? Did you hear her or look in on her? She didn't wake up sometime during the night?'

'No, she always slept like a rock,' said Peter, vigorously shaking his head. 'She always slept with the door closed, and we didn't look in on her once we'd said good night. There were never any problems with Nea in terms of sleeping, even when she was a baby. She loves her bed . . . loved her bed.'

His lower lip quivered and he blinked several times.

'I was up by six in the morning,' said Peter. 'I tiptoed around so I wouldn't wake Eva or Nea. I made myself sandwiches to take with me, and I'd already made coffee the night before, so all I had to do was heat it up. And then . . . then I left.'

'You didn't notice anything out of the ordinary? Was the front door closed and locked?'

Peter paused before saying, 'Yes, it was closed.' His voice broke again, and he began sobbing. Bengt reached out to stroke his back. 'I would have noticed if it hadn't been. If it was open, I definitely would have noticed.'

'What about the door to Nea's room?'

'Same thing. It was closed. I would have remembered.'

Gösta leaned towards Peter.

'So everything was normal? Nothing seemed the least bit different? You didn't see anything odd outside the house? Any people? Any cars passing by?'

'No. Nothing. When I got outside, it felt like I was the only one awake in the world. All I heard were the birds chirping, and all I saw was the cat, who came over to rub on my leg.'

'And then you left? Do you know about what time it was?'

'I had set the alarm for six, and I spent maybe twenty minutes in the kitchen. So it must have been about six twenty or six thirty.'

'And you didn't return home until the afternoon, right? Did you meet anyone? See anyone? Talk to anyone?'

'No. I was out in the woods all day. Several acres of woodland were included when we purchased the farm, and it needs looking after and . . .'

His voice trailed off leaving the sentence unfinished.

'So no one can confirm where you were during the day?'

'No, but . . . What do you mean?'

'Are you accusing Peter of something?' asked Bengt. His face flushed. 'Now wait just a minute—'

Gösta held up his hand. He'd been expecting this. Everyone reacted the same way, and he fully understood why.

'We have to ask. We have to rule out Peter and Eva from our investigation. I don't think they're involved, but it's my job to rule them out, according to police procedure.'

'It's okay,' said Eva faintly. 'I understand. Gösta is only doing his job, Bengt. The faster and better he does it . . .'

'Okay,' said Bengt, but he was still sitting ramrod straight in his chair, ready to defend his son.

'No, I didn't meet anyone all day,' said Peter. 'I was deep in the woods, and there's no mobile reception, so I couldn't get or make any calls. I was all alone. Then I drove home. I was back by quarter to three. And I know the exact time because I checked my watch as I drove into the yard.'

'Okay,' said Gösta. 'What about you, Eva? What was your morning and the rest of the day like? Can you give me a run-down?'

'I slept until nine thirty. I know the precise time because the first thing I always do when I wake up is look at the clock, if I didn't set the alarm, that is. And I remember being surprised . . .'

She shook her head.

'Surprised about what?' asked Gösta.

'Surprised it was so late. I hardly ever sleep past seven. I usually wake up automatically. But I guess I was so tired . . .'

She rubbed her eyes.

'I got up and looked in on Nea and saw she was gone. But that didn't worry me. I wasn't worried at all.'

She gripped the edge of the table.

'Why weren't you worried?' asked Gösta.

'She often went along with Peter,' said Ulla.

Eva nodded.

'Yes, she loved going out in the woods with him, and she usually got up early too. So I assumed she'd gone with him.'

'What did you do after that? During the rest of the day?'

'I spent a long time over breakfast reading the newspaper, and then I got dressed. Around eleven I decided to drive to Hamburgsund to do some shopping. I rarely have time for myself.'

186

'Did you meet anyone there?'

Gösta took a sip of coffee, but it had gone cold, so he set the cup down.

'I'll get you some more,' said Ulla, standing up. 'It must be cold by now.'

He didn't object, just gave her a grateful smile.

'I walked around looking in the shops,' said Eva. 'There were a lot of people, but I didn't see anyone I knew.'

'Okay,' said Gösta. 'Did anyone drop by the farm either before or after your shopping trip to Hamburgsund?'

'No, no one dropped by. I saw a few cars on the road. And several joggers. And right before I left I saw Dagmar out walking, like she always does in the morning.'

'Dagmar?' asked Gösta.

'She lives in the red house nearby. She takes a walk every morning.'

Gösta nodded and accepted the refilled coffee cup Ulla handed him.

'Thanks,' he said taking a sip of the steaming hot coffee. 'Okay. Was there anything in particular that caught your attention? Anything out of the ordinary?'

Eva frowned as she paused to think.

'Take your time. Even the smallest detail might be important.'

She shook her head.

'No. Everything was the same as usual.'

'What about phone calls? Did you talk to anyone on the phone during the day?'

'No, not that I can remember. Wait, I rang you, Ulla, when I got home.'

'That's right, you did.'

Ulla looked surprised that it was only yesterday her life had been perfectly normal. Without the least premonition everything was about to fall apart.

'What time was that?'

'Do you remember?' Eva looked at Ulla. She wasn't shaking any more. Gösta knew this relative calm was only temporary. There would be brief spells when her brain would push aside what had happened. But the next second it would all come back to her. He'd seen this happen so many times during his time as a police officer. The same grief. Different faces. Different reactions, and yet they were so similar. It never ended. There were always more victims.

'I think it was around one o'clock. Bengt, you heard when Eva rang. Wasn't it around one? We'd been down to La Mata for a swim and had not long come home for lunch.'

She turned to Gösta.

'We always have a very light lunch in Torrevieja. Some mozzarella and tomatoes, which are so much better in Spain, and—'

She raised her hand to her mouth, realizing that for a few seconds she had forgotten what had happened and was talking as if everything was normal.

'We got back to the flat shortly before one,' she went on quietly. 'Eva rang not long after. And we talked for maybe ten minutes.'

Eva nodded. Tears had appeared in her eyes again, and Gösta handed her another piece of household paper.

'Did you talk to anyone else yesterday?'

He knew it must sound crazy that he kept asking them about phone calls and who they'd met. But as he'd already explained, he needed to rule them out from the investigation and see whether they could establish any sort of alibi. He didn't for a moment think that Eva and Peter were involved. But he wasn't the first police officer in history to have a hard time believing parents would harm their own child. And unfortunately, in some cases they had. Accidents happened. And horrifyingly enough, sometimes it wasn't an accident.

'No, just Ulla. Then Peter came home, and I realized Nea was missing, and then . . . then . . .'

She was crushing the piece of paper so tightly in her hand that her knuckles were white.

'Is there anyone who might want to harm your daughter?' asked Gösta. 'Have you thought of any possible motive? Someone you used to know in the past? Do you or your family have any enemies?'

Both shook their heads.

'We're completely ordinary people,' said Peter. 'We've never been mixed up in anything criminal, nothing like that.'

'No ex-spouses wanting revenge?'

'No,' said Eva. 'We met when we were fifteen. There's never been anyone else.'

Gösta took a deep breath before asking the next question. He couldn't put it off any longer.

'I know this is a terribly insulting thing to ask, especially given the situation, but are either of you having an extramarital affair? Or have you ever had an affair? I'm not trying to embarrass you. I just need to find out, because it might provide a motive. Maybe somebody thought Nea was in the way.'

'No,' said Peter, staring at Gösta. 'My God. No. We spend all our time together, and we'd never . . . No.'

Eva shook her head vigorously.

'No, no, no. Why are you wasting your time on things like this? Why are you here with us? Why aren't you out looking for the murderer? Is there anyone around here who—'

Her face paled when she realized what she was about to ask, and what those words implied.

'Was she . . . Had she been . . . Oh, dear God . . .'

Her sobs echoed off the kitchen walls, and Gösta had to fight to stay seated and not run out of the room. It was unbearable to see the look on the faces of Nea's parents when they realized there was one question they didn't want answered.

And Gösta had nothing to tell them, no solace to offer, because he didn't know.

'Sorry, but it's sheer chaos out there.'

Jörgen turned to look at the young assistant who'd spoken. A blood vessel was throbbing at his temple when he replied, 'What the hell do you want? We're working here!'

He shoved aside a cameraman who had come too close and was about to back into a table in the living room set they'd created. A vase teetered for a moment and nearly toppled over.

Marie almost felt sorry for the assistant, who was blinking nervously. They were about to film the fourth take, and Jörgen's mood had been rapidly worsening.

'I'm sorry,' said the assistant. Marie thought his name was Jakob. Or was it Jonas?

The young man coughed.

'I can't fend them off much longer. There's a huge crowd of journalists out there.'

'They're not supposed to be here until four. That's when we scheduled the interviews.'

Jörgen looked at Marie, who threw out her hands. She hoped it wasn't going to become a habit for him to speak to her in that tone of voice. Or else it was going to be a very long and uncomfortable filming.

'They're talking about a dead girl,' said Jakob/Jonas uneasily. Jörgen rolled his eyes.

'Yeah, we know. But they'll just have to wait until four.'

The young man's throat flushed crimson, but he didn't budge.

'That's not the girl they're talking about. It's a different girl. And they want to speak to Marie. Now.'

Marie looked around the small film set. The director, cameramen, script girl, make-up artist, and assistants were all staring at her. The same way everyone had stared at her thirty years ago. Strangely enough, there was a certain feeling of security in the familiar situation.

'I'll go talk to them,' she said, straightening her blouse and reaching up to smooth her hair.

Photographers would undoubtedly be present as well.

She turned to the nervous assistant.

'Take them to the break room,' she said and then looked at Jörgen. 'We'll reverse the schedule and do the interviews now. Then we can shoot the scene at four, and we won't lose any time.'

On a film set, the shooting schedule was God, and Jörgen looked as if his whole world had crashed.

Standing in the doorway to the small break room, Marie paused for a moment. The crowd of reporters was impressive. She was glad she was dressed as Ingrid, in white shorts with buttons on both sides, a white blouse, and a scarf tied around her hair. The clothes suited her and would look good in any photographs. Excellent PR for the film.

'Hello!' she said in the slightly husky voice that had become her signature. 'I heard you had some questions you wanted to ask little old me.'

'Do you have any comment about what's happened?'

A young man with the hungry eyes of an evening paper reporter gave her an eager look.

The others in the room were staring at her with equal intensity. She perched on the arm of a sofa that took up most of the space in the room and crossed her long legs, showing them off to good advantage.

'Forgive me, but we've been shut up in the studio all day. Could you tell me what has happened?'

The young reporter leaned forward.

'The little girl who disappeared yesterday has been found. She was murdered. The girl who lived on the same farm as Stella.'

Marie pressed her hand to her chest. She pictured a little girl with reddish blond hair. She was holding a big ice-cream cone in her hand, and the soft ice was dripping down the cone on to her fingers.

'That's horrible,' she said.

An older man sitting next to the reporter stood up and went over to the table to fetch a glass of water, which he handed to Marie.

She nodded and took several sips.

The man with the hungry eyes wasn't about to let up.

'The police just held a press conference, and according to Police Chief Bertil Mellberg, you and Helen Jensen are considered persons of interest in their investigation. What do you have to say about that?'

Marie looked at the tape recorder he had thrust towards her. At first, all words deserted her. She swallowed hard several times. She recalled a different room, a different interview. And the man who had looked at her with suspicion.

'I'm not surprised,' she said. 'The police quickly came to false conclusions thirty years ago.'

'Do you have an alibi for the time in question?' asked the man who had handed her the glass of water.

'Since I have no idea when we're talking about, it's impossible for me to give you an answer.'

The questions now came fast and furious.

'Have you had any contact with Helen since you returned?'

'Isn't it a little strange that a girl from the same farm should die just as you came back here?'

'Have you and Helen kept in touch over the years?'

Usually, Marie loved being the centre of attention, but right now it was almost too much for her. She'd made use of her background to build her career; it had given her an edge over all the other thousands of ambitious young women fighting for acting roles. Yet the memories from those dark, loathsome years had taken their toll on her.

And now she would be forced to relive everything again.

'No, Helen and I have not had any contact. We've lived completely separate lives since we were accused of a crime we didn't commit. Staying in touch would have meant keeping those terrible memories alive. As children we were friends, but we're not the same people as adults. We haven't been in contact since I arrived back in Fjällbacka, or before that either. No contact at all since I was sent away, and the lives of two innocent children were ruined.'

The photographers were frantically snapping pictures. Marie leaned back.

'So what do you think about the coincidence of the two murders?' asked the young reporter. 'The police seem to think there's a connection between them.'

'I can't answer that.' She frowned apologetically. She'd had another Botox injection a month ago, giving her enough time to regain control of her facial features sufficiently before the film shoot began. 'But no, I don't think it's a coincidence. And that only serves to reinforce what I've been saying all these years: while police focused on us, the real murderer was allowed to go free.'

The cameras started flashing again.

'So you're blaming the Tanumshede police for causing Linnea's death?' asked the older journalist.

'Is that her name? Linnea? Poor thing . . . Yes, I'm saying that if they'd done their job properly thirty years ago, this would not have happened.'

'But it's still rather odd that a new murder should be committed only days after you came back here,' said a woman with dark hair cut in a pageboy style. 'Could your return be a factor in triggering the murderer to strike again?'

'That's possible. Don't you agree, it's a reasonable assumption?'

What headlines that would prompt in tomorrow's paper. The financial backers of the film would be over-joyed by all the publicity. If nothing else, it would guarantee that the project could continue.

'I'm sorry, but I'm truly shaken by the news of what's happened. I need time to take it all in before I can answer any more questions. For the time being, you'll have to talk to the film company's PR division.'

Marie stood up, surprised to notice that her legs were shaking. But she wasn't going to think about that now. She refused to think about the dark memories that kept turning up.

It was crowded at the top in her profession, and if she wanted to sustain her star position, she had to keep delivering. Behind her, she heard the reporters rushing out of the room, headed for their cars and computers to make the next deadline. She closed her eyes, picturing again a smiling little girl with reddish blond hair.

'You're lucky your mother is gone so much.'

Nils lit a cigarette. He blew the smoke towards the ceiling in Vendela's bedroom, then flicked the ash into an empty soft drink can on her night table.

'I know, but yesterday she tried to make me go with her to the garden centre,' said Vendela, reaching for Nils's cigarette.

She took a drag and then handed it back to him. He wiped off Vendela's lipstick from the filter before taking another drag.

'I have a hard time picturing you planting a bunch of fucking flowers.'

'Could I have one too?' asked Basse, who was slouched in a red bean chair.

Nils tossed him the pack of Marlboros, which Basse caught in both hands.

'What if somebody saw me there? I'd be a joke in school.'

'No way. Your tits are too nice for you to be a joke.'

Nils squeezed Vendela's boobs, and she slapped him on the shoulder. Not hard though. He knew she actually liked it.

'Did you see how big her tits were? That pig of a girl?' said Basse, unable to suppress a hint of longing in his voice.

Nils threw a pillow at him.

'Don't tell me you were ogling that pig's tits! My God, didn't you see how ugly she was?'

'Course I did. But she still has fucking big tits.'

He used his hands to sketch them in the air, and Vendela sighed.

'You're crazy.'

She looked up at the pale patches on the ceiling. A while ago Nils had told her that he thought One Direction was for kids. The next day she'd taken down all the posters.

'Do you think they're sleeping together?'

Nils blew a smoke ring at the slanted ceiling. He didn't need to say who he was talking about.

'I always thought he was gay,' said Basse, trying without success to blow smoke rings. 'With all that make-up he wears. It's hard to believe his father puts up with it.'

When they were younger, they'd all looked up to James Jensen, a real-life war hero. But now the man was starting to look old and haggard. He was nearly sixty, after all. Maybe it was because James seemed so awesome that they'd started teasing Sam at school. James was everything Sam was not.

Nils reached for the can and dropped his cigarette inside, creating a sizzling sound. He sighed. The old restlessness was back.

'Something had better happen, and soon.'

Basse looked at him.

'Or else you'll make it happen.'

THE STELLA CASE

Leif slowly opened the door. He'd encountered Larry and Lenita on numerous occasions over the years. And their sons. But never their daughter. Until now.

'Hello,' he said simply as he stepped into the room.

Larry and Lenita turned to face him, but Marie didn't look in his direction.

'The police are always dragging us over here to the station as soon as anything happens,' said Larry. 'By now we're used to it. We get blamed for everything. But when you force Marie to come over here for some sort of interrogation, you're bloody well going too far.'

Scorn spewed through the gaps in his teeth. He'd lost three front teeth in various brawls. Whether it was a local dance, a rock concert, or an ordinary Saturday-night gathering, Larry always turned up, drunk and ready for a fight.

'This is not an interrogation,' said Leif. 'We want to have a talk with Marie, that's all. So far we know only that Marie and Helen were the last ones to see Stella alive, and it's important for us to map out the time they spent with the girl.'

'"Map out",' said Lenita with a snort, shaking her head and making her bleached-blond, permed hair flutter.

'Frame her for the murder, that's what you're after. But remember, Marie is only thirteen.'

With a look of outrage she lit a cigarette, and Leif couldn't bring himself to tell her smoking wasn't allowed anywhere in the station.

'We want to hear how the girls spent their time with Stella. That's all.'

He studied Marie, who hadn't yet said a word as she sat between her parents. What must it be like to grow up in a family like hers? Constant rows and drunkenness, with the police coming over to deal with reports of domestic abuse.

Leif thought about one Christmas Eve when the girl was only a baby. If he remembered right, it was the older boy who had rung the police. How old was he back then? Nine? When Leif arrived, he found Lenita lying on the kitchen floor, her face covered in blood. Larry had slammed her head against the cooker, which was spattered with blood. The two boys were in the living room, hiding behind the Christmas tree as Larry ran through the house, cursing and shouting. The older boy was holding his baby sister in his arms. Leif would never forget it.

Lenita had refused to file a report. And through all the years of beatings and bruises, she had steadfastly defended Larry. Occasionally Larry would end up with a couple of bruises himself, and once he even got a nasty bump on the head when Lenita clobbered him with a cast-iron bucket. Leif knew that's what happened because he was actually present when she did it.

'It's okay,' said Marie calmly. 'Ask me whatever you like. I assume you've already talked to Helen, right?'

Leif nodded.

'I saw them arrive here,' said Marie, clasping her hands in her lap.

She was very pretty, and no doubt Lenita had also been a real beauty in her day.

'Tell me in your own words everything you did yesterday,' said Leif, giving Marie a nod. 'I'm going to tape our conversation and also take notes. I hope that's all right.'

'Sure.'

She sat quietly with her hands clasped. She wore jeans and a white camisole, her long blond hair hanging loose and reaching halfway down her back.

Calmly and methodically she described the day. Without ever veering from the topic, her voice steady and composed, she described hour by hour the time they had spent with Stella. Leif found himself mesmerized as he listened to her account. She had a slightly husky voice that was both captivating and made her seem older than her thirteen years. Growing up in the midst of such a chaotic household may have had its effect.

'Are these times correct?'

He repeated what Marie had reported, and she nodded.

'So you dropped her off at the farm when you saw the car belonging to Stella's father parked there? But you didn't actually see him?'

Marie had already said as much, but it was a crucial detail, and Leif wanted to make sure he'd heard correctly.

'Yes, that's right.'

'And then you and Helen went swimming?'

'Yes. Helen wasn't supposed to go swimming, because of her parents. We're not allowed to hang out together.'

Lenita snorted again.

'A right couple of snobs, always got their noses in the air,' she said. 'Think they're so far above everyone else. But as far as I know, they shit just like the rest of us.'

'Are the two of you good friends?' asked Leif.

'I suppose,' said Marie, shrugging. 'We've been friends

since we were kids. Or at least until we were told not to hang out together.'

Leif put down his pen.

'How long has that been? Since you weren't supposed to spend time together?'

Leif wasn't sure he would have wanted his own daughter to have anything to do with the Wall family. He was probably a snob too.

'About six months. They found out that I smoke, so they said their little princess couldn't see me any more. I'm a bad influence.'

Larry and Lenita shook their heads.

'Is there anything else you'd like to add?' asked Leif, looking Marie in the eye.

Her expression was inscrutable, but then she frowned.

'No. I just want to say that I think it's horrible, what happened to Stella. She was so sweet. I hope the police catch whoever did it.'

'We're doing our best,' replied Leif.

Marie nodded calmly.

It felt good to sit in his office with the door closed for a moment. They'd been out searching all night and then everything had come to a halt when Nea's body was found. His eyelids were so heavy it was all he could do to keep them open, and if he didn't get some rest soon, he'd end up falling asleep at his desk. But Patrik couldn't yet allow himself to lie down on the cot in the station's break room. First he had to make several phone calls and then Erica would be coming over to tell them what she knew about the Stella case. And he was looking forward to that. Regardless what Mellberg had said at the press conference, Patrik and his colleagues all thought there was some connection between the two cases. The big question was: What was the link? Had a murderer returned? Was it a copycat killing? What was behind the child's death?

He picked up the phone and made the first call.

'Hi, Torbjörn,' he said when the experienced crime technician answered after a few seconds. 'Do you have any preliminary information for me?'

'You know the procedures as well as I do,' replied Torbjörn.

'Yes, I know you have to meticulously go through all the evidence, but we're talking about a dead little girl in this case, and every minute counts. So was there anything that caught your attention? Anything on the body? Or anything found in the area?'

'I'm sorry, Patrik, but there's nothing I can tell you yet. We collected a lot of things, and we still have to go through it all.'

'Okay, I understand. It was worth a try, though. Please tell the guys to put a rush on it, and let me know as soon as you have anything concrete. We need all the help we can get.'

Patrik glanced at the clear blue sky outside. A large bird was gliding on the updraught until it abruptly dived and disappeared from sight.

'Could you pull the files on the Stella case?' he said. 'We need them for comparison.'

'I've already done that. I'll send them over via the secure email system.'

Patrik smiled.

'You're a gem, Torbjörn.'

He ended the call and took a few deep breaths before making the next one. Fatigue was making him shake.

'Hi, Pedersen. Hedström here. How's it going with the post-mortem?'

'What can I say?' replied the head of forensics in Gothenburg. 'It never gets any easier.'

'I know what you mean. Kids are always the worst. That must be especially so for you.'

Tord Pedersen murmured agreement. Patrik didn't envy him his job.

'When do you think you'll have something for us?'

'Maybe next week.'

'Seriously? Damn. Next week? Can't you get to it any faster?'

The pathologist sighed.

'You know what it's like in the summer—'

'I know. Because of the heat. I know the death statistics always rise. But we're talking about a four-year-old. Surely, you must be able to . . .'

He could hear the plea in his voice. He had complete respect for rules and regulations, yet he kept seeing Nea's face in his mind, and he was prepared to plead and beg if there was any way to speed up the investigation.

'At least give me something we can work from. How about a preliminary cause of death? You must have taken a brief look at her by now . . .'

'It's far too early to say for certain, but she did have a wound on the back of her head. I can tell you that much.'

Patrik made a note of this as he clamped the phone between his ear and shoulder. He hadn't noticed the wound when they lifted the girl up.

'Okay, but you don't know what might have caused it?'

'No, unfortunately I don't.'

'I understand. But please speed up the post-mortem as much as you can, and ring me as soon as you have anything. Okay? Thanks, Pedersen.'

Patrik put down the phone, frustrated. He wanted the results, he wanted them now. But resources were limited, and there were a lot of bodies. That's how it had been during most of his years on the police force. At least he'd found out one thing, even if it was only preliminary information. Though still he wasn't much the wiser. He rubbed his eyes. There was no hope of getting any sleep anytime soon.

Paula couldn't help shuddering as they drove past the farm where Nea lived. Her own son, Leo, was three years old, and the thought of anything happening to him made her feel sick.

'There's a police car over there,' said Martin, pointing. 'Gösta must be talking to the parents.'

'I don't envy him that job,' she said quietly.

Martin didn't say a word.

They looked at the white house they were heading towards. It was within walking distance of Nea's farm and could probably be seen from the barn, though not from the farmhouse.

'Shall we try this place?' asked Martin, and Paula nodded.

'Yes, this is the closest neighbour, so it seems only logical,' she said, realizing her words sounded sterner than she'd intended.

But Martin didn't seem to take offence. He turned on to the driveway and parked. There was no sign of anyone inside the house.

They knocked on the front door, but no one came. Paula tried again, knocking harder. She called 'Hello' but received no answer. She looked for a doorbell but didn't find one.

'Maybe nobody's home.'

'Let's check out back,' said Martin. 'I think I can hear music coming from there.'

They walked around the side of the house. Paula couldn't help admiring all the flowers in the small garden that merged almost seamlessly with the woods. Now she heard the music too. In the backyard they found a woman briskly doing sit-ups on the deck with the music playing loudly.

The woman gave a start when she caught sight of them.

'Sorry to bother you,' said Paula. 'We knocked on the front door.'

The woman nodded.

'It's okay. I was a little startled, that's all. I was so into my . . .'

She turned off the music and stood up. She wiped her sweaty palms on a towel and then shook hands, first with Paula and then with Martin.

'I'm Helen. Helen Jensen.'

Paula frowned. The name sounded familiar. Then the penny dropped. Bloody hell. That Helen. She'd had no clue she lived so close to the Berg family.

'So what are the police doing here?' asked Helen.

Paula glanced at Martin. She saw from his expression that he'd realized who they were talking to.

'Haven't you heard the news?' asked Paula in surprise.

Was Helen pretending not to know? Could she really have missed seeing the commotion in the woods all night? That was all anyone could talk about.

'Heard what?' asked Helen, looking from Martin to Paula. Suddenly she froze. 'Has something happened to Sam?'

'No, no,' said Paula, holding up her hand.

She assumed Sam must be either a son or her husband.

'It's the little girl who lives on the next farm. Linnea. She disappeared yesterday afternoon, or rather, that's when her parents realized she was missing. And I'm afraid that she was found dead this morning.'

The towel slipped out of Helen's hand and landed on the deck. She didn't bother to pick it up.

'Nea? Nea's dead? How? Where?'

She raised a hand to her throat, and Paula could see a vein throbbing under her skin. She swore silently. The plan was for them to talk to Helen after Erica had come to the station to brief all of them on the Stella case. But it couldn't be helped. They were here now and couldn't simply leave and come back later. They'd have to make the best of the situation.

She glanced at Martin, who nodded.

'Could we sit down over there?' he asked, pointing to the vinyl patio furniture a few metres away.

'Of course. Sure. Sorry,' said Helen.

She headed for the open terrace door, which led to the living room.

'Excuse me. I just want to put on a shirt,' she said. She was wearing only a sports bra and leggings.

'Okay,' said Paula.

She and Martin sat down on the patio chairs. They exchanged glances. She could tell Martin was also unhappy about the way the situation was developing.

'This is the kind of garden I'd like to have,' said Martin, looking around. 'Lots of roses and rhododendrons and hollyhocks. There's some peonies over there too.'

He pointed at one side of the garden. Paula hadn't a clue which flowers he meant. Gardens were not her thing. She was happy living in a flat and had no wish to own either a house or a lawn.

'Yes, they're doing so well,' said Helen, who had returned, now wearing a lightweight jogging suit. 'I replanted them last year. They used to be over there.'

She pointed to a shadier part of the garden.

'But I thought they'd probably do better in the spot where they are now. And I was right.'

'You do your own gardening?' asked Martin. 'If not, I happen to know that Sanna, who owns the garden centre, is very good at—'

He stopped abruptly, realizing what the connection was between Helen and Sanna. But she merely shrugged.

'Oh, I do all the gardening myself.'

She sat down at the patio table across from them. She seemed to have taken a quick shower, because her hair was damp at the back of her neck.

'So, tell me what happened to Nea,' said Helen, her voice quavering slightly.

Paula studied her. Her distress seemed genuine.

'Her parents reported her missing yesterday. Do you mean that you and your family didn't hear the search parties who were out all last night? There was a lot of commotion right around the corner from you.'

It was strange that Helen hadn't heard all those people searching the woods only a few hundred metres from her home.

Helen shook her head.

'No, we went to bed early. I took a sleeping pill and could have slept through a world war. And James . . . well, he was sleeping in the basement. He thinks it's cooler down there, and you can't hear anything from outside.'

'You mentioned someone named Sam,' said Martin.

Helen nodded.

'Our son. He's fifteen. He was probably up late, playing loud music on his earphones. And once he does fall asleep, nobody can wake him.'

'So none of you heard a thing?'

Paula knew she sounded sceptical, but she couldn't hide her surprise.

'No. At least, not as far as I know. James and Sam didn't say anything about it this morning.'

'Okay,' said Paula. 'I'm sure you'll understand that we'll need to speak to your husband and son too.'

'Of course. They're not home right now, but you can come back or phone.'

Paula nodded.

'Did you see Linnea at all yesterday?'

Helen paused to think as she studied her fingernails, which were not manicured or polished. She had the hands of someone who frequently dug in the soil and pulled weeds.

'I don't remember seeing her. I go for a run every morning, and if she's outside, she usually waves. I think she waves to everybody who passes by. But I don't think I saw her yesterday. I'm not sure. I can't really remember. I'm very focused when I'm running. I get into the zone, I'm in a world of my own.'

'Do you run for exercise, or do you compete in races?' asked Martin.

'I run marathons,' she told him.

That explained why she looked so thin and trim. Paula tried not to think about all the extra kilos she was carrying. Every Monday morning she thought about working out and changing her diet, but taking care of two small children plus working as a police officer, she never had enough time or energy. And she didn't feel especially motivated, since she knew Johanna loved her the way she was, love handles and all.

'So you ran past their farm yesterday?' asked Martin.

Helen nodded.

'I always take the same route. Except on my two rest days, when I don't run at all. But that's Saturday and Sunday.'

'And you don't recall seeing Nea?' Paula repeated.

'No, I don't think so.'

Helen frowned.

'How . . . what . . .?' she began, then fell silent for a moment before trying again. 'How did she die?'

Paula and Martin exchanged glances.

'We don't know yet,' he said.

Helen again raised her hand to her throat.

'Poor Eva and Peter. I don't know them very well, but they're our closest neighbours, so we do talk now and then. Was it an accident?'

'No,' said Paula, carefully watching Helen's reaction. 'Nea was murdered.'

'Murdered?'

She shook her head.

'A little girl the same age, from the same farm? I can understand why you're here.'

'Actually, we came here by chance,' said Martin honestly. 'We were planning to speak to the nearest neighbours, to find out if anyone saw anything. We didn't know you lived here.'

'I thought I remembered hearing that your parents sold their house and moved away,' said Paula.

'Yes, they did,' said Helen. 'They sold the house right after the trial and moved to Marstrand. But the person who bought it, James, was a good friend of my father. And well, when James and I got married, he wanted us to live here.'

'Where is your husband?' asked Paula.

'He's out doing errands,' she said, shrugging.

'And your son?' asked Martin. 'Sam?'

'I have no idea. It's the summer holidays. He was gone when I came home from my run, and his bicycle was gone too. So he probably biked into town to see some friends.'

For a moment no one spoke. Helen looked at Paula and Martin, her eyes flashing.

'Is everybody . . . is everybody going to think we did it?'

She moved her hand from her throat to her hair.

'The newspapers? People will . . . I assume the whole thing is going to start all over again.'

'We're looking at all possibilities,' said Paula, feeling some sympathy for the woman sitting across from them.

'Have you been in contact with Marie since she came back?' asked Martin.

He couldn't help asking the question, even though he knew they should wait with any further questions regarding the old case.

'No, no, we have nothing to say to each other,' replied Helen, shaking her head.

'So you haven't seen each other or spoken on the phone?' asked Paula.

'No,' said Helen. 'Marie belongs to a different time, a different life.'

'Okay,' said Paula. 'We'll need to talk to you again later, but for now we're just interviewing you since you're a neighbour of the Berg family. Did you see or hear anything out of the ordinary over the past few days? Cars? People? Anything that struck you as odd or didn't feel right? Anything at all?'

Paula was trying to speak in broad terms, since they didn't know exactly what to ask about.

'No,' said Helen after a moment. 'No, I can't say that I've seen or heard anything strange recently.'

'As I mentioned, we'll need to ask your husband and son the same questions,' said Martin as he stood up.

Paula added: 'Yes, and we'll need to come back to ask you other questions, as well.'

'I understand,' said Helen.

When they left she was still sitting at the table on the deck, against that backdrop of glorious roses and peonies. She didn't look up.

Erica gave Patrik a quick kiss when he met her in the reception area at the station. Annika's face lit up, and she got up from her desk to come out and give Erica a hug.

'Hi!' she said warmly. 'How are the boys? How's Maja?'

Erica returned the hug and then asked about Annika's family. She was fond of this woman who ran the police station, and she respected her more with every passing day. Occasionally they managed to have dinner together, but not as often as they would have liked. Since both of them had young children, the weeks and months flew by, and any social life had to take a back seat to family matters.

'We'll be in the conference room,' Annika told Erica, who nodded.

She'd been to the station countless times before, so she knew where to find the room.

'I'll be right there,' Annika called after Erica and Patrik as they headed down the corridor.

'Hi, Ernst!' cried Erica happily when the big dog came

towards her, his tongue hanging out and his tail wagging.

As usual, he'd been asleep under Mellberg's desk, but he came rushing out at the sound of Erica's voice. The dog greeted her by licking her hand, and Erica rewarded him by scratching behind his ears.

'Warning, civilians present,' said Mellberg glumly from where he was standing in the doorway to his office. He'd obviously been having a nap.

Despite the dour greeting, Erica could tell he was glad to see her.

'I heard you handled the press conference brilliantly,' she said without a hint of sarcasm.

Patrik gave her a sharp poke in the side. He knew she was teasing, but Bertil Mellberg beamed with delight.

'Well, I've been an expert at such things for a long time now. In a backwater like this, they're not used to seeing someone with my experience holding a press conference, and maintaining such a high level of professionalism. Those reporters were practically eating out of my hand. When you can handle the press corps the way I do, they can be a very useful tool in an investigation.'

Erica nodded solemnly as Patrik glared at her.

They went into the conference room. The file folder in Erica's briefcase suddenly seemed so heavy. She took it out and placed it on the table in front of her. As she waited for Patrik and Mellberg to take their seats, she went around the table to say hello to Gösta, Paula, and Martin.

'Patrik mentioned that you would help me go over the case details,' she said to Gösta.

'We'll have to see how much I can remember,' he replied, scratching the back of his neck. 'It was thirty years ago, after all.'

'I'd be grateful for any help you can give me.'

Annika had put up the big whiteboard and brought a good supply of marker pens. Erica took some papers out of the thick file folder and fastened them to the board using little silver magnets. Then she picked up a pen, wondering where to begin.

She cleared her throat.

'Stella Strand was four years old when she disappeared from her parents' farm. Two thirteen-year-old girls, Marie Wall and Helen Persson – now Helen Jensen – were supposed to babysit Stella for a few hours while Stella's mother, Linda, and her big sister, Sanna, drove to Uddevalla to go shopping.'

She pointed to the two school photos she'd put up on the whiteboard. One of them showed a dark-haired girl with a serious expression; the other a blonde girl with mischievous eyes, but even back then she was so lovely it could take your breath away. Helen had the undefined features of a teenager, while Marie already had the gaze of a grown woman.

'Both girls lived near the Strand farm. That was how they knew Stella and her family. They had babysat for her many times before, though not on a regular basis, but there was nothing unusual about that.'

No one else said a word. Everyone knew bits and pieces about the case, but this was the first time they were getting a complete overview.

'The girls went over to the Strand farm around one o'clock. No one was ever able to pinpoint the exact time, but it was approximately one. When Linda and Sanna left for Uddevalla, the girls were playing with Stella outside in the yard. A short time later they began walking to Fjällbacka with Stella in a little pushchair. They'd been given money for ice cream, so they went to the kiosk. After a while they walked back to the farm.'

'That's a long way to walk,' said Martin. 'I don't know I would have allowed two young girls to go all that way with a four-year-old in tow.'

'Things were different back then,' said Erica. 'People didn't worry about safety the same way they do now. When we were kids, my sister and I used to stand between the seats while my father was driving. We didn't wear seatbelts. It's hard to comprehend nowadays, but no one thought anything of it at the time. So, the girls walked back to the farm, with Stella in the pushchair. They got back around four. They'd agreed with Linda that they would hand Stella over to Anders at four thirty, but seeing his car parked in the yard, they assumed he'd come home from work early, and so they just dropped Stella off.'

'But they didn't see him?' asked Paula, and Erica nodded towards Gösta.

'He was inside the house,' he explained.

Erica glanced at the whiteboard before going on.

'Leif Hermansson was the chief of police here in 1985. I went to see his daughter this morning to find out if she remembered anything about her father's investigation of the case. She couldn't recall much about it, and she and her siblings didn't find any material when they cleared up his estate. However, she did say that during the last few years of his life, he mentioned he had doubts about the guilt of the two girls.'

Patrik frowned.

'Did he say what his doubts were based on?'

Erica shook her head.

'No, not that his daughter could recall. Gösta, do you have anything to add?'

Gösta scratched his neck.

'No, I can't remember Leif ever expressing any doubt about the outcome of the investigation. I know he thought it was tragic – we all did. So many lives were ruined, not just the lives of Stella and her family.'

'But what about while Leif was working on the case?' queried Martin. 'Did he ever express any doubts?'

'No, not that I can recall,' said Gösta. 'After the girls confessed, it seemed an open-and-shut case. Leif's attitude was, the girls retracting their confessions when they realized the seriousness of the situation didn't change a thing, the case was solid.'

He looked down at the table, searching his memory. It was clearly news to him that Leif had begun to have doubts during the last few years before he died.

'What happened next?' asked Patrik impatiently. 'After the girls dropped Stella at the farm because they thought her father was there.'

'Was the father ever a suspect?' asked Paula.

'Anders Strand was questioned several times,' replied Gösta. 'Leif turned his statement inside out, checking the chronology over and over. He also interviewed the mother and sister to see if . . .'

He hesitated, and Martin chimed in: 'To see if there were any problems at home, such as abuse or assaults.'

'Yes,' said Gösta. 'It's never pleasant when you have to ask those kinds of questions.'

'We do what we have to do,' said Patrik in a low voice.

'Nothing of that sort was found,' said Erica. 'There was never any indication of problems. They were an ordinary, loving family. No sign that things weren't as they should be. So the investigation entered the next phase: looking for someone outside the immediate family.'

'And that produced no results whatsoever,' said Gösta. 'No strangers had been seen in the vicinity of the farm, either before the murder or around the time Stella was killed. We found no known paedophiles in the area. Nothing.'

'What was the cause of death?' asked Paula as she absent-mindedly scratched Ernst behind the ears.

'Blunt trauma to the head,' said Erica, pausing a moment before she fastened another photo to the whiteboard.

'Oh, dear God,' said Annika, blinking away tears.

Gösta had to look away. He had seen these pictures before.

'Stella had suffered repeated blows to the back of the head. The post-mortem report stated the blows had most likely been inflicted long after she was dead.'

'With two different weapons,' said Patrik. 'I had a quick look at the post-mortem report Pedersen sent over, and that detail caught my eye.'

Erica nodded. 'Yes, there were traces of both stone and wood in the wounds. One theory was that she was hit with both a tree branch and a rock.'

'That was one of the reasons Leif began to suspect two perpetrators,' said Gösta, looking up.

'When the girls didn't arrive with Stella, as planned, her father started getting worried,' Erica went on. 'By the time Linda and Sanna returned home at five thirty, Anders was a nervous wreck. He got a phone call from KG, who said that Helen and Marie had dropped Stella off at the farm almost half an hour earlier. Linda and Anders went out looking for her in the woods and along the road, but soon gave up. They called the police around six fifteen, and an official search party was immediately launched. Just like this time, a large number of volunteers from the area turned up to help.'

'I heard the same man who found Stella also found Nea,' said Martin. 'Isn't that something we should look into?'

Patrik shook his head.

'No, not in my opinion. It was actually fortunate that he decided to do a more thorough search of the area where he'd found Stella.'

'Seems odd the tracker dogs didn't find her,' said Paula as she continued to scratch Ernst behind the ear.

'The dog patrols hadn't yet covered that particular area,'

explained Patrik with a grimace. 'So tell us more about the two girls.'

Erica knew what he was getting at. She always put a lot of effort into researching the individuals involved in a case, and she was convinced that was one of the reasons her books were so popular. For most of her readers these were names they'd read in the papers, figures seen in grainy photos under the headlines; Erica's aim was to flesh them out, give a sense of their character.

'Well, so far I haven't managed to do as many interviews as I'd like with everyone who knew Helen and Marie back then. But I've talked to some of the people, and I can at least partly describe some of the circumstances surrounding them and their families.'

Erica cleared her throat.

'Both families were well known in the community, but for completely different reasons. Helen's family was, to all appearances, perfect. Her mother and father were prominent figures in Fjällbacka's business and cultural community. Her father was chair of the Rotary Club, her mother was involved with the Home and School Association. They led an active social life, and they were in charge of a number of cultural activities in town.'

'Any siblings?' asked Paula.

'No, Helen was an only child. A conscientious and quiet girl who did well in school. That was how she was described. A talented pianist, and her parents were always eager to show off her skill, according to what I've heard. Marie, on the other hand, came from a family that I'm guessing was all too familiar to the police, even before the murder.'

Gösta nodded. 'You can say that again!'

'Fights, drunkenness, burglaries, you get the picture . . . And it wasn't only the parents. Marie's two older brothers were frequently in trouble. She was the only daughter, and she had no police record before Stella's death. But the names of her brothers often appeared in police records, long before they turned thirteen.'

'No matter what the crime – stolen bicycles, break-ins at a kiosk, etcetera – the first thing we always did was pay a call on the Walls,' said Gösta. 'And nine times out of ten, we'd find the bicycle thief, or whatever, right there. They weren't very bright.'

'But Marie was never involved, was she?' asked Patrik.

'No, she wasn't. Except we did receive a report from her school saying they suspected she was being abused. But she always denied it. Said she'd fallen off her bike, or something along those lines.'

'Couldn't you have intervened regardless?' asked Paula, frowning.

'Yes, although that was a rare occurrence in those days.'

Gösta shifted position. Erica noticed he looked uncomfortable. Presumably he knew that Paula was right.

'Those were different times. Bringing in the social services was a last resort. Leif handled the matter by going to see Marie's father and giving him a stern lecture. After that we didn't receive any more reports from the school. Of course, we can't be certain he stopped beating her, or whether he was just more careful about not leaving any visible marks.'

Gösta coughed into his clenched fist and fell silent.

'Despite coming from such different backgrounds,' Erica continued, 'the two girls became very good friends. They spent all their time together, even though Helen's parents didn't approve. At first they chose to ignore the friendship, hoping it wouldn't last. But eventually they became more and more annoyed at their daughter's choice of friend, and they forbade Helen to see Marie. Helen's father is dead, and I haven't been able to speak to her mother yet, but I did talk to others who knew them back then. They all say there was a huge row when Helen was told she could no longer see Marie. With two pre-teen girls, you can imagine the drama. But in the end they were forced to comply, and they stopped hanging out with each other in their free time. Helen's parents couldn't prevent them from seeing each other at school, of course. They were in the same class.'

'Yet Helen's parents made an exception when they were asked to babysit Stella,' said Patrik pensively. 'I wonder why? Seems odd, given they were so adamant about the girls not seeing each other?'

Gösta leaned forward. 'Stella's father was president of the Fjällbacka bank, which meant he held one of the most prestigious positions in the community. And since he and his wife, Linda, had already asked the girls if they could babysit Stella together, KG Persson probably didn't want to antagonize Anders Strand. So they made an exception.'

'How long did it take before the girls confessed?' asked Paula.

'A week,' said Erica, frowning at the photos on the whiteboard.

She kept coming back to the same question. Why had the girls confessed to committing a brutal murder if they didn't do it?

THE STELLA CASE

'This is crazy. Marie has been through enough!'

Lenita fluffed her thick blond hair. Marie sat calmly at the table with her hands in her lap, her long hair framing her lovely face.

'These are questions we have to ask. I'm sorry, but it's necessary.'

Leif never took his eyes off Marie. Her parents could say whatever they liked, he was convinced the girls were not telling the whole truth. The police had interviewed Anders Strand several times and turned the family history inside out, but they'd found nothing. It was the two girls who would provide an opening in the case. He was certain of it.

'It's okay,' said Marie.

'Could you tell me again what happened when you went into the woods?'

'Have you talked more with Helen?' asked Marie, looking at him.

Leif was once again struck by what a beauty she was growing into. He wondered how Helen felt about that. From his own daughter, he knew quite a bit about the dynamics of friendships between young girls, and it wasn't always easy to be the invisible one next to the pretty

219

one. Helen seemed quite plain beside the dazzling looks of Marie, and he was curious as to how that had affected their relationship. They were an odd pair in so many ways, it was hard to see what had drawn them together. Try as he might, he couldn't understand it.

Leif put down his pen. It was now or never. He looked at Marie's parents.

'I'd like to speak to Marie alone.'

'Out of the question!'

Lenita's shrill voice echoed off the walls in the small interview room of the police station.

'Sometimes a person's memory is better if there's not as much tension, and I think this situation is proving very stressful for Marie,' said Leif calmly. 'If I could ask her some questions about their walk in the woods, we might come up with information that would lead to a breakthrough in the investigation. And then this whole matter could be resolved in no time.'

Larry rubbed one of the many tattoos on his arm as he glanced at his wife.

'In our family, nothing good has ever come from separate conversations with the police,' snorted Lenita. She turned to her husband: 'Remember that time Krille came home with a black eye after the police took him to the station?'

Her voice was growing more shrill by the minute.

'He didn't do anything. He was out having fun with his pals, and for no reason at all the police picked him up and took him in, and he came home with a black eye.'

Leif sighed. He knew the incident she was talking about. It was true that Krille had been out having fun with his buddies. But he was drunk as a skunk, and when some guy started flirting with his girlfriend Krille went after him with a broken beer bottle. It took three officers to get the boy into the patrol car, and on the way to the holding cell he'd been throwing punches at the policemen so they'd had to use force to subdue him. That was how he'd ended up with a black eye. But Leif knew it would be useless to argue. Especially if he was to have any hope of getting Marie's parents out of the room.

'Most unfortunate,' he said now. 'If you'd like, I could look more closely into the matter for you. There might even be grounds for some sort of compensation. Payment for pain and suffering. But before I can do that, I need you to allow me to talk to Marie alone. She's in good hands.'

He gave them a big smile, noticing that the mention of compensation had made Lenita's face light up.

She turned to look at Larry.

'Of course we should allow the police to have a few words with Marie alone. She's a witness in a murder investigation, after all. I don't know why you're being so stubborn.'

Larry shook his head.

'I'm not sure—'

Lenita stood up, cutting off any further discussion.

'Come on, we need to let the police do their job. Then we can talk about the other matter as soon as they're done here.'

She took Larry by the arm and dragged him out of the room. She paused for a moment in the doorway.

'Don't disgrace yourself, Marie. You should try to be a little more like your brothers.'

She looked at Leif.

'The boys are going to do great things some day. But this girl has given me nothing but headaches and problems ever since she was born.'

Then she left, closing the door behind her, and silence settled over the room. Marie was still sitting with her hands clasped on her lap and her chin resting on her chest. Slowly she raised her head. Her expression was unexpectedly dark.

'We're the ones who did it,' she said in that husky voice of hers. 'We killed her.'

✿

James opened the fridge. He had to give Helen credit: she kept it well stocked and organized. He took out the butter and set it on the kitchen worktop. There was a glass next to the sink. Sam must have forgotten to put it away. James clenched his fist, disappointment flooding through him at the thought of the boy. Sam, who looked like a freak. Sam, who hadn't managed to find a summer job, who couldn't seem to do anything successfully.

But the boy could shoot; that much James had to admit. On a good day, Sam was actually a better shot than he was. Yet Sam was probably going to spend the rest of his meaningless life sitting around and playing computer games.

When Sam turned eighteen, James planned to throw him out. Helen could say what she liked, but he had no intention of supporting a grown man who was lazy and good-for-nothing. Then Sam would see how hard it was to find work with all that black make-up and dreary clothing he wore.

Someone knocked on the door, and James gave a start. Who could that be?

The sun came shining in when he opened the door,

and James had to raise one hand to shade his eyes in order to see who it was.

'Yes?' he said.

A man who looked to be about twenty-five stood on the front porch. He cleared his throat.

'Are you James Jensen?'

James frowned. What was this about? He took a step forward, and the other man immediately backed up. James frequently had that effect on people.

'Yes, that's me. What's this all about?'

'I'm a reporter from *Expressen*. And I'm wondering whether you have any comment about your wife's name being once again linked to a homicide investigation.'

James stared at the man. He had no idea what this guy was on about.

'What do you mean "again"? What are you saying? If you're talking about the murder that my wife was unjustly accused of committing, we've had absolutely nothing to say about it for years. And you know that!'

A blood vessel began throbbing at his temple. Why was somebody dredging up that old story again? For years they'd been plagued by requests for interviews, someone would show up wanting to 'give Helen a chance to present her version of what happened', but things had died down eventually. It had been at least a decade since they'd been bothered.

'I'm talking about the fact that a little girl who lived on the same farm as Stella was found murdered this morning. The police held a press conference this afternoon, and your wife and Marie Wall were both mentioned.'

What the hell?

'So, I'm wondering what you think about Helen being considered a possible suspect again after thirty years. I know she has always claimed she was innocent. Is she home, by the way? If I could just have a few words with her as well, that would be great. It's important to hear her side of the story, before people start rushing to judgement.'

The blood vessel was throbbing harder. These damn hyenas, couldn't they leave them alone? Were they going to descend on the house again, like they did when Helen's parents lived here? KG had told him how the journalists used to sit in their cars with the headlights switched off. They had pursued the family relentlessly, knocking on the door and phoning. Until it was as if the house was under siege.

James saw the reporter's lips continuing to churn out words. He assumed the man was asking more questions, trying to persuade him to talk. But James wasn't hearing a word. The only thing he heard was a loud roaring inside his head, and the only way to silence the sound was to make the mouth in front of him stop talking.

He clenched his fists harder and took a step towards the reporter.

They had stopped to have a swim after the morning meeting. They talked about Bill's enthusiasm and laughed at the thought of the insane project in which they'd agreed to participate. Learning to sail. No one they knew had ever sailed or even been on board a sailboat. And now they were supposed to compete in a race in only a matter of weeks.

'We'll never do it!' said Khalil, closing his eyes as they sat in the Jacuzzi.

He loved heat. In Sweden the warmth was only on the outside; a cold gust of wind might sweep in at any moment and bring goosebumps to his skin. He missed the stifling, dry heat. The heat that never dissipated entirely, merely letting up a bit so that the evenings were blessedly cool. And the heat had a very specific scent. In

Sweden the heat smelled of nothing at all. It was as empty and meaningless as the Swedes. But that was not something he dared say aloud.

Karim was always quick to admonish him whenever he complained about Sweden. Or the Swedes. He said they should be grateful. This was their new homeland; they'd been given refuge here, and they were allowed to live in peace. He knew Karim was right. It was just so hard to like the Swedes. They radiated suspicion and looked at him as if he were of lower status. And it wasn't only the racists. Those types were easy to deal with. They openly showed how they felt, and their words bounced off him. It was the ordinary Swedes who were more difficult to take. The ones who were basically good people, who considered themselves to be broad-minded and generous. The ones who read the news about the war in Syria and were shocked by how terrible the situation was, who gave money to aid organizations and donated to clothing drives. But they would never dream of inviting a refugee into their homes. Those were the people he would never get to know. So how was he supposed to get to know this new country? He couldn't bring himself to call Sweden his 'homeland' the way Karim did. It was not a home. It was merely a country.

'Hey, check out those girls,' said Adnan, and Khalil turned to see who he meant.

A blonde and two dark-haired girls about their own age were splashing noisily at one end of the swimming pool.

'Shall we go talk to them?' asked Adnan, nodding in their direction.

'It'll only cause trouble,' said Khalil.

During one of the Swedish lessons, Sture had discussed how to behave with Swedish girls. It was actually best not to talk to them at all. But Khalil couldn't help thinking about how nice it would be to meet a Swedish girl. Then he could learn more about this country and improve his spoken Swedish.

'Come on, let's go talk to them,' said Adnan, tugging at his arm. 'What could happen?'

Khalil pulled his arm away.

'Remember what Sture told us.'

'Oh, that old fogey. What does he know?'

Adnan climbed out of the Jacuzzi and dived into the swimming pool. With a few quick strokes, he swam over to the girls. Khalil reluctantly followed. This was not a good idea.

'Hello!' he heard Adnan call, and he realized he had no choice but to go along.

At first the girls looked suspicious, but then they smiled and answered in English. Khalil relaxed. Maybe Adnan was right and Sture was wrong. The girls didn't seem offended that they wanted to talk to them. They introduced themselves, saying they were staying in a holiday resort with their families. That's where they'd met each other.

'What the hell do you think you're doing?'

Khalil flinched.

A man in his fifties came over to them.

'Sorry, no Swedish,' he said, throwing out his hands. All he wanted was to be far away from here.

The blonde girl glared at the man and rattled off a few sentences in Swedish. Khalil understood from the way they were talking that he must be the girl's father.

'Leave the girls alone and go back where you came from!'

The man was shooing them away, a man wearing swim trunks with the Superman logo, which would have been comical if the situation hadn't felt so unpleasant.

'Sorry,' said Khalil, backing away.

He didn't dare look at Adnan. His hot temper often got him in trouble, and Khalil could almost feel the anger radiating from his friend.

'We don't need people like you here,' said the man. 'You're nothing but trouble!'

Khalil glanced at the man's face, flushed with anger. He wondered what he would say if he knew they'd been out all night searching for the little girl named Nea. But that probably wouldn't matter. People like that had already made up their minds.

'Come on,' he said now in Arabic, pulling Adnan away.

They might as well leave. The blonde shrugged, looking apologetic.

It was five thirty by the time Erica had finished discussing her notes on the Stella case at the police station. Patrik had noticed how worn out everybody looked. No one had had any sleep. After hesitating for a moment, he had ordered all his colleagues to go home for the night. It was better for them to be rested and alert the next day so they wouldn't make any mistakes out of sheer fatigue, mistakes that might be difficult to undo later on. The same applied to himself. He couldn't remember experiencing such longing for a good night's sleep.

'Don't forget the children,' said Erica as they drove to Fjällbacka.

She smiled at him, leaning her head on his shoulder.

'Darn, I thought I'd got away with it!' he joked. 'Couldn't we "forget" them until tomorrow, leave them at Dan and Anna's place for the night? What do you say? I'm completely knackered, and it's been ages since we've had a whole night to ourselves without someone climbing into bed between us.'

'I don't think this is the right time to forget them,' said Erica, smiling as she patted his cheek. 'Why don't you sleep in the guestroom tonight? I'll take care of the kids so you can sleep.'

Patrik shook his head. He hated sleeping without Erica. Besides, there was something so cosy about hearing the approach of little feet in the night, and then one or more of the children climbing in to cuddle up next to them. Especially now, when he needed to know his family were close by and safe. He was more than willing to give up a bit of sleep for that peace of mind. And considering how tired he was at the moment, they probably wouldn't wake him anyway.

They dropped by at Anna and Dan's and picked up three happy kids who had clearly eaten too much sugar. They were all invited to stay for dinner, but after a quick glance at Patrik, Erica had declined. He didn't know whether he even had enough energy to eat.

'Pappa, Pappa, we had ice cream,' said Maja happily from the back seat of the car. 'And sweets. And cake.'

She made sure her little brothers were properly strapped in. She seemed to feel that her parents weren't capable of taking care of her brothers without her help.

'Great, sounds like you've had something from all the food groups,' he replied, rolling his eyes at Erica.

'It's okay,' she said, laughing. 'Next time we're babysitting for Dan and Anna, we'll take our revenge and stuff their kids with sugar.'

Oh, how Patrik loved to hear her laugh. In fact, if he was perfectly honest, he loved everything about her. Even her bad habits. Without them, Erica wouldn't be the same. He'd felt so proud as she carefully and methodically went over all the research she'd done for her book. He would be the first to admit that, in all probability, she was far brighter than he was. She had a brilliant mind, and he couldn't help but admire her dedication and professionalism. Sometimes he wondered how his life would have turned out if he hadn't met Erica, but he always dismissed such thoughts. She was here, she was his, and they had three wonderful kids sitting in the back seat. He reached for her hand as he continued driving towards their home in Sälvik. She rewarded him with the smile that always made him feel warm inside.

When they arrived home, the kids were practically bouncing off the walls from too many sweets. To get them to calm down before bedtime, Patrik and Erica decided to let them snuggle up on the sofa to watch a film. He was prepared for trouble, since choosing a film usually resulted in a battle between three strong-willed children. But apparently Maja had carried out high-level negotiations on the drive home, because she told her father in a sensible tone of voice:

'Pappa, I know they're not really supposed to watch *Frozen*, because it's too scary, and only big kids are allowed to watch it this late at night . . . But I told them you might consider making an exceptional this time, and . . .'

Then she gave him an exaggerated wink. Patrik could hardly keep from laughing. She was a sneaky one, that girl. No doubt she got it from her mother. And she sounded so grown up, even though she'd said 'an exceptional' instead of 'an exception'. He didn't have the heart to correct her, and he forced himself to look serious. The twins were watching him expectantly.

'Hmm . . . I don't know . . . Daytime is one thing, but like you said, the film is a little too scary for small kids at night. But, all right, we'll make an exceptional. Just this one time!'

The twins cheered, and Maja looked pleased. Good lord, what was that girl going to be like when she grew up? Patrik had visions of the prime minister's official residence in Stockholm.

'Did you hear all that?' he asked, laughing, when he joined Erica in the kitchen.

She gave him a big smile. She was standing at the worktop chopping vegetables for a salad.

'I certainly did. What's to become of her?'

'I was thinking she'd make a good prime minister,' he replied, putting his arms around Erica from behind and nuzzling her neck.

He loved the scent of her.

'Sit down. Dinner will be ready in a minute,' she said, giving him a kiss. 'I've poured you a glass of red wine, and one of your mother's homemade lasagnes is in the oven.'

'I suppose we shouldn't really complain about her spoiling us,' said Patrik as he sank on to a kitchen chair.

His mother, Kristina, was always worrying that the children – as well as Erica and Patrik, for that matter – would die of malnutrition from eating too many ready-made dinners. At least once a week she would stop by with some homemade food to put in their freezer. And even though they muttered that it was time she started treating them like adults, on occasions like this, her food was a lifesaver. Besides, Kristina was a great cook, and the lasagne smelled delicious.

'What do you think? Was my report of any help?' asked Erica as she sat down across from Patrik and poured herself some wine. 'Have you made any progress in the investigation?'

'So far there's nothing concrete to go on,' said Patrik as he swirled the wine in his glass.

The flames from two candles were reflected in the red wine, and for the first time in nearly forty-eight hours, he allowed his shoulders to relax. But he wouldn't be able to relax completely until they found out what had happened to Nea.

'Have you heard anything from Helen or Marie?' he asked.

Erica shook her head. 'No, nothing yet. Much will depend on what advice Marie's received from the publisher she's negotiating with, and whether they think she should agree to an interview with me or not. Personally, I think my book would actually help promote hers and boost sales, but the publisher may feel differently.'

'What about Helen?'

'She hasn't answered either. I think it's fifty–fifty whether she'll agree. Most people have an innate need to unburden themselves. Yet Helen has managed to create a new life for herself here in Fjällbacka, even though she's done it by staying in the shadows. I'm not sure she would voluntarily step into the spotlight again. Although, after what just happened, she may be forced to. Everyone is going to be looking at her and Marie.'

'What's your view of it all?' asked Patrik as he got up to open the oven and check on the lasagne.

It was bubbling but still needed some time for the cheese to turn brown. He sat down again and looked at Erica, who was frowning. After a moment she said:

'I honestly don't know. When I started the research for this book, I was convinced they were guilty. The fact that they both confessed weighs heavily against them, even though they later retracted their confessions and have maintained their innocence ever since. I had planned to write a book in which I tried to understand how such young girls could kill a four-year-old. But now I'm not so sure . . . When I found out that Leif Hermansson thought they were innocent, I began looking at everything from a different angle. After all, he was the person most involved with the case. And the whole thing was based on the confessions of the two girls. The police didn't look any further. When the girls retracted their confessions, there was no interest in re-opening the case. Not even Leif wanted to do that. Any doubts he had came later.'

'So what do you suppose made Leif change his mind and believe in their innocence?'

'I have no idea,' said Erica, shaking her head so the blond locks fell softly around her face. 'But I'm going to find out. I'll start by interviewing people who knew Marie and Helen thirty years ago, while I wait to hear back from them.'

Erica got up to take the lasagne out of the oven.

'I rang Helen's mother, and she was willing to let me come over to ask her some questions.'

'What do you think Helen will say about that?' asked Patrik. 'The fact that her mother is going to talk to you?'

Erica shrugged.

'According to what I've heard about Helen's mother, she mostly cares about herself. I doubt she'd even give a thought to whether or not she had her daughter's approval.'

'What about Marie's family? Her parents are dead, but she has two brothers, doesn't she?'

'Yes. One lives in Stockholm and is apparently a junkie. The other brother is in prison for armed robbery in Kumla.'

'I'd rather you stayed away from those two,' said Patrik, even though he knew his words would fall on deaf ears.

'Uh-huh,' said Erica, since she knew that Patrik knew he couldn't control her.

They silently agreed to change the subject as they began eating their lasagne.

From the living room they heard 'Let It Go' playing full blast on the TV.

THE STELLA CASE

Leif tried to gather his thoughts before he entered the small interview room. It made sense. And yet it didn't. It was Marie's composure that had convinced him more than anything else. Her voice hadn't quavered at all when she confessed to the murder.

Marie was a child. She could never manage to dupe an experienced police officer. How could a child possibly lie about such an unimaginable crime? Calmly and matter-of-factly she had recounted the whole story from beginning to end while her mother sobbed and screamed and her father roared at her to shut up.

As her girlish voice recounted step by step what happened, Leif had looked at the clasped hands on her lap and her blond hair lit by a ray of sunlight from the window. It was hard to believe someone who so resembled an angel could have done something this evil, but he had no doubt she was telling the truth. Now all he needed to do was put the last puzzle pieces – or rather, puzzle piece – in place.

'I'm sorry to keep you waiting so long,' he said as he went into the other interview room, closing the door behind him.

KG nodded curtly, placing his hand on his daughter's shoulder.

'We're getting a little tired of all this,' said Harriet, shaking her head.

Leif cleared his throat.

'I've just had a talk with Marie,' he said.

Helen slowly raised her head. Her eyes had a slightly veiled look, as if she were somewhere else.

'Marie has confessed. She said the two of you did it.'

KG gasped for air, and Harriet put her hand to her mouth. For a moment Leif thought he saw surprise on Helen's face. But it vanished as quickly as it appeared, and later he wasn't sure he'd seen it at all.

For several seconds she didn't say a word. Then she nodded.

'Yes, we did it.'

'Helen!'

Harriet reached out her hand, but KG sat motionless. His face was a mask.

'Should we be contacting a lawyer?' he asked.

Leif hesitated. Much as he wanted to get to the bottom of things, he couldn't deny them the right to have a lawyer present.

'You're entitled to do that, if you wish,' he said.

'No, I want to answer the questions,' said Helen, turning to look at her father.

A silent battle seemed to take place between them. Much to Leif's surprise, Helen came out the winner.

'What do you want to know?' she asked, looking at Leif.

Point by point he went over Marie's account. At times Helen merely nodded, and then he had to remind her to answer verbally for the sake of the tape recorder. She displayed the same unnatural calm as Marie, and he couldn't decide what to make of her composure. Over the years he had questioned many criminals. Everything from bicycle thieves to wife-beaters to a woman who had drowned her newborn child in the bathtub. They had shown a wide range of emotions. Anger, sorrow, panic, rage, resignation. But never had he interviewed anyone whose demeanour was completely neutral. Let alone two such suspects. He wondered if it was because they were children; maybe they were too young to fully understand what they'd done. Their lack of emotion as they recounted their horrifying story had to be based on something other than evil.

'So afterwards you went swimming, is that right? Marie said you needed to wash off the blood.'

Helen nodded.

'Yes, that's right. There was blood on us, so we went swimming.'

'What about your clothes? Wasn't there blood on them too? How did you get rid of the bloodstains?'

She bit her lip.

'We rubbed off most of it in the water. Our clothes dried fast in the sun. And Mamma and Pappa didn't get a good look at my clothes when I came home. I slipped inside and changed before dinner. Then I threw the clothes in the washing machine.'

Behind her, Harriet was weeping with her face buried in her hands. Helen didn't look at her. KG was sitting as if turned to stone. He seemed to have aged twenty years.

Helen's incredible air of calm made her seem more like Marie. They no longer seemed such an odd pair. They moved the same way, talked the same way, and Helen's expression reminded Leif of Marie's. There was a nothingness to her face. A silent emptiness.

For a moment Leif shuddered as he stared at the child sitting in front of him. Something had been set in motion that would echo for many years to come, maybe for the rest of his life. His questions had been answered, but they had led to other, bigger questions. Questions that would probably never be fully answered. Helen's gaze was unfathomable and blank as she looked at him.

'You'll send us to the same place, won't you? We'll get to be together, right?'

Leif didn't reply. He simply stood up and went out to the corridor. He was suddenly finding it very hard to breathe.

♣

Karim was sitting on a smooth rock, but he still kept shifting position. The sun felt warm, yet he shivered now and then. There were so many strange terms to learn all at once that his head was spinning: *in irons, tiller, running downwind, beam reach, close haul.* Left and right were replaced with port and starboard. It wasn't even ten o'clock, and he was already feeling exhausted.

'If you end up in irons, it means the front of the boat, the bow, is heading straight into the wind.'

Bill was wildly gesturing as he used both Swedish and English words. Farid translated everything he said into Arabic. Karim was glad to see that the others looked as bewildered as he felt. Bill pointed at the boat he was standing next to, moving the sail this way and that. All Karim could think was that the boat looked awfully small and flimsy against the vast blue backdrop. The slightest gust of wind and it would capsize, and they'd all end up in the water.

Why had he agreed to participate? He knew why. It was an opportunity to get out into the Swedish community, to meet Swedes and find out how they operated, and maybe put an end to all the suspicious looks directed at him.

'When a boat is in irons, the sail merely flutters, but you are in a no-go zone, and the boat stops moving.' Bill illustrated by tugging on the sails. 'The boat has to be at an angle of at least thirty degrees in order to move at any speed. And speed is good, since we're going to be competing in a race!'

He waved his arms about.

'We must find the fastest way for the boat. Use the wind!'

Karim nodded even though he didn't really under-stand. He felt a prickling at the back of his neck and turned around. Sitting on a rock a short distance away were three teenagers, staring at them. A girl and two boys. Something about their posture unnerved Karim, so he turned his attention back to Bill.

'You adjust, or trim, the sails by using the sheet. That's what it's called when you pull the sail closer to the boat or let it out.'

Bill pulled on what Karim had so far called the rope, and the sail tightened. There was so much to learn; they'd never be able to manage it between now and the race. If ever.

'If you want to sail into the wind without ending up in irons, you do so by tacking. Beating to windward.'

Karim heard Farid sigh.

'Like a zigzag.' Bill waved his arms to demonstrate what he meant. 'You turn the boat and then turn it again, back and forth. That's called beating.'

Bill pointed at the small boat again.

'Today I was thinking you should each take a turn going out in the sailboat with me, just for a brief run, so you'll get a feel for how it's done.'

He pointed at the boats moored nearby. At the begin-ning of the class, Bill had told them the boats were called Laser Class sailing dinghies. They looked ridiculously small.

Bill smiled at Karim.

'I thought Karim could go first, and then you'll be next, Ibrahim. The rest of you can look through these photocopies to review the terms I mentioned. I found them on the Internet in English, so we can start there. Then you can learn the Swedish terms later. Okay?'

The others nodded, but Karim and Ibrahim exchanged looks of alarm. Karim was thinking about the journey from Istanbul to Samos. The seasickness. The surging waves. The boat up ahead that had capsized. The people screaming. The drowned bodies.

'Here's a life vest,' said Bill cheerfully, unaware of the storm raging inside Karim.

Karim pulled on the life vest, which was nothing like the one he had purchased for a large sum before making the journey across the sea.

Again he felt that prickling sensation on the back of his neck. The three teenagers were still watching them. The girl giggled. Karim didn't like the look in the eyes of the blond boy. He resisted an urge to say something to the others because they were already feeling tense.

'All right,' said Bill. 'Let's make sure the life vests are properly fastened, and then we can take off.'

He pulled the straps tight and nodded approvingly. He glanced behind Karim and laughed.

'Looks like we've got visitors. The young people have turned out in support!' Bill waved at the teenagers. 'Come on over here!'

The three teens clambered down from the rock and came towards them. The closer they got, the more the expression on the blond boy's face made Karim's skin crawl.

'This is my son, Nils,' said Bill, placing his hand on the shoulder of the boy with the creepy expression. 'And these are his friends Vendela and Basse.'

Nils's friends shook hands with everyone, while he merely continued to glare.

'Be polite and say hello,' said Bill to his son.

Karim held out his hand. After several seconds Nils took his hand out of his pocket and shook hands with Karim. His hand was ice-cold, but his expression was even colder. Suddenly the sea seemed like a warm and welcoming refuge.

Helen bit the inside of her cheek, as she always did when she was trying to concentrate. Cautiously she shifted position as she stood on the small stool. If she took too big a step, she'd fall. She probably wouldn't hurt herself, but she'd disturb James, who was sitting nearby reading the paper.

She arranged all the tins and cartons on the top shelf of the fridge to make sure the labels were facing forward. She could feel James watching her. A single sigh from him when he opened the fridge was enough to make her stomach clench. So she was taking pre-emptive action in order to avoid his wrath.

She had learned to live with James. His need to control. His moods. There was simply no alternative, she knew that. She'd been so scared during those first years, but then she'd had Sam. And she stopped being afraid for herself; it was for his sake that she was frightened. Most mothers dreaded the day when their children moved away from home. She was counting the seconds to the day when he would be free. And safe.

'How does it look?' she asked, turning to face the table.

Breakfast had been cleared away long ago, the dishwasher was quietly humming, and every surface shone.

'It'll do,' he said, without looking up from his newspaper.

James had started wearing reading glasses. She'd found

it rather surprising to discover he had any weaknesses. He'd always taken pride in being flawless. Both when it came to himself and to those around him. That was what made her so worried about Sam. In her eyes he was perfect. But even as an infant, Sam had proved to be a disappointment to his father. He was a sensitive boy, timid and nervous. He enjoyed playing quiet games. He didn't climb high or run fast, he didn't like fighting with other boys. He preferred to stay in his room, where he spent hours creating fantasy worlds with his toys. When he got older he loved taking things apart and putting them back together. Old radios, tape recorders, an old TV he'd found in the garage – he could dismantle anything and then reassemble it. Strangely enough, James didn't discourage this hobby. He even allowed Sam to work in a corner of the garage. That was at least one pastime he could understand.

'What else do you need me to do today?' Helen asked as she got down from the stool.

She put it away at the end of the kitchen island. Lined up with the other stool, with approximately two centimetres in between so they were both centred.

'There's some laundry in the basket. And my trousers were not properly pressed. You'll have to do it over.'

'Okay,' she said, bowing her head.

Maybe she should iron all his shirts at the same time. She might as well.

'I'm going grocery shopping later,' she said. 'Is there anything else you want besides the usual?'

James turned the page in the newspaper. He was still reading the morning issue of *Bohusläningen*. Then he had the newspapers *DN* and *Svenska Dagbladet* left. He always read them in the same order. First *Bohusläningen*, then *DN*, then *Svenska Dagbladet*.

'No, just the usual.'

Now he looked up.

'Where's Sam?'

'He rode his bike into town. He was going to meet a friend.'

'Who's the friend?'

He peered at her over the rims of his reading glasses. Helen hesitated.

'Her name is Jessie.'

'*Her* name? You mean a girl? Who are her parents?'

He lowered the newspaper as a glint appeared in his eyes.

Helen took a deep breath. 'He didn't say. But somebody told me he was spending time with Marie's daughter.'

James took several controlled breaths. 'Do you think that's a good idea?'

'If you want me to tell him not to see her any more, I will. Unless you prefer to tell him.'

Helen kept her eyes down. The knot in her stomach was back. So many things that should have been left in the distant past were being dug up again.

James turned back to his paper.

'No. We'll let it be. For now.'

Her heart raced, and there was nothing she could do about it. She wasn't sure that James had made the right decision. But it wasn't up to her to decide. Nothing had been left to her to decide since that day thirty years ago.

'Have you made any progress with the reports? Have you found anything worth investigating further?' Patrik asked Annika.

She shook her head.

'No, other than the guy who was taking videos of kids at the beach, I haven't come up with a single incident that has the slightest hint of targeting children. But I haven't made it through the whole stack yet.'

'What time frame are you looking at?'

Gösta reached for a slice of bread, which he spread with butter. Annika had laid on an assortment of breakfast items this morning, having guessed that everyone would skip breakfast in their eagerness to get to work.

'I've gone back as far as May, as we discussed. Do you want me to go back even further?'

She glanced at Patrik, who shook his head.

'No, May's a good starting point for now. But if you don't find anything relating to children, we may have to consider broadening our search and look at reported incidents of sexual assault and rape.'

'Is there any indication the murder was sexually motivated?' asked Paula, taking a bite of her cheese-and-ham open-face sandwich.

Ernst was sitting at her feet, giving her a pleading look, but she ignored him. He was starting to get fat from all the treats Mellberg fed him.

'Pedersen hasn't finished with the pathology exam yet, so we don't know. But Nea was naked when her body was found, and the two most common motives when children are murdered are either sexual or . . .'

He hesitated.

Gösta helped him out.

'Or the guilty person is someone close.'

'So, what's your feeling about this case?' asked Paula, pushing aside Ernst's muzzle, which he was trying to rest on her knee.

'As I said before, I have a hard time picturing Nea's parents as having anything at all to do with her death. But I can't be a hundred per cent sure. When you've been on the police force as long as I have, you realize nothing can be ruled out.'

'It does seem one of the least likely scenarios,' said Patrik.

'I agree. I also think we should explore any possible links to the murder of Stella,' said Martin, getting up to fetch the coffee pot and refill everyone's cup. 'The similarities are striking, even though it was such a long time ago.'

'You and Paula talked to Helen yesterday,' said Patrik. 'Could the two of you have a chat with Marie today? And I'll pay Helen a visit. I want to know if either of them has an alibi.'

'An alibi for when, though?' asked Paula. 'Nea's parents didn't see her after she went to bed, so we don't know whether she disappeared in the morning or was kidnapped during the night.'

'Were there any signs of a break-in?' said Martin as he took his seat again.

'I'll check with her parents if anyone could have got in at night without them noticing,' said Gösta. 'The nights have been so hot, a lot of people in the area sleep with the windows open.'

'Okay,' said Patrik. 'I'll leave that to you, Gösta. And you're right, Paula. We need to check alibis from Sunday evening onward.'

'Okay. We'll go see Marie and find out what she says.'

'Talk to her daughter too,' said Patrik. 'As I recall, Marie has a teenage daughter named Jessie. I'm hoping to see not only Helen but also her son, Sam, and her husband. He's that UN soldier who looks like he chews barbed wire for breakfast.'

He got up to put the milk away in the fridge so it wouldn't spoil in the summer heat. They had no air conditioning in the small yellow-painted kitchen, only an old fan, and it was almost unbearably hot in there, even though the window was open wide.

'By the way, has anyone seen Mellberg?' he asked.

'His office door is closed, and no one answered when

I knocked. He's probably sound asleep,' said Gösta with a wry smile.

It wasn't worth getting annoyed with Mellberg. As long as he stayed in his office and napped, the others could do their jobs in peace.

'Have you heard anything from Torbjörn or Pedersen?' asked Paula.

'I phoned both of them yesterday,' said Patrik. 'As usual, Torbjörn won't commit himself until his report is finalized, but he did send over the technical reports from the Stella case. And after a bit of coaxing, Pedersen revealed that Nea had a wound on the back of her head. I don't yet know what that signifies, but at least it's something.'

'Is it possible that Helen and Marie were innocent?' asked Paula, looking at Gösta. 'Or do you think maybe one of them killed Stella and has struck again?'

'I don't know,' replied Gösta. 'Back then I was totally convinced of their guilt. But now I've heard that Leif had doubts, I'm beginning to wonder. It sounds like a long shot – what motive would they have for killing another little girl, especially after a thirty-year gap?'

'It could be a copycat killer,' said Martin, tugging at his shirt to cool off.

His reddish hair was plastered to his head with sweat.

'Well, at the moment we can't rule out anything,' said Gösta, looking down at the table.

'How's it going with tracking down the old interview transcripts?' asked Patrik. 'And all the other investigative materials.'

'I'm working on it,' said Annika. 'But you know how haphazard the archiving of files has been in this place. Some documents have been moved. Others have disappeared. And some have been destroyed. But I'm not giving up. If there's any material at all left from the Stella case, I'm determined to find it.'

She gave Patrik a smile.

'By the way, have you asked your wife? She's usually better than we are at locating old investigative material.'

'Don't I know it!' said Patrik, laughing. 'She's given me access to everything she has collected so far, but it's mostly photocopies of newspaper articles. She hasn't managed to get hold of any investigative documents.'

'I'll keep looking,' said Annika. 'If I find anything, I'll let you know at once.'

'Great. Okay, looks like we've got a lot of work ahead of us today,' said Patrik. He was trying to remain objective, but it was difficult. Bordering on impossible.

A voice boomed from the doorway.

'So there you all are, loafing around drinking coffee!' Mellberg peered at them drowsily.

'It's a good thing somebody does any work in this place. Come on, Ernst! Your master is going to show them how things get done.'

Ernst happily followed his master out of the room. They heard Mellberg stomping along the corridor, and then the door to his office slammed shut. He was undoubtedly going back to resume his morning nap. No one bothered to comment. They had work to do.

Jessie was savouring the calm feeling that came over her as she listened to Sam's steady breathing. It was something new: this serenity and security. Knowing she was seen.

She turned over in bed, trying not to disturb Sam. But his arm around her tightened. Nothing she did seemed to bother him.

Cautiously she stroked his stomach under the black T-shirt he was wearing. It felt so strange, being this close to another person. A guy. Touching him without being mocked or rejected.

She raised her head to look at him. Those etched cheeks, those sensual lips, those long black lashes.

'Have you ever hooked up with anybody?' she asked him quietly.

He blinked once, then closed his eyes again.

'No,' he said after a moment, opening his eyes. 'Have you?'

She shook her head and leaned close to rub her chin on his chest.

She didn't want to think about that humiliating episode the previous spring at the boarding school in London. There had been a brief moment when she thought Pascal wanted to sleep with her. He was the son of a French diplomat and so handsome he took her breath away. He'd started by sending her texts – wonderfully sweet messages. Then he'd texted an invitation to the school dance, and she'd hardly been able to sleep at the thought of how everyone would gape when she turned up on Pascal's arm. And they'd kept on texting. He had coaxed her more and more out of her shell as they flirted, joked, and slowly approached the border of what was forbidden.

One evening he asked her for a picture of her breasts. He said he wanted to sleep with the image in his mind. He said she must have the most beautiful breasts in the world, and he longed to caress them. So in her room she lifted up her shirt and took a picture of her breasts, not wearing a bra, completely exposed.

The next day the picture had spread through the whole school. Everybody had known what Pascal and his pals were planning. They had deliberately laid a trap for her, and together they'd written all those messages to her. She wanted to die, to disappear from the earth.

'No,' she said. 'No, I've never had a boyfriend.'

'We've been smart enough to wait for the right person,' said Sam gently, turning to face her.

She looked into his blue eyes and knew that she could trust him. They were like two scarred veterans who had been through the same war and didn't need words to communicate about everything they'd endured.

What their mothers had done had taken its toll on both of them.

'I hardly know anything about what happened back then. Thirty years ago.'

'What do you mean?' asked Sam. 'Nothing?'

'Well, okay, I know what you can find on Google. But so much was written about it at the time, things you can't find on the Internet. But I've never asked Mamma . . . it's not something we talk about.'

Sam stroked her hair.

'Maybe I can help you. Would you like that?'

Jessie nodded. She rested her head on his chest, allowing calm to flow through her body, almost making her sleepy.

'In a year I'll be able to escape from all this,' said Sam.

He was talking about school. She knew that's what he meant even though he hadn't said so. They were so alike.

'What will you do?'

He shrugged.

'I don't know. I don't want to be part of the rat race. Running around with no purpose.'

'I want to travel,' said Jessie, wrapping her arms around him. 'I'll take along only what will fit in a backpack and go wherever I like.'

'You can't do that until you're eighteen. And it's such a fucking long way off. I don't know if I can stand it that long.'

'What do you mean?' asked Jessie.

He turned his head away.

'Nothing,' he said quietly. 'I don't mean anything.'

Jessie didn't say a word, just continued stroking his

stomach, as if she could somehow smooth away the knot she knew was inside. The same knot she always had in her own stomach.

She felt something under her fingers and pulled up Sam's shirt.

'What's that?' she said, touching the circular mark.

'A burn mark. Fuck. Basse and a few of the other guys in class held me down while Nils pressed a lit cigarette against my skin.'

Jessie closed her eyes. He was her Sam now. She wanted to heal all his wounds.

'What about this?'

She let her hand move along his back and pressed lightly so he would turn on to his side and show her his back. Long streaks formed an irregular pattern on his skin.

'Is that from Nils too?'

'No. My father. From a belt. When the gym teacher asked me about it, I lied and said I tore up my back on some thorns. Nobody dares fuck with James. But from then on he was smart enough not to do anything that would leave a mark. And three years ago he totally stopped that sort of punishment. I don't know why.'

'Do you have other scars?' asked Jessie, feeling a certain fascination as she touched the streaks on his back.

Her own scars were all on the inside. But that didn't mean they hurt less than if a belt had torn open the skin on her back.

Sam sat up in bed. He rolled up his trouser legs to show her his knees. They were both scarred. She reached out her hand to stroke them as well. They felt knobby under her fingertips.

'How did you . . . what happened?'

'I had to kneel on the floor when it was covered with sugar. It may not sound especially painful, but believe me, it hurts. And that's how I got these scars.'

Jessie leaned forward and kissed his knees.

He turned his back to her and pulled down his trousers to show her his buttocks.

'Do you see it?'

She did. Yet another circular scar, but this one didn't look like a burn mark.

'It's from a pen. That old trick when somebody shoves a sharp pen underneath you just as you're sitting down. The pen went in a couple of centimetres, then broke off. The whole class laughed so hard I thought they'd all pee their pants.'

'Shit,' said Jessie.

She didn't want to hear anything else. She didn't want to see any more scars. She was all too aware of her own invisible scars, and she had no wish to see more of Sam's. She leaned forward and kissed him on the buttocks. He turned on to his back and slowly pulled down his trousers without looking at her. She heard how his breathing changed; he was breathing harder now. Tenderly she kissed his hips, his thighs. He reached up to stroke her hair. For a second she shivered as she recalled the photos of her that had been circulated at school and the way she'd felt afterwards. Then she opened her lips and pushed the pictures out of her mind. She wasn't there now. She was here. With her soul mate. The person who would be able to heal her wounds.

'My God, it's hot.' Martin was panting like a dog as they headed for the police car. 'You're not even sweating, are you?'

Paula laughed and shook her head.

'I'm Chilean. This is nothing.'

'But you've hardly even lived in Chile,' said Martin with a laugh as he wiped the sweat from his brow. 'You're as Swedish as I am.'

'Nobody can be as Swedish as you, Martin. You're the biggest Swede I know.'

'You say that as if you think it's a bad thing,' said Martin, smiling as he opened the car door and got in.

The next second he jumped back out.

'Wait a minute. We've got it all wrong. She's probably at the studio.'

'Oh, right,' said Paula, shaking her head. 'And it's only a stone's throw away from here.'

'Might be kind of fun to see a film studio,' said Martin as he began walking towards the industrial area where the Ingrid Bergman film was being shot in one of the abandoned buildings.

'I don't think it's as flashy as you imagine.'

Martin turned to look at Paula, who was shorter and had a hard time keeping up with him. He gave her a mischievous wink.

'We'll see about that. No matter what, it's going to be exciting to meet Marie Wall. She's a real looker, considering her age.'

Paula sighed.

'Speaking of women,' she said, 'how's it going with the woman you met the other day?'

Martin felt himself blushing.

'Oh, I don't know. I only talked to her for a few minutes at the playground. I don't even know her name.'

'But I thought you said the two of you hit it off.'

Martin groaned. He knew Paula wasn't about to let the subject go. The more uncomfortable he got, the more amused she was.

'Well, I mean . . .'

He searched frantically for some witty retort but couldn't think of anything.

'Let's drop it,' he said, shaking his head. 'We've got work to do.'

'Okay,' said Paula, giving him a smile.

The film studio was located in an industrial building with a distinctly unglamorous facade. A fence ran around the entire perimeter but when Martin reached for the gate, he discovered it wasn't locked, so they were able to enter the area with no trouble. A door stood open, probably for the sake of ventilation, and they hesitantly entered. The place was the size of an aircraft hangar: one enormous room with a high ceiling. In front of them, sofas had been arranged to form a seating area, and with lots of clothes hanging from racks to one side, presumably the wardrobe area. On the left were several doors that led to toilets and an improvised make-up room. On the right, fake walls with windows had been erected to give the illusion of a real room. The set was surrounded by dozens of lights.

A blonde came towards them. Her hair was pulled into a topknot and held in place with a fine brush. Around her waist she wore a carpenter's belt filled with cosmetic brushes and applicators.

'Hi. Who are you looking for?'

'We're police officers, and we'd like to speak to Marie,' said Paula.

'They're shooting a scene, but I'll tell her you're here as soon as they're done. Is it urgent?'

'No, that's okay. We can wait.'

'Great. Have a seat and help yourself to coffee.'

They sat down after getting coffee and some snacks from the table next to the sofa.

'So, you're right. It's not very glamorous,' said Martin, looking around.

'Uh-huh,' said Paula, tossing some nuts into her mouth.

They looked in the direction of the stage set, where they could vaguely hear the sound of voices delivering lines. After a while they heard a man's voice shout: 'Cut!'

Several minutes later the woman with all the make-up paraphernalia came towards them, accompanied by the star, Marie Wall. The room suddenly seemed significantly more glamorous. She wore a white shirt and tight shorts, and she had a white ribbon in her hair. Martin couldn't help noticing what great legs she had for someone her age, but he forced himself to focus on the task at hand. He'd always been easily distracted by beautiful women. Before he met Pia, that had caused a number of problems for him, and there were still certain places in Tanumshede he avoided so as not to run into one of his exes.

'How lovely to see such a handsome man in uniform this morning,' said Marie in that husky voice that brought goosebumps to Martin's arms.

It was easy to see why she'd gained a reputation as one of Hollywood's most famous man-eaters. He wouldn't mind falling under her spell.

Paula gave him an annoyed look, and Martin realized to his embarrassment that he was staring with his mouth open. He cleared his throat while Paula stood up to make the introductions.

'I'm Paula Morales, and this is my colleague, Martin Molin. We're from Tanumshede police station, and we're investigating the murder of a little girl who was found dead in Fjällbacka. We'd like to ask you some questions.'

'Of course,' said Marie, sitting down on the sofa next to Martin.

She shook hands with him, holding his hand a few seconds too long. He had no objection, but he was conscious of Paula glaring at him.

'I assume you want to talk to me because of what happened thirty years ago.'

Martin again cleared his throat and nodded. 'There are such striking similarities between the two cases, we felt we had to talk to you. And to Helen.'

'I understand,' she said calmly. 'But I'm sure you know that Helen and I have maintained our innocence all these years. And for most of our lives, we've had to suffer the consequences for something we didn't do.'

She leaned back and lit a cigarette. Martin gazed at her, hypnotized, as she crossed one leg over the other.

'We may not have landed in prison, but in the eyes of society, that didn't make any difference,' she went on. 'Everybody was convinced we were guilty of murder. Our pictures were in all the newspapers, I was taken away from my family, and our lives were never the same.'

She blew a smoke ring as she looked Paula in the eye. 'If that's not a prison, I don't know what is.'

Paula didn't say a word.

'First of all, we need to ask whether you have an alibi from eight p.m. on Sunday until Monday afternoon,' said Martin.

Marie took another drag on her cigarette before replying.

'Sunday evening I was out with the entire crew. We had an impromptu get-together at the Stora Hotel.'

'When did you get home?' asked Martin, taking out a notebook and pen.

'Hmm . . . Actually, I stayed overnight at the hotel.'

'Is there anyone who can confirm that?' asked Paula.

'Jörgen? Darling? Come over here.'

Marie called to a tall, dark-haired man who was talking loudly and waving his arms on the set. He stopped abruptly when he heard Marie call his name and came over to them.

'This is Jörgen Holmlund. The director.'

He nodded and shook hands, then cast an enquiring look at Marie, who seemed to be enjoying the situation.

'Darling, could you tell the officers where I was Sunday night and early Monday morning?'

Jörgen clenched his jaw. Marie took a drag on her cigarette and blew out the smoke.

'Don't worry, darling. I don't think they have any intention of ringing your wife.'

He snorted and said:

'The crew got together at the Stora Hotel on Sunday evening, and afterwards Marie stayed overnight in my room.'

'When did you get home in the morning?' Paula asked Marie.

'I didn't go home. Jörgen and I came to the studio together. We got here around eight thirty and at nine I was having my make-up done.'

'Is there anything else?' Jörgen asked. He turned on his heel and left when they answered in the negative.

Marie seemed amused by his discomfort.

'Poor Jörgen,' she said, pointing her cigarette at the back of the retreating director. 'He spends way too much time trying to make sure his wife doesn't find out about his little escapades. He's one of those men possessed of an unfortunate combination of guilty conscience and an insatiable libido.'

Marie leaned forward to put out her cigarette in a soda can on the table.

'Anything else? No questions about my alibi, I assume.'

'We'd also like to speak to your daughter. Since she's a minor, we need your permission.'

Martin gave a little cough because of the cloud of smoke now surrounding them.

'Sure,' said Marie with a shrug. 'Look, I'm well aware of the seriousness of the situation, but if you don't have any more questions for me, I really need to get back. Jörgen is going to break out in hives from stress if we don't stick to the shooting schedule.'

She stood up and shook hands with them. Then she

reached for Martin's notebook and pen. She wrote something down before handing them back with a smile before striding off towards the set.

Paula rolled her eyes. 'Let me guess. She gave you her phone number.'

Martin looked at the notebook and nodded. He couldn't hide a foolish smile.

BOHUSLÄN 1671–72

During the days following the visit, it was as if no one could talk of anything else but Lars Hierne and the witch-craft council. Britta's relish for the topic was in stark contrast to Preben's obvious distaste for the task ahead of him, but soon daily life resumed and the talk faded. Everyone had duties to perform, both the servants on the farm and Preben, who was responsible for church business in both Tanum and Lur parish.

The winter days came and went with monotonous regularity, broken only by the occasional visitor to the vicarage, and Preben's comings and goings as he travelled around the parish on church business. He brought home stories of conflicts that needed to be resolved, glad tidings to be celebrated, and sorrows to be mourned. He officiated at weddings, christenings, and funerals; he offered advice on matters regarding God and family. Elin sometimes eavesdropped when he talked to members of the congregation, and she always found his advice wise and thoughtful, though it tended to be somewhat cautious. He was not a daring man, not like her Per had been, and he also lacked the proud stubbornness her husband had possessed. Preben was not as sharp-edged, and his eyes were gentler. Per had always harboured a darkness inside, which at times had made his outlook gloomy, while Preben seemed to have no trace of despondency whatsoever. Britta frequently moaned that she had married a child, nagging him for coming home with his clothes soiled from working with the livestock or toiling alongside the farm labourers. He merely smiled and shrugged and carried on as before.

Märta had begun her lessons with the parish clerk along with the other children. Elin was uncertain how to respond to the eagerness and joy her daughter displayed as she attempted to master all the strange squiggles that she herself found so incomprehensible. She agreed it was a gift to learn to write, but of what use would such knowledge be for the child? Elin was a poor servant, and that meant Märta would be the same. For the likes of them, there was no other option. She was not Britta. She was Elin, the daughter their father had never loved, widow of a man who had been lost at sea. These were facts that could not be changed by a pastor who insisted Märta should learn to read. Her daughter would have greater use for the skills that had been passed on to Elin by her maternal grandmother. Though they would not put food on the table or earn in payment in *riksdaler*, they would bring her respect, and that was not without value.

Elin was often summoned to attend a birth, or to aid someone suffering from toothache or melancholy. She was the first person to be summoned whenever anyone fell ill, easing any number of ailments with her herbs and words of supplication. People called upon her help when heartsick from unrequited love or plagued by unsought wooing, as well as more mundane matters such as illnesses afflicting livestock. Surely that should be the role Märta aspired to. Far better than being filled with learning she could never use, knowledge that would give her dangerous ideas about being superior to others.

Yet for all her healing skills, Elin's concoctions seemed to have no effect on Britta. Month after month the bleeding still came, and each time it did her sister grew more resentful. She insisted that Elin must have done something wrong, that she was not as skilled as she claimed. One morning Britta threw the tankard at the wall when Elin offered her the concoction to drink, and the green liquid slowly ran down the wall to form a puddle on the floor. Sobbing, Britta collapsed in a heap.

Elin was not a bad person, yet she could not help taking some little pleasure in her sister's despair. Britta was often mean, not only to the servants but also to Märta. And sometimes Elin wondered whether it was the meanness inside Britta that was preventing a child from growing in her womb. Inevitably she would curse herself for harbouring such bad thoughts. Elin did not want to seem ungrateful. Who knew where she and Märta would have ended up if Britta had not taken pity on them and brought them under her protection. Only a few days earlier, Elin had heard that Ebba of Mörhult had landed in the poorhouse with her two youngest children. Without Britta, she and Märta would have been destined for the poorhouse too.

But it was not easy to behave in a god-fearing manner when it came to Britta. There was something so hard and cold about her, and not even a good man like Preben could make her mend her ways. Elin thought that he deserved a better wife, someone with a warm heart and a cheerful disposition, instead of a shrew with a beautiful face and billowing dark hair. But it was not her place to judge.

Elin would often catch Preben secretly looking at her. She tried to avoid him, but it was not easy. He moved as confidently among the servants as if he were one of them, and he was often to be found in the barnyard or out in the pastures tending to the animals. He had a real knack for dealing with all living creatures, and Märta always followed close on his heels, clasping her hands behind her back as she tried to take big steps to keep pace with him. Whenever Elin begged forgiveness because her daughter was such a bother, he merely laughed and shook his head, saying he would be hard pressed to find more pleasant company. It was true that Preben and Märta always seemed to have much to talk about, for they were constantly conversing. Elin had tried asking her daughter what they discussed, but Märta had merely shrugged and said they talked about everything. About animals, about God, and about what Märta was reading. Preben was in the habit of constantly lending her books from his library at the vicarage. As soon as the girl finished with her chores, if she was not following Preben around, she would be found sitting down with a book he had lent her. Elin was amazed that all those squiggles on the pages could be of such interest to Märta, but she reluctantly allowed her to keep reading, even though she was convinced nothing good would ever come of it.

And then there was Britta. For every passing day, she became more sullen as she saw how much interest Preben took in the child. Many times Elin caught her looking out the window and jealously observing the two. She had heard several heated discussions between husband and wife on this matter, but for once Preben refused to give in to his wife. Märta was allowed to accompany him wherever he went. And Viola followed. The kitten had grown during the winter, and she went everywhere with her mistress, just as Märta went with Preben. They were a cheerful trio, walking about the farm, and Elin couldn't help but smile at the sight even though she knew there was gossip about the master's interest in the girl. She cared little for what the maids or farmhands might think;

regardless how much they might whisper behind her back, as soon as they had a headache or toothache, they would turn to her. And when they murmured their query about what payment she wanted for her trouble, she would always ask for something for her daughter. An extra portion of food. A pair of discarded shoes. A skirt she could remake into a dress. Märta was her whole world; if she was happy, Elin was happy. Britta could think whatever she liked.

When Märta came to her, crying that the mistress had pinched her or pulled her hair, Elin could only bite her tongue. She told herself these cruelties were a small price to pay for having a roof over their heads and food in their bellies. When she and Britta were growing up, her sister had often pinched her, and she had endured it with no lasting harm done. Preben would protect Märta. He would also protect Elin. She was confident of that, because of the way his kind eyes would often rest on her when he thought she would not notice. And sometimes when their eyes met, for only a second though it seemed an eternity, she would feel the ground sway beneath her feet.

Erica could feel her excitement growing as she approached Marstrand. She'd read so much about Helen's parents, and in her mind she'd created an image of them, based on the interviews they'd given. Helen's father, KG, had died long ago, but she was at least going to be able to interview her mother.

Though Erica always did her best to rid herself of preconceived notions about her subjects, it was a struggle in Harriet Persson's case, given the way she and her husband had placed all the blame on Marie while painting Helen as a victim. The Perssons had belonged to the upper echelons of society; KG owned a chain of office supply stores, while Harriet had been a fashion model before she married; he was rich, she was beautiful – the usual combination. In their world, appearances were everything. They had gone from being the envy of Fjällbacka to the reviled parents of little Stella's murderer.

Erica drove into the car park at Koön. It was a hot, sunny day, and she was looking forward to this excursion. She hadn't been out to the island in a long time, and she was struck by how lovely the little coastal community looked.

She enjoyed the short crossing to Marstrand, but as

soon as she stepped ashore, she focused all her attention on the interview. The questions she wanted to ask began whirling through her mind as she walked up the hill towards Harriet's home. When she found the right address, she paused for a moment to catch her breath and admire the house. It was enchanting. Painted white, trimmed with beautiful old carvings in the wood, with dazzling roses and pink and lavender lupins out front, and a big terrace facing the sea. Erica surmised that if Harriet ever wanted to sell the house, she'd get millions for it. Double-digit millions.

She opened the wooden, white-painted gate and followed the narrow gravel path to the front door. There was no doorbell, just an old-fashioned knocker in the shape of a lion's head, which she let fall against the wooden panel. The door was opened almost at once by a stylish woman in her sixties.

'Erica Falck! How nice to meet you at last! Oh, I've read *all* your books, and I think you're such a gifted writer. I'm glad you've had such success abroad too.'

She ushered Erica into the entryway without letting her get a word in.

'I hope you'll stay for coffee. I don't often have such a celebrated visitor,' she said, leading the way to the terrace through a spacious living room.

Erica was no interior design expert, but she recognized furniture from Josef Frank, Bruno Mathsson, and Carl Malmsten. It had the look of a place that had been put together by a skilled interior designer; Erica doubted whether Harriet had chosen any of the pieces herself.

'Thank you for seeing me,' said Erica as she sat down on the chair Harriet indicated.

'You're welcome. After all these years of waiting for the truth to come out, for poor Helen's sake, I'm delighted a writer of your calibre has decided to write about the case. Especially after friends in Stockholm told me that horrible person is planning to release her own book.'

'But would that be such a bad thing?' asked Erica cautiously, nodding when Harriet held up the coffee pot. 'Like Helen, Marie has always maintained her innocence, so her book might actually reinforce Helen's version of what happened.'

Harriet pursed her lips as she poured the coffee, which looked distressingly pale.

'I don't believe for a moment she's innocent. I think she's the one who killed that poor little girl, and then she tried to pin the blame on Helen.'

'Even though Marie was the first to confess to the murder?'

Erica took a sip of the coffee, which was definitely too weak.

'That was part of her plan all along!'

Harriet's voice had suddenly turned shrill, and she swallowed hard several times.

'She wanted to trick Helen into confessing,' she said. 'Helen was always so easily led, so gullible, and that Marie was a sly girl from a horrible family. From the beginning we were worried about the bad influence she would have on Helen. Our daughter changed so much after she started spending time with that girl. Against our better judgement, we allowed them to be friends. We didn't want to be accused of snobbishness, and of course it's important for children to be exposed to different types of people, but that family . . .' She shuddered at the recollection. 'We should have put a stop to it right away. I said as much to KG. But you know how men are, they won't listen once they've got some idea in their heads, so he refused to intervene until it was too late. And look what it led to! Over the years he said to me so many times: "Why didn't I listen to you, Harriet?"'

265

She paused to catch her breath and took a sip of coffee.

'I don't know whether you've heard,' Erica hurried to interject, 'but a little girl from the same farm where Stella lived has been murdered. And her body was found in the same place as Stella's.'

'Yes, I heard. Too dreadful.'

Harriet shivered, making her jewellery clink. She wore a wide gold chain necklace, heavy gold bracelets, and a discreet little Chanel brooch on her blouse. It was obvious from the way she carried herself that she had once been a model. Despite her age, she'd maintained her good posture, and her hair had been professionally coloured with blond highlights that hid any hint of grey. She looked closer to fifty than sixty. Erica sat up straighter. She had a tendency to slump like a sack of hay – an occupational hazard, the result of spending so many hours sitting in front of a computer.

Harriet refilled her cup with the weak coffee. Inwardly cringing at the prospect of having to drink it, Erica waited for Harriet to finish pouring and continue the conversation.

'This latest murder only proves what I was saying: Helen is innocent. It can't be a coincidence that a little girl dies right after Marie returns. She must be the one who did it.'

She fixed her gaze on Erica.

'But why do you think Helen confessed?' asked Erica. 'Why would a thirteen-year-old girl confess to a murder she didn't commit?'

Harriet took her time answering. She tugged nervously on her necklace as she stared at Carlsten, the stone fortress on Marstrand. When she turned to face Erica again, she had a strange look in her eyes.

'Helen was a fragile girl. She'll always be fragile. And KG spoiled her. We didn't have any other children, and she was her father's daughter. He protected her from everything and gave her anything she wanted. I have to admit, sometimes I felt a bit excluded. They could spend hours together, just the two of them. It was as if they had their own little world. I was also my father's daughter when I was growing up, so I understood and didn't try to interfere. But when Marie came into the picture, she was like a force that Helen couldn't resist. I saw how fascinated she was with Marie. That girl was beautiful, and even at the age of thirteen she had a worldly air about her and . . . I'm not sure what to call it, but she had some sort of survival instinct. I think Helen, who was scared of everything, felt safe with Marie. Helen changed after they met. She withdrew from us. KG noticed it too, and he made an effort to spend more time with her. Neither of us thought they should be friends. After a while, we tried to keep them apart, but Fjällbacka is a small place and it's hard to separate two people here. What were we supposed to do – keep her company in school all day long?'

Harriet kept on tugging at her necklace, which clinked against her tanned skin at the neckline of her blouse.

'So why do you think Helen confessed? Was she afraid of Marie?'

Harriet's reply had strayed from the original question, and Erica was determined to steer her back on track.

'I think she wanted to go along with whatever Marie did. When the police told her Marie had confessed, she wanted to do the same. That's how Helen was. Is. She never wants to go against the flow. When Marie later retracted her confession, Helen did too. But the damage had been done.'

Her voice quavered. She pushed a plate of cinnamon buns towards Erica.

'Help yourself. They're freshly baked. I bought them at the bakery this morning.'

Erica reached for a bun.

'Thank goodness the girls couldn't be sentenced to prison time. The Social Welfare system stepped in and determined what would be in their best interest. As you'd expect, that ghastly Wall family were deemed unsuitable guardians for Marie. But Helen was allowed to come home to us after a brief stay at a youth home. And quite right too. Nothing that happened was our fault, there was absolutely nothing wrong with the way Helen had been brought up or with our parenting methods. If she'd never met that miserable girl, none of this would ever have occurred.'

Her voice was becoming shrill again.

'You moved away from Fjällbacka soon afterwards, didn't you?' asked Erica calmly.

Harriet nodded.

'Naturally, it was unbearable for us to live there any longer, what with all the whispering and gossiping. It wasn't nice, suddenly finding ourselves treated like pariahs. They even removed KG as chair of the Rotary Club. As if what happened was in any way his fault!'

She took a few deep breaths. The old wounds had clearly never healed completely. Erica noted that Harriet seemed more upset about her and KG's fall from the social elite than about the trauma her daughter must have experienced.

'But Helen chose to move back, didn't she?'

'Yes. I've never understood why. James, who bought the house from us, didn't want to move away from Fjällbacka when he married Helen, and KG supported his decision, so what could I say?'

'From what I understand, James and your husband were close friends. And Helen was very young when she married a man who was the same age as her father. How did you and your husband feel about the marriage?'

Erica leaned forward, eager to hear what Harriet would say. During the months she'd spent doing research for her book, she'd often wondered about this.

'KG was thrilled. He and James were childhood friends, they'd grown up together in Fjällbacka, and KG had always admired him. So he encouraged the relationship right from the start. Personally, I didn't see any harm in it. I've known James ever since KG and I got married, so he was more or less part of the family. When James brought up the matter right before Helen's eighteenth birthday, we told him that it was up to Helen, but we had no objection to the marriage.'

Erica thought she caught something in Harriet's expression that didn't mesh with her words. Could the woman really have been so positively inclined towards a friend of the family, a man old enough to be her daughter's father, when he suddenly began courting Helen and then married her? She didn't buy it. There was something here that didn't make sense, but she realized she wasn't going to get anything more from Harriet on that subject, so she changed tack.

'I've tried to contact Helen many times, but she has never replied. I don't think she wants to be interviewed by me. It would be very valuable for the book, though, if I could hear Helen's version of the story. Do you think you could persuade her?'

Harriet nodded.

'Of course she'll see you. I know she's afraid that everything is going to be stirred up again, and I had the same thought myself at first. I thought talking to you would bring it all back. But then I realized this is the chance we've been waiting for, an opportunity to restore our reputation once and for all. Even after all this time, people still look at me askance, and year after year I feel more excluded from social events here on the island. And I have so much to offer!'

She swallowed hard.

'So, yes, I'll talk to Helen. I know she'll see you.'

'Thank you,' said Erica.

'I'll ring her today,' said Harriet, nodding decisively. 'I don't want her to miss out on this chance to clear our name.'

When Erica left, Harriet was still sitting on the terrace.

At midday it was always calm. People were out on the water or in town having lunch outdoors in the sunshine. They didn't feel like walking up and down the aisles of the garden centre, looking at flowers and bushes when the heat was at its height. That suited Sanna fine. She felt happiest inside a greenhouse, so the shimmering heat from the sun at its zenith didn't bother her, even though her head ached, as it always did in the morning. This pause in the day gave her a chance to tend to her plants. They were really soaking up water these days, and she made sure not to ignore even the smallest thirsty plant.

She also had time to set upright any pots that had been toppled by careless customers, and she could have a little chat with the hydrangeas and gossip with the roses. Cornelia could mind the cash register. The quality of summer hires varied from year to year, but Cornelia was a real gem.

If anyone ever asked Sanna who her closest friends were, she would have said they were her plants. Not that there was anyone else to choose from. She had a hard time letting anyone into her life. In secondary school she'd made clumsy attempts to become friends with some of the other students. She'd tried to do what she saw everyone else doing. Drink coffee together, talk about boys, have a light-hearted chat about the shoes she'd recently bought, or try a serious discussion about the greenhouse effect on the climate. She had tried to be normal. But she didn't understand other people. It was a miracle she'd managed to get together with Niklas. Plants – now there was something she understood. Unlike people, they understood her. They were all the company she needed.

Gently she burrowed her face in a big lavender hydrangea, breathing in its fragrance. It was the best scent in the world. It made her soul feel calm, and for a brief moment she was able to relax. It pushed away all memories, all thoughts, and made room only for a quiet humming.

It was different when she was a child. Stella was the one who had loved the woods and always went there to play. Sanna had kept to the farm, avoiding the woods with all their strange scents.

After what happened to Stella, she'd had even less reason to seek out the woods. After what Helen and Marie had done.

Something stirred inside Sanna every time she thought about Marie. A need to take action. Thirty years of brooding and thinking had piled up, hardening into a rock-solid lump over the years. A pressure in her chest that got stronger with every passing day.

Soon she would have to do something about it.

'Excuse me, can you tell me where the herbs are?'

Sanna gave a start, her face still buried in the hydrangea. She looked up. A woman with a small child impatiently tugging at her hand was giving her an enquiring look.

'Let me show you,' said Sanna, leading the way towards the section she'd reserved for herbs and vegetables.

She had already guessed the woman was a basil type. She was never wrong.

Her life had been like a rollercoaster for many years, but at last Anna felt she had solid ground under her feet.

Even so, knowing how fast it could all fall apart, she was scared to take the next step. The years she'd spent married to Lucas had fundamentally changed her. His kicks and punches had eroded her self-confidence to the point that, years later, she was still struggling to find her way back to who she used to be.

Before she met Lucas, she had believed herself to be invincible. Largely thanks to Erica. As an adult, she realized that her sister had been over-protective and had spoiled her, perhaps in an attempt to compensate for everything they'd never received from their parents.

Anna had long ago forgiven their mother, Elsy. It had been painful to find out the secret she'd lived with, yet Anna was glad Erica had discovered the bloodstained garment in the attic of their childhood home. Because of that, they had gained a new family member. Both she and Erica tried to visit their half-brother, Göran, as often as they could.

There's a reason for everything, thought Anna as she overtook an old tractor. The sun was blinding, so she reached for her sunglasses without taking her eyes off the road. She'd never been a particularly daring driver, but since the accident she was more cautious than ever. Especially when she could hardly fit behind the wheel because of her bulging stomach. Presumably she'd have to give up driving pretty soon. Dan had offered to be her chauffeur today, but she had firmly but politely declined. This was something she wanted to do on her own. She didn't want anyone interfering. She would make her own decision.

Anna allowed herself to regard this short drive as a relaxing interlude from her daily chores at home. In many ways the summer holidays were a wonderful invention – for the children. Not always for the adults though. At least, not when she was feeling so tired, sweaty, and hugely pregnant. She loved the kids, but trying to keep them occupied all day required a real effort, and since there was such a big age gap between her kids and Dan's, they had to put up with everything from childish squabbles to teenage outbursts. In addition, she had a hard time saying no whenever Erica and Patrik asked for help. Dan was forever scolding her, saying she needed to think about herself. But she was extremely fond of her sister's three children, and she also saw it as a chance to repay Erica for everything she'd done for her when they were growing up. Babysitting Maja and the twins once in a while seemed the least she could do, no matter what Dan said. She would always be available to help her big sister.

Anna was playing a Vinyl 107 CD, and she enjoyed singing along. After having kids, she'd completely lost track of the latest music. She knew that Justin Bieber was popular, and she could hum along to some of Beyoncé's tunes. Apart from that, she was clueless. But when Vinyl played 'Broken Wings' with Mr Mister, she would sing along at the top of her lungs.

In the midst of the refrain, she stopped singing abruptly, and swore. Damn it. The car approaching in the oncoming lane was all too familiar. Erica. Anna would recognize her old Volvo estate car anywhere. She considered ducking down behind the wheel but realized Erica would recognize her car. Yet she knew that Erica was hopeless when it came to cars and could hardly tell the difference between a Toyota and a Chrysler, so she was hoping her sister wouldn't react when she saw a red Renault rushing past.

Her mobile rang. It was fastened to the dashboard with a magnet. Shit, shit, shit. The call was from Erica. So she must have recognized her car. Anna sighed, but since she didn't like talking on the phone while she was driving, she had a little while to work out what she would say.

She didn't like lying to her sister. She'd done that far too often over the years. But right now she had no choice.

The child's swing was swaying back and forth, even though Gösta couldn't feel the slightest breeze in the oppressive heat. He wondered when Nea had last used it. Gravel crunched under his feet. The hopscotch lines were almost gone.

His stomach clenched as he went up to the door, which opened before he could knock.

'Come in,' said Bengt.

Bengt gave him a slight smile, but Gösta could sense the aggression below the surface.

Gösta had phoned ahead to warn them he was coming. They were all sitting at the kitchen table, waiting for him. He surmised that Peter's parents would probably be staying at least until after the funeral, whenever that might be. Until the post-mortem had been completed, Nea could not be laid to rest. Or maybe Eva and Peter would choose cremation. He put the thought out of his mind along with the images it conjured, and said yes to a cup of coffee. Then he sat down next to Peter and placed a hand on his shoulder.

'How are you holding up?' he asked, nodding his thanks to Eva when she set a piping hot cup of coffee in front of him.

'We're taking it second by second, minute by minute,' Eva said quietly as she sat down across from him, next to her father-in-law.

'The doctor gave them some sleeping tablets, and that helps,' said Peter's mother. 'At first they didn't want to take them, but I persuaded them to try. It won't help matters if they don't get any sleep.'

'Yes, that's probably a good idea,' said Gösta. 'Make use of all the help you can get.'

'Have you heard anything? Is that why you're here?'

Peter looked at him with eyes that seemed devoid of all life.

'No, I'm afraid not,' said Gösta. 'But we're working nonstop and doing everything we can. I'm here to find out if anyone could possibly have slipped inside the house while you were sleeping. Did you notice any windows open?'

Eva looked at him.

'It's been so hot, and we always sleep with the windows open. But they were fastened on the inside. Everything was as usual.'

'Okay,' said Gösta. 'The last time I was here, you said the front door was closed and locked. But maybe there are other ways for someone to get in. A basement door, for example, that you might have forgotten to lock?'

Peter slapped his forehead and pointed at the door.

'Oh my God, I forgot to mention it to you last time! We have a security system. We switch it on every night before we go to bed. We once had a break-in at our flat when we lived in Uddevalla. That was before we had Nea. Someone tossed a tear-gas canister through the letter box, and broke down the door. We didn't have any valuables worth stealing, but it didn't feel safe knowing that somebody had the nerve to come into our flat when we were home and asleep in bed. Since then, we've always had a security system. It was one of the first things we installed when we moved here. It seemed a wise precaution, given the remote location . . .'

His voice faded away, and Gösta knew what he was thinking. Danger had encroached nevertheless. The security system had undoubtedly made them feel protected, but it hadn't done any good.

'So you switched it on when you went to bed?'

'Yes, I did.'

'And did you switch it on again before you left?'

'No,' said Peter, shaking his head. 'It was morning and bright daylight, so . . .'

He looked up, realizing what Gösta was saying.

'So Nea couldn't have left the house before six thirty.'

'Exactly. She must have disappeared after that time, otherwise the alarm would have sounded. Does anyone else know the code for turning off the alarm?'

Now it was Eva's turn to shake her head.

'No. Besides, we receive notifications on our mobile phones about any activity related to the alarm system.'

She got up to fetch her iPhone, which was being charged on the worktop. She tapped in her password, scrolled through some files and then held up the phone towards Gösta.

'See, this is that night. We switched on the alarm when we went to bed around ten, and it wasn't turned off until three minutes past six when Peter got up in the morning.'

'I can't believe we didn't think of that,' said Peter in a low voice.

'I'm the one who should have thought of it,' said Gösta. 'The security pad is right there on the wall. But in these situations . . . well, in situations like this all logic goes by the wayside. At least we now know that we can rule out anyone breaking into the house during the night.'

'Have you investigated those people in Tanumshede?' asked Bengt.

Ulla tugged at his arm and leaned forward to whisper something to him. Angrily he pulled his arm away.

'If nobody else dares mention it, I will!' he said. 'There's been a lot of talk about criminal elements at that place in Tanumshede. And some of those men apparently took part in the search. Don't you realize what a golden opportunity it would have been for them to destroy any evidence? I heard one of them was even present when she was found. Don't you think that's a strange coincidence?'

Gösta wasn't sure what to say. He hadn't counted on the discussion taking a turn like this even though over the past few years he'd realized more and more that people who harboured animosity towards foreigners could no longer be identified by their shaved heads and boots. Sometimes they looked like perfectly ordinary retirees. He wondered whether Eva and Peter shared Bengt's views.

'We're not ruling out anything, but there has been no indication whatsoever that we should direct our attention to anyone at the refugee centre.'

'But is it true? Are there criminal elements at that place?'

It was hard to tell whether Peter was asking the question based on his personal conviction or as a desperate man grasping at straws.

'Shouldn't the local police do a background check on those people when they arrive here? There might be murderers, thieves, rapists, even paedophiles among them!'

Bengt raised his voice, and his wife again tugged at his arm.

'Hush, Bengt. This is not the right time to—'

But her husband was not about to be stopped.

'I don't know what's wrong with this damn country. It's precisely because of Swedish naivety that we moved to Spain! People are pouring across the borders, and we're supposed to give them food and clothing and a roof over their heads, and then they have the gall to complain about their living quarters! They claim to be fleeing from war and torture, yet they moan because there's no Wi-Fi!'

'Please excuse my husband,' said Ulla, tugging even harder at his sleeve. 'But nobody knows for sure what sort of people are living at the centre, and when we've gone into town to buy groceries . . . well, there's a lot of talk. Everyone's afraid that more children will go missing.'

'We have other leads that we consider a priority,' said Gösta.

He felt genuinely sickened by the turn the conversation had taken.

'Are you talking about what happened thirty years ago? With Helen and that actress who's back here now? Do you really think there's a connection?' Eva looked up and met Gösta's eye. 'We know Helen. She's our neighbour, and she would never harm Nea. And that actress? Good lord, why would she want to hurt our child? Those girls were kids when it happened. No, I don't believe it for a moment. If anything, I'm more inclined to believe . . . what Bengt is saying.'

Gösta paused, trying to formulate a reply. He found he had nothing to say. Given the desperate situation Nea's parents found themselves in, this was not the time to get into a discussion about ideologies.

'We're not ruling out anything, but it would be dangerous to leap to conclusions,' he said. 'The investigation is at an early stage. We're waiting for the pathology report and the technical analysis. Believe me when I say that we're not locked into any one theory, but it won't help matters if we waste our time following up on baseless rumours. So I beg you not to make things more difficult for us by . . . well, by causing people to jump to the wrong conclusion.'

'We hear what you're saying,' replied Peter, his hands clasped tightly on the table before him. 'But promise us that you won't rule out things for the wrong reasons. If someone has a bad name, and people are talking about him, there may be a reason for it. No smoke without fire.'

'I promise,' said Gösta, but the sick feeling of apprehension was getting worse.

He had an unpleasant feeling that something had been set in motion, and it would be very difficult to stop. The last thing he saw before he left was the dark, dead look in Peter's eyes.

BOHUSLÄN 1672

The last of the snow melted away, making the streams ripple with life and turning the vegetation lush. The farm was emerging from winter too, and they spent an entire week cleaning in order to welcome the warmer half of the year. All the feather beds and mattresses were washed and hung outside to dry. The rag rugs were beaten and the floors scrubbed. The windows were washed so the sun could seep into the small rooms and chase out the shadows from the corners. Warmth settled into everyone's chests, thawing the frost still lingering from the long winter nights. And Märta's legs seemed filled with dance as she ran around the farm with Viola in tow. Elin found herself humming as she knelt on the floor scrubbing the wooden planks, and even Britta seemed in a kinder mood.

News of the witches who had been burned at the stake in the Bohuslän area had contributed to a feeling of exhilaration in the whole community, and stories spread from house to house, to be told and retold in the candle-light. Tales about evil women journeying to Blåkulla mountain for the witches' sabbath, and cavorting with the devil were embroidered with more details every time the stories were told. The maids and farmhands with whom they shared their living quarters competed to describe the devilish goings on at these gatherings: dinners served in reverse order, upside-down candles, flying cows and goats, and children who were lured away by witches to serve Satan. Elin would look on indulgently as Märta listened, wide-eyed. She could not deny that the stories were exciting, but she secretly wondered how much was true. They reminded Elin of the fairy tales her grandmother used to tell her when she was a child. But she did not intervene. People needed stories to endure the hardships of life, and Märta's eager expression gave her joy. Who was she to take away her happiness? Märta would learn soon enough the difference between fairy tales and real life, and the longer she could stay in the fairy-tale world, the better.

Britta had been unusually kind towards Märta over the past few days. She had stroked the girl's blond hair, offered her sweets, and asked if she might pet Viola. Elin could not put her finger on why it should be so, but this made her uneasy. Perhaps it was because she knew her sister too well. Britta never did anything out of the goodness of her heart. But the child welcomed any kindness shown to her and, beaming with delight, she had shown her mother the sweets she had received from her mistress. So Elin tried to push all anxious thoughts to the back of her mind. Especially because on this particular day they had more work to do than usual. Britta's Aunt Ingeborg was coming to visit, which meant the spring cleaning they had already begun must now be hurried along so that everything would be ready by the time she arrived.

Elin had been so busy scrubbing and cleaning, she had not seen Märta all day. In the afternoon she began to worry about her daughter. She called the girl's name as she walked about the farm, looking in the servants' quarters, the barn, and the other buildings belonging to the vicarage, but Märta was nowhere in sight. Her stomach clenched with fear, and she called louder and louder. She asked everyone she saw, but no one had seen the girl.

The door to the house flew open.

'What is the trouble, Elin?' asked Preben as he came running out with his hair standing on end. He was tucking his white shirt into his trousers.

Distraught, Elin ran over to him as she scanned the farm area, hoping to see her daughter's fair plaits.

'I cannot find Märta, and I have looked everywhere!'

'Calm yourself, Elin,' said Preben, placing his hands on her shoulders.

She felt the warmth from his hands through her dress, and she could not stop herself from collapsing in his arms. She stood like that for several seconds before tearing herself away and wiping her tears on her sleeve.

'I have to find her. She is so little, and she is the dearest and most precious thing I have.'

'We will find her, Elin,' said Preben, and he strode resolutely towards the stable.

'I have already looked there,' said Elin in despair.

'I saw Lill-Jan in there. And he, more than anyone else, knows everything that goes on here at the farm.'

He opened the stable door and went inside. Elin lifted her skirts and ran after him. In the dim light of the stable, she heard the murmuring voices of the two men, though the only word she could make out was 'Britta'. Her heart began pounding. She forced herself to wait while Preben and Lill-Jan finished their conversation, but when she saw Preben's face, she knew that her fears were justified.

'Lill-Jan saw Britta take Märta into the woods some time ago.'

'The woods? What would they be doing there? Britta never goes into the woods. And why would she take Märta?'

She could hear how shrill her voice sounded, and Preben hushed her.

'Now is not the time for hysterics. We must find the girl. I saw Britta in the library. I will go and speak to her.'

Preben dashed inside the house. Feeling at a loss, Elin waited outside. Memories from her childhood washed over her. Everything she had ever held dear her sister had taken from her, with their father's blessing. The doll her mother had given her was found in the mire of the privy with its hair cut off and the eyelashes torn away. The puppy the farmhand had given her simply disappeared, but she knew in her heart that Britta was somehow involved. There was something rotten inside her sister. She could not bear for anyone to have anything she herself did not possess. She had always been that way.

And now Britta had no child, while Elin had the dearest of little girls. A girl whom Britta's husband looked at with love in his eyes, as if she were his own. Elin had known that this did not bode well, but what could she do? She lived at the mercy of her sister, and there was nowhere else she and her daughter could go. Not after the words she had spoken, which caused many to regard her with hatred and contempt. Britta had been their only salvation. And now it may have cost Elin her daughter.

Preben came running back, his expression dark.

'They went to the lake,' he said.

Elin had no thought for what must have played out inside the vicarage. Her only concern was that Märta was at the lake, and she did not know how to swim.

With her heart pounding, and murmuring prayers to God, she raced after Preben as he ran into the woods and headed for the lake. If the Lord had any mercy at all, He would allow them to find Märta alive. If not, she might as well perish in the dark waters along with her child.

Nils put the cigarette to his lips and took a deep drag. Next to him Vendela also lit a cigarette. Basse rustled the bag of sweets he'd bought from Eva at the Centrum Kiosk.

They were sitting at the top of the ridge, at the viewpoint above the local landmark called Kungsklyftan. Below, a group of tourists was taking pictures of the cleft which was the entrance to Fjällbacka.

'Do you think your father will succeed?' asked Basse. 'Teaching the Arabs to sail, I mean?'

He closed his eyes and turned towards the sun. His freckled face would soon turn beet red if he sat there much longer.

'I don't know, but he's completely obsessed,' replied Nils.

His father had always been like that. If he wanted something badly enough, he would work 24/7 to make it happen. He seemed to have unlimited energy. On the walls at home there were photographs of Bill carrying Nils's older brothers on his shoulders, teaching them to sail, and reading to them.

But when it came to Nils, half the time his father couldn't even be bothered to ask him how he was.

Vendela was distracted, staring at her mobile. She spent

most of her waking hours looking at her phone; she might as well have it grafted on to her hand as a permanent fixture.

'Hey, look how cute she was,' she said now.

She held up her phone towards the boys. They squinted to see the display in the sunlight.

'Fucking cute,' said Basse, devouring the photo with his eyes.

It was a picture from the early 1990s of Marie Wall standing next to Bruce Willis. Nils had seen the film several times. She was really hot back then.

'So how come she has such an ugly daughter?' he asked, shaking his head. 'Jessie's father must have been someone she met in a horror movie.'

'Hell, at least she's got big boobs,' said Basse. 'Bigger than her mother's. I wonder what it's like to fuck her? Ugly girls compensate by being awesome in bed.'

He pointed his cigarette at Vendela.

'Could you google Jessie too? See what you can find about her.'

Vendela nodded. As she fiddled with her mobile, Nils lay down on his back and turned his face towards the sky.

'Holy shit!' said Vendela, reaching out to shake his arm. 'You've got to see this!'

She held up the phone towards Nils and Basse.

'Are you kidding?' said Nils, feeling excitement race through him. 'Is that on the Internet?'

'Yup. It was super easy to find,' said Vendela.

'Huh. Fuck. Good.'

Basse gasped.

'What should we do? Should we put it on Snapchat?'

Vendela smiled at Nils.

He paused to give himself time to think. Then a big smile spread across his face.

'We don't do anything. Not yet.'

At first Basse and Vendela looked disappointed. Then he told them his plan, and Basse laughed loudly. It was brilliant. Simple, but brilliant.

The children peppered Karim with questions when he sat down at the kitchen table, but he didn't have the energy to answer. He merely grunted. So much information had been stuffed into his head in such a short time. He hadn't felt this mentally exhausted since his first year at university. Sailing itself wasn't that complicated – he'd studied far more difficult subjects – but it wasn't easy to grasp when it was being taught in a language he hadn't yet mastered, and when all the terminology and techniques involved were completely alien. And frightening.

Memories of the voyage across the Mediterranean had come back with a force that had surprised him. Only now did he realize how scared he'd been on the boat. While it was happening, there was no time or space for fear. He and Amina had been too focused on keeping the children safe and sound. But this morning, out in the dinghy with Bill, he'd remembered every wave, every scream from those who landed in the water. And he saw once more the eyes of those who suddenly stopped screaming and quietly slipped below the surface, never to come up again. He had repressed it all, telling himself the only thing that mattered was that they were now safe. They had a new country. A new home.

'Do you want to talk about it?' asked Amina, stroking his hair.

He shook his head. It wasn't because he didn't think he could confide in her. He knew she wouldn't judge him or doubt him. But she had been strong for such a long time. During that last period in Syria, and during the long journey to Sweden. Now it was his turn to be strong.

'I'm just tired,' he said, helping himself to more of her baba ganoush.

It was as good as his mother's had been, though that was not something he would ever have said to his mother. She had been as hot-tempered as Amina.

His mother died while Karim was in prison, and after that they'd been forced to leave. They hadn't dared tell anyone. Syria was now a country built on informers, and you never knew who might try to save his own skin by turning in someone else. Neighbours, friends, family members – you couldn't trust anyone.

He was astounded by the naivety of those Swedes who believed they had left Syria in the hope of finding a life of luxury. How could they believe anybody would leave everything behind in the belief that he would be swimming in gold in the West? He wished people would understand that they had been forced to leave their homes in order to save the lives of their families. And now they wanted to contribute everything they could to this country that had taken them in.

Amina stroked the scars on his arms, and he looked up from his plate. He realized he hadn't eaten anything because he'd been so immersed in memories he thought he had repressed.

'Are you sure you don't want to talk about it?' She smiled at him encouragingly.

'It's difficult,' he said.

Samia kicked Hassan, and Amina gave them a stern look. That was usually enough.

'There was so much new information,' said Karim. 'So many strange words, and I'm wondering whether he might be slightly crazy.'

'Bill?'

'Yes. I don't know, but maybe he's a crazy person who wants to do something impossible.'

'Everything is possible. Isn't that what you always tell the children?'

Amina put her hand on his knee. It was unusual for them to show affection in front of the children, who were now looking wide-eyed at their parents. But she seemed to sense that he needed her right now.

'Are you going to use your husband's own words against him?' he said, brushing a lock of hair back from her face.

Her thick, black hair fell halfway down her back. It was one of the many things he loved about her.

'My husband has such wise things to say,' she replied, kissing his cheek. 'At least sometimes.'

He laughed loudly for the first time in a long while and felt himself relax. The children didn't understand the joke, but they too began to laugh, because he was laughing.

'You're right. Everything is possible,' he said, patting her backside. 'Move now so I can get to the food. It's almost as good as my mother's.'

Without a word, she gave him a little slap on the shoulder. Then he reached for another dolma.

'Are you going to phone Marie?' asked Paula, smiling at Martin as he shifted gears ahead of a bend. 'I've heard cougars are the new big thing. And a little birdie tells me that this wouldn't be your first near-cougar experience . . .'

It was no secret that Martin had gone through a lot of women in his younger days, many of them significantly older than him. Paula hadn't known him then. She met him after he'd settled down with Pia, the love of his life, and she'd seen how much he loved her – and how he had lost her. All the stories from his bachelor days were tall tales to Paula, but she still enjoyed teasing him. And Marie's blatant flirting with him had left the door wide open.

'Oh, come on,' he said, blushing.

'There it is,' said Paula, pointing as they drove past the luxury villa on the water.

Martin heaved a sigh of relief. She'd been teasing him for nearly twenty kilometres.

'I'm going to park at Planarna,' he said unnecessarily, since he'd already turned into the big cement dock area and was parking the car.

Across from them towered Badis, the former seaside hotel, and Paula was glad the old building had been renovated a couple of years ago. She'd seen pictures of the way it had looked before, and it would have been a real shame if it had been allowed to deteriorate beyond repair. She'd heard how it had previously been the setting for so many parties and nightclubs, and no doubt a number of Fjällbacka's residents had Badis to thank for their existence.

'She might not be home,' said Martin as he locked the car. 'But let's knock and find out.'

He headed towards the beautiful house that Marie had rented, and Paula followed.

'Jessie is a teenager, yet she has access to a house like this?' she said. 'My God, if I were in her shoes I'd never leave the place.'

Paula shaded her eyes with her hand. Right in front of them was the dazzling sea.

Martin knocked on the door. They could have phoned in advance to see if Jessie was home, but they preferred to talk to people who were not forewarned. Denied the opportunity to think over what questions might be asked and how best to answer them, they were more likely to tell the truth.

'Doesn't look like anyone's home,' said Paula, stamping her feet. Patience was not her greatest virtue, unlike Johanna who was patience personified.

'Wait a sec,' said Martin, knocking again.

After what seemed like an eternity, they heard footsteps approaching inside the house. Then the door opened.

'Yes?' said a teenage girl.

She wore a black T-shirt promoting some hard rock band and a pair of short shorts. Her hair was tousled, and it looked as if she'd dressed in a hurry.

'We're from the Tanumshede police station, and we'd like to ask you a few questions,' said Martin.

The girl, who had opened the door only a couple of centimetres, seemed reluctant to open it any further.

'My mother—'

'We've just spoken with your mother,' Paula cut in. 'She knows we're here to talk to you.'

The girl still looked sceptical, but after a few seconds she took a step back and pulled open the door.

'Come in,' she said, leading the way into the house.

Paula could feel her pulse surge at the sight of the room they entered. The view was spectacular. Big glass doors stood open to a dock, and the entire approach to Fjällbacka was visible. Good lord. To think people actually lived like this.

'What do you want?'

Jessie sat down at a kitchen table made of solid wood without saying a proper hello. Paula silently wondered whether this breach of courtesy was due to poor upbringing or simply teenage truculence. After meeting Jessie's mother, she tended to think it was the former. Marie hadn't struck her as the warm, maternal type.

'We're investigating the murder of a little girl. And it's . . . well, we've had reason to speak with your mother about it.'

Paula saw that Martin was struggling to find the right words. They weren't sure how much Jessie knew about her mother's past.

She answered that question herself.

'Yeah, I heard about that. A girl was found in the same place as the other girl, the one people say Mamma and Helen killed.'

Her eyes wavered, and Paula gave her a smile.

'We need to know where your mother was from Sunday night until Monday afternoon,' she said.

'How would I know?' Jessie shrugged. 'She went to some party with the film crew on Sunday night, but when or whether she came home afterwards, I haven't a clue. It's not like we share the same bedroom.'

Jessie drew her feet up to the edge of her chair and tugged her T-shirt over her knees. Paula couldn't see much resemblance between mother and daughter, but maybe the girl took after her father, whoever that might be. She had googled Marie to find out as much as possible about her background, but according to what she'd read, no one knew who Jessie's father was. She wondered if the girl knew. Or whether Marie herself did, for that matter.

'This isn't a huge house, so even if you don't share a room, you should have heard her come in,' said Martin.

He's right, thought Paula. The renovated boathouse was definitely luxurious, but it wasn't particularly big.

'I play music while I'm sleeping. With a headset on,' said Jessie, as if stating the obvious.

Paula, who needed her bedroom to be ice-cold, dark and totally quiet, wondered how anyone could sleep with music pounding in their ears.

'So that's what you did then? All Sunday night and Monday morning?' asked Martin, refusing to give up.

Jessie yawned.

'It's what I always do.'

'And you have no idea what time your mother came home? Or whether she came home at all? Was she here when you got up?'

'No, she usually leaves early for the studio,' said Jessie, pulling her T-shirt even further over her knees.

That T-shirt was never going to regain its original shape. Paula tried to read what it said on the front, but the letters were shaped like some sort of strange flashes, so it was impossible. She probably wouldn't know the band anyway. She'd had a brief period as a Scorpions fan when she was a teen, but she didn't know much about hard rock music.

'Don't tell me you think my mother drove out to that farm and killed some kid. Are you serious?'

Jessie was picking at the cuticles on her left hand. Paula cringed when she saw how badly bitten the girl's fingernails were. In some places she had even chewed the skin at the side of the nail, leaving a wound.

'Have you any idea what it's been like for their families? For us? How much shit we've had to take because our mothers were convicted of a crime they didn't commit? And now you come here and ask questions about another murder that has nothing to do with them!'

Paula silently studied Jessie, stopping herself from pointing out that her mother had built her whole career on talking about that childhood trauma.

Martin looked at Jessie.

'*Our*?' he said. 'Are you talking about Helen's son? Do you know each other?'

'Yes, we know each other,' said Jessie, tossing her hair. 'He's my boyfriend.'

A sound from upstairs startled all of them.

'Is he here?' asked Paula, looking towards the steep stairs leading to the first floor.

'Yes, he is,' said Jessie, as crimson patches appeared on her throat.

'Could you ask him to come downstairs?' said Martin in a friendly tone of voice. 'One of our colleagues was supposed to talk to Helen and her family, but if he's here . . .'

'Okay,' said Jessie. She called upstairs: 'Sam? The police are here. They want to talk to you!'

'How long have you been together?' asked Paula, noticing how proud the girl looked at the question.

She guessed there hadn't been many boyfriends in her life.

'Not that long,' replied Jessie, squirming a bit, though Paula noticed she wasn't averse to talking about it.

She recalled the joy she'd felt the first time she'd been with someone. As a couple. Although for her, it hadn't been a Sam but a Josefin. And they definitely hadn't dared make their relationship known. She didn't come out until she was twenty-five, and then she wondered why it had taken her so long. The sky hadn't fallen, the earth hadn't collapsed, lightning hadn't struck the ground. Her life had not been destroyed. On the contrary. At long last she had felt free.

'Hello.'

A lanky teenager sauntered down the stairs. He was bare-chested, wearing only a pair of shorts. He pointed at Jessie.

'You've got my T-shirt.'

Paula studied him with interest. Most people in town knew his father – there weren't many UN soldiers in the vicinity – and it hadn't occurred to her that James Jensen's son would look like this. His hair was dyed raven-black. He wore kohl eyeliner and a defiant expression, which she instinctively knew must hide something else entirely. She'd seen it many times in kids she'd run into during the course of her work. There were rarely nice things or good experiences hidden behind such an expression.

'Would you mind having a chat with us?' asked Paula. 'If you want, you can ring your parents to ask their permission.'

She exchanged glances with Martin. It was actually against rules to question a minor without the parents being present. But she decided to regard this as a simple conversation rather than an official interview. They weren't planning to interrogate them; it was merely a matter of asking a few questions. It would be stupid not to take advantage of the situation, since he happened to be here anyway.

'We're investigating the murder of Nea, the little girl who lived at the farm next to yours. And for reasons that I'm sure we don't have to explain, we need to know where your mothers were during the time Nea went missing.'

'Have you talked to my mother?' he asked, sitting down next to Jessie. She smiled at him, her whole appearance changing. She seemed to radiate happiness.

'We've met your mother, yes,' said Martin, getting up and going over to the worktop. 'Is it okay if I have a glass of water?'

'Sure,' said Jessie with a shrug. She didn't take her eyes off Sam.

'So what did she say?' asked Sam, running his fingers over a knot in the wooden table.

'We'd prefer to hear what you have to say,' replied Paula, giving him a smile.

Something about the boy touched her. He was at that halfway stage between a child and an adult, and she could almost see the two sides battling each other. She wondered whether even he knew which side he wanted to be on. It couldn't have been easy, growing up with a father like James. She'd never cared much for professional soldiers and macho men, no doubt because they'd never cared for the likes of her.

'So what do you want to know?' Sam asked with a shrug, as if it were of no importance.

'Do you know what your mother was doing on Sunday night until Monday afternoon?'

'I don't really keep track of the time – or of my mother for that matter.'

He continued to rub his fingers over the knot in the wood.

Martin came back to the table with a glass of water.

'Tell us what you remember,' he said, sitting down. 'Start with Sunday evening.'

He drank half the water in one gulp.

Paula was thirsty too. A fan was whirring from the side of the room, but it did little good. The oppressive summer heat made the air in the room shimmer. Though the doors were open wide, there was no cooling breeze. The water in the harbour was mirror-smooth.

'We had an early dinner,' said Sam, looking up at the ceiling as if trying to picture Sunday evening. 'Meatballs and mashed potatoes. My mother made them from scratch. My father hates instant potatoes. Then he left on some business trip, and I went upstairs to my room. I have no idea what my mother did. I usually keep to myself in the evening. And in the morning I slept until . . . I don't know. It was late. But I assume Mother went out running. That's what she does every morning.'

Paula got up and went to get a glass of water too. Her tongue felt like it was sticking to her gums. She turned around as she ran the water from the tap.

'But you didn't see her?'

He shook his head.

'Uh-uh. I was asleep.'

'When did you see her later in the day?'

Martin drank the rest of the water and wiped his mouth on the back of his hand.

'Don't know. Maybe at lunchtime? It's the summer holidays. Who keeps track of things like that?'

'We went out in your boat later,' said Jessie. 'I think it was around two by then. On Monday.'

She still hadn't taken her eyes off Sam.

'Oh, that's right,' he said, nodding. 'We went out in my boat. Actually, the boat belongs to my parents. It's the family boat. But I'm mostly the one who uses it. My mother doesn't know how to steer it, and my father is almost never home.'

'How long has he been home this time?' asked Paula.

'A few weeks. He's going back soon. Sometime after school starts, I think.'

'Where's he going?' asked Martin.

Sam shrugged.

'Don't know.'

'Can either of you recall anything else about Monday?'

Both shook their heads.

Paula exchanged glances with Martin, and they got up.

'Thanks for the water. And for talking to us. We might have more questions later on.'

'Sure,' said Sam. He shrugged again.

The teenagers didn't bother to see them out.

BOHUSLÄN 1672

When Elin heard Märta's screams she ran faster than she had ever run before. She saw Preben's white shirt up ahead among the trees. He was quicker than she was, and the distance between them lengthened. Her heart was pounding, and she could feel her dress snagging on branches, ripping the fabric. She caught a glimpse of the lake and increased her pace even more as Märta's screams got closer.

'Märta! Märta!' she shouted, and when she came to the edge of the small lake, she dropped to her knees.

Preben was on his way out to the girl, wading through the dark water, but when the water came up to his chest, he swore loudly.

'My foot is stuck! I cannot pull it free!' He gave her a wild look as he struggled in vain to get loose. 'You will have to swim out to Märta. She cannot hold out much longer!'

Elin stared at him in despair. Märta had now fallen silent and looked as if she was about to slip below the surface, which was as black as night.

'I cannot swim!' she cried, but then she looked around for some other solution.

She knew that if she recklessly threw herself into the

lake in an attempt to save her daughter, Märta would certainly drown. And she would drown along with her.

She ran around to the other side of the lake. It was small but deep, and now she could see only the top of Märta's head sticking up above the gleaming surface. A big branch hung out over the water, and she threw herself out on to the limb and crawled forward. Yet there was still more than a metre to the girl, and she shouted for Märta to keep fighting. The little girl seemed to hear her because she flailed her arms and began splashing about. Elin's arms ached as she moved further out on the branch. She was getting close enough to Märta that she could try to grab her.

'Take my hand!' she yelled, reaching out as far as she could without losing her grip on the branch.

Preben also shouted loudly.

'Märta! Take Elin's hand!'

The girl struggled desperately to grab her mother's hand, but she had a hard time catching hold and she kept swallowing water.

'Märta! Oh, please, dear God, take my hand!'

And as if by a miracle, Märta grabbed hold. Elin held on with all her might and slowly began backing up along the tree branch. She was weighed down by the girl, but somehow she mustered the strength she needed. Preben had finally managed to pull his foot loose and swam towards them. As they got close to the shore, Preben reached Märta and took her in his arms so Elin could let go. Her muscles ached, but she felt such enormous relief that tears streamed down her cheeks unhindered. As soon as she felt solid ground under her feet, she threw her arms around Märta and at the same time embraced Preben, who was now crouching down as he held the girl in his arms.

Afterwards Elin had no idea how long they'd sat there, the three of them holding on to each other. It was only when Märta began shivering that they realized they had to make their way back to find dry clothes for her, and for themselves.

Preben lifted up Märta and gently carried her through the woods. He was limping, and Elin saw that he had lost one shoe, no doubt when his foot got caught on something at the bottom of the lake.

'Thank you,' she said, her voice trembling, and Preben turned to give her a smile.

'I did nothing. You were the one who found a way to save her.'

'I did it with God's help,' said Elin quietly, feeling that what she said was true.

It was with the help of God that her daughter had been able to grasp her hand, of that she was convinced.

'Then we must offer even more prayers to the Lord this evening,' said Preben, holding the girl closer.

Märta's teeth were chattering, and her lips were blue.

'Why would Märta go out to the lake? She does not know how to swim.'

Elin tried not to sound reproachful, but she could not understand it. Märta knew she was not to go near water.

'She said Viola was in the water and about to drown,' murmured Märta.

'Who? Who said Viola was in the water?' asked Elin, frowning.

But she knew what the answer would be. She met Preben's eyes over the girl's head.

'Was it Britta who told you that?' asked Preben.

Märta nodded.

'Yes, and she went with me to show me where the lake was. Then she said she had to go back, but I must stay and save Viola.'

Elin gave Preben a furious look, and she saw that his eyes had turned as black as the lake.

'I shall speak to my wife,' he said quietly.

They were approaching the vicarage by this time. Much as she longed to storm in there and claw and strike at her sister, Elin knew she must listen to Preben. If she were to lash out at Britta she would only bring misfortune upon both herself and her daughter. So she took several deep breaths and prayed to the higher powers for enough strength to remain calm. But inside she was seething.

'What happened?'

Lill-Jan came running, followed by more farmhands and maids.

'Märta went down to the lake, but Elin pulled her out of the water,' said Preben, striding purposefully towards the vicarage.

'Take her to our quarters,' said Elin. She did not want Märta to be anywhere near Britta.

'No. Märta shall have a hot bath and dry clothes.' Preben turned to the youngest of the vicarage maids. 'Could you prepare a bath for her?'

She curtseyed and ran ahead into the house to begin heating the water.

'I will fetch dry clothes for her,' said Elin.

Reluctantly she left Preben and Märta, but not before stroking the girl's hair and kissing her ice-cold forehead.

'I will be back in no time,' she told Märta, who whimpered in protest.

'What is going on here?' asked Britta indignantly from the doorway. She had heard all the commotion in the yard.

When she caught sight of Märta in Preben's arms, she turned as white as a sheet.

'What . . . what . . .?'

Her eyes grew big with surprise. Elin was silently praying, frantically praying as she had never done before, that she would have the strength not to strike Britta dead, right there on the spot. And her prayers were heard. She managed to keep still, but for safety's sake she turned on her heel and went to fetch dry clothes for her daughter. She did not hear what Preben said to his wife, but she did see the look he gave her. And for the first time in her life, she saw her sister was afraid. But behind the fear lurked something else that terrified Elin. A hatred that burned as hot as the fires of hell.

The children were playing downstairs. Patrik was at the police station, and Erica had asked Kristina to stay for a while so she could work undisturbed. She had tried to work when she was alone with the kids, but it was impossible to concentrate when a child's voice was constantly calling her, wanting something every five minutes. One of them was always hungry or needed to pee. But Kristina had been more than willing to stay with the children, and Erica was deeply grateful for that. Whatever else she might say about her mother-in-law, Kristina was great with the kids and never hesitated to offer to babysit. Sometimes Erica wondered what sort of grandparents her own parents would have been. Since they'd died before the children were born, Erica would never know, but she thought her kids might have been able to make her mother soften a bit. Unlike Anna and herself, perhaps they could have penetrated the hard shell she'd spent all those years hiding behind.

After learning her mother's story, Erica had forgiven Elsy, and she had decided to believe she would have been a warm and playful grandmother to her children. And Erica didn't doubt for a minute that her father would have been an amazing grandfather. Just as amazing as he'd been as her pappa. Occasionally she would imagine him sitting in his favourite chair on the porch with Maja and the twins, puffing on his pipe as he told them eerie stories about ghosts out on the islands. He probably would have scared the daylights out of the kids with his tall tales, just as he had done with her and Anna. But they would have loved it too. And they would have loved the smell of his pipe and the heavy knitted jumpers he wore because Elsy had always insisted on saving on their heating bill.

Erica felt the sting of tears in her eyes, so she had to stop thinking about her parents. She looked at the big bulletin board that covered one wall of her home office. She'd gone through the stacks of papers on her desk and pinned up all the copies, printouts, photos, and notes. That was step one in the process when she was writing. After the chaos of gathering material and piling up documents so she could take it all in, this was where she set about establishing structure and order. She loved this phase of her work. This was when the fog would start to clear, and what had initially seemed an unfathomable story would start to take shape. Every time she started work on a book, it was as if she would never be able to make sense of it. But somehow she always did.

This time, however, there was more than a book at stake. This was no longer a retelling of an old tragedy; it was also the story of a new murder investigation, the death of another little girl, and more grieving friends and relatives.

Erica clasped her hands behind her head, squinting as she tried to find connections between the bits and pieces posted on the bulletin board. These days it required more of an effort to read from this distance, but she refused to acknowledge that she needed glasses.

She studied the photos of Marie and Helen. They were so different, both in appearance and personality. Helen was dark-haired and plain, with a cowed air about her. Marie was blonde, beautiful, and always composed as she looked into the camera. It was frustrating that the police hadn't been able to find the old interview transcripts. No one knew where they were, and it was possible they might have been destroyed. Erica knew from experience that the filing system at the Tanumshede police station hadn't always been the best. The fact that Annika now kept everything in pristine order unfortunately didn't help when looking for files from the time before she started as the station secretary. The interview transcripts would have been useful for understanding the girls' relationship, what actually happened on that day, and what might have prompted their confessions. Newspaper articles from the period did not give much background information that could answer the question: 'Why?' And since Leif was dead, she couldn't ask him for help either. Erica had hoped her visit to his daughter would produce results, but Viola hadn't called back. She didn't know for sure whether Leif had saved any investigative materials, but she had a feeling he had, based on the fact that he hadn't been able to let go of the Stella case. And that was something Erica kept returning to. He was the one who had heard the confessions of Marie and Helen, and he was the one who had informed the newspapers that the case had been solved. So why had he later changed his mind? Why, so many years later, was he no longer convinced the girls had killed Stella?

Erica squinted again, trying to bring the words into sharper focus. From downstairs she heard the children playing hide-and-seek with their grandmother, which was always the twins' opportunity for some creative counting: 'One, two, ten – here I COME!'

An article from *Bohusläningen* suddenly caught her attention. She got up and went over to take it down from the bulletin board. She'd read it many times before, but now she picked up a pen to underline one sentence. The article was from the days after the girls had retracted their confessions, and a reporter had managed to get Marie to answer a question.

'Someone followed us into the woods,' she was quoted as saying.

The statement had been dismissed as a lie, a child's way of trying to cast blame on someone else. But what if the girls had been followed that day? What would that mean for the current investigation?

Erica took a yellow Post-it note and wrote: 'Someone in the woods?' Then she stuck the note on top of the article and pinned both up on the bulletin board. She stood there for a moment, staring at the words, her hands on her hips. How should she proceed? How could she find out whether someone had been following Helen and Marie? And if so, who was it?

Her mobile, lying on the desk, pinged. She turned around to look at the display. She saw an unfamiliar phone number but no name. Yet the message made it clear who had sent the text.

I understand you've talked to my mother. Shall we meet?

Erica smiled and put down the phone after sending a brief reply in the affirmative. Maybe now she'd be able to get answers to at least some of her questions.

Patrik finished writing his report about his conversation with Helen and James and pressed the 'print' button. They were both home when he went out to their farm, and they'd been willing to answer all his questions. James had confirmed Helen's statement that no one in the family had heard anything of the search conducted in the woods on Monday night and early Tuesday morning. He had been away on a business trip, arriving at his hotel in Gothenburg on Sunday evening. He'd been in meetings until four o'clock on Monday afternoon. Afterwards he got in his car and drove home. Helen said she went to bed around ten on Sunday night. She took a sleeping tablet and slept the whole night through until nine the next morning. Then she got up and went for her usual run.

Patrik wondered whether anyone could confirm Helen's statement.

He was pulled away from these speculations by the shrill ring of his phone. He distractedly took the call, trying to keep the contents of his pen holder, which he had accidentally bumped, from spilling across his desk. When he heard who was on the phone, he picked up a pen and reached for a pad of paper.

'So you managed to move us ahead in the queue,' he said with relief, prompting a muttered reply from Pedersen.

'Well, it wasn't easy. You owe me one. But when it comes to a case involving a child . . .' Pedersen sighed, and Patrik could tell the pathologist had been as affected by Nea's death as he was. 'I'll get right to the point. I don't have a final report, but we've been able to establish that cause of death was a head wound.'

'Okay,' said Patrik, making a note of it.

He knew that Pedersen would send over a detailed report after they finished talking, but taking notes helped him keep his thoughts in order.

'Any evidence of what might have caused it?'

'No, except there was dirt in the wound. Apart from that, her body was clean.'

'Dirt?' Patrik made another note, frowning.

'Yes. I've sent samples to the forensics lab. With a little luck, we'll get a reply in a couple of days.'

'What about the object that caused the wound? There must have been dirt on that too, right?'

'Yes . . .' Pedersen said hesitantly.

Patrik knew the pathologist did that whenever he was unsure about something and didn't want to commit himself.

'I'm not sure,' he said, again pausing. 'But judging by the wound, it was either something very heavy, or . . .'

'Or what?' asked Patrik.

Pedersen's lengthy pauses were making his blood pressure rise.

'Or, it might have been caused by a fall.'

'A fall?'

Patrik pictured the glade where Nea had been found. There was no place to fall from, unless the girl had fallen out of a tree. But if that had been the case, who had hidden her body under the tree trunk?

'I think the girl might have been moved,' said Pedersen. 'There are signs that she lay for a long time on her back, but when you found her body, she was in a foetal position. She was moved and placed in that position, but only after she'd been lying on her back for a number of hours. It's difficult to say exactly how long.'

'Have you found any similarities with the Stella case?' asked Patrik.

He got ready to write more notes.

'I've looked at the old post-mortem report,' said Pedersen. 'But I found no similarities, other than the fact that both girls died from injuries to the head. In Stella's case, there were traces of wood and stone in the wounds. It was also clear that she died in the glade close to the pond where she was found. Did Torbjörn find any evidence of where this little girl was killed? She could have been killed somewhere close to the tree and then hidden in the place you found her.'

'That would point to the wound being caused by a blow to the head and not a fall, assuming it would have been a fall from sufficient height to have killed her. There was nowhere she could have fallen from in that glade – the ground is almost perfectly level. I'll ring Torbjörn and check with him. But when I was there, I saw nothing to indicate Nea was killed where her body was found.'

Patrik again pictured the glade in his mind. He hadn't seen any bloodstains, but Torbjörn and his tech team had gone over the area with a fine-tooth comb. If there was anything to be found, he was confident they would find it.

'Do you have anything else to report?' asked Patrik.

'No. The girl was a healthy four-year-old. She was well nourished, and there were no injuries except for the wound to her head. The contents of her stomach were a mixture of chocolate and biscuits. My guess is, her last meal was a Kex chocolate wafer bar.'

'Okay, thanks,' said Patrik.

He ended the call and put down his pen. After a moment he rang Torbjörn Ruud. It took so long for someone to answer that he was about to give up, but then he heard Torbjörn's brusque voice say, 'Hello?'

'Hi. It's Patrik Hedström. I was wondering how you're doing with the Nea Berg evidence.'

'We're not finished yet,' Torbjörn replied curtly.

He always sounded cross, but Patrik was used to his tone of voice. Torbjörn was among the best in his field in Sweden. Both the Stockholm and Gothenburg police districts had offered him a job, but he had strong ties to his hometown of Uddevalla, and he saw no reason to move.

'When do you think you'll be finished?' asked Patrik, picking up his pen.

'Impossible to say,' muttered Torbjörn. 'We want to make sure we do everything by the book with this investigation. Not that we don't do that with every investigation, but, well . . . you know how it is. That little girl didn't get to have a very long life. It's . . .'

He cleared his throat and swallowed hard. Patrik fully understood, but the best thing he could do for the girl was to keep a clear head and remain as professional as possible. And find out who was guilty.

'Is there anything you can tell me right now? Pedersen did the post-mortem, and he says she died from a wound to the head. Is there anything to indicate something found at the site could have been used to deliver the blow? Or any signs that she was killed near the spot where her body was found?'

'No . . .' said Torbjörn reluctantly.

Patrik knew he didn't like to give out information until his team had completed their work. But he also under-stood Patrik's need to have any information that might help move the investigation forward.

'We found nothing to indicate she was killed in the glade. There were no traces of blood, nor did we find blood on any objects we recovered from the area.'

'How big an area did you search?'

'We examined a large area surrounding the glade. I can't tell you exactly. That will be in my final report, but we were very thorough. And, as I said, no sign of blood. Head wounds bleed profusely, so one would expect to find a great deal of blood.'

'Yes. It definitely sounds like the glade is a secondary crime scene,' said Patrik, jotting down a few notes. 'So our primary scene has yet to be found.'

'What about the girl's home? Should we look for blood traces there?'

Patrik paused before answering:

'Gösta is the one who interviewed the family. He thinks there's no reason to suspect them, which means so far we haven't followed up on that theory.'

'Hmm . . . I don't know,' said Torbjörn. 'We've seen what can happen in families. Sometimes it's an accident. Sometimes it's not.'

'You're right,' said Patrik with a grimace.

He had an uneasy feeling that they'd made a mistake. A naive and stupid mistake. He couldn't afford to be either sentimental or naive. They'd seen far too much over the years. They should have known better.

'Patrik?'

A discreet knock on his office door made him look up. He'd finished the phone call with Torbjörn and was sitting at his desk, staring into space as he pondered his next move.

'Yes?'

Annika stood in the doorway. She looked uncomfortable.

'There's something you ought to know. We're starting to get phone calls . . . of a very unpleasant type.'

'Unpleasant, how?'

Annika took a few steps into the room to stand in front of his desk with her arms crossed.

'People are accusing us of not doing our job. We've even received a few threats.'

'But why? I don't understand.'

Annika took a deep breath. 'They're saying we should be investigating the people at the refugee centre.'

'Why? There's no evidence pointing in that direction.'

Patrik was genuinely mystified. Why were people phoning about the refugee centre?

She held up her notepad and read from her notes.

'Well, according to one gentleman who prefers to remain anonymous, "some damn wog at the refugee centre" was responsible for Nea's murder. And according to one woman, who also wants to remain anonymous, it's "scandalous that none of those criminal types have

310

been brought in for interrogation". She went on to say, "None of them have fled from any war, that's just an excuse to come here and sponge off the Swedish people." I've had at least a dozen calls along the same lines. Everyone wants to remain anonymous.'

'Good lord,' said Patrik, sighing heavily.

This was the last thing they needed.

'Well, now you know,' said Annika, heading for the door. 'How would you like me to deal with them?'

'Same way you always do,' replied Patrik. 'Be polite and vague.'

'Okay,' she said, leaving the office.

He called her back.

'Annika?'

'Yes?'

'Could you ask Gösta to come and see me? And ring the district prosecutor in Uddevalla. We need a warrant to search a home.'

'I'll do it right now,' she said.

She was used to not asking any questions. In due course she'd find out what it was all about.

Patrik leaned back in his chair with a sigh. Gösta was not going to be happy, but this was necessary. And it should have already been done.

Warmth filled his heart when Martin looked at Tuva in the rear-view mirror. Pia's parents had been taking care of her, and he'd driven over to pick her up. She was going to stay with her grandparents for another night, but he'd felt such an overwhelming yearning to see her that he'd asked Patrik for an hour off. He needed to see his daughter in order to continue working on this case. He knew that his longing for Tuva was no doubt tied to his longing for Pia, and with time he'd be able to relinquish his hold on his daughter and give her more freedom.

But right now he always wanted to have her near. Pia's parents and Annika were the only ones he could imagine leaving Tuva with, and even then only if his job required it. His own parents were not particularly interested in young children. They were happy to come over for coffee to see him and Tuva once in a while, but they never offered to babysit, and he had never asked them.

'Pappa, I want to go to the playground,' said Tuva from the back seat. He met her eyes in the rear-view mirror.

'Sure, sweetie,' he said, giving her an air kiss.

Truth be told, he'd been hoping she would say that. He hadn't been able to stop thinking about the woman at the playground, and even though he knew the odds of her being there were slim, he had no other way of contacting her. He promised himself that if he was lucky enough to see her again, he'd be sure to get her name this time.

He parked next to the playground and unbuckled Tuva from her car seat. By now he could strap her into the seat in his sleep, but in the beginning, when Tuva was very small, he'd struggled with the task. He had panted and cursed as Pia stood nearby, laughing at him. So many things had seemed difficult back then, things he now took for granted. And so many things had seemed so easy but were now very hard. Martin stole a hug as he lifted Tuva out of the seat. The times when she wanted to snuggle with him were fewer and further between. There was too much for her to discover in the world, too few hours to play. Now it was only when she hurt herself or she was tired that she would crawl on to his lap for a hug. He accepted and understood this change, but occasionally he wished he could stop time.

'Pappa, the baby you kicked is here!'

'Thanks for reminding me, sweetie,' he said, patting Tuva on the head.

'You're welcome, Pappa,' she said politely. Then she

ran over to the baby boy, who was about to stuff a fistful of sand in his mouth.

'No, no. Don't eat sand,' she told him, gently taking his hand and brushing the sand away.

'What a good babysitter I have,' said the woman, giving Martin a smile.

The sight of her dimples made him blush.

'I promise not to kick your child this time.'

'I'd appreciate it,' she said, giving him another smile that made his ears turn bright red.

'Martin Molin,' he said, reaching out to shake her hand.

'Mette Lauritsen.'

Her hand was warm and dry.

'Are you Norwegian?' he asked, unable to place her accent.

'Yes, originally, although I've lived in Sweden for the past fifteen years. I'm from Halden, but I married a guy from Tanumshede. The one you heard me arguing with on the phone the other day.'

She gave him an apologetic look.

'Did you get everything worked out?' he asked, keeping an eye on Tuva as he did so. She was chatting happily to the toddler.

'No, I can't say I did. He's still too preoccupied with his new girlfriend to have any time for Little Man.'

'So his name is Little Man?' Martin joked, even though he already knew her son's name.

'No, of course not,' said Mette, laughing. She gave her son a loving look. 'His name is Jon, after his father, but I call him Little Man. My hope is I'll stop doing that well before he's a teenager.'

'That's probably wise,' said Martin, feigning seriousness. His heart began turning somersaults when he noticed how her eyes were shining.

'What sort of work do you do?' she asked him.

For a moment he thought she sounded quite flirty, but he couldn't decide whether that was merely wishful thinking on his part.

'I'm a police officer,' he said, hearing the pride in his voice.

And he *was* proud of his profession. He was making a difference. He'd wanted to join the police force ever since he was a kid, and he'd never had any doubts about that choice. The job had been his salvation when Pia died, and his colleagues at the station were more than his co-workers. They were his family. Even Mellberg. Every family needed one dysfunctional member, and Bertil Mellberg filled the role to a T.

'A policeman? Cool,' she said.

'What about you?'

'I'm a financial assistant at an office in Grebbestad.'

'Do you live here?' asked Martin.

'Yes. Jon's father lives here. But if he's not planning to be involved, then I'm not sure . . .'

She cast a long look at her son, whom Tuva was hugging.

'She hasn't learned yet about not being so forward,' said Martin with a laugh.

'Some of us never learn that,' she replied with a big smile.

Then she hesitated.

'So . . . If this isn't too presumptuous . . . How about having dinner one evening?'

She looked as if she instantly regretted her words, but Martin felt his heart turning somersaults again.

'That'd be great!' he said a little too emphatically. 'On one condition.'

'What's that?' asked Mette dubiously.

'That it's my treat.'

Her dimples reappeared, and Martin felt something inside him beginning to thaw.

'Where are Martin and Paula? Aren't they back yet?' asked Gösta as he sat down on the chair in front of Patrik's desk.

He thought they were all supposed to meet when Annika asked him to go to Patrik's office, but so far it was only the two of them.

'I sent them home for a while. Martin had to pick up Tuva, and Paula needed to say hi to her kids, but they'll be back later.'

Gösta nodded. He waited for Patrik to say why he wanted to see him.

'I've talked to both Pedersen and Torbjörn again,' said Patrik.

Gösta sat up straighter. It had felt as if they were merely treading water since the girl was found, so it would be invaluable to get even the smallest bit of information to help the investigation.

'What did they say?'

'The post-mortem is finished, and I received a preliminary report. Torbjörn and his team aren't quite done yet, but I persuaded him to give me an initial report.'

'And?' said Gösta, feeling his heart beating faster. He badly wanted to give Nea's parents some answers, some form of closure.

'The girl was most likely not killed in the glade in the woods. That's probably a secondary crime scene, and we need to find the primary site ASAP.'

Gösta swallowed. He had assumed Nea was killed in the glade. It changed everything to hear that she was killed somewhere else and then taken there, even if right now they couldn't say exactly what had happened.

'So where do we start looking?' he asked.

As soon as he asked the question, he knew what the answer would be.

'Oh,' he said quietly.

Patrik nodded.

'Yes, that's the logical place to begin.'

Patrik watched him anxiously. He knew how much empathy Gösta felt for the girl's family. Even though they were strangers, from the very start he had shared their grief and felt connected.

'No matter how much I'd like to object, I know it has to be done,' he said now, feeling his heart sink.

He looked at Patrik.

'When?'

'I'm waiting to hear about the search warrant from the district prosecutor in Uddevalla. But there shouldn't be any problem. I'd like to get started early tomorrow morning.'

'All right,' said Gösta. 'Did they tell you anything else?'

'She died from a wound to the back of her head. It might have been caused by a fall, or a blow to the head. If that's the case, it's unclear what sort of weapon was used. Dirt was the only thing found in the wound.'

'They should be able to do a more detailed analysis of the dirt,' said Gösta.

'Yes,' agreed Patrik. 'They've turned in everything for further analysis. But it will take a while to get the results.'

For a moment neither of them spoke. Outside, the sun had started to set, and the bright yellow rays had been replaced by subtle shades of red and orange. The temperature inside the station was almost comfortable now.

'Is there anything else we can do tonight?' asked Gösta, picking at an invisible thread on his uniform shirt.

'No. Go home and rest. I'll keep you posted about tomorrow. Martin and Paula are coming in tonight to write up their report about the interviews they did today. And I heard from Annika that you've written down the conversation you had with Nea's parents.'

'Yes, that's right. I'm also helping Annika go through all the reports we've received about sexual assaults and the like. But I can take some of the files home with me.'

He stood up and pushed the chair into place in front of Patrik's desk.

'Do that,' said Patrik. After a moment he added, 'Did you hear about the phone calls we've been getting? About the refugee centre?'

'Yes,' said Gösta. He thought about what Peter's parents had said, and decided not to mention it to Patrik. 'It's fear,' he sighed. 'Fear of the unknown. People have always blamed outsiders for any misfortune. It's easier to do that than face up to the fact a crime might have been committed by someone they know.'

'Do you think it's going to become a problem?' asked Patrik.

Gösta took his time before answering. He thought about all the headlines in the evening newspapers over the past few years, the growing support for the far-right political party Sveriges Vänner, in spite of all the scandals. He wanted to say no, but instead he heard himself confirming what Patrik already knew.

'Yes, it's going to become a problem,' he said.

Patrik merely nodded. He could think of nothing else to say.

Gösta left the room and went to his own office to get the papers he wanted to take home with him. For a moment he sat at his desk and stared out the window. Outside it looked as if the sky was on fire.

Vendela cautiously opened the window as she listened to the sound of the TV downstairs. Even though her room

317

was on the first floor, it had been a long time since she'd tried to climb down. The roof of the porch was right below her, and she could crawl out on to it and then clamber down the big tree next to the house. As an extra precaution, she had locked her bedroom door and turned up the volume of the music full blast. If her mother knocked, she would simply assume that Vendela couldn't hear her.

As she climbed down the tree, she peeked in the living room window. She saw the back of her mother's head as she sat alone in the middle of the sofa, watching some dreary detective show, as usual, with a glass of wine in her hand. It was still so light outside that her mother would see her if she turned around, but Vendela quickly reached the ground and then dashed across the front of the house. Her mother tended not to notice anything when she was drinking. In the past she used to drink wine one evening a week, mostly while holding a photo of Stella in her hand. She always complained of a head-ache the next day, as if she didn't know what the cause could be. Since Marie Wall had returned to Fjällbacka, her mother had started drinking every night.

Marie and Helen. The women who had killed her mother's sister and turned her mother into a boxed-wine alcoholic.

Around the corner, she found Nils and Basse waiting for her. Vendela pushed aside all thoughts of Marie and Helen and their children Sam and Jessie.

Nils gave her a hug, pressing his body close to hers.

He and Basse had cycled over, and Vendela hopped on to the back of Nils's bike. They headed towards Fjällbacka, passing the Tetra Pak factory and the big open car park with the small fire station. They raced past Pizzeria Bååhaket and the square with the patch of lawn. When they'd made their way up the slope of Galärbacken, they stopped, and Vendela wrapped her arms tighter around Nils's waist, aware of his smooth, hard stomach.

Then they started down. The hill was steep, and Nils didn't brake. The wind made it impossible to hear anything as it blew her hair back, making it flutter behind her. Her muscles clenched when they hit small holes in the asphalt, and she had to fight back her fear.

They passed Ingrid Bergman Square, and Vendela breathed a sigh of relief when the ground levelled out. There were a lot of people at the square, and some teenagers, all dressed up, had to jump out of the way as they zoomed past. She turned to see them raising their fists in anger, but she merely laughed. Stupid tourists. They came here for a few weeks every year and thought they owned Fjällbacka. They would never dream of coming here in November. No, they just sailed in with their rich families, on holiday from their fancy homes and schools, always trying to push ahead in the queue and talking loudly about the 'yokels'.

'Did you bring your swimsuit?' asked Nils over his shoulder.

They were slowly cycling out to the small pier facing Badholmen, so now she was able to hear what he said.

'No. Shit. I forgot. But I can still go swimming.'

She stroked his thigh, and he laughed. Vendela had quickly learned how to please him. The wilder she behaved, the more excited he got.

'Somebody's already here,' said Basse, pointing at the old diving tower.

'Damn. It's only some shitty kids from the class below us. They'll take off when we get there. Believe me.'

Vendela could sense Nils smiling in the dusk. There was something about that smile of his that always gave her butterflies in her stomach. They laid their bicycles on the gravel right next to the old bathhouse and walked over to the diving tower where three boys were splashing and shouting in the water. They fell silent when they saw who was coming and began treading water.

'Get lost. We want to swim,' said Nils calmly, and the three boys swam over to the ladder without a word.

Moving as fast as they could, they climbed the ladder and made their way over the rocks to one of the changing rooms. This was an old spa bath, so people changed under open skies, with only a few wooden walls offering privacy. But Nils and Basse didn't bother with that. They simply threw off their clothes.

Nils and Basse began climbing the diving tower, while Vendela took her time undressing. The diving tower was not her thing. It probably wasn't Basse's either, but he always did whatever Nils did.

Vendela went over to the ladder and climbed down a way, then launched herself backwards, allowing the water to flow over her body. Underwater, she couldn't hear a thing, but that simply made it easier to enjoy a few marvellous moments when she was cut off from everything else. From the image of her mother holding a glass of wine in one hand and a picture of Stella in the other. Eventually she was forced to resurface. She floated on her back, peering up at the diving tower.

Basse was dithering, as usual, while Nils stood next to him, grinning. The tower wasn't particularly high, but it was tall enough to make your stomach clench when you stood at the top. Basse moved closer to the edge but still hesitated. Then Nils gave him a shove in the back.

Basse screamed the whole way down.

Nils followed with an elegant cannonball. When he came up to the surface, he bellowed at the sky.

'What the fuck! That was great!'

He grabbed Basse's head and pushed him under, but let him come back up after a few seconds. Then he swam over to Vendela with elegant, strong strokes. He pulled her close in the water, pressing his groin against her as he trod water. His hand slipped inside her knickers, and he pushed a finger inside her. Vendela closed her eyes. She thought about that fucking Marie's fucking daughter Jessie, who probably did the exact same thing with Sam. She responded by kissing Nils.

Suddenly Nils pushed away.

'Shit!' he swore. 'A bloody jellyfish!'

He swam over to the ladder and climbed up. His right thigh had bright red streaks.

When Vendela got out of the water, she realized she'd forgotten to bring a towel. The air, previously so warm, was now icy cold.

'Here,' said Basse, handing her his T-shirt to dry off.

He had climbed out too. His pale face was almost luminescent.

'Thanks,' she said, drying off the salt water.

Nils had already put on his clothes. He kept clutching his thigh, but the pain seemed to egg him on. When he turned to face them, she saw the glint in his eye that always appeared right before he caused havoc in someone's life.

'What do you say? Should we do it?'

Vendela glanced at Basse. She knew he wouldn't dare say no.

She felt a jittery sensation in her chest.

'What are we waiting for?' she said, and headed towards the bicycles.

BOHUSLÄN 1672

A strange mood settled over the farm during the following week. Hatred and anger boiled inside Elin, but good sense won out. If she accused Britta of something when she had only a child's word to offer in evidence, they would both be sent away. And then where would they go?

At night she lay awake, holding Märta close when nightmares tormented her young body. Now and then the child would toss and turn as she muttered about the things haunting her. And there was no trace of Viola. Märta's joy had disappeared along with her cat. She no longer ran about the farm, nor did she protest in a childish way over her allotted chores. Elin's heart ached when she looked into her daughter's eyes, which were now as dark as the water in the lake, but there was nothing she could do about it. Her grandmother's teachings offered no remedies for a broken heart or fear, and not even her own maternal love could cure what ailed Märta.

She wondered what Preben had said to Britta. After carrying Märta inside the house, he'd allowed the child to stay for two nights in his own bed while he slept in the room meant for guests. And Britta had not once dared look Elin in the eye. They simply went about their usual routines. Nothing changed in terms of practical matters, and their conversation was confined to discussing the tasks Britta wished her to do, as it had been ever since Elin and Märta came to the vicarage. But Britta carefully avoided looking at Elin. Only once, when Elin turned around after shaking out Britta's feather bed, did she catch her sister staring at her. And the hatred in Britta's eyes nearly knocked her over. She realized her sister had now become an even bigger enemy. But it was better if Britta directed her loathing at her instead of at Märta. She had Preben to thank for that. Whatever he had said to his wife, it had worked. Britta would not dare go after Märta again. But he could not mend the anguish the girl's soul had suffered. A child's trust was one of God's most fragile gifts, and it was this gift that Britta had stolen.

'Elin?'

Preben's voice from the kitchen doorway nearly made her drop the vessel she was washing.

'Yes?' she said, turning around as she dried her hands on her apron.

They had not spoken all week, and she suddenly pictured how he had looked when he ran ahead of her through the woods: his white shirt visible among the trees, his desperate expression when Märta's face slowly slipped beneath the dark surface of the water, and the tenderness in his eyes as he carried the little girl home. Elin suddenly found it hard to breathe. Her hands were shaking so much she hid them under her apron.

'Come with me, please,' he said eagerly. 'Is Märta in the servant quarters?'

Elin frowned, wondering what he might want. A lock of blond hair had fallen over his forehead, and she had to clasp her hands so as not to step forward to brush the hair out of his eyes.

She nodded.

'Yes, she is,' she replied. 'At least, she was when I last saw her. She does not go out as she used to.'

She immediately regretted her words, which were a much too blunt reminder of what had happened. A reminder of the dark water and Britta's malicious actions. His wife's malicious actions.

'Well, come along. What are you waiting for?'

Reluctantly Elin followed him out of the house.

'Lill-Jan? Where are you?' he called when they entered the farmyard. His face lit up when he saw the farmhand coming towards him, carrying something in his arms.

'What is it?' Elin asked.

She looked around uneasily. The last thing she wanted was for Britta to see her out here in the middle of the yard talking to her husband. But it was impossible to ignore Preben's joy as he carefully took something from Lill-Jan.

'I understand that Märta is missing Viola. So when Pärla had puppies last night, I thought Märta might like to have one of them.'

'That is much too dear a gift,' said Elin sternly, hastily turning away to hide her tears.

'Not at all,' said Preben, holding out a white puppy with brown spots.

The tiny creature was so adorable, Elin could not resist reaching out her hand to gently scratch behind the dog's long, soft ears.

'I need help raising this little rascal to become a good herding dog, and I thought Märta might lend a hand. Pärla will not be able to protect the sheep for many more years, so we will need another dog to take over. I believe this pup will make a good shepherd's dog. What do you think, Elin?'

Again he held out the puppy, and she knew she could not object. The dog's brown eyes looked at her with such trust as it stuck out a paw towards her.

'Yes, as long as Märta learns what is needed to raise

the dog, I suppose it will be fine,' she said, trying to maintain her stern tone though her heart was melting.

'Then I humbly thank Märta's mother for permission,' said Preben with a teasing smile. He started towards the servants' quarters.

After a few metres he turned and gave her an encouraging nod.

'Come. I thought you would like to see the child receive the puppy.'

He briskly set off again, and Elin hurried after him. This was not something she wanted to miss.

They found Märta lying in bed. Her eyes were open as she stared up at the ceiling. Not until Preben knelt down next to the bed did she turn to look at him.

'May I ask a favour of you, Märta?' said Preben gently.

The girl nodded, her expression solemn.

'I need your help taking care of this little creature. She is weaker than the other puppies, and her mother refuses to accept her. If she does not find another mother, she will starve to death. And I thought to myself, who would be better able to help her than Mistress Märta. If you have the time and inclination, of course. It will be a hard job, I cannot lie. She will need food at all hours of the day and night, and all sorts of care. And she needs a name, too. The poor thing does not even have a name.'

'I can do it!' said Märta, immediately sitting up with her eyes fixed on the puppy, who was struggling to get out of the cloth wrapped around her.

Preben loosened the cloth and placed the dog on the bed next to Märta, who instantly burrowed her face in the animal's soft fur. The puppy began licking her face, its tail wagging from side to side.

Elin felt herself smiling, and she had not done that in a long time. And when she felt Preben's hand clasp hers, she did not pull away.

❖

The pillow felt lumpy under her head, but Eva didn't feel like changing position. Another sleepless night. She couldn't remember when she'd last slept. A fog had settled over her life. Her meaningless life. What was the point of getting out of bed? Or talking to each other? Or breathing? Peter couldn't give her any answers. His eyes were as empty as hers, his touch just as cold. During those first hours they had tried to comfort one another, but Peter was now a stranger. They moved about in the same house without touching, each wrapped in their own grief.

Peter's parents were doing what they could, making sure she and Peter ate something and went to bed when they should. The few times she'd looked out the window, Eva was surprised to see the flowers still looking so lovely. The sun was shining as it had before, the carrots were flourishing in the garden, and the tomatoes were gleaming red on their stalks.

Peter sighed next to her. She'd heard him quietly crying in the night, but she couldn't bring herself to reach out and take his hand.

She heard Bengt's heavy footsteps nearing the stairs down below.

'Someone's coming,' he called.

Eva nodded to herself. With an effort she sat up and swung her legs over the edge of the bed.

'Your father says someone is coming,' she said, looking at her feet.

'Okay,' said Peter in a low voice.

The bed creaked behind her as he sat up. For a moment they sat there in silence, their backs to each other and a shattered world between them.

Slowly she got up and went downstairs. She'd slept in her clothes, the same clothes she'd worn on the day Nea disappeared. Ulla had tried many times to get her to change, but these were the clothes she'd had on the last time she thought everything was normal, the clothes she'd imagined herself wearing when she hugged Nea, played with Nea, made dinner for her.

Bengt was standing at the kitchen window.

'I can see two police cars,' he said, craning his neck. 'Maybe they've made a breakthrough.'

Eva merely nodded. She pulled out a chair and sat down. What did it matter now? Nothing in the world would give her Nea back.

Bengt went to the front door to let the police in. They spoke quietly in the hall, and she could hear Gösta's voice. Thank goodness they'd sent him.

Gösta was the first to enter the kitchen. He looked from her to Peter, who had come downstairs and was sitting at the table. She could see at once that something was troubling him.

Bengt was standing next to the cooker. Ulla stood behind Peter with her hands on his shoulders.

'Have you found out anything?' asked Bengt.

Gösta shook his head, still with the same troubled expression on his face.

'No, I'm afraid there's nothing new to tell you at the

327

moment,' he said. 'But we're going to have to search your house.'

Bengt turned red with fury and took a few steps towards Gösta.

'You must be joking. Isn't it enough that their lives have been completely destroyed?'

Ulla went over to him and put her hand on his arm. He pulled his arm away, but didn't say anything more.

'Let them do it,' said Eva.

Then she got up and went back upstairs. She could hear angry voices in the kitchen, but none of it mattered to her any more.

'Are we going to get a lot of visits from the police?'

Jörgen was leaning against a bench in the make-up area. Marie frowned as she looked at him in the mirror. Her make-up was done, and her hair had been styled. She was just doing a few touch-ups of her own.

'How would I know?' she asked, wiping off a bit of eyeliner that had gathered at the corner of her right eye.

Jörgen snorted and turned away. 'I should never have got involved with you.'

'What's this all about? Is it because you found it unpleasant when the police asked you about my alibi? Or are you thinking about your wife and kids back home?'

Jörgen's expression darkened.

'My family has nothing to do with this.'

'Precisely.'

She smiled at him in the mirror.

Jörgen stared at her without speaking, then he stormed out, leaving her alone.

Men! They were so predictable. Much as they wanted to sleep with her, they never wanted to deal with the consequences of their actions. She'd seen how her father had treated her mother. The bruises left by his blows when he didn't get what he wanted. In the first family Marie was placed with, the father of the house had shown her exactly what he thought she was good for.

Helen hadn't been placed with strangers. She'd been allowed to return home to her parents because they offered 'a stable home environment'. But Marie wasn't envious. She knew the sort of pressure Helen was subjected to at home.

She realized that people had viewed her and Helen as an odd pair, but in reality they belonged together like two puzzle pieces. Each had found in the other the thing that they were lacking, and it had given them a reason to live. They had shared their worries, making them so much easier to bear.

When they were forbidden to see each other, they hadn't let that stop them. It had turned into an exciting game, finding ways to meet in secret. It was the two of them against the world. How naive they had been. Neither of them had understood how serious the situation was. Not even on that day in the police interrogation room. She'd been surrounded by an armour she thought would protect her and keep anything from happening to them.

But then it had all fallen apart. And Marie had ended up in the foster-home circus.

A few months after she turned eighteen, Marie packed a suitcase and never looked back. At long last she was free. From her parents. From her siblings. And from the long series of foster families.

Her brothers had tried to contact her several times – when her parents died and when she got her first role in a Hollywood film. A minor role, but it was still big enough news to make the Swedish papers. According to her brothers, they were family after all, and she was no longer merely a shitty brat. Via her attorney she let them know she wanted nothing to do with them. They were as good as dead to her.

She heard Jörgen swearing loudly somewhere. Let him sulk. Thanks to her and all the articles in the papers over the past few days, the financial backers no longer had any doubts, and any questions about whether the film would get made had now been resolved. She had no reason to worry about his misgivings. She also knew that this wasn't the first time he'd been unfaithful to his wife while on location; it had happened on every movie he'd ever made. That had nothing to do with her. Keeping his trousers zipped was his problem.

Again she pictured Helen's face.

She had seen her at the Hedemyr supermarket yesterday afternoon. Marie had gone there after the day's filming ended. She turned a corner, and there was Helen, holding a grocery list in her hand. Marie quickly backed away. She didn't think Helen saw her.

The sneer on Marie's bright lips slowly faded. Helen had looked so old. That was probably the most difficult thing for her to accept. Marie didn't dare even think about the fortune she'd spent over the years on beauty treatments and plastic surgery, while Helen had simply let the years take their toll.

Marie looked at herself in the mirror. For the first time in a long while, she truly saw herself. But she didn't dare meet her gaze when it was no longer protected by the security of caring only about herself. Slowly she turned away. She no longer knew who the woman in the mirror was.

'Are you sure this is a good idea?' asked Anna, placing her hands on her belly. 'How do we keep a straight face if the dress turns out to be awful?'

'I'm mentally preparing myself for something salmon-coloured,' said Erica, driving towards Grebbestad.

'For us too?' said Anna, horrified.

'Well, probably not for you. I'm sure they'll find some kind of eight-man tent and rework it to fit you. You'd better be prepared to see the Fjällräven logo somewhere on your dress.'

'Ha, ha. That's *so* funny. I didn't know my big sister was a comedian.'

'Yup. Think how lucky you are!' said Erica, smiling.

She got out of the car and slammed the door.

'Hey, wait a minute,' she said. 'I forgot to ask you. Wasn't that you I saw yesterday when I was driving home from Marstrand?'

'What? No.'

Anna groaned. How stupid could she be? She'd thought up a good explanation, but the impulse to deny the encounter had come faster than her ability to spout the story she'd made up.

'But I'm sure it was your car. And I saw a woman behind the wheel. Did you lend the car to someone?'

Anna felt her sister giving her a searching look as they entered the main shopping street. The wedding gown boutique was a few hundred metres away. They had agreed to meet Kristina there.

'Oh, how stupid of me. Sorry. It's the pregnancy and the heat and all of this . . .' Anna managed a smile. 'I went to see a new client yesterday. I simply couldn't stand sitting at home any longer.'

It was the best explanation she could come up with, but Erica looked sceptical.

'A new client? Now? When the baby is just about to pop out? How will you find the energy?'

'Oh, it's not a big assignment. Only a little something to keep me busy while I'm waiting for the birth.'

Erica looked at her suspiciously but decided to drop the subject. Anna gave a sigh of relief.

'Here it is,' said Erica, pointing at a shop with wedding gowns on display in the window.

Through the glass they could see that Kristina had already arrived and was in full swing, discussing her wants and needs.

'Does it have to be so low-cut?' they heard her say shrilly as they went inside. 'I don't remember it looking like that the last time I saw it. I can't possibly wear that! Good lord, I'd look like the madam of a brothel! You must have redone the neckline!'

'We haven't touched it,' said the shop clerk.

The woman looked stressed, and Anna gave her a sympathetic smile. She liked Erica's mother-in-law. Anna didn't believe Kristina had a mean bone in her body, but it was true she could be somewhat . . . overwhelming at times. Especially if you weren't used to her.

'Maybe you should try it on again, Kristina,' said Erica. 'Sometimes clothes look different on than they do hanging up.'

'Why would they do that?' said Kristina impatiently as she kissed first Erica and then Anna on the cheek. 'Good heavens, you're big!'

For a second Anna wondered how best to reply, then decided not to say anything at all. When it came to Kristina, you had to choose your battles.

'I don't see why a dress should look different on a hanger,' said Kristina. 'But I'll try it on to prove I'm right. Something must have been done to the neckline.'

She turned on her heel and went into the dressing room.

'I hope you're not planning to stay in here while I change,' Kristina told the shop assistant, who had hung the dress in the room. 'I don't get undressed for anyone but my husband, thank you very much.'

She shooed the woman out and pulled the curtain closed with a magisterial gesture.

Anna was fighting so hard to hold back the laughter that her eyes filled with tears. When she glanced at Erica, she saw her sister was struggling too.

'Sorry,' Erica whispered to the shop assistant.

The woman gave a shrug and whispered back:

'I work in a shop selling wedding gowns. Believe me, I've seen worse.'

'How on earth does anyone expect me to pull up the zipper?' Kristina hissed, shoving the curtain aside.

She had put on the dress and was holding it up by clutching the front to her chest. With the patience of an angel, the assistant stepped behind her and pulled up the zipper. Then she took a few steps away and allowed the future bride to look at herself in the mirror.

For a few seconds Kristina didn't say a word. Then she murmured in surprise:

'It's . . . it's actually wonderful.'

Erica and Anna went over to stand next to her in front of the mirror.

Anna smiled.

'It's lovely,' she said. 'You look fabulous.'

Erica nodded, and Anna saw she had tears in her eyes. The three of them stood there in silence, taking in every detail. Kristina had chosen a silvery-grey, form-fitting gown. It was definitely not too low-cut; it was perfect, with a beautiful heart-shape neckline. The sleeves were short with a simple hemmed edge. The skirt was slightly shorter in the front than in the back, emphasizing Kristina's figure to perfection.

'You look smashing,' said Erica, discreetly wiping away her tears.

Kristina suddenly leaned forward to give her a hug. That was unusual. She was not a demonstrative person, except with her grandchildren, whom she showered with kisses and hugs. So this was an exceptional moment, though it didn't last long.

'So, let's see what we can find for you girls. Anna, you're going to be a challenge. My God, are you sure you're not having twins?'

Anna gave Erica a desperate look behind Kristina's back.

But her big sister merely grinned and whispered: 'The Fjällräven logo.'

James scanned the treetops. There was no wind, and the only sound was the cawing of crows and an occasional rustling in the bushes. If it had been hunting season, he would have been more alert, but right now he was sitting here mostly to get away. Deer hunting wouldn't begin for a few more weeks, but he could always find something else to shoot, just for practice. A fox or a dove. One time he'd even shot a snake out of a tree.

He had always loved the woods, for much the same reason he felt so comfortable in the military: it allowed him to leave emotions aside and focus instead on strategies and logistics. Threats came from outside rather than within, and the answers were not to be found in talk but in action. James and his men never entered the picture until all possibilities for talk had been exhausted.

The only person he'd ever felt close to was KG. His late father-in-law had been the only one who understood him. Well, actually, they had understood each other, and that was not something he had experienced since.

When Sam was young, James had tried to take him hunting, but like everything else connected with his son, it had gone all wrong. The boy was three years old and unable to sit still or keep quiet for more than a few minutes at a time. Eventually James could stand it no more; he grabbed Sam's jacket and tossed him to the ground. And the damn kid broke his right arm. He shouldn't have suffered any harm at all, since kids were so malleable and agile. But typically, Sam landed on a stone jutting out of the ground. James told the doctor and Helen that Sam had fallen off the neighbour's horse. And Sam knew better than to contradict him. He merely nodded and said, 'Stupid horse.'

If he could choose, James would spend all his days out in the field. The older he got, the less reason he saw to go home. The military was his home. This did not mean he looked upon his men as family; anyone who thought soldiers regarded their comrades as brothers couldn't be more wrong. The troops serving under him were pawns, a means to an end. And that was what he longed to return to. Logic. Pure, simple lines. Easy answers. He was never involved in the process that required difficult questions. That was politics. That was power. And money. Nothing ever had to do with humanity, aid, or even peace. Everything had to do with who had power over whom, and to whom the flood of money would be steered through political manoeuvring. That was the extent of it. People were so naive, always wanting to ascribe nobler motives to their leaders.

James adjusted his knapsack and headed further up the path. The naivety of people had played right into their hands. No one suspected the truth about Helen, or what she was actually capable of.

Torbjörn turned away from the big barn belonging to the Berg family.

'What does the search warrant cover?' he asked.

'All the buildings on the property, including the barn and the garden shed,' said Patrik.

Torbjörn nodded and issued instructions to his team,

which today consisted of two women and one man. They were the same technicians who had searched the glade where Nea was found, but Patrik was better at remembering faces than names. He couldn't for the life of him recall what their names were. Everyone on-site, whether forensics or police officers, was wearing plastic coverings on their shoes, and their expressions were grim. The role of Patrik and his colleagues was mostly to observe, as well as keep other people away. The fewer people trudging through the area, the better. With that in mind, Patrik thanked heaven that Mellberg had decided to stay at the station this time. Though it wasn't like him to forgo an opportunity to be in the centre of the action, the heat combined with his girth and lack of fitness had apparently persuaded Bertil to opt for the comfort of his office where the fans whirred nonstop and he could doze in peace.

Patrik pulled Gösta aside as they stood in front of the farmhouse. He had allowed the older man to speak to the family while he remained outside, listening to the agitated voices within.

'How's the family doing?'

'They've calmed down now,' said Gösta. 'I explained that it's standard procedure in cases like this. That we need to rule out all possibilities.'

'And they accepted that?'

'They realize they have no choice. But it doesn't make me feel any better.'

'I know,' said Patrik, patting his arm. 'We'll do what we have to as fast and efficiently as we can. Then we can leave them in peace.'

Gösta took a deep breath as he watched Torbjörn and his team begin carrying equipment into the house.

'I found something last night,' he said, 'while I was going through those reports about crimes of a sexual nature.'

Patrik raised his eyebrows.

'Tore Carlson, a sex offender who lives in Uddevalla, was visiting Tanumshede in early May.' Gösta went on: 'According to the report, he tried to molest a five-year-old girl in the shopping centre toilets.'

Patrik shuddered. 'Where is he now?'

'I talked to our colleagues in Uddevalla. They're going to check up on him,' replied Gösta.

Patrik nodded and then looked at the house again.

The techs had decided that rather than split up the team, they would work together, moving from room to room. Patrik felt restless as he stood in the blazing sun. He heard Torbjörn instructing the family to leave the house. Peter came out first, followed by his parents and Eva. From the way she blinked at the light, Patrik surmised she hadn't been outside since Nea was found.

Peter slowly walked over to Patrik, who was now standing in the shade of an apple tree.

'Will this never end?' he said quietly, sitting down on the grass.

Patrik sat down next to him. He saw Peter's parents angrily talking to Gösta a short distance away. Eva was sitting on a patio chair with her hands clasped, staring down at the tabletop.

'We'll be done in a couple of hours,' said Patrik, but he knew that wasn't what Peter meant.

He meant the grief. And Patrik could do nothing to help him with that. He had no consoling words to offer. He and Erica had experienced a brush with grief after the horrible car accident. But that was nothing compared to the deep abyss in which Nea's parents now found themselves. It was beyond imagining.

'Who could have done something like this?' asked Peter as he mechanically pulled up blades of grass.

The lawn hadn't been watered in a few days, and patches of it were turning yellow and dry.

'We don't know, but we're doing all we can to find out,' said Patrik, hearing how meaningless and clichéd the words sounded.

He never knew what to say in these kinds of situations. Gösta was much better at dealing with family members, while he merely felt clumsy and stupid and often found himself delivering one platitude after another.

'We didn't try to have any other children,' said Peter. 'We thought it was enough with Nea. Maybe we should have had more. In reserve.' He let out a hollow laugh.

Patrik didn't reply. He felt like an intruder. The small farm was so peaceful, so beautiful, and they were swarming over it like Old Testament locusts, ripping away the last vestiges of peace. But he had learned the importance of probing beneath the surface. Things were seldom what they seemed at first glance, and the fact that someone was in mourning did not mean he or she was innocent. Sometimes he missed that naive belief in the goodness of people he'd had at the start of his career; since then he'd seen far too many examples of the darkness inside every individual, waiting for the trigger that would allow it to emerge and overpower them. It was undoubtedly inside him too. He was convinced that everyone was capable of murder; it was merely a matter of breaching their threshold.

'I can still see her,' said Peter, lying down in the grass, as if his tall body had given up.

He looked up at the sky without blinking, even though rays of the sun were seeping through the leaves and should have blinded him.

'I can see her. I can hear her. I forget that she's not coming home. And when I think about where she is now, I worry that she's cold. That she's all alone. That she is longing for us and wondering where we are and why we don't come to fetch her.'

His voice sounded drowsy, dreamlike. His words hovered over the grass, and Patrik felt his eyes sting with tears. The other man's grief weighed on his heart. As they sat there together, they were not a police officer and the next of kin of a murder victim. They were fathers, equals. Patrik wondered whether anyone ever stopped feeling like a parent. Did the feeling change if you lost your only child? Did you forget as the years passed?

He lay down next to Peter. Quietly he said: 'I don't think she's alone. I think she's with you.'

As he said those words, he realized he believed absolutely in what he was saying. When he closed his eyes, he thought he could hear a bright child's voice and a laugh rising to the sky. Then there was only the rustling of the leaves and the shrill cry of a bird. Next to him Peter's breathing slowed. Soon he was sound asleep beside Patrik, maybe sleeping for the first time since Nea disappeared.

BOHUSLÄN 1672

The spring was a blessed time, but there was a great deal of work to be done, and everyone was busy from early morning until late at night. The livestock and other animals needed tending. The fields had to be prepared for planting. And all the buildings on the farm needed to be carefully examined for signs of decay. Every vicar's family lived in fear of the wooden beams rotting and sending the roof crashing down. Whenever a vicar died, an inspection was carried out to determine how well he had cared for his farm; if the rot was deemed to be worse than expected, the widow would have to pay a fine. On the other hand, if the farm was found to be exceptionally well maintained, the widow might receive a reward. So there was good reason to examine all the living quarters and barns, as well as the vicar's residence. The cost was shared by the vicar and the congregation. And Preben was meticulous about ensuring the farm was kept in good condition, so the sound of pounding hammers echoed across the yard.

No one spoke of what had happened at the lake, and Märta seemed to be almost herself again. The puppy was named Sigrid, and she followed Märta as faithfully as Viola had done.

Preben was often away from the farm. He would rise

early in the morning and not return home until after dusk. Occasionally he would be gone for several days. Many members of the congregation asked for his advice or were in need of God's word in order to make their lives more bearable, and Preben took very seriously his role as a spiritual guide. This did not please Britta, and sometimes he would leave the house with harsh words resounding after him. But even Britta's mood lightened as the springtime sun caused everyone on the farm to seek the warmth of nature.

Britta's bleeding continued to arrive as regularly as the moon turned full each month. She had stopped taking Elin's concoctions, and this was not something Elin chose to discuss with her. The mere thought of Preben's child growing in Britta's womb filled her with loathing. She had managed to maintain the attitude demanded of her position with regard to the vicar's wife, but her hatred for Britta burned with ever hotter flames. She had no idea what had gone on between Preben and Britta after Märta nearly drowned. She had not asked, and he had not said a single word on the subject. But ever since, Britta had been very friendly towards Märta, often ensuring that the girl received extra portions from the kitchen, or even giving her sweets she had brought home from her excursions to Uddevalla. Several days a month Britta would go there to visit her aunt, and on those days it felt as if the whole vicarage breathed more easily. The servants stood taller and walked with lighter steps. Preben hummed and frequently spent the days with Märta. Elin would steal glances at them as they sat in the library with their heads together, immersed in their conversation about some book he had taken from the shelf. It warmed her heart in a most special way. She had not thought she would ever feel like that again. Not since the day when Per disappeared into the deep. That day when Per took her harsh words with him when he died.

'My God, did you run all the way here?'

Erica gave Helen an alarmed look. She got out of breath chasing the kids around the living room. The thought of running all the way from Helen's house made her sweat.

'Oh, that's nothing,' said Helen with a crooked smile. 'Just a little warm-up.'

She put on the thin hoodie she had tied around her waist and sat down at the kitchen table, gratefully accepting a glass of water.

'Would you like some coffee?' asked Erica.

'That would be great.'

'Do you get a stitch in your side if you drink anything?' asked Erica with interest as she poured coffee for Helen and then sat down across from her.

The kids had gone to a friend's house while she and Anna went to Grebbestad. When she got the text from Helen, she decided to let them stay there a while longer. She'd take over a bottle of wine for the parents or some other sort of bribe when she went to pick up the children.

'No, my body is used to running, so it doesn't affect me.'

'Personally, I'm of the belief that people should have been born with wheels. So far I've avoided exercise like the plague.'

'Running after kids is no easy job,' said Helen, sipping her coffee. 'I remember when Sam was a toddler and I had to keep chasing after him. It feels so long ago now, like a different lifetime.'

'Sam is your only child?' asked Erica, pretending not to know everything there was to know about Helen's family.

'Yes, it turned out that way,' said Helen, her expression shutting down.

Erica dropped the subject. She was grateful that Helen had agreed to talk to her, but she knew she had to be careful. Helen could decide to flee at the first question she didn't like. This wasn't a new situation for Erica. During the research for her books, she always met one or more people who seemed to teeter between a desire to talk and a wish to remain silent. Then it was a matter of proceeding cautiously, step by step, getting them to open up and preferably say more than they had planned to tell her. Helen had come to see her, but her whole body was signalling her reluctance. Clearly she was already regretting her decision to be interviewed.

'Why did you agree to talk to me?' asked Erica, hoping the question wouldn't spark Helen's flight reflex. 'I've sent you so many requests, but up until now you didn't seem interested.'

Helen sipped her coffee for a moment. Erica placed her mobile phone on the table to show she was recording their conversation. Helen merely shrugged.

'I thought, and still think, that the past should remain the past. But I'm not naive. I realize I can't stop you from writing this book, and that has never been my intention. Plus I know Marie is considering writing about what happened, and she hasn't exactly been silent over the years either. We both know, you and I, that she has built her whole career on our . . . tragedy.'

'Yes, because it was a tragedy, wasn't it?' said Erica, picking up the thread of the conversation. 'It wasn't only Stella's family members who had their lives destroyed by what happened. Both of you girls, and your families, suffered too.'

'Most people wouldn't share that view,' said Helen, and a hard glint appeared in her grey-blue eyes. 'Most people have chosen to believe the first version of what happened. When we confessed. Everything after that lost all importance.'

'Why do you think that was?' Erica discreetly checked to make sure her mobile was still recording.

'Probably because there was no other answer. No one else to blame. People want simple solutions tied up in a nice, neat package. By retracting our confessions, we shattered their illusion that they were living in a safe world where no one would harm them or their children. By continuing to believe we were the ones who did it, they could also hold on to their belief that everything was fine.'

'What about now? When a little girl from the same farm was found in the same place? Do you think it's a copycat murder? Has someone been reawakened after lying dormant so long?'

'I don't know,' said Helen, shaking her head. 'I honestly have no idea.'

'I read an interview in which Marie says she saw someone in the woods that day. What about you? Do you remember anything like that?'

'No,' said Helen quickly, looking away. 'No, I didn't see anyone.'

'Do you think she did see somebody, or do you think she made it up? To divert interest to someone else, perhaps? To reinforce her story when she retracted her confession?'

'You'll have to ask Marie,' said Helen, picking at a loose thread on her black running tights.

'But what do you think?' Erica persisted as she got up to refill their cups.

'All I know is that I didn't see anyone. Or hear anything. And we were together the whole time.'

Helen was still picking at the loose thread. She seemed very tense, so Erica changed the subject. She had more questions and didn't want to drive Helen away before she could work through her list.

'Can you describe the relationship you had with Marie?'

For the first time since she'd arrived, Helen's face lit up with a smile. It seemed to Erica that ten years vanished in an instant.

'We clicked right from the start. We came from very different families and had been raised differently. She was an extrovert, while I was shy. We shouldn't have had much in common at all. Even today I can't understand why Marie chose to be my friend. Everybody wanted to be around her, even though they teased her about her family. It was all in fun, though. Everyone wanted to be near her. She was so beautiful, so daring, so . . . wild.'

'Wild. That's not something I've heard about Marie before,' said Erica. 'Tell me what you mean.'

'What should I say? She was like a force of nature. Even back then she was already talking about becoming an actress, making films in the States, and being a Hollywood star. I mean, lots of people talk about things like that when they're kids, but how many actually succeed? Do you realize what determination a person has to have?'

'Yes, the success she's had is amazing,' said Erica, though she couldn't help wondering what the cost must have been.

In all the articles she'd read about Marie, the actress

345

had seemed a tragic figure, wrapped in a resounding loneliness and emptiness. She wondered whether Marie, as a child, could have imagined that would be the price she'd have to pay to achieve her dream.

'I loved being with Marie. She was everything I was not. She gave me security, she gave me courage. With Marie I dared to be someone I would never have dared otherwise. She brought out the best in me.'

Helen's face was radiant, and it was as if she had to force herself to hold back her emotions.

'How did the two of you react when you weren't allowed to see each other?' asked Erica, studying her face.

A thought was forming in the back of her mind, but it was still so hazy that she couldn't quite capture it.

'We were in despair, naturally,' said Helen. 'At least, I was. Marie immediately started working out how we could get around it.'

'So you kept on seeing each other?' asked Erica.

'Yes. We saw each other in school every day, but we also met secretly in our free time, as often as we could. It felt a little like a Romeo and Juliet story, two people unjustly treated by the rest of the world. But we didn't let that stop us. We were each other's world.'

'Where did you meet?'

'Mostly in the barn on the Strand family's farm. It was empty. They didn't keep any animals, so we would slip inside and go up to the hay loft. Marie would swipe cigarettes from her brothers, and we'd lie there and smoke.'

'How long did you keep up your friendship in secret? Before . . . well, before it happened.'

'I think about six months or so. I don't remember exactly. It was such a long time ago, and I've tried not to think about it all these years.'

'So how did you react when the Strand family asked you girls to babysit for Stella together?'

'Well, Stella's father asked my father, and I think he was a little taken aback and said yes without thinking about it. Appearances were important, you know, and Pappa didn't want to seem like a narrow-minded person who would judge a child to be an undesirable playmate because of her family. That wouldn't have looked good.'

Helen grimaced.

'But Marie and I were thrilled, even though we realized it didn't mean anything would change. Remember, we were only thirteen. We took one day at a time and hoped that some day we'd get to be together, without having to hide in the barn.'

'So you were looking forward to being Stella's babysitters?'

'We were,' said Helen, nodding. 'We liked Stella. And she liked us.'

She fell silent, pressing her lips tight.

'I have to go home soon,' she said, downing the rest of her coffee.

Erica felt slightly panicked. There was so much more she wanted to ask, so much more she needed to find out. She had questions about all sorts of details and events and feelings. She needed significantly more than this brief interview to bring the story to life. But she also knew that pressuring Helen would be counter-productive. If she made do for now with what she'd learned so far, that would increase her chances of getting Helen to agree to further conversations. So she forced herself to smile cheerfully.

'That's fine,' she said. 'I'm glad you could take time to talk to me. But could I ask you one more thing?'

She glanced at her mobile to make sure it was still recording.

'Okay,' said Helen reluctantly. Erica sensed that mentally she was already on her way home.

But of all the questions she wanted to ask, this was perhaps the most important.

'Why did you confess?' she asked.

Helen fell silent. She sat motionless at the kitchen table and Erica could almost see the thoughts whirring through her mind. After a moment, she took a deep breath and then exhaled, as if thirty years of accumulated tension were suddenly released.

She looked Erica in the eye and said quietly:

'So we could be together. And it was a way of telling our parents to go to hell.'

'And now trim the sail!' shouted Bill into the wind.

Karim strained to understand. Bill had a tendency to start out in English and then automatically slip into Swedish. Certain words had begun to sink in, and now Karim knew 'trim the sail' meant pulling on the line attached to the sail.

He pulled until he received a nod of approval from Bill.

Adnan shouted when the boat began to lean and reached out to cling to the side. They had each taken separate turns on a test run with Bill in a small boat, but they were now all gathered in a big white sailboat that Bill called *Samba*. At first they were wary when they saw it was completely open in the back, but Bill had assured them it wouldn't take on water. Apparently it had been used for handicapped sailors, and the idea was that it would be easier for them to be pulled into the boat from the water. That explanation alone made Karim uneasy. If it was so safe, why did they have to be pulled out of the water?

'No worry!' shouted Bill to Adnan, giving him a big smile and nodding eagerly.

Adnan responded with a sceptical look and gripped the side even harder.

'The boat is supposed to lean, then it moves better through the water,' said Bill in English, continuing to nod. 'It's supposed to do that,' he added in Swedish.

The wind drowned out some of his words, but they understood what he was trying to say. How strange. 'What if someone said the same thing about driving a car?' Karim muttered. He still wasn't convinced this whole project was a good idea. But Bill's enthusiasm was so contagious that he and the others were willing to give it a chance. And it was a welcome break from the tedium of the refugee centre. If only the sense of dread would subside a bit when they got on board the boat.

He forced himself to breathe calmly and checked for the fifth time that all the straps on his life vest were securely fastened.

'Tack!' yelled Bill, and they stared at each other in bewilderment. They didn't understand what Bill meant.

Bill began waving his arms as he shouted:

'Turn! Turn!' he cried in English.

Ibrahim, who was at the wheel, used all his strength to turn it to the right, which threw everybody towards the side of the boat. The boom swiftly swung across, and they barely managed to duck out of the way. Bill almost toppled into the water but managed at the last second to grab the side of the boat and stay on board.

'Bloody fucking hell!' he screamed, and those were all words they understood.

Swear words were the first ones they'd learned in Swedish. They'd heard 'damn roaches' as soon as they arrived at the train station.

'Sorry, sorry,' shouted Ibrahim, letting go of the wheel as if it were a cobra.

Bill threw himself towards the back of the boat as he

continued to swear. He took over the wheel from Ibrahim, and when the sailboat was once again stable, he took a deep breath. Then he smiled.

'No worries, boys! No worries! It's nothing compared to the storm when I crossed the Biscay!'

He began whistling merrily as Karim, for safety's sake, once again checked to make sure his life vest was properly fastened.

Annika stuck her head in the door.

'Bertil, there's someone who insists on talking only to you. An unknown phone number, and their voice sounds very odd. What do you think? Shall I put the call through?'

'Okay, go ahead,' said Mellberg, sighing heavily. 'It's probably some bloody telemarketer who thinks he can sell me something I absolutely can't live without, but we'll see about that.'

He leaned down to scratch Ernst behind the ear while he waited for the light on his phone to go on. When it did, he answered in an authoritative voice: 'Yes? Hello?' If there was one thing he knew how to do, it was dealing with sales people.

But the person on the line was not interested in selling him something. At first the distorted voice made him suspicious, but what he heard was undeniably startling information. He sat up straighter in his chair and listened intently. Ernst noticed the change and raised his head with his ears pricked.

Before Mellberg was able to ask any pertinent questions, he heard a click and the caller was gone.

Mellberg scratched his head. What he'd just heard made him view the whole case from a different angle. He reached for the phone to ring Patrik but then changed his mind. The other team members were all busy searching the Berg house and farm. And this information was of such magnitude that someone senior ought to take care of the matter. So it would be simpler and safer if he saw to it himself. Later on, when he was showered with gratitude by the public because he had successfully solved the case . . . well, that was something he could deal with, since he was police chief, after all, and constantly in the spotlight, solving the most complicated cases.

He got up. Ernst eagerly raised his head to look up at his master.

'Sorry, old boy,' said Mellberg. 'Today you'll have to stay here. I have important matters to tend to.'

He ignored Ernst's pitiful whimpers and hurried from the room.

'I'm going out for a while,' he told Annika as he passed her in the reception area.

'What was the phone call about?' she asked.

Mellberg groaned. What a trial it was these days, with staff forever sticking their noses in things instead of showing proper respect for their superiors.

'Er, it was one of those darn telemarketers. Just like I thought.'

Annika gave him a dubious look, but he knew better than to tell her where he was going. Quicker than he could blink an eye, she would be ringing Hedström, who would undoubtedly insist on tagging along. Power was intoxicating – that's what he'd learned over the years, and he was always having to fend off the attempts of his younger colleagues to upstage him when he was on the verge of a breakthrough or dealing with the media. It was tragic the way they carried on.

He grunted when he got outside. If this greenhouse effect keeps heating things up like this, I might as well move to Spain, he thought. Not that he was especially

351

fond of winter. Spring and autumn were more his cup of tea.

When he got into the police car, the heat inside nearly took his breath away. He was going to have to talk to the idiot who had left the vehicle parked in the sun. It was like stepping into a sauna! He hurried to switch on the AC but the temperature still hadn't noticeably dropped by the time he arrived at the refugee centre, and his shirt was drenched with sweat.

Mellberg hadn't told anyone he was coming. He didn't know the director of the centre, so he couldn't rely on the man not to tip off the individuals in question. It was best to handle these types of situation without any advance warning. That was why the police used to conduct dawn raids in the past. To have the element of surprise on their side.

He headed for the reception area and pulled open the door. It was blissfully cool in here. Mellberg wiped his right hand on his trouser leg before he shook hands with the man in the lobby.

'Hi. I'm Bertil Mellberg from the Tanumshede police station.'

'Hi. My name is Rolf. I'm the director of the centre. To what do we owe the honour?'

He gave Mellberg an uneasy look. Mellberg let him sweat for a moment, not because he had any reason to do so, but simply because he could.

'I need to have access to one of your residences,' he said.

'Oh?' said Rolf, startled. 'Which one? And why?'

'Who lives in the house furthest away? The one facing the sea?'

'That's Karim and his family.'

'Karim? What do you know about him?'

Mellberg crossed his arms.

'Well, he's from Syria. Came here a couple of months ago with his wife and two children. A journalist. Very quiet and calm. Why do you ask?'

'Did he participate in the search party when the little girl disappeared on Monday?'

'I think so.' Rolf frowned. 'Yes, he did. What's this all about?' He too crossed his arms.

'I need to have a look at where he's living,' said Bertil.

'I'm not sure I can allow that,' said Rolf, but there was a hesitancy in his voice.

Mellberg took a chance, knowing that most Swedes were unaware of their rights.

'This is a government-run place, so we have the right to gain access.'

'Oh, er, if that's the case . . . I'll show you the way.'

'This is police business, so I'd prefer to do this alone,' said Mellberg. He wasn't keen on having an anxious director looking over his shoulder. 'Just point out the house.'

'Okay,' said Rolf, following him out the front door. 'It's the last building, over there.'

Mellberg once again struggled through the infernal summer heat. No doubt the refugees thrived in these high temperatures. It probably felt like home to them.

The small white-painted house looked well-maintained. Toys were neatly stacked up outside and pairs of shoes were lined up in front of the steps. The door stood wide open, and he could hear children laughing inside.

'Hello?' he called, and a beautiful woman with long dark hair appeared, holding a saucepan and a dishtowel.

She gave a start when she saw him and immediately stopped drying the pan.

'What you want?' she said in English.

She spoke with a strong accent, and her voice sounded cold and hostile.

Mellberg hadn't thought about the language problem. If he was being honest, English was not his strong suit. And maybe the woman didn't really speak English. She kept talking in a language he didn't understand at all. Good lord, how hard can it be to learn the language of the country where she'd ended up?

'I have to . . . see in your house . . .' he managed.

Trying to find even a few words in English made his tongue feel thick and clumsy.

The woman looked at him, uncomprehending, and threw out her hands.

'I have some . . . information . . . that your man is hiding something in the house,' he said, and tried to push past her.

The woman crossed her arms and blocked the doorway. Her eyes flashed as she burst into an angry tirade.

For a moment Mellberg felt a flicker of doubt. But he was used to dealing with angry females at home, so he wasn't about to be frightened off by this young woman. He realized he should have brought along an interpreter, but decided there wasn't time to fetch one now. No, he needed to be cunning. As cunning as a fox. Even though a warrant wasn't required in Sweden, he knew that was not the case in many other countries. He had a flash of genius and reached in his breast pocket to pull out a piece of paper, which he carefully unfolded.

'I have permission to look in your house,' he said, holding up the paper with an authoritative expression. 'You know this? A permission?'

Frowning, he waved it in front of her eyes. She stared at the paper and began looking uncertain.

Then the woman stepped aside and nodded. Pleased, he stuffed Ernst's veterinary certificate back in his breast pocket. When it came to important business like this, any means were permitted.

BOHUSLÄN 1672

One of the things Elin's grandmother had taught her was how to follow the seasons of the year. Late spring was when she had to gather the herbs and flowers she would need for the rest of the year, so whenever she had some time to herself she would go out into the fields. Today she'd won two hours for herself by bribing the youngest maid, Stina, to take over her chores with the promise that she would help her say the proper words of supplication to entice a suitor.

There were plenty of plants to choose from. The early spring days had been rainy, followed by many sunny days, and now everything was in bloom. It was lovely roaming over the land belonging to the vicarage and for the first time in a long while she felt something akin to happiness. There were meadows, pastures, marshy areas, and forests. Everything looked so lush, and Elin hummed to herself as she put in her basket the best specimens of those plants with the properties needed to heal and cure, offer comfort and solace. On her return, she would carefully dry the contents of her basket in the small space allotted to her in the servants' quarters.

The rough terrain was hard to traverse, and even though she was strong and healthy, she was out of breath.

She stopped at the old cowshed and sat down for a moment. The air smelled so good, the sun was so warm, and the sky was so blue, that she persuaded herself it would do no harm to allow her soul to rest. She lay down in the grass with her arms outstretched and her gaze fixed on the sky. She knew that God was present everywhere, but she could not help thinking that He must be even closer at this moment. He must be sitting right here with all the colours of the earth, painting the day.

Her body grew heavier. The fragrance of the grass and flowers filled her nostrils. The clouds were slowly gliding across the blue sky. The softness of the ground embraced her. Everything lulled her to sleep. Her eyelids kept trying to close until she could no longer resist and let them fall shut.

She awoke when something tickled her nose. She reached up to rub her nose and heard a muted laugh beside her. Hastily she sat up. Preben was sitting next to her, holding a blade of grass in his hand.

'What is the vicar doing!' she said, trying to sound angry, but she could hear that her voice was filled with mirth.

He smiled and his blue eyes drew her in, closer and closer.

'You looked so peaceful sleeping there,' he said, running the blade of grass along her cheek to tease her.

She wanted to stand up, brush off her skirts, and pick up her overflowing basket to march home. That would be the proper thing to do. That was what she ought to do. But as they sat there in the grass next to the abandoned cowshed, they were not master and servant. Or even brother-in-law and sister-in-law. They were Elin and Preben, and above them God had painted the bluest of colours, while beneath them He had painted the greenest of green. Elin wanted one thing, then she wanted something else. She knew what she should do, and she knew what she could do. And she could not get up and leave. Preben was looking at her in a way no one had looked at her since Per was alive. She pictured him with Märta, holding the puppy in his arms. She saw him with the lock of hair falling into his eyes, with his hand gently stroking Stjärna's muzzle when the cow was ill. And without knowing what had come over her, she leaned forward and kissed him. At first he gave a start. She could feel his lips stiffen against hers as his body warily drew back. Then he softened and moved close. Even though it should have felt so wrong, it was as if God were watching them. And smiling in all His omnipotence.

'We're finished with the farmhouse.'

Torbjörn came over to Gösta and pointed towards the barn.

'We'll continue over there.'

'Okay,' said Gösta. He still felt a great aversion to this whole process, and he couldn't bring himself to join Patrik and Peter, who were lying in the grass a short distance away. He'd wanted to speak to Eva as she sat on the patio chair outside the house, but she had such a remote look in her eyes that he hadn't wanted to disturb her. Peter's parents were angry and unwilling to listen to any sensible arguments at the moment, so he left them alone.

The forensic technicians were working hard, which only made Gösta feel all the more superfluous and at a loss. He knew his presence here was necessary, but he would have preferred to be doing something practical instead of merely standing about, supervising. Patrik had asked Paula and Martin to take a closer look at the background of the Berg family, and he would have gladly exchanged assignments with them. Yet Gösta realized that he was needed here, since he was the one who'd had the most contact with the family.

He watched Torbjörn's team as they carried their equipment to the barn. A grey cat ran out when they opened the big doors.

A wasp buzzed close to his right ear, and he forced himself to stay still. He'd always been afraid of wasps, and it didn't matter how many times people told him not to run around and frantically flail his arms, he just couldn't help it. Some sort of primitive instinct caused an adrenalin rush and made his heart scream 'Run!' as soon as a wasp got near. But this time Gösta was in luck because the wasp found something sweeter and more interesting to attack and flew off without causing him to lose his dignity in front of everyone else on the farm.

'Come over and join us,' called Patrik, waving to him.

Gösta acquiesced and sat down in the grass next to Peter. It felt odd to be sitting there with him while the forensic team turned his home upside down, but Peter seemed to accept the situation. He appeared calm and composed.

'What are they looking for?' he asked now.

Gösta surmised Peter had a need to distance himself from everything in order to cope. He had to pretend none of the activity had anything to do with him. Gösta had seen the same thing many times before.

'I'm afraid we can't tell you what we're doing or what we're looking for.'

Peter nodded. 'Because we're potential suspects, right?'

There was a resigned tone to his voice, and Gösta felt that honesty was the best way to respond.

'Yes, I'm afraid so. I realize how awful that must feel. But I assume you want us to do everything in our power to find out what happened to Nea. Unfortunately, that includes considering even the most unlikely possibilities.'

'I understand. It's okay,' said Peter.

'Do you think your parents will understand?' asked Gösta, turning to look at Bengt and Ulla, who were standing some distance away.

Peter's father was gesticulating wildly, and his face was bright red under his suntan as they argued.

'They're worried. And sad,' said Peter, pulling up fistfuls of grass. 'Pappa has always been like that. If he feels anxious about something, he reacts by getting angry. But it's not as bad as he makes it sound.'

Torbjörn came out of the barn.

'Patrik?' he called. 'Could you come over here?'

'I'll be right there,' replied Patrik, getting up with an effort.

His knees creaked as he stood up, and Gösta thought his own knees would probably sound even worse. He frowned as he watched Patrik cross the stretch of gravel. Torbjörn was holding his mobile, and he began speaking intently with Patrik, who looked concerned.

Gösta got up.

'I'm going to go over and find out what Torbjörn wants,' he told Peter, shaking his right leg, which had fallen asleep.

He limped over to join his colleagues.

'What is it? Have you found something?'

'No, we haven't yet started on the barn,' said Torbjörn, holding up his phone. 'But I got a call from Mellberg, ordering us to stop everything and head over to the refugee centre immediately. He says he's found something.'

'Found something?' said Gösta, puzzled. 'How can that be? He was asleep in his office when we left.'

'He's obviously up to some mischief,' muttered Patrik. Then he turned to Torbjörn. 'I'd rather we finished up here, but Mellberg is in charge and I can't countermand his orders. We'll cordon off the area here, drive over to the centre, and then come back later.'

'It's not advisable to cut short this type of search,' said Torbjörn, and Gösta knew what he meant.

But he had to agree with Patrik. Mellberg was officially their boss and the one with the ultimate responsibility for the station. Even if they all knew this was more in theory than in practice, they had to obey his orders.

'We'll follow you,' Torbjörn said, receiving a nod of confirmation from Patrik, who had taken out his phone and was trying in vain to reach Mellberg.

Gösta went over to the family and told them they'd return later, but he left their questions unanswered.

The fact that Mellberg had gone out on his own could only spell trouble. What could he possibly have found at the refugee centre? Gösta climbed into the car with a sense of impending disaster growing inside him.

The children were in no hurry to go home, but Erica knew that if she ever wanted to leave them here for another play date, it would be best if they didn't stay much longer. She took the twins by the hand, and Maja went on ahead, skipping happily. What a wonderful child. Always happy, always so considerate and positive. Erica reminded herself to spend more time with her daughter. It was so easy to let the rambunctious twins demand all her attention.

While Noel and Anton merrily chattered about everything they'd done during the day, her thoughts returned to Helen. There were still so many unanswered questions, but she knew her instinct had been right: had she tried to put any pressure on Helen, she'd have clammed up. And Erica desperately needed more meat on the bone in order to complete this book. Her deadline was 1 December, and she hadn't yet written a single sentence. That was actually par for the course, since she always spent most of her time on the research and then wrote the manuscript in about three months. But if she was going to finish on time, she needed to start writing in early September, at the latest. And right now her carefully laid plans had been turned upside down.

She had no idea how the murder of Nea would affect the book and its publication. Regardless whether Helen and Marie were involved or not, she would be forced to write about the similarities between the two cases. And since the murder of Nea was still unsolved, it was impossible to know what should or could be included in the book. It felt a little cold-hearted to be thinking about a book when a child's life had been taken, plunging her family into unthinkable grief. But ever since Erica wrote the book about the murder of her childhood friend, Alexandra, she'd disciplined herself to separate her feelings from her work. She reminded herself of the letters she'd received from families of victims, telling how her books had helped them to achieve some form of closure. There had also been occasions when she had contributed to solving a case, and she was determined that she would be of assistance to the police in this investigation too – by digging into the previous homicide.

With an effort, she set aside thoughts about the book. Her New Year's resolution had been to try to be as present as possible whenever she was with her children. Not think about work, not sit with her eyes glued to the mobile display or the computer screen. Instead she wanted to give the kids her full attention. These early childhood years wouldn't last long.

Even though the infancy stage was not her favourite, she was wholeheartedly looking forward to Anna's new baby. Being able to borrow a baby was the best – playing games and snuggling with stuffed animals, then handing the little one back to the parents as soon as he or she smelled bad or cried. She couldn't wait to find out whether

362

this baby was a boy or a girl. Dan and Anna hadn't wanted to know ahead of time, they said it didn't matter either way. But for some reason Erica had a feeling it would be a girl. Maybe that would be for the best, since the unborn child they had so tragically lost was a boy. Anna's body and face still bore scars from the car accident that had nearly killed her, but she seemed to have started to accept the physical changes. At least, Erica hoped so; it was a long time since Anna had mentioned them.

Erica stopped abruptly. Thinking about Anna reminded her of the bachelorette party. She'd completely forgotten her suggestion that they should arrange a party for Kristina. Although her mother-in-law sometimes got on her nerves, she was always willing to help with the children when asked. So the least Erica could do for Patrik's mother was to organize something that she would enjoy. Not the usual nonsense, like selling kisses while wearing a bridal veil – that seemed undignified for a woman her age. But a fun day with Kristina in the spotlight. What could she come up with? And when? There wasn't much time left. Maybe on the weekend? If she was going to make this happen, she'd better start right away.

A notice on the bulletin board in front of the camping area made her stop. Now there was an idea. A really good idea. Brilliant, even if she did say so herself. She got out her phone and took a picture of the notice. Then she rang Anna.

'Hey, remember I was talking about organizing a bachelorette party for Kristina? How about Saturday? I'll make all the arrangements if you'll promise to reserve the date. Can Dan take care of the kids?'

Anna gave a curt reply, not sounding as enthusiastic as Erica had hoped. But maybe she was having a hard day because of her pregnancy, so Erica decided not to be put off.

'I'm not a hundred per cent sure what I'll think up, but I saw a notice on the bulletin board at the camping area, and it gave me an idea . . .'

Still no reaction from Anna. That was odd.

'Is everything all right, Anna? You sound a little . . . strange.'

'It's nothing. I'm tired, that's all.'

'Okay, okay. I won't nag. Get some rest, and I'll give you all the details once I work them out.'

They ended the call, and Erica pensively stuck the phone in the pocket of her shorts. Something wasn't right with Anna. She knew her sister so well, and she was convinced Anna was hiding something from her. And considering Anna's unerring ability to attract misfortune, Erica felt uneasy. After all the adversity and problems, it had seemed as if Anna had finally landed on her feet and was beginning to make sensible decisions, but maybe that was merely wishful thinking on Erica's part. The question was, what was her sister hiding? And why? Erica shivered in the summer heat. She wondered if she would ever stop worrying about her little sister.

Patrik had driven in tense silence the whole way to Tanumshede. He was an even worse driver when he was upset, and he was aware that Gösta was clinging tightly to the grab-handle above the car door.

'Bertil's still not answering?' he asked.

With his free hand, Gösta held his mobile to his ear, then shook his head.

'No reply.'

'Damn it, we can't leave him alone for even a minute. He's worse than the kids.'

Patrik stomped harder on the accelerator.

The road was straight at this point and Tanumshede would soon come into view. His stomach lurched as they raced over the hills, and he noticed that Gösta's face was starting to turn green.

'I'm not happy that we had to abandon the search of the farm. Even though we cordoned off the area, there's a risk the forensic examination might get compromised,' muttered Patrik. 'Are Paula and Martin on their way?'

'Yes. I talked to Martin, and they'll meet us at the centre. They're probably already there.'

Patrik was surprised by his own anger. Mellberg had an unfailing ability to make a mess of things, usually in the hope of covering himself in glory. This time Patrik simply couldn't permit him to derail their investigation. Not when they were dealing with the murder of a child.

When they pulled up to the refugee centre, they saw Paula and Martin waiting for them in the car park. Patrik parked next to their vehicle and got out, slamming the door behind him.

'Have you seen him yet?' he asked.

'No. We thought it best to wait for you. But we did speak to the centre's director, and apparently Mellberg went to the furthest house.' Paula pointed behind them.

'Okay. Well, let's go over there and find out what he's got himself into this time.'

Patrik turned at the sound of more cars pulling in. Torbjörn and his team had arrived.

'Why does he want Torbjörn here?' asked Martin. 'Do you know? Has anybody talked to him?'

Patrik snorted. 'He's not answering his phone. The only thing we know is that he told Torbjörn to get here fast. He said he'd found something and that he'd "locked up this bloody case like a tin of sardines".'

'Do we even want to know?' asked Paula gloomily. Then she nodded to the others. 'We might as well get this over with.'

'Should we bring our equipment or not?' asked Torbjörn.

Patrik hesitated.

'Sure, what the hell. Bring the equipment. Mellberg says he found something.'

Patrik motioned for Gösta, Paula and Martin to come with him, and they set off for the house in question. Torbjörn and his team began taking their gear out of the cars. They'd follow in a few minutes.

All around, people were watching them. Some were peering out of windows, others had come outside and were standing in front of the houses. But no one said a word. They simply watched, with worried expressions.

From a distance, Patrik heard a woman screaming, and he moved faster.

'What's going on here?' he asked when they reached the house.

Mellberg was talking to a woman. He was gesticulating wildly and using his most authoritative voice.

In broken English he kept repeating: 'No no, cannot go in house. Stay outside.'

He turned to Patrik.

'I'm glad you're here!'

'What's going on?' Patrik repeated. 'We've been trying to get hold of you ever since you rang Torbjörn, but you're not answering your phone.'

'No, I've had my hands full. She's hysterical, and the kids are crying. But I had to shoo them out of the house so they wouldn't destroy any evidence.'

'Evidence? What sort of evidence?'

Patrik heard his voice rise to a falsetto. His feeling of uneasiness was growing by the minute, and he had an urge to grab Mellberg by the shoulders and shake him until he wiped that smug look off his face.

'I received a tip,' said Mellberg proudly, then paused for dramatic effect.

'What kind of tip?' asked Paula. 'From whom?'

She took a step towards Mellberg as she cast a concerned look at the crying children. But Patrik realized that she too wanted to size up the situation before taking any action.

'Well, it was . . . an anonymous tip,' said Mellberg. 'Saying there was evidence that would lead to the girl's killer.'

'Here? In this particular house? Or connected to the people who live here? What exactly did this anonymous caller say?'

Mellberg sighed and began enunciating his words slowly and clearly, as if speaking to a child. 'The caller gave very precise information about this house. Described the layout. But didn't mention any names.'

'So you drove over here?' asked Patrik with rising annoyance. 'Without telling any of us?'

Mellberg snorted and glared at him.

'Yes. You were busy with other things, and I knew it was important to act fast so the evidence wouldn't disappear or get destroyed. It was a well-thought-out decision on my part.'

'And you didn't consider waiting for a search warrant from the prosecutor?' asked Patrik.

He was struggling to stay calm.

'Well . . .' said Mellberg. For the first time he looked a little uncertain. 'I didn't think it was necessary. As the chief, I made the decision. It was a matter of securing evidence in a homicide investigation, and in that situation, you know as well as I do that we don't have to wait for official permission.'

Putting emphasis on every word, Patrik said:

'So you relied on an anonymous tip and forced your way in here without consulting anyone else. Is that what you're saying? And the woman who lives here let you in? Without asking any questions?'

Patrik cast a glance at the woman standing nearby.

'Well, I mean, I know that in many countries you have to show some sort of document, so I thought it would be easier if I did too, so—'

'A document?' queried Patrik, not sure he wanted to hear the explanation.

'Yes, she can't speak Swedish, and she doesn't seem to know English either. And I had a veterinary certificate for Ernst in my breast pocket. I took him to the vet the other day. He's been having stomach trouble, you know, and—'

'Am I understanding you right?' Patrik interrupted. 'Instead of waiting for backup or an interpreter, you forced your way into the residence of a traumatized refugee family by showing the woman a veterinary certificate, pretending it was a search warrant?'

'Yes, but bloody hell, didn't you hear what I said?' Mellberg's face was bright red. 'It's a matter of getting results! And I found something! I found the little girl's knickers. The ones with the *Frozen* illustration that her mother mentioned. They were behind the toilet. With bloodstains!'

No one said a word. The only sound was the crying of the children. Off in the distance they saw a man running towards them. He ran faster the closer he got.

'What is happening? Why are you talking to my family?' he shouted in English as soon as he was close enough to be heard.

Mellberg took a step towards him to grab his arm and twist it behind his back.

'You are under arrest.'

Patrik glanced behind him and saw the woman staring at them while the children kept crying. The man did not resist.

* * *

368

She'd done it. She was standing here outside Marie's house. She still wasn't sure she was doing the right thing, but the pressure in her chest had begun to feel worse and worse.

Sanna took a deep breath and knocked on the door. It sounded like a gunshot, and Sanna realized how tense she must be.

Relax.

Then the door opened and there was Marie. The inimitable Marie. She gave Sanna a puzzled look. Her lovely eyes narrowed.

'Yes?'

Sanna's mouth was dry, her tongue felt thick. She cleared her throat and forced herself to speak.

'I am Stella's sister.'

At first Marie simply stood in the doorway, one eyebrow raised. Then she stepped aside.

'Come in,' she said and led the way inside.

Sanna followed her into a big, open room. Beautiful French doors had been thrown open, facing a dock with a view of Fjällbacka's harbour. The evening sun was glinting off the water.

'Can I get you anything? Coffee? Water? A drink?'

Marie picked up a glass of champagne from a bench and sipped her drink.

'No, thank you,' said Sanna.

She couldn't think of anything else to say.

Over the past few days she had been mustering her courage and planning what she'd say. But now all the words had vanished.

'Let's sit down,' said Marie, going over to a big wooden table.

From upstairs came the sound of cheerful pop music, and Marie looked up at the ceiling.

'My teenage daughter.'

'I have one too,' said Sanna, sitting down across from Marie.

'Strange creatures, teenagers. You and I never had the experience of being a teenager.'

Sanna looked at her. Was Marie comparing her childhood to hers? Sanna's teenage years had been stolen from her, and Marie was the one who'd done it. She'd also stolen her own teenage years. But Sanna didn't feel the anger she'd imagined or thought she should feel. The person sitting across from her seemed no more than a shell. A glossy, perfect exterior, but resoundingly empty inside.

'I heard about your parents,' said Marie, taking another sip of her drink. 'I'm sorry.'

The words held no emotion, and Sanna merely nodded. It was all so long ago now. She had only vague memories of her parents. The years had swept them away.

Marie set down her glass.

'Why are you here?' she asked.

Sanna felt herself shrinking under Marie's gaze. All the hatred she'd felt, all the anger and rage now seemed like a distant dream. The woman before her was not the monster who had been chasing her in her nightmares.

'Did you do it?' she heard herself ask. 'Did the two of you murder Stella?'

Marie stared down at her hands, seeming to study her fingernails. Sanna wondered if she'd heard the question. Finally Marie looked up.

'No,' she said. 'No, we didn't do it.'

'Then why did you say you did? Why did you say you killed her?'

The music upstairs had stopped, and Sanna had a feeling that someone was listening up there.

'It was so long ago. What does it matter?'

For the first time there was some emotion in Marie's eyes. Weariness. Marie looked as tired as Sanna felt.

'It does matter,' said Sanna, leaning forward. 'Whoever did it, took everything from us. We didn't just lose Stella, we lost our family, we lost the farm . . . and I was left all alone.'

She straightened up.

The only sound was the water lapping against the posts of the dock.

'I saw somebody in the woods,' said Marie at last. 'On that day. I saw somebody in the woods.'

'Who?'

Sanna didn't know what to believe. Why would Marie say this if she and Helen were guilty? She wasn't naive enough to think Marie would speak the truth when she'd been professing her innocence for thirty years, but she'd thought she could read the truth in Marie's reaction, if only she asked the question face to face. But Marie's face was a mask. Nothing was genuine.

'If I knew, I wouldn't have had to spend thirty years claiming I was innocent,' said Marie, getting up to refill her glass.

She took a half-empty bottle from the fridge and held it up.

'Sure you won't have any?'

'No, thank you,' said Sanna.

A memory stirred deep in her subconscious. Somebody in the woods. Someone she used to be scared of. A shadow. A presence. Something she hadn't thought about in close to thirty years, but now it had been conjured back into existence by Marie's words.

Marie sat down again.

'So why did both of you confess?' asked Sanna. 'I mean, if you didn't kill her?'

'You wouldn't understand.'

Marie looked away, but Sanna saw her face contort with pain. For a second it made her look like a real human being instead of a beautiful doll. When Marie turned back to look at Sanna, all trace of pain had disappeared.

'We were children. We didn't understand the seriousness of the situation. And when we did, it was too late. Everyone thought they had the answer, and they refused to listen to anything else.'

Sanna didn't know what to say. For so many years she'd dreamed of this moment, tried to picture it, turned and twisted the words she would speak, the questions she would ask. But it turned out there were no words, and the only thought in her mind right now was the distant memory of something in the woods. Someone in the woods.

When Sanna let herself out the front door, Marie was standing at the worktop, refilling her glass. Upstairs the music was once again playing. When Sanna stepped outside, she noticed a girl in the window upstairs. She waved, but the girl merely stared. Then she turned around and was gone.

'Bill! Wake up!'

He awoke with a start when he heard Gun calling him. He must have forgotten to set the alarm clock before he took his afternoon nap.

'What's happened?' he managed to say.

Gun never woke him from his nap.

'Adnan and Khalil are here.'

'Adnan and Khalil?'

He tried to rub the sleep from his eyes.

'They're waiting downstairs. Something has happened . . .'

Gun didn't meet his eye, which immediately alarmed Bill. She almost never lost her composure.

He went downstairs and caught sight of Adnan and Khalil pacing back and forth in the living room.

'Hello, boys!' he said first in Swedish, before switching to English. 'What has happened?'

They both started talking at once in English, and Bill had to strain to understand what they were saying.

'What? Karim? Speak slower, boys. Slowly!'

Adnan nodded to Khalil, who explained, and Bill was suddenly wide awake. He looked at Gun, who looked as outraged as he felt.

'That's madness! The police took him in? They can't do that!'

Adnan and Khalil again began talking at once. Bill held up his hand.

'Calm down, boys. I'll take care of this. This is Sweden. The police can't just arrest anyone they please. This isn't some banana republic!'

Gun nodded, and that warmed his heart.

They heard a creaking sound from above.

'I told you.'

Nils came downstairs. He had a gleam in his eye that Bill hadn't seen before, a look he didn't want to see.

'Didn't I tell you it had to be one of those roaches who did it? Everybody's been talking about it, saying that somebody at the centre must have read about the old case and then seized the opportunity. Everybody knows what sort of people are staying there. Swedes are so naive! Those refugees don't need help, they're just looking for a soft life or else they're criminals!'

Nils's hair was sticking straight up, and he was so agitated that his words came spilling out. The look he gave Adnan and Khalil practically robbed Bill of breath.

'You're a fool if you think it's a matter of offering human-itarian help while we let rapists and thieves pour across our borders. You've let them take advantage. What bloody idiots you are. I hope you realize how wrong you were. I hope that filthy wog who killed a kid rots in jail, and—'

Gun's hand slapped Nils's cheek with a sound that echoed through the whole living room. Nils gasped and gave his mother a shocked look. Suddenly he was a child again.

'Go to hell!' he shouted and ran upstairs with his hand pressed to his cheek.

Bill looked at Gun who was studying her hand. He put his arm around her and then turned to face Adnan and Khalil, who didn't know how to react.

'Sorry about my son. Don't worry. I will fix this.'

This whole thing made him sick. Bill knew his home town and the people who lived here. Anyone foreign or different had never been welcomed with open arms. If one of the men from the refugee centre was suspected of murdering a little girl from here, all hell would soon break loose.

'I'm going over to the police station,' he said, sticking his feet into a pair of summertime loafers. 'Tell Nils that he and I need to have a serious conversation when I get back,' he added.

'You'll have to take your place in the queue behind me,' said Gun.

When he drove off with Adnan and Khalil, Bill looked in the rear-view mirror and saw Gun standing in the doorway, her arms crossed and her expression grim. For a moment he almost felt sorry for Nils. But when he registered the fear in Adnan's and Khalil's eyes, all sympathy with his son evaporated.

James ran up the steps. The rumour circulating in town had lifted his spirits and given him energy.

He threw open the front door.

'I knew it!' he said, looking at Helen who flinched as she stood at the worktop in the kitchen.

'What's happened?'

The colour had drained from her face, and as usual he was struck by how weak she was. Without him, she would have been lost. He had taught her everything, protected her against everything.

He sat down at the kitchen table.

'Coffee,' he said. 'Then I'll tell you.'

Helen had just started a fresh pot, and the coffee was already seeping through the filter. She took out his cup, filled it from the pot, and added some milk. Not too much, not too little.

'They've arrested someone for the murder of the little girl,' he said as Helen picked up the pot to wipe off the coffee machine.

The sound of the pot striking the floor startled James so much that he spilled coffee on the front of his shirt.

'What do you think you're doing?' he shouted, jumping up from his chair.

'Sorry. I'm sorry,' stammered Helen, dashing to get the broom and dustpan.

While she swept up the pieces, James reached for the kitchen roll and wiped off his shirt.

'Now we'll have to buy a new coffee pot,' he said, sitting back down. 'We're not made of money, you know.'

Helen silently continued to sweep up the glass. This was something she'd learned over the years: it was best not to say anything.

'I was over at the town square when I heard about it,' he said. 'It was one of those guys from the refugee centre. Nobody's at all surprised.'

Helen paused for a moment, her shoulders slumped. Then she began sweeping again.

'Are they sure?' she asked, dumping the shards of glass into an empty milk carton, which she carefully placed in the bin.

'I don't know the details,' he said. 'All I heard was

that they've arrested a guy. The Swedish police may not be especially efficient, but they don't pick up people without cause.'

'Right,' said Helen, wiping off the worktop with a rag, which she wrung out and hung neatly from the tap.

She turned to face James.

'So, it's over.'

'Yes, it's over. It has been for a long time. I'll take care of you. That's what I've always done.'

'I know,' said Helen, lowering her eyes. 'Thank you, James.'

The sound of the door splintering was what woke them. The next second they were inside the bedroom, grabbing his arms, dragging him away. Karim's first instinct had been to resist, but when he heard the children screaming, he relented. He didn't want them to see him get beaten to a pulp. That's what had happened to so many others, so he knew it would do no good to offer resistance.

After that he was left to lie on a cold, damp floor in a windowless room, unable to tell whether it was day or night outside. He could still hear the children's screams ringing in his ears.

The blows had rained down on him, and they had asked the same questions over and over. They knew he'd found documents stating who in Damascus was working against the regime, and they wanted those documents. Now. To begin with, he had refused, insisting that, as a journalist, he could not be forced to reveal his sources. But days of torture followed, and at last he'd given them what they wanted. He gave them names, he gave them places. When he slept, briefly, uneasily, he dreamed of the people he'd named, he pictured them being dragged from their homes while their children screamed and their spouses wept.

Every waking minute he scratched at his arms in order to keep from thinking of all the lives he had destroyed. He scratched until the blood ran, leaving wounds that became dirty and infected.

After three weeks they released him, and only a day later he and Amina packed up what few possessions they owned. Amina had cautiously touched the wounds on his arms, but he never told her what he had done. It was his secret, his shame, which he could never share with her.

Karim leaned his head against the wall. Even though the room where he now found himself was cold and bare, it was clean and the sun shone through a small window. But the feeling of powerlessness was the same. He didn't think the police were allowed to beat prisoners in Sweden, but he wasn't sure. He was a foreigner in a foreign country, and he didn't know the rules.

He thought he'd left everything behind when he came to this new land, but now the children's screams were once again ringing in his ears. His fingers dug into the scars on his arms. Slowly he pounded his forehead against the wall in the small cell, while sounds from the street outside came in through the barred window.

Maybe this was his fate, his punishment for what he'd done to those who still haunted his dreams. He'd thought he could flee, but no one could escape the all-seeing eyes of God.

THE STELLA CASE

'What will happen to the girls?'

Kate was using her strong, supple fingers to knead the dough. Leif loved watching her do that. For forty years he had watched her standing at the kitchen worktop with flour on her face and a cigarette hanging from her lips. Always ready with a smile. Viola had inherited her smile and sunny disposition. And her creativity. The boys were more like him. They took life a little too seriously. Roger, the oldest, had become an accountant, while the youngest, Christer, worked as an administrator at an employment agency. Neither of them seemed to have much fun.

'They're too young to be sent to prison, so the matter will be handled by social services.'

'Humpf. Sounds so clinical when you say it like that. We're talking about two children here.'

Flour was whirling around Kate. Behind her the sun shone through the kitchen window and lit up the short, fluffy down of her hair. Her scalp looked translucent and ethereal in the light, with the blood vessels pulsing under her skin. Leif had to restrain himself from getting up to put his arms around his wife. She detested being treated as weak.

Kate had never been weak. And after a year of chemo-therapy, she was still the strongest person he knew.

'You should stop smoking,' he said mildly as she tapped the ash from her cigarette just before it would have landed on the bread.

'No, you should stop smoking,' she said, and he laughed and shook his head.

She was impossible. They'd had this discussion so many times before. She was always more worried about him than about herself. Even now. The absurdity of the situation only made him love her more. And he didn't think that was possible.

'So what's going to happen?' she persisted.

'Social services will determine what would be best for the girls, and I have no idea what their recommendation will be.'

'But if you had to make a guess?'

'If I had to make a guess, I think Helen will be allowed to remain with her family while Marie will be placed in foster care.'

'And do you think that would be the right decision?' she asked, taking another drag on her cigarette.

Leif pondered her question. He wanted to say yes, but something was bothering him. It had been bothering him ever since he'd interviewed the girls, but he couldn't put his finger on it.

'Yes, I think that's the right decision,' he said.

Kate stopped kneading the dough. 'You don't sound too convinced. Do you have doubts about their guilt?'

'No, I see no reason why two thirteen-year-old girls would confess to a murder if they didn't do it. It's the right decision. Helen has a stable home environment, while Marie's home . . . well, it was probably what set her on this path, turned her into the instigator.'

'Instigator?' said Kate, her eyes filling with tears. 'She's a child. How can a child be . . . an instigator?'

How should he explain this to Kate? How could he tell her about the eerily calm manner in which Marie had confessed to killing Stella and described step by step what had happened? Kate always saw the good in everyone.

'I think this will be best. For both of them.'

'You're probably right,' said Kate. 'You've always been a good judge of character. That's what makes you such a good police officer.'

'You're the one who makes me a good police officer. Because you make me a good person,' he replied simply.

Kate stopped what she was doing. Her strong hands suddenly began to shake. She raised a floury hand to her head. Then she burst into tears.

Leif got up and put his arms around her. She was as thin as a bird. He pressed her head to his chest. They had so little time left. Maybe only a year. Nothing else mattered. Not even the two children who were about to enter the social services system. He'd done his job. Now he needed to focus on what was most important.

'I've called this meeting because we need to get to the bottom of what happened.'

Patrik looked at his colleagues as Mellberg patted his stomach.

'Okay, I can see you're all a little surprised,' said Mellberg. 'You obviously haven't been keeping up with developments. But that's how it is with solid police work. If you do the groundwork, sooner or later you get to that decisive moment when it's a matter of being in the right place at the right time. And if I say it myself, I happen to have a talent for doing precisely that.'

He fell silent and surveyed the others. No one spoke. Mellberg furrowed his brow.

'Would it kill you to offer a few words of praise? Not that I expect a standing ovation or anything, but this blatant display of jealousy isn't very becoming.'

Patrik was seething. He was so angry he didn't trust himself to speak. Even for someone of Mellberg's monumental stupidity, this latest exploit beggared belief.

'Bertil. First of all, it was a flagrant blunder not to inform your colleagues that you'd received an anonymous phone call. We can all be reached by mobile phone, so you could easily have contacted one of us. Second, I don't understand how you could drive to the refugee centre without any sort of backup or at least an interpreter. I'm dumbfounded that someone with your experience could make an error like that. Third: waving a veterinary certificate and forcing your way into a woman's house when she has no idea what you're saying is so . . . so . . .'

Patrik stopped himself. He clenched his fists and took a deep breath. Then he looked around the room.

It was quiet enough to hear a pin drop. All the others had their eyes fixed on the table, not daring to look at either Patrik or Mellberg.

'What the hell!' exploded Mellberg. His face was white with fury. 'I deliver a child killer on a silver platter, and I get stabbed in the back by my own colleagues! Don't think I don't know why you're doing this. Sheer jealousy, all because I'll be the one who'll get the credit for solving the case! Well, let me tell you: I deserve the credit! While you lot were hounding the child's own family, even though it was perfectly obvious to everybody around here that we have a whole damned centre filled with criminals right around the corner, I relied on my policeman's instinct to lead me straight to the guy who did it. That's what none of you can stand: I did what you couldn't do. You always have to be so damned politically correct, but sometimes a spade is a spade! You can all go to hell, the whole lot of you!'

Mellberg jumped up from his seat, his comb-over dangling over his left ear, and stormed out of the room, slamming the door so hard that the windows rattled.

For a moment no one spoke. Then Patrik took a deep breath.

'So, that went well,' he said. 'How shall we proceed? We're sitting here with a big mess on our hands, and we need to sort it out somehow.'

Martin held up his hand, and Patrik nodded for him to speak.

'Do we have any reason to hold Karim?'

'Yes, we do, since we found a pair of knickers in his home that match the description Eva Berg gave. However, despite the fact they have the *Frozen* illustration on them, we have no proof as yet that they belonged to Nea, or that Karim was the one who hid them there. We need to proceed cautiously. From the way Karim and his wife reacted when we brought him in, it's obvious they've been through a traumatic time in their own country.'

'But what if he really is the perpetrator?' said Paula.

Patrik paused for a moment before replying.

'It's possible, but the fact that the tip-off came from an anonymous caller raises doubts in my mind. The murderer could have put the knickers there in order to shift the blame to someone else. We need to stay objective and make a thorough job of the police work. Everything has to be done by the book.'

'Before we get started,' said Gösta, 'I need to update you on a phone call that came in from Uddevalla regarding the sex offender Tore Carlson. According to his neighbours, he hasn't been home the past few weeks, and nobody knows where he is.'

Everyone exchanged glances.

'Let's not get ahead of ourselves,' said Patrik. 'It could be just a coincidence. Uddevalla need to keep looking for Tore Carlson while we work on the leads we have here.

'Annika, find out all you can about this anonymous caller. Since he called the station, we'll have it on tape; we need to listen to what was said and see if it gives us any ideas. Gösta, take a picture of the knickers found in Karim's home and show it to Eva and Peter. We want to know if they can identify the knickers as belonging to Nea. Martin and Paula, see what you can find out about

Karim's background. Does he have a criminal record? What do the others at the centre say about him? And so on.'

Once he had given them their assignments, Patrik tried to make himself relax by lowering his shoulders. Anger had made his body as taut as a violin string, and his heart had been beating too fast. Stress and tension could have fateful consequences for him, and the last thing he wanted was to land in hospital again. They simply couldn't afford that.

His heart rate now slowed to a more normal rhythm, and Patrik breathed a sigh of relief.

'I'm going to see if I can get Karim to talk. He's in shock, but with a little luck, he'll be able to help us get to the bottom of all this.'

He looked around at the discouraged faces. 'I know exactly how you all feel, but do your best and we'll get this investigation back on track. Mellberg has pulled stunts like this before, and no doubt he'll do it again. We have no choice but to deal with it as best we can.'

Without waiting for a reply, he picked up his notepad and headed for the part of the station where the holding cell was located. As he passed the reception area, the doorbell rang, and he opened the door. Outside stood an indignant Bill Andersson. Patrik sighed inwardly. As he'd feared, all hell was about to break loose.

Erica had put the kids to bed early. Now she was comfortably settled on the sofa with a glass of red wine and a bowl of nuts. She was hungry and should have found something more substantial to eat, but she found it so boring to cook dinner just for herself. Patrik had sent a text saying he probably wouldn't get home until after she'd gone to bed.

She had brought downstairs several folders from her

desk so she could go through them again. It took time to process all the material. Her method was to reread the articles and printouts many times, while she also looked at photos, trying to see everything with new eyes.

After pondering how to start, she reached for the file labelled 'Leif'. He would inevitably be one of the main figures in her book, but she still had questions in need of answers. Why did he change his mind? Why did he start out firmly convinced that Helen and Marie had killed Stella, but later begin to have doubts? And why did he kill himself? Was it merely depression after the death of his wife, or was there some other reason?

She picked up the copies of the post-mortem report and the photos taken of Leif at death. He was leaning over his desk in his home office, with a whisky glass next to him and a gun in his right hand. His face was turned towards the gun, and blood had gushed from his head to form a big, congealed pool. A wound was visible at his temple, his eyes were wide open and glassy. According to the post-mortem report, he'd been dead about twenty-four hours when one of his sons found him.

His children had stated that the gun was his, and the registration number confirmed this. Leif had applied for a gun permit because after retiring he had taken up shooting as a hobby.

Erica leafed through the documents, looking for a ballistics report, but she didn't find one. She frowned. That worried her, because she knew she'd gathered all the material related to his death. Either no analysis had been done on the bullet and gun, or the report had been lost. Erica reached for her notepad and jotted down the words 'ballistic report' followed by a question mark. She had no reason to believe there was anything amiss about the investigation into Leif's suicide, but she didn't like it when pieces of a puzzle went missing. It was worth looking into, but Leif had died fifteen years ago, so it was going to take a major stroke of luck to locate any of the individuals who had worked on the technical and forensic aspects of the investigation.

No matter, it would have to wait until tomorrow. It was too late in the evening to do anything about it now. She leaned back on the sofa cushions and propped her feet on the coffee table, on top of the files and documents. The wine tasted divine, but maybe she ought to abstain from drinking for a month after the summer holidays were over. She knew she was not alone in finding excuses to have a daily glass of wine during the summertime, but that didn't make it any better. She would definitely abstain for a month. In September.

Pleased with herself for having taken such a healthy decision, she allowed herself another sip of wine and savoured the warmth coursing through her body. She wondered what had happened to make Patrik stay at the station so late, but she knew it would do no good to ask him until he came home.

Erica leaned forward again to look at the pictures of Leif, lying there with the blood like a red halo around his head. She couldn't help wondering why he had killed himself. She knew that people often lost the will to live when a beloved spouse died. But he'd had his children, and several years had passed since his wife's death. And why get involved in an old case if he didn't want to go on living?

Bill slammed his fist against the steering wheel as they left the police station in his car. Karim sat next to him in silence, staring out the window. The twilight hour made the sky shimmer with lilac and pink, but Karim could see only the darkness he himself had created. What happened today proved that it was impossible to escape the fact he was guilty, that God had seen what he'd done and was punishing him for it.

Karim didn't know how many lives he had on his conscience. The people he had named disappeared without a trace, and no one knew what became of them. Maybe they were alive, maybe they weren't. The only certainty was that their spouses and children cried themselves to sleep at night.

Karim had saved his own skin by betraying others. How could he ever have believed this was something he could live with? He'd got lost in their flight to Sweden, in the thoughts of building a new life far away. But the old life, the old country, the old sins, had continued to live inside him.

'It's a scandal, but don't you worry, I will sort this out for you. Okay?'

Though he couldn't understand everything he said, it was obvious that Bill's voice was seething with emotion, and Karim was grateful that somebody believed in him and was on his side. But he didn't deserve it. Bill's words were drowned out by the Arabic voices in his head, repeating over and over: 'Give us the truth.'

Cockroaches had swarmed across the floor, scurrying over the bloodstains from those who had occupied the cell before him. He had given the interrogators everything they wanted. Sacrificed courageous people to save himself.

When the Swedish police officer said he would have to come down to the station, he hadn't offered any resistance. He was guilty, after all. Guilty before God. He had blood on his hands. He was not worthy of this new country. He was not worthy of Amina and Hassan and Samia. Nothing could change that. And he couldn't understand how he'd ever been able to fool himself into believing anything else.

When Bill dropped him off at his home, Amina was

standing in the doorway, waiting. Her dark eyes were filled with the same fear as on that morning in Damascus when the police had dragged him away. He couldn't look at her as he walked past her and lay down on the bed.

He stared at the wall, his back to the door. An hour later he heard her get undressed and then lie down next to him. Cautiously she placed her hand on his back. He didn't shake it off, pretending to be asleep.

Karim knew he wasn't fooling her. He felt her body shaking with sobs, and he heard her murmuring a prayer in Arabic.

Rita came into the hallway as Mellberg slammed the front door shut.

'Shh,' she told him. 'Leo's asleep on the sofa, and Johanna is downstairs putting Lisa to bed. What's happened?'

Mellberg smelled chilli cooking in the kitchen, and for a moment his anger subsided as his stomach took over. Then he remembered the humiliation he'd suffered and his rage surged.

'My so-called colleagues stabbed me in the back today,' he said, kicking off his shoes so they landed in the middle of the hall rug.

A glance from Rita made him lean down and pick them up. Then he placed them neatly in the shoe rack to the left of the door.

'Come in and tell me what happened,' said Rita, heading for the kitchen. 'I've got something on the hob, and I don't want it to burn.'

Muttering to himself, Mellberg followed. He sank down on to a kitchen chair, sniffing at the air. Something smelled awfully good.

'So tell me,' she said. 'But keep your voice down so you won't wake Leo.'

She waved a wooden spoon at him.

'Maybe I should have something to eat first. I'm so upset. I've never been so badly treated in my whole career. Well, there was that time back in 1986 in Gothenburg when my boss—'

Rita held up her hand.

'The chilli will be ready in ten minutes. Why don't you go snuggle with Leo while you're waiting? He looks so sweet, sleeping on the sofa. Then you can tell me everything while we eat.'

Mellberg did as she said and went into the living room. He never had to be asked twice to see to the little boy who was his godson. He'd been present at Leo's birth, and ever since they'd had a special relationship. The sight of the slumbering child on the sofa made his blood pressure drop. Leo was the best thing that had ever happened to him. Well, besides Rita, of course. Mind you, she was lucky too. Not everyone had such a commendable man at their side. Sometimes it seemed as if she didn't fully comprehend or appreciate that fact. But no doubt she would as the years passed. He was the sort of man who improved with the passage of time.

Leo stirred in his sleep, and Mellberg gently moved him to make room on the sofa. The boy was sunburned and his hair had turned a lighter shade from the sun. He reached out to brush back a lock of hair that had fallen over Leo's face. What a sweet child he was. Mellberg could hardly believe they weren't actually related. But there had to be something to what people said about the strong influence of those you surrounded yourself with in life.

Rita called from the kitchen to tell him dinner was ready, so Mellberg got up without waking Leo. Then he tiptoed to the kitchen and sat down at the table. Rita tasted the food in the saucepan one last time and took two bowls from the cupboard.

'Johanna will come up to eat as soon as Lisa falls asleep. But we might as well start. Where's Paula?'

'Paula?' Mellberg snorted. 'Well, that's the thing. Wait till you hear this.'

He told her all about the meeting, about how he'd made a professional and well-thought-out decision to investigate the matter himself, how he'd come up with the idea of using Ernst's veterinary certificate to get inside the house, how he'd found the child's knickers hidden behind the toilet, how he'd expected a standing ovation for his excellent police work. And how shocked he was by the atrocious way he'd been treated by his colleagues. Mellberg paused to catch his breath and looked at Rita, expecting to be rewarded with sympathy and the big bowl of chilli she was dishing up.

But Rita didn't say a word, and he didn't like the look in her eyes. Then she picked up his bowl and dumped the food back in the saucepan.

Five minutes later Mellberg was standing outside on the street. Something came sailing down from their balcony on the third floor and landed with a thump on the pavement. A bag. From the sound of it, the bag probably contained no more than a toothbrush and a pair of underpants. From the balcony he heard a long, loud series of Spanish swear words. Apparently it was no longer important to keep quiet so as not to wake Leo.

With a heavy sigh, Mellberg picked up the bag and began walking away. The whole world seemed to be against him.

Patrik was bone-tired when he opened the front door. But stepping into the hallway was like stepping into a warm embrace. Outside the porch, the view of the sea was ablaze with an evening sunset, and he could hear the crackling of a fire in the living room. Some people

390

might call him and Erica nuts for lighting a fire in the fireplace on these warm summer nights, but they thought a cosy atmosphere was more important, and they simply opened a couple of windows when it got too hot.

He saw light from the TV was flickering as he went into the living room. If there was ever a time when he needed to snuggle up to Erica, it was an evening like this one.

Her face lit up when she saw him. He sank on to the sofa next to her.

'Bad day?' she asked, and he merely nodded.

The phone had been ringing nonstop. Annika had taken one call after another from the media, from 'concerned citizens', and from crackpots. They'd all asked the same question: was it true the police had arrested someone from the refugee centre for the murder of the little girl? The evening papers had been especially aggressive, and for that reason Patrik had called a press conference for eight tomorrow morning. He wasn't going to get much sleep tonight because he needed to prepare and work out what exactly he wanted to say. The alternative would be to push Mellberg in front of a bus, but they always stuck together at the station. That's just the way it was. For better or worse.

'Tell me,' said Erica, resting her blond head on his shoulder.

She held a glass of red wine towards him, but he shook his head. He needed to be as clear-headed as possible tomorrow.

He told her the whole story, holding nothing back.

'You've got to be joking!' she said, sitting up straight. 'What are you going to do? How are you going to deal with this?'

'I've never felt so ashamed as when I went to the holding cell. Karim had scratched his arms to shreds, and his expression was completely blank.'

'You have nothing to be ashamed of,' said Erica, patting his cheek. 'Has the gossip already started?'

'Yes, I'm afraid so. Right now we're getting a good look at the dark side of humanity. Everyone is saying they "knew all along it had to be one of those foreigners who did it".'

Patrik massaged his forehead.

Everything was suddenly so very complicated. He loved this place and the people who lived here, but he also knew how easily fear could take hold. In Bohuslän, people clung to tradition and the region had always been a breeding ground for suspicion and distrust of other people. Sometimes he thought nothing much had really changed since the days of Henrik Schartau, the pietistic Lutheran pastor of the eighteenth century. At the same time, people like Bill were proof that there was good in the community too.

'What do the girl's parents say?' asked Erica, turning off the TV so the only light in the room came from the candles and the fireplace.

'They don't know yet, at least not from us. Though they've probably heard about it from others by now. But Gösta is going to drive over there to talk to them first thing in the morning. He's going to show them a picture of the knickers to see if they recognize them.'

'How did the search go at their place?'

'We only managed to search the farmhouse before Mellberg summoned all of us and Torbjörn's team to the refugee centre. The techs were about to start on the barn, but now that will have to wait. Maybe it's no longer necessary.'

'What do you mean? Do you think Karim might be guilty, after all?'

'I don't know,' said Patrik. 'There are too many things that seem a little too convenient. Who made the phone call? How did that person know where the knickers had been hidden in Karim's home? We've listened to the tape, and even though the caller's voice was distorted in some way, we could clearly hear that the person spoke Swedish without an accent. Which immediately makes me suspicious about the caller's motive regarding Karim. But maybe I'm being cynical.'

'No, I'd think the same thing,' said Erica.

Patrik could practically see the gears turning inside her head.

'Was Karim one of the guys from the centre who joined the search party?'

Patrik nodded.

'Yes, he was one of the three men who found her body. And it would have presented a good opportunity to erase any evidence. If we find footprints, fibres, or any other evidence pointing to him, he can simply say that they got there after the body was found.'

'It doesn't sound like the actions of a first-time criminal, if he had thought through everything that carefully.'

'No, I agree. The problem is, we don't know anything about his background except that he came here as a refugee. We know only what he has told us himself, plus anything that might exist in Swedish documents after he arrived here. Which is zero. And I came away with a good impression of him after our conversation. When he understood what it was about, he said that his wife could give him an alibi, and that he had no idea how the knickers ended up in his home. Since his wife and children were so upset, I let him go after he promised to appear for a hearing tomorrow.'

Erica took a sip of her wine. Pensively she twirled the glass in her hand.

'What's this?' he asked, reaching for a colourful advert lying among the papers and file folders spread over the coffee table.

He was too tired to discuss the case any further. He wanted to think about something else before he had to start preparing for the press conference.

'It's an advert for a gallery opening tomorrow. Leif Hermansson's daughter, Viola, is exhibiting some of her paintings. She phoned me a while ago, saying she might have something to tell me, and she asked me to meet her at the gallery.'

'Sounds exciting,' he said, putting down the advert.

The paintings were nice, but art was not really his thing. He preferred photographs, especially in black and white. His favourite was a big framed poster with a black-and-white picture of 'The Boss' in action at Wembley Stadium during the 'Born in the USA' tour. That was something worth looking at. That was art.

Erica placed her hand on Patrik's knee and got up.

'I'm going to bed. Coming with me? Or are you going to stay up for a while?'

She gathered up all the papers and files from the coffee table and stuffed them under her arm.

'You go ahead, sweetheart. I need to work for a couple of hours. I've called a press conference for eight in the morning.'

'Yippie,' said Erica dryly, blowing him a kiss.

The display on Patrik's mobile lit up. He'd turned off the ringer, but when he saw the name *Gösta*, he reached for the phone.

Gösta spoke rapidly, sounding upset, and Patrik felt his heart sink.

'I'm coming,' he said, ending the call.

A minute later he was in his car. As the Volvo roared off towards Tanumshede, he caught a glimpse of the lights in his house in the rear-view mirror. And the silhouette of Erica standing in the doorway, watching him go.

* * *

A man jumped right in front of him and shot him in the chest.

Khalil blinked. His eyes were dry and irritated, not only from all the video games they'd been playing, but also from the wind that had blown in his face during the long sailing lesson. Even though he was still scared, he was looking forward to the practice sessions. At least they were different from everything else he'd ever done.

'I saw Karim come home,' said Adnan, shooting an enemy soldier in the head. 'Bill gave him a lift.'

They had turned off all the lights, and the glow from the TV screen was all that lit up the room.

'Do you know why the police took him in?' asked Adnan.

Khalil thought about the children crying and Amina, who had given them all a proud look before closing the door.

'No idea,' he said. 'We'll have to ask Rolf in the morning.'

Another enemy soldier fell, and Adnan pumped his fist in victory. He'd just won lots of points.

'The police here aren't like back home,' said Khalil, though he could hear how uncertain he sounded.

He didn't actually know much about the Swedish police. Maybe they were as lawless here as they'd been in Syria.

'But what could they have on Karim? I don't think—'

Khalil interrupted Adnan.

'Shh! Listen!'

He turned off the sound of the video game, and they both listened intently. They heard screams coming from outside.

'What could that be?'

Khalil put down the game console. They heard more screams. He looked at Adnan, who tossed aside his console as well. Together they ran out of the room. The screams got louder.

'Fire!' someone shouted, and they saw fire rising into the sky fifty metres away. From Karim's home.

The flames were racing towards them.

Farid came running with a fire extinguisher, but he soon threw it down in frustration.

'It doesn't work!'

Khalil grabbed Adnan's arm.

'We need to fetch water!'

They turned and shouted to everyone they met to bring water. They knew where the hose was that Rolf used to water the lawn around the office building, and that's where they ran, but they could find no containers to hold the water.

'Fetch saucepans, buckets, basins, everything you have!' shouted Khalil. He dashed into the room he shared with Adnan and grabbed two saucepans.

'We need to ring the fire department!' yelled Adnan, and Khalil nodded as he turned on the water.

At that moment they heard sirens approaching.

Khalil turned around, lowering the saucepan he was holding. He let the water spill out. The wind had caused the flames to spread quickly across the dry old wooden buildings, and an entire row was now on fire. A child was screaming shrilly.

Then he heard Karim bellow and saw him come running out of the blazing house. He was dragging someone out. Amina.

Women wept, raising their hands to the night sky where flames and sparks created their own starry firmament. As the fire engines arrived, Khalil sank to the ground and hid his face in his hands. Karim was still bellowing as he held Amina in his arms.

Once again everything was gone.

BOHUSLÄN 1672

They had been avoiding each other all week. What they had experienced had been so intense, so overwhelming for both of them, that afterwards they had simply put on their clothes, brushed off the grass, and hurriedly returned home, taking separate paths. They had not dared look at each other for fear that God's lush vegetation and sky might be reflected in their eyes.

Elin felt as if she were standing on the edge of an abyss that was pulling her forward with irresistible force. She felt dizzy from peering down into the depths, but the mere sight of Preben, seen from a distance as he worked on the farm wearing his white shirt, made her soul long to throw itself in.

Then Britta left for Uddevalla. She would be away for three days. As soon as she was gone, Preben came to Elin in the kitchen and stroked her hand. He looked into her eyes, and after a moment she nodded. She knew what he wanted, and her whole body and soul wanted the same.

Slowly he backed out of the kitchen and headed across the farm towards the meadow. She waited a suitable amount of time so as not to draw attention before heading in the same direction. Then she quickly made her way over to the old cowshed where they had met before. The day was just as lovely and sunny as the previous week, and she felt beads of sweat running down her chest, both from the heat of the sun, from the effort it took to dash across the grass in her heavy skirts, and from the thought of what lay ahead.

He was lying in the grass, waiting for her. His eyes shone with a love so great that she almost flinched. She was frightened, yet she knew this was meant to be. He was in her blood, her limbs, her heart, and in her belief that God had a purpose for everything. Surely the Lord could not have given them this gift of love if He did not mean for them to make use of it. Her God could not be so cruel. And Preben was a man of the church. He, if anyone, must know how to interpret God's will, and he would have stopped if he did not also know this was meant to be.

With fumbling fingers she began to undress. Preben watched her, his chin propped in his hand, never taking his eyes off her even for a second. Finally she stood naked and trembling before him, though without any sense of shame or any desire to hide.

'You are so lovely,' he said, breathlessly.

He held out his hand towards her.

'Help me out of my clothes,' he said as she slowly sank down beside him. Eagerly she began unbuttoning his shirt as he pulled off his trousers.

At last they lay naked together. Gently he ran his finger over the curves of her body. He stopped at the birthmark she had below her right breast and laughed.

'It looks like a map of Denmark.'

'Yes. Maybe Sweden will take it away from me,' she said with a smile.

He caressed her face.

'What are we going to do?'

Elin shook her head. 'Let us not think of that now. This is God's will. Of this I am convinced.'

'You truly believe so?'

His eyes were sorrowful. She leaned forward and kissed him, stroking him at the same time. He groaned and opened his lips to her, and she felt him respond to her touch.

'I know it,' she murmured before slowly sinking down to receive him.

Preben's gaze was fixed on her as he put his hands on her waist and drew her close. As they clung to each other, the sky and sun overhead exploded in light and heat. This must be God's work, thought Elin before she dozed off with her cheek resting against his chest.

'How's Amina doing?' asked Martin when he and Paula entered the waiting room.

Patrik stretched and shifted position on the uncomfortable chair.

'In a critical condition,' he said, getting up to fetch a cup of coffee.

It was his tenth cup. He'd been drinking the disgusting hospital coffee all night in order to stay awake.

'What about Karim?' asked Paula after he sat down again.

'Minor smoke damage to his lungs and burns on his hands from dragging Amina and the children out of the house. The children seem to be fine, thank goodness. They inhaled a lot of smoke and have been treated with oxygen. The doctors are keeping them here for twenty-four hours for observation.'

Paula sighed. 'Who's going to take care of them while their parents are in hospital?'

'I'm waiting for someone from social services to get here. Then we'll find out what they recommend. But they have no relatives, no family at all, from what I understand.'

'We can take them,' said Paula. 'Mamma took the

summer off so she could help us with the baby, and I know she'd say the same thing if she was here.'

'Sure, but what about Mellberg?' said Patrik.

Paula's face darkened.

'When he told Mamma what he'd done, speaking with such pride and claiming to be a victim, Mamma threw him out.'

'She did what?' said Martin.

Patrik stared at Paula. 'Rita threw Bertil out? So where's he staying?'

'I have no idea,' said Paula. 'But as I said, the children can stay with us. Provided social services give their approval.'

'I can't see any reason why they'd object,' replied Patrik.

A doctor came down the corridor towards them, and Patrik stood up. It was Anton Larsson, the consultant who was treating Amina.

'Any news?' asked Patrik, downing the rest of his coffee with a grimace.

'No. Amina's condition is still critical. She inhaled a lot of smoke and suffered third-degree burns to large parts of her body. She's on a respirator and an IV drip to replace the fluid loss caused by the burns. We've been working on her injuries all night.'

'What about Karim?' asked Martin.

'Well, as I told your colleague, he has injuries to the skin on his hands, and his lungs suffered minor smoke damage, but apart from that he is relatively unscathed.'

'Why was Amina much more affected than Karim?' asked Paula.

As yet they knew little about last night's events at the refugee centre. Fire experts were still investigating the cause of the blaze, but arson was suspected.

'That's a question you'll have to put to Karim. He's

awake now, so I can ask him whether he feels up to talking to you.'

'We'd appreciate that,' said Patrik, sitting down again.

The three of them waited in silence until the doctor returned and motioned them to follow.

'I didn't think he'd talk to us,' said Martin.

'Me neither. If I was in his shoes, I'd never want to talk to the police again,' said Paula, standing up.

They walked over to the room where Dr Larsson was waiting and hesitantly stepped inside. Karim was lying in the bed next to the window. When he turned towards them, his face was furrowed with fatigue and fear. His hands, wrapped in gauze, rested on top of the covers.

The tube leading to the bed hummed as it pumped oxygen.

'Thank you for agreeing to speak to us,' said Patrik quietly, pulling a chair over to the bed.

'I want to know who did this to my family,' said Karim groggily, his English more fluent than Patrik's.

He coughed and his eyes filled with tears, but he kept his gaze fixed steadily on Patrik.

Martin and Paula stayed in the background, having silently agreed to let Patrik steer the conversation.

'They say they're not sure whether Amina will survive,' said Karim, suffering another attack of coughing.

Tears ran down his cheeks. He fumbled with the nasal tube delivering oxygen to him.

'They're doing their best to save her,' said Patrik.

The lump in his throat forced him to swallow several times. He knew exactly how Karim was feeling. He was thinking about the time after the car accident that nearly took Erica's life. He would never forget how scared he'd felt.

'What will I do without her? What will the children do without her?' said Karim. This time he didn't cough.

He fell silent, and Patrik didn't know what to say. Instead he asked: 'Can you tell us what you remember about last night? What happened?'

'I . . . I'm not sure,' said Karim, shaking his head. 'It all happened so fast. I was dreaming . . . At first I thought I was back in Damascus and a bomb had exploded. It took a few seconds before I realized where I was . . . Then I ran to get the children. I thought Amina was right behind me. I heard her scream when I awoke. But after I'd carried the children outside, I didn't see her. So I picked up a towel lying on the ground and put it over my mouth and then ran back inside . . .'

His voice faded, and he started coughing again. Patrik handed him a glass of water that was on the bedside table, helping Karim to drink the water through a straw.

'Thank you,' he said, leaning back against the pillows. 'I ran to our bedroom, and she . . .' He held back a sob and went on. 'She was on fire. Amina was on fire. Her hair. Her nightgown. I lifted her up and ran outside and rolled her on the ground. I . . . I could hear the children screaming . . .'

Tears ran down his face as he raised his eyes to look at Patrik.

'They say the children are doing fine. Is that true? They're not lying to me, are they?'

Patrik shook his head.

'No, they're not lying. The children are fine. They're keeping them here for . . .' Frantically he searched for the English word and then realized it was the same as in Swedish. 'For observation.'

For a moment Karim looked relieved, but then his expression once again darkened.

'Where will they stay? The doctors say I have to stay here for several days, and Amina . . .'

Paula took a step forward.

She pulled a chair up to the bed and said quietly: 'I'm not sure whether you'll like this idea, but I suggested the children could stay with me until you're well enough to be discharged. I . . . My mother is a refugee. Like you. From Chile. She came to Sweden in 1973. She understands. I understand. I live with my mother, my two children, and . . .' Paula hesitated. 'And my wife. We'd be happy to take care of your children. If you'll let us.'

Karim studied her face for a long moment. Paula silently waited. Then he nodded.

'Yes. I don't have much choice.'

'Thank you,' Paula said.

'You didn't see anyone last night?' asked Patrik. 'Or hear anything? Before the fire started?'

'No.' Karim shook his head. 'We were tired. After . . . everything. So we went to bed and I fell asleep at once. I didn't see or hear anything. Doesn't anyone know who did this? Why would anyone do something like this? Is it connected to the charges against me?'

Patrik couldn't meet his eye.

'We don't know,' he said. 'But we plan to find out.'

Sam reached for the phone on the bedside table. His mother hadn't come to wake him, which was what James always made her do. Instead, he'd awakened because of nightmares. He used to have them only once or twice a month, but now he was waking up every night drenched in sweat. He couldn't remember a time when he wasn't afraid or haunted by anxiety. Maybe that's why his mother was always going out running, to tire out her body so she wouldn't have any energy left to think. He wished he could do the same.

The faces he'd seen in his dreams were still tormenting him, so he focused his attention on the display of his mobile. Jessie had sent him a text. He felt warmth spread through his groin at the mere thought of her. For the first time in his life someone saw him for who he was and didn't flinch at the darkness she'd discovered.

He was filled with something black that was getting stronger every day. They'd made sure of that. He sensed more than felt the notebook hidden under the mattress. Neither James nor his mother would find it there. The notebook was not meant for anyone's eyes but his own, yet to his surprise he'd been toying with the idea of showing it to Jessie. She was as broken as he was. She would understand.

She would never find out why he'd taken her along on the boating excursion on Monday. He'd decided not to think about that ever again. But it kept returning in his dreams, joining the other demons that plagued him. Yet none of that mattered now. His future was laid out in his notebook. The road was straight and wide, like Highway 66.

He no longer thought about being afraid of what might be hiding around the corner. He knew he could show her the notebook. She would understand.

Today he'd take along everything to show Jessie. All that he'd gathered over the years. He'd already put the files and folders in a bag and placed it by the door.

He sent a text asking her to meet him in half an hour and received an 'okay' in reply. He quickly dressed and slung his backpack over his shoulder. Before he headed for the door to pick up the heavy bag, he turned and looked at his bed. He could almost make out the shape of the notebook hidden there.

Then he swallowed several times, went over to the bed, and lifted the mattress.

Jessie opened the door to find Sam standing there, smiling. The smile he reserved for her alone.

'Hi,' she said.

'Hi.'

He'd brought a backpack, and he was carrying a bag in his hand.

'Wasn't it hard to cycle with all that stuff?'

Sam shrugged.

'It was fine. I'm stronger than I look.'

He set the backpack and bag on the floor and then put his arms around her. He breathed in the scent of her freshly washed hair. She loved knowing that he liked the way she smelled.

'I've brought a few things to show you,' said Sam, going over to the big kitchen table. He started taking items out of the two bags. 'I promised to show you more – about our mothers and the case.'

Jessie looked at the files and folders he'd set on the table. They were labelled with 'Maths' and 'Swedish' and other school subjects.

'James and Mamma thought these files were for school,' said Sam, sitting down on a chair. 'I was able to collect all this material without them noticing.'

Jessie sat down across from him, and together they opened the 'Maths' folder.

'Where did you get all this information?' she asked. 'Aside from the Internet, I mean.'

'Mostly from the newspaper archives at the library.'

Jessie was looking at pictures of her mother, Marie, and Sam's mother, Helen. School photos of the two girls.

'Imagine – they were younger than we are now,' she said.

Sam ran his index finger over the article.

'They must have been carrying a darkness inside them,' he said. 'Just like you and I do.'

Jessie shivered. She leafed through the other material

in the folder and caught sight of a photo showing a smiling Stella.

'But what made them do it? How could anyone get so angry at . . . a child?'

Jessie tapped on the photo, and Sam stood up. His face was flaming red.

'Because of . . . the darkness, Jessie! Bloody hell, don't you understand? Why can't you UNDERSTAND?'

Jessie flinched. All she could do was stare at him. Where was this sudden anger coming from? She couldn't keep back her tears.

The anger faded from Sam's face. He knelt down in front of her.

'I'm sorry, so sorry,' he said, hugging her legs as he buried his face in her lap. 'I didn't mean to lose my temper. I'm just so damn frustrated. I have all this fury boiling inside me, and sometimes it gets so bad I want . . . I want to blow up the whole world.'

Jessie nodded. She knew exactly what he meant. There was only one person in the world she cared about, and it was Sam. Everyone else seemed to want to humiliate her, make her feel small and powerless.

'I'm sorry,' he repeated, wiping away her tears. 'I would never do anything to hurt you. You're the only one I don't want to harm.'

The wooden planks of the dock felt warm against her legs, almost hot. The ice cream was melting faster than Vendela could eat it. But Basse was having even more trouble than she was. He was frantically licking the chocolate ice cream from his arm. Sometimes he seemed such a child.

Vendela couldn't help laughing. She leaned closer to Nils, who put his arm around her. When she was this close to him, everything seemed good again. It made her forget the images she'd seen on the Internet this morning. The buildings on fire. How did it get so out of hand? That couldn't possibly have anything to do with them, could it?

Basse had finally had enough of the melting ice cream and threw the rest in the water, where a seagull instantly dived after it.

He turned away from the bird to look at them.

'Mamma and Pappa won't be coming home this weekend, like they planned,' he said. 'They'll be away for another week.'

'Time to party,' said Nils, smiling at Basse, whose face took on that uncertain look, which could be so annoying.

Vendela sighed, and Nils grinned.

'Hey, come on! Think of it as a pre-celebration to the school dance next Saturday! We'll invite over some people, get some booze, and make a bonfire.'

'I don't know . . .'

But Nils had already won. Vendela knew that.

Again she pictured the smouldering ruins. She wanted to erase it from her mind, along with the headline that screamed: 'Woman seriously injured.' And suddenly she knew what she wanted to do.

Nils had wanted to wait to post Jessie's naked picture until school started, in order to get maximum attention. But what if they put it up a little early?

'I have an idea,' she said.

Bengt came out to the yard to meet Gösta as he parked the police car. He took a deep breath before getting out of the vehicle. He already knew what direction this conversation would take.

'Is it true that you've arrested one of those refugees?'

Bengt was pacing back and forth.

'I heard he even participated in the search party!

They've got no bloody conscience at all, those guys. You should have listened to me from the start!'

'We don't know anything for certain yet,' replied Gösta, heading for the house.

He felt his stomach lurch, as it always did, when he saw Nea's clothes still hanging on the line to dry at the side of the house. He found the spiteful glee on Bengt's face unpleasant, especially now, after the fire, yet he felt a certain empathy for the grieving man. And he also understood the human desire for a simple solution. The problem was that simple answers were rarely the right ones. Reality had a tendency to be more complicated.

'Mind if I go in?' he asked Bengt, who opened the front door for him.

'Could you ask Peter and Eva to come downstairs?' Bengt said to his wife, who nodded.

Peter appeared first, followed a minute later by Eva. They looked half-asleep.

Peter sat down and motioned for Gösta to do the same.

It was starting to feel very familiar, sitting at this kitchen table. Gösta wished he could come here with news that the case had been solved. Instead, once again he was about to disappoint them. And their faith in him had suffered as a result of yesterday's search. He no longer knew how to approach the family. He was as upset as Patrik about the fire and the way Mellberg had treated Karim and his family. Yet he could not rule out the possibility that they'd found conclusive evidence in Karim's home and that he might be the perpetrator. Everything was so muddled and confusing.

'Is it true?' asked Peter. 'About the man at the refugee centre?'

'We don't know anything for sure at the moment,' Gösta replied cautiously. He saw Bengt's face turning red, his mouth opening to interrupt, and hurried to finish what he had come to say: 'We've found something, but because of certain . . . technicalities, we're not sure at the moment what it might signify.'

'I heard you found Nea's clothes at his place. Is that true?' asked Peter.

'People have been ringing us,' said Bengt. 'We find out things from other people, but not from you. It's—'

He had raised his voice again, but Peter held up his hand towards his father and then said calmly, 'Is it true that you've found Nea's clothes at the home of someone living at the refugee centre?'

'We've found one item of clothing,' said Gösta, taking a plastic folder out of his bag. 'But we need your help to identify it.'

Eva whimpered, and Ulla patted her arm. Eva didn't seem to notice as she kept staring at the folder in Gösta's hand.

'Do you recognize this item of clothing?' he asked, placing several photographs on the kitchen table.

Eva gasped.

'Those knickers belong to Nea. Her *Frozen* knickers.'

Gösta looked at the pictures of the blue knickers with the blonde princess and asked again: 'Are you sure? Do these knickers belong to Linnea?'

'Yes!' said Eva, nodding vigorously.

'And you let him go!' said Bengt.

'There are certain problems with the way this piece of clothing was found.'

Bengt snorted. '*Certain problems*? You have a foreigner who comes here and kidnaps a little girl and kills her – and you're talking about problems?'

'I understand why you're upset, but we have to—'

'We don't have to anything! I told you from the beginning that it had to be one of them, but you wouldn't listen. You've been wasting time and keeping us wondering what happened to Nea, and now you've let the killer go free! What's more, you've turned this house upside down and treated my son and his wife like suspects. Have you no *shame*?'

'Pappa, calm down,' said Peter.

'How can it not be him if you found her knickers there? We heard about a fire. Was he trying to hide more evidence? Since you let him go, it's only logical that he'd try to erase all traces. That must be why he joined the search party in the first place.'

'The cause of the fire has not yet been determined.'

Gösta considered telling them that Karim had been injured and his wife was in intensive care and it wasn't known whether she'd ever regain consciousness. But he chose not to say anything. He didn't think they'd be receptive to anyone else's sorrow at the moment, and besides, Fjällbacka's highly efficient gossip grapevine would ensure they were soon informed.

'Are you positive these are the knickers she was wearing when she disappeared?' Gösta asked, looking at Eva.

She hesitated for a second but then nodded.

'She had five pairs like that, in different colours. The others are here at home.'

'Okay,' said Gösta.

He put the photos back in the folder and stood up.

Bengt clenched his fists.

'Make sure you arrest that damn wog soon, or I'll take matters into my own hands.'

Gösta looked at him. 'You have all my sympathy for what you're going through. But nobody, I repeat *nobody*, should do anything that will make the situation worse.'

Bengt merely snorted, but Peter nodded.

'His bark is worse than his bite,' he said.

'I hope that's true. For his sake,' said Gösta.

As he drove away from the farm he saw Peter standing in the doorway, watching him. Something was nagging at Gösta. Something was bothering him, but he couldn't for the life of him work out what it could be. It was something he'd missed, but the more he tried to identify it, the more it slipped away. He cast another glance in the rear-view mirror. Peter was still standing there, watching him drive away.

'Hello? Is anyone here?'

It was Rita's voice that woke him. Mellberg opened his eyes, not sure where he was. Then he saw Annika standing in the doorway.

'Oh, it's you,' he said, getting up.

He rubbed his eyes.

'What are you doing here?' asked Annika. 'You nearly scared the living daylights out of me when I heard a noise coming from in here. Why are you here so early?'

She crossed her arms over her ample breasts.

'Well, er, you might say I'm actually here very late . . .' said Mellberg, trying to smile.

He didn't want to tell Annika what had happened, but the news would soon spread through the station like wildfire, so he might as well.

'Rita threw me out,' he said, pointing to his bag.

Rita hadn't packed his favourite flannel pyjamas, so he'd had to sleep in his clothes. And the minuscule room here at the station was meant only for a few hours' rest, not an overnight stay, so it was as stuffy and hot as a steam bath.

He looked down at his sweaty and wrinkled clothes.

'Well, I would have done the same thing!' said Annika before turning on her heel and heading for the kitchen. Halfway there, she paused and shouted: 'I assume you've been sound asleep and haven't heard what happened, right?'

'I can't say I got a good night's sleep,' said Mellberg, limping after her. 'That camp bed is terribly uncomfortable, and there's no air conditioning, and my skin is very sensitive, so it itches if the bedclothes aren't good quality, in fact it felt like they were made of cardboard, so I . . .'

He paused and tilted his head to one side.

'Could you get me a cup of coffee, dear, if you're going to make a fresh pot?'

He realized he'd said the wrong thing the second the word 'dear' crossed his lips, and he steeled himself for Annika's reaction, but she merely sat down at the kitchen table.

'Someone set fire to the refugee centre last night,' she said in a low voice. 'Karim and his family are in hospital.'

Mellberg clutched his chest. He sank heavily on to a chair across from Annika.

'Was it because . . . because of what I did?'

His tongue felt big and thick in his mouth. It was all he could do to look her in the eye.

'We don't know. But yes, that may well be the reason, Bertil. People have been ringing the station nonstop, so I switched the phone over to my home last night, and I've hardly slept. Patrik is with Martin and Paula at the hospital. Karim's wife is in a medically induced coma. The burns she suffered are so serious that the doctors don't know whether she'll survive, and Karim injured his hands when he pulled her out of the burning building.'

'What about the children?' asked Mellberg, dread growing inside him.

'They're being kept under observation at the hospital until tomorrow, but they seem to be fine. No one else was injured, thank goodness. Those whose homes were destroyed have been evacuated to the community centre.'

413

'Good lord,' said Mellberg, his voice barely above a whisper. 'Do we know who did it?'

'No, so far we don't. But we've received plenty of tips, so we need to go through them as quickly as possible. The callers have ranged from crackpots who think the refugees set fire to the place themselves in order to gain sympathy, to people who claim right-wing extremists are behind the arson. The fire seems to have divided the town into two camps. There are still a lot of people who think it's what the refugees deserve. On the other hand, we have people like Bill Andersson, who've spent the night mobilizing resources and ferrying refugees left homeless by the fire to the community centre. People have been bringing them all sorts of things they might need. You might say the situation is showing people at their best and at their worst.'

'But I . . .' Mellberg shook his head, hardly able to go on. 'I didn't mean to . . . I didn't think . . .'

'No, that's just it, Bertil,' said Annika with a sigh. 'You don't think.'

She stood up and began making coffee.

'Did you say you'd like a cup?'

'Yes, please,' he said.

He swallowed hard.

'What are the chances?'

'Of what?' asked Annika, sitting down across from him again as the coffee maker began chuffing.

'That his wife will make it.'

'Not good, from what I understand,' said Annika quietly.

Mellberg didn't say a word. He knew he'd made a huge mistake. All he could do now was hope that he'd be able to make amends.

BOHUSLÄN 1672

Towards the end of the summer, Elin began to worry. At first she thought it was a late summer ailment that was making her run behind the barn to vomit. Yet she knew better. The same thing had happened when she was expecting Märta. Every night she prayed to God. What was His purpose behind this? What sort of test was she being asked to endure? And should she tell Preben or not? How would he react? She knew that he loved her, but deep in her heart she had misgivings about his fortitude. Preben was a good man, but he was also ambitious and eager to please – that much she had learned about him. All her questions about what this might lead to and how it could go on had always been silenced with kisses and love-making, but not before she glimpsed the anxious look in his eyes.

And there was Britta to consider. She had become increasingly surly and suspicious. They had done their best to hide their feelings for one another, but Elin knew there were moments when she and Preben, in Britta's presence, had caught sight of each other and were unable to conceal how they felt. She knew her sister all too well. She knew what Britta was capable of. Even though it was a topic she had never discussed with anyone, Elin had not forgotten how Märta had nearly drowned in the lake. Nor had she forgotten who was responsible.

As the days grew shorter and everyone worked even harder on the farm to make preparations for winter's arrival, Britta withdrew more and more. She stayed in bed longer in the morning, refusing to get up. All strength seemed to be seeping out of her.

Preben asked the cook to make Britta's favourite foods, but she refused to eat, and every evening Elin had to remove the untouched food from the bedside table. At night Elin caressed her stomach, wondering how Preben would react if she told him she was carrying his child. She could only think he would be glad. He and Britta seemed unable to have children, and he did not love Britta the way he loved her. What if Britta had now contracted some fatal illness? Then Elin and Preben would be able to live together as a family. When she had such thoughts, Elin would pray even more fervently to God.

Britta grew inexplicably weaker day by day. Finally, Preben summoned a doctor from Uddevalla. Elin was overcome with tension and concern as they awaited the doctor's arrival. She frantically tried to convince herself it was concern for her sister, but the only thing she could think about was if Britta should be taken badly, there would suddenly be a future for her and Preben. Even though they would be met with suspicion and whispers if they should marry so soon after Preben became a widower, the talk would subside over time. Of that she was certain.

When the wagon bringing the doctor arrived, Elin kept away and prayed. She prayed harder than she had ever prayed before. And she hoped God would not punish her for the entreaties delivered in her prayers. Deep in her soul she believed that God wanted her and Preben to be together. Their love was too great to be mere chance.

The fact that Britta was now ill had to be part of God's plan. The more she prayed, the more convinced she became. Britta would not live much longer. Elin's unborn child would have a father. They would be a family. She put her trust in God.

Her heart pounding, Elin went back to the vicar's house. None of the other servants had said anything, so she assumed they had not yet heard. Gossip usually travelled fast on the farm, and she knew there had been whispering about her and Preben. Nothing escaped the servants' notice on such a small farm. And they had been talking for days about the fact that the doctor had been summoned from Uddevalla to find out what was ailing their mistress.

'Have you heard anything, Elsa?' Elin asked the cook who was preparing the evening meal.

'No,' said Elsa as she continued to stir the big pot. 'I think the doctor is still with her.'

'I will go and see if I can find out more,' said Elin, without meeting the cook's eyes. 'She is my sister, after all.'

She was afraid the woman might be able to see from her appearance what she had been praying for, or that her pounding heart might make itself heard. But the cook merely nodded and did not turn around.

'Do that. When the mistress does not eat my pancakes, I know things are not right. But we must trust in God that it is nothing serious.'

'Yes, we must trust in God,' said Elin, hurrying to the door.

For a long moment she hesitated outside Britta's bedchamber. She was not sure she dared knock. Then the door opened, and a thickset man with a bushy moustache came out carrying a doctor's bag.

Preben shook his hand.

417

'I cannot thank you enough, Dr Brorsson,' he said, and Elin was surprised to see that he was smiling.

What news could the doctor have delivered to make Preben smile so his eyes gleamed in the dark of the hall? A hard knot formed in Elin's stomach.

'This is Britta's sister, Elin,' said Preben, introducing her to the doctor.

Warily she shook his hand. She was still having trouble deciphering the expression on the faces of the two men. Behind them she saw Britta sitting in bed, her dark hair spread out on the pillows.

She looked like a cat who had swallowed the cream, and Elin felt even more bewildered.

Dr Brorsson said with a sly look:

'It would seem congratulations are in order. She is only a few weeks along, but there is no doubt Britta is with child. Her condition is taking its toll on her, so you must see to it she takes in enough fluids and as much sustenance as she can tolerate. I have recommended that she should be given bouillon for the next few weeks until the discomfort has passed and her appetite returns.'

'I am certain Elin will be most helpful,' said Preben, beaming with joy.

Why did he look so happy? He did not want to be with Britta, he wanted to be with her. That was what he had said. He had told her he had chosen the wrong sister. It had been God's will that his seed refused to grow inside Britta.

But now he stood there with a big smile, promising Dr Brorsson that Elin would offer her best nursing skills. Britta gave her a maliciously gleeful look. She reached up to brush back her hair and whimpered:

'Preben, I am feeling ill again.'

She held out her hand, and Elin watched as he rushed to Britta's side.

'Is there anything I can do? You heard what the doctor said. Rest and bouillon. Shall I ask Elsa to make you some bouillon?'

Britta nodded. 'Not that I have any appetite to speak of, but for the sake of our child, it is best I try to eat something. But please do not leave me. Ask Elin to speak to Elsa and bring the bouillon. I am certain she will gladly do that. She wants her little nephew or niece to be born with the best possible health.'

'I am certain that is true,' said Preben. 'But I must see to it that Dr Brorsson takes his leave before I can stay with you.'

'No, no, I can certainly find my own way out,' laughed the doctor, heading for the door. 'Take care of the little mother, then I will know that I have done my job properly.'

'Very well,' said Preben, nodding as he clasped Britta's hand in both of his.

He looked at Elin, who still stood in the doorway as if frozen in place.

'Please be quick about arranging the food for Britta, she must follow the doctor's orders.'

Elin nodded, lowering her eyes.

Keeping her eyes fixed on her shoes was the only thing she could do to prevent herself crying. If she was forced to look at Preben's happy face and Britta's triumphant expression for even a moment longer, she would fall apart. She turned on her heel and swiftly made her way to the kitchen.

The mistress was with child and needed bouillon. And God in His omnipotence was laughing at poor, foolish Elin.

Erica wasn't exactly sure how to dress for a gallery opening, so she had opted for something tried and trusted: a pair of plain white shorts and a white blouse. It was only because she'd left the children with Kristina that she dared wear white. If there was one thing she'd learned as the mother of three young children, it was that white clothing acted like an irresistible magnet to sticky little fingers.

She double-checked the time on the invitation she'd received from Viola, though it wasn't necessary, since she could see a stream of people making their way into the small gallery. Erica looked around when she stepped inside. The room was bright and airy, and Viola's paintings had been nicely hung on the walls. On a table in the corner she saw glasses of champagne and vases with flowers that friends and acquaintances had brought. Erica suddenly felt so stupid. Maybe she should have brought something too.

'Oh, Erica! I'm so glad you could come!'

Viola came forward, giving her a big smile.

She looked fabulous in a beautiful dark blue kaftan, with her grey hair pulled back in a stylish chignon. Erica had always admired people who could wear a kaftan without making it look like a costume. The few times she'd tried on that sort of garment, she'd felt as if she were in a fancy dress costume. But Viola looked radiant.

'Here, have some champagne. You're not driving, are you?' she said, handing Erica a glass.

Erica thought over her plans for the rest of the day and concluded no driving was involved, so she accepted the glass.

'Have a look around,' Viola told her, 'and if you see anything you might like to purchase, just tell that nice girl over there, and she'll put a red dot on the label next to the painting. She's my granddaughter, by the way.'

Viola pointed to a girl in her late teens who stood next to the door holding a strip of red-dot stickers. She seemed to be taking her assignment very seriously.

Erica took her time looking at all the paintings. A few red dots had already appeared, and that made her happy. She liked Viola. And she liked her paintings. She knew nothing about art and didn't feel drawn to any sort of artwork that wasn't representational. But here she saw lovely watercolours with recognizable subjects – mostly people depicted in everyday situations. She stopped in front of a painting showing a blonde woman kneading bread with flecks of flour on her face and a cigarette hanging from her lips.

'That's my mother. All the paintings in the gallery are of people who have been important to me, and I chose to show them in day-to-day situations. No fancy poses. I wanted to paint them the way I remembered them. My mother was always baking. She loved to bake, especially bread. We had fresh bread every day, but with hindsight I've often wondered how much nicotine my siblings and I ingested along with the bread, since my mother always smoked like a chimney when she kneaded the dough. But that wasn't something anyone gave a second thought to in those days.'

'She was beautiful,' said Erica, and she meant it.

The woman in the painting had the exact same glint in her eye as her daughter, and she guessed the two women must have looked very much alike at the same age.

'Yes, she was the most beautiful woman I knew. The most fun too. I'd be satisfied if I was even half as good a mother to my children as she was to me.'

'I'm sure you are,' said Erica, having a hard time thinking otherwise.

Someone tapped Viola on the shoulder, and she excused herself.

Erica stayed where she was, looking at the portrait of Viola's mother. It made her both happy and sad. Happy because she wished everyone could have a mother who radiated such warmth. Sad because that was far from what she and Anna had experienced when they were growing up. Their mother had never baked bread or smiled or hugged her children or said she loved them.

Erica suddenly felt guilty. She'd vowed she would be the direct opposite of her mother. Always warm, fun, and loving. Yet right now she was working on her book, and she'd arranged for Kristina to babysit the children. But she did give her kids lots of love, and they enjoyed being with their grandmother or spending time with their cousins at Anna's home. It was not a hardship for them. And if she didn't work, she would no longer be Erica. She loved her children, and she also loved her job.

Slowly she moved from one painting to the next as she sipped her glass of bubbly. The gallery was an attractive, air-conditioned space, and it didn't feel crowded in spite of all the people. Occasionally she overheard someone whisper her name, and she'd seen several women giving their companions a poke in the side. That was something she still hadn't grown used to – the fact

422

that people recognized her and viewed her as some sort of celebrity. So far she'd been able to avoid the worst celebrity traps. She hadn't gone to any film premieres, hadn't wrestled with snakes and rats on the TV show *Fångarna på fortet*, hadn't spilled her heart out on the talk show *Hellenius Hörna*, or appeared on the TV show *På sporet*.

'That's my father,' said a voice next to Erica, who gave a start.

Viola had returned and was now pointing at a large painting in the middle of the wall. It had an entirely different aura to the portrait of her mother. Erica tried to put into words the feeling depicted and decided it had to be 'melancholy'.

'Pappa sitting at his desk. That's how I remember him, always working. As a child, I couldn't understand it, but as an adult I understand and respect his passion for his job, which could be both a blessing and a curse. As the years passed, it ate him up . . .'

The meaning of what she'd said hung in the air. Then she turned to Erica.

'Sorry. There's a reason I asked you to come here. I found Pappa's old diary. I don't know whether it will be of any use to you. He used abbreviations for everything, but I thought you might want to see it anyway. I brought it with me, if you'd like to have it.'

'Yes, I would,' said Erica. 'Thank you.'

She hadn't been able to stop thinking about why Leif would so drastically change his view about the girls' guilt. One way or another, she wanted to get to the bottom of this. Maybe his diary would provide a new lead.

'Here,' said Viola, coming back with a well-worn black diary. 'You can keep it.'

She handed it to Erica.

'I have Pappa here,' she said, pointing to her heart. 'I

can recreate him in my memory whenever I like. Sitting at his desk.'

She placed her hand lightly on Erica's shoulder, then left her standing in front of the painting. Erica studied it for a moment. Then she went over to speak to the girl holding the strip of red dots.

Khalil was sitting on a chair in the corner, watching an elderly woman as she handed blankets to Adnan. He couldn't forget the image of Karim dragging Amina out of the house. The way his hands had smouldered. The way he had screamed. And the way Amina had been so horribly silent.

After the fire, Bill, their Swedish teacher Sture, and more people that Khalil didn't know had turned up. Apparently, Rolf and Bill had joined forces to ferry them to the community centre. Bill had waved his arms about, talking too fast in his strange mixture of Swedish and English, as he pointed at the cars, but no one had dared get in until Khalil, Adnan and the others on the sailing team had each climbed into a car.

They had exchanged quizzical glances when they arrived at the red building at the other end of Tanumshede. How would things go in this place? But over the last half hour people had begun streaming in. Dumbfounded, they had watched car after car pull into the parking area in front of the big building, bringing blankets, Thermoses of coffee, and clothes and toys for the children. Some people simply dropped off what they'd brought and then left, while others had stayed and were now doing their best to chat.

Where had all these Swedes been before? They smiled, talked, asked the children their names, offered food and clothing. Khalil couldn't understand it.

Adnan came over to him, his eyebrows raised enquiringly. Khalil shrugged.

'Listen here, boys,' called Bill from a short distance away. 'I've talked to the folks at Hedemyrs supermarket, and they said they want to donate some food. Could you drive over there and pick it up? Take my car keys.'

Bill tossed the keys to Adnan, who caught them in mid-air.

'Sure, we'll go,' said Khalil.

When they got outside to the car park, he held out his hand.

'Give me the keys.'

'I want to drive,' said Adnan, holding the key ring in a tight grip.

'Forget it. I'm driving.'

Reluctantly Adnan opened the door on the passenger side. Khalil got into the driver's seat and looked first at the keys, then at the dashboard.

'There's nowhere to put in the key.'

'You just press the start button,' said Adnan with a sigh.

Cars were his biggest interest other than video games, but he got most of his knowledge from YouTube.

Khalil looked sceptical as he pressed the button labelled 'Stop/Start'. The car started up with a rumble.

Adnan grinned.

'Do you suppose Bill knows neither of us has a driver's licence?'

Khalil found himself smiling, in spite of everything.

'Would he have given us his car keys if he knew?'

'This is Bill we're talking about,' said Adnan. 'Of course he would. You do know how to drive, don't you? If not, I'm getting out right now.'

Khalil began backing up.

'Don't worry. My father taught me.'

He reversed out of the car park and turned on to the road. It was only a few hundred metres to Hedemyrs.

'Swedes are so strange,' said Adnan, shaking his head.

'What do you mean?' asked Khalil, pulling into the car park behind the supermarket.

'They treat us like lepers, they say all sorts of shit about us, they throw Karim in jail, and they try to burn us alive. But then they want to help us. I don't get it.'

Khalil shrugged.

'I don't think everyone is going to bring us blankets,' he said, pressing the stop button. 'There are probably a lot of people who wish we'd all died in the fire.'

'Do you think they'll come back and try again?' asked Adnan.

Khalil got out and closed the car door. He shook his head.

'People who sneak around and set fires under the cover of night are cowards. Too many people are watching now.'

'Do you think this would have happened if the police hadn't taken Karim in?' asked Adnan, holding open the supermarket door for Khalil.

'Who knows? The anger has probably been smouldering for a while. Maybe that's all that was needed to make words turn into action.'

Khalil looked around. Bill hadn't said who they were supposed to talk to, so after a moment he went over to a young man who was unpacking tinned goods in one of the aisles.

'You should probably talk to the boss,' he said. 'He's in his office.'

The young man pointed to the back of the shop.

Khalil hesitated. What if the man knew nothing about donating food? Maybe Bill hadn't talked to the right person. What if the boss thought they had come here to beg?

Adnan took his arm.

'Come on. Might as well talk to him, now we're here.'

Ten minutes later they were filling the boot of the car with sandwiches, soft drinks, fruit, and even some sweets for the children. Khalil again shook his head. The Swedes certainly were strange.

It felt as if her feet were flying across the gravel. This was the routine that had kept her alive. Getting up each morning, putting on her running clothes, lacing up her shoes, and going out to run.

Over the years Helen had improved. Oddly enough, marathons didn't discriminate in terms of age. The younger runners had an advantage when it came to energy and strength, but the older runners compensated for this with experience. It was always amusing to see cocky young runners on their first marathon get outrun by a woman old enough to be their mother.

Helen felt the warning signs of a stitch in her side, which forced her to calm her breathing. She had no intention of giving in today.

The police had taken into custody the man from the refugee centre, and then someone had set fire to the place. Helen was horrified when she saw the pictures, but almost immediately it had crossed her mind that now she and Marie would come under scrutiny again. One of them would be suspected. Or both.

She and Marie had both had so many dreams, so many plans. When they turned eighteen they were going to leave everything behind and buy one-way tickets to America, where all sorts of wonderful things would await them. Marie had actually gone there. She had fulfilled her dreams, while Helen had stayed here. Dutiful. Obedient. All those traits that had made her a victim from the start. Marie would never have accepted Helen's fate. She would have fought hard against it.

But Helen was not Marie. All her life she had done what others told her to do.

She had followed Marie's career, read about her life and her reputation for being difficult, cold, and at times even nasty. A bad mother who sent her daughter to boarding schools all over the world and was constantly photographed partying with different men. But Helen saw something else. She saw the girl who was never afraid of anything, who always tried to protect her, who would have given her the sun and the moon.

That was why Helen had never been able to tell her. How could she? Marie had been powerless, a mere child. What could she have done?

She thought she'd caught a glimpse of Marie when she was grocery shopping yesterday. She'd seen only a slight movement in her peripheral vision, but Marie's presence was so strong. When Helen looked up, she saw only an elderly man with a cane, but she could have sworn Marie had been there, looking at her.

The gravel road passed swiftly as her feet rhythmically pounded the ground. Her right foot forward, her right arm back. She glanced at her pulse watch. She was making better time than ever, maybe because the rhythmic pace forced out everything else.

There were so many memories she tried to avoid. And there was Sam. Her wonderful Sam. He had never had a chance. He was condemned before he was even born, infected by her sins. How could she have believed that the years would make everything disappear, that it would all slip into the dark water of forgetfulness? Nothing ever disappeared. She, more than anyone, should have known that.

Helen ran with her gaze fixed on the horizon. She was thirteen when she started running. And she didn't dare slow down now.

* * *

Jessie pushed aside the last folder containing articles about Helen, Marie, and Stella. She looked at Sam. His expression could be so open one moment, so closed the next. In the very back of the folder he had included a handwritten sheet with his thoughts about the murder. Reading them was like seeing her own thoughts in print. But there was a difference. He had taken everything one step further.

What should she say to him now? What did he want to hear?

Sam reached for his backpack.

'There's something I'd like to show you,' he said.

He took out a worn notebook and leafed through it. All of a sudden he looked so vulnerable.

'I . . .' Jessie began.

That was as far as she got. A loud knock on the door made both of them jump.

When Jessie opened the door, she took a step back in surprise. Vendela was standing on the porch. She didn't look at Jessie. Her eyes were fixed on her shoes, and she was nervously shifting her weight from one foot to the other.

'Hi,' she said in a low voice, sounding almost shy.

'Hi,' Jessie managed to say.

'I . . . I don't know what Sam has told you about us, but I thought that . . . maybe . . .'

Jessie heard Sam give a snort behind her. He was leaning against the wall in the entryway. His expression was almost wickedly dark.

'Oh hi, Sam,' said Vendela.

Sam didn't reply, so Vendela turned her attention back to Jessie.

'I was wondering if you'd like to come over to my place and hang out for a while. It's only ten minutes away by bike. Do you have a bike?'

'Yes, I have a bike.'

Jessie could feel her cheeks burning. Vendela was one of the most popular girls. One look at her was enough to tell you that. And none of the popular kids had ever come to see her like this. Or asked her to come over and hang out.

'Don't tell me you're buying any of this,' said Sam.

He was still glaring at Vendela, and Jessie was starting to feel annoyed. It was a big deal that Vendela had come to see her, and this was an opportunity for both Jessie and Sam to ensure that their school days would be more tolerable. What did he think she should do? Slam the door in the girl's face?

Vendela held up her hands.

'Believe me, I'm really ashamed of what we did to Sam. Nils and Basse are too, but they didn't dare come over here to apologize. You know how boys are . . .'

Jessie nodded. She turned to Sam.

'Let's meet later. Okay?' she said in a low voice.

Why couldn't he drop his stupid pride and tell her it was okay, that of course she should go hang out with Vendela? But his eyes narrowed. Then he went over to the table and gathered up all the folders and stuffed them in his backpack and bag. She thought she saw him wipe away a tear from his cheek as he tossed the worn notebook into his backpack.

He walked past Jessie without saying a word, but then he paused in the doorway, standing very close to Vendela.

'If I hear that you guys treat her badly . . .'

He fell silent but gave her one last stare before he went over to his bicycle. Then he took off.

'You'll have to excuse Sam . . . He . . .'

Jessie searched for the right words, but Vendela merely shook her head.

'I get it. We've been mean to Sam since he was a kid,

so it's only natural he's cross. I would be too. But we're older now, and we understand things we didn't get before.'

Jessie nodded.

'I know exactly what you mean. Actually.'

Did she? Jessie wasn't sure, but Vendela clapped her hands.

'Okay!' she said. 'Hop on your bike, and let's get going!'

Jessie went over to her bicycle. It had come with the house and looked shiny and new and expensive, which made her happy when she saw Vendela's envious look.

'Nice place you live in!' she said as they cycled towards Hamngatan.

'Thanks!' called Jessie, feeling butterflies in her stomach.

Vendela was so . . . perfect. Jessie could have killed to be wearing short denim cut-offs like Vendela had on.

They passed the town square, which was bustling with people. She caught a glimpse of Marie behind the film cameras. She was talking to the director. Jörgen. Marie occasionally mentioned him.

Jessie had a sudden idea.

'My mother's over there,' she called to Vendela. 'Want to say hi?'

Vendela looked at her. 'If it's okay with you, I'd rather go home and hang out. I don't want to be rude or anything, but . . .'

Jessie felt her heart skip a beat. This was the first time, except with Sam, that someone didn't care who her mother was. If only Sam had been here now, he would have seen how honest and sincere Vendela was.

As she pedalled hard up the steep slope of Galärbacken, she had a feeling she couldn't identify. Then she worked out what it was. This must be what happiness felt like.

* * *

Sanna's head was pounding when she unlocked the front door and went in. It seemed worse than usual. She went over to the worktop in the kitchen and poured herself a big glass of water. She loved to eat among the flowers in the garden centre, but today she'd forgotten to bring a lunch, so she decided to go home. Cornelia could hold down the fort for an hour.

When Sanna opened the fridge she wanted to cry. Aside from a tube of tomato purée and a jar of mustard, there were only a few sad-looking vegetables that had definitely passed their sell-by date.

She knew what was haunting her. It was all her thoughts about Marie and Helen. About Stella and that little girl named Nea. About the shadow in the woods. The one that had scared her so badly. Last night these thoughts had tormented her. Thoughts about the man who had come and asked her about the shadow in the woods, and who it was Stella had played with. Had she lied to him? She couldn't remember. Didn't want to remember. Then he'd vanished, and her dreams were all about the girl with the green eyes.

At least he hadn't come back to ask her more questions.

Sanna gave a start when she heard girls' voices approaching. Vendela was rarely home. She spent most of her time running around with those two boys from her class, and she definitely didn't have any friends who were girls. But here she was now, wheeling her bike across the lawn, as usual, but this time with a big blonde girl walking alongside.

Sanna frowned. There was something familiar about that girl, but she couldn't put her finger on what it was. Probably one of the girls Vendela had been friends with when she was younger. Sanna had never managed to keep track of all of Vendela's friends.

'Hi!' said Vendela. 'You're home?'

'No, I'm back at the garden centre,' said Sanna, immediately regretting her words.

She should be the grown-up here. No need for sarcasm. But Vendela had looked so disappointed to see her.

'Hi,' said the big girl, holding out her hand. 'I'm Jessie.'

'Sanna. Vendela's mother,' she said, looking at the girl.

She did look familiar. Could she be the one whose mother was a teacher at the school? Or was she the one who lived in the house where the road turned? The one who had played with Vendela when they were kids?

'So, have you and Vendela been friends long?' Sanna asked. 'You've all grown so big that I hardly recognize any of you.'

'Mamma . . .'

'I just moved here,' said Jessie. 'My mother is working here, so we'll be staying for a while.'

'I see. How nice.'

Sanna could have sworn she knew this girl.

'We're going up to my room,' said Vendela, already halfway up the stairs.

'Nice to meet you,' said Jessie, following Vendela.

A door slammed and soon music started blasting away. Sanna sighed. So much for a peaceful lunch break.

She opened the freezer to see what she could find. It was a little more promising than the fridge. She found some frozen beef hash in the very back. She got out a frying pan, added a big dab of butter, and then put in the hash.

A short time later she was sitting at the kitchen table with a cup of coffee. She cast a pensive glance up at the ceiling where she now heard dance music pounding from her daughter's bedroom. Where had she seen that girl before?

She reached for a tabloid that lay on the table and

began leafing through it. An issue of *Veckans Nu*. A trashy publication Vendela insisted on bringing home. Page after page of meaningless news about meaningless celebrities. She turned the page and there was Marie, smiling. And suddenly Sanna knew who the girl was.

Black spots danced before her eyes. Jessie. Marie's daughter. The girl she'd seen in the window at Marie's place. She had Marie's eyes. Those same green eyes that Sanna had seen so many times in her dreams over the years.

From upstairs came the sound of girlish laughter above the music. Sanna's mouth had gone dry. Marie's daughter was here, in her house. Should she do something? Should she say something? The girl was not to blame for what her mother had done. That was obvious. But the walls were closing in on her, and her throat tightened.

Sanna grabbed her car keys and rushed out of the house.

'All right. There's something we need to decide,' said Patrik, clasping his hands over his stomach and staring at his shoes.

No one said a word.

'What do you think? Should Mellberg be included in the meeting?'

'He realizes he brought this on himself,' said Annika in a low voice. 'I'm not usually the one to come to Bertil's defence, but in this case, I actually think he realizes his mistake and genuinely wants to help.'

'Sure, but wanting to help and being able to help are two different things,' said Paula dryly.

'He's the station's chief of police,' said Patrik, standing up. 'Whatever we may think about it, that's the reality.'

He was gone a few minutes before returning with a subdued Mellberg. Ernst padded a few steps behind his master, hanging his head as if he too had fallen into disfavour.

'So,' said Patrik, sitting down again. 'Now we're all here.'

Mellberg took his seat at the foot of the table, and Ernst lay down on the floor beside him.

'From now on, I'd like all of us to work together in the same direction. We will do our job in a professional manner and not allow emotions to get the better of us. We need to focus on two things. First, the ongoing investigation into the murder of Linnea Berg. And second, the matter of who set fire to the refugee centre.'

'How should we proceed?' asked Martin.

'Yes, how do you want to divide up the work?' said Gösta.

'There are a number of things we need to do. Annika, will you take notes?'

Annika held up her pen in confirmation.

'First, we need to interview everyone from the refugee centre. We'll start with the people who lived closest to Karim and his family. From what I understand, those whose homes were destroyed have been given shelter at the community centre until permanent housing can be found for them. Paula and Martin, could you take this assignment?'

They both nodded.

'Gösta, what did Eva and Peter say about the knickers? Could they identify them as Nea's?'

'Yes,' said Gösta. 'They said she had those kind of knickers, and they could very well be the ones she had on the day she disappeared. But . . .'

'But what?' asked Patrik, pricking up his ears.

Gösta was the most experienced of his colleagues, and it was always worth listening to what he had to say.

'Well, I don't know . . . It's nothing specific, but there's something bothering me. I just can't work out what it is . . .'

'Keep thinking about it and see what you can come up with,' said Patrik. He checked his notes and continued:

'At the top of my list is contacting Torbjörn again. It's been bothering me that we abandoned the search of the Berg family's property halfway through. I discussed this with the prosecutor this morning, and she wants us to finish the search, in spite of what was "found" at Karim's home.'

'I agree,' said Gösta.

Patrik gave him a surprised look. Gösta had been reluctant about the search to begin with. What could have happened to make him so eager for it to be resumed?

'Good,' he said curtly. 'I'll ring Torbjörn and we'll drive out there as soon as we can. With a little luck, we can go today or tomorrow, depending on Torbjörn's caseload.'

'Are they working on the fire?' asked Paula.

Patrik shook his head.

'No, the fire department's arson experts are handling that. But until we know more, the preliminary information is that a Molotov cocktail was thrown through Karim's window.'

'What are we doing about the recording of the anonymous phone call?' asked Paula.

'Annika has it,' said Patrik. 'Feel free to listen and let me know if anything strikes you. The voice is distorted, but I'm going to send it off for analysis today. Hopefully they can do something about the distortion or at least isolate some background sound that will help us identify the caller.'

'Okay,' said Paula.

'What about Helen and Marie?' asked Martin. 'We still don't know whether there's any connection with the Stella case.'

'No, but we've already talked to them, and right now I have nothing concrete that would warrant questioning them further. We'll just have to wait until we know more. I still think there has to be a connection.'

'In spite of what was found at Karim's home?' asked Paula.

'Yes, in spite of what was "found",' said Patrik, and he couldn't resist casting a glance at Mellberg.

Bertil had his eyes fixed on the table. He hadn't said a word during the meeting.

'I think it's a false lead,' Patrik went on. 'But at the moment we can't rule anything out. It feels too convenient that we should get an anonymous phone call and then for Mellberg to make that discovery. If Karim was guilty, who else would know that the knickers were there? Who would be in a position to tip us off?'

Gösta had been sitting quietly for the past few minutes, lost in his own thoughts. Just as Patrik was about to end the meeting, he looked up.

'I think I know what's been bothering me.'

BOHUSLÄN 1672

Elin's despair grew worse with every passing day. Preben devoted all his free time to Britta and paid no mind to her whatsoever. It was as if nothing had ever taken place between the two of them. He was not unfriendly, but he had simply forgotten what had once been. Britta and her child now captured all his attention. Even Märta held no interest for him now. The girl dashed around in bewilderment, with Sigrid at her heels. Elin's heart ached to see her daughter's confusion and dismay at Preben's sudden indifference, and Elin had no idea how to explain to the child this adult madness.

How could she explain something to her daughter when even she did not understand?

Yet one thing was clear. She could no longer contemplate telling Preben about the child she was carrying. Nor could she keep it. She would have to get rid of the child. If she did not, then she and Märta would be left homeless. They would end up starving or begging. Or they would suffer some other terrible fate, which struck women who had nowhere to go. She could not allow that to happen to her and Märta.

She possessed no knowledge about how to rid her body of the child, but she knew someone who did. She knew who others went to in this situation – those women who had no husband to fend for mother and child. She knew who could help her. Helga Klippare.

A week later the opportunity presented itself when Britta asked her to go to Fjällbacka on an errand. As she rode in the wagon, Elin felt her heart sinking more and more. She thought she could feel the child moving inside her, even though she knew it was much too early. Lill-Jan, who was driving the wagon, soon gave up trying to talk to her. She was not in the mood for any sort of conversation and merely sat in silence as the wheels steadily lumbered over the road. When they reached Fjällbacka, Elin climbed down from the wagon and went on her way without saying a word. Lill-Jan had errands to run for the master, so they would not set off for home until evening. Plenty of time to do what she needed to do.

Eyes were watching her as she made her way along the street. Helga lived in a house at the very end. Elin hesitated before knocking, but finally she rapped her knuckles against the worn wood of the door.

Elin had been given home-brewed alcohol for the pain, but in truth she had nothing against feeling bodily pain. The worse it felt in her body, the more dulled the pain would be in her heart. She felt her body contracting. Rhythmically. Methodically. The way it had when Märta was born. But this time without the joy and anticipation she had felt when she knew what would come from all the hard labour. This time she felt only sorrow awaiting her at the end of the searing pain and blood.

Helga offered no sympathy. Nor did she judge. Silently and methodically she did what had to be done. Her only display of concern was when she occasionally wiped the sweat from Elin's brow.

'It will soon be over,' Helga said tersely after peering

between Elin's legs as she lay on the floor on a filthy rag rug.

Elin looked out through the small opening next to the door. By now it was later afternoon. In a couple of hours she would have to get back in the wagon with Lill-Jan and head home to the vicarage. The road was bumpy, and she knew that every jolt would hurt. But she would have to put on a good face. No one must find out what had happened.

'Bear down now,' said Helga. 'With the next contraction, you must bear down, and it will come out.'

Elin closed her eyes and grabbed the edges of the rag rug. She waited until the contractions increased, and when the pain was at its worst, she pushed with all her might.

Something slid out of her. Something small. A lump. There was no cry. No sign that it was alive.

Helga worked briskly. Elin heard the sound of something landing in the bucket next to her.

'It was just as well,' said Helga dryly, getting up with an effort as she wiped her bloodstained hands on a towel. 'It was not as it should be. It would not have gone well.'

She picked up the bucket and set it next to the door. Elin felt a sob form in her chest, but she forced it back, fiercely holding it in until it became a tiny ball inside her heart. So she was not to be allowed even the image of a lovely little son or daughter with Preben's blue eyes. The child was not as it should have been. They would never have been a family, except in her own naive dreams.

At that moment the door was yanked open, and Ebba of Mörhult stepped inside her sister's house. She stopped abruptly when she saw Elin lying on the floor. Open-mouthed, she took in the entire scene. Elin with her bloodied legs spread apart, the contents in the bucket next to the door, and Helga wiping Elin's blood off her hands.

'So,' said Ebba, her eyes flashing. 'She has come here for your help. Yet to my knowledge Elin has not married again. Has she been lying with one of the farmhands? Or has she started whoring at the local inn?'

'Hush,' Helga admonished her sister, who merely pursed her lips.

Elin could not bring herself to reply. All strength had seeped out of her, and Ebba's views were nothing she need care about any longer. She would get in the wagon with Lill-Jan, go back to the vicarage, and forget this had happened.

'Is this it?' asked Ebba, kicking at the bucket.

She peered down and then wrinkled her nose.

'It looks like one of nature's abominations.'

'Keep quiet, or I may find myself giving you a box on the ear,' snapped Helga. Then she grabbed her sister's arm and ushered her out the door. When Ebba was gone, she turned back to Elin.

'Pay no mind to her. She has always been a wicked one, ever since we were small. Sit up carefully now and wash yourself.'

Elin did as she said. She sat up, leaning heavily on one arm. Her womb ached, and there was blood between her thighs.

'You are fortunate. You will not have to be stitched. And you have not lost a lot of blood, but you must rest for a few days.'

'There is no question of that,' said Elin, taking the wet rag Helga handed to her.

It stung when she washed herself. Helga placed a bowl of water next to her so she could wring out the rag.

'I . . .' Helga hesitated. 'I heard your sister is with child.'

At first Elin did not reply. Then she nodded.

'Yes, she is. This winter a child's cries will be heard at the vicarage.'

'I suppose some doctor from Uddevalla will tend to the vicar's wife when it is her time, but if needed, you may send word to me.'

'I will tell them,' said Elin.

She could not bear to think of Britta's child. She could not even bear to think of her own, lying in that bucket.

With great effort she stood up and pulled down her skirts. It was time to head for home.

'Don't slam the door!'

James stared at Sam, who was standing in the front hall.

'I didn't slam the door, damn it,' said Sam, taking off his shoes.

The familiar anger surged inside James. Always this sense of disappointment. The black nail polish and black eye make-up were his son's way of spitting in his face. He knew that. He clenched his fist and pounded it against the flowered wallpaper. Sam flinched, and James felt the tension in his body ebb away.

He'd been forced to find an outlet for all the anger he'd felt towards Sam when the boy was younger, whenever they were out in the woods. On those few occasions when Helen had been away. Accidents happened so frequently. But then Helen had discovered them. Sam was crouching on the floor as James raised his fist. Sam's lip was split and bleeding, and James realized how it must have looked. But Helen had over-reacted. Her voice trembled with fury when she told him what would happen if he ever touched Sam again.

And James had controlled himself ever since. That was three years ago.

Sam stomped up the stairs, and James wondered what was making the boy so furious. Then he shrugged. Teenage problems.

He longed to be able to leave again. Two weeks to go. He was counting the minutes. He didn't understand his colleagues who longed for home, who wanted to go back to all the daily dreariness and to their family. But the military insisted that everyone should take 'leave' once in a while. It was probably some psychological bullshit. He didn't believe in that stuff.

He went into his home office and walked over to the gun cabinet behind his desk. He entered the combination and heard the lock click open. These were the guns he owned legally, but in the wardrobe upstairs he'd hidden row upon row of guns that he'd collected over a period of nearly thirty years – everything from simple pistols to automatic weapons. It wasn't hard to get hold of guns if you knew where to go.

Here in this cabinet he kept his Colt M1911. It was a real gun. There was nothing elegant or lightweight about it. A .45 calibre.

He put the gun back. Maybe he should take Sam out for some target practice this afternoon. It was ironic that shooting was the only thing Sam was any good at, aside from computers, but it was something he'd never have use for. Skill as a sharpshooter wouldn't give extra points for someone working as a desk-jockey. And that was the future James envisioned for Sam. A desk-jockey at some sort of IT company. Dreary, meaningless, superfluous.

James carefully closed the cabinet. The door clicked shut, automatically locking. He glanced up. Sam's room was directly above. He didn't hear anything, but that just meant Sam was sitting at his computer with his headset on, with that wretched music blaring in his ears. James sighed. The sooner he could report for duty again, the better. He couldn't stand this much longer.

Erica asked to have the painting sent to her home after the gallery opening was over, and then she said goodbye to Viola. When she stepped outside her mobile pinged, and she quickly read the text message. Wonderful. The plans she'd made were now booked and confirmed, so all that remained was to 'kidnap' Kristina. Erica rang Anna's number, hoping she would have an idea how to do that. The only thing she could think up at the moment involved a slightly sadistic humour, which wasn't something her mother-in-law would appreciate.

She listened to the phone ringing as she surveyed the town square, noting that they seemed to be filming there. She craned her neck and thought she caught a glimpse of Marie Wall beyond the cameras, but it wasn't easy to see anything because of the big crowd of curious onlookers.

'Hello?' said Anna, giving Erica a start.

'Oh, hi. It's me. So, everything's all set for tomorrow. We have to be at the hotel at noon. But the question is, how to get Kristina there without arousing her suspicions. Have you got any ideas? I'm pretty sure you wouldn't approve of my plan to rent a couple of guys dressed as terrorists to rush in and fetch her.'

Anna laughed. In the background, sirens were wailing.

'What's going on, is that the police?' asked Erica.

Anna didn't reply.

'Hello? Are you still there?'

Erica glanced at the display, but there was no indication the call had been ended.

'Yes, I'm still here. No, it was an ambulance going past.'

'An ambulance? I hope everything's okay with your neighbours.'

'They're fine. I'm not home at the moment.'

'Oh? Where are you?'

'In Uddevalla.'

'What are you doing there?'

Why hadn't she mentioned this when they were helping Kristina try on wedding gowns?

'It's for a doctor's appointment.'

'But why?' asked Erica, frowning. 'Your doctor isn't in Uddevalla.'

'It's a special test that they can only do at the Uddevalla hospital.'

'Anna, I get the feeling you're not telling me something. Is something wrong with the baby? Or with you? Are you ill?'

Worry clutched at her heart. After the car accident, Erica no longer took anything for granted.

'No, no, Erica. Everything's okay. They want to be a little extra cautious, considering . . .'

Anna didn't finish her sentence.

'Okay, but promise you'll tell me if there's anything wrong.'

'I promise,' said Anna and then swiftly changed the subject. 'I'll think of something by tomorrow. Noon at Stora Hotel, right?'

'Yes. I have the rest of the day and evening all planned. You can stay as long as you feel like it. Hugs.'

Erica ended the call, but the worrying feeling wouldn't go away. Anna wasn't telling her something, she was sure of it.

She walked over to the square to watch the filming. Yes, that was Marie Wall over there. They were just finishing up a scene, and Erica was impressed by Marie's sheer radiance. She didn't need to look through a camera lens to know the actress would be lighting up the screen. She was one of those people who looked as if she walked about in her own spotlight.

446

When they finished filming, Erica turned to head for home. Then she heard someone call her name and turned, trying to pinpoint who it was. Marie waved when she saw Erica looking in her direction. Erica went over to join her.

'You're Erica Falck, aren't you?' said Marie. Her voice sounded as husky as it did in her films.

'Yes, that's right,' said Erica, feeling uncharacteristically shy.

She'd never met a film star before, and she found herself star-struck to be standing in front of someone who'd hung out with George Clooney.

'Well, you know who I am,' said Marie, with a casual laugh, taking a pack of cigarettes from her purse. 'Would you like one?'

'No, thanks. I don't smoke.'

Marie lit her cigarette.

'I understand that you'd like to talk to me. I've seen your letters . . . I have a break right now, while they take stock photos, so if you'd like we could sit down and have a drink and talk.'

Marie pointed her cigarette at the tables outside Café Bryggan.

'Absolutely,' said Erica, a little too eagerly.

She had no idea what stock photos were, but she didn't dare ask.

They sat down at a table near the edge of the dock, and the waitress came running. She was so excited about waiting on Marie that she looked as if she might have a heart attack at any moment.

'Two glasses of champagne,' said Marie, waving away the girl, who smiled broadly and then hurried inside the restaurant. 'I know I didn't ask what you'd like to have, but only boring people refuse champagne, and my impression is that you are not a boring person.'

Marie blew a cloud of smoke towards Erica as she steadily studied her.

'Er, well . . .'

Erica couldn't think of a suitable reply. Good lord, she was behaving like a twelve-year-old. Hollywood stars were just people like everybody else. She tried to use a trick her father had taught her whenever she was nervous about giving a speech at school. In her mind she pictured Marie sitting on the toilet with her knickers around her ankles. Unfortunately, this didn't work as well as Erica had hoped. Somehow Marie managed to look as elegant as ever, even in that situation.

The waitress came back and set two glasses of champagne on the table.

'We might as well order two more while you're here, honey,' said Marie. 'These will be gone in a second.' And she dismissed the waitress again.

She picked up her glass and raised it towards Erica.

'*Skål*,' she said, gulping down half the champagne at once.

'*Skål*,' said Erica, though she made do with a sip.

If she kept on drinking bubbly in the middle of the day like this, she'd end up tipsy.

'What would you like to know?' asked Marie, downing the rest of her drink.

She glanced around for the waitress, who came running with two more glasses.

Erica took a few more sips as she pondered how to begin.

'Well, the first thing I'd like to know is why you changed your mind about talking to me. I've been trying to get an interview for quite a long time.'

'I can understand why you'd ask, since I've talked openly about my background during my entire career. But as you may have heard, I'm considering writing my own book.'

'Yes, I've heard the rumours.'

Erica finished her glass of champagne and reached for the second. It was too amazing to be sitting here in the warm sunshine on the dock, drinking champagne with an international film star, for her to listen to common sense.

'I still haven't decided how to go about it. But now that Helen has already talked to you . . .' Marie shrugged.

'Yes, she dropped by yesterday,' said Erica. 'Or rather, she ran by.'

'I've heard she's obsessed with running. We haven't spoken, but I've seen her out running in town. I hardly recognized her. Thin as a whippet. I've never understood the purpose of all that exercise. All anyone has to do to stay trim is to avoid carbs like the plague.'

She crossed one long, slender leg over the other. Erica looked at her slim figure with envy, but she shuddered at the thought of a life without carbs.

'Have the two of you had any contact over the years?' she asked.

'No,' said Marie curtly. Then her expression softened. 'We made a few half-hearted attempts to reach out to each other right after it happened. But Helen's parents quickly put a stop to that. So we gave up. And it was probably easier to try to forget everything and put it all behind us.'

'How did the two of you deal with everything? The police? The newspapers? The public? You were only children. It must have seemed overwhelming.'

'We didn't understand how serious it all was. Helen and I both thought it would blow over and things would go back to normal.'

'But how could you think that? A little girl was killed, after all.'

Marie didn't answer immediately. She sipped her champagne, gazing out at the view.

'You have to remember that we were also children,' she said. 'We knew it was us against the world. We were living in a bubble no one else could enter. How did you view the world when you were thirteen? Did you see the nuances? The grey zones? Or was everything black and white?'

Erica thought back to how she was at that age. Naive, inexperienced, full of clichés and simple truths. It was only when people got older that they began to realize how complicated life was.

'I see what you mean,' she said. 'I asked Helen why you confessed and later retracted your confessions, but she avoided giving me an answer.'

'I don't know if I can give you an answer either,' said Marie. 'There are things we don't want to talk about. Things we won't talk about.'

'Why?'

'Because certain things should be left in the past.'

Marie stubbed out her cigarette and lit another one.

'But you've been so open about almost everything related to the case. About your family and your foster families. I don't get the impression you've tried to hide any details.'

'It's not wise to reveal everything,' said Marie. 'Maybe I'll discuss it in my own book. Maybe I won't. Probably I won't.'

'Well, at least you're honest about the fact you're not telling the whole truth. Helen wouldn't go that far.'

'Helen and I are totally different. We always have been. She has her demons, and I have mine.'

'Have you had any contact with your family? I know both your parents are dead, but what about your brothers?'

'My brothers?' Marie snorted, tapping the ash from her cigarette. 'They tried to reconnect with me after my career

450

took off and my name started appearing in the newspapers. But I cut them off very quickly. They've both thrown away their lives, and I've never felt any need to have them in my life. They tormented me when I was a child, and I can't imagine they've become any nicer as adults.'

'You have a daughter, don't you?'

'Yes, my daughter Jessie is fifteen now. A teenager through and through. Takes more after her father than me, unfortunately.'

'According to the tabloids, he's never been in the picture. Is that true?'

'Yes. My God, it was only a quickie on his office desk to get a part in a film.' Marie laughed hoarsely. She gave Erica a wink. 'And yes, I got the part.'

'Does Jessie know about your background?'

'Of course she does. Kids these days have access to the Internet, and I'm sure she has googled everything ever written about me. Apparently her classmates have harassed her because of me.'

'How does she handle that?'

Marie shrugged. 'I have no idea. I suppose that's something kids these days have to put up with. And to a certain extent she has only herself to blame. If she paid more attention to her appearance, she'd probably have an easier time in school.'

Erica wondered if Marie was really as cold as she sounded when she talked about her daughter. Personally, she didn't know what she would do if anybody was mean to Maja or the twins.

'So what's your theory about what happened here the other day? The murder of little Nea. It seems too much of a coincidence that you should come back here and then a child is killed and found in the same place as the girl you were found guilty of murdering.'

'I'm not stupid. It doesn't look good, I realize that.'

Marie turned to summon the waitress. Her glass was empty again. She gave Erica an enquiring look, but Erica shook her head. There was still champagne in her second glass.

'The only thing I can say is that I'm innocent,' said Marie, gazing out at the sea again.

Erica leaned forward. 'I recently found an interview in which you said you saw someone in the woods that day.'

Marie smiled.

'Yes. I told the police about it too.'

'But not at first. You waited until after you retracted your confession, didn't you?' said Erica, studying Marie to see her reaction.

'Touché,' said Marie.

'Do you have a theory about who it was?'

'No,' said Marie. 'If I did, I would have told the police.'

'So what are the police saying now? Do you think they believe that you and Helen are involved?'

'I can't say what they think about Helen. But I've told them I have an alibi for when the girl disappeared, so they can't possibly suspect me. Helen isn't involved either. She wasn't back then. Neither was I. And she's not involved now. The bitter truth is, the police failed to follow up on the lead when I told them about seeing someone in the woods. And now the same person has probably struck again.'

Erica thought about the gallery opening.

'Did you ever hear again from the police officer who was in charge of the investigation into Stella's death? Leif Hermansson?'

'Hmm . . .' said Marie, with only minimal furrowing of her brow, which made Erica suspect Botox. 'Now that you mention it, yes, I did. But that was years ago. He tried to contact me through my agent. Left several messages saying he wanted to get in touch with me. And finally I decided to reply. But when I phoned him, I was told he'd committed suicide.'

'Okay,' said Erica, frantically pondering her next question. If Marie was telling the truth, and he hadn't been able to contact her, he must have discovered something that threw a new light on the old investigation. But what could it have been?

'Marie?'

A tall man that Erica surmised must be the director was calling Marie and motioning for her to come.

'Time to work. You'll have to excuse me.'

Marie stood up. She downed the last of her champagne and smiled at Erica.

'We can talk more another time. Be a dear and pay the bill.'

She strode off to join the film crew, with everyone's eyes fixed on her.

Erica motioned for the waitress and paid the bill. Clearly, they hadn't been drinking cheap champagne, so Erica finished off what was left in her glass. It had cost too much to let it go to waste.

It meant a great deal that Marie had agreed to talk to her. Erica planned to make an appointment for next week so she could conduct a real interview with Marie. She also needed to talk to Helen again. The two of them held the key to her book about the Stella case. Without their input, the book would never be a success.

But there was one more person who was important to the story. Sanna Lundgren. She had spent her whole life living with the consequences of the murder which had shattered her family. When Erica wrote her books, she wanted to discuss the murder itself as well as the victim and the perpetrator. But just as important was the story of those who had been affected by the crime. The families whose lives were wrecked, people who suffered such distress that they were never able to recover. Sanna would also be able to tell her about Stella. She was only a child when her little sister was murdered, and it was possible her memories had become hazy over the years. But she was still the one who possessed the greatest treasure trove of stories about Stella. And that was always at the very heart of Erica's books. She wanted to make the victim come to life. She wanted the reader to understand that the victim was a real person with dreams, feelings and thoughts.

She needed to contact Sanna as soon as possible.

When Erica passed the crowd watching the filming she felt someone touch her arm. It was a woman wearing a belt filled with make-up paraphernalia, who kept a watchful eye on Marie as she leaned close to Erica.

'I heard Marie say that she had an alibi for the time when the little girl disappeared,' she whispered. 'She said she was sleeping with Jörgen in his hotel room . . .'

'Oh?' said Erica, anxious to hear more.

'It's not true,' whispered the woman, who Erica assumed must be the film company's make-up artist.

'How do you know that?' she asked.

'Because I was with Jörgen that night.'

Erica looked at the woman. Then she turned to look at Marie, who was in the midst of playing a scene. She was certainly a superb actress.

Karim was groggy from all the medicines they'd pumped into him. Painkillers. Sedatives. Even the humming of the oxygen made him drowsy. He could hardly stay awake. Whenever Karim realized where he was, tears would fill his eyes. He asked the nurses about Amina, pleaded to be taken to her, but they merely murmured that he needed to stay where he was. The children had come to his room to see him. He recalled their warm cheeks whenever he found himself weeping into his pillow. A doctor told him they would be discharged tomorrow, but could he trust anyone? The police? The others living at the refugee centre? He no longer knew who was friend or foe.

He'd had such high hopes when he came to this new country. He would work and contribute. He would watch his children grow up to be strong and confident and intelligent Swedes. The sort of people who made a difference.

Now all that was gone. Amina was lying in this hospital in a foreign country, surrounded by a team of strangers fighting to save her life. Maybe she would die here, in a country thousands of kilometres from home. And he was the one who had brought her here.

She had been so strong during the long journey. She was the one who had encouraged him and the children on the voyage across the stormy sea, as they passed through customs and crossed borders, as they listened to the clacking of train rails and the lethargic sound of tyres on tarmac as the bus raced through the night. He and Amina had whispered to the children when they couldn't fall asleep, reassuring them that everything would be fine. He had failed them. He had failed Amina.

Uneasy dreams tormented Karim. Dreams about the people he had betrayed mixed with dreams about Amina's hair on fire, the devastated look on her face as she asked him why he had brought this misfortune upon them, why he had dragged her and the children to this god-forsaken land where no one would look them in the eye, no one wanted to welcome them and reach out a hand, and someone wanted to see them burn.

Karim let the drugs carry him back to sleep. He had finally come to the end of the road.

* * *

'There,' said Gösta, pointing to the turn-off.

They were halfway to Hamburgsund, and the road became narrow and winding as they turned off the paved road.

'Does he live in the middle of the forest?' asked Patrik, swerving to miss a cat that ran right in front of the car.

'When I rang, he said he's temporarily living with his grandfather. But I know Sixten slightly. He's getting frail, and I'd already heard in town that his grandson had moved in to help him. I just didn't realize it was Johannes Klingsby.'

'That's pretty common,' said Patrik, increasing speed on the gravel road. 'A grandchild stepping in to help the old folks, I mean.'

'It's this way,' said Gösta, clutching the grab-handle above the door. 'Slow down, would you! Being driven around by you has probably cut several years off my life.'

Patrik smiled as he pulled into a small, well-kept farmyard with various vehicles parked in front of the farmhouse.

'Looks like someone is fond of anything with a motor,' he said, looking at the row of boats, cars, jet-skis, and bulldozers.

'Stop drooling and come on,' said Gösta, slapping him on the shoulder.

Patrik tore himself away from all the vehicles and went up the stone steps to knock on the door. Johannes opened it immediately.

'Come in, come in. I'm making coffee,' he said, stepping aside to allow them in.

Patrik was reminded of the previous occasion when they'd met, and he was grateful that this time it was under more pleasant circumstances, even though the business at hand was equally serious.

'Grandpa, they're here!' called Johannes, and Patrik

heard someone mumble a reply from upstairs. 'Wait a minute and I'll come help you down. You know what we talked about. You're not supposed to take the stairs without help!'

'Nonsense,' said the voice from above, but Johannes quickly disappeared up the stairs.

He soon reappeared, firmly gripping the arm of a stooped man wearing a worn cardigan.

'It's hell getting old,' said the man, shaking hands with Patrik and Gösta.

He peered at Gösta. 'I know you.'

'Yes, you do,' said Gösta with a smile. 'I see you've got yourself a good helper.'

'I don't know what I would have done without Johannes. I wasn't keen at first – I don't think someone his age should be keeping an old man company – but he insisted. He's a good boy, my Johannes, though he hasn't always seen the best in people.'

He patted his grandson's cheek. Johannes shrugged, looking embarrassed. Then he led the way to the kitchen.

They sat down in a bright little country kitchen, like so many Patrik had visited over the years. It was clean and tidy, but had never been updated. There was linoleum on the floor, the cupboards were original from the 1950s, and the tiles were bright yellow. Hanging on the wall was a big gilded clock steadily ticking, and the table was covered with an oilcloth decorated with red raspberries.

'Don't worry, I'm not making coffee the old-fashioned way on the cooker,' said Johannes with a smile as he went over to the worktop. 'Soon as I arrived, I threw out the old pot and brought in a real coffee maker. You have to admit you think the coffee is better now, right, Grandpa?'

Sixten grunted agreement. 'I suppose we have to give in to certain modern conveniences.'

'Here you are,' said Johannes, pouring coffee for their guests. 'And help yourself to sugar if you like.'

Then he sat down and his expression turned serious.

'So you're interested in what I videotaped. Is that right?' he asked.

'Yes,' replied Patrik. 'Gösta said he saw you filming at the farm before you set off with the search party. We'd like to see what you got.'

'I didn't know we weren't supposed to take pictures. I wasn't being a ghoul, I wanted to record how many volunteers had turned up to help out.'

Johannes looked a little nervous.

'But I stopped filming as soon as Gösta told me not to, and I didn't post anything on Facebook or anywhere else. I swear I didn't.'

Gösta held up his hands to reassure him. 'It's not a problem, Johannes. In fact, you might be able to help us with the investigation. We'd like to have a look at the video. Is it on your mobile?'

'Yes. I also saved it on a memory stick. You can take my phone, if you need to, but I'd rather you didn't because I need it for my job and so . . .' He blushed but went on: 'So my girlfriend can reach me.'

'He's met such a nice girl,' said Sixten, winking at Johannes. 'They met in Thailand, and she's a real beauty with dark hair and dark eyes. I told you that you'd meet somebody sooner or later, Johannes. Didn't I tell you?'

'Yes, you did,' said Johannes, looking even more embarrassed. 'Well, as I said, you can take my phone, but the whole video is on the stick, so maybe that will do?'

'That will do,' Patrik assured him.

'But is it possible for us to have a look at it right now?' asked Gösta, pointing to the mobile lying on the table.

Johannes nodded, picked up the phone, and began scrolling through the videos.

'Here. Here it is.'

He slid the phone across to Gösta and Patrik with the display turned in the right direction. They leaned forward to focus on the video. It felt weird to look at the images now that they knew what the outcome of the search would be. When Johannes made the video, everyone had been filled with hope. That was evident in the eager expressions on people's faces, the way they talked and gesticulated, forming groups and heading purposefully into the woods. Patrik caught a glimpse of himself, noticing how determined he looked. He also saw Gösta, who was talking to Eva, with his arm around her shoulders.

'Nice camera,' said Patrik, and Johannes nodded.

'Yeah. It's the latest Samsung model. The video function is really high quality.'

'Hmm . . .'

Gösta squinted as he focused on the video. The camera panned across the whole farmyard and over to the barn, then back to the yard and finally over to the farmhouse.

'There!' said Gösta, pointing at the image.

Patrik pressed the pause button, but had to go back a ways since they'd already missed the sequence Gösta wanted to see. At last he was able to pause in the right place, and they both leaned closer to look at the display.

'There,' said Gösta, pointing.

Patrik saw what he meant. And it cast everything in a new light.

THE STELLA CASE

Life was so empty without Kate. Leif wandered about the house, not sure what to do with himself. All the years that had passed since they had laid his wife to rest had done nothing to ease his sense of loss. His loneliness actually seemed even worse. The children came to visit him – Viola dropped by practically every day. They did their best, but they had their own lives, families to look after and demanding jobs, it wasn't right that they should be burdened with a grieving old man on top of all that. So he tried to put on a good face for them. He told them everything was fine, talked about how he spent his days taking walks, listening to the radio and solving crossword puzzles. And it was true, he did all those things. But still he missed Kate so much it took everything he had to keep going.

He missed his job on the police force too. He missed feeling he had a purpose in life.

Now that he had so much time on his hands, he'd begun to wonder about certain things, both major and minor. About people. About crimes. About things that had been said over the years. And about things that had not been said.

But above all, he thought about the Stella case. Which

was actually rather strange. He'd been so convinced those two girls were guilty. But Kate had sown doubt in his mind; she had always questioned their account of what happened. And towards the end of her life, it became increasingly clear that she had been plagued by doubt. Just as he was now.

At night when sleep refused to come, he thought about every word, every statement, every detail. And the more he thought about the case, the more he sensed that something wasn't right. Something had fallen between the cracks, and his eagerness to solve the case, to give the families closure, had meant he'd never looked into what that might be.

But he could no longer ignore his failure. He still didn't know the how or where or when. But he knew he'd made a terrible mistake. And somewhere out there, Stella's killer was still on the loose.

'Rita, honey?'

Mellberg knocked on the door for the fifth time, but the only reply was a lengthy tirade of Spanish swear words. At least, that's what he thought he was hearing. He had only a passing knowledge of the Spanish language, but judging by Rita's tone of voice, they were not words of endearment.

'Sweetheart? Sweetie? Rita, honey?'

He made his voice as gentle as he could and knocked again. Then he sighed. Why did it have to be so hard to apologize?

'Sweetie, could you let me come in, please? Sooner or later we need to talk. Think about Leo. He's going to miss his grandpa.'

Mellberg heard a few grumbling noises, but no more harangues. It seemed he'd hit upon the right approach at last.

'Couldn't we have a little talk? I miss you. I miss all of you.'

He held his breath. Complete silence inside. Then he heard the lock turn. Relieved, he picked up his bag from the floor and cautiously stepped inside when Rita opened the door. He knew it was possible he might still get hit over the head. Rita's hot temper could make things fly through the air. But this time she settled for standing there with her arms crossed, glaring at him.

'I'm sorry. I know my behaviour was reckless and stupid,' Mellberg said, and he had the satisfaction of seeing Rita's mouth fall open.

This was probably the first time she'd ever heard him apologize.

'I heard what happened,' said Rita. The tone of her voice was still harsh and angry. 'Do you realize that what you did may have led to the fire?'

'Uh, er, yes, I know. And I feel really bad about that.'

'Have you learned anything from all this?' she asked, studying him intently.

He nodded. 'Yes, Rita. And I'll do anything to put things right.'

'Good! You can start by packing up everything I've cleared out of the bedroom.'

'Pack up? I thought you said—'

Panic surged inside him, and it must have been evident in his expression, because Rita quickly explained:

'I cleared out some of your clothes. And some of mine. To give to the refugees from the centre. You can pack up what's lying on the bed and then follow me. From what I've heard, Bill Andersson is doing a fantastic job getting people to help the refugees who lost their homes.'

'What are you giving—' asked Mellberg, but he stopped himself in time. Even he understood this was not the time to raise objections. And if some of his favourite clothes had slipped in, he could always discreetly slip them back in the wardrobe.

As if reading his mind, Rita said: 'If you put back even one garment that I've cleared out, you'll have to sleep somewhere else again tonight! And every night from now on.'

Bloody hell. Rita's always a step ahead of me, he thought as he headed for the bedroom. The pile on the bed was awfully big. And on the very top was his favourite shirt. He could admit it had seen better days, but it was still wearable, and he doubted anybody ever noticed the holes here and there. He picked it up and glanced over his shoulder. Maybe she wouldn't notice if—

'Give it here!'

Rita was standing behind him, holding an open bin bag in her hand. With a sigh, he placed the shirt in the sack, and then added the rest of the clothes. Her pile was only half as big as his, but he realized it wouldn't be a good idea to point that out. He filled two bin bags, tied them closed and set them down in the front hall.

'Okay, let's go,' said Rita, coming out of the kitchen with two shopping bags filled with groceries.

He followed her out the door, setting down the bags so he could lock up behind them.

'By the way,' she said, 'we'll be having guests staying with us as of tomorrow.'

'Guests?' he said, wondering who she could have invited now.

Rita was at times too generous.

'Karim's children are going to stay with us until he's discharged from hospital. It's the least we can do, considering all the trouble you've caused.'

Mellberg opened his mouth to say something, but immediately closed it again and picked up the bags. Sometimes it was best to choose his battles.

'Hi, Bill. What an amazing turnout!' said Paula, looking around the community centre.

More and more people had arrived, and the old

464

building was bustling with activity. Everywhere she looked there were Swedes and refugees chatting, and the sound of laughter rose to the ceiling.

'I know. I've never seen anything like it!' said Bill. 'Everyone's been so generous! So involved! Who would have thought it?'

'Well, it looks as if at least something good has come of this,' said Paula sternly.

'You're right. Of course we're all thinking about those who are still in hospital.' He bit his lip.

Bill's wife, Gun, came over and hooked her arm through his.

'Have you heard anything more?' she asked.

Paula shook her head. 'Last we heard, they're planning to keep Karim and Amina's children for observation until tomorrow. Karim will need to stay a couple more days because his hands were badly burned, and Amina . . . well, the doctors don't know yet whether she's going to pull through.'

Gun clutched Bill's arm even harder. 'If there's anything we can do . . .'

'You're already doing more than anyone would have believed possible,' said Martin, looking around the room.

'I've told Karim the children are welcome to stay with me,' said Paula.

'That's so good of you,' said Gun. 'But if it doesn't work out, we'd be happy to take them.'

'No, no,' said Paula. 'Leo is going to be thrilled to have playmates, and my mother will be helping to look after them when I'm at work.'

Martin cleared his throat. 'We need to have a word with some of Karim and Amina's neighbours. To find out if they heard or saw anything. Do you happen to know who . . .?'

He glanced around at all the people.

'Of course,' said Bill. 'I'm beginning to figure out who's

who, and that couple you see over there lived next door. Why don't you start with them, and I'll find out who else you should talk to.'

'Thanks,' said Paula.

She and Martin made their way through the crowd to speak to the couple Bill had pointed out. But the conversation proved to be disappointing. As were their talks with other residents of the refugee centre. No one had seen or heard anything. Everyone had been asleep in bed until they were woken by screams and smoke. When they dashed outside, everything was chaos.

Paula sat down on a chair in the corner, feeling a growing sense of hopelessness. Would they ever catch the person who set the fire? Martin sat down next to her and began talking about what they needed to do next. Suddenly he stopped mid-sentence. Paula saw who he was looking at, and a big smile spread across her face.

'Is that . . .?'

She gave Martin a poke in the side, and he nodded. He didn't need to reply. The crimson on his cheeks was telling enough, and Paula smiled even more.

'She's cute.'

'Oh, be quiet,' he said, blushing even more.

'So when are you taking her out?'

'Saturday,' said Martin without taking his eyes off the woman and her child.

'What's her name?' asked Paula.

She looked very nice. She had lovely eyes, although she had the stressed expression of a toddler's parent – the same look Paula now saw every time she looked at herself in the mirror.

'Mette,' said Martin curtly. His face was now so red it nearly matched his hair.

'Martin and Mette,' said Paula. 'That has a nice ring to it.'

'Cut it out,' he said, standing up when Mette glanced in their direction.

'Wave to her,' said Paula.

'No, no,' said Martin nervously, but Mette was already on her way over, carrying her son in her arms.

'Hi!' she said happily.

'Hi!' replied Paula.

'It's so awful, what happened,' said Mette, shaking her head. 'How could anyone be so evil as to do something like that? With children living there, and everything.'

'Yes, it never ceases to amaze me what people are capable of,' Paula said.

'Do you know who did it?' Mette looked at Martin, who blushed again.

'No, not yet. We've been talking with some of the refugees, but unfortunately nobody saw anything.'

'Then it might just end up in the statistics as one more burned refugee centre,' said Mette.

Neither Paula nor Martin replied. They were afraid she was right. At the moment they had no evidence to go on. All across Sweden, refugee centres had been set on fire, and in most cases no one had been arrested. There was a good chance the same thing would happen here.

'We came over to donate some of Jon's old toys,' said Mette, kissing her son's cheek. 'We have to go now, but I'll see you tomorrow evening, right?'

'Yes, absolutely!' said Martin. Even his throat was crimson.

He waved to Mette and Jon as they made their way to the door, and Paula also raised her hand to wave.

'You definitely have my approval!' she said with a grin, and Martin sighed.

Then it was his turn to grin.

'Hey, looks like Bertil has had his sins forgiven . . .'

Paula glanced towards the door and rolled her eyes

467

when she saw her mother and Mellberg come in carrying two grocery bags and two bulging bin bags.

'I thought he'd be in the doghouse for at least a week this time,' she said with a sigh. 'Mamma is too nice . . . But I suppose he doesn't mean to cause trouble. Not really.'

Martin grinned. 'I wonder who's being too nice now.'

Paula didn't reply.

Sam ignored Jessie's first five text messages, but then he had to reply. He wasn't really angry. He understood her. If he hadn't known Vendela and the others so well, he might have reacted the same way. He was actually more worried than angry. Worried about what they were planning. Worried Jessie would get hurt.

For a few minutes Sam simply sat there, holding his mobile. Then he texted:

Meet me in the woods behind my house. By the big oak tree. You can't miss it.

After sending the text, he went downstairs. James was sitting at his desk, staring at the computer screen. He glanced up when Sam came in, with the same furrow between his brows that always appeared whenever he looked at his son.

'What do you want?' he asked.

'I was thinking of doing a little target practice. Could I borrow the Colt?'

'All right,' said James, getting up and going over to the gun cabinet. 'I was thinking we could do some target practice this afternoon.'

'I'm going to meet Jessie.'

'So you shoot with your girlfriend?'

James stood in front of the cabinet so Sam couldn't see him enter the combination. The lock clicked and he opened the door.

'She's not like the others,' said Sam.

'Okay.' James turned around and handed Sam the gun. 'You know the rules. Bring it back in the same condition you received it.'

Sam merely nodded.

He stuck the gun in his belt and left the room. He could feel his father's gaze burning the back of his neck.

When Sam walked past the kitchen, he saw his mother standing at the worktop, as usual.

'Where are you going?' she asked. Her voice was shrill and quavering.

'Target practice,' he said, avoiding her gaze.

They were for ever circling around each other, both of them afraid to speak. Both of them afraid that some word might prove too much. His mother had mentioned that Erica Falck wanted to talk to him, but he hadn't yet decided what to do. What he wanted to tell her. Or could tell her.

The air smelled of newly mown grass as he reached the back of their property. He'd mowed the grass last night. James made him mow it three times a week.

He glanced to the right and saw the barn next to Nea's house. He'd didn't particularly care for young children. Most of them were wild with snot running from their nose. But Nea had been different. She'd been like a smiling ray of sunshine. He felt his stomach clench, and he had to look away. He didn't want to think about it.

When he entered the woods, his shoulders relaxed. Here he felt calm. Here no one cared what he looked like or how he talked. In the woods he could simply be Sam.

He closed his eyes and tilted his head back, breathing through his nose. He smelled the leaves and pine needles, he heard birds singing and small animals rustling through the undergrowth. Sometimes he imagined he could even hear the beating wings of a butterfly or the sound of a beetle scuttling up a tree trunk. Slowly, very slowly, he spun around, keeping his eyes shut.

'What are you doing?'

Sam gave a start and almost lost his balance. He opened his eyes.

'Nothing,' he said.

Jessie merely smiled, and he felt a warm sensation spread through his chest.

'That looks fun,' she said, closing her eyes.

She leaned her head back and slowly began spinning. She giggled and stumbled. Sam stepped forward to catch her.

He buried his nose in her hair, then put his arms around her, feeling her soft skin under his hands. He wished she would see herself the way he saw her. He wouldn't change a single thing about her even if he could. The two of them were so alike. Broken inside. And no words could fix that.

She looked at him with those lovely, serious eyes of hers.

'Are you angry?' she asked.

He brushed a lock of hair out of her face.

'No,' he said, realizing he meant it. 'I don't want you to be disappointed, that's all. Or hurt.'

'I know,' she said, hiding her face against his chest. 'I know you've had a different kind of experience with Vendela than I have. But she was super nice when I went over to her house. I don't think it's an act.'

Sam didn't reply. He could feel his hands clench into fists. He knew what Vendela was like. And Nils and Basse too. He'd seen how much they enjoyed tormenting him.

'I'm invited to a party at Basse's house tomorrow night,' said Jessie. 'You're welcome to come too.'

Her eyes shone, and Sam wanted to scream at her not

to go. But people had been bossing her around her whole life. She didn't need him to start doing it too.

'Be careful,' he said, stroking her cheek.

'I'll be fine. But if you're worried, you could come with me.'

'I don't want to see those guys, but you go ahead. I would never tell you what to do. You know that, don't you?'

He held her face between his hands and cautiously kissed her on the lips.

As always, she took his breath away.

'Come on!' he said, taking her hand and pulling her along.

'Where are we going?' she asked, jogging to keep up with him.

'I want to teach you something.'

He stopped and pointed at the target fastened to a tree a short distance away.

'Are you going to shoot?' she asked.

There was a gleam in her eyes that he'd never seen before.

'You are too,' he said.

Jessie didn't take her eyes off the gun when he removed it from his belt.

'I can't believe your parents let you have a gun.'

Sam snorted.

'My father actually encourages it. Shooting is the only thing he thinks I'm good at.'

'Are you good at it?'

'Very.'

And it was true. It was as if his body knew exactly what to do in order to fire the bullet at a precise target.

'I'll show you first, then I'll help you do it. Okay?'

She nodded and gave him a smile.

He loved seeing himself through her eyes. He became

a better person. He became everything his father never thought he could be.

'Take up a stance like this. Plant your feet firmly. Are you right-handed?'

'Yes.'

'So am I. Hold the gun in your right hand like this . . . Rack the slide and the bullet goes into the chamber.'

'Okay.'

'Now you're ready to fire. Keep your hand steady. You should be able to see whatever you're aiming at in the sight. If you can hold the gun steady, you'll hit the intended target.'

He took up position, squinted, aimed, and pulled the trigger. Jessie jumped and screamed. Sam laughed.

'Did I scare you?'

She nodded, but she had a big smile on her face. He motioned for her to stand next to him.

'Now it's your turn.'

He handed her the gun, then stood behind her and put his arms around her.

'Hold it like this.'

He wrapped her fingers around the butt and moved her feet into the correct position.

'Now you're standing like you should and holding the gun properly. Do you have the target in sight? Are you aiming for the middle of it?'

'Yup. I am.'

'Good. I'm going to step away. I want you to squeeze the trigger. Do it gently, don't pull too hard, no sudden movements. You need to caress it.'

Jessie stood straight, with her feet firmly planted, holding the gun as she should. She was breathing calmly.

Sam's shoulders hunched as he waited for the gun to fire.

The shot hit the target, and Jessie jumped up and down.

'Hey, watch out. You can't jump around with a loaded gun!' he shouted, but he was relieved to see how happy she was.

Jessie set down the gun and turned to give him a smile. She'd never looked more beautiful.

'You're so fierce,' he said.

He put his arms around her and pulled her close. He held her tight, as if she were the only thing keeping him in this world. And that was probably true.

'I love you,' he gasped.

For a moment she didn't speak. She looked up at him, a look of uncertainty in her eyes. As if she were wondering whether those words were truly meant for her. Then she smiled that wonderful smile of hers.

'I love you too, Sam.'

'Hi, Kristina!' called Erica, a little too enthusiastically.

She was clearly feeling the effects of all the champagne she'd had, and she reminded herself to pull herself together. For safety's sake she'd chewed menthol gum all the way home, and when she tested her breath by holding her hand in front of her mouth, she hadn't smelled even a trace of alcohol.

'So, I see you've had a couple of drinks,' said Kristina when she came into the front hall.

Erica sighed. Her mother-in-law had a nose like a bloodhound. It was a wonder Patrik didn't make use of her when the police needed help tracking a criminal.

'Oh, you know. They offered me a glass at the gallery opening,' she said.

'One glass?' Kristina snorted and went back to the kitchen.

A wonderful aroma was coming from the oven.

'As usual, I could find nothing but that horrible ready-made food in the house, full of toxic ingredients. The children are going to end up growing tails if you insist on feeding them such rubbish. If you'd only do some real cooking once in a while . . .'

Erica stopped listening. Instead, she went over to the oven and opened the door. Kristina's lasagne. Four casserole dishes, so there would be enough to freeze for later use.

'Thank you,' she said, impulsively giving her mother-in-law a hug.

Kristina looked at her in surprise.

'Definitely more than one glass . . .' She took off her apron, hung it up, and went out to the hall. 'The children can eat when the lasagne is ready. They've been playing nicely, except for a little incident with a toy lorry, but we worked it out just fine, Maja and I. She's such a sweet girl, so like Patrik when he was her age. He never made a fuss. He could sit on the floor for hours and play all by himself . . . But I've got to rush home now. There are so many things to do before the wedding, and Gunnar isn't being much help. He wants to help, but he doesn't really know how, so it's better if I do it all myself. And they phoned from Stora Hotel, insisting that I go over there tomorrow to select the china I want them to use for the wedding dinner. And here was I thinking they only had one kind of china! Nothing about this wedding is proving to be easy, and I have to manage everything myself. I'm supposed to meet someone there at noon, but I hope it won't take long. I asked them to text me photos of the china, but they said it was essential that I see the dishes in person. I'm going to have a heart attack before this is over.'

Kristina sighed. She was standing with her back to Erica as she put on her shoes, so she didn't see Erica smiling. Anna had certainly come up with a good ploy to get Kristina to the hotel.

She waved to her mother-in-law and then went to find the children in the living room. The room looked unusually tidy, and Erica felt a mixture of gratitude and shame. It was a little embarrassing that Patrik's mother felt the need to do some cleaning whenever she came over to their house, but there were certain things Erica prioritized above having a perfectly neat home. Of course she was happy to see everything so orderly, but in her mind that took third place compared to getting her work done or being a mother. And she also needed time to be a wife and maybe even to be Erica. And to manage all that, she sometimes had to prioritize watching an episode of *Dr Phil* instead of tidying up. But the fact that she occasionally simply let things go might be what prevented her from slamming into the proverbial wall.

The timer rang, and she went back to the kitchen to take the four pans of lasagne out of the oven. Her stomach growled loudly. She called the children, got them settled at the kitchen table, and served them and herself a big helping of the wonderfully aromatic food. She enjoyed chatting with the kids. As always, they had lots of questions and she'd learned that 'because' was no longer a sufficient reply.

After dinner the children were eager to go back to playing, so she cleaned up the dishes and put on some coffee. Five minutes later she could finally sit down to look at the diary Viola had given her. She began leafing through it. The diary was filled with scribblings and notes. She had a hard time deciphering the old-fashioned writing style, and she also discovered that Viola was right when she said her father had mostly used abbreviations. But he seemed to have recorded everything that happened each day, from meetings to weather reports. It felt strange to sit there holding the written account of a stranger's life in her hands. Weekdays and weekends, day after day, with details both major and minor recorded in blue ink. Until she finally came to a blank page. She looked at the date of the last entry. It was the day he died.

Pensively she ran her hand over the page. She wondered what had made him decide that this particular day would be the last day of his life. There were no clues in the notes for that day. Nothing but a simple recording of sunshine, a light breeze, a walk to Sälvik, grocery shopping. The only thing that stuck out was the number 11. What could that refer to?

Erica frowned. She went back a few pages to see if she could find the same number somewhere else. No, that was the only time it appeared. But she did find a note for the previous week that caught her attention. She saw the number 55, followed by the note '2 p.m.'. Was 55 a code for someone he was supposed to meet at two? If so, who could it be? And had they met?

Erica put down the diary. Outside the light was changing from yellow to orange, and the sun was sinking below the horizon. It would soon be evening, but only the gods knew when Patrik would come home. She had a vague feeling there was something she should have remembered to tell him, but it had slipped her mind. She shrugged. It probably wasn't important.

Patrik looked around the conference room as he stood at the whiteboard with a marker in his hand.

'We've had some very long and intense days,' he said. 'But considering the latest developments, I want us to go over everything together and then divide up the tasks for tomorrow.'

'Do you think it's time to call in reinforcements?' said Paula. 'From Uddevalla or Gothenburg?'

Patrik shook his head. 'I've already checked with them.

Resources are limited because of cutbacks. So I'm afraid we'll have to handle matters ourselves.'

'Okay,' said Paula, looking resigned.

Patrik could understand her dismay. Her children were even younger than his, and giving up so much family time was a strain.

'Did you find out anything at the community centre?' he asked. He wondered why Paula grinned at Martin when he asked that question.

'No, nothing,' said Martin, without meeting Paula's eye. 'No one saw anything. They were all asleep and were suddenly awakened by the screaming and commotion.'

'Okay, thanks for trying. Gösta, can you tell us what you found out today?'

'Of course,' he said, with a certain pride.

And rightfully so, Patrik thought to himself. Gösta had done some excellent police work.

'I had a feeling there was something wrong about that anonymous tip about the knickers that were so conveniently found in Karim's home.'

Gösta avoided looking at Mellberg, who in turn kept his eyes angrily fixed on a knot in the tabletop.

'And I knew I'd seen something pertinent . . . but I'm not twenty any more, and . . .'

He smiled wryly.

Patrik could see how tense everyone looked. They had realized something was afoot when he and Gösta returned to the station, but Patrik had wanted to wait until they were all gathered before briefing them.

'The thing is, according to her mother, Nea was wearing a pair of knickers with an illustration from the Disney film *Frozen*. She'd bought a pack of five, and each one was a different colour. The knickers found in Karim's home were blue, and there was something about them that I couldn't get out of my head. And then it came to me, but I wasn't sure how to prove I was right. You see, I wasn't one hundred per cent—'

'Good lord, get to the point,' muttered Mellberg, earning himself icy glares from his colleagues.

'I remembered that Johannes Klingberg, who was part of the group that found Nea, had used his mobile to video what was going on before he joined the search party. So Patrik and I went to see him, and we got a copy of the video. Patrik, would you like to show everyone?'

Patrik tapped on the computer keyboard he'd set up on the table. Then he turned the monitor at an angle so everyone could see.

'What are we looking for?' asked Martin, leaning forward.

'Have a look and see if you can tell what it is. If you don't see it, we'll run the video again and point it out,' said Patrik.

Everyone stared intently at the screen. The camera panned over the farm, back and forth, filming the house, the gravel yard, the barn, and all the people who had gathered.

'There,' said Gösta. 'On the clothes line. Do you see?'

They leaned even closer.

'Blue knickers!' exclaimed Paula. 'They're hanging on the line!'

'Exactly!'

Gösta clasped his hands behind his head.

'Nea couldn't possibly have had those knickers on when she disappeared, because they were hanging on the clothes line while we were searching for her.'

'In other words, someone stole them and planted them in Karim's house. And then they made an anonymous phone call, which Mellberg answered.'

'Yes,' said Patrik grimly. 'Someone tried to place the

478

blame on Karim, and my guess is that Karim wasn't necessarily the specific target. I think whoever made the call just wanted to direct suspicion at someone at the refugee centre.'

Paula sighed. 'There's been a lot of talk in town about how one of the refugees must be the killer.'

'And then somebody had the brilliant idea of taking matters into their own hands,' said Patrik. 'I think we can assume the motive was racist. The question is, was the same individual – or group – responsible for setting the fire.'

'There have been arson attacks on refugee centres all over Sweden,' said Gösta gloomily. 'Some people think they're above the law.'

'Considering how many voted for Sveriges Vänner in the last election, I'm not surprised,' said Patrik, shaking his head.

Sweden wasn't alone in witnessing a surge in popularity for right-wing parties opposed to immigration. The same thing was happening all over Europe. People were even turning against second-generation immigrants, like Paula. But Patrik had never thought the tide of hatred would reach Fjällbacka.

'I suggest that we separate this arson investigation from the investigation into Nea's murder. I no longer think the two cases are related, and I don't want to confuse things by mixing apples with oranges. We've already lost valuable time.'

'It wasn't that easy to work out,' muttered Mellberg, but then he realized it was best to keep a low profile and fell silent.

'Paula, I'd like you to take charge of the arson investigation, with help from Martin. Keep talking to the refugees, not only about when and how the fire was set, but also when the knickers might have been planted in

Karim's home. Did any of them see someone at the refugee centre who didn't belong, and so on.'

'It's hard to know what time period we should be asking about,' said Paula.

Patrik paused to think about this.

'There must be a connection with the timing of the anonymous phone call. That came in around lunchtime on Thursday,' he said. 'Start there and work your way back in time. Gösta has checked with Nea's family, and they have no idea when the knickers disappeared from the clothes line. So the only thing we know for sure is that they were there when the search party started. They could have been stolen from the farm at any time afterwards.'

Paula turned to Gösta.

'Did you ask the family whether they'd noticed anyone who shouldn't have been there?'

'Yes, but they didn't see anyone. It's not hard to sneak on to the property from the woods and discreetly swipe something from the clothes line. It's behind the house, near a wall with no windows.'

'Okay,' said Paula, jotting down a note. 'I'd like us to check with our sources within the anti-immigrant organizations in the area. Maybe it wouldn't be wise for me to do that, given my own "ethnic background". Martin, could you do it?'

'Definitely,' he said.

Patrik hoped that Martin wouldn't feel he'd been passed over because Paula had been put in charge instead of him. But he thought Martin was smart enough to know his time would come soon.

'Good. Sounds like you're on top of the situation, with regard to the investigation of the fire and the attempt to blame Karim. Stay in contact with the hospital as well, and keep me updated about what happens. How are the children doing, Paula? Have you been given permission to take them home?'

'Yes, and everything's set on the home front.'

Mellberg had been unusually quiet, but now his face lit up.

'It'll be fun for Leo to have some playmates.'

'Good,' said Patrik curtly.

He forced himself not to think too much about Karim and his family. Right now there was nothing he could do, other than attempt to catch the person who had harmed them.

'So now we need to talk about the homicide case. As you know, I'm not happy that we had to break off the search of the Berg family's farm. I've spoken to Torbjörn, and his team will be available tomorrow afternoon so we can complete the search. We cordoned off the area, and we can only hope that nothing was compromised in any way. We'll have to assume that's the case.'

'Yes, not much we can do about it,' said Gösta.

Patrik knew he found it unpleasant to have to invade the Berg family home for a second time.

'How's it going, comparing the current homicide case to the old investigation?' asked Patrik. Annika looked up from her notes.

'I still haven't managed to locate the old interview files in the archives, but I've gone through the forensic and technical reports again, plus all the material we received from Erica. There's not much new for us to go on. You've all read the post-mortem report, you've seen the material from the crime scene, and you've heard what Erica had to say about Marie and Helen.'

'Yes, and our conversations with Helen and Marie didn't produce anything either. They claim they didn't kill Stella, which means someone else did. And in theory that could be the same person we're looking for now.

Marie has an alibi. Helen doesn't, but there's nothing pointing at her.'

Martin reached for a Ballerina biscuit. The chocolate filling had melted in the heat, and he had to lick it off his fingers.

'We'll start with the search at the Berg farm tomorrow. Then we'll go from there,' said Patrik.

There were far too many blind alleys and too few leads for his liking. If they didn't find more to go on, the investigation could easily grind to a standstill.

'What about the chocolate found in Nea's stomach? Could that give us some kind of lead?' asked Paula.

Patrik shook his head. 'Apparently it was from an ordinary chocolate bar, sold in every shop. We'd never be able to trace it. But since there was no chocolate found in the Berg home, Nea must have got it somewhere else that morning. Or someone gave it to her.'

'What do you think about the fact that, at the end of his life, Leif had begun to doubt the girls were guilty?' asked Gösta.

'I know Erica is looking into that. I only hope she'll find something.'

'Civilians doing the work of the police,' muttered Mellberg, scratching Ernst behind the ear.

'And doing a better job than some people I might mention,' said Martin.

Patrik cleared his throat. 'We need to work together. We all have to be on the same page,' he said. 'All of us.'

Clearly embarrassed, Martin swiftly changed the subject: 'When will we get the analysis of the anonymous phone call? Do you think it'll take a long time? And what can we expect it to tell us?'

'I'm not sure what's possible,' replied Patrik. 'My hope is they'll be able to wipe away the filter so we can hear the caller's real voice. And if we're lucky there might be something in the background that will help us identify them.'

'Like in the films, where there's always the sound of a train whistle or a church bell tolling?' teased Martin.

'Right. It's possible we'll get some crucial information from the recording,' said Patrik.

He looked around the room and noticed Gösta stifling a yawn.

'I think we'll call it a night now – we all need to get some rest. So go home, spend time with your family, eat, sleep, and then we'll start fresh in the morning.'

Everyone gratefully got up. He could see the enormous stress of the past few days etched into their faces. They needed to be with those who were near and dear to them tonight. They all did. He hesitated and then turned to Gösta, but Martin beat him to it.

'Could you come over and have dinner with me and Tuva tonight? She'd love to see you.'

'Sure,' Gösta said with a shrug. But he couldn't hide how happy that made him.

Patrik stayed behind as, one by one, his colleagues left the room. They were a family. In many ways a dysfunctional, demanding, and unruly family. But at the same time a family that was loving and considerate.

BOHUSLÄN 1672

Her body had recovered faster than she had thought possible. It ached and stung for a few days, but then it was as if nothing had happened. Yet she felt the loss. She went about her duties and carried out her tasks, but without joy.

Märta was uneasy and slept close to Elin at night, as if trying to warm her mother with her body. She gave Elin little gifts to make her smile again. Small bouquets of flowers she picked in the meadow, a lovely white stone she found on the gravel path, a handful of yellow mica in a jar. And Elin did try. She smiled at Märta and thanked her for the presents as she patted the child's soft cheek. But she was aware that her smile never reached her eyes. And her arms felt stiff and clumsy when she pulled Märta close.

Preben no longer spoke to her or to Märta. The girl had finally accepted the situation and made no further effort to attract his attention. She continued her reading lessons with the parish clerk, but it felt as if all the time she had spent in the library with Preben had never happened. The news that Britta was with child had changed everything, and Preben treated his wife like a fragile porcelain doll.

Now that she had her husband's full attention, Britta's power grew ever stronger. Yet the resentment she felt towards Elin also grew. Elin constantly felt her sister's watchful eyes on her, even though there was no longer any reason for her to keep watch. Elin did what she was told to do. On those occasions when she was not at Britta's beck and call, she did her best to avoid her. It was a constant reminder and torment to see Britta's stomach grow, while her own was flat and barren.

One morning Britta decided she needed to go into Fjällbacka. It was mostly because she was tired of staying in bed, and now that the doctor had said she might get up, she needed a change of scene.

Elin stood and watched as her sister left. Britta had spent an hour getting dressed, which Elin regarded as wasted effort, since she was only going to Fjällbacka. But Uddevalla was too far for someone in her condition, so Britta had to settle for Fjällbacka, and she clearly enjoyed getting out of her nightgown and donning her finery.

The day passed quickly. It was wash day, and everything at the vicarage had to be taken out to be scoured and scrubbed, hung outside in the sun to dry, and then carried back indoors. It felt good to be so busy that there was no time to think. And Elin was happy that neither Britta nor Preben was home. Preben was in Lur on church business and would be gone for two days, while Britta was expected home in the evening.

For the first time since getting rid of the baby, Elin found herself humming.

Märta looked at her in surprise. Her little face lit up with such joy that Elin felt a pang in her heart. She was ashamed she had allowed her daughter to suffer for her sake. She dropped the rug she was scrubbing and pulled Märta close as she kissed her blond hair. It would be all right. They had each other.

Everything else had been a dream. A childish, impossible dream. Elin had tried to convince herself that God was on their side, that He was with her and Preben, but her pride had been knocked out of her. God had punished her in the way He found most suitable. And who was she to question His will? Instead, she should be grateful for what she had. Her daughter Märta. Food to eat and a place to live. Many people did not have even a fraction of what she possessed, and it would be presumptuous of her to wish for more.

'Shall we take a walk this evening? Just you and me?' she asked as she squatted down in front of Märta, keeping her arms around the child.

Märta nodded eagerly. Sigrid was running around at her feet, jumping and leaping, seeming to sense that her mistress was happy.

'I thought we could take along a basket, and I could teach you a little of what my grandmother taught me. And what she in turn learned from her mother. How you can help others, the way I sometimes do.'

'Oh, Mother!' cried Märta, throwing her arms around Elin's neck. 'Does this mean I am a big girl now?'

'Yes!' Elin laughed. 'It means you are a big girl now.'

Märta beamed and then ran off with Sigrid at her heels. Smiling, Elin watched her go. It was a couple of years earlier than she had planned, but Märta had been forced to grow up quickly, so it seemed only right.

She leaned down and began scrubbing the rug again. The muscles in her arms ached from the heavy work, but her heart felt lighter than it had in a long time. With the back of her hand she wiped the sweat from her forehead and then looked up when she heard the sound of a wagon coming into the yard.

She squinted into the sun. Britta had returned home, and her expression was dark as she climbed down from the wagon. She strode over to Elin, her skirts swinging, and came to a halt right in front of her. Everyone on the farm had stopped what they were doing. Britta's expression made Elin take a step back. She could not understand what was happening until she felt Britta's hand strike her cheek. Then Britta turned on her heel and stormed inside the house.

Elin lowered her eyes. She could feel that everyone was staring at her. Now she knew what had happened. Britta had found out why Elin had gone to Fjällbacka. And she was smart enough to have put two and two together.

Her cheeks burning with shame, and still feeling the sting of the slap Britta had given her, Elin squatted down to continue the scrubbing. She had no idea what would happen now. But she knew her sister. Something evil was in the offing.

'Why do you think your mother agreed to let me talk to you?' asked Erica, studying the teenager sitting across from her.

She had been surprised when Sam phoned, but also very happy. Sam might be able to give her a new perspective on Helen as a person and how it had felt to grow up in the shadow of a crime.

He shrugged.

'I haven't a clue. But she talked to you herself.'

'Yes, but I had the feeling she wanted to keep you out of it.'

Erica slid the plate of cinnamon buns towards Sam. He took one. She noticed his fingernails were painted black, although the polish was beginning to flake off. There was something touching about his attempt to look older than his years. His skin was still downy and oily in patches. His body was gangly and did not yet possess the control of an adult. He was a child who desperately wanted to be grown up; he wanted to be different, and yet he also wanted to belong. Erica was suddenly filled with a great tenderness for this boy. She saw his loneliness and uncertainty, and she also sensed the frustration lurking behind his defiant expression. It couldn't be easy for him, growing up in the

shadow of his mother's history, being born into a community rampant with whispered gossip and rumours. Though
the talk had died down over the years, it had never ceased
entirely.

'She couldn't keep me out of it,' said Sam gloomily,
as if confirming what Erica was thinking.

Like the teenager he was, he seemed reluctant to meet
her eye, but she saw that he was listening intently to
everything she said.

'What do you mean?' asked Erica.

The recording function on her mobile was capturing
every word and inflection.

'I've heard about it ever since I was little. I don't
remember how it began, but people would ask me about
things. Their kids would taunt me. I don't know how old
I was when I started finding out more details. Maybe
when I was nine? I did a search on the Internet, looking
for articles about the case. It wasn't hard to do. And after
that I collected whatever I could find. I have folders at
home filled with newspaper clippings.'

'Does your mother know?'

Sam shrugged. 'No, I don't think so.'

'Has she ever talked to you about what happened?'

'No, not a word. We've never talked about it at home.'

'Did you want to talk about it?' asked Erica gently as
she got up to pour herself more coffee.

Sam had said yes to her offer of coffee, but she saw
now that he hadn't touched his cup. She guessed he
would rather have had a can of Coke or something but
didn't want to seem childish.

Again Sam shrugged. He cast a longing glance at the
plate of buns.

'Help yourself,' said Erica. 'Take as many as you like.
I'm trying not to eat so many sweet things, so you'll be
doing me a favour. If they're not there, I won't be tempted.'

'Oh, you look great. You shouldn't worry about that,' Sam said magnanimously, with the innocence of a child.

She smiled as she sat back down. Sam was a nice boy. She wished he could let go of the burden he'd been forced to carry all his life. He hadn't done anything wrong. He hadn't chosen to be born into a web of guilt, accusations, and sorrow. The sins of his parents were not his burden to bear. Yet she could see how it weighed on his shoulders.

'Would it have been easier if you and your family could have talked openly about what happened?' asked Erica.

'We don't talk. Not about anything. We . . . we're not that kind of family.'

'But was it something you would have wanted?' she persisted.

He raised his eyes and looked at her. The black eye make-up made it hard for her to focus on his gaze, but somewhere inside a light was gasping for oxygen.

'Yes,' he said at last. 'Yes, that's what I would have wanted.'

Then he shrugged. The gesture was his armour. His defence. His indifference was a cloak of invisibility behind which he could hide.

'Did you know Linnea?' asked Erica, changing the subject.

Sam gave a start. He took a big bite of cinnamon bun and looked down as he chewed.

'Why do you ask?' he said. 'What does that have to do with Stella?'

'I'm just curious. My book is going to deal with both cases, and since you're a neighbour of the Berg family, I thought you could tell me a little about what Nea was like. What you thought of her.'

'I saw her often,' said Sam, his eyes filling with tears.

'That's not so strange, since we lived so close to each other. But she was only a kid. I can't say I knew her. I liked her, and I think she liked me. She used to wave when I cycled past their farm.'

'But you can't tell me anything else about her?'

'No. What would I say?'

Erica shrugged. Then she decided to ask the question she really wanted an answer to.

'Who do you think murdered Stella?' she asked, holding her breath.

Did Sam think his mother was guilty? She still hadn't decided what her own opinion was on the matter. The more she read, the more she talked with people, and the more she checked the facts, the more confused she felt. So it was important to hear what Sam would say.

He paused for a long time before answering. He drummed his fingers on the table. Then he raised his eyes and the flickering light in his gaze steadied as he looked at her.

His voice was barely above a whisper when he said, 'I have no idea. But my mother didn't murder anyone.'

When Sam left on his bike a little while later, Erica stood in the window and watched him go. Something about him had touched her deeply. She felt such sympathy for the black-clad boy who hadn't been allowed the upbringing he deserved. She wondered how it would shape him. What sort of man he would become. She sincerely hoped that the pain she saw emanating from him wouldn't set him on the wrong track, and that along the way he would meet someone who would fill the hole created by the past.

She hoped someone would love Sam.

'How do you think she's going to react?' asked Anna. 'Do you think she'll be cross?'

They were standing in the dining room of the Stora Hotel, waiting for Kristina to arrive.

Erica hushed her. 'She could be here any minute.'

'Yes, but Kristina isn't exactly fond of surprises. What if she gets angry?'

'It's a little late to be worrying about that,' Erica hissed. 'And stop pushing me.'

'Sorry, but I can't do anything about my stomach,' Anna retorted.

'Okay, girls, keep it down or she's going to hear us.'

Kristina's closest friend Barbro was giving them a stern look, so Erica and Anna stopped talking. A small but valiant group had gathered for Kristina's bachelorette party. In addition to Erica and Anna, four other women were present. Erica had met them only briefly, so in the worst-case scenario, this could turn out to be a very long afternoon and evening.

'She's coming!'

Anna waved excitedly to the others. They heard Kristina's voice at the front desk. The receptionist had been given instructions to tell Kristina to go to the dining room.

'Surprise!' they all shouted when she came in.

Kristina jumped and pressed a hand to her chest.

'Good lord! What's all this?'

'It's your bachelorette party!' cried Erica with a big smile, although she was quaking a bit inside.

What if Anna was right?

For a moment Kristina didn't say a word. Then she started laughing.

'Bachelorette party! For an old woman like me! You're out of your minds! But okay, let's do it! Where do I start? Selling kisses in a booth?'

She winked at Erica, who felt overwhelmed with relief. Maybe this wouldn't be a complete disaster after all.

'No, you don't have to sell kisses,' said Erica, giving her mother-in-law a hug. 'We've planned something else. First you have to change your clothes. I've put your new outfit in this bag.'

Kristina looked alarmed as she eyed the bag Erica held out to her.

'You don't have wear it anywhere else. It's for our eyes only.'

'Okay . . .' said Kristina warily, but she took the bag. 'I'll just slip into the ladies and get changed.'

While Kristina was gone, the receptionist brought in six glasses and a bottle of champagne in a bucket. Anna cast an envious glance at the bottle but then picked up a glass of juice instead.

'Cheers,' she said and took a few sips.

Erica put her arm around her sister's shoulders. 'It won't be long now . . .'

She poured champagne for the other women and then filled a glass for herself as they waited for Kristina to return. Everyone gasped in unison when she appeared in the doorway to the dining room.

'What on earth were you thinking?'

Kristina threw out her hands, and Erica had to hold back a giggle. Yet she had to admit that her mother-in-law looked amazing in the short red dress with fringe and sequins. And what legs! thought Erica jealously. She'd give anything to have legs half as nice as Kristina's.

'What are you planning for me to do, dressed like this?' asked Kristina, but she allowed herself to be ushered into the room.

Erica handed Kristina a glass of champagne. Her mother-in-law nervously downed half of it at once.

'You'll see,' said Erica, taking out her mobile and sending a text: *Come now.*

While she waited for an answer, she shifted from

one foot to the other. This could go either way. Fun or fiasco.

They heard music coming from upstairs. Hot Latin rhythms slowly approaching. Kristina drank the rest of her champagne. Erica hurried to refill her glass.

A plump figure wearing a black suit appeared. Gripping a rose in his teeth, he dramatically threw out his arms. Anna giggled, and Erica poked her in the side.

'Oh, my! Gunnar?' said Kristina in surprise.

Then she too began to giggle.

'My beautiful lady,' he said, taking the rose out of his mouth. 'May I?'

He went over to Kristina and with a flourish handed her the rose. She was now laughing hard.

'What on earth is all this!' she exclaimed, accepting the rose.

'You're going to learn to dance the cha-cha,' said Erica with a smile.

She pointed to the doorway.

'And we've brought in some expert help.'

'What? Who?' said Kristina, suddenly looking nervous again.

But Gunnar was beaming. He could hardly contain himself.

'We've hired an expert. Someone you admire on the TV show *Let's Dance*. Someone you watch every Friday.'

'Not Tony Irving?' said Kristina, startled. 'I'm terrified of Tony!'

'No, no, not Tony. Someone else who's usually very stern.'

Kristina frowned as she thought hard. The sequins on her dress rustled when she moved, and Erica reminded herself to take pictures. Lots of pictures. They would be prime blackmail material for years to come.

Then Kristina saw who came into the room, and she shouted:

'Cissi!'

Erica had a big smile on her face. Kristina's look of joy told her this had been a brilliant idea. Everyone who knew Kristina was aware that she was a huge fan of *Let's Dance*, so when Erica caught sight of an advert announcing that Cecilia 'Cissi' Ehrling Danermark from *Let's Dance* would be offering a course at TanumStrand, she'd instantly made a phone call.

'Okay, let's get started!' exclaimed Cissi enthusiastically after saying hello to everyone.

Kristina looked nervous again.

'Do I have to dance in front of everybody? I'll make a total fool of myself.'

'No, no. Everybody's going to dance,' said Cissi firmly.

Erica and Anna exchanged terrified looks. That wasn't part of the plan. She thought Kristina and Gunnar would have a dance lesson while everyone could watch and drink bubbly. But she knew better than to protest. Giving Anna a long look, she went over to Cissi. She wasn't about to let Anna off the hook by claiming she was too pregnant to dance.

Two hours later Erica was sweaty, tired, and happy. Cissi had gone over the basic steps with an energy that was infectious but eventually wore them all out. Erica could only imagine how her whole body was going to ache in the morning. But it had been so much fun to see Kristina's joy as she moved her feet and hips, shaking the fringe on her dress. Gunnar also seemed to be enjoying himself immensely, though he was sweating buckets in his dark suit.

'Thank you,' Erica said to Cissi, impulsively giving her a hug.

This was one of the most fun things she'd ever done. But now it was time to move on to the next item on the agenda. She had planned the day down to the last detail, and besides, they only had use of the dining room at Stora Hotel for two hours.

She refilled everyone's glass.

'Now it's time for the groom to leave us,' she said. 'For the rest of the afternoon and evening, gentlemen are not invited. We've booked a suite on the top floor so we can get ready. We have an hour to rest, and then it's time for cooking lessons.'

Kristina gave Gunnar a kiss. Apparently he'd got a real taste for the dancing, because he elegantly dipped her, and everyone cheered. The mood couldn't have been better.

'Nice job,' whispered Anna, patting Erica's arm. 'Although you're awfully stiff. Even the old ladies were better at shaking their hips than you were.'

'Oh, shut up,' said Erica, swatting at her sister, who merely grinned.

When they went upstairs to the Marco Polo suite, Erica realized she hadn't thought about her work for even a second since the bachelorette party began. That was wonderful. A much-needed break. But she couldn't believe how her feet ached.

'How are all of you holding up?'

They gave Bill a bewildered look, which reminded him for the thousandth time that he had to speak simple Swedish or English.

'Are you okay?' he asked in English.

They nodded, but their expressions were tense. He understood. It must feel as if it would never end. So many of the refugees he'd talked to at the community centre told him the same thing. They had thought that if only they could get to Sweden, everything would be all right. But the locals looked at them with suspicion, and they encountered lots of red tape and far too many people who hated everything they were and stood for.

'Adnan, could you take over?' said Bill, motioning towards the helm.

Adnan took his place with a glint of pride in his eyes. Bill sincerely hoped he'd be able to show them a different picture of the country he loved. Swedes were not evil. They were afraid. That was what made society more harsh. Fear. Not evil.

'Could you trim the sails, Khalil?'

Bill tugged on an imaginary line and pointed.

Khalil nodded and perfectly trimmed the sails, precisely according to the rule book, just enough so the sail grew taut and stopped fluttering.

The boat picked up speed and began leaning a tad, but this no longer caused panicked looks among the crew. Bill wished he felt equally calm. The regatta was fast approaching, and there was so much more he needed to teach them. But as things now stood, he was just happy they were willing to continue. He would have understood if they'd decided to throw in the towel and give up on the whole project. But they'd said they wanted to keep going for Karim's sake, and he'd noticed a new determination when they arrived at the boat club this morning. They were taking it more seriously, and this was evident in the way they sailed, the way the boat moved through the water.

People who were into horseback riding talked about how important it was to communicate with the horse, and for Bill the same thing was true of boats. They were not dead, soulless objects. Sometimes he thought he understood boats better than people.

'We need to tack in a moment,' he said, and they knew what he meant.

For the first time they felt like a team. Something good always comes from something bad, as his father used to say. And that seemed to apply to this situation. But the cost had been high. He had rung the hospital in the morning to hear how Amina was doing, but they refused to give out any information to anyone who was not a family member. For now he hoped that no news was good news.

'Okay, tack now.'

When the sail filled and grew taut with wind, he had to restrain himself from shouting with joy. It was the best they'd done so far. They were sailing the boat like a well-oiled machine.

'Great, boys,' he said emphatically, giving them a thumbs up.

Khalil's face lit up, and the others sat up straighter.

They reminded Bill so much of his older sons. He'd taken them out sailing too. Had he ever done that with Nils? He didn't think so. He'd never given the boy the same amount of attention he'd given to Alexander and Philip. And now he was paying the price.

Nils was a stranger to him. Bill didn't understand how Nils's attitude and anger could have been fostered in the home he and Gun had created, a home where their guiding principles were tolerance and consideration. Where had Nils got all his ideas?

Last night when he came home, Bill had decided to have a talk with Nils. A real talk. Open up old wounds, lance the abscesses, lay it all out and ask for forgiveness, allowing Nils to let loose his disappointment and anger. But Nils had locked the door to his room, and he refused to open it when Bill knocked. He had merely turned up the volume so the music was soon pounding through the whole house. In the end, Gun put her hand on Bill's shoulder and asked him to wait. Give Nils some more time. And no doubt she was right. Everything would work out eventually. Nils was young and still developing.

'Let's head for home,' he said now, pointing towards Fjällbacka.

Sam was slumped over his bowl of yogurt, focusing all his attention on his mobile. Helen's heart ached as she looked at him. She wondered where he'd been in the morning.

'You're spending a lot of time with Jessie these days,' she said.

'Uh-huh. And?'

Sam pushed back his chair and went over to the fridge. He poured himself a big glass of milk and chugged it down. He suddenly looked so young. It seemed to Helen as if only a few weeks had passed since he was tottering around in shorts, with his beloved and battered teddy bear under his arm. She wondered what had happened to the bear. James had probably thrown it out. He didn't like them to hold on to things they no longer used. Saving something for its sentimental value was not part of his world.

'I just meant that it might not be wise,' she said.

Sam shook his head.

'I thought we weren't supposed to talk about that.'

The world began spinning before her, as it always did when she thought about it. She closed her eyes and managed to make the spinning stop. She'd had many years of practice. She'd spent thirty years living in the eye of a storm, until finally she'd grown used to it.

'It's just that I don't know whether I like the two of you spending so much time together,' she said, and she could hear the pleading in her voice. 'I don't think your father would like it either.'

In the past, that argument had sufficed.

'James.' Sam snorted. 'Isn't he going back on duty soon?'

'Yes, in another week,' she said, unable to hide her relief.

They'd have months of freedom ahead of them. Respite. The absurd thing was that she knew James felt the same way. They were prisoners in a prison of their own making. And Sam had become their shared hostage.

Sam set down his glass.

'Jessie is the only one who has ever understood me. That's something you'll never understand, but it's true.'

He put the milk carton back in the fridge, on the shelf intended for butter and cheese.

She wanted to tell Sam that of course she understood. She understood all too well. But the wall between them merely got higher and higher with all the secrets. They were strangling him and he couldn't know why. She should have been able to set Sam free, but she didn't dare. And now it was too late. Her inheritance, her guilt, had trapped him in a cage, and it was just as impossible for him to escape as it was for her. Their fate in life was intertwined and could not be separated, no matter how much she wished it could.

But the silence was unbearable. His facade was so impenetrable, so hard. He must have so much inside that could explode at any moment.

She decided to make a try.

'Do you ever think about—'

He interrupted her. His expression was so cold, so like James's.

'I already told you, we don't talk about that.'

Helen fell silent.

The front door opened, and they heard James come stomping inside. Before she could even blink, Sam had disappeared upstairs to his room. She got up, pushed in her chair, and put the plates and glasses in the dishwasher. Then she hurried over to the fridge to move the milk to its proper place.

*　　*　　*

'So, here we go again,' said Torbjörn dryly. Patrik felt his stomach knot.

Everything having to do with this search of the Berg family's property had been such a muddle, and he wasn't sure how that might affect the results. The only thing they could do was roll up their sleeves and get going.

'Yes. We didn't find anything of interest in the house, so now we're going to tackle the barn,' he said.

'And then the shed and the rest of the property, if I understood correctly when we spoke yesterday.'

Patrik nodded.

'Yes, that's right.'

Torbjörn peered at him over the rims of his glasses. He'd started wearing them a few years ago. A reminder that they were both getting older.

'So, I heard it was Mellberg who made a real mess of things.'

'Who else?' replied Patrik with a sigh. 'But we have to make the best of the situation. At least it's a relief not to have the family here this time.'

Patrik surveyed the deserted farm, grateful for Gösta's help. He'd had a long phone conversation with Peter, explaining why they needed to complete the search of the family's property. He'd suggested that it might be a good time for the family to leave the farm for a few hours. Apparently they had listened to his advice, because they were gone when Patrik and Gösta and the tech team arrived.

'Can I come with you?' Patrik asked Torbjörn, hoping he would say yes.

It was always important that as few people as possible were present at the place to be searched, but he didn't know what else he would do. For whatever reason, Gösta had disappeared into the woods.

'Okay,' said Torbjörn. 'But stay back as much as possible – and you have to wear the full protective suit. Okay?'

'Absolutely,' said Patrik, although he felt sick at the thought of how hot it would be inside the Tyvek suit.

This summer was beating all records for high temperatures, and he sweated enough in his ordinary clothes.

Just as he'd thought, it felt like being in a steam bath when he put on the protective suit. Yet it was cooler inside the barn than outdoors. He'd always liked barns. There was something special about the way the light seeped through the cracks in the boards in the walls. It felt somehow like a sacred place. A barn breathed peace and calm. So in a way it felt wrong to be invading that calm with rustling plastic suits, equipment, fluids, and the low murmuring of technicians as they worked.

Patrik took up position in one corner and looked around the barn. It was big, and someone had kept it in good repair. It didn't seem to be on the verge of collapse like so many barns out in the country. Nor had it been converted to a storage room. It was not filled with old cars, tractors, or junk. It was empty and neat and tidy. A ladder led up to the hayloft at one end, and Patrik was itching to climb up there.

He gave a start. Something had rubbed against his leg, and he looked down. A grey cat meowed and wound its way between his legs. He leaned down to scratch under its chin. The cat began purring loudly, turning its head with contentment.

'What's your name?' he babbled, petting the cat. 'What a fine cat you are.'

The cat was so happy it rolled on to its back and allowed Patrik to tickle its belly.

'Patrik?'

'Yes?'

He straightened up. At first the cat looked offended and disappointed, but then it got up and sauntered off.

'Could you come up here?'

Torbjörn motioned to him from the loft.

'There's nothing here,' said Torbjörn when Patrik climbed up. 'Except for this.'

He held up a Kex chocolate bar wrapper.

Patrik frowned.

'Pedersen thought it was Kex chocolate that Nea had in her stomach when she was found,' he said, feeling his pulse rise.

It could be a coincidence. But he rarely believed in coincidences.

'We'll try to get fingerprints off of it,' said Torbjörn. 'With the naked eye I can see there are some excellent prints. The wrapper was wedged in between two loose boards up here. It was sheer luck that I found it, because apart from that the place is clinically clean. Almost too clean.'

Torbjörn gestured towards the loft.

'Could you come back down?' said one of the techs who was working below the hayloft. 'We need to black out the barn now.'

Torbjörn climbed down with the Kex wrapper in a bag, and Patrik followed.

'The next part of the search has to be done in total darkness,' Torbjörn explained. 'So we have to cover all the walls with dark cloth. It can take quite a while, so you might as well wait outside.'

Patrik sat down on a patio chair and watched as the techs went in and out of the barn. Then they closed the doors, and silence descended.

After what seemed ages, Torbjörn called to him. Hesitantly Patrik got up and went over to open the door. He stepped inside the dark barn. It took a moment for his eyes to adjust, but then he saw several dark shadows some distance away.

'Come over here,' said Torbjörn, and Patrik cautiously headed towards his voice.

503

As he got closer, he saw what Torbjörn and the other techs were studying with such interest. A bright blue patch on the floor. After witnessing many crime scene inspections, he knew what that meant. The techs had sprayed the area with Luminol, which showed traces of blood that could not be seen with the naked eye. And this was a big patch.

'I think we've found the primary crime scene,' he said.

'Don't go jumping to conclusions,' said Torbjörn. 'Don't forget this is an old barn, and they've probably kept animals here. So this could be an old bloodstain.'

'Or not. The stain, combined with the chocolate wrapper you found, makes me think we've found the place where Nea died.'

'I think you're right. But I've been wrong before, so it's always best not to latch on to any one theory until we have the facts to prove it.'

'Can we take samples to compare with Nea's blood? So we can get a definite match?'

Torbjörn nodded.

'Do you see the gaps in the floor? I'm guessing the blood ran down into the cracks, so even if someone tried to give the place a real good scrub, we'll find blood if we tear up the floorboards.'

'So let's do it,' said Patrik.

Torbjörn held up his gloved hand.

'First we need to document everything very carefully. Give us a while, and I'll holler when we're ready to pull up the floor.'

'Okay,' said Patrik, retreating once more to a corner of the barn.

The grey cat came over to rub against his leg again, and he obediently squatted down to pet it.

Even though it felt like an eternity, it actually took no more than fifteen minutes before the techs turned on the lights, and Torbjörn said they were ready to pull up the floorboards. Patrik stood up so quickly that the cat was frightened and raced off. He went over to the place on the floor that had now been documented from all angles. Samples had been taken and bagged. The only thing remaining was to see what was underneath.

The barn door opened, and Patrik turned around. Gösta came towards them, holding his mobile in his hand.

'I just talked to our colleagues in Uddevalla.'

'The ones who are supposed to be checking on the sex offender Tore Carlson?'

Gösta shook his head. 'It wasn't about that. I'd asked them some questions about the Berg family when I rang them last time. They told me they still talk about the Bergs at the station.'

Patrik raised an eyebrow.

'And?'

'Well, apparently Peter Berg had a reputation for turning violent when he was drunk.'

'How violent?'

'Extremely violent. Lots of brawls at the local pub.'

'But no reports of domestic abuse?'

Gösta shook his head.

'No, nothing like that. And no reports were ever filed against him. That's why we never found anything on him.'

'Okay. Good to know. Thanks, Gösta. We'll have another talk with Peter.'

Gösta nodded at the techs.

'What's going on here? Have you found something?'

'A Kex chocolate bar wrapper up in the loft. But more importantly, we've found traces of blood. It's been cleaned up, but it was visible when the techs sprayed Luminol. Right now we're going to pull up the floorboards because Torbjörn thinks blood may have run underneath.'

'My God,' said Gösta, staring at the floor. 'So you think—'

'Yes,' said Patrik. 'I think Nea died here.'

For a moment no one spoke. Then they began pulling up the first board.

BOHUSLÄN 1672

A commotion outside the door woke Elin. For the first time in weeks she had slept soundly. It had done her good to take a long walk with Märta yesterday, just as the sun was setting over the meadows. And it had almost chased away her uneasy feeling about what Britta might do. Britta cared about appearances, so she would not want to live with the shame if people knew what had gone on between her husband and her sister. This was what Elin had managed to tell herself right before she fell asleep. The whole thing would blow over. Britta would be fully occupied caring for a baby in the house, and time had a way of making even the most overwhelming matters fade until they eventually vanished completely.

She was having such a lovely dream about Märta when all the commotion jolted Elin from her slumber. She sat up, rubbing her eyes. She was the first of the maids to awake, so she swung her legs over the side of the bed she shared with Märta.

'I am coming,' she said, hurrying to the door. 'What an awful tumult so early in the morning.'

She opened the heavy wooden door. Outside stood Sheriff Jakobsson, a grim expression on his face.

'I am looking for Elin Jonsdotter.'

'I am Elin,' she told him.

Everyone was now awake, and she could tell they were listening tensely.

'You are accused of witchcraft, and you must come with me to the gaol.'

Elin stared at him. What was he saying? Witchcraft? Had he lost his senses?

'There must be a misunderstanding,' she said.

Märta had slipped forward and was now holding on to Elin's skirts. She pushed the child behind her.

'There is no misunderstanding. We are here to take you into custody, and later you will be charged before the court.'

'But this cannot be right. I am no witch. Speak with my sister. She is the vicar's wife. She can affirm—'

'It is Britta Willumsen who has accused you of witchcraft,' the sheriff interrupted her, taking a firm grip on Elin's arm.

She fought against him as the sheriff dragged her outside. Märta screamed and held on to her skirts. Elin gasped when Märta fell to the ground behind her. As she watched the others rush forward to help her daughter, the sheriff gripped her arm even harder. Everything was whirling before her eyes. Britta had accused her of being a witch.

Jessie's hand shook slightly as she stood in front of the mirror in Vendela's room. She didn't want the mascara to clump.

Behind her, Vendela was trying on a fourth dress, but she soon took that one off too, exclaiming with frustration, 'I have nothing to wear! I'm getting fat!'

Vendela pinched the nonexistent flab at her waist. Jessie turned around to look at her.

'How can you say that? You've got a gorgeous figure. I could never compete.'

It was more a statement than a complaint. Now that Sam loved her, she didn't find her weight as repulsive as she used to.

Her stomach rumbled. She hadn't eaten anything all day. It was as if everything had turned around for her after coming to Fjällbacka. She'd been so scared things would be even worse here, and then she'd met Sam, and now she'd become friends with Vendela, who was . . . Well, Vendela was so perfect and cool and worldly. She was like a human key to a world Jessie had always longed to be part of. All the harsh words and sly digs, all the scornful remarks, all the pranks and humiliations had now vanished. She was going to draw a line through all of what had been and forget the person she used to be. She was a new Jessie.

Vendela seemed to have decided on the dress she was now wearing. A tight, knitted red dress that barely covered her knickers.

'What do you think?' she said, doing a pirouette in front of Jessie.

'You look awesome,' Jessie said, and she meant it.

Vendela looked like a doll. Jessie saw her own reflection behind Vendela, and her new-found self-confidence abruptly disappeared. The blouse she wore looked like a sack, and her hair was stringy and oily, even though she'd washed it in the morning.

Vendela must have noticed her dejected expression. She placed her hands on Jessie's shoulders and pushed her down on to the chair in front of the mirror.

'You know what? I could fix you up so you look really cute. Shall I have a try?'

Jessie nodded. Vendela got out some bottles and jars, as well as three different curling irons and a straightening iron. Twenty minutes later Jessie had a whole new hairstyle. She looked at herself in the mirror and could hardly believe her eyes.

She was a new Jessie, and she was going to a party. Life couldn't get any better.

Martin sat down next to Paula at the kitchen table in the station.

'When are we going to hear about the tape?' he asked.

'The tape?' said Paula. A second later she realized he was talking about the recording of the anonymous phone call.

Good lord, she thought, my brain can't function in this heat. And she'd hardly slept a wink all night. Lisa had been fussy and woke up so often that it almost didn't seem worth it for Paula to go back to bed in between times. In the end she'd given up and settled down to do some work. But now she was so tired she couldn't keep her eyes open.

'We should hear something this week,' she said. 'But I don't think we should have very high expectations.'

'So are the children settling in okay?' asked Martin, pouring her a big cup of coffee.

It would be her eighth cup of the day – not that she was keeping count.

'Yes, they're doing fine. They arrived this morning. Patrik picked them up at the hospital and drove them over to our place.'

'Did he find out anything more about Amina? Or Karim?'

'Amina's condition is unchanged,' said Paula. 'But Karim will be discharged soon.'

'Is he going to be staying with you too?'

'No, no, we don't have room,' said Paula. 'The plan is for the municipality to arrange some sort of emergency housing for those who were affected by the fire. They reckon they'll have a place for Karim by the time he's discharged. Some of the refugees have already moved out of the community centre and into new accommodation. But I must say I've been happily surprised. People have opened their homes, offering their guestrooms and summer cottages. One couple even moved in with an aunt so they could lend their flat to a refugee family.'

Martin shook his head.

'One extreme to another. People are strange. Some want only to destroy, while others are ready to do whatever they can to help strangers. Just look at Bill and Gun. They've been over at the community centre every day from early morning until late at night.'

'I know. It gives me hope for humanity.'

Paula got up to fetch some milk from the fridge. She added a little to her coffee. She couldn't drink it without milk.

'I'm going home now,' said Mellberg, sticking his head in the door. 'Rita can't handle all those kids on her own. I'll stop by the bakery on the way and buy some cinnamon buns.'

For a moment he looked confused.

'They do eat cinnamon buns, don't they?'

Paula rolled her eyes at Martin as she sat down at the table again.

'Yes, they eat cinnamon buns, Bertil. They're from Syria, not outer space.'

'There's no need to be rude just because I asked a simple question,' said Mellberg, offended.

Ernst tugged at his lead, eager to get going.

Paula nodded and then gave Mellberg a smile.

'I think the cinnamon buns will be a great success,' she told him. 'But don't forget to buy some Wienerbröd for Leo.'

Mellberg snorted.

'Do you think I'd forget that Grandpa's little darling prefers Wienerbröd?'

He left the room, taking Ernst with him.

'What did I ever do to deserve him?' said Paula as he disappeared down the corridor.

Martin shook his head.

'I'll never understand that man.'

Paula's expression turned serious. 'Have you checked on the racist factions?'

'I phoned some of my informants from the past, and they all denied knowing anything about the fire.'

'Not surprising,' said Paula. 'We can't exactly expect somebody to raise his hand and say: "We're the ones who did it."'

'No, but they're not the smartest people in the world, so sooner or later somebody's bound to talk. And maybe someone will feel an incentive to gossip . . . It's possible, anyway. I'll keep rattling their cages, and we'll see what happens.'

Paula took a sip of her coffee. Fatigue was making her body feel heavy and clumsy.

'Do you think the search at the Berg family farm will produce any results?'

'No,' he sighed. 'We found nothing inside the house. I don't think the family had anything to do with it. So probably not.'

'We're going to run out of leads pretty soon,' said Paula. 'We have no witnesses, no physical evidence, and we haven't found any connection to the Stella case, in spite of the similarities. I'm actually beginning to think there is no connection. The Stella case is so well known in the area – everybody knows all the details, including where she was found. There are no secrets about it. Anybody could copy the murder. The only question is, why would they?'

'What about the fact that Leif ended up doubting the girls were guilty? What made him suddenly change his mind? And why did he then kill himself?'

'I don't know,' said Paula wearily, rubbing her eyes. 'It feels as though we're treading water. And on top of everything else we have the arson investigation. Do you think we'll ever get to the bottom of all this?'

'Of course we will,' said Martin, getting up.

Paula merely nodded. She wanted to believe him, but fatigue was making her feel hopeless. She wondered if her colleagues felt the same way.

'I've got to go now. There's something I have to do,' said Martin, shifting from one foot to the other.

At first Paula didn't know what he meant. Then she gave him a big smile.

'Oh, right. Today's the big day. Dinner with the woman from the community centre.'

Martin looked embarrassed.

'Er, well . . . It's just dinner. Then we'll have to see what happens.'

'Uh-huh,' said Paula with a knowing look. Martin's response was to give her the finger.

She laughed and called after him as he headed for the front door: 'Good luck! Remember – it's like riding a bike!'

His only answer was to slam the door behind him. She glanced at her watch. Another hour of work, she decided, and then she'd call it a day.

Basse lived in an older house with bay windows and lots of nooks and crannies. Jessie thought she would enjoy being in a house that was so different from anywhere else she'd ever lived. But when a complete stranger opened the door and she caught a glimpse of the crowd inside, she was suddenly nervous.

Almost everyone at the party was drunk but also self-assured in a way that Jessie was not. She was never welcome at these kinds of parties. She wanted to back away and run home, but Vendela took her hand and pulled her over to a table at the far end of the living room. It was crammed with bottles of beer, wine, and a variety of spirits.

'Does all that belong to Basse's parents?' asked Jessie.

'No, that would never work,' said Vendela, tossing her long, blond hair. 'Everybody usually brings whatever they can to the party.'

'I could have brought some champagne,' murmured Jessie, feeling stupid.

Vendela laughed. 'Don't worry about it. You're new. A guest of honour. What would you like?'

Jessie surveyed the bottles on the table.

'I've only ever had champagne,' she said.

'Then it's time you had a proper cocktail. I'll mix it for you.'

Vendela reached for a big plastic cup. She poured from various bottles and then added a little Sprite.

'Here!' she said, handing the full cup to Jessie. 'This should be super!'

Vendela took another plastic cup and filled it to the brim with white wine from a box.

'*Skål!*' she said, tapping Jessie's cup with her own.

Jessie took a sip and forced herself not to grimace. It tasted strong, but she'd never had a cocktail before, so maybe that's how it was supposed to taste. And Vendela seemed to know what she was doing.

Vendela nodded towards the other end of the room.

'Nils and Basse are over there.'

Jessie took another sip of her drink. It tasted better than the first sip. There were so many people, and none of them was giving her a scornful or contemptuous look. Instead, they seemed curious. But curious in a good way. At least, that's how it felt.

Vendela again took her hand and led her past all the people who were talking, dancing, and laughing.

The boys were slouched on a big sofa, each holding a beer. They nodded at Jessie, and Vendela sat down on Nils's lap.

'Shit, you guys are so late,' said Nils, pulling Vendela close. 'How long does it take to put on make-up and get dressed?'

Vendela giggled when Nils brushed her hair aside and kissed her on the back of the neck.

Jessie sat down on a big white armchair next to the sofa, trying not to stare too much at Nils and Vendela as they kissed.

She leaned towards Basse.

'So, where are your parents?'

The music was now pounding full blast.

'They're out sailing,' said Basse, with a shrug. 'That's what they always do in the summer. But the last two summers I haven't gone with them.'

Vendela stopped kissing Nils and gave Jessie a smile.

'They think he has a summer job,' she said.

'Oh.'

It's true that Jessie's mother wouldn't even notice if she was gone for three weeks, but this was different. Imagine thinking up that sort of lie.

'They said I had to work if I was going to stay home,' said Basse, taking a swig of beer. He spilled a little on his shirt but didn't seem to notice. 'I told them I got a job at TanumStrand. They don't know anyone there, so they can't check up on me.'

'But won't they wonder what happened to your pay?'

'They have a huge wine cellar with lots of expensive wine that they don't keep track of, so while they're away, I sell a few bottles.'

Jessie gave him a surprised look. She hadn't thought Basse was that smart.

'Nils usually helps me,' he added.

Jessie nodded. That explained things. She took another sip of her drink. It burned her throat but did nothing to calm the happy butterflies in her stomach. Was this what it was like to belong? To be part of a group?

'Too bad Sam didn't want to come,' said Nils, leaning back against the sofa.

Jessie felt a sudden pang. Why did Sam have to be so stubborn? They clearly thought they had behaved badly.

'He couldn't make it tonight. But we're both coming to the party at the community centre next Saturday.'

'Oh, cool!' said Nils, raising his beer bottle in a toast.

Jessie took her mobile out of her purse and sent a quick text to Sam:

Everything's fine, everyone is cool, and I'm having a great time.

He instantly texted back a thumbs up emoji with a smiley. She smiled and put her mobile back in her purse. She could hardly believe how wonderful it all was. This was the first time in her life that she felt . . . normal.

'Do you like your drink?' asked Nils, pointing his beer bottle at her cup.

'Sure. It's great!' she said, taking a few more sips.

Nils shoved Vendela off his lap and swatted her on the rear.

'Go make another drink for Jessie. She's almost done with that one.'

'Okay,' said Vendela, tugging down her short dress. 'I'm almost done with my wine, so I'll get both of us more drinks.'

'Bring me a beer too,' said Basse, setting his empty bottle on the table.

'I'll try to carry it all.'

Vendela made her way through the crowd to the drinks table at the other end of the room. Jessie didn't know what to say. Sweat had started running down her back, and she probably had big patches under her arms. She wanted to run away, but she kept her eyes fixed on the rug.

'So what's it like having a film star for a mother?' asked Basse.

Jessie inwardly cringed, but she was grateful someone else had started up a conversation. Even though it was not her favourite topic.

'I don't know. My mother is just my mother. I don't really think of her as a film star.'

'But you must have met tons of cool people.'

'Sure. But they're just ordinary colleagues for my mother.'

Should she tell them what it was really like? That she'd hardly ever been part of Marie's life. That she'd been left at home with an endless stream of nannies when she was little while Marie was shooting films or attending various functions. As soon as she was old enough, Jessie had been sent to boarding schools all around the world, wherever Marie happened to be filming. When she was at school in England, Marie had been gone for six months, making a film in South Africa.

'Refills for everyone,' said Vendela, setting glasses and bottles on the table.

She looked at Jessie.

'Taste it and see if it's as good as the first one. I made you a different cocktail this time.'

Jessie took a sip. Again it burned her throat, but this time it tasted of Fanta soda, and she liked it better. She gave it a thumbs up.

'I hardly put any alcohol in it, so you don't have to worry about getting drunk.'

Jessie gave Vendela a grateful smile and took another sip. She wondered what a drink with lots of alcohol would taste like, considering how this one was burning her stomach. But it was nice of Vendela to think of her. Happiness spread through her. Were they going to be her friends? That would be amazing. Along with Sam. Wonderful, awesome, lovely Sam.

She raised her glass to the trio sitting on the sofa and took another big sip. What a marvellous burning sensation in her chest.

Marie carefully wiped off her make-up. Film make-up was the worst kind for her skin because of the thick layers required. She would never dream of going to bed without taking it off so her skin could breathe. She leaned forward and studied her face in the mirror. Tiny crow's feet at her eyes and a few fine lines around her mouth. Sometimes she felt as if she were a passenger on a train racing towards a precipice. Her career was all she had.

At least it looked as if this film was going well, and if it turned out to be a commercial success she would have bought herself a few more years. In Sweden, at any rate. Her days in Hollywood were coming to an end. She was no longer the box office draw she'd once been. The roles were getting worse, and they were now few and far between. These days she was reduced to playing someone's mother, not the hot female lead. She was being pushed aside by young starlets with hungry eyes who were willing to sleep with directors and producers to get a role.

Marie picked up the jar of expensive face cream and began smoothing it on her face. Then the jar with cream for her eyes. She smeared it on her neck too. Many women paid attention only to their face, but the wrinkles on their neck gave away their age.

She glanced at the clock. Eleven forty-five. Should she wait up for Jessie? No, she'd probably come home in the wee hours of the morning, or else she'd stay overnight. And Marie needed her beauty sleep before another long day of filming.

Marie met her own eyes in the mirror. Her face was now devoid of all make-up. Her outward appearance had been her armour ever since she was a child. It prevented everybody from having access to what was inside. No one had ever seen her, really seen her. Not since Helen. She'd managed to keep away all thoughts of her during most of the years that had passed. She had never looked back. Never cast even a glance over her shoulder. What good would that have done? They had been forced apart. And ever since . . . Helen had refused to see her.

She had been waiting for the day they would both be

eighteen. She had reached that age a year before Helen, and it wasn't until four months later, in October, that they had finally talked to each other again. Marie expected they would make new plans. They no longer had to suffer that awful sense of longing every second.

Marie had phoned her in the morning. She had wondered what she would say if Helen's parents answered, but she needn't have worried. Helen's voice filled her with such happiness. Marie wanted to banish the intervening years, erase them, and start fresh. Together with Helen.

But Helen had sounded like a stranger. Cold. Distant. She explained that she didn't want to have any contact with Marie. That she would soon be marrying James, and Marie belonged to the past she was trying to forget. Marie had sat silently holding the phone in her hand. Her longing was mixed with disappointment. She hadn't asked any questions. She merely hung up the phone and decided that no one would ever be allowed into her heart again. And she had kept that promise. From then on she made a point of thinking about only one person. Herself. And she had achieved everything she wanted.

But now, in the darkness of this house by the sea, she looked into her own eyes and wondered whether it had been worth it. She was empty. Everything she had acquired was nothing but show.

The only thing that had ever had any value in her life was Helen.

For the first time Marie allowed herself to think about how things might have been. And she saw with surprise that the woman in the mirror was crying. Thirty-year-old tears.

THE STELLA CASE

His conversation with her had steered his thoughts in a whole new direction. Leif's gut instinct told him he was on the right track. Yet it meant he was forced to acknowledge to himself, and eventually to others, that he'd made a mistake. A mistake that had destroyed the lives of many people. And it wasn't good enough to defend himself by saying he had believed in the decisions he'd made. Back then he could have discovered the same answer if he'd only kept looking; instead he'd succumbed to what was easiest and most obvious. It was only later in life that he'd learned things often were not as simple as they seemed. He'd also learned that life could change in a second. Kate's death had given him a humility that he'd lacked back then, when it was truly needed.

He'd found it difficult to look her in the eye. Because when he did, he saw only loneliness and pain. And he didn't know whether he was doing her a disservice by stirring up the past. Yet he had an obligation to put things right, as best he could. There was so much that could not be repaired. So much that could not be given back.

Leif parked in front of his house but didn't get out of the car. The house was so empty. So filled with memories. He knew he should sell it and buy a flat instead. But he couldn't bring himself to do that. He missed Kate. He'd missed her for so many years now, and it was a torment to keep living without her. Especially when he no longer had a job to keep him busy. He'd tried to fill the emptiness with his children and grandchildren, and it did help keep the loneliness at bay. But Kate had been so imprinted in every cell of his body – she'd been the reason he lived and breathed. Life without her had no meaning.

Reluctantly he got out of the car. The silence in the house was deafening. The only sound was the ticking of the kitchen clock. The clock from Kate's childhood home. Yet another reminder of her.

Leif went into his home office. Only there did he feel any sense of peace. He made up the sofa every evening so he could sleep in his office. He'd done that ever since he retired.

His desk was neat and tidy, as usual. He took pride in having an orderly desk, just as he had all the years of his working life. He'd kept his desk at the police station equally neat. It helped him to sort his thoughts. To create structure and order from seemingly random facts.

He got out the file folder with the documents from the case. For the umpteenth time he went over everything. But this time he was seeing it all from a new perspective. And yes. It fit. Far too much of it fit. Leif slowly put down the papers. He'd been wrong. So terribly wrong.

Vendela swayed on her high heels as she stood in the doorway to Basse's parents' bedroom. The wine had created a lovely buzzing inside her head, and everything seemed so pleasantly hazy. She pointed at Jessie, who was lying on the bed.

'How the hell did you get her up here?'

Nils grinned.

'Basse and I had to carry her together.'

'That girl really can't hold her alcohol,' said Basse, nodding at Jessie.

He was already slurring his words, but he took another swig of beer.

Vendela looked at Jessie. She was completely out of it, sleeping so heavily she almost seemed dead. But her chest rose intermittently. Looking at her, Vendela was filled with anger, as always. Jessie's mother had killed someone, and yet nothing bad had happened to her. She'd become a Hollywood star while her own mother drank away the pain every night. And Jessie had lived all over the world while Vendela had been rotting away here in Fjällbacka.

Someone knocked on the door, and Vendela turned to open it. From downstairs she heard Flo Rida's 'My

House', along with laughing and shouting as people at the party tried to make themselves heard.

'What are you guys doing?'

Three of the boys from the Strömstad school stood in the hall, their eyes glazed.

'We're having a private party here,' said Nils with a sweeping gesture. 'Come on in.'

'Who's that?' asked the tallest of the boys.

Vendela thought his name was Mathias.

'A sick bitch who tried to put the move on me and Basse,' said Nils, shaking his head. 'She's been trying to get some cock all night, so we carried her up here.'

'What a whore,' muttered Mathias, standing in the middle of the room and staring at Jessie.

'Look, here's the kind of pictures she posts,' said Nils, taking out his mobile.

He scrolled to the picture of Jessie showing her breasts, and the boys tried to focus their drunken gazes on the image.

'God, they're big,' one of them said, grinning.

'She's fucked everybody,' said Nils, downing the rest of his beer.

He waved the empty bottle.

'Who wants more to drink? It's not a party if we're not drinking.'

They mumbled a reply, and Nils looked at Vendela.

'Go get us some more, okay?'

She nodded and tottered out of the room.

She managed to make it down to the kitchen, where Basse had hidden more bottles, some of which now stood on the big worktop. She picked up a box of white wine in one hand and a big bottle of vodka in the other. She also grabbed a couple of extra plastic cups, which she carried in her teeth.

On her way upstairs, Vendela stumbled several times.

Eventually she made it and managed to use her elbow to knock on the bedroom door. Basse let her in.

Basse sank down on the bed next to Nils, who was sitting beside Jessie, still passed out. Mathias and the other boys sat on the floor. Vendela handed out the cups and began filling them with a mixture of wine and vodka. Nobody even noticed the taste any more.

'Somebody should teach a bitch like that a lesson,' said Mathias, taking a couple of big swigs of his drink.

He swayed a bit as he sat there.

Vendela met Nils's eyes. Should they go through with it? She thought about her mother and all the dreams she hadn't been allowed to realize. About how her life had been destroyed on that day thirty years ago.

She and Nils nodded to each other.

'Maybe we ought to mark her in some way,' said Nils.

'I have a pen,' said Vendela, taking it out of her purse. 'It's a permanent marker.'

The boys from Strömstad sniggered. The shortest boy nodded enthusiastically.

'Fucking great idea. Let's mark the whore.'

Vendela went over to the bed. She pointed at Jessie.

'First we have to undress her.'

She began unbuttoning Jessie's blouse, but the buttons were tiny and she was so drunk that her fingers fumbled, and she couldn't manage to undo even one. Frustrated, she grabbed hold of the fabric and ripped it open.

Nils laughed.

'That's my girl!'

'Here, take off her skirt,' Vendela told Mathias, who sniggered as he came over and began pulling it off Jessie.

She had on ugly white cotton knickers, and Vendela grimaced. Why wasn't she surprised?

'Help me roll her on to her side so I can undo her bra,' she said.

A whole bunch of willing hands reached out to help. 'Wow!'

Basse was staring at Jessie's breasts. She stirred a little when they placed her on her back again. She murmured something incomprehensible.

'Here! Have a refill!'

Nils handed Mathias the vodka bottle, which was then passed around. Vendela sat down next to Jessie.

'Here, give me the bottle.'

Nils handed her the vodka bottle. She put her hand under Jessie's head and raised it off the bed. With the other hand she poured vodka into her open mouth.

'She has to be part of the party!' she said.

Jessie coughed without waking.

'Wait, I have to take a picture of this!' said Nils. 'Pose with her.'

He fumbled for his phone and began snapping photos. Vendela leaned over Jessie. Finally it was her family that had the power. The four other boys also got out their phones to take pictures.

'What should we write?' asked Basse, who couldn't take his eyes off Jessie's breasts.

'Let's take turns,' said Vendela, taking the cap off the pen. 'I'll go first.'

She wrote 'SLUT' across Jessie's stomach. The boys cheered. Jessie squirmed a bit but didn't wake up. Vendela handed the pen to Nils, who paused to think. Then he pulled off Jessie's knickers and drew an arrow pointing to her pubic hair with the words 'Glory Hole'. Mathias hooted and Nils did a triumphant fist pump and then handed the pen to Basse, who looked uncertain. But then he took a big swig of vodka, moved to the head of the bed, and wrote 'WHORE' on Jessie's forehead.

She was soon covered with words. Everyone was

frantically taking pictures on their mobiles. Basse still couldn't stop staring at her.

Nils grinned at him.

'Hey, everybody, I think Basse would like some alone time with Jessie.'

He ushered everybody out of the room and then gave Basse a thumbs up. Vendela pulled the door closed, but before she did, she saw Basse starting to unbutton his trousers.

Patrik checked the clock. He was surprised that Erica wasn't home yet, but he was happy to think they must be having a fun time. He knew her well enough to realize that she would otherwise have thought up some excuse to leave early.

He went into the kitchen to clear up after dinner. The children had been tired after another play date with friends, so they'd fallen asleep earlier than usual. The house was nice and quiet. He hadn't even switched on the TV. He needed peace and quiet to mull over the day. At the moment it felt as if thoughts were tumbling through his mind without any pattern or structure. They had made an important discovery today – he only wished he knew what it meant. The fact that Nea had died on the family farm meant they would have to give serious consideration to the possibility that someone in the family was the killer. And for that reason they had told Eva and Peter they could not return to the farm, since the police now needed to inspect the whole property and the shed.

Patrik turned on the dishwasher and took a bottle of red wine from the cupboard. He poured himself a glass and went out to the deck. He sat down on one of the wicker chairs and gazed out at the sea. It was still not completely dark, even though it was close to midnight. Instead, the sky was purple with streaks of pink, and he could vaguely hear the waves rolling on to the shore below. He and Erica both considered this their favourite place in the house, but he realized how little time they'd spent out here the past few years. Before the children were born, they'd spent many evenings on the deck, talking, laughing, sharing dreams and hopes, making plans for their future together. That was all so long ago. These days, after they put the kids to bed, they were too tired to make plans, let alone dream. Instead they often ended up sitting in front of the TV watching some insipid show. And then Erica would give him a poke as he sat on the sofa snoring, and she'd say maybe it would be better if he went up to bed to sleep.

He wouldn't trade the life they had with the children for anything, but he wished there was more time for . . . well, for their love. It was always there, but it was frequently limited to a loving glance while they each tied the shoelaces of one of the twins, or to a hasty kiss at the worktop as Erica made sandwiches for Maja and he heated up the boys' oatmeal. They were a fine-tuned machine, a train confidently chugging along the rails they had laid during those earlier evenings they'd spent on the deck. But he wished there was time to stop the train occasionally and enjoy the view.

He knew he ought to get some sleep, but he didn't like going to bed without Erica. It felt so sad to crawl into his side of the bed when her side was empty. And for many years they'd had the same routine when they went to bed. Provided it wasn't one of their rare intimate nights, they would always kiss each other good night and then hold hands under the covers as they fell asleep. So he preferred to wait up for her, even though he knew he'd have to get up early in the morning. He would only toss and turn if he went to bed now.

It was almost one in the morning when he heard

someone at the front door. Someone was cursing and fumbling with a key in the lock. He pricked up his ears. Was it possible his dear wife was slightly tipsy? He hadn't seen Erica drunk since their wedding night, but judging by the trouble she was having unlocking the door, she seemed to be drunk again. He set down his wine glass and went through the living room, almost falling over the painting Erica had brought home from the gallery. Then he went into the front hall. She still hadn't managed to get the door open, and the curses he could hear on the other side of the door were worthy of a sailor. He turned the lock and pulled on the handle. Erica stood there, holding the key in her hand and peering with surprise, first at him, then at the open door. After a moment her face lit up.

'Hi, sweeeeeetheart!'

She threw her arms around his neck and he had to brace himself not to fall over. He shushed her as she started laughing.

'Not so loud. The kids are asleep.'

Erica nodded solemnly and pressed a finger to her lips as she struggled to stay on her feet.

'I'll be sooooo quiet . . . The kids are sleeeeeeping . . .'

'Exactly, the little tykes are asleep,' he said, putting a supportive arm around his wife.

He led Erica to the kitchen and sat her down on a chair. Then he filled a carafe with water and set it in front of her, along with a glass and two ibuprofen.

'Drink the water, and take the ibuprofen. Otherwise you're going to feel terrible in the morning.'

'You're so nice,' said Erica, trying to focus her gaze on him.

Apparently there had been plenty to drink during the bachelorette party. He wasn't sure he even wanted to know what condition his mother was in.

'Soooo . . . Kristina, your mother . . .' said Erica, before downing the first glass of water.

Patrik instantly refilled it.

'Yes, I know who Kristina is.'

This was really entertaining. If he'd dared, he would have videoed it, but he knew Erica would kill him if he did.

'She is sooooo lovely, your mother,' she said, nodding.

She drank another glass of water, and he refilled it from the carafe.

'Such amazing legs,' said Erica, shaking her head.

'Who has amazing legs?' he asked, trying to make sense of the thoughts whirling inside Erica's head.

'Your mother . . . Kristina. My mother-in-law.'

'Oh, you mean my mother has amazing legs. Okay. Good to know.'

He got her to drink one more glass of water. Tomorrow was going to prove challenging for Erica. He had to go to work, and he suspected that their regular babysitter, meaning Kristina, would not be in any shape to look after the kids.

'And she can dance! They should invite her to be on *Let's Dance*. Not me, though. I can't dance . . .'

Erica shook her head and drank the last glass of water, swallowing the two ibuprofen that Patrik handed to her.

'But it was fun! We danced the cha-cha. Can you believe it? The cha-cha!'

She hiccupped and got up to put her arms around Patrik.

'Erica, honey, I don't think you're in any shape to do the cha-cha right now.'

'But I want to! Come on . . . I'm not going to bed until we've danced the cha-cha.'

Patrik weighed his options. Carrying Erica upstairs was not one of them. The best thing would be to do what she wanted and then persuade her to go upstairs to bed.

'Okay, sweetie. Let's do the cha-cha. But we'd better go in the living room. Otherwise I'm afraid we'll knock everything on to the floor here in the kitchen.'

He ushered her into the living room. She stood in front of him, placed one hand on his shoulder and took his left hand in hers. She swayed a couple of times then regained her balance. She cast a glance at the portrait of Leif leaning against the wall right next to them.

'Leif, you can be our cha-cha audience.'

She laughed at her own joke. Patrik gave her a little shake.

'Come on. Focus. The cha-cha, right? And after that: bed. Okay? That's what you promised.'

'Sure, we'll go to bed and . . . Do a little more than sleep . . .'

She looked him deep in the eyes. He felt tears fill his eyes from the alcohol fumes on her breath, and he had to restrain himself from coughing. This was probably the first and last time he wasn't enticed by such an invitation.

'Cha-cha,' he reminded her.

'Oh, right,' said Erica, stretching. 'So, this is how you move your feet. One, two, cha-cha-cha. Get it?'

He tried to watch her feet, but there didn't seem to be any pattern to how she was moving them. It didn't get any easier when she stumbled a few times.

'And then the right . . . And then the left . . .'

Amused, Patrik tried to follow, though he was preoccupied with wondering how long he would have to keep doing this.

'One, two, cha-cha-cha, then right, then left . . .'

She stumbled again, and Patrik caught her. She fixed her gaze on Leif's portrait, trying to focus. She frowned.

'Right . . . and left . . .' she muttered.

She gave Patrik a hazy look.

'Now I know what doesn't fit . . .'

She rested her head on his shoulder.

'What? What doesn't fit? Erica?'

He gave her a little shake, but she didn't answer. Then he heard her begin to snore. Good lord. How was he going to get her upstairs now? And what did she mean something didn't fit? He had no idea what she was talking about.

BOHUSLÄN 1672

The gaol stood on a hill, right next to the inn. Elin had given it only a cursory glance until now. No doubt she had some idea what a gaol looked like, but she could not have imagined how dark and damp it would be. Tiny creatures crept and crawled through the dark, nudging her hands and feet.

The gaol was small, used mostly for those who indulged too much at the inn, or for husbands to calm down and sleep off the drink before returning to their families.

She was all alone here.

Elin wrapped her arms tightly around herself, shivering in the raw cold. Märta's screams still rang in her ears, and she could still feel her daughter's fingers clinging to her skirts.

They had seized her possessions from the servants' quarters. Her herbs and concoctions. The book with pictures that her grandmother had left her. Instructions for what to mix together and how to do it, illustrated by someone who could not write. Elin had no idea what they had done with all these things.

What she did know was that she was in serious trouble.

Preben was due to return home in two days' time, and he would not allow this lunacy to continue. As soon as he came back from Lur, he would sort everything out. He knew the sheriff. He would speak to him. And he would also put Britta right. No doubt she merely wanted to teach Elin a lesson and frighten her. Surely she did not mean for her to die.

Yet she thought about the incident at the lake in the woods. And Märta's terrified expression when she was about to slip beneath the dark water. And her cat Viola, who disappeared and never came back. Perhaps Britta did intend for her to die, but Preben would never allow that to happen. He would not treat Britta kindly when he heard what she had done. If only Elin could hold out for two days, she would be able to return home. To Märta. She did not know where they would go after that, but they could no longer remain under Britta's roof.

She heard a rattling sound, and the sheriff appeared in the doorway. Hastily she stood up and brushed off her skirts.

'Is it truly necessary for me to sit here, imprisoned like a criminal? I have a daughter, and there is nowhere for me to go. Could I not stay at home under my own roof until we sort this out? I promise to answer all your questions, and I know that many people will testify that I am not a witch.'

'You are not going anywhere,' said the sheriff, pompously squaring his shoulders. 'I know what the likes of you are capable of, and with what enticing tones you brides of Satan can speak. I am a god-fearing man, and no incantations or devilish spells will have the slightest effect on me.'

'I don't know what you are talking about,' said Elin with growing bewilderment.

How had it come to this? How had she landed here? What had she done to the sheriff for him to look at her with such revulsion? Of course she had sinned. She had been weak in both flesh and soul, but she had paid a price for that. She could not understand why God would demand from her even greater penance. In despair, she sank to her knees on the filthy floor, clasping her hands and fervently praying.

The sheriff stared at her with loathing.

'Your play-acting does not fool me,' he said. 'I know what you are up to, and soon everyone else will know it too.'

As the door closed and the cell was once again shrouded in darkness, Elin continued to pray. She prayed until her legs went numb and her arms lost all feeling. But no one was listening.

Erica opened her eyes and squinted at the light. Maja was standing in front of her.

'Why are you sleeping on the sofa, Mamma?' she asked.

Erica glanced around. Yes, why was she sleeping on the sofa? She had no memory of coming home.

The sofa cushions underneath her felt lumpy, so she propped herself on one hand and tried to sit up, but her head felt like it would explode. Maja moved closer, waiting for an answer to her question.

'Mamma has a tummy ache. It was better for me to sleep here so that Pappa wouldn't catch it,' Erica explained.

'Poor Mamma,' said Maja.

'Yes, poor Mamma,' Erica agreed, wincing.

Good lord, she hadn't had a hangover since the day after their wedding, and she'd totally repressed how much like a near-death experience it could be.

'So the corpse awakens,' said Patrik a little too cheerfully as he came into the living room, carrying a twin in each arm.

'Just shoot me,' said Erica, struggling to sit up.

The room spun and her mouth was as dry as tinder.

'It must have been a successful bachelorette party yesterday,' said Patrik with a laugh.

Erica could tell he was laughing at her and not with her.

'We actually had an amazing time,' she said, holding her head. 'But we had a lot to drink. Your mother is probably feeling the effects today.'

'I'm so glad I didn't have to see that. It was enough to see you when you came home.'

He set the twins down in front of the TV and turned on the kids' programme.

Maja sat down next to Noel and Anton and told her brothers sternly: 'Mamma is sick so we have to be very nice to her.'

The twins nodded but then went back to watching the kids' show.

'When did I get home?' Erica asked, desperately trying to fill her lungs.

'Around one. And then you wanted to dance. You insisted on teaching me the cha-cha.'

'You're kidding.'

Erica put her hand to her forehead. She knew she'd be hearing about this for a long time to come.

Patrik's expression turned serious. He sat down next to her on the sofa.

'You said a strange thing before you passed out. You were looking at the portrait of Leif, and you said something about right and left and that you understood what didn't fit. Do you recall?'

Erica tried to remember, but her mind was blank. The last thing she recalled was a Long Island Iced Tea being set down in front of her. She should have known better than to drink things like that. But hindsight never helped. Goodness knows how she'd made it home afterwards. Looking down at the pitch-black soles of her feet, she concluded that she must have walked home barefoot.

'No, I don't remember a thing. Unfortunately,' she said, with a grimace.

'Keep trying. Right. Left. That's what you said. It seemed to trigger something in your mind.'

Erica tried, but her head was pounding so badly she couldn't think.

'No. Sorry. But maybe it'll come back to me.' She gave a start and frowned. 'But there *is* one thing I remember – from the day before yesterday! Sorry, but there was so much happening with the bachelorette party that I forgot all about it.'

'What is it?' asked Patrik.

'I'm sure this is super important, and I should have told you earlier, but you came home so late, and then I was busy with the party. I met Marie on Friday, just by chance. I was walking past the film set at the harbour, and they were taking a break. Marie called me over and said she'd heard I wanted to talk to her. So we went to Café Bryggan and talked about what happened to Stella. But that's not the most important thing. As I was leaving, the make-up artist from the film company came over and said that Marie didn't have an alibi for Sunday night, because *she* was the one who'd spent the night with the director, not Marie.'

'Oh, shit,' said Patrik. Erica could see the gears starting to turn in his mind.

She massaged her forehead.

'There's one more thing. Marie says she saw or heard somebody in the woods right before Stella disappeared. The police didn't believe her, and maybe that's not so strange since she didn't mention it until after she'd retracted her confession. Regardless, she thinks the same person may have struck again.'

Patrik shook his head. It sounded like a long shot.

'I know, the last bit sounds like speculation on her part. But I thought I should tell you anyway,' said Erica. 'How's it going with the investigation?'

She was struggling to talk because her tongue felt like it was glued to her gums.

'Did you do the rest of the search yesterday?'

'Yes, we did.'

When he told her what they'd found in the barn, Erica's eyes widened. It was hard to know what the discovery meant, but she realized this was a major breakthrough in the investigation.

'When will you get back the results from forensics?'

'Not until the middle of the week,' said Patrik with a sigh. 'I wish we could have had the results yesterday. It's incredibly frustrating not to know, especially when it has a bearing on what our next step should be. But I have to bring in the parents for questioning today, so we'll see if that gives us any new leads.'

'Do you think one of them did it?' asked Erica. She wasn't sure she wanted to hear the answer.

Crimes committed by parents against their children happened all too often, but she simply couldn't understand how anyone could do such a thing. She glanced at her kids sitting on the floor in front of the TV and knew with all her soul that she would do anything to protect them.

'I don't know,' replied Patrik. 'That's been the problem the whole time. There are so many possible scenarios, but no evidence to support or rule them out. And now you're telling me that Marie doesn't have an alibi. Which opens the door to even more possibilities.'

'I know you'll work this out,' she said, stroking his arm. 'And who knows? In a few days the report may give you more useful information.'

'That's true,' he said and stood up.

He nodded towards the children.

'Will you be able to manage, given the state you're in?'

Erica would have liked to tell him that she definitely could not manage, but she refrained. Since this hangover was self-inflicted, she'd simply have to deal with the consequences. But it was going to be a long day. And it was going to take a lot of kids' TV and bribes if she was to survive.

Patrik kissed her on the cheek and left for work. Her head pounding, Erica looked at the painting leaning against the wall. What had she meant? But no matter how hard she tried, she couldn't remember. Her mind was still in a fog.

Patrik pressed the record button and stated the day, date, and the names of the people present in the interview room. Then he fell silent for a few moments, staring at Peter. The man sitting across from him looked as if he'd aged ten years in the past week. Patrik was flooded with sympathy for him, but he reminded himself to remain objective and professional. It was so easy to be fooled by what he might want, or not want, to believe about others. He'd made that mistake before, and he'd learned that human beings were seldom straightforward. Nothing was a given.

'How often do you use the barn on your property?' he asked.

Peter's eyes narrowed.

'I . . . um . . . the barn? We don't use it at all. We don't have any animals except for the cat, and we don't use it for storage. We don't believe in collecting a lot of junk.'

He gave Patrik a long look.

'When was the last time you were in the barn?'

Peter scratched his head.

'It must have been when we were looking for Nea,' he said.

'What about before that?'

'I'm not sure. Maybe a week ago. I went there to look for her. Nea was the only one who ever went in the barn. She thought it was so cosy inside. She used to spend a lot of time in there playing with the cat. For some reason she called it a black cat.'

Peter laughed, but stopped abruptly.

'Why are you asking about the barn?' he asked, but Patrik didn't reply.

'Are you sure the last time you were in the barn was a week before she disappeared? Can you be more precise?'

Peter shook his head.

'No, I really have no idea. My guess is it was a week ago.'

'What about Eva? Do you know when she was last inside the barn? Aside from when you were looking for Nea, that is.'

Peter again shook his head.

'No, I haven't a clue. You'll have to ask her. But she had no reason to go there either. We don't use the barn.'

'Have you ever noticed anyone near the barn?'

'No, never. Or rather, one time I thought I saw something moving about inside, but when I went to look, the cat came out. So it must have been the cat I saw.'

He raised his eyes to look at Patrik.

'Do you think somebody was in there? I don't understand where these questions are leading.'

'How often did Nea go to the barn? Do you know what she did there?'

'No, only that she loved going to the barn to play. She was always so good about entertaining herself.' His voice broke, and he coughed. 'She often said: "I'm going to

541

the barn to play with the black cat." So I assume that's what she did. She played with the cat. It's a very affectionate animal.'

'Yes, I noticed,' said Patrik with a smile. 'So what about the morning when she disappeared? Did you notice anything in or around the barn? The smallest detail might be of interest.'

Peter frowned. He shook his head.

'No, it was a perfectly ordinary morning. Very quiet.'

'Do you ever go up in the hayloft?'

'No. I don't think we've been up there since we bought the place. And we forbade Nea to go up there. There's no railing, and no hay to break her fall if she got too close to the edge. She knew she wasn't supposed to go up there.'

'Was she an obedient child?'

'Yes, she is . . . she was. Not like some children who do the opposite of what they're told. If we said she wasn't to go up in the loft on her own, she wouldn't do it.'

'How was Nea with other people? With strangers? Would she trust someone she didn't know?'

'I'm afraid we probably didn't teach Nea enough about the fact that some people aren't very nice. She loved everybody and thought all people were good. Everyone she met was her best friend. She also said all the time that the black cat was her best friend, so I suppose I should add that both people and animals were her best friends.'

Again his voice broke. Patrik saw him clench his jaw so as not to lose control. He curled his hands into fists, not sure how to ask the next question.

'We've had some reports from the Uddevalla police.'

Peter gave a start. 'What do you mean?'

'About your violent outbursts when you . . . when you were drinking.'

Peter shook his head.

'That was years ago. When I was having . . . problems at work.'

He looked at Patrik and shook his head even harder.

'Do you think that I . . .? No, I would never do anything to hurt Nea. Or Eva. They're my family. Don't you understand? Nea was my family.'

He hid his face in his hands. His shoulders shook.

'What is this? Why are you asking me about things I got up to years ago? Why are you asking so many questions about the barn? What did you find in there?'

'I'm afraid I can't tell you that at the moment,' replied Patrik. 'We may have to ask both of you more questions. As you know, Gösta is speaking to Eva, asking her the same questions I've asked you. We're grateful for your cooperation, but right now you'll just have to trust me when I say we're doing everything we can.'

'Are you positive it wasn't . . . him?' Peter wiped his eyes. 'I know my father has strong opinions, and it's easy to get swept up . . . Everybody has been talking about it too. About the refugee centre. And after a while, well . . .'

'The man you're talking about was definitely not involved in any way. Someone stole Nea's knickers from the clothes line after she disappeared, and then tried to frame the man.'

'How are they doing?'

Peter avoided looking at Patrik.

'Not great, to be honest. The doctors aren't sure whether the wife will recover, and Karim – that's his name – suffered serious burns to his hands.'

'What about the children?' asked Peter, finally raising his eyes.

'They're fine,' Patrik assured him. 'They're staying with one of my colleagues until their father is discharged from the hospital.'

'I'm sorry that we . . .'

He couldn't finish the sentence.

Patrik nodded.

'It's okay. People have different opinions. And, unfortunately, the refugees are convenient scapegoats at the moment. For all sorts of things.'

'I shouldn't have . . .'

'It doesn't matter. We can't change what happened, but we're trying to find out who set the fire at the refugee centre at the same time as investigating your daughter's murder.'

'We need to know who did it,' said Peter, desperation shining in his eyes. 'Otherwise we can't go on. Eva won't be able to go on. Not knowing will break us.'

'We're doing everything we can,' said Patrik.

He consciously chose words that would not imply any promises. Right now he wasn't convinced they would solve this case. He declared the interview over and switched off the tape recorder.

Nausea was the first thing she noticed. Then the lumpy surface underneath her. Her eyelids felt glued shut, and it was a struggle to open her eyes. She didn't recognize the ceiling spinning overhead, and the nausea got worse. The room had blue-and-white striped wallpaper that she couldn't remember ever having seen before. The nausea was making her shake all over. Panicked, she turned her head to the side. Vomit splashed on to the floor next to the bed. It tasted disgusting and stank of alcohol.

Jessie whimpered. When she touched her chest, she realized she had already thrown up on herself.

Her panic grew. Where was she? What happened?

Slowly she sat up. She was shivering, and the nausea nearly overwhelmed her again, but she was able to stop from vomiting. She looked down at her body and at first couldn't process what she saw. She was naked, but covered with black lines. It took a few seconds for her to understand she was looking at words written on her body. One by one she read what they said.

Whore. Slut. Fatso. Slob.

Her throat closed up.

Where was she? Who had done this to her?

A memory slowly surfaced. She was sitting in an armchair. Drinking cups of alcohol.

Basse's party.

She wrapped a blanket around her and surveyed the room. It seemed to be his parents' bedroom. A framed photo on the bedside table showed a smiling family. And there was Basse, grinning as he stood between a man and a woman with very white teeth.

The nausea surged again as she realized this had been their plan from the beginning. It was all a con: Vendela knocking on her door and wanting to hang out with her, the rest of them pretending to be her friends. None of it was genuine.

It was the same crap she'd fallen for in England – and she'd let herself be taken in again.

She drew her knees up. She no longer noticed the stink. The only thing she was aware of was the feeling of a gaping hole in her chest.

She felt an aching sensation between her legs and reached down to touch herself there. Something was sticky, and even though she had no experience, she knew what it was. Those bastards.

With an effort she swung her legs over the edge of the bed. When she stood up, she swayed, and this time she couldn't hold back the vomit.

Then she wiped her mouth on the back of her hand and stepped over the mess on the floor. She managed to make it to the bathroom adjoining the bedroom.

Tears filled her eyes when she saw herself in the mirror. Her make-up was smeared, and there were traces of vomit on her neck and chest. And it said 'whore' across her forehead. Her cheeks were also covered with ugly words.

Tears ran down her face. Sobbing, she leaned over the sink, standing there for several minutes. Then she went over to the shower and turned on the water full blast. When steam started forming, she stepped in and let the hot water pour over her. It was so hot that her skin was turning bright red, making the black letters stand out even more.

The words screamed at her, and her abdomen felt tender and raw.

Jessie found a bottle of liquid soap and poured it over her body. She washed between her legs until all trace of the foul stuff was gone. She vowed never to let anyone touch her there again. It was tainted, ruined.

She rubbed and rubbed at her skin, but the words refused to come off. She was marked, and she was determined to mark those who had done this to her.

Standing there under the scalding water, Jessie came to a decision. They were going to pay. Every single one of them. They were going to pay.

Erica realized that taking care of children while hungover should be relegated to the same level as punishments for aggravated assault. She had no idea how she was going to make it through the day. The kids, sensing her weakness, were taking the opportunity to act up. Well, Maja was her usual calm self, but the twins shrieked, they fought, they climbed on all the furniture, and if Erica admonished them in any way, they responded with ear-splitting howls that made her head feel as if it would explode.

When her mobile rang, she hesitated to take the call because the noise level in the house precluded any sensible conversation. But then she saw on the display that the call was from Anna.

'Hi! So how are you feeling today?'

Anna sounded so alert and cheerful, Erica immediately regretted taking the call. The contrast with her own situation was too great. She consoled herself with the thought that if Anna wasn't pregnant, she would be in even worse shape.

'Did you get home all right? You were still there when I left, and I was a little worried about how you were going to get home.'

Anna laughed, and Erica sighed. Yet another family member who would be teasing her about this until her dying day.

'Of course I got home okay, though I can't remember how I got here. Judging by my feet, I seem to have walked home barefoot.'

'My God, what a night! Who would have thought the old ladies could party like that! What stories they told! For a while I thought my ears were going to fall off!'

'I know. I'm never going to look at Kristina in the same way again!'

'The dancing was fun too.'

'Uh-huh. Apparently I tried to teach Patrik the cha-cha when I got home.'

'Really?' said Anna. 'I'd give anything to have seen that.'

'And then I fell asleep with my head on his shoulder in the middle of the dance lesson, so he had to put me to bed on the sofa. And now I admit I'm suffering the consequences. And naturally the boys can sense my weakness, so they've been on the attack.'

'You poor thing,' said Anna. 'I could babysit them for a while if you need a rest. I'm just sitting here at home, doing nothing.'

'No, that's okay,' said Erica.

Tempting as the offer was, the self-critic inside her thought she had only herself to blame for landing in this situation.

Erica had roamed about the room as she talked to her sister, but now she stopped in front of the portrait of Leif. Viola had truly captured her father, judging by the photograph Erica had seen. But the painting added something more. It portrayed his personality and gave the impression that he was peering back at her. Straight-backed and proud, he sat at his desk, where everything was neatly stacked. A pile of papers in front of him, a pen in his hand, a glass of whisky nearby. Erica stared at the painting. Suddenly the fog lifted. She knew exactly what it was she'd discovered before she fell asleep on Patrik's shoulder.

'Anna, can I take you up on that offer after all? Could you possibly come over here for a while? I need to go to Tanumshede.'

Karim turned his head towards the window. The loneliness here in hospital was numbing even though he'd had several visitors. Bill had dropped by along with Khalil and Adnan. But Karim hadn't known what to say. Even with them in the room, he'd felt so alone and abandoned. With Amina at his side, he'd always felt at home no matter where he was. She was his whole world.

At first he had been reluctant to allow the children to stay with the police officer, since it was the police who had started this whole business. But Paula had such kind eyes. And she didn't really belong either.

This morning he'd talked to the children on the phone, and he could tell they were doing okay. They were anxious to know how their mother was and how long he'd have to stay in hospital, but then they'd told him about their new playmate named Leo and all the toys he had. They also told him there was a baby in the family and that Rita was a very good cook, although the food didn't taste like their mother's.

Their happy voices made him happy, but their anxiety made him sad. The doctors looked more and more worried each time he asked about Amina. He'd been allowed to visit her once. Her hospital room was so hot, about 32 degrees Celsius, he was told. A nurse explained that the body temperature of badly burned patients goes down due to loss of fluids, so the room temperature had to be kept very high.

The smell had brought tears to his eyes. This was his beloved Amina who smelled so awful. She lay motionless in the bed. He had reached out his hand towards her, wanting to touch her, but he didn't dare. Her head had been shaved, and he couldn't hold back a sob when he saw the exposed, burned skin. Her injured face glistened with Vaseline, and much of her body was swathed in bandages.

Amina was being kept in a medically induced coma, and she was hooked up to a respirator to help her breathe. People had moved about the room the whole time he was there. Their focus was on Amina, and almost no one even glanced at Karim. He was grateful for that, grateful that they were doing everything possible for Amina.

All he could do was wait. And pray. Swedes didn't seem to believe in prayer, while he prayed for Amina day and night, asking that she might stay with him and the children, and that God might be willing to let them keep her for a little while longer.

Outside the window the sun was shining, but it was not his sun. This was not his country. Did that mean he had also left behind his God when he fled?

When he heard the doctor's footsteps slowly approaching

his room, Karim knew what the man was about to tell him. One look at the doctor's face was enough for him to realize that now he was all alone.

'There are several new developments we need to consider,' said Patrik, who had remained standing in order to get everyone's attention.

Annika had arranged for a morning snack. On the table was a loaf of Skogaholm rye bread, butter, cheese, slices of tomato, and coffee.

This was exactly what Paula needed, since she'd had time to grab only a piece of crisp bread, and then only because Johanna insisted she eat something. Paula glanced at Martin as he made himself a sandwich. He looked tired, as if he'd hardly slept at all, though not in that 'I tossed and turned all night' kind of way. It was more like 'I've been rolling in the hay all night'. She gave him a knowing grin, and his face turned bright red. She was happy for him, but she also hoped this new love of his wouldn't lead to angst and heartache. He'd had enough of both.

She turned her attention to Patrik.

'As all of you know, we made several important discoveries yesterday when we were searching the Berg family farm,' said Patrik. 'In the barn the tech team found a Kex chocolate bar wrapper, stuck in a gap between the floorboards. We don't know how or when it got there, but Nea had the remains of chocolate and biscuit in her stomach, so it's likely there's a connection. Especially considering what else we found.'

No one said a word. The news of their discovery had hit his colleagues like a bomb yesterday. It had given them hope and blown fresh life into the investigation, which had begun to feel so hopeless.

'When will we know whether it's Nea's blood?' asked Martin.

'Mid-week, according to Torbjörn.' Patrik took a sip of juice and went on. 'But now I'm coming to something that none of you has heard yet. Torbjörn just phoned to tell me they've made another discovery. I left the farm after the techs were finished with the barn. They were about to go over the whole property. Torbjörn thought it would take them the rest of the afternoon and evening. Neither of us thought the search would turn up anything more, but we were wrong.'

Patrik paused for effect.

'In the tall grass outside the barn, one of the techs found a watch. A child's watch with a *Frozen* illustration. I didn't know about this when I interviewed Peter this morning, but I rang their home, and Eva confirmed that Nea had a watch like that. She wore it almost every day. Even though her parents haven't yet identified the watch as hers, I think we can assume it belonged to Nea.'

Paula took a deep breath. Like her colleagues at the station, she realized what this meant.

'The strap was broken, the glass was smashed, and the watch had stopped at eight o'clock. As always, we need to be careful about jumping to conclusions, but it seems likely that we have now discovered both the primary crime scene and the approximate time of death.'

Mellberg scratched his scalp.

'So she died at eight in the morning and was then transported to the site where she was found?'

'That seems the most likely scenario, yes,' replied Patrik.

Martin raised his hand. 'Does this change anything with regard to Marie's alibi or Helen's?'

'No, not really,' said Patrik. 'Helen has never presented an alibi that can be substantiated, either for Sunday night or Monday morning. She says she took a sleeping pill and slept soundly until nine a.m., when she went out for a run. But no one has been able to confirm this; her husband was out of town, and her son didn't see her until lunchtime. Marie has consistently maintained that she has an alibi for both the night and morning, but this morning Erica told me she happened to run into Marie on Friday, when the film crew were shooting on location in town. As she was passing by the film set after her chat with Marie, the make-up artist told Erica that Marie's alibi was a sham. Apparently she was the one who spent Sunday night with the film director. Not Marie.'

'Oh, shit,' said Martin.

'Can that be true?' said Paula. 'Do you think the make-up artist made up the story out of jealousy?'

'We'll have to ask Marie. And we need to speak to the director again, as well as this woman. If what she told Erica turns out to be true, then Marie certainly has a lot of explaining to do. For instance, why did she feel the need to lie about her alibi?'

'Jörgen confirmed that Marie was with him,' said Martin. 'Why would he do that if she wasn't?'

Paula looked at him and sighed. He was a good police officer, but sometimes he seemed terribly innocent and naive.

'Marie is the star of a film with a multimillion kronor budget. A film they're hoping will be a commercial success. I think Jörgen would be prepared to say anything rather than put the film in jeopardy.'

Martin stared at her. 'Oh, shit. I didn't think of that.'

'You're a little too nice to think of something so devious,' said Paula.

Martin looked deeply insulted at this, but no one challenged Paula's assessment. Not even Martin himself. In his heart he knew Paula was right.

'We'll begin by finding out what Marie has to say about this,' said Patrik. 'Gösta, I'd like you to come with me.

We'll go as soon as this meeting is over. But since Marie was already sitting in make-up in Tanumshede by nine o'clock, I don't see how she could have committed a murder at eight.'

'Okay,' said Paula. 'Let's go back to the chocolate wrapper. When will we get the lab results? There may be fingerprints and saliva on the wrapper.'

'That's what we're hoping,' said Patrik. 'Torbjörn has assured me they'll treat this case as a priority, but you know how these things go.'

'So as of now, we're looking at mid-week before we get the results, right?'

'I'm afraid so.'

'Did you find anything else? Footprints? Fingerprints? Anything at all?'

Paula finished eating her sandwich and began making another. She hadn't slept much last night, and lack of sleep was making her hungry.

'No. It looks as if the barn had been thoroughly cleaned. Torbjörn found the chocolate wrapper only because it had slipped into a crack. Presumably, whoever did the cleaning missed it.'

Martin raised his hand again. His bloodshot eyes matched his hair.

'When will Pedersen be done with his final report?'

'Every time I ask him, he says "in a couple of days",' said Patrik. His frustration was evident in his voice. 'They've got a backlog, and he's working as fast as he can.'

'What are the parents saying?' said Mellberg, concentrating hard on assembling a towering sandwich with six slices of bread and several kinds of filling. 'You know how I always say we should start by looking at the closest family members.'

Paula had to chuckle. Mellberg invariably went home

to Rita in the evening and claimed he was starving because he'd hardly eaten a thing all day. And then he'd add that he couldn't understand how he could be putting on weight when he ate like a bird.

'We haven't yet told them what we've found,' said Gösta. 'They both say they never used the barn and that Nea was the only one who ever went inside. And they didn't notice anyone hanging around or going into the barn on the morning Nea disappeared. Or during the whole time they've lived there, for that matter.'

Gösta gave Patrik an enquiring look and then added: 'Well, there was one occasion when Peter thought he saw someone inside the barn, but when he went over to have a look, he found only the cat. So it was probably nothing, but I thought I should mention it.'

'Is it possible someone was hiding in the barn and they attacked Nea?' asked Paula. 'Was there any evidence of sexual assault? Any trace of sperm?'

Crimes involving the sexual molestation of children were her worst nightmare. Much as she hated to ask the question, it had to be done.

'We'll find out when we get the post-mortem report,' said Patrik. 'Our killer could have been waiting for Nea in the barn. Maybe he bribed her with the chocolate and . . . Well, only the gods know what happened next.'

'I went into the woods behind the house to have a look around,' said Gösta. 'I wanted to see if it was possible for anyone to come from that direction and steal the knickers from the clothes line without being seen from the house. Which is what I think the individual in question did. Crossing the open yard would have left them too exposed. Anyway, I discovered it *is* possible to sneak out from the bushes and over to the side of the house to the clothes line without getting caught. And there are plenty of hiding places where you could keep an eye on the yard and no one would know. Someone may have been watching Nea and taking note of her routines, including the fact that she often played in the barn. That individual could also have seen Nea's father drive off, so they'd have known her mother was the only other person on the farm. If the perpetrator is a man, he might view a woman as much less of a threat than the father.'

'It's not unusual for sexual predators to observe their victim for a while before committing the crime,' Paula remarked quietly.

Suddenly her appetite had vanished. She pushed her sandwich away, struggling to swallow the last bite she'd taken.

'The tech team also searched the woods behind the house yesterday,' said Patrik. 'But they didn't find anything of significance. They collected a few odds and ends, but nothing of particular interest.'

He looked at Paula.

'What about the fire? And the attempt to frame Karim? Have you found out anything?'

She wished she had more to tell her colleagues, but their enquiries kept coming to one dead end after another. No one knew anything. No one wanted to claim responsibility or take the blame. A few people had muttered that the refugees 'got what they deserved', but that was a long way from an admission of guilt.

'No, we haven't made any progress, but we're not giving up. Sooner or later somebody will let something slip.'

'Do you have the impression this was something planned?' asked Mellberg. 'Or could it have been some teenager acting on impulse?'

He'd been unusually quiet during the meeting, possibly because he still felt ashamed of the role he'd played.

Paula paused for a moment before replying.

'The only thing I'm sure of is that it was an act of hatred. But I can't say at this stage whether it was planned or not.'

Mellberg nodded. He patted Ernst, who was lying at his feet, and didn't ask any other questions. Paula was grateful to see he was taking the matter so seriously. And she thought she knew why. He'd spent all morning playing with Samia and Hassan and Leo, chasing them around the flat, pretending to be a monster, and tickling them to make them laugh. Presumably laughing in a way they hadn't done in a long time. That was why, deep in her heart, and in spite of everything, she loved this man with whom her mother had chosen to share her life. She would never admit it out loud, but Bertil had become a sort of grandfather to her children. Because of that side of his personality, she was willing to forgive him for all his pompous stupidity. She would probably find him annoying until he took his last breath, but she knew he would give his life for her children.

Someone tried to come in the front door, so Annika went to open it. She returned with an out-of-breath Erica, who gave everyone in the room a brief nod before she turned to Patrik.

'I remember what I discovered yesterday: Leif Hermansson didn't commit suicide. He was murdered.'

Everyone looked at her in stunned silence.

BOHUSLÄN 1672

Two days had passed. Every time Elin heard someone approach the door, she anxiously waited to see who it might be. She had not been given any food since she arrived, only a little water. The chamber pot had not been emptied. If she turned slightly, the stench was over-whelming. The only thing that made the situation bearable was knowing that Preben would soon return home and put everything right.

Finally a key rattled in the lock and the door opened. And there he stood. She wanted to throw her arms around his neck, but she was ashamed of her filthy attire.

She could see he was sickened by the stench.

'Preben!' she attempted to cry, but his name came out as hardly more than a croak.

She had not spoken in two days, and her voice sounded hoarse and brittle. Hunger tore at her, but she knew that now she would soon be released. She was yearning to feel Märta's soft arms around her, and her small body pressed close. As long as they were allowed to be together, it did not matter if they were forced to go on their way and beg to stay alive. So long as she had Märta with her, hunger and cold were of no importance.

'Preben,' she said again, and this time her voice was firmer.

He fixed his eyes on the floor as he turned his hat in his hands. Uneasiness clutched at Elin's stomach. Why did he not speak? Why did he not berate the sheriff and take her away from here, back to Märta?

'Have you come to fetch me home?' she asked. 'Britta took against me because of what you and I did. She found out about us when she went to town. Then she called me a witch to exact revenge. But no doubt she has calmed down by now, and I have been punished enough. It has been terrible to sit here in this gaol. I have spent day and night asking God to forgive us for our sins, and I will ask forgiveness from Britta as well. I promise you that. If Britta so desires, I will kiss her feet and beg forgiveness, and then Märta and I will take our leave and she need never see us again. Preben, please. Will you not speak to the sheriff so that we can go home?'

Preben continued to turn his hat in his hands. Behind him she now glimpsed the parish clerk and the sheriff. She realized they had been standing there the whole time and must have heard what she said.

'I have no idea what you are talking about,' Preben said warily. 'My wife and I have been kind enough to open our home to you and your daughter because you were part of our family, and yet this is how you repay us. It was a shock to return home and hear that Britta had discovered her sister is a witch. And it was no doubt you who caused all the difficulties she has had to conceive a child . . . It is a great shame, how you have acted against us. That you should now speak lies about your own sister's husband . . . It merely confirms how evil and wicked you are. It demonstrates all too clearly that you are in the clutches of the devil.'

Elin could only stare at him. She sank to her knees

and buried her face in her hands. The betrayal was so enormous and so shattering that she could not even feel anger. How could she defend herself against such accusations? Preben was a man of the church. His position and his words carried great weight. If he joined forces with those who declared her to be a witch, then she would never get out of here, at least not alive.

Preben turned on his heel and left, with the parish clerk right behind him. The sheriff came into the cell and gave Elin a scornful look as she lamented her fate.

'You will have your chance to prove the accusation wrong. Tomorrow we will conduct the water test. But I would not hold out much hope, if I were you, Elin. In all likelihood, you will float.'

Then he closed the door, and once again darkness filled the room.

❧

Sam walked slowly along the path. When he'd woken up that morning and reached for his mobile, he was overwhelmed by a feeling of doom the instant he saw the text message from Jessie. His heart felt like it would break. She hadn't wanted to come to his house, so they'd agreed to meet in the wooded glade at the edge of the property. He took along a bag with the things Jessie had asked for: his mother's bottle of acetone, which she used to remove nail polish, as well as some tissues and towels. He'd also brought paracetamol, a big bottle of water, some sandwiches, and clean clothes that he'd borrowed from his mother's wardrobe.

His notebook was still in his backpack. He hadn't yet been able to show it to her.

Jessie was waiting for him in the glade. He hesitated when he caught sight of her. She did not look at him. She seemed to be staring into space. She had on long jogging trousers and a hoodie with the hood pulled up.

'Jessie,' he said softly as he went over to her.

She didn't move or look up. He put his hand under her chin and turned her face towards him. The shame in her eyes was so enormous, it felt as if he'd been punched in the gut.

Sam put his arms around her and pulled her close. She didn't hug him back. She didn't cry, didn't move a muscle.

'They're scum,' he said in a low voice.

He tried to kiss her cheek, but she turned away. He hated them for destroying her like this.

He got out the bottle of acetone and some tissues.

'Do you want to eat something first?'

'No, just take it off. Take all of it off.'

Cautiously he pushed back the hood, and brushed her hair out of her face. He tucked her hair behind her ears and stroked her head.

'Stand very still so you won't get any acetone in your eyes.'

Gently he began rubbing at the words. For Jessie's sake he stayed calm, but inside he was raging. He'd thought he hated them because of how they'd treated him all these years. But that was nothing compared to what he felt now, after what they'd done to Jessie. To his lovely, warm-hearted, fragile Jessie.

The ink came off, but it left her skin red and chapped. When he'd removed all the words from her face, he started on her neck.

Jessie pulled down the neckline of her shirt to help him get to the words.

'Could you take off your shirt? You don't have to, but . . .'

He didn't know what was the right thing to say or do.

She took off the hoodie and then pulled off her T-shirt. She wore no bra, and he saw all the words on her breasts, stomach, and back. They covered her whole body.

He looked up at Jessie's face. Her eyes were blazing.

Sam went back to rubbing at the words, and slowly the black ink disappeared. She stood still, swaying a bit when he pressed too hard. After a while he had finished her torso, and he gave her an enquiring look. She didn't say a word, merely took off the jogging trousers. She wasn't wearing knickers underneath, so now she stood naked in front of him. Sam knelt down, unable to meet her gaze, which was both hate-filled and distressingly blank. The words danced before his eyes as he rubbed at her skin. There were four or five different kinds of handwriting. He had so many questions, but he didn't dare ask them. And he wasn't sure she'd be able to answer.

'They did other things too,' she said quietly. 'I don't remember what, but I can feel it.'

For a moment he stopped drying off her skin with a tissue. Part of him wanted to lean his head against her thigh and weep. But he knew he needed to be strong for both of them.

'They were sleeping like pigs when I left,' she said. 'How could they sleep? How could they do something like this and then just go to sleep?'

'They're not like us, Jessie. I've always known that. We're better than them.'

He knew what they needed to do now. To everybody who had done this, and to everybody who had let it happen.

'You didn't drive here, did you?' asked Patrik, giving Erica a stern look.

She rolled her eyes.

'Hey, I'm not stupid! I took the bus.'

'Why isn't she supposed to drive?' asked Martin, peering at Erica.

'Because my dear wife came home . . . pickled – and that's putting it mildly.'

'Pickled?' snorted Erica. 'Are we still in the 1950s or what?'

She turned to Martin.

'We had a bachelorette party for Patrik's mother yesterday, and we may have had . . . a little too much to drink.'

Mellberg hooted, but after a warning look from Erica, he didn't say a word.

'Now that we've got all that interesting information out of the way, could we possibly focus on something a bit more important?'

Patrik nodded. He'd lain awake in the night, pondering what Erica could have meant. She rarely made superfluous claims, and when she had an idea, it was worth listening to.

'So you're saying Leif Hermansson was murdered?' he said now. 'What makes you think that?'

Erica looked a little pale, and he motioned towards an unoccupied chair.

'Sit down before you faint. A sandwich and a cup of coffee would probably be a good idea too.'

Gratefully she sank on to a chair near the window. Paula pushed a cheese sandwich across the table to her, and Annika got up to pour her some coffee.

'Leif's daughter, Viola, is an artist,' Erica began. 'As you know, I went to see her to find out whether Leif had left behind any material from the Stella case. I was hoping for notes or something like that. While I was there, she couldn't recall anything, but afterwards she did find something – Leif's diary. One of those small diaries people use to take notes. I haven't looked through the whole thing, but he seems to have recorded the weather conditions and bits and pieces about what happened each day. At any rate, Viola gave me the diary when I went to the gallery opening on Friday. While I was there, I was so taken by one of her paintings that I decided to buy it. The painting is a portrait of her father, Leif.'

She paused to take a sip of coffee and a bite of her sandwich. Then she went on.

'There was something about the painting that's been bothering me, but I couldn't work out what it was. I've read all the material about the Stella case, and I've also studied the documents and looked at all the photographs pertaining to Leif's suicide. The whole time I've had a vague feeling that something didn't fit.'

She took another sip of coffee. Tiny beads of sweat had formed at her temples; the hangover had obviously taken its toll. Patrik felt sorry for her, but he also admired her determination. The bus trip over here could not have been much fun.

'Yesterday I discovered what it was.'

'Although this morning she had no memory of it at all,' Patrik couldn't help interjecting.

'Thanks for that,' said Erica. 'But finally I did recall what it was. Right and left.'

'Right and left?' said Paula, puzzled. 'What do you mean by right and left?'

'Look at this.'

Erica rummaged in her bag and then placed on the table a series of photos taken by the police photographer after Leif's suicide. She pointed to his temple.

'See the bullet wound – in his right temple. And his gun is in his right hand.'

'So?' said Patrik, leaning forward to look at the pictures.

After all his years on the police force, he still found it unnerving to look at a dead body.

'Don't you see it?' Erica got out her mobile and began scrolling through all her photos. 'I took pictures of the painting because it was too big to bring with me. Do you see now?'

She pointed at the portrait of Leif. Everyone leaned

close to study the painting on the phone display. Paula was the first to see what she meant.

'He's holding the pen in his left hand! He was left-handed!'

'Exactly!' Erica exclaimed so loudly that Ernst raised his head in alarm. But after ascertaining that everything was all right, he lay down again at Mellberg's feet.

'I don't understand how the police and his family could have missed something like that. So I phoned Viola for confirmation. She said Leif was definitely left-handed. He would never have used his right hand to write or to shoot.'

She gave Patrik a triumphant look.

At first he felt a prickle of excitement in his gut, but then he thought one step further ahead and sighed.

'Oh, no. Don't tell me what you're thinking.'

'Yes,' said Erica. 'You'll have to ring whoever it is you need to contact for permission. Because you're going to have to get Leif's body exhumed.'

Bill and Gun were sitting at the kitchen table when the front door opened. They hadn't said much to each other while they ate a late breakfast. Bill had taken out his mobile several times and read the text that had come in the middle of the night: *Staying over at Basse's.*

He got up and went out to the front hall, where he saw his son taking off his shoes. Bill wrinkled his nose.

'You stink to high heaven of alcohol,' he said, even though he'd told himself to remain calm. 'And sending a text in the middle of the night is not acceptable. You know you're supposed to tell us in advance where you're going.'

Nils shrugged. 'I've stayed over plenty of times before,' he said. 'And yes, we had a few beers yesterday, but I'm fifteen now. I'm not a kid any more!'

Bill was so angry he didn't trust himself to reply. He turned to Gun, who was leaning against the doorjamb. She pointed upstairs.

'Go up and take a shower,' she told Nils. 'And while you're up there, I want you to find yourself a better attitude. When you've done that, you can come back down and we'll have a talk.'

Nils opened his mouth to say something, but Gun merely pointed upstairs again. He shook his head and climbed the stairs. A few moments later they heard the sound of the shower.

Bill went into the living room and stood staring out the window at the sea. It looked so inviting right now.

'What are we going to do with him?' he asked. 'Alexander and Philip never acted like this.'

'Oh, they had their defiant periods too, but you always had to hurry off to your boats whenever some incident occurred.' She sighed. 'But you're right. They were never this bad. I know, I know. We were too old to have another child.'

The look in her eyes made his chest ache with guilt. He knew Gun was doing her best. It was his fault things had gone wrong. His absences, his indifference. No wonder Nils hated him.

He sank on to the big, floral-patterned sofa.

'So what should we do?' he asked.

He turned to look out the window again. It was going to be a fine day for sailing, but he'd lost all interest. Besides, Khalil and Adnan were going to look for a new place to live today.

'He's so angry,' said Bill, keeping his gaze fixed on the sea. 'I don't understand where all that anger comes from.'

Gun sat down next to him and squeezed his hand.

He'd been wrestling all night with a thought that kept nagging at him. He didn't want to say it out loud, but he'd shared everything with Gun for forty years, and force of habit proved too strong to resist.

'Do you think he was involved?' he whispered. 'With setting the fire, I mean?'

Gun's silence told him he was not the only one who'd had dark thoughts in the night.

Sanna feverishly picked up one pot after another. She forced herself to breathe evenly, to stay calm. Roses were sensitive flowers no matter how thorny the bushes were, and she didn't want to risk harming the plants. But she was so angry she hardly knew what to do with herself.

How could she have believed Vendela when she said she would be staying at her father's place after the party? Niklas and his family lived closer to Basse, so it would have been easier for her to stay with them. It had sounded so sensible that she hadn't bothered to check with Niklas.

But this morning Vendela hadn't answered her phone, and when Sanna rang Niklas, she found out Vendela hadn't spent the night there after all. Niklas said she hadn't mentioned a word to him about coming over. 'Should I be worried?' he'd asked.

'No, you should be furious,' she'd told him before ending the call.

Sanna left a dozen messages on Vendela's voicemail, and if she didn't turn up soon, she'd leave another dozen.

The soil flew up when Sanna set down a rosebush. A thorn snagged her glove, which came off, and she got a long scratch on her hand.

She swore so loudly that several customers turned to stare. Sanna smiled at them and forced herself to breathe. So much had happened lately, her whole world seemed off-kilter. Nea's death. Marie's return. And Marie's daughter Jessie had been inside her home. She realized that what happened thirty years ago was not the girl's fault. Her logical, rational adult mind knew that. Yet it was unsettling to see the girl in her house, with her daughter.

Sanna hadn't been able to sleep last night. Instead, she'd lain in bed staring up at the ceiling, haunted by images she hadn't seen in decades. Stella talking about the green man, the friend she had in the woods. During the investigation, Sanna had talked to her parents about the green man and mentioned him to the police. But no one had listened. She realized now it must have sounded like a fairy tale. And it probably was. Something Stella had simply dreamed up. And why re-open old wounds? The case had been solved. Everybody knew who had killed her little sister. Nothing good would come from digging everything up all over again.

'Why did I have to come over here? Why couldn't we meet at home?'

Sanna jumped. With her arms crossed, Vendela was standing right in front of her. She was wearing big sunglasses, and her clothes didn't look clean. Even though she seemed to have taken a shower, she reeked of alcohol.

'Don't tell me you're hungover.'

'What? I haven't been drinking. We were up late, and I'm tired, that's all.'

Vendela refused to look at her mother. Sanna clenched her fists.

'It's obvious you're lying, just as you lied to me about staying at your father's place.'

'I did not!'

Sanna could feel all the customers staring at them, and Cornelia was looking concerned as she worked at the cash register. But it couldn't be helped.

'You told me you were going to stay with your father, but he never heard a word about it!'

'I have my own key, so why should I have to tell him

anything? It was super late, and the others were worried about me. They didn't want me to go out that late, so I slept on the sofa.'

Her voice quavered: 'I do everything right, and you still get mad at me. It's so bloody unfair!'

Vendela spun on her heel and dashed out. The customers were whispering all around Sanna. She took a deep breath and went back to tending the pots of roses. She knew she'd been defeated.

'What did he say?' asked Gösta, trying to keep up with Patrik as they headed for the film studio.

'I think I've worn him down with all my requests for exhumations over the past few years,' said Patrik with a crooked smile. 'He just sighed and signed the papers when I presented all the relevant forms. He agreed this is a matter that should be further examined.'

'So when will the exhumation take place?'

'Permission has been granted, so as soon as the practical details are taken care of, it can go ahead. It could be as early as Tuesday.'

'Wow,' said Gösta, impressed.

Things usually took significantly more time, but he could sense how restless Patrik was. He wanted to make some progress in the case and get closer to a resolution. Gösta could always tell when his colleague had shifted into high gear. At times like this he was unstoppable, so it came as no surprise that Patrik had managed to get the administrative and judicial wheels to turn faster.

'How do you want to handle Marie? The usual interviewing procedures? Do we go on the attack?'

'I'm not sure,' replied Patrik. 'I have the impression she won't be easily intimidated or sweet-talked. We'll have to play it by ear.'

Gösta pressed the buzzer on the intercom attached to

the studio gate. After explaining they were police officers, they were allowed in. They walked over to the studio building and stepped through the open door. The place was teeming with people, spotlights, and props. A woman holding a notepad shushed them, so Gösta gathered they had arrived in the middle of filming. He turned to the right because he could hear voices, but the filming was happening behind stage sets, so he couldn't see anything.

Cautiously they moved closer and heard the actors speaking their lines more clearly, but they still couldn't see anything. It sounded like a scene between two women – some sort of confrontation, with raised voices and emotional outbursts. Finally they heard a man shout: 'Cut!' Only then did they dare venture around the corner. Gösta gaped. Within the plywood walls a real room had been created in all its detail. It was like travelling back in time to the 1970s. Everything about the room brought back memories.

Two women were talking to the director. Gösta recognized Marie as the older of the two, made up to look haggard and ill. This scene must be towards the end of Ingrid Bergman's life, when cancer had taken hold. He wondered who the younger woman was supposed to be; maybe one of Ingrid's daughters.

Marie caught sight of them and stopped in mid-sentence. Patrik motioned to her. She said a few words to the woman and the director before briskly striding over to join them.

'You'll have to excuse my appearance,' she said, taking off the shawl covering her hair.

Her complexion had been given a greyish tinge, and wrinkles and lines had been drawn on her face. Somehow this only made her even more beautiful.

'So how can I be of service to you today?' she asked tonelessly, pointing to a cluster of sofas a short distance away.

After they were seated, Patrik looked at Marie.

'We've been given new information relating to your alibi.'

'My alibi?' she said. The only reaction Gösta could see was that her eyes narrowed slightly.

'Yes,' said Patrik. 'We've learned that you were not telling the truth. So we're primarily interested in hearing where you really were at eight o'clock on Monday morning.'

'I see,' said Marie, delaying her answer by lighting a cigarette. She took a couple of drags and then said: 'Who told you my alibi was a lie?'

'That's not something we're going to reveal. And you haven't answered the question. Do you still claim that you spent the night with Jörgen Holmlund, and that the two of you left his hotel room together at eight o'clock Monday morning?'

Marie didn't reply. She took a few more drags on her cigarette. Finally she sighed.

'Okay, I confess.' She held up her hands and laughed. 'I took home some eye-candy from the party, and . . . I thought you might latch on to the story, so I decided to tell a white lie.'

'A white lie?' said Gösta. 'Don't you realize this is a murder investigation?'

'Of course I do. But I also know that I'm innocent, and that my director would be furious if I got involved in something that might delay filming. So that's why I asked him to give me an alibi when I heard about the little girl getting killed; I was afraid you'd start poking around in my personal life.'

She gave them a smile.

Gösta felt a surge of irritation. Treating this situation so lightly was not only arrogant, it was insensitive and cruel. Now they'd once again have to waste valuable time confirming her alibi. Time they could have spent on something else.

'So this young man you spent the night with . . . does he have a name?' asked Patrik.

Marie shook her head.

'That's what's so embarrassing. I have no clue what his name is. I called him darling, and that was good enough for me. To be perfectly honest, I was more interested in his body than his name.'

She tapped the ash from her cigarette into an overflowing ashtray on the table.

'Okay,' said Patrik, fighting to remain patient. 'You don't know his name, but could you tell us what he looks like? Or do you know anything else that might help us identify him? Do you know the names of any of his friends?'

'I'm afraid I don't. He was at the hotel with a bunch of young guys his age, but he was the only one who was good-looking enough to grab my attention, so I didn't bother to talk to the others. Well, I didn't bother to talk much to him either. I suggested he come home with me, which he willingly did, and that was that. Since I had a film shoot the next day, I kicked him out, and there's really not much more to tell you.'

'What did he look like?' persisted Patrik.

'Oh, good lord, he looked like most young men in their twenties who hang around here in the summertime. That blond, blue-eyed type, with slicked back hair, expensive brand-name clothes, and a slightly snobbish attitude. Probably living off his pappa's money.'

She waved her cigarette.

'So you don't think he was from around here?' asked Gösta, coughing from the smoke.

'No, he talked like someone from Gothenburg. Probably a tourist from Gothenburg on a sailing holiday. But that's only a guess.'

She leaned back and took one last drag on her cigarette.

Gösta sighed. A nameless guy in his twenties from Gothenburg, here on a sailing holiday. It didn't exactly narrow down the possibilities. The description fit thousands of young men who passed through Fjällbacka in the summer.

'Did your daughter happen to see him?' he asked.

'No, she was in bed asleep,' said Marie. 'You know how teenagers are. They sleep half the day.'

Patrik raised his eyebrows.

'My wife tells me you mentioned seeing someone in the woods, right before Stella disappeared.'

Marie smiled.

'Your wife is a very intelligent woman. And I'll tell you, just like I told her: the police never bothered to follow up on the lead. Because of that, the murderer has struck again.'

Patrik stood up.

'If you think of anything that might help us find the young man to confirm your alibi, be sure to give us a call,' he said. 'Otherwise we have only your word that you were with someone on Sunday night. And that is not good enough.'

Gösta stood up too, giving Marie a surprised look. She was smiling and didn't seem at all concerned about the serious situation in which she now found herself.

'Of course,' she said sarcastically. 'Anything to help out the police.'

Someone called her name from the stage set, and she got to her feet.

'Time for another take. Are we finished here?'

'For now,' said Patrik.

As they left the cool air of the studio and stepped outside into the summer heat, they paused for a moment at the gate.

'Do you believe her story?' asked Gösta.

Patrik took his time before replying.

'The part about her taking home some young guy and not even knowing his name rings true. But it seems implausible that she'd lie about it because she didn't want us poking around in her personal life.'

'I'm sceptical too,' agreed Gösta. 'So the next question is, what is she hiding? And why?'

THE STELLA CASE

All of a sudden Marie was simply gone. They thought they'd be able to steer the situation, work it to their advantage, that they could still have an impact and make decisions. But gradually they realized they had no control over anything. And then Marie was sent away.

Sometimes Helen envied Marie. Maybe things were better where she was now. Maybe she'd found a good home with nice people who liked her. That was her hope, at any rate, even though the thought filled her with jealousy.

In the meantime, she had ended up in a prison far worse than any with bars on the windows. Her life was no longer her own. In the daytime her parents watched every move she made. At night her dreams haunted her, with the same scenes playing over and over. She was never free even for a second.

She was thirteen years old, and her life was over before it had even started. There was nothing but lies. Sometimes she longed for the truth, but she knew she could never allow the truth to cross her lips. It was too big, too overwhelming. The truth would destroy everything.

But she missed Marie. Every minute, every second. She missed her the way she would miss an arm or a leg, a part of herself. It had been the two of them against the world. Now she was all alone.

It had felt so liberating to work out what had been bothering her about the painting. Now Patrik and his colleagues could take over. Even though Erica realized it was necessary to re-examine Leif's body, she was doubtful they'd find anything after all these years. Bodies deteriorated so rapidly.

Viola was shocked when Erica rang to tell her what they'd discovered and what had to be done. She said she needed to speak to her two brothers first, but after ten minutes she phoned back to say they supported the police decision to exhume their father's body. They too wanted to know what really happened.

'You're not looking so hot,' said Paula, refilling Erica's coffee cup.

The two of them were still sitting in the station kitchen, going through Leif's diary. They were helping each other to decipher his scribblings. Of most interest was the mysterious '11' from the day he died. Leif's handwriting was typical of his generation: hopelessly elaborate, with sweeping loops and flourishes. He also had a fondness for odd abbreviations, which made the notes in his diary resemble coded entries.

'Could it be a temperature?' wondered Paula, squinting

her eyes, as if that might make it easier to work out what was written.

'Hmm . . .' said Erica. 'He wrote "55" the week before, so I don't think he's referring to the weather.'

She groaned.

'Maths and numbers have always been my Achilles' heel, and I'm not exactly at my most alert today. I forgot how bad a hangover could be.'

'I hope you at least had a good time.'

'It was great! I've been trying to ring Kristina, but she must be in bed with her head under the covers.'

'Maybe you should do the same.'

'You're probably right,' muttered Erica as she continued to stare at the notes in the diary.

Gösta came into the kitchen.

'Hi, girls. Are you still here? Don't you think you should go home to bed, Erica? You're looking a bit peaky.'

'I'd feel a lot better if everybody would quit reminding me how lousy I look.'

'How did it go?' Paula asked Gösta. 'What did Marie say?'

'She claims she took some young guy home with her that night, but she doesn't know his name. And she got her director to lie for her because she wanted to come up with a quick alibi to stop us sniffing around her private life.'

'Do you believe her?' asked Paula.

'Patrik and I are both sceptical,' he said, pouring himself a cup of coffee.

He went over to stand behind Erica and looked down at the open diary.

'Are you getting anywhere?' he asked.

'No. It seems to be some incomprehensible code. Can you understand what "55" and "11" might signify?'

Erica showed Gösta the cryptic notes.

'What do you mean, "55" and "11"?' he replied. 'It says "SS" and "JJ".'

Paula and Erica stared at him. Gösta laughed at their surprised expressions.

'I realize it's a little hard to see, but that's the same handwriting as my mother's. Those are letters of the alphabet, not numbers. My guess is they're somebody's initials.'

'You're right!' exclaimed Erica. 'They're letters!'

'SS and JJ . . .' said Paula.

'James Jensen, maybe?' said Gösta.

'That's possible,' Paula replied. 'But the question is, why would Leif write down the initials of Helen's husband in his diary? Were they supposed to meet? Did they meet?'

'You'll have to ask James Jensen,' said Erica. 'What about the SS? Who could that be? Viola said that the Stella case was the only thing of importance on Leif's mind before he died, so I imagine these initials are somehow connected.'

'Seems plausible,' Gösta agreed.

'I'll phone Viola and check, just to be sure. We may be making too much of this. It could be she'll recognize immediately what these initials stand for.'

'While we're waiting to solve this puzzle, let's hope that a new examination of Leif's body will produce results,' said Gösta.

'Yes. It's always difficult trying to work on a case from so long ago,' said Paula. 'People forget, evidence is destroyed, and, to be honest, the exhumation is a real long shot. At any rate, we have no idea whether it might lead us to finding proof that Leif was murdered.'

Erica nodded.

'Leif must have been facing the same challenges when he decided to re-examine the Stella case. So many years had passed. And we still don't know whether he found out any new information or discovered anything in the old case files. I so wish I'd had access to transcripts of those original interviews with Marie and Helen.'

She ran her hand through her hair.

'If JJ does stand for James Jensen, maybe he could at least explain why they were supposed to meet on the day Leif died,' said Gösta. 'And whether they did meet or not.'

He looked at Paula.

'What do you say? Shall we drive over to Fjällbacka and have a talk with James Jensen? We can drop you off at home on the way, Erica. Unless you'd rather take the bus back . . .'

'No, thanks. I'd be happy if you'd drive me,' said Erica, feeling sick at the mere thought of another bus ride.

'We'll phone ahead, to see if he's home. But let's not say why we want to talk to him. We'll leave in a few minutes. Okay?'

Paula and Erica both nodded.

'We have barf bags in the back seat of the police car, in case you need one, Erica.'

'Oh, shut up,' she said.

Paula grinned and got up to make the phone call.

Basse woke with the sun on his face. Cautiously he opened one eye. That simple movement made his head feel as if it would explode. His mouth felt sticky and dry. He managed to open his other eye and then forced himself to sit up. He was on the sofa in the living room, and he must have been lying at an odd angle because his neck hurt.

He rubbed the back of his neck and looked around. Outside, the sun was high in the sky. He glanced at his watch. Twelve thirty. How long had the party lasted?

Basse stood up but immediately sat back down. People were sleeping everywhere. Two lamps lay on the floor, broken. The parquet floor was scratched up. The sofa he was sitting on was littered with food and half-empty beer bottles. The upholstery was completely ruined. The white armchair was covered with red-wine stains, and the shelf that used to hold his father's whisky collection was empty.

My God. His parents would be home in a week, and he'd never be able to fix up the house in time. They were going to kill him. He'd never planned to invite so many to the party. He didn't even know half the people who were sprawled around the living room. It was a miracle the police hadn't turned up.

It was all Vendela's and Nils's fault. It was their idea. At least part of it. He couldn't really remember now. He needed to find them. They'd help him sort this out.

His socks got wet as soon as he took a few steps on the carpet, which was sticky and damp and smelled of stale beer. The smell was sickening, and he gagged but was able to keep himself from vomiting. He didn't see Vendela or Nils anywhere. One boy's fly was open, and Basse wondered whether he should cover him up with something, but he had bigger problems to deal with than some guy's exposed cock.

He dragged himself up the stairs. Even the slightest effort brought out a cold sweat. He refused to look over his shoulder because he didn't want to see more of the devastation below.

Three people were sleeping in his bedroom, but Vendela and Nils weren't among them. The whole room reeked. Someone had barfed on his keyboard, and the contents of his desk were scattered on the floor.

In his parents' bedroom the destruction was less, but the stench of vomit was overwhelming. The sheets and blanket were covered with dark stains.

Basse stopped abruptly. Images appeared in his mind, like pale Polaroid photographs. They'd been in here. He pictured Nils grinning at Vendela, who was holding a plastic cup. And he heard boys' voices. Who else had been here? The more he strained to remember, the more the images faded.

He stepped on something hard and swore. A marker was lying on the floor, without its cap, and it had left a stain on the light-coloured wood that his mother loved so much. A marker. Jessie. Vendela's plan. What was it they'd intended to do? What had they done? He pictured bare breasts. White and big and voluptuous. He was lying on top of someone, with his eyes right above those breasts. He'd grabbed them. He shook his head in an attempt to clear his mind, but his skull felt as if it would split in two.

He felt his mobile vibrating in his trouser pocket, and he fumbled to get it out. A text from Nils. Lots of pictures. And with each picture he saw, his memory came back to him. Pressing his hand to his mouth, he dashed for his parents' bathroom.

Patrik was sitting in his office at the station writing a report about the bizarre meeting with Marie. But his thoughts kept wandering to what he'd heard about the notes in Leif's diary. Gösta had briefed him about their theories, and now even Patrik was wondering about the mysterious initials. He'd immediately given his okay for Gösta and Paula to have a talk with James. It was a long shot, but sometimes these types of guesses proved right and allowed an investigation to move forward.

His mobile rang, snapping him out of his brooding. He reached for the phone.

'Pedersen here,' said a brisk voice. 'Are you busy?'

'No. Nothing that I can't put aside for a moment. Are you working on a Sunday?'

'Can't take much time off in the summer. We set a record for the number of bodies in July, and August isn't looking much better. The old record had stood for thirty years.'

'Shit,' said Patrik.

But his curiosity was piqued. Whenever Pedersen phoned, he usually had something substantial to report. And physical evidence was what they were definitely lacking at the moment. All they had were hypotheses and speculation, gossip and assumptions.

'By the way, I heard you've arranged to have another body brought over here. Something about an old suicide?'

'Yes. Leif Hermansson. He was in charge of investigating the Stella case. We're exhuming his body the day after tomorrow to see what we can find.'

'That'll take time,' said Pedersen. 'As for the little girl, I'll be finished with my final report this week, probably on Wednesday. That's what I'm hoping, at least. But I wanted to talk to you about something. I think it may be of help.'

'Yes?'

'I've found two fingerprints on the body. On her eyelids. Her body had been washed, so there was nothing there. But whoever washed her forgot about the eyelids. My guess is that the perpetrator closed her eyes.'

'Oh . . .' said Patrik, pausing to consider what he'd just heard. 'Could you email me the prints? At the moment we have nothing to compare them with, but we found fingerprints at the primary crime scene, and I want Torbjörn Ruud to have a look at both sets.'

'I'll send them right over,' said Pedersen.

'Thanks. And thanks for taking the time to call me. I know you're swamped. I hope it lets up soon.'

'I do too,' said Pedersen with a sigh.

Patrik put down the phone and stared impatiently at

his computer screen. Why was it that the more anxiously you were waiting for something, the longer it seemed to take? But finally Pedersen's message came through via the secure email server.

Patrik opened the attached file. Two pristine finger-prints.

He immediately rang Torbjörn.

'Hedström here. Hey, I'm on my knees begging you for help with some evidence Pedersen's just found. There were two fingerprints on Nea's body, and I'd like you to compare them to the ones on the chocolate wrapper found in the barn.'

Torbjörn grunted. 'Can't it wait? I'd like to get through the rest of the search results, then check the fingerprints against the police database.'

'I understand, but my gut instinct is telling me the fingerprints will match.'

There was silence at the other end of the line. He only hoped Torbjörn was considering his request.

At last Torbjörn said morosely, 'All right. Send them over and I'll set about comparing them as soon as possible. Okay?'

'Thanks!' said Patrik. He was about to say more, but Torbjörn had hung up.

'Hello?' Erica called as she stepped inside.

Anna was talking on her phone in the kitchen. When she caught sight of her sister, she swiftly ended the call.

'Hi!'

Erica gave her a suspicious look.

'Who were you talking to?'

'Nobody. Well, er . . . it was Dan,' said Anna, blushing.

Erica felt her stomach knot. Of one thing she was certain – Anna had not been talking to Dan, for the simple reason that she herself had just been speaking to him on the phone. She wanted to confront Anna and ask her what she was hiding, yet she also wanted to show her little sister that she trusted her. Anna had fought hard to repair her misstep, and they had all put it behind them. Questioning Anna or letting on that she knew she was lying would destroy the trust they had built. Her sister had been so fragile for so long. Now that she seemed whole again, the last thing Erica wanted was to risk a setback. So she took a deep breath and put her suspicions aside. At least for now.

'So how are you feeling, you poor thing?' asked Anna.

Erica dropped on to a kitchen chair.

'Terrible, but it's my own fault. And it hasn't helped that everyone insists on pointing out how awful I look.'

'Well, I have to say you've certainly looked better,' said Anna, giving Erica a crooked smile as she sat down across from her.

She pushed a plate of cinnamon buns towards her sister. Erica stared at them as she fought an internal battle. But she decided if there was one day she deserved an excess of carbs, it was today. Besides, her whole body was screaming for pizza, so that meant a trip to Bååhaket tonight. The kids would be overjoyed. Patrik would pretend to object, but inside he'd be turning cartwheels.

She picked up a bun and ate half in one bite.

'What did they say about your theory that it wasn't suicide?'

Anna also ate a bun, and Erica noted that her baby bump made an excellent crumb collector.

'They agreed. Patrik has already made arrangements to have Leif's body exhumed. They're hoping to do it day after tomorrow.'

Anna coughed.

'Day after tomorrow? That fast? Is that possible? I thought there'd be a lot of red tape.'

'He got the prosecutor to put through an emergency request to the court, so with luck they'll open the grave on Tuesday. Based on that assumption, Patrik is making all the practical arrangements. In other words, it hasn't been approved yet, but the prosecutor didn't think there'd be any problem.'

'I suppose by now they're used to Patrik wanting to dig up bodies,' said Anna. 'They probably have a standing request filled out in his name, just to be on the safe side.'

Erica couldn't help grinning.

'It'll be interesting to see what a new examination shows,' she said. 'And the family is supporting the effort, which is great.'

'In their shoes, I'd do the same. If it wasn't suicide, the police need to start looking for whoever was responsible.'

While Anna reached for another bun, Erica glanced around the kitchen. Only now did she realize how quiet it was in the house.

'Where are the kids? Are they taking a nap somewhere?'

'No, they're at the neighbours' house,' said Anna. 'And Dan's at the beach with our kids, so I can hold down the fort here a little while longer. Why don't you have a lie down? You don't look too good, as I already mentioned.'

'Thanks a lot,' said Erica, sticking out her tongue.

But she was grateful for the offer. Her body was shouting that she was no longer twenty. Yet it took a while for her to fall asleep. She couldn't help speculating about who Anna had been phoning. And why she had ended the call so quickly when her sister came home.

BOHUSLÄN 1672

The morning was cool and hazy. Elin had been given permission to wash herself with a rag and a bucket of water brought to her cell. She had also been given a clean white shift to wear. She had heard rumours of the witch test but did not know what the procedure would be. Would they toss her off the wharf and leave her to flail in the water as best she could? Did they want her to die from drowning? Would her body float to the surface in the springtime?

The guards roughly escorted her to the edge of the wharf. A crowd had gathered to watch, and she wondered whether it had been decided to do this in Fjällbacka in order to inflict upon her as much humiliation as possible.

When Elin looked around, she discovered many familiar faces. Everyone appeared to be in high spirits. Ebba of Mörhult stood a few metres away. Her eyes gleamed with anticipation.

Elin turned away from Ebba, not wanting the woman to see how frightened she was. She peered down at the water. It was so dark and deep. She would drown if they threw her in, of that she was certain. She was going to die here, on the wharf in Fjällbacka, while old friends, old neighbours, old enemies looked on.

'Tie her up,' said the sheriff to the guards. She looked at him in alarm.

If she was tied up she would have no chance whatsoever in the water. She would sink to the bottom and die among the crabs and weeds. She screamed and tried to pull free, but they were stronger and forced her down on to the wharf. They wound a coarse rope around her feet and then bound her hands behind her back.

Elin caught sight of a familiar skirt very near. She raised her head. In the middle of the crowd stood Britta. And Preben. He was again nervously turning his hat in his hands, the way he had done when he visited her at the gaol. But Britta had a big smile on her face as she looked at Elin lying there bound and wearing a white shift. Preben turned away.

'Now we shall see if she floats!' said the sheriff, speaking to the crowd.

It was clear that he was enjoying all the attention and the excited mood. He wanted to make the most of it.

'If she floats, she is without a doubt a witch. If she sinks, she is not, and we will try to pull her out.'

He laughed, and the spectators followed suit. Elin prayed to God as she lay on the wharf, bound with ropes that chafed at her hands and feet. It was the only way for her to keep the panic under control, but her breathing was rapid and shallow, as if she had been running. She heard a roaring in her ears.

When they lifted her up, the rope cut into her skin, making her scream. A scream that was abruptly cut short when she landed in the water, which instantly filled her mouth. The cold, salty water was a shock to her body, and she expected to disappear below the surface and sink to the bottom. But nothing happened. She lay face down but was able to lift her head to gasp for air.

Instead of sinking, she bobbed in the water. On the

wharf above her, the spectators gasped. Then they began shouting all at once.

'Witch!' someone cried, and then another. 'Witch!'

Rough hands pulled Elin out the water, but she was no longer screaming. The pain was no longer part of her.

'There you see!' yelled the sheriff. 'She floated like a swan. She's a witch!'

The crowd howled. With a great effort, Elin raised her head. The last thing she saw before she fainted was Preben and Britta walking away. She felt Ebba of Mörhult spitting at her as she slipped into unconsciousness.

✣

James hadn't answered the phone when they rang, but Gösta and Paula decided to take a chance on finding him at home all the same.

'Oh, is that sweet old lady selling her house?' said Paula as they passed the red house next to the gravel road.

'Sweet old lady?' said Gösta, glancing at the house and seeing the 'For Sale' sign out front.

'Yes. Martin and I visited her when we were knocking on doors in the neighbourhood. She's over ninety and was watching the MMA on TV when we dropped by.'

Gösta laughed.

'Hey, why not? Maybe I'll be an MMA fan in my old age too.'

'It can't be easy, finding ways to pass the time when she lives in such a remote area and can't get out any more. She told us she mostly sits at her kitchen window and watches whatever goes on outside.'

'My father did the same thing,' said Gösta. 'I wonder why. Do you suppose it's a way of trying to maintain control when life starts feeling precarious?'

'Maybe,' said Paula. 'But I think it's a Swedish phenomenon. You're the only ones who allow the elderly to live all alone. In Chile, that would never happen. People take care of their ageing family members until they die.'

'So does that mean you and Johanna will have your mother and Mellberg living with you for the rest of their lives?' asked Gösta with a chuckle.

Paula stared at him in horror. 'When you put it like that . . . the Swedish model actually sounds rather enticing.'

'I thought you might say that,' replied Gösta.

They had reached the house where Helen and James lived, and Paula parked next to the family's car. Helen opened the front door as soon as they knocked. Her expression remained impassive when she saw them.

'Hi, Helen,' said Gösta. 'We'd like to speak to James. Is he home?'

Gösta thought he saw her gaze waver for a moment, but it happened so quickly, he might have imagined it.

'He's doing some target practice out back.'

'Can we go over there without putting our lives in danger?' asked Paula.

'Sure. Just give a shout to warn him you're coming. Then it'll be okay.'

Gösta and Paula headed towards the sound of scattered gunshots.

'Do I even dare count up all the laws he's breaking by doing target practice out here?' said Paula.

Gösta shook his head. 'No, it's best we don't mention that at the moment. But on some other occasion we should have a talk with him about how inappropriate this is.'

The shots got louder and louder as they approached.

Gösta raised his voice and called: 'James! It's Gösta and Paula from the Tanumshede police station. Don't shoot!'

The gunshots ceased. Just to be on the safe side, Gösta again shouted: 'James! Please confirm that you heard we're coming!'

'I hear you!' yelled James.

They picked up pace and soon caught sight of him up ahead. He had his arms crossed. He'd set his gun down on a tree stump. Even unarmed, there was something about his demeanour that Gösta found unnerving. Perhaps it was the man's fondness for dressing as if he were in an American war film.

'I know, I know. I'm not allowed to practise here,' said James, holding up his hands.

'You're right, but we can have a conversation about that some other time,' said Gösta. 'We're here about something else.'

'Let me just put my weapon away,' said James, picking up the gun from the stump.

'Is that a Colt?' asked Paula.

James nodded proudly.

'Yes. A Colt M1911. Standard sidearm used by the US military between 1911 and 1985. It was used in both world wars and also in the Korean and Vietnam wars. It's the first gun I ever owned. My father gave it to me when I was seven, and it's the one I used when I learned to shoot.'

Gösta refrained from commenting on how inappropriate it was to give a seven-year-old a gun. He didn't think James would understand.

'Have you taught your son to shoot?' he asked instead.

'Yes, he's an excellent shot,' said James as he carefully, almost tenderly, returned the gun to its case. 'Apart from that, he's not much good at anything. But he can shoot. He's been practising pretty much daily, in fact. He'd make a good sharpshooter, except he's too feeble to pass the military's physical tests.'

Gösta cast a surreptitious glance at Paula. Her expression revealed what she thought of the way James spoke of his son.

'So, what's this about?' James asked, setting the gun case on the ground.

'It has to do with Leif Hermansson.'

'The police officer who set my wife up for murder?' said James, frowning. 'Why do you want to talk about him?'

'What do you mean by "set up"?' asked Paula.

James stretched and again crossed his arms, which made them look gigantic.

'Look, I'm not saying he did anything illegal, but he worked awfully hard to prove my wife was guilty of a murder she didn't commit. And I don't think he seriously considered any other option.'

'Apparently he began to have doubts towards the end of his life,' said Paula. 'And we have reason to believe that he had contact with you on the day he died. Do you recall anything about that?'

James shook his head. 'It was a long time ago, but I don't remember being in contact with him that day. We had very little to do with each other. Why would we?'

'We thought he might have contacted you first,' said Gösta, 'in order to get in touch with Helen. I'm guessing she wouldn't have been favourably disposed towards him.'

'You're right about that,' said James. 'If he wanted to talk to her, it probably would have been easier to go through me. But he never did. And I'm not sure how I would have handled it. So many years had gone by, and we were trying to put the whole thing behind us.'

'It must be difficult, given the current situation,' said Paula, studying his expression.

He calmly met her eye.

'Yes. It's a tragedy. But it's much worse for the girl's family than for us. It would be presumptuous of us to complain, though it's obviously tempting to do so because of all the media attention. Reporters have even turned up at our house. But they won't be coming back.'

James smiled slyly.

Gösta decided not to ask why. He was inclined to take the view that journalists had only themselves to blame. They'd been getting steadily more intrusive, and all too often they overstepped the boundaries of common decency.

'Okay. There's nothing else we need to discuss right now,' said Gösta, glancing at Paula, who nodded in agreement.

'If I think of anything, I'll give you a call,' said James obligingly.

He pointed towards the house that was visible through the trees.

'I'll walk you out.'

He led the way as Gösta exchanged glances with Paula. Clearly she didn't believe a word James had said either.

As they passed the house, Gösta looked up at a window on the second floor. A teenage boy was watching him, his face expressionless. Something about his black-dyed hair and all the eye make-up made him look like a ghost. Gösta shivered. Then the boy was gone.

When Marie came home, Jessie was sitting on the dock. She had smeared her face and body with lotion she'd found in the bathroom. No doubt expensive stuff. Her skin was still bright red, but it didn't itch as much. Jessie wished she could have found some sort of lotion for her soul. Or whatever it was that had broken inside her.

She had washed her vaginal area several times, but it still felt dirty. And disgusting. She'd thrown out the clothes belonging to Basse's mother. Now she had on an old T-shirt and a pair of sweatpants. She was staring at the evening sun. Marie came over to stand behind her.

'What have you done to your face?'

'Sunburn,' she said tersely.

Marie nodded. 'Well, a little sunshine is probably good for spots.'

Then she went back inside. Not a word about the fact that Jessie hadn't come home yesterday. Had she even noticed? Probably not.

Sam had been wonderful. He'd offered to go home with her and stay over. But Jessie needed to be alone for a while. She needed to sit in one place and feel the hatred growing inside her. She was guarding it. Somehow it felt liberating to finally give in and hate without restraint. For all these years she'd fought against it, not wanting to believe the worst of people. She had been so naive.

Her phone had been flooded with text messages all day. She couldn't understand how they'd got her number. But it had probably been shared along with all the photos. She had opened only the first one, then pressed delete whenever more texts came in. They were all the same. Whore. Slut. Pig. Fatso.

Sam had received the same texts. And photographs. They'd started coming in while he was removing the last of the words from her body. He'd put away his mobile and kissed her. At first she'd pulled away. She felt so disgusting, so dirty. She knew her breath must stink from vomit even though she'd brushed her teeth in the bathroom belonging to Basse's parents. But Sam didn't care. He gave her a long kiss, and she felt the blazing ball of hatred surge between them. They shared it.

The question was, what should they do now?

As the sun turned red, Jessie raised her face to the glow. Inside the house she heard Marie opening a bottle of champagne. Everything was exactly the same. And yet everything had changed.

*　　*　　*

Patrik was on his third cup of coffee since he'd talked to Torbjörn Ruud. He still hadn't heard from the pathologist.

He sighed and looked out to the corridor where Martin was slowly approaching, holding a cup in his hand.

'You look a little tired,' he said, and Martin stopped.

Patrik had already noticed it at the morning meeting, but he hadn't wanted to say anything to Martin in front of the others. He knew Martin had been having a hard time sleeping since Pia passed away.

'Oh, I'm fine,' said Martin, coming into Patrik's office.

Patrik gave a start. Martin was blushing.

'What are you not telling me?' he asked, leaning back in his desk chair.

'It's . . . it's just . . .' stammered Martin, staring at his shoes.

He seemed to be having trouble deciding which foot to stand on.

Patrik studied him with amusement.

'Sit down and tell me all about it. What's her name?'

Martin sat down and gave him an embarrassed smile.

'Her name is Mette.'

'And?' Patrik persisted.

'She's separated from her husband. She has a son who's a year old. She's from Norway and works as a financial assistant in an office in Grebbestad. We had our first date yesterday, but I'm not sure what will come of it.'

'Judging by how worn out you look, the date must have gone well, in any case,' Patrik said, grinning.

'Er, uh . . .'

'How did you meet?'

'At the playground,' said Martin, squirming on his chair.

Patrik decided to give Martin a break and not ask any more questions.

'I'm glad you're dating again,' he said. 'And that you're

596

at least open to the possibility of meeting someone. Whatever happens, happens. And that's okay. No one can ever replace Pia. It will be something different.'

'I know,' said Martin, again fixing his eyes on his shoes. 'I actually think I'm ready.'

'All right then.'

The phone started ringing, and Patrik raised a finger to indicate Martin should stay.

'Well, you were right, Hedström,' grumbled Torbjörn.

'What are you saying? Are the prints from the same person?'

'Without a doubt. But I checked the database, and unfortunately there was no match. I also compared them to the parents' prints, and they didn't match either.'

Patrik sighed. Why had he allowed himself to think this would be easy? But if nothing else they could now rule out Nea's parents.

'At least we have something to go on now. Thanks.'

He ended the call and looked at Martin.

'The fingerprints on Linnea match the ones on the chocolate wrapper.'

Martin raised his eyebrows.

'So let's see if they're in the database.'

Patrik shook his head.

'Torbjörn has already checked and didn't find a match.'

He'd never believed the murderer had chosen his victim at random. This felt more deliberate, more personal. And the parallels with the Stella case were impossible to ignore. No, he wasn't surprised they hadn't found the owner of the fingerprints in the police files.

'There are a number of people we ought to check,' said Martin. Then he paused. 'I don't like saying this, but the girl's parents, for example. And—'

'And Helen and Marie,' Patrik interjected. 'Yes, believe me, I've thought of that, but we have to have a high degree of suspicion in order to request their fingerprints. We asked for Peter's and Eva's prints when we interviewed them about the barn, and Torbjörn has already checked. They don't match.'

'But don't we have Helen's and Marie's prints on file?' asked Martin. 'From the previous investigation.'

Patrik shook his head.

'No. They were children when the murder was committed. They were never sentenced, and their finger-prints are not on file. But I would certainly have liked to do a comparison. Especially now that Marie's alibi has gone up in smoke. And the mere fact that she lied to us makes me wonder . . .'

'Yes, I agree. Something isn't right,' said Martin. 'By the way, have you heard from Gösta and Paula?'

'Yes. Paula phoned. James is adamant that he never had any contact with Leif. Gösta and Paula aren't convinced he's telling the truth.'

'But without anything concrete to go on, we can't force the point.'

'Exactly,' said Patrik.

'Let's hope Leif has a few secrets to tell us. When will we hear back about the exhumation request?'

'Tomorrow morning,' said Patrik. 'In the meantime, there's nothing more we can do today, so let's sleep on it. If we rack our brains, maybe we can work out how best to make use of this information.'

He gathered up the printouts and placed them in a plastic folder, which he stuffed into his briefcase.

'So, have you arranged to see this Mette again?'

'Tonight,' said Martin. 'Her son is staying with her ex for two days, so we might as well . . .'

'Absolutely. But see if you can get a little more sleep tonight,' said Patrik, putting his arm around Martin's shoulders as they left the room together.

They had almost reached the front door when Annika called to them. They turned to see her holding up the phone and pointing.

'It's the hospital. They've been trying to get hold of you.'

Patrik glanced at his mobile and saw that he'd missed three calls from the same number.

'What do they want?' he said, but Annika merely motioned for him to come over and take the call.

She handed him the phone. He listened, replied with a few brief comments and then put the phone down. He turned to Annika and Martin, who were waiting tensely.

'Amina passed away a couple of hours ago,' he said. It took a lot of effort to keep his voice steady. 'The fire at the refugee centre is no longer an arson investigation. It's a homicide case.'

He turned on his heel and headed for Mellberg's office. They needed to ask Karim what to do about the children. Their mother was dead. And someone had to tell them.

They could hear the muted sound of a TV upstairs. Khalil looked at Adnan, who was wiping away his tears. They had asked to continue to be flatmates, and that hadn't been a problem. The municipality wanted as many people as possible to share living space so there would be enough temporary housing for everyone who needed it.

So here they were. In a small room in a dark basement in a house built in the 1950s. It smelled damp and mouldy and felt closed-in. But the woman who owned the house was nice. She had invited them to dinner, and that had been pleasant even though they didn't know many words in common, and the food, which she called mutton with dill sauce, had tasted quite strange.

After dinner the phone rang, and then they called others, hoping to find solace with friends. Beautiful, happy, temperamental Amina was dead.

Adnan again wiped away tears.

'Could we go visit Karim? Maybe Bill could drive us there.'

Khalil followed Adnan's hollow gaze. He was staring at the stained wall-to-wall carpet. He rubbed the toe of his shoe on some of the stains. They looked old. It seemed as if no one had been down here in a long time.

'He can't have visitors this late,' said Khalil. 'Maybe tomorrow.'

Adnan clasped his hands and sighed.

'Fine, we'll go tomorrow.'

'Do you think they've told the children?'

Khalil's voice echoed off the cold stone walls.

'I think they'll let Karim do that.'

'If he can bear to tell them.'

Adnan rubbed his face.

'How could this happen?'

Khalil didn't know whether the question was directed at him or at God.

Sweden. This rich and free country.

'Lots of people have been kind,' he said. 'People like Bill. Bill and Gun. And Rolf. And Sture. We shouldn't forget that.'

He couldn't look at Adnan when he said that. He rubbed his toe harder on the carpet stains.

'They hate us so much,' said Adnan. 'I don't understand it. They come in the night and try to burn us alive, even though we haven't done anything to them. And yes, I know what you always tell me: "They're scared." But if somebody tosses a burning torch into a house, hoping the family inside will be burned alive just because they come from a different country, that's not being scared. That's something else.'

'Do you regret coming here?' asked Khalil.

Adnan was silent for so long that Khalil knew he was

thinking about his cousin who he'd seen shot to death, and his uncle whose leg had been blown off in an explosion. Sometimes he shouted their names at night.

It should have been an easy question to answer. But not any more. Not after Amina.

Adnan swallowed hard.

'No, I don't regret it. There was no choice. But I've realized one thing.'

'What?' asked Khalil as they sat in the dark.

'I now know that I will never have a home.'

Upstairs, the happy music on the TV got a little louder.

BOHUSLÄN 1672

Elin moved like a sleepwalker as she was led into the courtroom. She still could not understand how she had been able to float during the water test. All the benches in the room were filled, and Elin realized that more spectators must have been turned away.

The sheriff had told her she would be brought before the court, but what did that mean? Was there some way her life might be spared? Was there *anyone* who could save her?

She was seated at the very front. Everyone fixed their eyes on her, making her feel even more humiliated. All those curious, frightened, and hateful stares. Britta was present too, but Elin did not dare look in her direction.

The judge pounded his gavel to silence the murmuring voices. Elin gazed at the solemn men before her. She recognized only Lars Hierne. The others were strangers and for that reason all the more frightening.

'We are here today to determine whether Elin Jonsdotter is a witch. We have seen her float, and we have been given a number of statements as to her actions, but Elin Jonsdotter also has the right to summon character witnesses to speak on her behalf. Do you wish to call anyone?'

Elin glanced at the people sitting on the benches. She saw the maids from the farm and neighbours from Fjällbacka. She saw Britta and Preben and all the women and men she had helped when they were suffering from toothache, headache, heartache, and other ailments. With pleading eyes she looked at them, one by one, but they all turned away. No one stood up. No one said a word.

No one would come to her defence.

Finally she turned to look at Britta, who had a smile on her lips as she rested her hands on her stomach which was not yet overly large. Preben sat next to her. He lowered his head, making locks of his fair hair fall into his eyes. How she had loved his hair, which she used to stroke when they made love. She had loved him. Now she no longer knew what she felt. Part of her remembered her love for him. Part of her hated him. Part of her felt such loathing at his weakness. He went wherever the wind took him and gave in at the slightest resistance. She ought to have seen that, but she had been blinded by his kind eyes and his concern for her daughter. She had allowed herself to dream and to fill in the gaps instead of realizing that something was lacking. And now she would have to pay the price.

'Since no one has come forward as a character witness for Elin Jonsdotter, we will now call those who can testify regarding her actions. The first person we call is Ebba of Mörhult.'

Elin snorted. This was no surprise. She knew Ebba had been waiting for a chance to seek revenge, the way a fat spider waits for a fly. She did not deign to look at Ebba as the woman took her place in the witness box.

After Ebba was sworn in, the questions began. She preened as she sat in the chair, waving her hands about as she spoke.

'The first thing we noticed was that she could do things

a human being should not be able to do. She had the women in the area running to her with all manner of problems, such as aching feet or aching stomachs. And the girls kept asking Elin to help them lure young men. But I saw at once that things were not as they should be. It is not in the nature of human beings to control such matters. No, that is the work of the devil. But would anyone listen to me? No. They kept running to that woman to seek help for their troubles. And she offered them liniments and potions and long incantations. Things a god-fearing woman would never know.'

She looked around. Many of the spectators nodded agreement, even some who had gladly accepted Elin's help.

'What about the herring?' said Hierne, leaning towards Ebba.

She nodded eagerly.

'When the herring stopped appearing, I knew it was Elin who had done it.'

'Done it?' asked Hierne. 'How do you mean?'

'One evening I saw her put something in the water. And everyone knows that if you put copper in the water, the herring will stay away.'

'But what reason would she have to do such a thing? She and her deceased husband made their livelihood from fishing.'

'That merely shows how evil she is, the fact that she would allow her own family to risk starvation simply because she had a quarrel with the rest of us. She argued with some of the wives of Per's crew the day before the herring stopped coming. Afterwards nothing went right with the fishing for herring.'

'And what about the customs official? What happened on that day when he left their home after reporting that Per's boat would be confiscated by the state because he had illegally smuggled a cask of salt from Norway?'

'I heard how she cursed the customs official as he rode away. She flung after him blistering oaths that only the devil himself could have put in her mouth. No one with God in her heart would say the words she hurled at him. And then, on his way home . . .'

She paused. The crowd waited with bated breath.

'The customs official will recount for the court what happened to him,' said Hierne. 'But we will allow Ebba to speak of it first.'

'On his way home, he was unseated from his horse, and he toppled into the ditch. I knew at once that Elin had done this to him.'

'Thank you, Ebba. As I mentioned, we will also hear from customs official Henrik Meyer.' He cleared his throat. 'This leads us now to the most serious accusation against Elin Jonsdotter – that she used her witchcraft to cause her husband's boat to sink.'

Elin gasped and stared at Ebba of Mörhult. She knew she would not be allowed to speak unless addressed directly, but she could not stop herself.

'Have you lost your wits, Ebba! Are you accusing me of sinking Per's boat? With his entire crew? That is madness!'

'Silence, Elin Jonsdotter!' roared Hierne.

Ebba of Mörhult pressed one hand to her chest and used the other to fan her face with a handkerchief.

Elin snorted at this play-acting.

'Pay no mind to the accused,' said Hierne, placing his hand on Ebba's arm to reassure her. 'Please continue.'

'Well, she was terribly angry with her husband, with Per. She was angry at him because of the cask of salt and because he wanted to take the boat out. I heard her say that if he did go out, then he might as well die.'

'Tell us what happened next,' said Hierne.

Everyone leaned forward. There was no telling when they would next encounter such marvellous entertainment.

'They went out in the storm, and I saw a dove fly over them. It was Elin. Somehow I was able to recognize her, even though she was not in human form. When she flew after the boat, I knew my husband would not be coming home again. And that is exactly what happened.'

She sobbed loudly and blew her nose on her handkerchief.

'He was such a good husband, a wonderful father to our five children, and now he is lying in the deep, eaten by fish because that . . . that witch was angry at her husband!'

She pointed at Elin, who could only shake her head. This was so unreal. Like a bad dream. At any moment she would awake. But then she caught sight of Britta again and saw the satisfied smile on her sister's face. And she saw Preben's bowed head.

Then she knew this evil was real.

'Tell us about the abomination,' said Hierne.

Nausea surged inside Elin. Was nothing sacred?

'She must have become with child after lying with the devil,' said Ebba. A gasp passed through the crowd. 'So she came to my sister to get rid of the abomination. I saw it myself. When I entered the room, I saw it in a slop bucket next to the door. It looked nothing like a child. It was the image of the devil himself, so ugly and disfigured that it turned my stomach.'

Several women cried out. Hearing talk of lying with the devil and then giving birth to the devil's spawn was beyond anything they had ever witnessed.

'Ebba's sister was the one who served as midwife to this abomination, and she will also offer her testimony about what took place,' said Hierne, nodding.

These were serious matters being discussed, and he

made a great effort to ensure his bearing suited the gravity of the occasion.

Elin shook her head. Her hands trembled as she clasped them on her lap, and the weight of these accusations bowed her head towards the wide wooden planks of the floor. Yet she had no idea what else awaited her.

Two days had passed as they waited with growing frustration. Even though the investigation had come to a standstill, Gösta still had plenty of work to do. Tips had continued to pour in, especially since the newspapers not only published big headlines about the murder case but also posted black-bordered placards about Amina's death. This had led to a rancorous debate about refugee policies in Sweden. Both sides tried to make use of the arson and Amina's death to argue their case. One side claimed the fire was the result of the hate-filled propaganda and hostile attitude towards refugees espoused by the Sveriges Vänner party. The other side claimed the fire had resulted from the frustration felt by the Swedish people because of an untenable refugee policy. And some insisted it was the refugees themselves who had set the fire.

Gösta was sickened by the whole debate. In his view the refugee policies and the question of immigration should, of course, be examined and debated, and certainly improvements could be made. It wouldn't work to open the borders completely and welcome an endless flood of people. There had to be a functioning infrastructure in place in order to integrate the immigrants into Swedish society. With that much he could agree. But he was repelled by the rhetoric of Sveriges Vänner and its supporters when they blamed the immigrants for the problem, making them out to be villains for coming to Sweden.

A number of rotten apples did turn up, and the police couldn't ignore that fact. But the overwhelming majority of the people who had come to Sweden simply wanted to save their own lives and the lives of their families. They wanted to build a better life in a new country. Only desperation would make someone leave his homeland and everything near and dear, knowing he might never be able to return. Gösta couldn't help wondering how all the Swedes who were now complaining about refugees coming in and straining the country's resources would have behaved if a war were raging in Sweden and their own children were in constant danger. Wouldn't they also do everything they could to save their families?

He sighed and put down the newspaper. Annika always placed the daily papers on the table in the kitchen, but he often couldn't stand to do more than skim the bad news. Yet the police did have to keep an eye on what was written about the homicide case. Speculation and false statements had damaged many a criminal investigation.

Paula came into the kitchen, looking more tired than usual.

Gösta gave her a sympathetic look.

'The kids having a tough time?'

She nodded, helped herself to coffee, and then sat down across from him.

'Yes. They can't stop crying. And they wake up at night from bad dreams. My mother took them to the hospital so Karim could tell them about Amina, and I don't know how she could bear it. But she's been amazing, and we're making arrangements so that Karim and his kids can rent a flat in our building when he's discharged. The flat right next to ours has been vacant for a while, so I think it would be a good option for them. The only problem is that the municipality thinks the rent is too high, so we'll have to see what happens.'

Paula shook her head.

'I heard it went well yesterday,' she said. 'I mean, with the exhumation.'

'Yes, it was done in a dignified manner, under the circumstances. Now we're just waiting for the results. But the bullet from the first post-mortem is still missing. It wasn't even mentioned in the report. They've looked through all the material that was saved, which wasn't much, but there's no bullet. Evidence is supposed to be saved for seventy years. I wish they had complied with regulations.'

'We don't know why they can't find the bullet,' said Paula diplomatically. 'But nobody suspected murder back then. His death was deemed a suicide, plain and simple.'

'It doesn't matter. Evidence should not disappear,' said Gösta.

Yet he knew he was being unfair. They did an incredible job at the Swedish National Forensic Centre, and at the forensic lab. Even with a budget that was too small and with too much work. But the missing bullet was yet another frustration in this investigation, which kept leading to blind alleys. He was convinced the death of Leif Hermansson, which was now presumed to be murder, was connected to the Stella case. He only wished they could find something soon that would prove his theory.

'So I'm guessing there's been no progress in locating Marie's young stallion?'

Gösta reached for a Ballerina biscuit and carefully separated the top from the bottom before licking off the chocolate filling.

'You're right. We've talked to a lot of people who were

at Stora Hotel, but nobody saw anything. And the film director has confirmed that he spent the night with the make-up artist and not with Marie. He claims Marie begged him to lie because she knew she would be a suspect if she didn't have an alibi. She also told him about the mysterious young man, but he didn't see them together that night.'

'Well, I seriously doubt that he even exists,' said Gösta.

'If we assume she's lying . . . Why would she do that? And if she has something to do with the girl's murder . . . Why? What's the motive?'

They were interrupted when Paula's mobile rang.

'Oh, hi, Dagmar,' she said, giving Gösta a puzzled look.

She listened intently, and then Gösta saw her face light up.

'No, good God, it doesn't matter that you forgot. What's important is that you've now remembered! We'll come right over.'

She ended the call and looked at Gösta.

'Now I know how we can work out what vehicles passed the Berg farm on the morning when Nea disappeared. Let's go.'

She stood up. Then she paused and a smile appeared on her face.

'Wait. I think I'll take Martin with me instead. I'll explain later.'

Patrik sat at his desk, trying to plan his work for the day. But how should they proceed when they kept hitting brick walls? He was pinning all his hope on the exhumation. Pedersen had promised to call first thing in the morning, and at eight o'clock the phone rang.

'Hello,' said Patrik. 'That was fast.'

'Yes. And there are two reasons for my call,' said Pedersen.

Patrik sat up a little straighter in his chair. This sounded promising.

'First and foremost, I've finished my report regarding Linnea Berg. You'll have it within the hour, although I don't have anything more to add to the preliminary reports, which, against my better judgement, I already gave you. And by the way, that needs to stay between you and me.'

'Of course. As always,' Patrik assured him.

Pedersen cleared his throat. 'Well, there's something I have to tell you about the body we received yesterday. Leif Hermansson's body.'

'Yes?' said Patrik. 'I realize you've barely started examining the body, so what's this about?'

'It's about the missing bullet,' Pedersen sighed. 'The one that disappeared without trace.'

'Yes . . .' said Patrik, feeling his excitement rising. He was going to burst if Pedersen didn't get to the point.

'We've found it.'

'Great!' exclaimed Patrik. It was about time they had some luck. 'Where was it? Hidden in the back of an evidence box?'

'Not exactly. It was in the coffin.'

Patrik gaped. Had he heard correctly? It made no sense whatsoever.

'In the coffin? How did the bullet end up in the coffin?'

He laughed, but Pedersen didn't laugh with him. Instead he said wearily:

'I know this may sound like a joke, but as usual, the human factor came into play. The pathologist who carried out the post-mortem was going through a divorce and custody battle at the time, so he was drinking a little too much. His situation eventually got sorted out, but it turns out there were certain . . . flaws in my predecessor's work during that year when his personal life was in shambles.'

'So you're saying—'

'I'm saying that the pathologist never removed the bullet. It was still embedded in the head wound, and when the soft tissues disintegrated, the bullet rolled out.'

'You're kidding,' said Patrik.

'Believe me, I wish I was,' said Pedersen. 'Unfortunately, there's no one around to yell at, because the pathologist in question died from a heart attack last year, while going through his third divorce.'

'But you have the bullet?'

'No, I don't have it here. I immediately sent it over to Torbjörn in Uddevalla. I thought you would want to have it analysed as soon as possible. Give him a call and see if you can get a report this afternoon. As for this failure to follow the proper protocol, I can only apologize. This should never have happened.'

'No, but the important thing is that we have the bullet,' said Patrik. 'Now we can compare it to Leif's gun and determine whether his death was a suicide or not.'

Basse sank on to the sofa, which still had a few stains left. Despite his having spent two days cleaning the house, it looked like shit. Dread was making his throat close up. When his parents phoned, Basse had assured them that everything was fine, but his knees shook as he ended the call. He'd be grounded for a year. At least. Maybe he'd never be allowed to go out ever again.

And this was all Nils's and Vendela's fault. He should have known better than to listen to them, but ever since they were kids, he'd done whatever they told him. That was why they let him hang out with them. Otherwise he might have been the one they tormented instead of Sam.

They hadn't helped him with the house cleaning. Nils had merely laughed at him when he begged for help, and Vendela hadn't even bothered to respond. And it wasn't just the damage to the furniture. His mother's jewellery box was missing, along with his father's cigar box. Someone had even taken the big angel made from stone that his mother had set on the lawn as a birdbath.

Basse leaned forward, rested his arms on his thighs and groaned. Soon his parents would arrive home. He'd thought about running away, but where would he go? He'd never be able to get by on his own.

In his mind he pictured Jessie's body and whimpered. Every time he closed his eyes, he saw her. He had nightmares about her. And he kept remembering more details. He heard his own panting breath as he thrust inside her again and again, bellowing when his body exploded.

He recalled the feeling of pleasure at doing something forbidden, and because of her complete helplessness. The power he'd felt at doing whatever he liked with her. Even now the emotions he had were so contradictory it sickened him.

Everyone had been sent pictures. He'd lost count of how many texts he'd received. Nils and Vendela were satisfied because their plan to humiliate Jessie once and for all had worked.

No one had either seen or heard from Jessie. Nothing but silence. Also from Sam. Nobody else seemed to think that was odd. He was the one sitting in a ruined house with a sinking feeling in his stomach that grew worse every day. Whatever Nils and Vendela said, this was not the end of it. It was too quiet. Like the calm before the storm.

Erica backed out of the car park, thinking what luck she'd had lately. She'd worked hard on her book while the kids played, and now it felt as if the puzzle pieces were finally falling into place.

She'd hardly dared hope that Sanna would talk to her. All the same, she'd taken a chance and phoned her as soon as Kristina left with the children for the amusement park in Strömstad. There had been a moment of silence after she made the request, and Erica had held her breath until Sanna's voice came over the line agreeing to an interview. So now Erica was on her way to the garden centre to meet one of the people who had known Stella best.

And something told Erica that she would soon find out who was behind the initials 'SS'.

She looked around as she parked the car in a gravel parking area and then got out to walk towards a rose trellis that seemed to function as the entrance to the garden centre. It was only ten minutes from Fjällbacka, but Erica had never had any reason to come here. She had no interest in gardening, and after several valiant attempts to keep alive an orchid that was a gift from Kristina, she had given up pretending to have green fingers. It seemed unlikely any flowers or shrubs would survive the wild romping of the twins, so their own yard was more a playground than a garden.

Sanna came forward to greet her, pulling off a pair of soiled gardening gloves. They'd run into each other in town over the years and said hello, the way people do in a small community where everyone knows everyone else. But this was the first time they'd properly introduced themselves.

'Hi,' said Sanna, shaking Erica's hand. 'Let's sit in the arbour. Cornelia will watch the shop.'

She headed for some ornate white patio chairs surrounded by bushes and roses. Erica was taken aback when she happened to glance at the price tag on the furniture. Tourist prices.

'I supposed it's about time we met,' said Sanna, studying Erica as if trying to read her thoughts.

Erica shifted position a bit nervously under Sanna's intense scrutiny, but she was used to dealing with scepticism. Family members often had to fend off ghouls drawn by their tragic situation. Sanna had every reason to suspect that Erica was no different.

'You know that I'm writing a book about the Stella case, right?' said Erica. Sanna nodded.

Erica had taken an instant liking to her. There was something so down-to-earth, so grounded, about Sanna. Her blond hair was pulled back in a casual ponytail, and she wore no make-up. Erica surmised that even on festive occasions she would be reluctant to use much make-up. The clothing she wore suited her occupation. Boots, jeans, and a loose-fitting denim shirt. There was nothing frivolous or superficial about Sanna.

'What do you think about me writing this book?' asked Erica, getting right to the point.

This was often the key question in her interviews. She needed to know how the person would react to the project.

'I have nothing against it,' said Sanna. 'Though it's not something I'm in favour of either. I'm . . . neutral. It's not important to me. Stella is not your book. And I've lived so long with what happened back then, whether you write the book or not doesn't matter.'

'I will try to do her justice,' said Erica. 'And I would really value your help. I want to describe Stella as vividly as possible for the reader. And you're the one who can best do that.'

Erica got out her mobile and held it up for Sanna to see.

'Is it okay if I record our conversation?'

'Sure, go ahead,' said Sanna.

She frowned. 'What do you want to know?'

'Just tell me in your own words,' said Erica. 'About

Stella, about your family. And, if you can bear to talk about it, I'd like to hear what the whole experience was like for you.'

'Thirty years have passed,' said Sanna brusquely. 'Life has gone on. I've tried not to think too often about what happened. The past can so easily consume the present. But I'll try.'

Sanna talked for two hours. And the more she talked, the more Stella became a real person for Erica. Not just the victim she'd read about in the investigative documents and newspaper articles. She was a real, live four-year-old who loved to watch the kids' TV show *Five Ants Are More Than Four Elephants*. She had a hard time getting up in the morning, and she never wanted to go to bed at night. She liked hot rice cereal with sugar and cinnamon. She liked to wear her hair in two pigtails, not a ponytail. At night she liked to crawl into her big sister's bed, and she'd given every one of her freckles a name. Her favourite was Hubert, the freckle on the tip of her nose.

'She was a real pest sometimes, but she was also the most fun person you'd ever meet. She often got on my nerves, because she was such a little snoop. Her favourite game was sneaking up on people and eavesdropping. Then she'd run off and tell everybody what she'd heard, and once in a while that made me want to strangle her.'

Sanna stopped abruptly, clearly regretting her choice of words. She took a deep breath.

'I was always being sent off into the woods to look for her,' she went on. 'I never dared go very far. I thought it was a creepy place. But Stella was never scared. She loved the woods and went there whenever she could. That was probably why it was so hard to comprehend that something horrible had actually happened. She'd been gone so many times, but she always came back – no

617

thanks to me, because I never made a proper search. I would only go far enough into the woods so my parents thought I was looking for Stella. Instead of searching, I would sit down next to a big oak tree right behind the house, maybe only fifty metres inside the woods, and I'd wait. Sooner or later Stella would show up. She always found her way home. Except that last time.'

Sanna suddenly laughed.

'Stella didn't have many friends, but she did have an imaginary playmate. Strangely enough, that's what has been haunting my dreams lately. I've dreamed of him several times.'

'Him?' asked Erica.

'Yes. Stella called him the green man, so I'm guessing it was some moss-covered tree or bush that had captured her imagination. She could create entire worlds in her head. Sometimes I wonder if there were as many imaginary people in her world as real people.'

'My eldest child is the same way,' said Erica with a smile. 'Most often it's her imaginary friend Molly who thinks she should have cakes and sweets whenever Maja has some.'

'Ah, yes. A brilliant way to get twice the treats,' said Sanna. Her smile softened her features. 'Personally, I have a teenage monster at home. I'm starting to wonder whether teenagers ever become human.'

'How many children do you have?' asked Erica.

'Just the one,' said Sanna with a sigh. 'But sometimes it feels like there are twenty of her!'

'I'm dreading those years. At the moment it's so hard to imagine them as stroppy teens, storming up to their bedrooms and calling me a bitch because they can't get their own way.'

'Oh, believe me, I've been called much worse,' chuckled Sanna. 'Especially because I'm clearly ruining her life by making her work here in the garden centre. We had a little incident over the weekend that required some sort of punishment, and forcing her to do a day's work is child abuse in her eyes.'

They both laughed, but then Sanna's expression turned serious. 'So what do you think?' she asked. 'Is it a coincidence that the little girl who lived on our old farm has been murdered too?'

Erica didn't know what to say. Common sense said one thing. Her gut instinct said another. If she was careful about how she answered, she might be able to find out whether her suspicion was correct about the identity of 'SS'.

'I believe there's a connection,' she said at last, 'but I don't know what it is. I think it's too easy to point fingers at Helen and Marie. I don't want to re-open old wounds, because I know your family felt the case was solved when Marie and Helen were found guilty. But there are still a number of questions unanswered. And Leif Hermansson, the officer in charge of the investigation, told his daughter a short time before he died that he had begun to have doubts. But we don't know why.'

Sanna fixed her gaze on her feet. Some idea seemed to be forming in her mind. She raised her head and looked at Erica.

'It's been a long time since I thought about this, but what you're saying reminded me of something. Leif contacted me, and we met for coffee, not long before he died.'

And with that, another piece of the puzzle fell into place. At the police station they had thought of Sanna as Sanna Lundgren. But for Leif, she would have been Sanna Strand.

'What did he want to talk about?' asked Erica.

'That's what was so strange. He asked me about the

green man. I had mentioned the imaginary friend back when Stella died. And now, all these years later, a police officer suddenly wanted to talk about him.'

Erica stared at her. Why had Leif wanted to know about Stella's imaginary friend?

'Hello! Anybody home?' called Paula as she cautiously opened the door.

They'd knocked several times without getting any response. She'd noted with satisfaction that Martin had looked at the 'For Sale' sign when they drove up to the house.

'I'm here! Come on in!' they heard a hoarse voice call from inside the house. They took off their shoes and placed them on the doormat before going in.

Dagmar was sitting in her usual place at the kitchen window. She looked up from the crossword puzzle she was doing.

'There you are again!' she said. 'What fun!'

'So you're selling the house?' asked Paula. 'I saw the sign out front.'

'Yes, I think it's best. Sometimes it takes a while for a stubborn woman like me to make up her mind. But my daughter is right. It's off the beaten track, and I'm not twenty any more. And I should count myself lucky that I have a daughter who wants me to come and live with her. It seems like most people can't wait to throw their old parents into some nursing home.'

'I know. I was saying to my colleague only the other day that Swedes aren't very good about taking care of the elderly. Has there been much interest in your house?'

'No prospective buyers yet,' said Dagmar, motioning for them to sit down. 'Most people don't want to live way out here. Too rural and old-fashioned. Everything has to be new and in the thick of things, and no crooked walls or slanting floors. But I think that's a shame. I love this house. There's a lot of love in these old walls, let me tell you.'

'I think it's marvellous,' said Martin.

Paula bit her tongue to keep from saying anything. Certain things needed to take their time.

'So, enough about an old woman's crazy philosophies. I assume you came here to talk about my notebook, not about my house. I just can't understand how I forgot to tell you about it last time.'

'It's easily done,' said Martin. 'The news about Nea must have come as a terrible shock. It's hard to think rationally when you're hit by something like that.'

'What's important is that you did remember and you phoned us,' said Paula. 'So tell me, what sort of notebook is it?'

'Well, I remembered that you wanted to know if I saw anything out of the ordinary on the morning when Nea disappeared. I still can't recall anything, but this morning I realized you might be better at seeing a pattern than I am. So I thought you could have a look at the notes I write down, just to pass the time. They help me to focus on my crossword puzzles. If I only do one thing at a time, I have real trouble concentrating. I need some type of distraction. So I jot down notes about what goes on outside my window.'

She handed the notebook to Paula, who quickly found the page from the morning when Nea disappeared. There weren't many items. Nothing that jumped off the page at her. Three cars had driven past and two cyclists. The cyclists were described as: 'Two fat German tourists out for a bike ride.' So Paula dismissed them at once. That left the cars. Dagmar had merely noted the colour and make of each vehicle, but it was better than nothing.

'Could I take this back to the station?' she asked, and Dagmar nodded.

'Take it. Be my guest.'

'I was just wondering when your house was built,' Martin said.

'In 1902. My father built it himself. I was born on a kitchen bench next to that wall.'

'Have you had a survey done?' asked Martin.

Dagmar gave him a sly look and said, 'You're certainly asking a lot of questions.'

'Just wondering,' replied Martin.

He avoided looking at Paula.

'A surveyor's been round. He said what needs fixing most urgently is the roof. There's also some mould in the basement, but he said that could be dealt with later. The estate agent has all the paperwork. But if anyone is interested, they're welcome to have a look around.'

'Hmm . . .' said Martin, looking down.

Dagmar studied him for a moment. The sun was shining on her face, revealing all the friendly wrinkles etched into her skin. She put her hand on his arm and waited for him to look up and meet her eye.

'This house is a fine place to start fresh,' she said. 'And it needs to be filled with life again. And love.'

Martin quickly turned away. But Paula saw that his eyes had filled with tears.

'There's someone from forensics on the phone, it's about the tape of the anonymous tip-off. Shall I ring Paula? She and Martin are handling the investigation.'

Annika had stuck her head in Mellberg's office, waking him from a deep slumber.

'What? What is it? Oh, the phone call,' he said, sitting up. 'No, put it through to me.'

In a fraction of a second Mellberg was wide awake and determined to get his mitts on the bastard who had started this whole thing. If somebody hadn't tried to frame

Karim, the fire would never have happened. He was sure about that.

'Mellberg,' he said authoritatively when he picked up the phone.

To his surprise, he heard a woman's voice speaking. Since this was a technical matter, he had expected to talk to a man.

'Oh, hi, I'm calling regarding the audio file you needed help with.'

Her voice was bright and girlish, and Mellberg suspected she was hardly more than a teenager.

'That's right. And I suppose you're going to tell me you couldn't do anything with it.'

He sighed. They must really be short-staffed if they let some young girl take on such a difficult and important task. He'd probably have to ring her boss and ask for someone more competent to handle the matter. Preferably a man.

'Well, actually, I did solve the problem. The sound was a little rough, but I was able to adjust . . . well, I won't bore you with the technicalities. But I think I've got as close to the original voice as it's possible to get, given current technology.'

'Oh, well, er . . .'

Mellberg didn't know what to say. In his mind he'd already carried on an entire conversation with her boss.

'So, let's hear it,' he said. 'Who's hiding behind the anonymous identity?'

'Would you like me to play the conversation for you right now on the phone? Then I can email you the file afterwards.'

'Sure.'

'Okay. I'll play the recording now.'

Mellberg heard a voice on the phone, speaking the

same words he'd heard before. But now the anonymous voice was no longer deep and fuzzy but bright and clear. Mellberg frowned as he tried to listen for anything that might tell him the caller's identity. He couldn't honestly say he recognized the voice, but that was probably expecting too much.

'Okay, email it to me,' he said after the brief recording ended.

He rattled off his email address and only a moment later his computer pinged to announce the file had arrived. He played it several more times. An idea began to take shape in his mind. For a moment he considered checking with Patrik first, but he and Gösta had gone out for lunch and it would be a shame to disturb them. Besides, his idea was brilliant, so why would Patrik have any objections? Far better to wait until the meeting Patrik had called at two o'clock and present them all with his findings. Mellberg was already looking forward to the praise he would receive for taking the initiative. This was the sort of thing that separated a good police officer from a great police officer. Thinking outside the box. Coming up with a new way of looking at things. Trying new approaches and making use of modern technology.

With a satisfied smile, Mellberg tapped in a number he'd saved on his mobile. Now things were really going to take off.

'You're getting better,' said Sam, making a slight adjustment to Jessie's stance. 'But you're still squeezing the trigger a little too hard and too fast when you fire. You need to caress the trigger.'

Jessie nodded. She kept her gaze focused on the target fastened to the tree. This time she did caress the trigger, and the bullet struck close to dead centre.

'Awesome!'

He meant it. She was a natural. But shooting at a fixed target wasn't enough.

'You need to practise firing at moving targets too,' he said, and she nodded.

'Yeah, I know. How are we going to do that? How did you learn?'

'Animals,' he said, with a shrug. 'James had me shooting squirrels, mice, birds. Whatever turned up.'

'All right. Let's do it.'

The steely glint in Jessie's eyes made him want to put his arms around her and hold her close. All trace of softness was now gone. He knew she wasn't eating properly. In the few days since the weekend, her face had lost some of its roundness. He didn't care. He loved her no matter what. He had loved her naivety, but now her way of seeing the world more closely resembled his own view.

He had the same hard core inside, and that's what would see them through this. He'd already crossed the line. Any form of retreat was gone, he could never turn back. Everything had a breaking point. Even people. He'd passed his first one, and now Jessie was following. Now they were both in the same borderland.

It felt amazing not to be there alone.

He knew he would have to tell her everything. He had to place his darkest secrets at her feet. That was the only thing that still scared him. He didn't think she would judge him, but he wasn't sure. Part of him wanted to continue to forget, while another part knew he needed to remember, because that would help him to move forward. He could not stand still. He could not stop. It was no longer possible for him to be merely a victim.

He took off his backpack and pulled out the notebook. It was time to tell her his deepest secrets. She was ready.

'There's something I want to show you,' he said. 'Something I have to do.'

BOHUSLÄN 1672

A long series of witnesses followed. The customs official recounted how Elin had hurled incantations after him, and how the wind had blown his horse off the road. Neighbours from Fjällbacka and folks from Tanumshede testified that she had used devilish sorcery to heal and cure. Then it was Britta's turn. She was pale and beautiful as she glided through the room to take her seat up front. She looked sorrowful, but Elin knew she was pleased with what she had done. After all these years she finally had Elin where she wanted her.

Britta's eyes were downcast, her dark lashes lying like fans on her cheeks. The slight curve of her stomach could be glimpsed under the fabric of her gown, but there was still nothing maternal in her face. It was as narrow and finely chiselled as always.

'Could you tell us about yourself?' said Hierne, giving her a smile.

Elin saw that he was as enchanted by Britta today as he had been on that evening at the vicarage.

And she understood there was no help to be found. Nothing could save her. Whatever Britta said would make no difference. Yet she also knew that Britta would never give up this moment to speak.

'I am Elin's sister. Her half-sister,' she added. 'We have the same father but not the same mother.'

'And Elin has lived with you since her husband's death? You and your husband, the vicar Preben Willumsen, generously offered shelter to Elin and her daughter Märta. Is that correct?'

Britta smiled modestly.

'Yes, we agreed that we should help Elin and sweet little Märta after Per drowned. We are family, after all. That is what families do.'

Hierne's eyes brightened as he looked at her.

'A truly generous and loving offer. And neither of you knew . . .'

'No, we did not.' Britta shook her head vigorously and let out a sob.

Hierne pulled a handkerchief from his waistcoat pocket and handed it to her.

'When did you first notice anything?' he asked.

'It took some time. She is my sister, and I did not want to believe . . .'

She sobbed again, dabbing the handkerchief to her eyes. Then she straightened her back and lifted her chin.

'She began giving me concoctions every morning, to help me to conceive. And I was grateful for her help. I knew she had aided other women in the surrounding area. Every morning I drank that loathsome sludge. Elin would mutter something over the drink before she handed it to me. But the months passed and nothing happened. I asked Elin many times if it was doing me any good, and she insisted it would help, so I did my best to keep drinking what she gave me.'

'But eventually your suspicions grew?'

Hierne leaned towards Britta, who nodded.

'Yes. I began to suspect that it was not God but darker powers assisting Elin. We . . . we had an animal that disappeared from the farm. A cat named Viola. I found it hanging by its tail behind our house, outside my bedroom window. And then I knew. So secretly I began pouring out the drink, behind her back. And as soon as I stopped taking that concoction, I was able to have a child.'

She stroked her stomach.

'That was when I understood that Elin did not want me to conceive. On the contrary. She did not want me to give birth.'

'And why was that?'

'Elin has always been jealous of me. Her mother died when she was little, and my mother was our father's favourite. And yes, I was the apple of my father's eye. I was not to blame, but Elin took against me. She always wanted to have whatever I had, and that became even clearer when I married a vicar while she had to settle for a poor fisherman. So I assume that Elin did not want me to have a child. I also think she had set her sights on my husband.'

Britta looked at the crowd in the courtroom.

'Imagine what a victory that would have been for the devil, if his woman succeeded in stealing a man of the church. Yet, as luck would have it, Preben is a strong person, and all her sly ploys and seductive tricks had no effect on him.'

She smiled at Preben, who briefly met her eye before again fixing his gaze on the floor. Elin was studying him intently. How could he simply sit there, listening to such lies? She had heard that he would not testify. The vicar would be spared that experience. And that was no doubt fortunate, because she did not know how she could have stood it if he were the one telling lies before the court, instead of allowing Britta to do it for her.

'Tell us about the devil's mark,' said Hierne.

The spectators were listening closely. They had heard about this. It was said that the devil left a mark on the bodies of his wives. A form of branding. Did Elin Jonsdotter have such a mark? If so, where was it? They eagerly waited to hear Britta's reply.

She nodded.

'Yes, she has a mark just below one breast. The colour of fire. It looks like a map of Denmark.'

Elin gasped. It had barely been visible when they were children. And she had never known it looked like such a map. There was only one person who could have made that comparison.

Preben.

He had given Britta this proof to use against her. Elin tried to make Preben meet her eye, but the coward merely stared at the floor. She wanted to stand up and recount everything that had happened, but she knew it was pointless. No one would believe a word she said. In their eyes, she was a witch.

All she could do now was try not to make things worse for Märta. The girl had no one except Britta and Preben. They were the only family she had left. Elin could only hope that Britta and Preben would allow Märta to grow up with them. So she kept silent. For Märta's sake.

As Britta continued to speak of the devil's mark on her body and tell a thousand other lies which one by one sealed her sister's fate, Elin longed for the trial to be over. She would go to her death. She knew that now. But she still had hope that her daughter might have a good life. Märta was everything. Nothing else mattered.

'Things are starting to come together,' said Patrik, feeling that familiar prickling sensation that came when all the knots in a case began to unravel. 'Pedersen called me earlier. You won't believe this, but the missing bullet was found inside the coffin. Because of an oversight on the part of the pathologist, the bullet ended up being left in the wound.'

'So that explains why no one could find it,' said Gösta.

'The bullet's been sent to Torbjörn, and I've just received his preliminary report. It's a full-jacketed .45 calibre bullet. I could go over what that signifies, but you probably know more than I do. The most important finding so far is that the bullet can be linked to a Colt.'

'So does this mean Leif did not commit suicide?' asked Martin.

'Leif was left-handed, but the bullet hole was in his right temple, and he was holding the gun in his right hand, not his left.' Patrik found it difficult to keep the excitement out of his voice as he continued: 'The gun in question was his own, a Walther PPK, .32 calibre. The .45 calibre bullet found in the coffin cannot have been fired by that particular gun. So we are dealing with murder, not suicide. And we also have a suspect.

Leif jotted down the initials "JJ" in his diary, and we know that James Jensen owns a Colt M1911, which is compatible with the .45 calibre bullet found with Leif's remains.'

'When we went to see him, James showed us a Colt M1911. Said his father gave it to him when he was seven,' said Paula grimly.

'So how can we link him to the bullet? And to Leif's murder?' asked Gösta. 'This is all supposition. There must be thousands of people in Sweden who have Colts in their possession, both legally and illegally. And it's pure guesswork that "JJ" refers to James Jensen. There's no proof.'

'We need to link the bullet to the gun,' said Patrik. 'I doubt we could get a search warrant from the prosecutor, based on what we have right now. So that's the big question – how can we find a way to link the bullet to the gun?'

Paula raised her hand. Patrik nodded.

'He's been doing target practice on public land. He was actually firing the Colt when Gösta and I found him in the woods. There must be plenty of bullets out there, and we could go and pick them up without needing a warrant.'

'Great,' said Patrik. 'You and Gösta can go collect the bullets, then we'll send them to the lab for analysis.'

Patrik glanced at his mobile. He had ten missed calls. What was going on? He didn't recognize any of the phone numbers, and he tried to think what might have led to such a flood of interest from the media. He took a minute to listen to his voicemail. When he was finished, he glared at Mellberg.

'Apparently we've appealed to the public to help us identify a voice. The audio file was posted on the *Expressen* website. Anybody know about this?'

Mellberg squared his shoulders.

'Yes. I received the file while you were out. It was a woman who solved the technical issues and removed the distortion filter. Can you believe it?'

He glanced around the room, but didn't receive the response he expected.

'Anyway. I didn't recognize the voice,' he went on, 'so I could tell we needed a little help, and the public can be a good resource. I took it upon myself to phone a contact of mine at the tabloid, and they were happy to help us! Now all we have to do is wait for the tips to come rolling in!'

He leaned back with a pleased expression.

Patrik silently counted to ten and then opted for the path of least resistance. He took a deep breath and said:

'Bertil . . .' But then he didn't know what to say next.

There was so much he wanted to say, but it wouldn't be productive.

He began again.

'Bertil. In that case, you're in charge of handling all the tips.'

Mellberg nodded and gave him a thumbs up.

'I'll let you know when I've nailed him,' he said cheerfully. Patrik managed a strained smile.

Then he gave Mellberg an enquiring look.

Mellberg looked puzzled and said, 'Yes?'

'Don't you think it would be a good idea if the rest of us heard the audio file?'

'Oh, sure,' said Bertil, reaching for his phone. 'I sent the file from my mobile. Did I tell you it was a female who solved the technical problem?'

'Yes, you mentioned that,' said Paula. 'So let's hear the recording.'

'Okay, okay. You're all so impatient,' said Mellberg.

He scratched his head.

'Now how do I play the file? These bloody modern phones . . .'

'Would you like some help from a female?' asked Paula sweetly.

Mellberg pretended not to hear and kept pressing buttons.

'There it is!' he said triumphantly.

Everyone listened intently to the conversation.

'So?' said Mellberg. 'Anybody recognize the voice? Or hear anything interesting?'

'Not really . . .' said Martin. 'But the voice sounds young. And judging by the dialect, I'd say it's someone from around here.'

'In other words, you have no clue either. It's lucky I've already asked for help from the public!' said Mellberg with satisfaction as he pushed the phone away.

Patrik ignored him.

'Okay, let's continue. Erica called. This morning she interviewed Sanna Lundgren for her book. Sanna Lundgren, née Sanna Strand. She told Erica that Leif made an appointment to speak to her a week before he died, so we now have confirmation that she was the "SS" in Leif's diary.'

'What did he want?' asked Gösta.

'Well . . .' Patrik wasn't sure he could make any sense of what Erica had told him, and he was uncertain how to present the information to his colleagues. 'It appears Leif wanted to know more about an imaginary friend that Stella had . . .'

Martin choked on his coffee. He looked at Patrik in disbelief.

'An imaginary friend? Why?'

'You might well ask,' replied Patrik. 'He wanted to know more about the imaginary friend Stella called the green man.'

'You're joking!' exclaimed Mellberg, laughing. 'The green man? An imaginary friend? That's insane.'

Again Patrik ignored him.

'According to Sanna, Stella often played in the woods, and she talked about seeing this "green man" there,' he went on. 'Sanna mentioned her sister's imaginary friend to the police right after Stella's body was found, but no one took it seriously. Many years later, Leif phoned Sanna and wanted to hear more. She couldn't remember the exact date when they met, but she thought it matched the day when Leif wrote "SS" in his diary. A week later she heard that he'd committed suicide. She didn't give it any further thought until Erica started asking questions about Stella.'

'Are we to go chasing after some make-believe story?' laughed Mellberg.

No one joined in with the laughter. Patrik glanced at his mobile. Twelve more missed calls. As if they didn't have enough problems.

'I think there must be something to it,' said Patrik. 'Let's keep an open mind. Maybe Leif discovered something important.'

'What do we do about James?' asked Gösta, reminding his colleagues they hadn't finished with that subject.

'Nothing for the moment,' replied Patrik. 'First, you and Paula need to pick up those bullets.'

He sympathized with their impatience. He would have liked to bring James in at once, but without any proof, they'd never be able to charge him.

'There's another important matter we need to discuss,' said Paula. 'I had a talk with an old lady who is a neighbour of the Berg family. During our previous visit she said she couldn't recall seeing anything out of the ordinary on the morning Nea disappeared. But then she realized we might have some use for the notebook in which she writes down everything that happens outside her kitchen window. Martin and I went to see her and picked up the notebook. At first glance it seems she was right. I can't see anything unusual.'

Paula hesitated.

'But I have the feeling something doesn't fit. I just can't work out what it might be.'

'Keep at it,' said Patrik. 'You know how it goes. Sooner or later it'll come to you.'

'Right,' said Paula doubtfully. 'I hope so.'

'And the motive?' asked Martin. When he had everyone's attention, he explained. 'I mean, if we're assuming James shot Leif. Why would he do that?'

No one spoke for a long time. Patrik had already spent the last couple of hours thinking about it, but hadn't come up with anything. Finally he said:

'For the time being, let's focus on linking James to the bullet. Then we'll take it from there.'

'We could leave now,' said Gösta, looking at Paula.

She yawned, then nodded.

'Be sure to follow regulations,' said Patrik. 'Paper bags, proper labels – document everything. We don't want anyone questioning our procedures later on.'

'Will do,' said Gösta.

'I can go with you,' said Martin. 'I'm not getting anywhere with my contacts in the anti-immigrant groups. Nobody knows anything about the fire. Or so they say.'

'Fine. Go ahead,' said Patrik. 'This is the best lead we have right now. I think there has to be something behind Leif's questions about Stella's imaginary friend. Gösta, do you recall anything about this? Anything from the original investigation?'

Deep furrows appeared on Gösta's face as he thought back to the Stella case. He seemed about to shake his head when his face suddenly brightened and he looked up.

'Marie. We talked about the fact that Marie claimed someone had followed them into the woods on the day Stella died. I know I may be making too much of this, but . . . could there be some sort of connection? Could Stella's imaginary friend be a real person?'

'Could it have been James?' asked Paula.

Everyone turned to look at her. She shrugged.

'Think about it. James is in the military. When Sanna says "the green man", I think instantly of green clothing. Military clothing. Could it have been James that Stella was meeting? And could it have been James that Marie says she heard in the woods?'

'That's just guesswork at this stage,' said Patrik.

He cast another glance at his phone, which now had twenty more missed calls.

'While everybody else is gathering evidence, you and I are going to have a little talk, Bertil,' he said with a sigh.

Anna was getting more and more nervous. There were too many variables, too many things that could go wrong. And she could tell that Erica was suspicious. She'd noticed her sister studying her, but even Erica hadn't said anything.

In the kitchen Dan was whistling as he fixed a late lunch. He'd taken on more of the household duties as her pregnancy progressed, but she knew he was glad to do it. They had come so close to losing everything, but now they had regained their daily life, their family, and each other. The scars in her heart and in his still existed, but they'd learned to live with them. And she had accepted the physical scars. Her hair had grown out, and the scars had slowly begun to fade. They would always be there, and she could cover them with make-up if she chose to do so, though she frequently did not. The scars were part of her.

Dan had once asked Anna how she managed not to turn bitter. Her life had turned out so different from Erica's. Sometimes it seemed as if misfortune constantly hounded her, while Erica's life was so harmonious. But Anna refused to fall into the trap of feeling sorry for herself and envying Erica; hard as it was to admit it, a lot of her troubles had stemmed from her own poor decision-making. She was the one who had chosen Lucas, the father of her children, ignoring Erica's warnings and misgivings about him. And the infidelity that had nearly destroyed the love she and Dan shared was her fault and hers alone. Everything else that had happened – the car accident that scarred her body and claimed the life of her unborn child – was just bad luck. Any time she felt like giving into the temptation of feeling bitter or jealous of Erica, she only had to remind herself of the way her big sister had taken care of her and watched over her ever since they were kids. Anna knew that she had been allowed to be a child at Erica's expense, and she had always been grateful to her sister for that.

But now she had broken a promise to Erica. A promise never to keep secrets from her. She listened to the clatter of plates as Dan set the table for lunch. He was singing along with the radio. She envied his carefree and cheerful attitude. Unlike him, she was a worrier. And she wondered whether she'd made the right decision. She was afraid of hurting Dan, and she knew she was already on thin ice because she'd had to lie to him. But it was too late to undo what was done.

With an effort she got up off the sofa. When she went into the kitchen and saw Dan's smile, she felt the warmth of his love and for a moment her worry was erased. In spite of everything she'd been through, she considered herself lucky. And when the children came streaming into the kitchen from different parts of the house and from playing outdoors, she knew she was truly blessed.

'Do you think James could have been the one who killed Stella?' asked Paula, studying Gösta's profile. 'And then he killed Leif because Leif was about to expose him?'

Gösta had asked to drive, and she had reluctantly given in, even though she knew he would go at a snail's pace all the way to Fjällbacka.

'I'm not sure what to believe,' he said. 'I don't recall his name ever coming up when we were working on the original investigation. It may be that Leif was so quick to focus attention on the two girls and when they confessed there was no reason to consider other possibilities. As for Marie's claim to have seen somebody in the woods . . . Well, she didn't mention it until after she retracted her confession, so we all thought it was a child's clumsy attempt to divert suspicion elsewhere.'

'Did you know who he was? Back then, I mean?' asked Paula, realizing she was pressing her right foot on an imaginary accelerator. Gösta was so painfully slow, she would have preferred Patrik's erratic driving.

'Of course. Fjällbacka's a small town, most people know each other. And James has always been something of a character. His big goal in life was to become a soldier. If I remember right, he signed up for some macho unit when he did his mandatory military service – he was a diver or paratrooper, something like that – and then he stayed on in the army.'

'It strikes me as very odd that he married his best friend's daughter,' said Martin from the back seat. 'Especially with such a big age difference.'

'You're not alone in that,' said Gösta, slowing down even more. Though there were no other vehicles in sight, he indicated before turning left on to the gravel road. 'No one had ever seen James with a girlfriend, so it came as a real surprise. And Helen was only eighteen. But you know how these things go. At first people can talk of nothing else, then another scandal comes along and they all lose interest. They had Sam and became just another family. And they've been married for all these years now, so the marriage must be working.'

They had decided not to tell James they were coming, so Gösta parked a good distance away from the house. They wanted to head straight for the target practice area in the woods without anyone spotting them.

'What do we do if he's there?' asked Martin.

'We'll have to tell him what we're doing. And hope there aren't any complications. We're within our legal rights to take anything we want from that area.'

'True, but I'm not too keen on standing face to face with a professional soldier and potential murderer while we're looking for evidence to use against him,' muttered Martin.

'Oh, come on. You could have stayed back at the station, you know,' said Paula, leading the way to the woods.

They stopped when they entered the glade. Paula was relieved James wasn't there, but it now dawned on her what they were up against. Years of target practice had left the entire area littered with bullets and casings. She was no gun expert, but it was obvious an arsenal of different weapons had been fired in this spot.

Gösta took in the scene and then turned to the others.

'Shouldn't all this give us reason to believe that James has illegal weapons in his home? We can link him to this spot – we've seen him using it for target practice. Judging by all these casings and bullets, he must have more guns in his possession than the ones registered to his name.'

'He has permits for a Colt, a Smith & Wesson, and a hunting rifle,' said Martin. 'I checked.'

'I'll phone Patrik and see whether he thinks this is enough to warrant a search of the house. Don't touch anything without photographing it in situ first.'

While Paula and Martin got busy taking photos, Gösta stepped aside to make the call.

'He's checking with the prosecutor,' Gösta reported as soon as he finished speaking to Patrik. 'But he thinks what we've found here plus the bullet from the coffin should be enough to justify a look inside James's house.'

'What do you suppose we'll find?' asked Martin. 'Sub-machine guns? Automatic weapons?'

He squatted down to study the pile of casings on the ground.

'Looks as though he has quite a collection,' said Paula as she snapped more photos.

'I can't say I'm thrilled about seeing James with an MP5,' said Gösta.

'It would have been difficult to claim it was suicide if he'd used a sub-machine gun,' said Paula. 'But I suppose it has happened.'

'Kurt Cobain killed himself with a Remington shotgun,' said Martin.

Paula looked at him in surprise. Who'd have thought Martin would know that.

Gösta's mobile rang, and he took the call.

'Hi, Patrik.'

He listened for a moment then held up his hand to indicate they should stop what they were doing. When he came off the phone, he told them:

'The prosecutor wants to bring in the tech team. We're to leave it to them to examine the area.'

'Okay,' said Paula, looking disappointed. 'Does that mean she's going to issue a search warrant?'

'Yes,' said Gösta. 'Patrik is on his way. He wants to be here when we go inside.'

'Is Mellberg coming too?' asked Paula uneasily.

'No. Apparently it's been sheer chaos ever since he turned over the audio file to *Expressen*. He's spending all his time giving interviews. And Annika is drowning in tip-offs from callers who think they recognize the voice. The list of names already runs to several pages.'

'Even so, the old guy might just have done something right for once,' muttered Paula. 'This might actually bring results. We wouldn't have had a chance of identifying the voice on our own.'

'What did Patrik say about James?' asked Martin as they slowly walked back to the car.

'We'll take him in for questioning after we search the house. But one of us will have to wait outside with him while we're doing the search.'

'I'll do it,' said Martin. 'I'm curious to find out about him.'

Nils nibbled at her ear. Usually it would make her shiver with pleasure, but right now Vendela felt only annoyance. She didn't want him here in her bed.

'So, when Jessie—' he began.

'What do you think Basse's parents will say when they get home?' she interrupted, pulling away from him.

She didn't want to talk about Jessie. It had been her idea, and everything had gone exactly according to plan. Yet somehow it didn't feel good. She had wanted to punish Marie. Wanted to punish her daughter. Why wasn't she happy?

'I think Basse's weekly allowance is going to get cut,' he said with a smirk.

He stroked her stomach, and she suddenly felt sick.

'Do you think he'll put the blame on us?' she asked.

'Never. He'll just clam up. He won't want his parents hearing all the details about what went on that night.'

They had closed the door to the bedroom and left Basse there with the unconscious Jessie. Back then, when Vendela was drunk, it had felt right, but now she'd sobered up . . . it felt like they were headed for disaster.

'Do you think she'll tell anyone? Her mother, maybe?'

That was what Vendela had wanted. To punish both of them.

'Are you crazy?' said Nils. 'She'll be too ashamed. The last thing she wants is even more people knowing.'

'I don't think she and Sam will show up on Saturday.'

At least she'd succeeded with that. Made it so Jessie would never want to show herself again.

Nils nibbled more on her ear and grabbed her breast, but she pushed him away. For some reason she didn't want to be with him tonight.

'She must have told Sam. Isn't it strange that he's not—'

Nils put a hand over her mouth and began pulling off his shorts with the other hand.

'Enough already! Stop talking and suck me.'

With a moan he pressed her head to his crotch.

Helen looked up as the cars appeared on the drive. The police. What did they want? Why were they here now? She went to the front door and opened it before they had a chance to knock.

Patrik Hedström stood there with Paula, Martin, and an older officer she hadn't previously met.

'Hi, Helen,' said Patrik. 'We have a warrant to search your house. Is James home? And your son?'

Her knees buckled, and Helen had to put a hand on the wall for support. She nodded as thirty-year-old memories flooded over her. The policeman's voice with the same tone as Patrik's. The solemn expression. The penetrating gaze that seemed to want to force the truth out of her. The air in the interview room, stifling and hard to breathe. Her father's heavy hand on her shoulder. Stella. Little Stella. The reddish blond hair bobbing in front of them as she scampered ahead, happy to be on an outing with two big girls. Always filled with curiosity. Always so lively.

Helen swayed, then realized Patrik was talking to her. She forced herself to remain calm.

'James is in his office, and Sam is in his room.'

Her voice sounded surprisingly normal even though her heart was hammering in her chest.

She stepped aside to let them into the front hall. They went to talk to James, while she called Sam.

'Sam! Could you come down here?'

She heard a surly reply, but after a minute he sauntered down the stairs.

'The police are here,' she said, meeting his eye.

His blue eyes rimmed with black were impassive. They were completely blank. She shivered, wanting to reach out a hand towards him, stroke his cheek and tell him everything would be fine. That she was here. Just as she always had been. But she merely stood there, her arms at her sides.

'We'd like you to step outside, said Paula, opening the front door for them. 'You won't be able to come back in until we're finished.'

'What . . . what's this about?' asked Helen.

'We can't discuss it at the moment.'

Helen felt her pulse slowly returning to normal.

'You can decide for yourself what to do,' Paula went on. 'You might want to visit a family member or friend – it could be a long wait.'

'I'm not going anywhere,' said James.

643

Helen didn't dare look at him. Her heart was pounding so hard she thought it would jump out of her chest. She gave Sam a nudge. He was standing motionless in the middle of the hall.

'Come on, let's go outside.'

In spite of the heat, the air felt refreshing as she stepped outside and took several deep breaths. She reached for Sam's arm, but he pulled away.

Standing in the sunlight, she looked at her son – really looked at him for the first time in a long while. His face was so white next to the black hair and all the black eye make-up. The years had passed so quickly. Where had the chubby tow-headed boy with the bubbling laugh gone? Deep down, she knew the answer. She had allowed James to sweep away all trace of that boy and the man he could have become. He had made Sam feel he was no good. The truth was that they were standing here because they had nowhere else to go. No friends. No family. Only her mother, who never wanted to hear about anything bad.

Helen and Sam. They had been living in their own bubble.

From inside the house she heard James's agitated voice. She knew she ought to be worried. The police were about to uncover one or all of the secrets that had served as the foundation for their life. She raised her hand to stroke Sam's cheek. He turned away, and she let her hand fall. For a second she saw Stella turn to look over her shoulder at her in the woods. Her reddish blond hair fiery against her white skin. Then she was gone.

Helen got out her mobile. There was only one place she could think of going.

'Jessie, I'm leaving!'

Marie stood at the bottom of the stairs for a few seconds, but there was no response. Jessie was going through a phase where she stayed in her room during the few hours she spent at home. By the time Marie woke in the morning, Jessie had already left the house. She had no idea where her daughter went.

At least she was starting to lose weight. That boy Sam actually seemed to be a good influence.

Marie headed for the door. The filming was going well. She'd almost forgotten how it felt to make a film that promised to be worth watching instead of something destined to be forgotten the second the credits rolled.

She knew that she was giving the performance of her life. She could see it in the eyes of the crew after each scene. No doubt this was partly because she felt a kinship with the woman she was playing. Ingrid Bergman had been a complex woman, strong and kind, yet she could also be ruthlessly driven. Marie could relate to that. The difference was that Ingrid had found love. She had loved. She had been loved. When she died, she was mourned not only by strangers who had seen her on the big screen, but also by those closest to her, showing how much she had meant to them.

There was no one close to Marie. Not since Helen. Maybe everything would have been different if Helen hadn't put down the phone that day. Maybe there would have been people in her life who would mourn her when she passed away, just as Ingrid had been mourned.

But there was no use crying over spilt milk. Certain things could not be changed. Slowly Marie closed the door to the house and set off for the second filming session of the day. Jessie would manage. Just as Marie had done at her age.

THE STELLA CASE

Helen was trembling as she stood on the courthouse steps in the gusty wind. She could no longer ignore it. She was scared. The way someone was scared when they knew they were doing something wrong. The label in the neckline of her simple dress from H&M scratched the back of her neck, but she didn't mind. It gave her something to focus her attention on.

She didn't know when it had been decided. Or when she had agreed. Suddenly it was a fact. In the evenings she'd heard her parents arguing about it. She hadn't been able to make out what they were saying, but then again she didn't need to. She knew what the argument was about. It was about her marrying James.

Helen's father, KG, had assured her this would be in her best interest. And he always knew what was best for her. She had merely nodded. That's how it was. KG took care of her. Protected her. Even though she didn't deserve it. She knew she ought to be thankful; she ought to admit that she was fortunate, that she did not deserve this concern.

Maybe the world would also be bigger if she did as she was told. She felt as if she'd lived her life trapped in a small cage. The house was her world, and the only people in it were her father, her mother – and James.

James was often abroad, fighting in other countries. Shooting blacks, according to her father. Whenever James was in Sweden, he spent as much time with them as in his own house. There was such a strange mood whenever he came to visit. James and her father seemed to have their own world, and no one else had access. 'We're like brothers,' KG used to say back then, before everything happened. Before they were forced to move.

Marie had phoned the house a few days ago. Helen had immediately recognized her voice, even though she sounded older, more mature. It was as if she'd been thrown back in time. To the thirteen-year-old whose life had revolved around Marie.

But what could she say? There was nothing she could do. She was going to marry James – after everything that had happened, there was no other option. After what James had done for her.

It did feel strange to be marrying someone the same age as her father, but James looked so handsome as he stood next to her in his uniform. And her mother was happy that for once she could dress up, even though on the night before the wedding, Helen had heard her parents quarrelling yet again. There was never any doubt who would win the argument; Pappa was the one who made all the decisions.

They had decided against a church wedding. It would be a quick civil ceremony, followed by dinner at the inn. Then she and James would spend the night at her parents' home before going to his house – or rather, their house – in Fjällbacka. The same house where her family had lived before being forced to move.

No one had asked Helen for her opinion, but how could she object? The noose around her neck was there day and night, reminding her of the thousand reasons why she should close her eyes and obey. But part of her longed to escape. Longed for freedom.

She cast a surreptitious glance at James as they approached the judge who would marry them. Would he be prepared to grant her a tiny sliver of freedom? She was eighteen now. An adult. No longer a child.

Helen reached for his hand. Wasn't that what people did? Hold hands when they got married? But he kept his hands tightly clasped by his sides. The label on her dress scratched as she listened to the judge's words. He asked them questions that she didn't know how to answer, but somehow she managed to say yes in all the right places.

When it was over, she met her mother's eye. Harriet turned away with a clenched fist pressed to her mouth.

The dinner was as brief as the ceremony had been. KG and James drank whisky, and Harriet sipped at her wine. Helen had also been given a glass of wine, her first. In that instant she had gone from child to adult. She knew her mother had made up the bed in the guestroom for them. The pull-out bed that became a double bed. Clean blue sheets and a blue blanket. During the whole dinner Helen kept picturing those sheets and the pull-out bed she was going to share with James. No doubt the food was good, but she didn't eat a thing, merely pushed the food around on her plate.

When they got home, her parents said good night. KG suddenly seemed embarrassed. He reeked of all the whisky he'd had at dinner. James also smelled rank and smoky, and he stumbled when they went into the guest-room. Helen undressed while James was in the bathroom; she could hear him emptying his bladder. She put on a big T-shirt and crawled under the blanket, close to the wall. Stiff as a board, she waited as James turned off the light, waited for what would happen next. Waited for the touch that would change everything for ever. But nothing happened. And after a few seconds she heard James's drunken snoring. When she finally fell asleep, she dreamed of the little girl with the reddish blond hair.

'I told you that you wouldn't find anything that hadn't been registered,' said James, leaning back in the chair in the small interview room.

Patrik had to fight the urge to wipe the arrogant look off James's face.

'I have permits for a Colt 1911, a Smith & Wesson, and a hunting rifle – a Sauer 100 Classic model,' James recited, calmly meeting Patrik's eye.

'Why are there bullets and casings from other weapons at your target practice site?' asked Patrik.

'How should I know? It's no secret that I go out there for target practice. Anyone could have gone there to use the target I set up.'

'Without you noticing?' asked Patrik, unable to hide his scepticism.

James merely smiled.

'I'm away for long periods of time. I can't possibly keep track of what goes on out there. Nobody would dare use the site when I'm home, but most people in town know when I'm gone and how long I'll be away. It's probably some kids, sneaking out there to shoot.'

'Kids? With sub-machine guns?' said Patrik.

'Kids today,' James sighed. 'What is the world coming to?'

'You think this is funny?' asked Patrik, annoyed with himself for letting James get under his skin. Jensen was the epitome of that smug, superior, macho type who thought Darwin's survival of the fittest was the highest principle a man could aspire to.

'Of course not,' said James, smiling even more.

They had searched the whole house, but the only weapons they found were the three guns registered to James. Yet he knew James was lying. There had to be a cache of weapons somewhere close by, so that they'd be easily accessible, but where the police wouldn't be able to find them. After searching the house, they had gone through a small garden shed. There weren't many other places on the property to look, but theoretically James could have hidden the guns anywhere. The police couldn't search the whole woods.

'So did Leif Hermansson contact you on the third of July, the day of his death?'

'As I told you before, I never had any contact with Leif Hermansson. The only thing I know about him is that he was the officer in charge of the investigation when my wife was accused of murder.'

'Accused and found guilty,' said Patrik, mostly to see what the man's reaction would be if he ticked him off.

'Based on a confession that she later retracted,' replied James.

No emotion. His gaze as steady as ever.

'But why confess if she wasn't guilty?' Patrik persisted.

'She was a child,' James sighed. 'She was confused and no doubt pressured to say things she didn't want to say. But what does that have to do with this? Why are you interested in the guns I own? You know what I do for a living. Guns are part of my life. It's not exactly strange for me to have guns in my possession.'

'You own a Colt M1911,' said Patrik, ignoring his questions.

'Yes, I do,' replied James. 'The jewel of my collection. A legendary gun. And I have the original model, not one of the later copies.'

'And you load it with full-jacketed .45 calibre bullets ACP, right?'

'Do you even know what that means?' sneered James. Patrik forced himself to count silently to ten.

'Weapons proficiency is part of police training,' said Patrik deliberately, not acknowledging that he'd been forced to ask Torbjörn a lot of questions on that very topic.

'Sure. And in the big cities I dare say they put that training to use. But out here in the sticks, the old school-book learning gets rusty real fast,' said James.

'You didn't answer my question,' said Patrik, refusing to rise to the bait. 'Do you load your weapon with full-jacketed .45 calibre bullets ACP?'

'Yes, I do. It's a first-class ABC.'

'How long have you owned the gun?'

'Oh, I've had it a very long time. It was my first. My father gave it to me when I was seven.'

'So you're a good shot?' asked Patrik.

James sat up straight.

'One of the best.'

'Do you keep an eye on your guns? Could anyone have borrowed the Colt without you knowing? For instance, when you're away from home?'

'I always keep my guns under lock and key. Why this interest in my Colt? And in Leif? If I recall correctly, he killed himself a long time ago. Something about his wife dying of cancer . . .'

'So you haven't heard?' Patrik asked.

He felt a flutter of satisfaction when he caught a glimpse of uncertainty in James's eyes.

'Heard what?' asked James. His tone of voice was so neutral, Patrik wasn't sure he'd seen correctly.

'We've dug him up.'

He purposely let the sentence hang in the air. For a long moment James didn't say a word.

Then he said: 'Dug him up?' as if he didn't understand what Patrik meant.

Patrik saw through the attempt to buy time in which to formulate an answer.

'Yes. New information came to light, so we opened the grave. It turns out Leif's death was not a suicide. He couldn't possibly have shot himself with the gun he was holding when his body was found.'

James was silent. The arrogance was still there, but Patrik thought he sensed an opening, a trace of vulnerability, and he decided to exploit it.

'We've also received information that you were in the woods on the day the little girl named Stella was murdered.' He paused and then made a statement that was such an exaggeration it could be classified as a lie: 'There's a witness.'

James showed no reaction, but a tiny blood vessel began throbbing at his temple as he weighed up his next move.

Finally he got to his feet.

'I assume you don't have enough to arrest me,' he said. 'So this conversation is over.'

Patrik smiled. He'd succeeded in wiping that smug grin off Jensen's face. Now they just needed to find proof.

'Come in,' said Erica, expectantly.

She'd been more than surprised when Helen phoned to ask if she could come over.

'Did you bring Sam with you?' she asked.

'No, I dropped him off at a friend's house,' Helen said, looking down.

Erica stepped aside to let her come in.

'Well, I'm glad you're here, at any rate,' she said, biting her tongue to keep from asking any questions.

Patrik had called to tell Erica they suspected James of being the green man. He'd probably been running around in the woods, dressed in camouflage gear, and that's where Stella had bumped into him when she went for a walk. According to Patrik, the police thought he might have been the person Marie heard in the woods on the day Stella died.

'Do you have any coffee?' asked Helen, and Erica nodded.

In the living room, Noel and Anton were quarrelling again, and they weren't paying any attention to Maja's scolding. Erica went over and in her most authoritative voice told them to stop. When that didn't work, she resorted to measures familiar to desperate parents in need of peace and quiet: she got ice lollies from the freezer and handed one to each of the kids. All three children sat down to eat their ice cream while Erica went back to the kitchen with a churning feeling in her stomach that she was a bad parent.

'I remember times like that,' said Helen with a smile.

She accepted a cup of coffee and the two of them sat down at the kitchen table. For a few minutes neither woman spoke. Then Erica got up to fetch some chocolate bars, which she set on the table.

Helen shook her head.

'No, thanks. Not for me. I'm allergic to chocolate,' she said, taking a sip of coffee.

Erica took a big bite, promising herself to give up sugar

next Monday. This week was already a lost cause, so it was no use beginning today.

'I've been thinking a lot about Stella,' said Helen.

Erica raised her eyebrows in surprise. Not a word about why Helen had suddenly turned up here. Not a word about what had happened. Because something must have happened. She could feel it in her whole body. Helen radiated a nervous energy that was impossible to ignore, but Erica didn't dare ask the cause for fear of scaring her off. She needed to hear Helen's story. So she didn't say a word, just sipped her coffee and waited for Helen to go on.

'I didn't have any siblings,' said Helen at last. 'I don't know why, and I would never have asked my parents. We didn't talk about things like that. So I liked being with Stella. We lived right next door, and she was always so happy to see me whenever I came over. I enjoyed playing with her. She had so much energy! She was always bouncing around. I can see her now, that reddish blond hair, those freckles. She hated her hair colour until I told her I thought it was more beautiful than any other colour. Then she changed her mind.

'Stella was always asking questions. About everything. Why was it so hot, why was there wind, why were some flowers white and others blue, why was the grass green and the sky blue and not the other way around? Thousands and thousands of questions. And she wouldn't give up until she heard an answer that was acceptable. You couldn't get away with saying "because" or offering some stupid reason. She would keep on asking until the answer sounded right to her.'

Helen was talking so fast that she ran out of breath and had to pause.

'I liked her family. It wasn't like mine. The Strands

hugged each other and laughed together. They used to hug me too when I came over, and Stella's mother would joke with me and stroke my hair. Stella's father used to say that I needed to stop growing so tall or I'd end up with my head in the clouds. Sometimes Sanna would play with us. But she was more serious, more like a mini-mother to Stella, and she usually followed her mother around, wanting to help with the laundry or cooking supper. She wanted to be a grown-up, while Stella's world was filled with games from morning to night. And I was so proud that I was allowed to babysit for her occasionally. I think her parents noticed, because sometimes it didn't seem like they actually needed a babysitter, but they saw how happy it made me.'

Helen stopped and looked at Erica.

'Would it be too rude to ask for more coffee?'

'Of course not.' Erica got up to refill Helen's cup. It seemed as if a dam had burst, and now everything was simply pouring out of her.

'When I made friends with Marie, it took a while before my parents reacted,' said Helen. 'They were so immersed in their own affairs – all their parties, clubs, and arrangements. They didn't have much time to wonder who I was spending my time with. When they realized Marie and I had become friends, they were wary, and as time went on and we grew closer, they got more and more disapproving. Marie was not welcome in our home, and we couldn't go to her house. Her house was . . . Well, it wasn't a pleasant place. But we still tried to see each other as often as we could. When my parents found out, they banned me from seeing her. We were thirteen and had no say in the matter. Marie didn't care what her parents thought, and they couldn't care less where she was or who she saw. But I didn't dare defy my parents. I wasn't strong like Marie. I was used to obeying my parents – I didn't know how to act any other way. So I tried to stop seeing Marie. I really tried.'

'But didn't the two of you have permission to babysit Stella together on that day?' asked Erica.

'Yes. Stella's father ran into my father and asked him. He had no idea we weren't supposed to see each other. For once, Pappa was caught off guard, so he said yes.'

She swallowed.

'We had so much fun that day. Stella loved our outing to Fjällbacka. She skipped and ran the whole way home. That was why we took the path through the woods. Stella loved the woods, and since she didn't want to sit in the pushchair, we thought we might as well go home that way.'

Helen's voice quavered as she looked at Erica.

'Stella was happy when we dropped her off at the farm. I remember that. She was so happy. We'd bought ice cream, and she'd held our hands, and she'd skipped all the way home. She was bubbling over with energy. We'd answered all her questions, and she hugged us like a little monkey. I remember how her hair tickled my nose. She thought it was so funny when I sneezed.'

'What about the man in the woods?' The words were out before Erica could stop herself. 'Stella's imaginary friend, the one she called the green man? Could it have been a real person, not just imaginary? Was it James? Was your husband the man in the woods? Was it James that Marie was talking about?'

Erica saw the panic in Helen's eyes, and she realized she'd made a big mistake. Helen's breathing was suddenly abrupt and shallow, and her expression was that of a hunted animal just before the shot was fired. She jumped up and dashed out of the house.

Erica remained sitting at the kitchen table, cursing herself. Helen had been so close to telling her something that could unlock the secrets of the past. But Erica's eagerness had ruined everything. Wearily she picked up the coffee cups and set them on the worktop. Outside she heard Helen's car pull away.

'These days they use 3D technology to analyse bullets,' said Gösta when Paula came into the station kitchen.

'How do you know that?' she asked, sitting down.

She placed Dagmar's notebook on the table.

Sometimes she wondered if they actually spent more time in the small, yellow-painted kitchen than in their own offices. Tossing around ideas with colleagues was one way to gain a new perspective on things. Besides, it was more pleasant to sit and work in the kitchen than in their cramped offices. Plus it was closer to the coffee pot.

'I read about it in *Kriminalteknik*,' he told her. 'That journal is a mine of information. Every issue is packed with the latest advances in forensics.'

'But even with this 3D technology, can they match a bullet with a specific gun? Or even two bullets from the same gun?'

'Well, according to the article, no two groove patterns are identical. All sorts of factors come into play: the age of the gun, the condition it's in—'

'So you're saying it *is* possible to get a match?'

'I think so,' replied Gösta. 'Especially with this new 3D technique.'

'Torbjörn said it looked as if someone had used a file on the Colt.' Paula shifted position to avoid the blazing sun coming in the window.

'*Someone!*' said Gösta with a snort. 'I'm sure James did that right after we asked him whether he'd been in contact with Leif. He's a shrewd guy – I'll give him that much.'

'He's going to have a hard time coming up with an explanation if the bullet that killed Leif matches the bullets we found in the woods near his property,' she said, sipping at her coffee.

She made a face. Gösta must have been the one who brewed the coffee. He always made it too weak.

'Yes, but I'm worried we might not get another chance to question him. He's due to go abroad again soon, and it's going to take a while to get the analysis back from the lab. We can't arrest him before we have the results.'

'But his family is here.'

'Do you get the impression he's particularly family-oriented?'

'No,' sighed Paula. She hadn't considered the possibility that James might skip the country.

'Can we link him to the Stella case?'

'Given that it was thirty years ago . . .' Gösta sounded as if he'd given up before they'd even started.

'Well, it seems Leif was right: the girls were innocent. They have must gone through hell.'

A phone was ringing in the background. The phones hadn't stopped ringing since the tape of the anonymous caller was released.

'I still don't get why Marie lied about her alibi for the night of Nea's disappearance,' said Gösta. 'At least we know that James wasn't in Fjällbacka then, so he couldn't have killed her.'

'No, his alibi is watertight,' said Paula. 'He left the night before, and the Scandic Rubinen hotel have confirmed that he stayed there. The staff remember checking him in and seeing him at breakfast. He was in meetings until late afternoon, and then he drove home. Assuming Nea's watch stopped at the time of her death, James was in Gothenburg when she was killed. Of course it's possible Nea died earlier, and the watch was damaged when she was moved at eight a.m., but James is still out of the frame because he was in Gothenburg from Sunday night until Monday afternoon.'

'I know,' said Gösta, scratching his head in frustration. Paula picked up the notebook.

'I don't seem to be making progress on anything today. I've read and reread Dagmar's notes and I can't work out what's troubling me about them,' she said. 'I thought I'd ask Patrik to have a look. Maybe a fresh pair of eyes will see it.'

'Do that,' he said as he stood up, his joints creaking. 'I think I'll head home. Don't stay too late. We'll give it another try tomorrow.'

'Hmm . . .' said Paula.

She kept leafing through the notebook and didn't even notice when Gösta left. What was it she'd missed?

James went into the bedroom. The police were a bunch of amateurs – they couldn't even search a house properly. He blamed all that Swedish red tape that insisted law enforcement officers had to tiptoe around, taking care not to upset anybody. Whenever James and his men received orders to carry out a search, they ripped the place apart and didn't stop searching until they found what they were looking for.

He would miss the Colt, but he didn't care about the two other guns. So long as the rest of his arsenal was still safely in place, in the cabinet behind a row of shirts and a removable panel in the wardrobe wall. The police hadn't even knocked on the wall to see if it was hollow!

James took his time surveying his guns, debating which ones he should take with him. He couldn't stay here much longer. He'd burned his bridges. He would put all this behind him. He felt no pang of conscience; everyone had played the role assigned to them. Played the game to the end.

The time had come to face the fact he was getting old. His military career was winding down anyway, so it wouldn't be such a hardship to quit. He had the financial means, thanks to the money he'd made on the side while serving his country – money that he'd had the foresight to stash in overseas accounts.

He gave a start when he heard Helen's voice at the door.

'What are you doing, sneaking around?' he demanded. She knew better. 'How long have you two been home?'

He closed the door to the gun cabinet and placed the panel back in the wall. He'd have to leave most of the guns here. That bothered him, but there was nothing he could do about it. Besides, he wouldn't need them.

'Half an hour. Me, anyway. Sam got home about fifteen minutes ago. He's in his room.'

Helen wrapped her arms around her thin torso and looked at him.

'You're going, aren't you? You're planning to leave us. Not just for military duty. You're leaving us for good.'

There was no sadness in her voice. No emotion at all. She was merely stating a fact.

At first James didn't reply. He didn't want her to know his plans, didn't want to give her the power. Then he reminded himself that he was the one with power in this house, not her. That hierarchy had been established long ago.

'I've done the paperwork, signing over the house to you. The two of you can get by for a while on the money in the bank account.'

She nodded.

'Why did you do it?' she asked.

He didn't have to ask what she meant. He closed the wardrobe door and turned to face her.

'You know why,' he said. 'For your father's sake. I promised him.'

'So none of it was ever my fault?'

James didn't answer.

'And Sam?'

'Sam,' he snorted. 'Sam was a necessary evil as far as I was concerned. I've never pretended anything else. If I'd cared about him, I would never have allowed you to raise him like this. A mamma's boy who's been clinging to your skirts since he was a baby. He's worthless.'

A scraping sound came from behind the wall, and they both looked in that direction. Then James turned his back on her.

'I'll stay until Sunday,' he said. 'After that, you're on your own.'

For a few seconds she didn't move. Then he heard her footsteps as she slowly walked away.

'I'm beat,' said Patrik, sinking on to the sofa next to Erica.

She handed him a glass of wine, which he gratefully accepted. Martin was on duty, so Patrik could treat himself to some wine with a clear conscience.

'How did it go with James?' she asked.

'We'll never be able to break him without some concrete evidence. And that's going to take time. We sent in the bullets for comparison, but there's a backlog at the lab – as usual.'

'Too bad you couldn't find a match for the fingerprints. But at least you got it confirmed that the prints on Nea's body match the prints on the chocolate wrapper.'

Erica leaned closer to give Patrik a kiss.

Her familiar soft lips made all the tension seep out of his body.

Patrik leaned his head back against the sofa cushion and let out a deep sigh.

'You've no idea how good it feels to be home. But I still have some work to do if I'm going to make sense of all this.'

'Try thinking out loud,' said Erica, brushing her hair back. 'Things usually seem clearer if you say them out loud. And by the way, I also have something to tell you about today . . .'

'Oh? What's that?' asked Patrik.

But Erica shook her head and took a sip of wine.

'No, you go first. I'm listening.'

'Well, the problem is some things seem clear, some things seem hazy, and some things I simply can't understand at all.'

'Explain,' said Erica.

'Okay. I have no doubt that James shot Leif with his Colt. He then placed Leif's gun in his right hand, since he assumed he was right-handed.'

He paused for a moment, then went on.

'This probably happened because Leif contacted him about the Stella case. James agreed to meet him, then shot him.'

'As I see it, there are two questions,' said Erica, holding up two fingers. 'One: What was his motive for shooting Leif? Did he do it to protect his wife, or to protect himself?'

'My guess is he did it to protect himself. We're fairly certain he was the one Stella used to run into in the woods. He's always been something of a lone wolf.'

'Have you asked Nea's parents if she ever mentioned something similar? Meeting someone in the woods?'

'They said she always played in the barn, not the woods,' said Patrik. 'And she didn't have an imaginary friend, she spent her time playing with a grey kitten – cute little thing; I met it when we were doing the search of their property. Although I suppose there was a bit of fantasy involved, because Nea called it the "black cat".'

'Okay,' said Erica, who seemed to be pondering rather than listening. 'Let's say you're right, and it was James who killed Stella, and then killed Leif to cover up the murder – that throws up more questions. Why did the girls confess? Why did James then marry Helen?'

'Now you see what I'm up against,' said Patrik. 'It feels like there's a lot more to this story that we still don't know. And I'm afraid we'll never be able to work it out. Gösta is convinced James will flee the country before we have a chance to arrest him.'

'Can't you prevent that from happening? Apply for a travel ban, or something? As they say in American films: "You are not allowed to leave town . . ."'

'I wish!' Patrik laughed. 'Unfortunately, without evidence, my hands are tied. I was hoping we would find some illegal weapons when we searched his house. That would have been enough to take him into custody for a while. So, what was the second? You said there were two questions.'

'Right. I'm wondering why he thought such a clumsily executed murder would go undiscovered. He couldn't have known that the pathologist would screw up. If the post-mortem had been done properly, they would have realized the bullet that killed him was a different calibre to the gun found with the body.'

'I wondered about that,' said Patrik, twirling his wine glass. 'But after meeting James, I reckon you can put it down to sheer arrogance. He thinks everyone involved in law enforcement is incompetent.'

'What about Nea's murder? How is it connected with Stella's? If James killed Stella and then murdered Leif in order to cover it up, how does Nea come into the picture?'

'That's the million-dollar question,' said Patrik. 'That's one murder that definitely wasn't down to James. He has a watertight alibi: he was in Gothenburg when she died.'

'So who could have done it? Whose fingerprints are on the chocolate wrapper and her body?'

'If I knew that, I wouldn't be sitting here, I'd be on my way to arrest Nea's killer.' Patrik realized how exasperated he sounded; it wasn't directed at Erica. She was only voicing the question that had been nagging at him all day. 'I'd like to compare the prints with Marie's and Helen's. But since I don't have enough evidence to detain them, I can't demand their fingerprints.'

Erica stroked Patrik's cheek then got to her feet.

'I can't help you with both. But I *can* help you with one of them.'

'What?' said Patrik.

Erica headed for the kitchen. She came back carrying a coffee cup, using a plastic bag to prevent her hand from touching it.

'Here – you wanted Helen's fingerprints.'

'What do you mean?' asked Patrik.

'She came over earlier. Yes, I know. I was surprised too. But she phoned, and I now realize this must have been while you were searching their house.'

'What did she want?' asked Patrik, staring at the cup that Erica set down on the coffee table.

'She wanted to talk about Stella,' said Erica, sitting down next to him again. 'Once she started talking, the words just came pouring out. It felt as if she was going to say something important, but like a total idiot, I interrupted her and asked whether James was involved . . . And then she more or less fled.'

'But you confiscated her coffee cup,' said Patrik, raising his eyebrows sceptically.

'Okay, okay. I just didn't get around to doing the dishes,' said Erica. 'But you wanted Helen's fingerprints, and here they are. I'm afraid you'll have to get Marie's on your own. If I'd known about this earlier, I could have swiped the champagne glass she drank from at Café Bryggan.'

'It's easy to think of things in hindsight,' said Patrik with a laugh. He gave Erica another kiss.

Then his expression turned serious.

'Paula asked me to help her with something. To cut a long story short, there's a charming old lady who lives in a house near the turn-off to the Berg farm and Helen and James's house. You know, that nice red house?'

'Sure. I know which one you mean. It's for sale, right?' said Erica, demonstrating once again her uncanny knack for keeping track of everything that went on in Fjällbacka.

'Exactly. She's in the habit of sitting at the window in the mornings and doing crossword puzzles. At the same time she jots down notes about everything going on outside. In this notebook.'

He picked up Dagmar's dark blue notebook and placed it on the coffee table.

'Paula says something didn't seem right when she went through it, but she can't for the life of her work out what it is. Maybe something about the cars? Dagmar jotted down only the colour and the make, not licence plate numbers, so we can't look up whose vehicles passed by. The thing is, Paula's been right through the notebook, and I have too, and neither of us can see anything that stands out.'

'Let me have a look,' said Erica, picking up the note-book with the crabbed handwriting.

She took her time. Patrik didn't want to stare at Erica while she was reading, so he sipped his wine and zapped through the TV channels. Finally she set the notebook on the table, open to the day Nea died.

'You've been focusing on the wrong things. You're looking for what stands out, not what's missing.'

'What do you mean?' asked Patrik, frowning.

Erica pointed to the notes from Monday morning.

'Here. Something is missing here. Something that was there every other weekday morning.'

'What?' said Patrik, staring at the notes.

He flipped the pages, going back a couple of weeks, and read the jotted notes. Only then did he see what Erica was getting at.

'On all the other weekday mornings, Dagmar made a note that Helen had run past. But on Monday, she didn't run past until lunchtime.'

'Right. That's odd, isn't it? I think that's what Paula's subconscious must have picked up on.'

'Helen . . .' he said, staring at the cup on the table. 'I'll send this cup over to the lab first thing in the morning. But it'll take a while before I know if the fingerprints match the ones on the chocolate wrapper and on Nea.'

Erica looked at him and raised her glass.

'Helen doesn't know that.'

He realized his wife was right. As she so often was.

BOHUSLÄN 1672

The witnesses had come and gone. Elin had fallen into a sort of daze and no longer took any notice of all the made-up stories about her devilish activities. She yearned for the whole thing to be over. But after breakfast on the third day, a murmuring passed through the spectators, and Elin was aroused from her torpor. What was causing such a stir?

Then she saw her. With her blond plaits and bright face. Her life. Her dear one. Her Märta. Holding Britta's hand, she came into the courtroom and looked around in bewilderment. Elin's heart skipped a beat. What was her daughter doing here? Were they attempting to humiliate her further by allowing Märta to listen to what was being said about her? Then she saw Britta lead Märta to the witness chair and leave her there. At first Elin didn't understand. Why would the girl be seated there and not among the crowd? Then she realized what was intended, and she wanted to scream.

'No, no, no. Do not do this to Märta,' she said in despair.

Märta looked at her in confusion, and Elin stretched out her arms towards the girl. Märta was about to get up and run to her mother, but Hierne grabbed her arm and firmly kept her in the chair. Elin wanted to tear him to pieces for laying a hand on her daughter, but she knew she had to restrain herself. She did not want Märta to see the guards drag her away.

So she held her temper and smiled at her daughter, though she could feel her eyes filling with tears. The child looked so small, and so defenceless.

'Am I correct in saying that she is your mother? Elin Jonsdotter?' asked Hierne.

'Yes. My mother's name is Elin, and she is sitting over there,' said Märta, her voice bright and clear.

'I understand you have told your aunt and uncle a few things about what you have done with your mother,' Hierne went on, looking at the gathered spectators. 'Would you tell us about that?'

'Yes, Mamma and I used to go to the witches' sabbath at Blåkulla,' said Märta excitedly.

Screams issued from the crowd, and Elin closed her eyes.

'We used to fly there with our cow Rosa,' she said happily. 'To Blåkulla. And there we had such fun and games. Everything was backwards. We sat at the table with our backs turned and we ate over our shoulders and the plates were turned upside down and the meal was served with dessert first. Oh, they were such fun dinners. I have never had anything like it.'

'Fun and games? My word,' said Hierne, with a nervous laugh. 'Could you tell us more about these feasts? Who was there? What did you do?'

Elin listened with growing amazement and horror as her daughter vividly described these journeys to Blåkulla. Hierne even succeeded in getting the girl to say she had seen her mother fornicate with the devil.

Elin could not understand how they had made Märta come up with such stories. She looked at Britta, who had a big smile on her face. She was wearing yet another fine dress. She waved and winked at Märta, whose face lit up as she waved back. Britta must have done her utmost to win over Märta after Elin was sent to gaol.

Märta clearly did not understand what she was doing. She smiled at Elin as she sat in the witness chair and happily told her stories. For Märta these were mere fairy tales. Encouraged by Hierne, she continued to talk of witches they had met at Blåkulla and children she had played with.

The devil had taken a particular interest in Märta. She had sat on his knee and watched as her mother danced without wearing a stitch of clothing.

'And the next room was called Vitkulla, and that was where angels played with us children, and they were so beautiful and lovely. I could hardly believe my eyes!'

Märta clapped her hands in delight.

As Elin looked around and saw everyone around her gaping, wide-eyed, her heart sank more and more. What could she possibly say to all this? Her own daughter was testifying about journeys to Blåkulla and seeing her mother fornicate with the devil. Her Märta. Her lovely, naive, innocent Märta. She looked at the girl's profile as she told her stories to an enthusiastic audience, and she felt her heart burst with longing.

When at last Hierne announced he had no more questions for Märta, Britta stepped forward to lead her away. Märta took Britta's hand and they headed for the door, but right before they left the little girl turned to give Elin a big smile and wave.

'I hope Mamma will soon come home!' she said. 'I miss you!'

At that moment Elin's strength gave out. She leaned forward and buried her face in her hands as she wept the tears of the condemned.

❖

'How are you doing in your new living quarters?' asked
Bill. To his relief he could now make himself understood
in Swedish if he spoke slowly and clearly.

'We're good,' said Khalil.

Bill wondered whether he was telling the truth. Both
Adnan and Khalil looked tired, and the rebellious teenage
spirit of Adnan seemed to have vanished.

Tomorrow Karim would be discharged from hospital.
He would go home to be with his children, but Amina
would not be there.

'Turn up in the wind,' he said in English, nodding to
port.

Adnan did as he said. They were much better sailors
by now. But their joy was gone. It seemed as if the wind
had been knocked out of their sails, which Bill realized
was an apt description, considering the circumstances.

He hadn't talked to Nils, and he knew it was because
he dreaded doing so. He had no idea what to say to his
son. There was such a distance between them. Even
Gun didn't know how to deal with him. Nils would
come sauntering home late at night and go straight up
to his room. Then the music would start pounding. The

nearest he came to conversing with them was a grunted acknowledgement as he passed by.

Bill carefully trimmed the sail. He should be offering more instructions, making use of the hour to teach them as much as possible before the Dannholmen race. But their faces looked grey against the white sails, and he suspected his own expression was equally resigned. Enthusiasm had always been his trademark, but now it eluded him, and he didn't know who he was without it.

When he gave an order to tack, they obeyed, silently and without protest. Without heart. Like a crew of phantoms.

For the first time since Bill began this project, he felt doubt. How could they sail without any joy? It took more than wind to sail a boat.

It was early in the morning when they knocked on the door of Helen and James's house. Patrik had phoned Paula the moment he got up, asking her to go with him. There was no way of knowing whether the plan he and Erica had devised would work, but if he'd read Helen right, they were in with a chance.

The door opened and Helen stood there, giving them an enquiring look. She was fully dressed, looking as if she'd been awake for hours.

'We need to ask you a few questions. Would you mind coming with us?'

Patrik held his breath, hoping James was not at home. He would undoubtedly object and send them on their way. They had no warrant allowing them to bring Helen in for questioning. Nothing that could force her to come with them. They were relying on Helen's good will.

'Sure,' she said, casting a glance over her shoulder.

It looked as if she wanted to do something, but then she changed her mind. She picked up a jacket from a hook in the hall and followed them. She didn't ask what they wanted, nor did she voice any anger or objections. She merely bowed her head and quietly got into the police car. Patrik tried to chat with her on the way to the station, but she answered only in monosyllables.

When they entered the station, he got two cups of coffee from the kitchen and led the way to an interview room. Helen remained silent, and he wondered what she was thinking. For his part, he caught himself yawning and had to make a real effort to remain clear-headed. He'd lain awake all night, going over everything, examining all the threads of the case – or rather, cases – and the insights he'd arrived at with Erica's help. Though he still couldn't fully grasp how those threads might be woven together, he was convinced that Helen had the answer.

'All right if I record our conversation?' he asked, pointing at the tape recorder on the table.

Helen nodded.

'We spoke to your husband yesterday,' he began. When Helen didn't react, he went on. 'We have evidence linking him to the murder of Leif Hermansson. I assume you recognize the name?'

'Yes, he was in charge of the investigation in the Stella case.'

'Exactly,' said Patrik, nodding. 'We think your husband killed Leif.'

He waited for her reaction. She didn't reply, but he noticed that she didn't seem surprised by the accusation.

'Do you know anything about that?' he asked, staring at her intently, but she merely shook her head.

'No. Nothing.'

'We also have reason to believe that your husband has weapons at home for which he has no permit. Are you aware of this?'

She shook her head but didn't say a word.

'I need to have a verbal response for the tape,' he said.

Helen hesitated but then said, 'No, I am not aware of that.'

'Do you know what motive your husband would have had for murdering the police officer who investigated the Stella case? A homicide that you and Marie were found guilty of committing?'

'No,' she said, her voice cracking. She cleared her throat and repeated: 'No. I have no idea.'

'You don't know why he did it?' asked Patrik.

'No. I don't know whether he killed Leif. So I have no idea what the motive would be,' she said. For the first time she looked him in the eye.

'But I'm telling you that we have evidence he did it. What's your reaction to that?'

'You'll have to show me the evidence,' said Helen. A sense of calm had settled over her.

Patrik paused for a moment and then said, 'Maybe we should talk about the murder of Linnea Berg.'

Helen looked him in the eye. 'My husband was out of town when that happened.'

'We know,' said Patrik calmly. 'But you were home. What were you doing that morning?'

'I've already told you. What I always do, every morning. I went for a run.'

Her gaze wavered briefly.

'But you didn't go running that morning, Helen. You killed a little girl. We don't know why. That's what we'd like you to tell us.'

Helen didn't speak. Her eyes were fixed on the tabletop. Her hands lay on her lap, motionless.

For a moment Patrik felt sympathy for her, but then he remembered what she'd done, and he went on, his voice steely.

'Helen. The search of your house we carried out yesterday is nothing compared to what we're going to do to find traces of how you murdered an innocent child. We're going to look everywhere. We're going to examine every detail of your life, your family's life.'

'You have no proof,' said Helen hoarsely.

But he saw her hands were trembling.

'Helen,' he said softly. 'We have your fingerprints on a chocolate wrapper we found in the barn. We have your fingerprints on the girl's body. It's over. If you don't confess, we're going to turn your whole world upside down until we find every little secret that you and your family are hiding. Is that what you want?'

He tilted his head to one side as he looked at her.

Helen stared at her hands. Then she slowly raised her head.

'I killed her,' she said. 'And I killed Stella.'

Erica looked at everything she had tacked up on the wall. All the photographs, articles and excerpts from the old technical and forensic reports, along with the transcripts of her conversations with Harriet, Viola, Helen, Marie, Sam, and Sanna. She looked at the picture of Stella next to the picture of Nea. The cases were finally closed. Their families had been given closure; sadly it had come too late for Stella's parents, but at least Sanna now knew what had happened to her little sister. When Patrik rang to say that Helen had confessed to both murders, Erica's first thought had been for Sanna. The one who had been left all alone.

Erica wondered how Nea's parents had reacted to the news. Whether it was worse knowing a neighbour had killed their daughter, a familiar face, someone they knew. Or whether it would have been worse if the killer had been a stranger. It probably made no difference. Either way, their child was gone. Erica also wondered whether they would continue to live on the farm. She didn't think she would have been able to do that. The place would be filled with memories of a lively, laughing child they would never see running about the property again. The farm would be a constant reminder.

She turned on her computer and opened Word. All the months of research, getting to know the people involved, tracking down facts and filling in holes in the story, had led to this moment. Now she could start writing the book. She knew exactly where to begin. With two little girls who had only a few years on this earth. She wanted to make them come alive for the reader, ensure their memory would linger in the mind long after finishing the book. Taking a deep breath, she set her fingers on the keyboard.

Stella and Linnea were alike in many ways. Their lives were filled with imagination and adventures. Their world was a farm next to a wooded area. Stella loved the woods. She went there as often as she could to play with her friend the green man. Whether he was real or imaginary, we may never know. All the questions have not been answered, and we can only surmise. Linnea's favourite place was the barn. In that dim and quiet space she played as often as she could. Her best friend was not an imaginary friend but the family's cat. For Stella and Linnea there were no boundaries. Their imagination could take them wherever they wanted to go. They were safe. They were happy. Until one day when they encountered someone who wanted to do them harm. This is the story about Stella and Linnea. This is the story about two little girls who learned much too soon that the world is not always a good place.

Erica lifted her hands off the keyboard. She would be fine-tuning the words and sentences many times over the next few months. But she knew this was where she wanted to begin; this was how she wanted to set up the story. Her books never confined themselves to black and white. She had occasionally been criticized for being too understanding towards those who had committed crimes, especially when the crimes in question were brutal and repulsive. But Erica refused to believe that anyone was born evil. Everyone was somehow shaped by their fate. Some became victims. Some became perpetrators. As yet, she hadn't heard the details of Helen's account of what happened, or what her motive was for taking the lives of these two little girls. In many ways it was incomprehensible that the soft-spoken woman who had sat in her kitchen only yesterday was the murderer of two children. Yet so much had now fallen into place. Erica now understood that the nervous energy emanating from Helen had been guilt. That was why Helen panicked when she'd questioned her about James's role in Stella's murder; she didn't want him to be blamed for something she had done.

A murder affected so many people. The effects spread like rings on the water, but those at the epicentre were hit the hardest. And their sorrow would be passed down through the generations. Erica wondered what would happen to Helen's son. Sam had seemed so vulnerable when she met him. Try as he might to appear hard, with his raven-black hair, his black clothing, black nail polish, and kohl-rimmed eyes, she'd seen how sensitive he was. When they talked, she'd felt his desperate need for someone in whom he could confide. Now he'd be left all alone, with only his father. Another child's life destroyed.

And one question kept going through Erica's mind: Why?

*   *   *

Gösta had gone to see the Berg family to give them the news. He didn't want to tell them on the phone. That felt too cold, too impersonal. Nea's parents needed to hear it from him, face to face.

'Helen?' said Eva in disbelief. She grabbed Peter's hand. 'But why?'

'We don't know yet,' said Gösta.

Peter's parents sat in silence. Their suntans had faded, and they had aged since the first time Gösta had seen them.

'I can't believe it,' said Peter, shaking his head. 'Helen? We've hardly had any contact with her family. We've exchanged a few words with her once in a while. That's all.'

He looked at Gösta as if he might conjure an explanation from him, but Gösta had no answer. He was asking himself the same questions.

'She has also confessed that she was the one who killed Stella. We're questioning her now, and we'll be searching her house again for more evidence. But we already have sufficient proof, and Helen's confession is the last piece in the puzzle, so to speak.'

'How did Nea die? What did she do?'

Eva's words were barely audible and not really directed at anyone.

'We don't know at this point, but we will keep you informed.'

'What about James?' asked Peter, puzzled. 'We heard you'd taken James in for questioning. So we thought . . .'

'That's a different matter,' said Gösta.

He couldn't tell Nea's family anything more. The police couldn't link James to Leif's murder until they had the lab results and actual proof. But he knew that Fjällbacka – in fact, the entire municipality – was buzzing with rumours. The search of Helen and James's home had not

678

gone unnoticed. And everyone also seemed to know that James had been taken to the station.

'That poor boy,' said Eva softly. 'Helen and James's son. He looks so lost. And now this . . .'

'You shouldn't worry about him,' said Peter in a low voice. 'At least he's alive. But Nea's not.'

For a moment no one spoke as they sat at the kitchen table. The only sound was the clock ticking on the wall. Then Gösta cleared his throat.

'I wanted to tell you in person. There's going to be a lot of talk in town. But don't pay any attention to wild speculation. I promise to keep you updated.'

Nea's parents did not reply, so he decided to broach a different subject.

'I also wanted to tell you that they're finished with . . . the post-mortem. You can have her back so you can make arrangements for . . .'

He couldn't finish his sentence.

Peter looked at him.

'The funeral,' he said.

Gösta nodded.

'Yes. For Nea's funeral.'

After that there was no more to say.

As Gösta drove away, he glanced back at the farm in the rear-view mirror. For a moment he thought he saw two little girls waving to him. He blinked, and they were gone.

'Fucking hyenas!' snarled James.

He flung the phone away and paced the floor in the kitchen. Sam watched him listlessly. Part of him enjoyed seeing his father thrown off balance. This man who always had to have complete control over everything, who thought he owned the world.

'Do they really think I'm going to sit back and give

fucking interviews?' he said. '"We'd like to hear your comments . . ." Shitheads!'

Sam leaned against the fridge.

'I only hope she has enough sense to keep her mouth shut,' said James, coming to a standstill.

He suddenly realized Sam was listening. He shook his head.

'When I think of everything I've done for you two. Everything I've sacrificed for your sake. And with no fucking gratitude.' James went back to packing. 'Thirty years of keeping everything in line. And now this.'

Sam heard the words and registered their meaning, but it was as if he found himself outside his body. Nothing could shake him any more. Everything was going to be set right. There would be no more secrets. He was the one who would clear them all up. Until now, he'd been inside a bubble, along with Jessie. Nothing outside had been able to affect them. Not the search of the house, which he had thought at first was because they had found out about his plans. Nor the fact that his mother was in custody at the police station. Nothing.

They were making their preparations now. Jessie had understood when she read his notebook. She understood what he wanted to do and why it had to be done.

He looked at James, who was now standing at the kitchen window, shaking with frustration.

'I know you despise me,' Sam said calmly.

James spun around and stared at him.

'What are you talking about?' he asked.

'You're a small man,' said Sam quietly, noticing how James clenched his fists.

The big blood vessel on the right side of his neck began throbbing, and Sam enjoyed seeing the reaction he had caused. He looked James right in the eye. For the first time in his life, Sam didn't avoid his gaze.

Sam had spent his whole life afraid, uneasy, fighting to remain indifferent and yet allowing himself to be hurt. Anger had been his worst enemy, but now it was his friend. He'd seized hold of the anger, and it had given him power. Only when a person was no longer afraid of losing something did he have real power. That was what James had never understood.

Sam saw James hesitate. A momentary wavering as he looked away, just for a second. And then the hatred. James surged forward, his hand raised, but as he did so there was a knock at the door. James gave a start. With one last look at Sam, he went to open the door. A man's voice was heard.

'Hello, James. We have a warrant to search your house again.'

Sam leaned his head against the fridge. Then he left the house by the back door leading to the deck. Jessie was waiting for him.

The whole community was buzzing. The news had spread like wildfire, the way it always does in a small town. Suddenly everybody knew.

Sanna was standing near the Centrum Kiosk when she heard. She hadn't felt like making her own lunch, so she decided on a quick sausage. As she waited in the queue, people had started talking. About Stella. About Helen. About Linnea. At first it wasn't clear to her what they were saying, so she'd asked the guy standing behind her. She recognized him as someone who lived in Fjällbacka. He'd told her that Helen had been arrested for the murder of Linnea. And she had confessed to killing both Nea and Stella.

Sanna stood there without saying another word. She realized that everyone knew who she was, and they were all staring at her, waiting to see her reaction. But she had nothing to give them. The news merely confirmed what she'd always known, that at least one of those girls had been responsible. It was so strange. She'd always pictured Marie and Helen as a pair. But at last she had a face. Now she knew who was responsible. The trace of doubt that had been nagging at her for thirty years was gone. She knew the truth. It was a feeling like no other.

She stepped out of the queue. She suddenly had no appetite. She headed for the water and went out on to the wharf closest to the tourist information office. She sat down cross-legged on the pontoon pier at the end. A light breeze ruffled her hair. She closed her eyes, enjoying the cool air. She heard people talking, seagulls screeching, dishes clattering at Café Bryggan, and a few cars driving past. And she saw Stella. She saw her running towards the woods with a mischievous look on her face as Sanna chased after her. She saw her hand raised in a wave and a smile showing the slightly crooked front tooth. She saw her mother and father, as they were back then, before everything happened, before all the grief and questions made them forget about her. She saw Helen. The thirteen-year-old Helen whom she had secretly admired. And the grown-up Helen with the evasive gaze and the cowed posture. Sanna knew she would soon start asking questions about why she'd done it, but not yet, not until the light breeze caressing her face had disappeared and the sense of relief at hearing the news slipped away.

Thirty years. Thirty long years. Sanna raised her face to the wind. Now, finally, the tears came.

BOHUSLÄN 1672

Three days after the trial ended, Lars Hierne from the witchcraft council came to the gaol. Elin was waiting in the darkness, dejected and alone. They had given her a little to eat, but not much. Rancid porridge that they slopped into a bowl with some water. She was weak and cold, and she had resigned herself to the rats nibbling at her toes in the night. Everything had been taken from her, so she might as well let the rats take the flesh off her bones.

She squinted at the light when the sheriff opened the cell door. There stood Hierne. He was elegantly dressed as always, and he held a white handkerchief to his nose because of the stench. She no longer noticed it.

'Elin Jonsdotter, you are accused of being a witch, but you now have the chance to confess to your crimes.'

'I am not a witch,' she said quietly, standing up.

She tried in vain to brush the dirt from her clothing, but it was everywhere. Hierne looked at her with distaste.

'The test has proven that you are. You floated like a swan. And we have also heard the testimony of witnesses at the trial. A confession is merely for your own sake, so that you might atone for your crimes and be accepted into the Christian community.'

Elin leaned against the cold stone wall for support.

It was a dizzying thought. To be allowed into heaven was the goal of this earthly life, to secure a place at God's side and be allowed to live for all eternity, without the travails associated with the daily toil of an impoverished person.

But she shook her head. It was a sin to lie. She was no witch.

'I have nothing to confess,' she said, tossing her head.

'So be it. Then we must continue this conversation,' he said, motioning to the guards.

They escorted her further down the corridor and shoved her into another room. Elin gasped for breath when she saw another man come in. A large man with a wild red beard peered at her. The room was filled with strange tools and equipment. Elin gave Hierne a puzzled look.

He smiled.

'This is Master Anders. We have worked together for many years to bring the work of the devil to light. He has forced witches all over this land to confess. You shall have the same opportunity. And so I ask you once more: Will you take this opportunity I am offering to confess to your crime?'

'I am not a witch,' whispered Elin as she stared at the objects in the room.

'So be it,' Hierne snorted. 'I will leave it to Master Anders to persuade you.'

And with that he left the room.

The big man with the wild red beard stared at her without saying a word. His gaze was impassive rather than unfriendly. And that was somehow more frightening than the hatred she was now so used to seeing.

'Please,' she said, but he did not react.

He reached for a chain fastened to the ceiling as Elin watched, wide-eyed.

She screamed and backed away until she felt the cold, damp stone wall at her back.

'No, no, no.'

Without speaking, he grabbed her wrists. She resisted, planting her feet on the stone floor, but it was hopeless. He bound her hands and feet. He held up a pair of shears in front of Elin, who screamed. She thrashed about on the floor, but he merely grabbed her long hair and began cutting it off. Lock after lock of her beautiful hair fell to the floor as she sobbed.

Master Anders then stood up and took a bottle from the table. When he removed the cork, she smelled alcohol. No doubt he needed to fortify himself in order to perform his duties. She hoped he would give her a swig to ease and deaden what was to come, but she doubted he would. To her surprise, instead of raising the bottle to his lips, he poured the liquid over her head.

Elin blinked hard as the alcohol ran into her eyes. She could no longer see anything and had to rely on what she could hear. A rasping sound. She thought it might be a flint. Then she smelled fire. Horror surged inside her, and she writhed even harder.

Then came the searing pain. Master Anders held the flame to her head, and the alcohol burned her scalp, even as it burned off the rest of her hair and her eyebrows.

The pain was so great that she felt as if she'd left her body and was looking at herself from above. When the flame went out, the smell of burnt hair stayed in her nostrils, and nausea welled up and spilled out of her mouth.

The vomit soiled her clothing. Master Anders grunted, but he said not a word.

She was hauled up on to her feet. Master Anders wrapped something around her hands and she was hoisted into the air. The pain from the fire was still making her gasp for breath, but now the chain tightened around her wrists and cut off the blood flow, making her scream.

At first Elin was unaware what he was smearing on her armpits. But then she smelled sulphur and again she heard the flint. She flailed frantically as she hung from the chain.

Elin howled when he touched the fire to the sulphur. When it burned out, she fell silent and hung with her chin resting on her chest. The pain was so great that all she could do was whimper.

She did not know how long she hung there. It could have been minutes or hours. Master Anders had calmly sat down at the table to eat his dinner. When he was finished, he wiped his mouth. Elin's eyes stung so much that she could see only shadowy shapes. The door opened and she turned her head in that direction, seeing only a dark figure. But she recognized the voice.

'Is she prepared to confess to her crime?' said Hierne, speaking slowly and clearly.

Elin waged an inner battle. She wanted to put an end to the pain. She certainly did. She wanted it to stop at all costs, but how could she confess to something she had not done? Was it not a sin to lie? What mercy would God have for her if she lied?

Elin shook her ravaged head and tried to formulate words with lips that would not obey her.

'I . . . am . . . not . . . a . . . witch.'

For a moment no one spoke. Then Hierne said in a measured voice.

'So be it. Master Anders will continue his work.'

The door closed, and she was once again alone with Master Anders.

'How did it go?'

Mellberg stuck his head out his office door as Patrik walked past. Patrik looked at him in surprise. It was rare for the door to Mellberg's office to be open. But there was something about this case, or cases, that had seized hold of everyone.

Patrik stopped and leaned against the doorjamb.

'We found remnants from Nea's clothing in the fireplace in the living room. Helen had managed to burn most of the fabric, but as luck would have it, Nea's clothes had some plastic bits that didn't burn. We also found cleaning implements with traces of blood, and several Kex chocolate bars in a kitchen cupboard. Lots of households would have that kind of chocolate on hand, so it can't be considered evidence. But the plastic bits and the blood on the cleaning implements will go a long way towards backing up her confession.'

'Has she said why she did it?' asked Mellberg.

'No. But I'm going to have another talk with her right now. I wanted to wait until we had the results from the house search. And I wanted her to sit and stew for a couple of hours. I thought she might be more willing to talk.'

'Okay. But she did manage to keep her mouth shut for thirty years,' said Mellberg sceptically.

'True. But it was her decision to confess now. I think she wants to talk.'

Patrik looked around.

'Where's Ernst?'

Mellberg grunted.

'Oh, Rita is so soft-hearted, it's ridiculous.'

He fell silent.

Patrik waited, but then said, 'And Ernst is . . .?'

Mellberg scratched his head in embarrassment.

'Oh, you know, they like him so much, those kids. And they've had such a tough time. So I thought Ernst could stay at home with them.'

Patrik stifled a laugh. Bertil Mellberg. Deep in his heart he was actually a big softie.

'Great,' he said, receiving only a snort in reply. 'I'm going to talk to Helen now. Don't tell the media about what I just told you, okay?'

'Why would I do that?' Mellberg pressed a hand to his chest, looking insulted. 'I'm Fort Knox when it comes to information!'

'Hmm . . .' said Patrik, and he couldn't help smiling as he turned away.

He motioned for Paula to come with him as he passed her office, and they both went into the interview room. Annika had brought Helen and made sure there were sandwiches and coffee. No one considered Helen to be violent or a flight risk, so she was being treated more like a guest than a criminal. Patrik had always believed in the philosophy that you could catch more flies with honey than with fly swatters.

'Hi, Helen. How are you doing? Would you like an attorney to be present?' he asked, switching on the tape recorder.

Paula sat down next to him.

'No, no, that's not necessary,' said Helen.

She looked pale but composed. She didn't seem to be nervous or upset. Her dark hair with its few streaks of grey had been pulled back into a simple ponytail, and she had clasped her hands on the table in front of her.

Patrik regarded her calmly for a few minutes. Then he said:

'We've found items at your home that corroborate what you've told us. Remnants from Nea's clothing that you tried to burn, and blood on a mop and a rag.'

Helen stiffened. She studied Patrik for a long moment, before seeming to relax.

'Yes, that's right,' she said. 'I burned the girl's clothes in the fireplace, and I scrubbed the floor in the barn. I suppose I should have burned the mop and rag too.'

'What we don't understand is why you did it. Why did you kill Stella and Nea?' Paula said gently.

There was no trace of anger in the room. Maybe it was the heat making them sluggish, maybe it was the sense that Helen had resigned herself to the situation. Paula was about to repeat the question, uncertain whether she had heard, when Helen started talking.

'Marie and I were so happy that we had the chance to be together. The weather was lovely, as it had been all summer. Although when you're young, all summers are sunny. At least, that's how it seems later on. We decided to take Stella into town to buy ice cream. She was really happy about that, but Stella was always happy. Even though we were much older, we liked playing with her once in a while. And she loved to sneak up on us. She thought it was great fun to jump out and scare us. And we let her do that. We liked her. Marie and I both did. We liked Stella so much . . .'

Helen fell silent and picked at a ragged cuticle. She

had been staring at her hands the entire time she was talking; anything to avoid meeting their gaze. Patrik waited.

'We took the pushchair along, and we practically had to force her to sit in it when we walked to Fjällbacka. We got her the biggest ice-cream cone we could buy. She chattered nonstop. And I remember the ice cream ran down her hand, so we had to get some paper napkins to wipe it off. Stella was . . . she was very intense. As if she was always bubbling over.'

Again she picked at her cuticle. It had started to bleed, but Helen continued to pick at it.

'She talked the whole way home too. She ran on ahead, and both Marie and I liked seeing the sun on her reddish blond hair. It was so shiny it gleamed. I've seen her hair so many times in my dreams . . .'

A tiny trickle of blood was now running down her finger. Patrik picked up a tissue and handed it to her.

'When we reached the farm, we saw the car belonging to Stella's father,' said Helen, wrapping the tissue around her finger. 'We told her she should go home, because her father was there. We . . . we wanted to get rid of her so we could have some time to ourselves. We saw her head towards the house, and we assumed she went inside. Marie and I left and went to the lake to swim. And talk. We'd missed that. Being able to talk to each other.'

'What did you talk about?' asked Paula. 'Do you remember?'

Helen frowned.

'I don't recall, but I suppose we talked about our parents, the way teenagers usually do. Complaining about how they didn't understand anything. How they were so unfair. We were feeling very sorry for ourselves at the time, Marie and I. We felt like victims and heroes in some great drama.'

'What happened next?' asked Patrik. 'What went wrong?'

At first Helen didn't answer. She began picking at the tissue wrapped around her finger, tearing it into tiny pieces. She took a deep breath, then sighed, before continuing her story in a low voice. They could hardly hear what she said, so Patrik pushed the tape recorder closer. Both he and Paula leaned forward to hear better.

'We dried ourselves off and got dressed. Marie headed off in one direction, and I was about to go home too. I remember worrying about how I would explain to my parents that my hair was wet. I decided I'd tell them we'd been playing in the sprinkler with Stella. And then Stella turned up. She had sneaked after us instead of going home. And she was cross because we'd gone swimming without her. Really cross. She stomped her foot and shouted. She had asked us if we planned to go swimming when we walked home, and we'd told her no. And she said . . .'

Helen swallowed. She seemed reluctant to continue. Patrik leaned even closer, as if to coax her to go on.

'She said she'd tell our parents that we'd been swimming. Stella wasn't stupid, and she had ears like antennas. She'd picked up on the fact that our parents wouldn't allow us to be together any more, and in her childish way she wanted to get back at us. And I . . . I can't explain how or why it happened. But I missed Marie so much, and I knew that if Stella said we'd gone off together, we'd never be able to see each other again.'

She fell silent and bit her lower lip. Then she raised her eyes and stared at them.

'Do you remember what it was like to be thirteen and a friend was your whole world, and you thought that's how it would always be? You thought the world would fall apart without that person? That's how I felt about

Marie. And Stella was standing there, shouting and shouting, and I knew she could wreck everything. And when she turned around to run home, I was so . . . I was so angry and panic-stricken, and all I wanted was for her to shut up! So I bent down and picked up a rock and threw it at her. I was only trying to make her stop yelling so I could persuade her not to say anything, or maybe bribe her so she wouldn't talk. But the rock hit her on the back of the head, and she stopped shouting and just toppled over. And I got scared and ran. I ran all the way home and rushed into my room and locked the door. And then the police came . . .'

The tissue was now shredded into tiny pieces. Helen was breathing hard, so Patrik waited for her to compose herself for a minute before he asked:

'Why did both of you confess? And why did you later retract your confessions? Why did Marie confess when she wasn't involved?'

Helen shook her head.

'We were children. We were stupid. The only thing we could think about was being together. Marie hated her family. She wanted nothing more than to get away from them. But I don't know why she confessed. We never had a chance to talk about it. Maybe she thought if we both confessed, we'd be sent to the same place. We thought we'd end up in prison, even though we were kids. And Marie would rather have been in prison with me than at home.'

She looked from Paula to Patrik.

'So now maybe you'll understand how awful her situation was. When we found out that we wouldn't be sent away together, we tried to take back what we'd said. But it was too late. I realized I shouldn't have retracted my confession. I should have explained what I'd done. But I was scared. All the grown-ups around me were so angry.

Everybody was shouting. I felt threatened. Everybody was upset and disapproving, and it was all so emotional that I didn't know what to do. So I lied and said I hadn't done it, I hadn't killed Stella. But it didn't matter . . . I could just as well have confessed. At the court hearing they decided we were guilty, and I've been viewed with suspicion ever since. Most people think I was the one who killed Stella. I know I should have told the truth so that Marie wouldn't be suspected, but we weren't given a sentence, and I actually think she was better off with a foster family than in her own home. Then, as the years went by, she seemed to make use of having this shadow hanging over her past. So I let it drop.'

Patrik nodded. His neck felt tight.

'Okay. Now I understand things better,' he said. 'But we also need to talk about Nea. Would you like to take a short break first?'

Helen shook her head.

'No, but I'd like some more coffee.'

'I'll get it,' said Paula, standing up.

Patrik and Helen waited in silence for Paula to come back. She brought a whole Thermos of coffee and a carton of milk. She refilled all three cups.

'Nea,' said Patrik. 'What happened?'

There was nothing accusatory about his voice. Nothing aggressive. They might as well have been talking about the weather. He wanted Helen to feel secure. And oddly enough, he didn't feel any anger towards her. He knew that he should, because she had murdered two children. Yet he felt a reluctant sympathy for this woman sitting at the table across from him.

'She . . .' Helen looked up as if trying to picture the scene. 'She . . . came over to our place. I was out in the garden and suddenly there she was. She did that some-times. She would sneak away from home and come over

693

to our house. I used to tell her to go back home so her parents wouldn't worry, but this time she wanted to show me something . . . And she was so eager, so happy. That's why I . . . I agreed to go with her.'

'What did she want to show you?' asked Paula.

She held up the milk carton, but Helen shook her head.

'She wanted me to go with her into the barn. She asked me if I would play with her, and I said no, I had things to do. But she looked so disappointed that I told her she could show me one thing, and then I'd have to go back home.'

'Didn't you wonder where her parents were? It was awfully early in the morning.'

Helen shrugged.

'Nea was often outside playing early in the morning. I suppose I thought they'd let her go outdoors after breakfast.'

'So what happened?'

Patrik cautiously urged her to go on.

'She wanted me to go inside the barn. There was a little cat there, a grey cat that rubbed on my legs. She wanted to show me the loft. I asked her if she was allowed up there, and she said she was. She climbed up the ladder first, and I followed. Then . . .'

She took a sip of coffee, carefully setting down her cup as if it were made of the most delicate porcelain.

'I turned my back, and . . . It was only a second . . . And somehow she fell. I heard only a muffled scream and a thud. When I looked down, I saw her lying there. Her eyes were open, and blood was running from her head. I knew she was dead. Just as I knew Stella was dead when I heard the rock strike the back of her head. I was in such a panic . . .'

'Why did you move her?' asked Patrik.

needed to breathe in the scent of his children; Amina's scent. He saw her in the features of his daughter's face, in his son's eyes. They were all he had left of her, and yet they were a difficult reminder of what he had lost.

Finally he released the children and stood up. They ran back into the living room and sat down on the sofa next to a little boy who was shyly peering at him, with a dummy in his mouth and a comfort blanket on his lap. All three kids turned their attention back to the children's programme on TV.

Karim set down his bag and looked around. It was a bright and pleasant flat, but he felt himself a stranger, and at a loss. Where would he go now? He and the children were on their own, without a place to live. They didn't have even the smallest essentials. They were dependent on the charity of people who didn't want them here. What if they ended up on the street? He'd seen beggars sitting outside the shops with poorly written cardboard signs and a blank, distant look in their eyes as they held out their hand.

It was his responsibility to take care of the children, and he'd done everything in his power to give them security and a better future. Yet here he now stood. In a stranger's front hall, with nothing left. He couldn't go on.

He sank to the floor and felt tears fill his eyes. He knew the children would be frightened to see him like this, and he shouldn't scare them. He should be strong, but he simply couldn't do it any longer.

He felt the weight of warm hands on his shoulders. The woman put her arms around him, and her warmth spread over him, loosening the pieces in his chest that had been lodged there ever since they left Damascus. She took him in her arms and rocked him, and he let her do it.

His longing for home was so sharp, and remorse tore apart all the hope he'd had for a better life. He was shipwrecked.

'Hello?'

Martin came to an abrupt halt when he saw who was standing in the reception area. He noted with amusement that for once even Annika was speechless. She was silently staring at Marie Wall.

'How can we help you?' asked Martin.

Marie seemed to hesitate. Her usual self-assured manner was gone, and she actually looked a little uncertain. Martin couldn't help thinking this changed attitude suited her. She looked younger.

'Someone at the film shoot said that you had arrested Helen. For the murder of the little girl. I . . . I need to speak to someone in charge. This can't be right.'

She shook her head and her gleaming blond hair, curled in a 1950s style, framed her face. Martin saw that Annika was still staring. Film stars didn't turn up at the Tanumshede police station very often. In fact, when he thought about it, this was the first time.

'You'll need to speak to Patrik,' he said, motioning for her to follow him.

He paused outside Patrik's office and knocked lightly on the open door.

'Patrik, there's someone here who wants to talk to you.'

'Can't it wait?' said Patrik, without looking up from the papers he was reading. 'I have to write a report about the interview with Helen, and then I—'

Martin interrupted him.

'I think you'll want to see this particular visitor.'

Patrik looked up. The only sign that he was surprised to see Marie was the slight widening of his eyes. He stood up and nodded curtly.

'Of course. Martin, would you please come with us?'

Martin and Marie followed as Patrik led the way to the room where Helen had been interviewed earlier. The shredded bits of tissue were still lying on the table. Patrik briskly swept them into his hand and tossed them in the rubbish bin.

'Please, have a seat,' he said, pointing to the chair closest to the window.

Marie looked around hesitantly.

'It's been a long time since I was in this room,' she said.

Martin realized this was where she must have been questioned thirty years ago, under other circumstances, though there were eerie similarities.

'Would you like some coffee?' asked Patrik, but she shook her head.

'No . . . I . . . Is it true that you've arrested Helen for the murder of Nea Berg? And that she has confessed to killing Stella?'

Patrik hesitated and cast a quick glance at Martin. Then he nodded.

'Yes, it's true. We haven't yet made an official announcement, but news travels fast in this town.'

'I just heard about it,' said Marie.

She held up a pack of cigarettes, and Patrik nodded. Smoking wasn't allowed in these rooms, but if ever there was a time to make an exception, it was now.

Marie carefully lit a cigarette and took a few drags before she began to talk.

'I have never believed that Helen killed Stella, and I still don't, no matter what she says. But above all, I know she couldn't have killed the other little girl.'

'How do you know that?' asked Patrik, leaning forward.

He pointed at the tape recorder on the table, and Marie nodded. The machine hummed as he switched it on, and he quickly rattled off the date and time. Even though this was not an official interview, it would be better to record too much rather than too little. The human memory was unreliable and sometimes directly misleading.

'She was with me when the girl died. You wanted to know where I was at eight in the morning on Monday, didn't you?' she said, her expression uncertain.

Martin coughed at the smoke. He'd always had sensitive lungs.

'So where were the two of you?' asked Patrik.

Her whole body seemed tense.

'At Helen's place. You were right. I lied about my alibi. I didn't take anyone home with me. I was with Helen at eight o'clock. She didn't know I was coming because I was convinced she would say no if I rang ahead.'

'How did you get there?' asked Patrik.

Martin glanced at her sky-high heels under the table. It seemed unlikely she would have walked.

'My rental house includes a car. A white Renault that's parked in the big space next to the house.'

'There's no car registered to the owners of the house you've rented. We've already checked.'

'It's in his mother's name. They borrow the car whenever they're in Sweden, so it was included when I rented the house.'

'There's a white Renault in Dagmar's notes for that morning,' Martin confirmed for Patrik.

'Helen didn't want to let me in, but I can be . . . very persuasive, and in the end she gave in. We'd spoken on the phone the night before, and she'd mentioned that her husband was out of town. I wouldn't have gone there otherwise. I had the feeling she told me he was away because subconsciously she wanted me to come over.'

'What about her son? Sam?'

Marie shrugged and took another drag on her cigarette.

'I don't know. He was either asleep or not at home. At any rate, I didn't see him. But I've met him when he was with my daughter. By some strange twist of fate, they've become friends. Maybe more than friends . . . They're both misfits.'

'Why did you go to see Helen?' asked Patrik.

He coughed discreetly. The smoke was getting to him too.

The vulnerable look on Marie's face returned. She stubbed out her cigarette.

'I wanted to know why she abandoned me,' she said quietly. 'I wanted to know why she stopped loving me.'

Silence descended over the room. The only sound was a fly buzzing at the window. Patrik's face was impassive. Martin tried to take in what Marie had just said. He glanced at Patrik, who was silently studying Marie without knowing how to follow up on her statement.

'The two of you were in love . . .' he said slowly.

Random phrases, vague hints, a facial expression, a glance, so many things suddenly took on meaning.

'Tell us,' he said.

Marie took a deep breath and exhaled slowly.

'At the time, we didn't understand what we were experiencing. You know how it is when you've grown up here, and . . . well, those were different times. A family consisted of a mother, a father, and children. I had never heard about women loving women, or men loving men. So it took a long time before we realized we'd fallen in love with each other. We'd never been in love before. We had hardly left childhood behind. We were teenagers and we talked about boys just like all the other girls did. Slowly we began pushing the boundaries. Touching each other, caressing each other. We played and explored, and the feeling was stronger than anything we'd ever experienced. We had a world that included only the two of us, and that was enough. We needed nothing more. But then . . . I think Helen's parents began to sense something was going on, something that was unacceptable to them, that would have caused talk in the social circles they moved in. So they decided to separate us.

'Our world collapsed. We cried for weeks. We were in despair. All we thought about was being together. And not being able to touch each other was . . . it tore us up. I know it sounds ridiculous. We were so young, just girls, not women. But people always say that first love is the strongest. And ours burned day and night. Helen stopped eating, and I quarrelled with everyone. My situation at home got worse than ever, and my family did their best to pound some sense into me. Literally.'

Marie lit another cigarette.

Patrik got up to open the window, and the fly that had been buzzing flew out.

'So you can understand what a special day it was when we were allowed to babysit Stella together. Oh, we'd managed to see each other in secret, but only a few times and only briefly. Helen's parents never let her out of their sight.'

'Helen told us that the two of you took Stella into town to buy ice cream, then walked back through the woods, and left her at the farm when you saw her father's car. Is that right? And then you went swimming?'

Marie nodded.

'Yes. We were in a hurry to drop Stella off so we could have some time to ourselves. We went swimming and we kissed and . . . Well, I think you get the picture. That was when I thought I heard someone else in the woods, and I had the feeling we were being watched.'

'What happened next?'

'We got dressed. I went home, and Helen did too. The fact that she says she killed Stella after I left . . .' She shook her head. 'I have a hard time believing it. Good lord, we were only thirteen! It must have been the person I heard in the woods. And I think I can guess who it was. James was horrible, even back then, and he was always hanging around in the woods. Sometimes we'd find dead animals, shot by James. He'd always been obsessed with guns and war and killing. Everybody knew. Everybody knew there was something wrong with him. Except for Helen's father. Those two were inseparable. Whenever James wasn't in the woods, he was visiting Helen's family. The fact that he ended up marrying Helen . . . well, it borders on incestuous.'

'So why did you confess?' asked Patrik. 'Why did you confess to a murder you didn't commit?'

He wondered whether Marie's answer would be different from Helen's.

'I was naive. And I didn't really understand how serious the situation was. Or how real. I remember thinking it was exciting. My plan was for us to be together. I had some romantic notion that Helen and I would both be sentenced and sent away together. Then I'd be rid of my family, and I'd be allowed to stay with Helen. And when we were released, we'd share the world. The fantasies of a thirteen-year-old, but I believed they would come true. I could never have imagined the consequences of my stupidity. I confessed and hoped that Helen would understand my plan and do the same, which she did. By the time I realized we wouldn't be sent to the same juvenile institution the way I'd imagined, it was too late. No one believed us. They had solved the case, everything was tied up nicely. Like a little gift box with a red ribbon. Nobody was interested in continuing the investigation.'

She paused and swallowed several times.

'They separated us. I ended up with various foster families while Helen moved to Marstrand with her family after a short stint at a youth home. But I was counting the seconds until we both turned eighteen.'

'What happened when you were eighteen?' asked Martin.

He couldn't take his eyes off Marie. The story issuing from her lips was incredible and yet completely plausible and clear. It filled in all the gaps that had had them mystified.

'I phoned Helen. And she brushed me off. She told me she was going to marry James and she didn't want any contact with me. She said the whole thing had been a mistake . . . At first I didn't believe her. But when I realized she was serious, I was heartbroken. I still loved her. My feelings were as strong as ever. For me, this was not some stupid teenage crush. Far from it; the passing of time and the circumstances had made me love her even more. But she didn't want anything to do with me. I couldn't understand it, but what could I do? The hardest part was accepting that she was going to marry James, of all people. It didn't seem right. Yet I had no choice but to let it go. Until now. It can't have been a coincidence that I got this role and was forced to come back here. I never forgot her. Helen was the great love of my life. And I thought I was hers.'

'So that's why you went to see her that Monday morning?' asked Patrik.

'Yes. I made up my mind, I was going to confront her.'

'After she let you in, what happened?' asked Patrik.

'We went out to the deck in back and talked. She was treating me like a stranger. Cold and pompous. But I could see that the Helen I had known was still there, no matter how hard she tried to hold her back. So I kissed her.'

'How did she react?'

Marie raised her fingers to her lips.

'At first she didn't react at all. Then she kissed me back.

704

It was as if thirty years melted away. She was my Helen. She clung to me, and I knew I'd been right all along: she had never stopped loving me. And I said that to her. She didn't deny it, but I never got a clear answer about why she abandoned me. Either she couldn't or didn't want to explain. I asked her about James. I told her I didn't believe she had ever wanted to marry him, but she insisted she had fallen in love with him. She said she chose him instead of me, and I would just have to accept that. But I knew she was lying. It made me so angry that after all these years she was still lying that I got up and left. She was still sitting there on the deck when I drove away. And I remember checking my watch because I was afraid I'd be late for the film shoot. It was twenty past eight. So if the girl died around eight, Helen couldn't have killed her. She was with me.'

'If that's true, why would she claim to have killed Nea?' asked Patrik.

Marie took a drag on her cigarette as she pondered the question.

'I think Helen has a lot of secrets,' she said. 'Only she knows the truth.'

She stood up abruptly.

'I have to get back to the film studio. My work is the only thing that means anything to me.'

'You have a daughter,' Martin said, unable to stop himself.

Marie looked at him. The naked and vulnerable expression had vanished.

'An on-the-job mistake,' she said tersely, and then she was gone, leaving them in a room filled with cigarette smoke and the heavy scent of perfume.

'You need to stand still, Bertil!' snapped Paula.

Trying to knot Mellberg's tie had turned out to be impossible. Muttering and cursing, Rita had eventually given up, and now they had to hurry if they were going to be on time for Kristina and Gunnar's wedding.

'Why the hell should we have to get all dressed up? Who was the idiot who decided that to look nice a man has to wear a noose around his neck?' said Mellberg, tugging at his tie and making the knot come undone again.

'It must have been the devil himself, damn it,' said Paula, instantly regretting her words when Leo's face lit up and he shouted: 'Damn it! Damn it! Damn it!'

Bertil chuckled and turned to Leo, who was sitting on the bed watching them.

'Good boy! You need to collect lots of swear words because you'll have use for all of them in life. Can you say "hell"? Can you say "bastard"?'

'Hell! Astard!' shouted Leo. Paula glared at Mellberg.

'You're like a big kid! What are you thinking of, teaching a three-year-old swear words!' She turned to Leo and said sharply, 'You may *not* say those words Grandpa is trying to teach you! Do you hear me?'

Leo looked disappointed but nodded.

Mellberg gave him a wink and whispered, 'Satan!'

'Satan!' Leo repeated with a giggle.

Paula groaned. This was impossible. And she wasn't talking about knotting his necktie.

'What do we do if Karim and his kids don't get the flat?' she asked as she made one last attempt to fix Mellberg's tie. 'I can tell that Karim thinks it's awkward to be staying with us, and in the long term it won't work. They need their own place. It would be perfect if they could have the flat next door, but I haven't been able to get hold of the owner so he can talk to the municipality about the rent. And the municipality can't seem to find any other housing for them.'

'Oh, I'm sure it will all work out,' said Mellberg.

'That's easy for you to say. I haven't seen you lift a finger to try and help Karim, and yet it's partially your fault things turned out this way!'

She bit her lip. She hadn't meant to be so harsh, but she was feeling frustrated because no one seemed prepared to help the family. It made her want to kick someone in the shins. Hard.

'You have your mother's temperament,' said Mellberg cheerfully, seemingly unaffected by her outburst. 'Sometimes that's a good thing, but both of you should practise having a little more patience and self-control. Try and learn from me. Things always get worked out. As they say in *The Lion King*: "Hakuna matata".'

'Hakuna matata!' cried Leo happily, bouncing on the bed.

The Lion King was his favourite film. Lately he'd been watching it five times a day, or at least it felt that way.

Paula angrily let go of Mellberg's tie. She knew she shouldn't let him get to her, but his nonchalance drove her mad.

'Bertil, you are an egotistical and selfish male chauvinist under normal circumstances. I've learned to live with that! But when you don't give a shit what happens to Karim and those two poor children who just lost their mother, it's . . .' She was so angry she was at a loss for words. '*Fuck you*, that's all I can say!'

As she stormed out of the bedroom, she heard a merry 'Fuck you' echoing from Leo. She'd have to have a serious talk with him later. Right now she was going to get hold of the damn building owner if she had to pound on his door all night. She gathered up the full skirt of her dress in one hand, swearing as she made her way down the stairs in her high heels. Dressing up was not her strong suit, and she felt ridiculous in this dress. It was also impractical, she thought as she nearly tripped again outside the owner's flat. She pounded her fist on the door. Just as she was about to try it again, the door opened.

'What's going on?' said the man. 'Is there a fire?'

'No, no,' said Paula, ignoring his look of surprise when he noticed her wearing a dress and high heels.

She straightened up to her full height, though it was hard to project authority wearing a flowery dress and pumps.

'It's about the flat for the refugee family who've been staying with us. I know there's a difference of a couple thousand kronor per month between what the municipality has offered and the rental price, but can't we find a solution? The flat is standing empty, and they really need a home. Since it's right next to ours, they wouldn't be lonely. We can vouch for them. I'll sign a form, whatever you need! Somebody has to show some bloody empathy for a family with kids in need of help!'

She put her hands on her hips and glared at him. He stared back in astonishment.

'But it's all been taken care of,' he said. 'Bertil came

708

to see me yesterday. He said he'd make up the difference for as long as needed. They can move in on Monday.'

Paula stared at him.

The building owner shook his head, looking puzzled.

'Didn't he say anything? I wasn't supposed to mention it to Karim if I ran into him. Bertil wanted you to tell him.'

'That fucking old man,' muttered Paula.

'Sorry?' said the owner.

'Nothing,' she said, waving her hands dismissively.

Slowly she went back upstairs to Mellberg and Rita's flat. She knew he was up there laughing himself silly at her expense. But it served her right. She would never understand that man. He could be the most annoying, irrational, narrow-minded, stubborn man to walk the earth. But he was also the person Leo adored most in the world. That alone made Paula forgive most of his stupidities. And now she would never forget that he'd made sure Karim and his children would have a home.

'Come here, you old bastard, and I'll fix that necktie!' she called when she stepped back inside the flat.

From the bedroom she heard Leo happily shout: 'Astard!'

'Do you think this makes me look fat?' asked Erica anxiously.

She turned to face Patrik.

'You look amazing,' he said, slipping behind her to put his arms around her. 'Mmmm, you smell good too.'

He nuzzled the back of her neck.

'Be careful of my hairdo,' she said with a laugh. 'It took Miriam an hour and a half to style it, so don't be getting any ideas.'

'I don't know what you're talking about,' he said, nibbling at her neck.

'Stop!'

She wriggled out of his grasp and looked at herself in the mirror.

'This dress actually looks quite nice, don't you think? I was afraid I'd have to wear something salmon-coloured with a big rosette on the rear, but your mother surprised us. Her dress is beautiful too.'

'I still think this whole wedding thing feels a bit strange,' muttered Patrik.

'You're being silly,' said Erica. 'Parents have their own lives. And I'm certainly planning to go on sleeping with you when you're seventy.'

She smiled at him in the mirror. Then went on:

'I'm looking forward to seeing how Anna looks. It was a real challenge for them to make a tent-dress for her.'

'She's definitely getting big,' said Patrik, sitting down on the bed to tie his shoelaces.

Erica put on a pair of earrings with glittering white stones and turned to face Patrik.

'So what do you really think about this Helen and Marie business? Can you make any sense of it?'

'I'm still as confused as ever as to who to believe,' said Patrik, rubbing his eyes. 'Helen denies ever having been in a romantic relationship with Marie. She says that's something Marie made up. She also maintains Marie wasn't with her the morning Nea died. Yet Dagmar's notes confirm that a white Renault passed by, which seems to indicate Marie is telling the truth. But we have only her word as to the time she left. And since we don't know whether Nea's watch stopped at the time of her death or later, not to mention whether it was fast or slow, we can't be sure she was killed at eight o'clock. Hopefully the lab results will give us a definitive time of death. In the meantime, we have enough to keep Helen in custody: the evidence in the barn, the chocolate she gave Nea, the clothing she tried to burn, the fingerprints . . .'

Erica saw that something was bothering him.

'But?'

'There are too many things that don't fit. For instance, Helen says she threw a rock at Stella's head, saw that she was dead, and then ran home. But according to the pathologist, Stella had suffered multiple blows to the head, and she was found in the water. So how did she get there?'

'It was thirty years ago. Helen may be misremembering what happened,' said Erica, casting one last look at herself in the mirror.

She twirled around in front of Patrik.

'You're incredibly beautiful,' he said, and he meant it.

He stood up and put on his jacket before imitating her pirouette.

'What about me?'

'So handsome, sweetheart,' she said, leaning forward to kiss Patrik on the lips.

Then she straightened up. Something Patrik had said was nagging at her. What was it?

Patrik put his arms around her, and the thought disappeared. He smelled so good today. She gave him a cautious kiss.

'So what about our little rascals?' he said. 'Do you think they're still neat and clean and dressed, or are we going to have to start all over with them?'

'Cross your fingers,' said Erica, leading the way downstairs.

Sometimes miracles do occur, she thought when she entered the living room. Noel and Anton were sitting on the sofa like little angels, looking so adorable in their white shirts, waistcoats, and bow ties. Presumably they had Maja to thank for that. She was standing in front of her brothers, watching them like a hawk. She'd been allowed to choose her own dress, and with a little coaxing she had selected a pink dress with a full tulle skirt. An added accessory was a pink flower in her hair, which Erica had laboriously managed to curl without singeing even a single strand. That alone was an achievement.

'All right!' she said, smiling at her family, all dressed up. 'Let's go to Grandma's wedding!'

By the time they reached the church, most of the guests had already arrived. Kristina and Gunnar had decided to get married in Fjällbacka, even though they lived in Tanumshede, and Erica could understand why. The Fjällbacka church was so beautiful, towering like a pillar of granite above the small town and the shimmering sea.

The boys dashed inside, and Erica left Patrik to look after them. Then she took Maja's hand and went to join Kristina. She looked around for Anna, who was also supposed to be part of the wedding procession, but she didn't see her or Dan anywhere. How typical of Anna to be late.

'Where's Emma?' asked Maja.

Anna's daughter Emma was her favourite cousin, and the fact that they were going to wear matching dresses was a wondrous and big event in Maja's life.

'They'll be here soon,' Erica assured her, stifling a sigh.

She went into the small room where the pastor and wedding party were supposed to wait until the guests had all taken their seats.

'Wow,' she said when she caught sight of her mother-in-law. 'You look amazing!'

'Thanks. You do too,' said Kristina, giving her a warm hug. Then she glanced at the clock with concern. 'Where's Anna?'

'Late, as usual,' said Erica, 'but I'm sure she'll be here any minute.'

She got out her mobile to see if there was a text from Anna. It said 'Anna' on the display.

Erica read the message and then gave Kristina a strained smile. 'You won't believe this, but they drove to Munkedal to fetch Bettina, and their car started overheating on the way back. Right now they're standing on the side of the road, waiting for the tow truck. And Anna has been trying to get a cab for the last half hour.'

'And she didn't try to get hold of you until now?' Kristina said shrilly.

Erica was thinking the same thing, but she forced herself to remain calm. This was Kristina's day, and she didn't want anything to spoil it.

'They'll be here. But if not, you should start without them.'

'You're right,' said Kristina. 'Everyone is waiting, and we can't be late for the luncheon at Stora Hotel. But I have to say, I don't know how she always manages to . . .'

She sighed, but Erica could see her annoyance was gone. Sometimes you simply had to accept the situation. And nobody was particularly surprised. Anna always made things more complicated in some way.

The church bells began to toll, and Erica handed the bridal bouquet to Kristina.

'It's time,' said Gunnar, giving his future wife a kiss on the cheek.

He looked very elegant in his dark suit, and his friendly face shone as he looked at his bride. This is so good, thought Erica. This is splendid and good and just as it should be. She felt tears well up in her eyes, but she made an effort to pull herself together. She was a sentimental fool when it came to weddings. It would be nice if the make-up she was wearing would last at least until they stood at the altar.

'All right, time for you to go in,' said the church warden, motioning them forward.

Erica cast a quick glance at the church door. No Anna. But they couldn't wait any longer.

The organist began playing the wedding march. Hand in hand, Kristina and Gunnar walked up the centre aisle. Erica took Maja's hand and had to smile when she saw how seriously her daughter was taking her role in the procession. She glided up the aisle, waving like a queen to all the guests.

At the altar, Erica and Maja took up position on the left while Kristina and Gunnar stepped in front of the pastor. Patrik was sitting in the front pew with Noel and Anton. He mouthed the words: 'Where's Anna?' Erica discreetly shook her head and rolled her eyes. How embarrassing. And Emma was so looking forward to being a bridesmaid.

The ceremony proceeded solemnly, and the bridal couple said 'I do' precisely as they should. Erica wiped away a tear but surprisingly managed to keep her composure. She smiled at Kristina as they waited for the music to start up before heading out of the church.

But instead the organist began playing the wedding march again. Astonished, Erica looked up. Was the cantor drunk? But then she saw them. And suddenly she understood. All her worry vanished, and tears streamed down her cheeks. She looked at Kristina, who smiled and winked. She and Gunnar had stepped to the side and were now standing across from Erica and Maja.

A quiet murmur passed through the crowd, and surprised looks followed the second bridal couple making their way to the altar. Anna turned to look at Erica as she passed. Erica was now crying so hard she could hardly breathe. Thankfully someone pressed a handkerchief into her hand, and when she looked up, she saw it was Patrik who had come over to her.

Anna looked so beautiful. She had chosen a white gown with embroidery at the middle, which emphasized rather than tried to hide her pregnancy. She wore her blond hair loose, and the veil was fastened to a simple tiara. Erica recognized the veil. It was the same one she had worn when she married Patrik. The one their mother had also worn on her wedding day. Dan was handsome in a dark suit with a simple white shirt and dark blue tie. He was like a Viking with his broad shoulders and blond hair, yet the formal attire looked unexpectedly good on him.

After the vows were said and they were declared husband and wife, Anna turned to look at Erica. And for the first time Erica saw something in her restless sister's eyes that she'd never seen before. She looked calm. And Erica realized Anna was wordlessly trying to tell her that she could let go now, that she no longer needed to worry. Anna had at last found peace.

The sun was still warm as Marie reclined in the Adirondack chair on the dock. The afternoon sun was making her feel drowsy, as usual. Jessie had gone out an hour ago, so the house was deserted. She was going over to see Sam again, and tomorrow there was some sort of party. Marie was amazed Jessie was going to a party. Things seemed to be improving for her daughter.

Marie was drinking more than usual, but it didn't matter. She wouldn't be needed on set again until tomorrow afternoon. Greedily she drank the last drops in her glass and then reached for the bottle on the small table. Empty. She tried to get up but immediately dropped back in the chair.

Finally she managed to stand up. Holding the empty bottle, she tottered into the kitchen. She opened the fridge and took out a cold bottle of champagne. The third bottle of the evening. But she needed it to dull the pain.

She'd thought that if she told the police everything, Helen would have to come out of hiding and tell the truth. Instead Helen had once again rejected her, refusing to confirm what she'd said about the two of them.

Marie was surprised that it could still hurt so much to be dismissed and humiliated that way. She had spent thirty years forgetting. She had lived well, shunning the use of brakes, limitations, or blinkers, and in the process she had achieved a level of success that Helen could only dream of. And all the while Helen had hunkered down here in her dreary life with her boring husband and her peculiar son. She'd remained in Fjällbacka where people whispered behind your back if you had a glass of wine on a Tuesday or tinted your hair a brighter shade than a lacklustre ash-blond.

How could Helen reject her?

Marie tumbled into her chair, spilling champagne on her hand, which she licked off. Then she poured herself another glass, adding some peach juice. She was drunk enough for her body to feel comfortably lethargic. She thought about what she'd said to that ginger-haired police officer, about Jessie being a mistake. It was true; she'd never planned to have a child. She'd taken every possible precaution so she wouldn't end up with a kid. And yet she got pregnant. All because of some short, fat slob of a producer. A married man, naturally. All of them were.

She had hated being pregnant and had seriously believed she would die in childbirth. The baby was sticky, red, cranky, and possessed of a voracious hunger. She'd relied on countless nannies, and then sent Jessie off to boarding school as soon as possible. She'd hardly had anything to do with the child at all.

She wondered what would happen to Jessie. According to the settlement, Marie received monthly payments from the fat producer that would continue until Jessie turned eighteen. At that point she would serve no further purpose in Marie's life. She tried to picture a life without Jessie. She welcomed the solitude and freedom. People were nothing more than disappointments. Love was nothing more than a disappointment.

It would be only a matter of time before the newspapers found out about her and Helen. She had no idea how news could spread so fast here; it was as if everybody shared some sort of collective consciousness. News, information, gossip, facts, lies – everything spread with the speed of the wind.

She wasn't sure it would be such a bad thing. These days it was actually considered cool. In artist and actor circles, it could enhance a career if it came out you'd slept with someone of the same gender. It would give her brand a new edge, a sense that she was keeping up with the times. The film investors would be cheering. A controversial star was a financial jackpot. First all the press about the murders. Something taboo, dark, and dangerous. That was always enticing. Then the love story. And the twist. Two young girls forced apart by an uncomprehending adult world. So banal. So dramatic. So effective.

Marie held up her nearly empty glass. The bubbles seductively danced before her eyes. This was the only thing that had stood by her side all these years. Her constant companion.

Again she reached for the bottle. She intended to keep drinking until dark fell and the alcohol had drowned out all her thoughts. About Helen and Jessie. About what she'd had, and about what she'd never had.

*   *   *

'Hello?'

Mellberg stepped away and covered his ear with one hand. There was such a din he could hardly hear.

'Yes?' he said, trying to work out what the person was saying on the phone.

He moved further down the corridor and finally the reception was good enough that he could hear his contact at *Expressen*.

'Have you received any tips? We've been inundated with calls. Everyone claims to recognize the voice. Everybody from the postman to my neighbour. What? A guy who gave them a ride? When? What? Talk louder!'

He listened intently. Then he ended the call and went back into the restaurant. He found Patrik sitting on a sofa talking to a woman who looked as if she'd passed her expiry date and also seemed to have helped herself to a generous amount of wine.

'Hedström. Could I have a word with you?'

Patrik gave Mellberg a grateful look and excused himself.

'Who was that old crone?'

'I'm not sure. Somebody related to my maternal grandmother's sister-in-law, or something like that. There are a lot of people here I didn't even know were part of the family.'

'That's the worst part about weddings, and why I'd never dream of getting married,' said Mellberg. 'Rita can beg and plead all she likes, it's never going to happen. Certain souls are too free to be shackled.'

'So, you had something important to tell me?' Patrik interjected.

They had gone over to the bar and were leaning against the counter.

'I got a call from *Expressen*. A man phoned with some very . . . interesting information. The night before we got

718

the anonymous tip about Karim, a man gave three teenagers a lift from Fjällbacka. Two boys and a girl. He dropped them off at the refugee centre. And he thought he heard them sniggering about something they planned to do. He didn't take it seriously. At least not at the time. But now, after what's been reported in the newspapers, he has begun to wonder.'

'Okay, that sounds interesting,' said Patrik, nodding.

'Wait,' said Mellberg. 'It gets better. He recognized one of the boys. It was Bill's son.'

'Bill? Sailor Bill?'

'Yup. Apparently the man's son had taken Bill's sailing class, and he recognized the boy.'

'What do we know about him?' asked Patrik, holding up two fingers to order beer from the bartender. 'Is it plausible?'

'So we're not going to do anything about it tonight?' asked Mellberg, pointing at the beers.

'No, not tonight,' Patrik confirmed. 'But on Monday, I'd like to have a talk with those kids. Want to come along?'

Mellberg glanced around. Then he pointed at himself in surprise.

'Me?'

'Yes, you,' said Patrik, taking a couple of swigs from his beer.

'You never ask me to go with you. You usually ask Martin. Or Gösta. Or Paula.'

'Well, I'm asking you now. You were the one who sorted this out. I might not have gone about it in the same way, but it worked. So I'd like to have you along.'

'By God, of course I'll go!' said Mellberg. 'You might need to have someone along with a little experience.'

'Definitely,' said Patrik, laughing.

Then he turned serious.

'Paula told me about Karim and the flat. I just want to say that I think that was bloody well done.'

He raised his glass.

'Oh, er,' said Mellberg. He raised his glass in return. 'Rita insisted. And you know what they say: "Happy wife, happy life!"'

BOHUSLÄN 1672

Master Anders picked up the bottle of alcohol. He pulled out the cork, and Elin began to pray. She feared that God had abandoned her, but she could not stop praying.

The liquid was poured over her back, and she shuddered as it cooled her skin. But now she knew what was about to happen. She had ceased fighting and struggling, since that merely served to flay the skin from her wrists. She took a deep breath when she heard the sound of the flint and smelled the flame. She screamed at the top of her lungs when her back was set alight.

When the fire eventually went out, she merely whimpered, sensing that unconsciousness was mercifully beginning to dim her mind. She hung from the ceiling like a piece of meat. All that was human about her was seeping away. The only thing she could think about was the pain and trying to breathe, just breathe.

When the door opened she knew without being able to see that it was Lars Hierne coming back to hear whether she was ready to confess. Soon she could bear no more.

But the voice she heard belonged to someone else. It was a voice she knew all too well.

'Oh, dear God!' said Preben, and a wisp of hope flickered in Elin's heart.

Surely he would relent when he saw her like this. Naked and desecrated and subjected to the most horrifying torment.

'Preben,' she managed to say, trying to turn her head in his direction, but the chain swung her the other way. 'Help . . . me.'

Her voice broke, but she knew he heard her. His breathing was rapid and shuddering, but he said not a word. After a silence that lasted too long, he said:

'I am here as your vicar, to counsel you to confess to the crime for which you have been sentenced. If you confess to your deeds of witchcraft, you will then atone for your crime, and I promise to personally see to your burial. But you must confess.'

As the words sank in and she heard the anxious tone of his voice, it was as if all sense left her. With a hoarse croaking sound, she slipped into insanity as she hung from the chain, burned and defiled. She laughed and laughed until the door finally closed. She had made her decision. She had no intention of confessing to something she had not done.

A day and a night later, Elin Jonsdotter confessed that she was guilty of witchcraft and carrying out the devil's work. Master Anders's skills had proved too much for her. He had tied weights to her feet and placed her face-up on a bed of nails; he had used a steel file between her fingers and crushed her thumbs in a vice; he had stuck pieces of wood under the nails of her fingers and toes. After that Elin could stand no more.

Her sentence was confirmed by the court in Uddevalla and by the Göta court of appeals. She was a witch and was condemned to death. First she would be decapitated and then her body would be burned at the stake.

'You need to eat something,' said Sam.

He opened the fridge and looked inside. Jessie was sitting at the kitchen table. She shrugged.

'I'll make us some sandwiches.'

He got out the butter, cheese, and ham. He took some bread from the breadbox and began making the sandwiches. He put two on a plate and set it in front of Jessie. Then he poured her a glass of O'boy chocolate milk.

'O'boy is for kids,' she said.

'O'boy is good.'

He looked at her as she sat leaning over the table, eating a sandwich. She was so beautiful that it hurt. He was prepared to follow her to the ends of the earth and back. He only hoped she felt the same way about him.

'You're not having second thoughts?'

Jessie shook her head. 'We can't back out now.'

'We need to double-check that we have everything we need,' he said. 'It has to be perfect. It has to be . . . elegant. Beautiful.'

Jessie nodded and ate the rest of the second sandwich.

Sam sat down next to her and pulled her close. He ran his finger along her jaw and then touched her lips. There was no outward sign that her body had once been covered with black ink, but inside was a different matter. There was only one way to wash it all away. He would help her do that. And at the same time he would wash away the blackness that was clinging to him.

'What's the time?' she asked.

He glanced at his watch.

'We should leave in half an hour. But almost everything is ready. And I've taken care of the guns.'

'So how does it feel?' she asked, pulling up her hood. 'Does it feel good?'

Sam stood up and took a long moment to think about it. In his mind he pictured James's surprised face.

Then he grinned.

'It feels fucking great.'

The music was pounding. With an annoyed expression, Sanna went upstairs and yanked open the door. Vendela and Nils were sitting on the bed and flew apart when they saw her.

'What do you think you're doing?' shouted Vendela. 'Can't I have any privacy in my own room?'

'Turn down the music. And from now on, leave the door open!'

'Are you crazy?'

'Turn down the music and leave the door open, otherwise you can forget about getting a ride to Tanumshede.'

Vendela opened her mouth to say something but then changed her mind. For a moment Sanna thought she almost looked relieved.

'Is Basse going too?' she asked.

Vendela shook her head.

'We don't hang out with him any more,' said Nils.

'Oh? Why not?'

Nils suddenly looked serious.

'People change. People grow and move on. That's all part of becoming an adult. Right, Sanna?'

He tilted his head to one side. Then he glanced at Vendela and smiled at her. Vendela seemed to hesitate before smiling back.

Sanna turned away to go back into the hall. She'd never liked Nils. Basse might be slightly stupid, but he seemed nice enough. Whereas there was nothing nice about Nils. It was hard to believe that Bill and Gun could have raised a child who was the very opposite of them in every way; they were such kind, considerate people. The sort of people who'd do anything to help.

She didn't like Vendela hanging out with him. And today she got the feeling Vendela didn't especially want to be with Nils either.

'Turn down the music. Leave the door open. We're going in ten minutes.'

'Do you know how to drive?' asked Jessie as Sam aimed the keys at the car and pressed the button to unlock it.

He opened the boot and put the package inside.

'Mamma taught me. We've driven around the farm.'

'But that's not the same thing as driving on the road, is it?' she asked.

'What do you suggest? Do you want us to take the bus?'

Jessie shook her head. He was right, of course. Besides, what did it matter?

'Do we have everything?'

'I think so,' said Sam.

'Did you leave the USB stick in the computer?'

'Yeah. It's impossible to miss.'

'What about petrol?'

'We've got all we need.' He closed the boot and gave her a smile. 'Don't worry. We've thought of everything.'

'Okay,' she said and opened the passenger-side door.

Sam got in behind the wheel and started up the car. He looked calm and confident as he sat there, and Jessie relaxed. She turned on the radio and searched for a channel playing happy music. She found some old Britney Spears tune, it wasn't what she'd have chosen, but it was cheerful and upbeat, and today she didn't really care. She closed her eyes and felt the wind ruffling her hair and caressing her cheeks. She was free. After all these years she was finally free. Free to be who she wanted to be.

Everything was set, planned, and arranged. Sam had carefully sketched it all out in his notebook, and he'd thought of every contingency. He'd spent hours in his room thinking about this particular evening, and he'd googled anything he didn't know. It turned out it wasn't all that difficult to work out how to do the greatest possible damage.

The destruction would be cleansing; it would reset the balance. Because they had all been participants, each in their own way – everyone who had remained silent all these years and looked on without saying anything. Everyone who had laughed and pointed, who had joined in with the back-slapping and shouting. Even those who had protested, but gone about it so quietly that no one would hear; they just wanted to feel they were good people, they didn't really give a damn about anyone else.

They too deserved to suffer some sort of consequences.

They arrived early. Inside the building, preparations were under way for the evening disco. No one noticed them. It wasn't hard to unload the car and hide what they needed without being seen. The jerrycans of petrol were heavy, but they each took one and shoved them in the bushes, pulling branches in front to hide them from view. The approaching twilight would help to conceal everything.

Sam dealt with the exits. He'd thought about this for a long time before deciding on a simple solution. Big padlocks. Of course they could always smash the windows, but he didn't think anybody would be that enterprising, or daring. They were all such cowards.

Sam and Jessie settled down to wait in the car. They didn't talk, just held hands. He loved the warmth of her hand in his. He would miss that. But it was about the only thing he would miss. It hurt too much. Life hurt too much.

Finally people began arriving. Sam and Jessie stared out the windscreen, studying who was there. They wouldn't begin until the most important players were in place.

At last they saw them. First Vendela and Nils. Then a while after that, Basse showed up. The trio seemed to have disbanded. Sam leaned towards Jessie and kissed her. Her lips felt dry and tense, but they softened at his touch.

The kiss didn't last long. They were ready to start. Everything had been said, everything had been done.

No one looked in their direction as they got out of the car. They approached in a wide arc so as to reach the back of the building without drawing attention. They dragged along the jerrycans and the bag. Nobody noticed as they crossed the lawn. It was dark inside the building. Most of the windows were covered with dark cloth or plastic. The music was blasting at full volume as they opened the back doors. Disco lights were pulsing on the dance floor in front of the stage.

They placed the cans and bag inside the door and then left, fastening a chain and padlock on the door handle outside. Now all they carried was the money for the entrance fee and another chain and padlock. They walked purposefully around the building and joined the queue at the entrance. No one paid any attention to them. Everyone was in high spirits and slightly intoxicated after partying somewhere else before coming here.

Sam and Jessie paid the fee and went in. By now the place was packed with a dancing, howling, many-headed crowd. Sam whispered to Jessie. She nodded. They walked along the wall. A boy and a girl were making out near the back exit. Sam recognized them from school. They were totally focused on each other, fumbling under each other's clothing and unaware of anyone else. Sam and Jessie opened the bag and quickly stuffed the guns under their clothes. They had taken care to wear loose, oversized clothing. They left the jerrycans where they were, since they weren't yet needed. They had to lock the entrance doors before the fun could begin.

They headed back to the front, and out of the corner of his eye Sam saw Vendela and Nils in the middle of the dance floor with a group of friends. But no Basse. Sam looked for him, and eventually spotted him at the other end of the room. He was leaning against the wall with his arms crossed, staring at Nils and Vendela.

There was still a ten-metre queue of lively party-goers waiting at the entrance. The ticket seller was standing just outside the doors. Sam went over to him.

'We need to make sure we can close the doors. It's a security measure. It'll only take two minutes.'

'Okay,' said the guy. 'Sure.'

Sam pulled the doors closed from inside and quickly attached the chain and padlock. He relaxed his shoulders and forced himself to take a deep breath. Focus. No one was leaving now. No one was coming in. They had total control of the place. He turned to Jessie and nodded. Someone had started pounding on the doors from outside, but he ignored them. The music was loud, so nobody else could hear the noise.

The cabinet with the electrical control panel was in a small hallway to the left of the entrance. He went over to it, threw one last look at Jessie, who was ready with her hands stuck under her clothing. He switched on the lights and pulled out the plug for the music. Now there was no going back.

As light flooded the room and the music stopped, there was a moment of stunned silence. Then someone started shouting, and a girl jeered. Soon lots of voices joined in. All the kids looked pale and pathetic in the glaring light. Sam felt his self-confidence surge. He allowed all the emotions he'd kept bottled up for years to pour out. He went over to stand with his back to the front doors, facing the dance floor so everyone could see him.

Jessie came over and stood next to him.

Slowly he took out the guns. They had decided they would each have two pistols. A shotgun would have been too cumbersome and hard to hide.

He fired a shot into the air and some of the girls began to scream. Everyone was staring at them. Finally the situation was reversed. He'd always known he was better than these kids with their petty lives and their banal thoughts. They would soon be forgotten. But no one would forget him or Jessie.

Sam walked towards the dance floor. Nils and Vendela were stupidly staring at him. Sam enjoyed seeing the terror in Nils's eyes. He could tell Nils knew what was going to happen. With a steady hand, Sam raised the gun. Slowly, wanting to enjoy every second, he squeezed the trigger. The bullet hit Nils right in the middle of the forehead, and he dropped to the floor. He lay on his back, with his eyes open. A trickle of blood ran from the perfectly round hole.

Adnan and Khalil walked and walked. Every night they went out walking. The air in the basement felt as if it would suffocate them, and the walls seemed to close in on them when it was time for bed. The sound of the TV upstairs continued until two or three in the morning. The old woman never seemed to sleep. The only thing that helped was to go out and walk. For hours. They walked until they were worn out and had inhaled enough oxygen to last them a whole night in the basement.

They didn't converse as they walked. The risk was always there that they would talk about what had once been, and that in turn might feed their nightmares about buildings in ruins and children who had been blown to pieces. There was also a risk they would start talking about the future and realize that for them it held no hope.

It felt as if the people inside the houses they passed were living in a different world.

On the other side of the windowpanes was that part of Sweden they wanted to know, and every evening they tried to learn more about it. They went into the centre of town and looked at the flats with the balconies that were so strangely decorative. No laundry hanging out to dry, no lanterns flickering, although a few of them were adorned with tiny lights. Someone had even set a yucca plant on their balcony. It was such a peculiar sight that Adnan had pointed it out to Khalil.

Tonight, after passing through town, they headed for the school. The Swedish school fascinated them. It looked so new. So fancy.

'Looks like a party going on in the red building,' said Adnan, pointing at the community centre.

Bill had tried to explain what a community centre was, but they couldn't come up with a comparable Arabic term, so all the refugees had simply dubbed it the 'red building' when they had stayed there after the fire.

'Should we go check it out?' Adnan asked.

Khalil shook his head.

'It looks like teenagers. And they've probably been drinking. Which means somebody will be looking to pick a fight with the likes of us.'

'Not necessarily,' said Adnan, touching Khalil's arm. 'And maybe we'll meet some girls.'

'Like I said: it'll be nothing but trouble if we go there,' Khalil sighed.

'Oh, come on.'

Khalil hesitated. He knew he tended to be overly cautious, but who could blame him after what he'd been through?

Adnan started heading for the building, but Khalil grabbed his arm.

'Listen!'

Adnan stopped to listen. Then he looked at Khalil, his eyes wide.

'Gunshots,' he said.

Khalil nodded. It was a sound they both knew well. And it was coming from inside the community centre. They stared at each other. Then they ran towards the sound.

'What a fabulous wedding that was,' said Erica, nestling closer to Patrik as they sat on the patio loveseat. 'I was so surprised when Anna and Dan came into the church yesterday. I had a feeling she was hiding something from me, but never in a million years would I have imagined she was planning a double wedding with Kristina.'

She was still in shock, but the wedding celebration had turned out to be the most fun of any she'd attended, and that included her own. Everyone had been so amazed by Anna and Dan's big surprise that a festive mood had started even before they left the church. After a marvellous dinner with plenty of speeches, the dancing had gone on all night.

Now Erica and Patrik were sitting out on the deck, watching the sun set and savouring the memories.

'You should have seen your face when Dan and Anna came in!' Patrik chuckled. 'I thought you were going to dissolve into a big puddle on the floor. I had no idea anyone could cry that hard. You were so sweet. Your make-up was running, and you looked like a cute raccoon. Or a cat. One of those black cats with a sweet little muzzle . . .'

'Oh great,' said Erica, but she had to admit he was right. She'd been forced to repair her make-up in the ladies' room as soon as they got to the hotel. Her mascara and eyeliner had smeared so badly that she looked like . . .

Erica froze. Patrik looked at her in surprise.

'What's wrong? You look as if you've seen a ghost.'

Erica got up abruptly. She thought of something else that had been bothering her. Something Patrik had said about Helen.

'Yesterday you mentioned something when you were talking about Helen. Something about the chocolate bar she gave to Nea. Do you remember what you said?'

'Well, Nea had chocolate in her stomach. It was the last thing she ate. Chocolate and biscuit, to be precise. So Pedersen thought she'd been eating a Kex chocolate bar. When I asked Helen about it, she said Nea had seen her eating a Kex and asked for a taste, so she split it with her. And we found a Kex wrapper in the hayloft, so—'

'Helen's lying. She couldn't have been eating chocolate – she's allergic. Was she the first to mention the Kex bar, or was it you?'

'I think it might have been me.'

'And who was it Nea said she played with in the barn?'

'The black cat,' said Patrik with a laugh. 'Kids are so funny.'

'Patrik,' said Erica, giving him a sombre look. 'I know how it all fits together. I know who did it.'

'Did what?'

Erica was about to answer when Patrik's mobile rang.

Patrik listened grimly, then ended the call and turned to her.

'I have to go,' he said. 'That was Martin. They've had reports of gunshots at the community centre in Tanumshede.'

'What do we know?' asked Martin, turning to look at Paula and Mellberg in the back seat. He'd been the officer on duty and had gone to pick them up after phoning Patrik. 'Do we know yet who the shooter is?'

Paula met his eye in the rear-view mirror.

'No,' she said. 'But I'm in contact with Annika. More calls have been coming in to the station, so hopefully we'll know more soon.'

'Could it be related to the refugees?' asked Mellberg. 'Again?'

'I don't think so,' said Martin, shaking his head. 'It seems there was some sort of dance tonight to celebrate the end of the school holidays. So we're talking about secondary school students.'

'Bloody hell. Teenagers?' said Mellberg. 'How much further?'

'Come on, Bertil. You've driven this way as often as I have,' said Martin impatiently.

'Do we need reinforcements?' asked Paula. 'Should I ring Uddevalla?'

Martin didn't need to check with Mellberg; he instinctively knew the answer. His gut told him this was bad. Really bad.

'Yes, ring Uddevalla,' he said, stomping on the accelerator. 'We're almost there. Do you see Patrik and Gösta anywhere?'

'No, but they're on the way,' said Paula.

733

When Martin pulled up in front of the community centre, he saw two young guys come running from the direction of the building. He parked the car and jumped out to stop them.

'What's going on?'

'Someone is shooting in there!' said one of the young men in English. Martin recognized him from the refugee centre. 'It's crazy! People are panicking!'

The words came pouring out of him as he mixed English with Swedish. Martin held up one hand to get him to slow down.

'Do you know who it is?'

'No, we couldn't see anything. We just heard shots and people screaming.'

'Okay, thanks. Get out of here now,' said Martin, motioning for them to leave.

He looked at the building and then turned to Paula and Mellberg.

'We need to find out what's happening. I'll go closer,' he said, gripping his gun.

'We're right behind you,' said Paula and Mellberg.

More young people came running towards them, but they didn't appear to have emerged from inside the building. The main doors were closed, as were the windows.

'Let's split up,' he said. 'Try to get as close to the windows as possible. We need to get an idea of what's going on in there.'

His colleagues nodded and the three of them approached the building in a crouched run. With nerves on high alert, Martin looked in one of the windows that wasn't entirely covered. He froze at what he saw.

He now knew what they were dealing with, but that didn't mean he knew how to handle the situation. Patrik and Gösta couldn't be far away, but it might take almost an hour before the reinforcements from Uddevalla arrived. And from what he'd seen, they couldn't wait that long.

The screams got louder. Sam fired a shot into the air.

'Shut up!'

Everyone fell silent, although muted sobbing could still be heard. Sam nodded to Jessie, and she walked past him to the back exit. With an effort she picked up the jerry-cans and carried them over, then placed them at Sam's feet.

'You,' said Sam, pointing to a big guy wearing a white shirt and brown chinos. 'Take that can and start pouring the petrol out over there.'

He pointed to the left wall.

'And you,' he said, nodding at a stocky black kid wearing a pink shirt. 'Take the other side. Make sure the window coverings get really soaked.'

He pointed at the pieces of cloth hanging in front of the panes.

Both boys remained where they were, as if paralysed, but when Sam raised his gun, they got moving. Each picked up a jerrycan and made their way to the windows on either side of the hall. Again they hesitated.

'Move it!' yelled Sam.

He turned to Jessie.

'Watch them – make sure they do it right. If they don't, shoot them.'

Sam looked at the pathetic group of kids in the room. Everyone was shaking and sobbing. Some had started looking for a means of escape, assessing their chances of making a run for it.

'The doors are locked. There's no way out,' he said, grinning. 'Don't try anything stupid.'

'Why?' cried Felicia, a girl from his class. 'Why are you doing this?'

She was one of the popular kids. Big boobs and lots of blond hair. Dumb as a doornail.

'Why do you think?' he replied.

He looked at Vendela, who hadn't moved from the spot where Nils was lying on the floor. She wore a short skirt and a skimpy camisole. She was shaking.

'Do you have a theory, Vendela? Any idea why we're doing this?'

He ran his eyes over the room, stopping when he saw Basse.

'What about you?'

Basse was silently crying.

'You shouldn't be standing there all by yourself,' said Sam. 'Come over to be with Vendela and Nils. You're all such good pals. Your old gang.'

Basse slowly came towards Vendela, who was staring straight ahead. He stood next to her without looking at Nils's body.

Sam tilted his head to one side.

'So, who do you think I should shoot first? You can decide, if you want. Or do you want me to decide? It's not an easy decision to make. Should I start with the slut who likes to boss everyone around, or should I go for the wimp who does everything he's told?'

They didn't answer. Vendela's cheeks were striped with black from her mascara running.

Control. It was all his now.

Sam raised his gun. And fired. Vendela fell to the floor without uttering a sound. Shrill screams echoed off the walls and he shouted:

'QUIET!'

But he couldn't stop the kids from sobbing, and a young boy from a lower class threw up. Vendela had landed to the right of Nils. Sam's aim had been a little off this time, and the bullet had entered Vendela's right eye. But the result was the same.

She was dead.

Erica was in the passenger seat next to Patrik as he drove faster than ever before. He knew it was against all regulations and also against his better judgement, but Erica had convinced him to bring her along. 'Teenagers' lives are in danger,' she'd said. 'You'll need lots of adults on the scene to offer comfort and support.' And she was right. Of course she was. He reached out to squeeze Erica's hand as he looked out at the beautiful summer landscape. There was normally something sleep-inducing about racing along these dark, deserted roads, but at the moment he'd never felt more awake.

When they reached the exit for the community centre he took the turn with screeching tyres and parked next to Martin's and Gösta's vehicles. He told Erica to stay in the car and then climbed out to get a report of the situation.

'It's Helen's son! And Marie's daughter!' said Martin. 'Sam and . . .'

'Jessie. Her name is Jessie,' Patrik told him.

'Sam and Jessie. They're armed and holding the kids hostage. We saw one person on the floor, not moving, but they were standing in front, so we couldn't tell how badly the person was injured. An ambulance is on the way, but it's going to take time.'

'What about reinforcements from Uddevalla?' asked Patrik.

'At least half an hour before they get here,' said Paula. 'I don't think we can wait that long.'

A shot was heard from inside the building, startling all of them.

'What do we do?' asked Gösta. 'We can't stand here waiting for reinforcements while they shoot more kids.'

Patrik thought for a second then opened the car door and asked Erica to step out. He told her what was going on.

'You have Sam's mobile number, right?' he asked.

'Yes, I got it when I interviewed him.'

'Can I have it? Our only chance is to try and get through to him. If we can talk to him and make him realize what madness this is, maybe we can end this.'

Erica told him the number, and he tapped it in, his hand shaking. It rang and rang, but no one picked up.

'Shit!' he said, feeling his panic grow. 'Maybe if we had Helen here, Sam would take a call from her. But it'll take too long to bring her.'

'Want me to try?' Erica asked quietly. 'Maybe he'll pick up if he sees it's me calling. When we met, I thought the two of us connected. He really opened up to me.'

Patrik gave her a sombre look.

'It's worth a try.'

Erica got out her mobile. He watched tensely as the call went through.

'Put him on speaker,' he said in a low voice.

'Why are you calling me?'

Sam's voice echoed, ghostlike, across the car park.

Erica took a deep breath.

'I was hoping you would talk to me,' she said. 'I know you think nobody listens to you, but I'm listening.'

No response. In the background they could hear sobbing and murmured voices. Someone was screaming.

'Sam?'

'What do you want?' he said. He sounded like an old man.

Patrik motioned for Erica to hand him the phone, and after hesitating a few seconds, she did.

'Sam? Patrik Hedström here. From the police.'

Silence.

'We just want to talk to you. Is there anyone inside who needs help? An ambulance is on the way—'

'It's too late for an ambulance.'

'What do you mean?' asked Patrik.

'It's too late . . .'

Sam's voice faded. They could hear Jessie telling someone to shut up.

Patrik hesitated and looked at Erica. If he said the wrong thing, it might make things worse. But they had to try to keep the conversation going – it was their only hope. They didn't have enough officers on hand to storm the building until reinforcements arrived, so in the meantime all they could do was talk.

'We know, Sam,' said Patrik. 'We know all about it. We know your mother tried to take the blame for what happened. Why don't you let the kids inside go? They haven't done any—'

'Haven't done anything? What the hell do you know about what they've done or haven't done?' Sam's voice rose to a falsetto. 'You have no idea. They're disgusting. They've always been disgusting, and they don't deserve to go on living.'

He tried to stifle a sob, and Patrik saw an opening, a crack. As long as Sam was feeling something, he might be able to reach the boy. People who had shut down were the most dangerous.

'What about Nea?' he said. 'What happened to her? Did she deserve to die too?'

'No. It was an accident.' Sam's voice was almost a whisper. 'I didn't mean to do it. I was . . . I saw . . . I saw Mamma kissing Marie. They thought they were alone, but I could see them from my hiding place in the barn. I wanted to be alone, but Nea wouldn't leave me in peace. She kept on chattering and saying we should play, until I lost my temper and pushed her. As soon as I realized she was right near the edge of the hayloft, I reached out to grab her, but she took a step back . . . and she fell.'

For a moment no one spoke. Patrik looked at Erica.

'And your mother helped you take care of the situation?' he said, even though he already knew the answer.

'I'm sorry,' Sam sobbed. 'Tell my mother I'm sorry about everything.'

Then he ended the call.

Patrik frantically tried to call him again, but this time he didn't pick up. Another gunshot, and they all jumped. Patrik looked at his watch.

'We can't wait. We have to go closer. Erica, you stay here with Mellberg. Under no circumstances are you to leave the car. Understood?'

Erica nodded.

'Paula, Martin, and Gösta, come with me. Mellberg, when reinforcements arrive I need you to brief them. Okay?'

Everyone nodded. Patrik cast a steely glance at the community centre and checked for his gun. He had no idea how to prevent the disaster that was unfolding, but he had to try.

It had unnerved Sam when the cop told him he knew what had happened in the barn. An image flashed into his mind: Nea's face as she teetered on the edge of the hayloft. He hadn't meant to hurt her. All he'd wanted was for her to leave him alone. Her expression when she fell was more surprised than scared. He'd lunged forward and tried to grab her, but it was too late. He looked down and there she was, lying on the floor below, a pool of blood forming around her head. She'd taken a few shuddery breaths, then her body seemed to deflate, and her gaze went blank.

If that hadn't happened, he wouldn't be standing here tonight. This had started out as a fantasy, planning his revenge and writing it all up in his notebook, telling himself he had the power to take control if he wanted to. It was only after what they did to Jessie that he decided to make it real. After what he'd done to Linnea, he had nothing left to lose.

'The police are outside,' he told Jessie now. 'It's time to put an end to this.'

Jessie nodded.

She went over to stand in front of Basse, her feet set wide apart the way Sam had shown her. Calmly she raised her gun and placed the muzzle against Basse's forehead. His eyes filled with tears and he tried to say 'I'm sorry,' but only sobs came out. Jessie's arm jerked when she fired the shot. Basse's head slammed backward and he too landed on the floor.

For a moment Sam and Jessie stared at the trio while screams started up all around them. By now all Sam had to do was raise his gun to make them shut up.

Jessie stuck her hand in her pocket and took out two lighters. She tossed them to the boys who had poured out the petrol.

'Light it,' said Sam curtly.

They didn't move. Just looked at the lighters they were holding.

Calmly Sam fired a shot into the chest of the big boy in the white shirt. He looked down in surprise as a red splotch formed. Then he sank to his knees and fell on to his stomach. The lighter was still in his right hand.

'You. Go get the lighter.'

Sam pointed to a small boy with glasses, who shook all over as he leaned down to pick it up.

'Light it,' said Sam, again raising his gun.

The boys held the lighters to the petrol-soaked cloths covering the windows. Flames quickly raced up the fabric towards the ceiling and out to the sides. There was no longer any point in trying to stop anyone from screaming. The kids rushed in panic for the doors.

Sam and Jessie now stood back to back, just as they'd practised. They raised their guns. He felt the warmth of Jessie's back against his own, then the rhythmic jolts in their bodies as they fired more shots. No one would be allowed to escape, no one deserved to escape. It was all or nothing. He'd known that from the beginning. That applied to him too. And to Jessie. For a brief moment he regretted dragging her into this. Then he pictured Nea falling.

The police had told them to go home. Khalil was more than ready to do just that, but Adnan grabbed hold of his shirt.

'We can't leave. We have to help!'

'But what can we do?' said Khalil. 'The police are here. How can we help?'

'I don't know, but those are kids inside there. Kids my age.'

'We're not supposed to be here,' said Khalil.

The police officers were stealthily approaching the building, heading for the corner where they could look inside.

'Go then, do whatever you want,' said Adnan, turning away.

Khalil realized he was heading for the rear of the building.

'Shit!' he said and followed.

The small glass panels in the doors had been covered with cloth on the inside, but there was a gap and they

742

could see the perpetrators. A boy and a girl. They looked so young. Two kids were lying on the floor. The girl went over to another boy. Khalil felt Adnan clutching at his arm. Without a trace of emotion, the girl shot the boy. His head jerked backward and then he collapsed on to the floor, next to the two other bodies.

'Why don't the police do something?' whispered Adnan, his voice thick with tears. 'Why don't they do something!'

He yanked on the chain fastened to the door handle.

'There aren't enough of them. They're waiting for reinforcements,' said Khalil, swallowing hard. 'Those two kids have probably secured the room. If the police go in, more kids might get shot.'

'But how can we just stand here and—'

Adnan gripped his arm even harder.

Another boy was shot. Then the gunman turned on a little kid wearing glasses.

'What are they doing now?'

'I think I know,' said Khalil.

He turned around and threw up. The vomit covered his shoes. He raised his hand to wipe off his mouth. Inside the building flames shot up. The kids were screaming, their terror and panic increasing by the second. They rushed towards the doors. Shot after shot was fired. Adnan and Khalil watched in horror as bodies fell to the floor.

Khalil looked around. He caught sight of a loose brick a short distance away. He picked it up and lifted it over his head. Again and again he slammed it against the door handle, and finally the chain broke so he could yank open the doors.

Fire billowed out towards them, along with terrified screams. The smoke was thick and black, stinging their eyes, but they could see people running.

'Over here! Over here!' they shouted, and then helped one person after another out the door.

Their eyes were practically sealed from the smoke, stinging and running with tears, but they kept on guiding the terrified kids to freedom. Khalil heard Adnan shouting close by. He saw him help a panic-stricken girl.

Then the fire reached Adnan. Khalil turned around when he heard him scream.

BOHUSLÄN 1672

A big crowd had gathered at the gallows hill. The executioner was waiting next to the block as Elin was lifted out of the wagon. The spectators gasped when they caught sight of her. She wore a new white shift, but her head was bald and covered with burns. Her hands were twisted and limp, hanging at her sides, and she could barely stay on her feet as the two guards practically dragged her forward.

At the block, she fell to her knees. Anxiously she looked at all those who were staring at her. There was only one thing she'd been able to think about after she had confessed and then was sentenced to death: Would Märta be present? Would the child be forced to watch her own mother die?

Much to her relief, she did not see Märta anywhere. Britta was there with Preben. Ebba of Mörhult stood a short distance from them, along with many other people with whom she and Per had lived side by side, as well as workers from the vicarage.

Lars Hierne was not present. He had moved on to other places, other witches, fighting against other abominations of Satan. For him, Elin Jonsdotter was merely an entry in the books. Yet another bride of the devil whom the witchcraft council had caught and executed.

Britta was now large with child. She looked so pleased, pressing her hands to her stomach. Her face radiated righteousness. Preben had his arm around her. His eyes were fixed on the ground, as he held his hat in his other hand. They were very close, only a few metres away. Ebba of Mörhult was chatting with the women around her. Elin heard her repeating select parts of her testimony. She wondered how many times Ebba had told her lies. She had always had a loose tongue. She had always been an inveterate gossiper and liar.

Hatred smouldered inside Elin. She had spent so many hours in the dark cell, going over everything again and again. Every word. Every lie. She had recalled Märta's laugh when she innocently said what she had been told to say. And Britta's satisfied look when she took Märta by the hand and led her out of the courtroom. How would Märta be able to live with that when she grew older and realized what she had done?

Rage surged inside Elin, becoming a storm. Just like the storm that had taken Per and turned her and Märta into blameless and obliging victims.

She hated them. Hated them with an intensity that made her shake all over. With a great effort, she rose to her feet. The guards took a step forward, but the executioner raised his hand to stop them. Her eyes blazing with fury, Elin stood there unsteadily in her white shift and fixed her gaze on Britta, Preben, and Ebba. They had all fallen silent as they looked at her uneasily. She was a witch, after all. Who knew what she might do, now that she was at death's door?

Not taking her eyes off those who had condemned her to death, those three people who stood there so self-righteously, Elin said in a strong and calm voice:

'You may have persuaded everyone to believe you have done God's will. But I know better. Britta, you are a false and loathsome person. You have been ever since you emerged from the womb of your equally false mother. Preben, you are a whoremonger and a liar, a weak and cowardly man. You know that you lay with me, not just once but many times, behind the back of your wife and behind the back of God. And Ebba of Mörhult: you are an evil, envious, gossiping crone who could never bear to see that your neighbour had even a breadcrumb more than you had. May you all burn in hell. And may your offspring suffer ignominy, death, and fire, for generation after generation. You may destroy my body today with steel and flames, but my words will live on long after my body has turned to ashes. This do I, Elin Jonsdotter, promise you on this day of Our Lord, the Almighty. And with that, I am now ready to meet my God.'

She turned towards the executioner and nodded. Then she fell to her knees and placed her head on the block, fixing her gaze on the ground. To the side of her, they lit the pyre on which her soon-to-be decapitated body would be placed.

When the axe fell, Elin Jonsdotter was saying her last prayer to the God she had invoked. And with all her soul she felt that He had now heard her.

They would suffer their punishment.

Her head was cleaved from her body and rolled to the ground. When it stopped, her eyes were staring up at the sky. At first there was silence, along with a few shocked gasps. Then jubilant cheers arose. The witch was dead.

✤

Patrik had been preparing himself all morning for this conversation with Helen. She had played so many roles in the story. As the mother of a dead teenage boy, she should have been left in peace to grieve. But as the mother of a murderer, she had to help the police with their investigation. Patrik realized he needed to choose the right approach. As a father, he wanted to leave her in peace. But as a police officer, he needed to get the answers which the families of the victims deserved. And there were so many victims. The headlines in all the papers were huge and pitch-black, screaming the news about the tragedy in Tanumshede.

When the first reports emerged about the mass shooting in Tanumshede, the political party Sveriges Vänner had been quick to claim on social media sites that the shooting was an act of terror by one or more foreign residents. 'What did we tell you?' The claim spread like the wind through websites and forums sympathetic to their cause. But it soon became clear that two Swedish teenagers had caused the unimaginable devastation, and the news flashed all around the world. When the media then reported that the heroes who had managed to save the lives of so many kids were Syrian refugees, Sveriges Vänner and their cohorts fell silent. Instead, a wave of respect and gratitude surged from the Swedish public. And sympathy for the people of Tanumshede streamed in from all directions. Sweden was a nation in shock. Tanumshede was a community in mourning.

But right now, all that Patrik could see was a grieving woman. Both her husband and her son were dead. How should he talk to a person who had suffered so much? He had no idea.

When the police went to Helen and James's house, they found James shot to death in front of a gun cabinet hidden behind a false wall in a wardrobe. The theory was that Sam had forced his father to open the cabinet where he stored the guns, and then he had shot him in the head.

When the police told Helen what Sam had done, and that he was dead, she had wept hysterically. When they told her James was dead, she said nothing.

They had left Helen in peace for half an hour, but now they could wait no longer.

'I'm sorry for your loss,' said Patrik. 'And I apologize, but we need to do this.'

Helen nodded. Her eyes were empty, her face pale. A doctor had been summoned to see to her, but she had refused medical help.

'I understand,' she said.

Her thin hands were trembling, but she did not cry. The doctor had said she was most likely still in shock, but he considered her to be lucid enough to answer questions. She had declined their offer to have a lawyer present.

'As I told you before, I killed Stella,' Helen said, looking Patrik in the eye.

Patrik took a deep breath. Then he got out several sheets of paper that he'd brought along and placed them on the table in front of her so she could read the text.

'No, you didn't,' he said.

Helen's eyes widened. Uncomprehending, she looked from him to the papers on the table.

'These are copies of a document we found in James's safe. He left documents about various matters, in case he should be killed on one of his missions abroad.'

Patrik went on:

'Most of these documents pertain to practical matters – the house, bank accounts, and his wishes regarding his funeral. But we also found this . . .' He pointed to the document on top of the pile. 'It's what you might call his last confession.'

'Confession?' said Helen.

She stared at James's handwriting on the pages, then pushed them aside.

'Tell me what it says.'

'You didn't kill Stella,' said Patrik sombrely. 'You thought you did, but she was still alive when you ran off. James . . . James had a relationship with your father, and he realized how disastrous it would be if Stella survived and told what had happened. So he killed her. And he let both you and your father believe that you did it. He hid the girl's body in order to help you. In that way he came across as your rescuer, and your father was in his debt. That was why your father allowed you to marry James.

'The military had started wondering about James; rumours were spreading. He needed a family to hide behind. So he convinced KG that it would be best for all parties if he married you. You were a front. Protection for a man who led a double life that could cost him his career.'

Helen stared at Patrik. Her hands were shaking harder, and her breathing was shallow, but still she said nothing. Then she reached for the papers. Slowly she crumpled James's account into a tight ball.

'He let me believe . . .' Her voice broke and she clutched the ball of paper in her hands. 'He let me believe that I . . .'

Her breathing was now rapid and jagged, and tears streamed down her face. Fury blazed in her eyes.

'Sam . . .' She could hardly get the words out. 'Because he let me think I was a murderer, Sam . . .'

She couldn't finish the sentence. Her voice was filled with so much anger that it felt as if the walls might explode in the small room at the police station.

'Sam could have escaped all of this! His anger . . . His guilt . . . It isn't his fault. You realize that, don't you? He's not to blame for any of this! He's not an evil boy. He's not wicked. Before this, he never tried to harm anyone. All his life he had to bear so much of my guilt that he just couldn't stand it any more.'

She let out a howl of grief as the tears spilled from her eyes. When her scream faded, she wiped her face on the sleeve of her shirt and stared wildly at Patrik.

'All of this . . . It was all a lie. Sam never . . . If James hadn't lied for all these years, Sam would never have . . .'

She clenched and unclenched her fists. Then she picked up the ball of paper and flung it against the wall. She pounded her fists on the table.

'All those kids yesterday! All those dead children! None of this would have happened if . . . And Nea . . . That was an accident. He didn't mean to hurt her! He would never . . .'

She fell silent and looked at the wall with a resigned expression. Then she went on, her voice now calm and infinitely sad.

'He must have been hurting so much to do something like that. He must have fallen apart because of all the burdens we placed on him. But no one is going to under-stand. No one will see my sweet boy. They will see a monster. They will paint him as a terrible person, a wicked boy who took the lives of their children. How can I make them see my sweet boy? The warm, loving boy who was destroyed by all our lies? How can I make them hate me and hate James, but not Sam? It wasn't his fault! He was the victim of our fear, our guilt, our self-centred obsessions. We let our own pain eat up everything we had and everything he had. How can I make them understand that none of this was his fault?'

Helen fell forward, holding on to the edge of the table. Patrik hesitated. His role as a police officer did not allow him to succumb to sympathy. So many lives had been destroyed. But the parent in him saw another parent's paralysing grief and guilt, and he could not deny that part of himself. He stood up and went around the table. He set a chair next to Helen's and took her in his arms. Gently he rocked her as her tears soaked his shirt. There was no perpetrator in this story. No winner. Only victims and tragedies. And a mother's sorrow.

She didn't get home until dawn. The fire engines. The hospital. The ambulances. The journalists. It was all a fog. Marie remembered the police questioning her, but she could hardly recall what she'd said. Only that she'd had no clue, didn't understand.

She hadn't been allowed to see Jessie. She didn't even know where her body had been taken. Or how much of it remained. How much damage the fire had done. And the bullets of the police.

Marie met her own eyes in the mirror. Out of sheer habit, her hands moved. A terry cloth band to hold back her hair. Three dabs of cleansing lotion on a cotton ball. Circular movements to rub in the lotion. The bottle of facial astringent. A new cotton ball. The cool, fresh feeling on her skin as she wiped off the sticky cleansing cream.

Another cotton ball. She wiped off her eye make-up, careful to remove the mascara without breaking any lashes. Finally her face was bare. Clean. Ready to be rejuvenated, renewed. She reached for the flat, round silver jar. Night cream from La Prairie. Insanely expensive but hopefully as good for her skin as the price indicated. She picked up the little spatula and dipped it in the jar. She smeared the cream on her fingertips and began rubbing it on her face. First her cheeks. The area around her mouth and nose. Then her forehead. Then another little silver jar. Eye cream. She mustn't rub too hard or it would damage the delicate skin around her eyes. A tiny dollop cautiously pressed into her skin.

So. Finished. A sleeping pill and then she could sleep while her skin cells were rejuvenated at the same time as memories were erased.

She couldn't start thinking about anything else. If she thought about anything other than the silver jars and her skin, which she needed to keep young and elastic so the new film investors would be willing to put their money on her, then the dam would burst. Her outward appearance had always been her salvation, the spotlights and glamour had prevented her from remembering all the filth and pain. Allowed her to have only one dimension, which provided a refuge from the memories of what she had lost and the memories of what she had never had.

Her daughter had existed in a parallel reality, floating around in a world she had allowed herself to visit only sporadically. Had there been moments when she'd felt love for Jessie? Her daughter would probably have said no. She knew that. She had always been aware of Jessie's longing for a single moment of tenderness from her. And there had been times when she'd wanted to give in. Like the first time she placed the infant to her breast. Jessie had been sticky and warm, but she'd had such a searching look on her face when she met her mother's eyes. And when Jessie took her first steps, with such a happy expression at mastering something that human beings had been mastering for millions of years. The pride Marie felt had almost knocked her cold, and she'd had to turn away and leave so as not to give in to it. Then her daughter's first day of school. The little girl with her blond ponytail, wearing a backpack, had scampered off, filled with anticipation about everything she was going to learn about the world, about life. Out on the pavement, holding the hand of her nanny, Juanita, Jessie had turned around to wave at Marie, who stood in the doorway of the beautiful house they had rented in The Hills. And Marie had almost relented. She had almost rushed out the door and picked up the little girl in her arms to hold her close and bury her nose in the blond hair that always smelled of lavender from the expensive children's shampoo. But she had resisted. The price would have been too great.

Everyone in Marie's life had competed to teach her the lesson that it would cost too much to care. Most of all Helen. She had loved Helen. And Helen had loved her. Yet she had betrayed Marie. She had chosen someone else. Chosen something else. She had thrown all love and all hope in Marie's face. That wouldn't happen again. No one would ever hurt her again.

Jessie had also chosen to leave her. She had chosen to walk right into the fire. In the end, Jessie had also betrayed her. And left her here all alone.

Marie noticed the smell of smoke in her nostrils. She picked up another cotton ball, soaked it with astringent, and carefully cleaned her nostrils. It stung and prickled, making her want to sneeze. Tears filled her eyes, but the smell refused to leave. She looked up, trying to make her eyes stop running. She took a tissue from the box of

Kleenex and frantically rubbed her eyes, but she couldn't stop the tears.

She didn't have to be on the film set for a few days. No one needed her right now. She was all alone, just as she'd always known she would be. But she couldn't let it break her. She had to be strong. The show must go on.

'Yesterday was a black day in the history of this town,' said Patrik.

Several of his colleagues nodded. Most were simply staring down at the table in the conference room, which felt so confining.

'What's the latest report from the hospital?' asked Gösta.

His face was grey and furrowed. None of them had slept a wink. The heartbreaking work of notifying the families had taken all night, and they'd been pestered throughout by increasingly aggressive journalists, hell-bent on finding out as much as possible about what had happened.

This was something people had been talking about for a long time. It was what they had feared. That the school shootings in the United States might spread to Sweden, that someone, sooner or later, would decide to take the lives of fellow students. Sam and Jessie hadn't done it at a school, but the pattern was the same, and the targets had been their classmates.

'Another girl died an hour ago. So we now have nine dead and fifteen wounded.'

'My God,' said Gösta, shaking his head.

Patrik couldn't compute those numbers. His brain refused. It was impossible to think that so many young people had died, or had been wounded and would be scarred for life.

'Ten dead, if we count James,' said Martin.

'What is Helen saying?' asked Gösta. 'And Marie? Did they notice anything? Were Sam and Jessie acting strangely? Did they give any clues?'

Patrik shook his head.

'They say they had no idea. But we found Sam's notebook at home, with a detailed plan of what they intended to do, including sketches of the community centre. He seems to have been planning this for quite a while, and then he somehow persuaded Jessie to join him.'

'Had she displayed violent tendencies before?' asked Paula.

'Not according to Marie. She says her daughter has always been a loner, that she might have been bullied at the schools she attended. I get the impression she never paid much attention to her daughter.'

'Nea's death must have been what triggered Sam,' said Martin. 'Imagine – being fifteen and having to carry that guilt. A boy with a domineering father and weak mother as parents. Add in the stigma of living in the shadow of Helen's shame, and . . . well, it couldn't have been easy for him.'

'For God's sake don't feel sorry for him!' said Mellberg. 'Lots of kids have had a far worse home life, but they don't go out and massacre their classmates.'

'That's not what I meant,' said Martin in a subdued voice.

'What does Helen say?' asked Gösta.

'She's in despair. Shattered. Her son and her husband are both dead. She's going to be charged with obstruction of justice and harbouring a criminal because of what she did after Nea died.'

Paula held up a newspaper.

'Adnan is being hailed as a hero in all the papers,' she said, changing the subject. 'The refugee who gave his life to save Swedish kids.'

'The bloody fool,' said Mellberg, but he couldn't hide the admiration in his voice.

Patrik nodded. What Adnan and Khalil had done was both terribly stupid and terribly brave. They had rescued thirty teenagers. Thirty kids who would undoubtedly be dead otherwise.

He had personally been struggling all night with the images that would be for ever etched into his memory. The fire and the gunshots had forced them to make a quick decision to enter the building. Patrik and Paula had been first through the front door after the fire fighters had smashed it open. There was no time for hesitation. They saw Sam and Jessie standing back to back in the middle of the burning room, shooting at kids who ran screaming for the back doors that Adnan and Khalil had managed to open. Patrik exchanged a quick glance with Paula, and she nodded. They raised their service weapons and fired. Sam and Jessie both fell instantly to the floor.

The rest was like a fog. Ambulances had shuttled back and forth all night. All the hospitals in the county had helped, and private individuals had shown up to transport the wounded.

More and more people had gathered outside the community centre. They lit candles and wept, hugging each other as they asked thousands of questions that might never be answered. Tanumshede had taken its place alongside the names of other towns in the history books – those communities that would for ever be linked to some great tragedy and would for ever summon images of death and evil. But no one was thinking about that now. Right now they were grieving for their sons and daughters, their siblings and friends, their neighbours and acquaintances. They could no longer convince themselves that just because they lived in a small town, they would be spared all the evil they read about in the papers.

From now on, they would lock their doors and go to bed at night with an uneasy feeling, an anxiety about what might happen.

'Are you okay?' asked Annika, looking at Patrik and Paula.

Patrik looked at Paula, and they both shrugged. What could they say?

'There was no other option,' said Paula heavily. 'We did what we had to do.'

Patrik merely nodded without speaking. He knew she was right. There was no doubt about that. The only way for them to save the hostages was to shoot Sam and Jessie. He knew it was the right decision, and no one would ever criticize them for what they'd done. But having to shoot a child . . . Both he and Paula would have to live with that for the rest of their lives. Because no matter what Sam and Jessie had done, they were two lost teenagers who had driven each other to do something that was so horrifying it was nearly impossible to comprehend. Patrik might never understand what had led them to do it. He might never understand how they were able to justify their actions to themselves.

Patrik cleared his throat.

'When the techs searched Sam's room this morning, they found a USB stick showing intimate photos of James with a man who has now been identified as KG Persson. Helen's father.'

'Could that have been the deciding factor for Sam?' asked Martin. 'Seeing his mother kissing another woman, and finding those pictures of his father?'

Paula shook her head.

'I don't know,' said Patrik. 'We'll probably never know the whole story. And there's another issue we need to discuss.'

He pointed at Mellberg.

'At the wedding dinner, Bertil told me that a tip had been received from a man who gave three teenagers a ride in his car. He dropped them off near the refugee centre about the time Nea's knickers were left inside Karim's house. The witness says one of the kids was Bill's son, Nils, along with a girl and a boy. All three were killed yesterday. I don't see any point in making this information public. Anyone have a problem with that?'

He looked around the room. Everyone shook their heads.

'As for the fire at the refugee centre, we'll continue with our investigation, but I think it's going to be difficult to find out who did it. Refugee centres all over Sweden are burning, and no one gets caught. But let's keep our eyes and ears open.'

Everyone nodded. Silence settled over the room. Patrik realized they should do a debriefing and go over everything that had happened, but fatigue was beginning to set in, and the heat in the room was making them even drowsier. They were sad, shocked, exhausted, and shattered. The phone in the reception area had been ringing nonstop for hours. Not only Sweden, but the whole world was focused on Tanumshede and the tragedy that had unfolded. And Patrik knew that everyone sitting in this small room at the Tanumshede police station felt that something had permanently changed. No one would ever be the same again.

Karim was afraid people would think that he was ungrateful, that he didn't appreciate all they had done for him. But it wasn't true. Karim had never thought that any Swede would open their home as they had for him and his children, that they would help him get his own place, that they would hug his kids and speak to him as an equal. He was happy he'd been able to experience this other side of Sweden.

But he couldn't stay here. They couldn't stay here. Sweden had taken too much from him. Amina was with the stars in the sky and the warm rays of the sun, and he missed her every minute, every second. He carefully placed the photographs of her in his suitcase, wrapping them in soft clothing. Most of the suitcase was filled with the children's clothes. He didn't have the strength to carry more than one bag, so he was packing only the essentials. He didn't need much. They needed everything. They deserved everything.

It was impossible to take along all the toys they had received from Rita, Bertil, and Leo. He knew the children would be sad, but there simply wasn't room. Once again they would have to leave behind things they loved. That was the price they had to pay for freedom.

He looked at his children. Samia was sleeping with a rabbit in her arms, a grey and white toy rabbit that Leo had given her. She refused to sleep without it. She would be allowed to take the rabbit along, but only that one. And Hassan was clutching a little bag of coloured marbles in his hand. The marbles gleamed through the black netting of the bag. Hassan could stare at them for hours. They would be coming along too. But there was no room for anything else.

Karim had heard about Adnan and Khalil. Everyone had phoned everyone else to talk about them with both horror and pride. The Swedes were calling them heroes. How ironic. Karim recalled how disappointed Adnan had been when he recounted how the Swedes looked at him as if he were from another planet. He was the one at the refugee centre who had most wanted to fit in. Wanted to be accepted. And now the Swedes were hailing him as a hero, but what was the point of that? Adnan would never know.

Karim looked around the flat. It was nice and bright.

Spacious. It could have been a good home for him and the children. If only his grief for Amina hadn't hurt so badly. If only he'd still had hope that this country would be able to offer him a future. But Sweden had caused him to suffer only sorrow and rejection. He had felt hatred and distrust directed at him, and he knew he would never feel secure here. He and the children would have to keep looking for a place where they could stay. Where they would feel safe and have faith in a future. Somewhere he would be able to picture Amina's smile without feeling grief stabbing his chest.

With an effort he picked up a pen in his injured hand. The bandages had been removed at the hospital, but his hands still hurt, and for a long time to come, maybe for ever, they would be stiff and scarred. He got out a piece of paper and then paused. He didn't know what to write. He was not ungrateful. He wasn't. He was frightened. And empty.

Finally he wrote down only a single word. One of the first Swedish words he had learned. 'Tack.' Thank you. Then he got up to wake the children. They had a long journey ahead of them.

✤

Almost a week had passed since the tragedy at the community centre. The grieving process had slowly entered a new phase, and daily life had started to take over. As it always did. At least for those on the periphery and not at the epicentre of what had happened. For those who had lost someone dear, there was still a long road to go before they approached anything resembling daily life.

Martin had been brooding all morning about what yesterday's strange conversation with the attorney could mean. He stared at the ceiling as Mette drowsily rolled on to his side of the bed and murmured: 'What time do you have to be there?'

'Nine,' he said, glancing at the clock.

He saw that it was almost time.

'What do you think it's all about?' he asked. 'Is somebody suing me? Do I owe someone money? What could it be?'

He threw out his hands in frustration, and Mette laughed. He loved hearing her laugh. Actually, he loved everything about her, though he hadn't dared say that yet. Not directly. They were taking things slow, one step at a time.

'Maybe you're a multimillionaire. Maybe some filthy rich unknown relative in the United States died and you're the only heir.'

'Ha! I knew it!' he said. 'You're only after my money!'

'Of course! What did you think? That it was because of your huge biceps, or something?'

'Very funny!' he said, and began tickling her.

She knew that he was sensitive about his not particularly muscular arms.

'You probably should think about getting dressed if you're going to get there on time,' she said. He nodded and reluctantly got up.

Half an hour later he was in his car, on his way to Fjällbacka. The attorney had refused to say what this was all about, merely repeating that Martin should be at his office at nine o'clock sharp.

He parked in front of the villa that housed the small legal firm, got out, and knocked on the door. A grey-haired man in his sixties opened the door and enthusiastically shook hands.

'Have a seat,' he said, pointing to a chair in front of his extremely neat desk.

Martin sat down. He was always suspicious of people who were overly tidy, and in this office everything seemed to be in its proper place.

'So, I'm wondering what this is about,' said Martin.

He could feel the palms of his hands had started to sweat, and he realized his face and neck had turned red, which he hated.

'It's nothing to worry about,' said the attorney. 'In fact quite the opposite.'

Martin raised his eyebrows. Now he was really curious. Maybe Mette was right about that American millionaire.

'I am the executor for Dagmar Hagelin's estate,' said the attorney. Martin gave a start.

He stared at the man.

'Dagmar?' he asked, confused. 'She's dead? But we talked to her only a week ago.'

He felt a pang in his chest. He had liked the old woman. Liked her very much.

'She died a few days ago, but it always takes a little time to work out these types of things,' said the attorney.

Martin had no idea what he was doing here.

'Dagmar had a very specific wish regarding you.'

'Me?' said Martin. 'We didn't really know each other. I met her only twice, on police business.'

'I see,' said the attorney, surprised.

Then he collected himself.

'In that case, you must have made quite an impression on those two occasions. Dagmar added a codicil to her will because she wanted you to inherit her house.'

'Her house? What do you mean?'

Martin was confused. Someone must be joking. But the attorney looked completely serious.

'According to Dagmar's will, she wants you to inherit the house. She wrote you a note to say that there are a few things that need to be repaired, but she thinks you'll like living there.'

Martin couldn't take in what the attorney was saying. Then something occurred to him.

'But she has a daughter. Won't she be upset? Won't she want the house?'

The attorney pointed to some papers lying on the desk in front of him.

'I have a document here stating that Dagmar's daughter has relinquished all claim to the house. When I spoke to her on the phone, she said she was too old to take on such a ramshackle house, and she didn't need the money. "I have what I need," she said. "If my mother decided this is what she wanted, I know it's for the best."'

'But . . .' said Martin, tears filling his eyes.

Slowly it began to sink in. Dagmar had gifted her lovely red house to him. The house he hadn't been able to stop thinking about. He'd been wondering how he could afford to buy that house for him and Tuva. He'd pictured the whole scene: where he would set up a swing set in the yard, where Tuva could plant a little vegetable garden, how they would have a fire in the fireplace in the wintertime, and how he would shovel the path to the front steps. He'd imagined a thousand and one things, but he'd never been able to work out how they could afford it.

'But why?' he said, no longer able to hold back the tears, because now he was thinking about Pia and how she had always wanted Tuva to grow up in a little red house out in the country, with swings in the yard and her very own garden patch.

He was crying not only because Pia wouldn't see this, but because he knew she would be happy for all the new things in his life, even though she was no longer here.

The attorney handed Martin a tissue and then said quietly:

'Dagmar said that you and the house needed each other. And do you know, I believe she was right.'

Bill and Gun had taken care of Khalil when he was discharged from hospital. When he was overcome with grief. They had given him a nice, bright guestroom on the ground floor. His belongings had already been brought over from his basement lodgings. Along with Adnan's things. Bill had promised to help him get a letter to Adnan's parents. Khalil wanted them to know that their son had died a hero. That every single person in his new country now knew his name and had seen his picture. He had become a symbol, a bridge to the Swedes. The prime minister had even mentioned his name in a speech on TV. He had talked about how Adnan had shown that human compassion was not about national borders or skin colour. Adnan hadn't thought about the nationality of the kids or their colour when he sacrificed his life to save so many of them. The prime minister had said much more. He had talked for a long time. But that was what Khalil wanted to say in the letter to Adnan's parents.

The prime minister had also talked about Khalil. But by then he had stopped listening. He didn't feel like a hero. He didn't want to be a hero. He just wanted to be one of them. At night he had nightmares about the faces of the kids. The fear in their eyes, their terror and panic. He'd thought he would never have to experience that again. But the fear in the kids' eyes was exactly the same as back home. There was no difference.

In the evening Bill and Gun sat in front of the TV. Sometimes they held hands. Sometimes they simply sat side by side as the glow from the TV lit up their faces. They hadn't yet been allowed to bury their son Nils. The police couldn't say when they would be finished with their investigation. Their older sons came to visit but then returned to their own homes, their own families. They couldn't ease their parents' sorrow, and they were dealing with their own grief.

Khalil had assumed they wouldn't enter the sailing competition. Not without Adnan. Or Karim. He missed him and wondered where he and the children were now. They had simply disappeared.

On the third morning in Bill and Gun's home, Bill told Khalil that he'd talked to the others, and they were going to meet at the sailboat at ten o'clock. That's all he said. He hadn't asked. He had just announced they would be sailing in the regatta. Without Adnan. And without Karim.

So here they were now, waiting for the starting gun. Several other classes of boats had already competed, and

Dannholmen was packed with spectators. The organizers had had great luck with the weather, and the sun was shining in a clear blue sky. Lots of people were there to witness Bill's project. Journalists and curiosity-seekers, local residents and tourists. It actually looked as if all of Fjällbacka and the surrounding area had gathered on the small, bare island. Khalil had read on the Internet that a Swedish film star used to live here. The same one whose statue stood in the little square in Fjällbacka. It wasn't someone he knew, but Bill and Gun had played a DVD of one of her films last night. A film called *Casablanca*. She was beautiful. A little sad but beautiful. In that cool, Swedish sort of way.

Khalil had seen the island before, but he'd never gone ashore. They had trained intensively during the few days left before the competition, trying out the stretch of water around the island. From the beginning, the regatta had been intended only for small boats, for the children and youths of the Fjällbacka sailing school. But when the competition was re-instituted a few years back, their class of boat had been added. Bill said it was called class C55.

Khalil looked at Bill as he stood at the wheel. They were moving back and forth along with the seven other boats in their class, eyeing the clock in order to get in the best possible position when the starting gun sounded. No one spoke of Adnan. Yet they all knew this was no longer just a competition, a way of spending time as they waited to find out whether they would have a new home in Sweden.

Three minutes left before the start, and Khalil again cast a glance at the island. The buzz of voices from people having coffee, from the children running around and chattering to each other, from the groups of photographers and journalists conversing, had suddenly stopped. Everyone had moved to the side of the island where the boats would start off. Grown-ups. Children.

Journalists. Residents of Fjällbacka. Tourists. Khalil saw some people from the refugee centre. Rolf was there. Gun was there with her two older sons. Familiar and unfamiliar faces. Several of the officers from the police station. Everyone stood there in silence, looking at their boat. Not a sound was heard other than the lapping of the water against the side of the boat and the sail fluttering in the wind. Bill was holding the wheel so tightly that his knuckles were white, and his jaw was clenched.

A young child started waving. Then another person waved. And another. Everyone on Dannholmen was now waving to their crew as they sailed past. Khalil felt it hit him right in the heart. This was not a language he had to struggle to understand. It was the same the world over. A universal gesture of love. He waved to show that they saw, that they understood. Ibrahim and Farid waved too, but Bill kept his eyes fixed ahead as he stood, straight-backed, in the stern. His tear-filled eyes were the only indication that he had noticed.

Then the signal flare went up. With perfect precision, they broke from the starting line. On Dannholmen the spectators continued to wave, and some cheered and whistled. The sound rose up to the clear blue sky. The sail filled with wind and grew taut, and the boat keeled and cut through the waves. For a moment Khalil thought he saw their faces in the crowd. Amina. Karim. Adnan. But when he looked again, they were gone.

'I'm glad you like the food,' said Erica, serving her sister another helping of potato au gratin.

Anna could apparently eat as much as a six-foot man when she was pregnant.

'You're not the only one,' said Patrik, reaching for the platter of fish filets. 'I'm finally getting my appetite back.'

'How are you doing?' asked Dan. 'We've all been

affected by the tragedy at the community centre, but for you it must be . . . awful.'

He nodded at Erica, who was holding up a bottle of Ramlösa mineral water towards him. She knew Dan didn't dare drink any wine in case he had to drive Anna to the maternity clinic.

Patrik put down his fork and knife. Erica knew he didn't want to answer that question. So many had lost so much, so many were grieving, and there were so many victims.

'We're getting counselling,' he said, twirling his wine glass. 'It feels strange to be talking to a psychologist, but then . . . well, maybe we shouldn't dismiss it so quickly.'

'I heard there's buzz the film might get a Guldbagge Award,' said Anna, wanting to change the subject. 'For Marie.'

'Well, considering all the media attention, I'm not surprised,' said Erica. 'But Marie seems to have changed since Jessie died. She hasn't given a single interview.'

'I heard she's going to publish her own book about what happened,' said Dan, reaching for the salad bowl.

'She says she wants to tell her own version,' said Erica. 'But she and Helen have promised to talk to me some more. Sanna too.'

'How is Sanna doing?' asked Patrik.

'I talked to her yesterday,' she said, thinking about the poor woman who had now lost her daughter too. 'What can I say? She's coping as best she can.'

'And what about Helen?' asked Dan.

'Presumably she'll be given a prison sentence for obstructing justice and harbouring a criminal,' said Patrik. 'I'm not sure how I feel about that. It seems to me she's as much a victim as many others in this tragic case. But the law is the law.'

'How are Nea's parents doing?' asked Anna, putting down her fork.

'They're going to sell the farm,' said Patrik tersely.

Erica gave him a sympathetic look. She knew how personally he had taken everything about this case, how many sleepless nights he'd tossed and turned, plagued by thoughts and memories that would never leave him. She loved him for that. He was compassionate. He was brave. He was strong and loyal. He was a better husband than she'd ever dreamed of having and an amazing father to their children. Their life together wasn't always rosy or romantic or easy. It was stress-filled and tumultuous, with all the little everyday conflicts that went with being parents to children who were at a stubborn age. They didn't get enough sleep, they didn't have enough sex; they had too little time for themselves and too little time to talk about things that were important. But it was their life. Their children were doing well, they were loved, they were happy. She reached out to take Patrik's hand and felt him squeeze her hand in return. They were a team. A unit.

Anna whimpered. She had eaten four helpings of pork and potatoes au gratin, so it wasn't strange if her stomach was protesting. But then her face contorted even more. Dan stiffened and looked at Anna, who slowly lowered her head to look down. She looked up again, breathing rapidly.

'I'm bleeding,' she said. 'Help me. I'm bleeding.'

Erica felt her heart stop for a second. Then she lunged for the phone.

BOHUSLÄNINGEN

THE WITCH'S CURSE

A coincidence? Or a witch's curse from nearly three hundred years ago that has once again claimed a victim?

The discoveries made by Lisa Hjalmarsson, aged fifteen, are guaranteed to make the reader's blood run cold. Lisa, a student in 9B at the Hamburgsund secondary school, has written an essay about Elin Jonsdotter of Fjällbacka – a woman who was convicted of witchcraft and executed in 1672. At the executioner's block, Jonsdotter hurled a vicious curse at her accusers: her sister Britta Willumsen, her brother-in-law Preben, and a woman by the name of Ebba of Mörhult.

Jonsdotter's gripping and bloody story has now been given a nasty but titillating sequel because of Lisa Hjalmarsson's research.

It turns out that descendants of the seventeenth-century accusers have been involved in every sort of unthinkable human tragedy: murder, suicide, and fatal accidents.

Tragedies that culminated in a horrifying event this past summer.

The tragedy in Tanumshede, which we reported in this newspaper, can be directly linked to Elin Jonsdotter's curse from more than three hundred years ago. Lisa Hjalmarsson has been able to prove that the teenagers who set fire to the community centre and shot to death so many young people were direct descendants of Preben and Britta Willumsen, as well as Ebba of Mörhult.

A coincidence?

Or is Elin Jonsdotter's curse still very much in force today?

ACKNOWLEDGEMENTS

Writing about the seventeenth century was both difficult and challenging, but also incredibly enjoyable. I've ploughed through a ton of books, read articles on the Internet, and consulted experts. Yet I have barely scratched the surface of this fascinating period, and all errors, both conscious and unconscious, are entirely my own. The same applies to the present-day story. I have taken certain liberties in order to make historical events and facts fit the story. That's the prerogative of authors and storytellers.

As always when I write a book, there are many people I'd like to thank. A book is not written in a vacuum; it requires teamwork, even though I'm the one sitting at the keyboard.

I'm always conscious of the risk I might leave out someone who played an important role, but I'd like to thank a number of key individuals, both in my professional and my personal life.

My Swedish publisher Karin Linge Nordh and my editor John Häggblom have done a tremendous job with the manuscript of *The Girl in the Woods* – a job that was more demanding than ever because of the sheer length of the book. With meticulous attention and love they have pruned the weeds from the flower garden and trimmed what needed more care. I am mindful of their amazing input, and I am immensely grateful. I would also like to thank Sara Lindegren at Forum publishing company, and Thérèse Cederblad and Göran Wiberg at Bonniers publishing company. I also received help with fact-checking from Niklas Ytterberg, Miriam Säfström, Ralf Tibblin, Anders Torewi, Michael Tärnfalk, Kassem Hamadè, Lars Forsberg and Christian Glaumann. Your help was invaluable!

I want to thank everyone who helps me keep my life on track. My mother Gunnel Läckberg, Anette and Christer Sköld, Christina Melin, Sandra Wirström, Andreea Toba and Moa Braun. And my amazing older children Wille, Meja and Charlie, who were always willing to lend a hand by washing dishes or babysitting for Polly when I needed to work. What wonderful, wonderful children!

Joakim and the gang at Nordin Agency: You rock! I look forward to more great things in the future.

I also want to thank my friend and sister (although not by birth) Christina Saliba, as well as Sean Canning who has become not only an amazing resource on my team but also a good friend. And my thanks to all your delightful and talented co-workers.

There are two more people I want to single out in particular. First, Johannes Klingsby, who inspired a key character in the book. At an auction in support of the charity Musikhjälpen, his winning bid gave him the opportunity to be included in the novel while it also contributed generously to the cause. Bidding against him was Fredrik Danermark, the fiancé of my friend Cecilia Ehrling, whom I met while appearing on the TV show *Let's Dance*. Fredrik lost out to Johannes, and he was so disappointed because he had planned to make it a wedding gift to Cecilia. So I decided that, as a wedding present from Simon and me, Cecilia would also have a minor role in the book. My thanks to both Johannes and Cecilia for lending a little extra authenticity and personality to my story.

Next, thanks to all my friends. As usual, I don't want to mention specific names, because there are so many of you, and you are all so wonderful I would feel terrible if I left out anyone. Yet, as always, I want to give an honourable mention to Denis Rudberg. We may not see each other often, but during my entire writing career you have been only a phone call away, offering me advice that is both wise and insightful. And speaking of insightful advice, I have to mention Mia Törnblom as well. Thanks for all the pep talks!

And now, my beloved Simon. Where should I start? Since I wrote my previous book we have had a lovely daughter, Polly. Our little sunshine and the darling of our entire family. I've written this novel during her first year. And that would never have been possible if you weren't the amazing man that you are. You are my rock. I love you. Thank you for all that you do for me and the children. Thank you for loving us.

Camilla
Gamla Enskede
Sunday, 5 March 2017